For everyone who's ever stood in their own way; t
me far too long to tell but I got there and you will t

And, of course, for my pal Caz, who's my biggest fan.

Introduction: Beginning at the End.	2
Part I: The Deep End.	5
Part II: A New Normal	77
Part III: Hunting 4XM	147
Part IV: Finding Joseph	205
Part V: Who Are These People?	251
Part VI: How I Used-To-Be	293
Part VII: And That's Why I Hate You	341
Part VIII: Love and War	401
Author's Note	476

Introduction: Beginning at the End.

It's the end of the fucking world. That's not hyperbole or overdramatisation. The world as we know it is over and it's only getting worse. It won't be long until it spreads beyond this country and the whole world is overrun. The entire human race will either be infected, enslaved, or destroyed and no one outside of this room stands a chance of stopping it.
Tomorrow I'm probably going to die and I'm wasting my last night listening to the only living people for hundreds of miles bicker between themselves about how we ended up here.
We're hiding in the heart of a dead city and it's so dramatically different from the world we once knew. I hadn't realised. Not until right now. That's stupid, given everything we've been through over the last few months, but I suppose I haven't been able to stop and think about it. I'm staring out of the window, and just trying to tune the argument out, and it strikes me that we're surrounded by nothing but ruins. I remember when this place was vibrant. It had been years since I'd spent any real time here, but once you've been to London you don't forget it. It was incredible, over-powering, even. The bright lights of the buildings blaring against the darkness of night, some of them constant beacons that were visible for miles around and kept the dark at bay. Now it's changed too much. The buildings are barely even recognisable. Now they're not vibrant and now they cower from the darkness, they don't hold it back. That is the world that we live in now. These monoliths that once stood at the heart of England's capital city are now just faded and sad. There used to be so much activity, so many humans, and now there are no signs of life anywhere except here in this room with us. I don't think it had dawned on me how far we'd fallen until right now, until this very moment. It was here where I finally let myself wonder if there was even a way back at all. This, right here, surrounded by all the people I had left to care about, was when, just for a second, I lost hope.
And so, I tuned back into their argument and found them still shouting over each other. I'd grown so tired of it that I'd let my mind wander but that was no good for anyone. I needed to stop this. They needed me to stop this. Years of arguing and fighting with each other and where had it got us? Here. To this. We were all to blame for this, me most of all, but here and

now it's not the time to go through it all again. There's no way we're all living through tomorrow, if any of us do, so now just isn't the time to behave like this. I know I'll never get them to act like one big happy family, there's too much collective trauma in this room, but for some of us this is the last night we'll ever get and it seems so stupid to spend it arguing over what are now insignificant little details.
I take a deep breath and look out at the dead city around us. There's so much trauma out there too, and I can feel it. Maybe that's why I've discovered this moment of hopelessness, because I can feel the tens of thousands of others who lost hope here. I can feel the pointless deaths just hanging in the air. I look at the room around me, at the faces of those I've known for both years and mere hours. A lot of them can probably feel it too, even if they're not as in tune as I am. I close my eyes and reach out. The energy around me feels electric, stronger than I think I've ever felt it. There's so much emotion and it's a little overwhelming, and for a second I let myself sink into it and let it carry me away. I focus on my breathing. I let it ground me in only this room. I tune into just these people with me now. There's so much emotion around us; fear, anger, anxiety, disgust, sadness, and even jealousy. They're all so loud. But I dig through it, still breathing, still focussing, and pull on the threads of positivity I find. There's joy, I don't know how, given where we're at, but it's there. There's tranquillity too. That's a nice feeling. There's curiosity; some people are looking at me with it, and some people are just wondering what will come next. There is happiness and joy. Some of these people are just happy to be alive and some are just clinging desperately to happy memories. Some of that is coming from him, and I take a little comfort in knowing that's there, despite everything we've been through.
I find hope, at last, and surprisingly there's a lot of it. They might be fighting, they might be arguing, they might be so angry and so scared but ultimately they all believe there's a way through this. I dive into that feeling and I push. I take their hope and I drag it to the surface. I open my eyes and they've all stopped because they can feel it too. I'm blanketing them in it. Some of them know what I'm doing, and others have been looking at me like I'm some kind of deity all night, so all their eyes turn to me. I'm not, by the way, I'm just some kid with way more power than he was ever supposed to have. It's weird to think back on it all now. That's what had started the argument; how we even got here and what's going to happen tomorrow. My sister's voice was the loudest but her voice is generally the

loudest in every argument, in every room, and even she is quiet now. They're all waiting for me to speak. I've stepped forward, without even noticing, so I think I am too. That sums up how we got here better than anything could, really, me stepping forward without any kind of plan, me stepping forward without even realising I was doing it.

I think of that stupid, stupid boy walking through the village one morning in Autumn. It was bright, and sunny, and warm. I wonder what that village looks like now. He was a postman, if you can fucking believe it, a stupid twenty-year-old postman doing his rounds. But it doesn't start with him, that stupid boy. Not really. If I have to pick a point where it starts then I'd say that it starts with Alex.

Part I: The Deep End.

Chapter One.

I didn't meet Alex but I've heard they were intense. The story starts with them. They're in a house in a small town in the north of England, called Endsbrough, hunched over a laptop as it scans through various bits of surveillance in the area. They're tired because they've been at this for a long, long time; weeks and weeks of scanning and watching suspected targets. Their dark curly hair is an unwashed mess and there's bags under their eyes. Their search has been obsessive, and it would probably be called an unhealthy obsession if it wasn't for the fact that it was this kind of behaviour that got them promoted to being a "Level 3" Agent. I know you need context about the different levels and what they mean, but I don't want to throw too much at you at once.
Alex is tapping their pen in frustration as they flick, almost hopelessly, between CCTV all over the town. Their patience is wearing thin, but suddenly they're offered a ray of hope as the facial recognition software they're running pings with a hit.
"I've got you." They say, a satisfied grin spreading across their face. "It worked. I've actually got you." They stand quickly and a little triumphantly, pushing aside a lot of the papers strewn across the desk and searching for something. They find a gun and grab it, holstering it on their belt and sprinting to the door. They make their way down the stairs of the house they've been staying in, practically tripping over their own feet in desperation to get out. They call out to the other occupants. "Chris? Lauren? Anyone? I need back-up now." They quickly realise that no one else in the team is home and as they reach the ground floor they pull out their phone, dialling a number quickly. It's answered and they frantically bark an instruction before the other person can even speak. "I'm sending you a location, get everyone and meet me there."

Somewhere, a couple of miles away, trainers thud rhythmically on the pavement. Jon Hamilton breathes steadily, entering the third kilometre of his post-work run. It's quiet, this little patch of pavement by the canal, but mostly quiet in a good way. He runs this way on Monday, Tuesday, and Thursdays after work. It helps him relax and clear his head because he, frankly, hates his job. Jon is in his late twenties and painfully aware that most people in their late twenties hate their job. But, it pays the bills and he doesn't really have the energy to look for another. He'll always look like a failure compared to his sister, Amy, and so, he doesn't really think there's a point. So he just runs, the same days every week, to help him cope with a shitty work day. Amy probably has a personal trainer and nutritional coach. He mentally chastises himself. He's so incredibly proud of his sister, it's just difficult not to feel like a failure in comparison. He decides to once again bury those feelings and lets his mind wander to a particularly difficult conversation he had with his manager earlier today, as he tried to feed back something Jon had done wrong. Feedback was a gift, apparently. Bullshit. Utter bullshit. God that man was the part of his hated job that he hated the most. The kind of manager who was completely absent when you needed something; but there like the fucking boogeyman the second you did something wrong. He tuned that out, and back into the thudding of his footsteps. He passes a warehouse, it's quiet because whatever happens there has obviously finished for the day but what he doesn't realise is that he's picked up on a CCTV camera. He continues, and passes through a dark tunnel with a road running over it. It always worried him a little bit, partly because the path took a sharp right just after, so you couldn't see if anything was coming in the opposite direction and he had a fear that he'd one day collide with a bike and end up in the river. There was also a little bit of him that was just scared because it was a dark tunnel. He makes it through to the other side though, and there's no collisions with cyclists or incidents with fairy tale trolls. He looks at the still empty path ahead of him, knowing it'll be time to turn back soon. Running is still a relatively new thing. He's trying to build up to ten kilometres, although the most he's managed so far is seven. Maybe he'll do at least a half marathon one day.

Suddenly, a figure sweeps past him and Jon nearly falls in surprise. He steadies himself, just, and looks around. It's another runner, clearly much faster and quieter than he is. Jon is very aware that he's heavy footed and probably loudly panting like a dog, but this guy was like a ninja and he didn't hear him coming. The other runner looks back at him, but it's not an apologetic look, it's more the kind of glare that says the near collision was all Jon's fault.

The other runner is skinny and a little gaunt in the face, and that makes him look a little menacing, but he's swift and quickly disappears from view around a bend. Jon shakes his head in wonder, and picks his pace back up. He realises it's getting dark; it's nearly October now, fully and properly

Autumnal and he's not sure if he'll keep up running when it's dark after work. That half marathon might have to wait, because he'll likely soon be back to his post-work ritual of eating dinner too early and vegging on the sofa. He could join a gym, he supposed. He decides he can think about that in a few weeks, when it's properly dark. Instead, he fumbles around in his pocket to check his phone. But that was it. His mistake. He took his eyes off the path just after he rounded the corner and he tripped, and fell hard to the ground, scraping his knee on the concrete.
"Ow." He shouted out, just holding back from swearing.
"That looked like it hurt," Came a voice; and Jon suddenly became aware of a figure looming over him. It's the same gaunt, skinny man from before. He extends his spindly hand and Jon takes it without hesitating.
"Yeah buddy, it doesn't feel great but I'll live." He says, trying for a friendly smile through gritted teeth as the stranger helps him to his feet.
"Humans are so fragile." He replies. It's to himself more than anything. Jon hears the words but can't process them before the stranger is speaking again. "You're Jonathan, right? Jonathan Hamilton?"
"Umm, yeah?" Jon says, trying to place the stranger's face. "Do we work together or something? Sorry, I'm terrible with faces." He doesn't want to be rude by outright asking who the hell this guy is, and he is terrible at remembering people sometimes. It can lead to some pretty awkward moments. The stranger chuckles and it sends a chill down his spine.
"No, no. I tracked you. I've been studying you for weeks and I've learned your running pattern. The same days every week. The same route. Did you know you even check your pace at the same point each time? I did. That made it easy to make sure you tripped." He says, and he gestures to a large branch that's been dragged across the path where Jon tripped. The stranger locks eyes with him and just stares. He must be kidding, Jon tells himself. He chuckles, nervously, and the stranger breaks his gaze to join in. But it's more than just a chuckle. He laughs and it booms through the air of their quiet surroundings.
"Good one, you nearly had me there." Jon replies, still trying to convince himself it was a joke. Then, without another word, the stranger smacks him across the side of his face. He's sent tumbling off the path and sliding down a hill, crashing into a tree half way down. There's a crack as he feels an indescribable pain in the side of his chest, from his ribs. He can feel straight away at least one is broken and yelps like a wounded animal.
"Stop, please!" He cries out as his attacker descends the slope after him.

"Why?"
"Because you deserve it." He spits, before stopping in his tracks. "Okay, no, look I know it's not that simple. Maybe you don't deserve it. But, it's part of the plan and we're sticking to the plan." In that moment of explanation he goes from menacing to sounding confused; like he's arguing with himself more than he's telling Jon, as if he'd broken character temporarily. Jon, grunting in pain, pulls himself up using the same tree he'd collided with but then realises that the reprieve was all too brief as his attacker darts forward and grabs him by the throat pinning him to the trunk of the very same tree. "I just have to do it because…"
"Stop!" Another voice calls from the path at the top of the hill. Jon doesn't recognise the voice or the person it belongs to, but he can see that his attacker does by the way he bites his lip and screws his face up in frustration, before turning to face them. Alex stands at the top of the hill, pointing a gun and wearing a stern expression on their face.

"Drop him and turn around," Alex demands of the creature, who's seconds away from claiming another life. He does as he's told, and turns to face them sticking his lip out like a petulant child.
"This again? Really?" He says, before rolling his eyes and raising his hands, because he knows that's the demand that will. They've done this before. Alex ignores him and looks over his shoulder to the human who looks a little dazed.
"Climb up to me. Carefully." The human, still looking dazed, obeys the command and makes his way back up the muddy slope. He slips a few times, particularly because his right knee looks hurt, but he makes it. Alex notices that he's looking at them gratefully, and waves him off before he starts asking questions they can't really answer. "Get out of here. Go home. Don't talk to anyone about this. You're safe. I'll find you later."
"Or I will, Jonathan Hamilton." The creature says, with a grotesque grin creeping onto his face.
"Ignore him. Go." Alex demands. Jonathan Hamilton's eyes flick quickly between the two of them for a moment, quite clearly trying to process what is going on, but he does what he's told and takes off at as brisk a pace as his injured leg will carry him. Alex's focus has never fully been off their target, they know better than that, but now that the human is safely gone he gets their full attention. "Where is she?"
"Who?" He responds playfully. Alex doesn't have the patience for this

game. They're too tired, and too close to ending this.
"You know who."
"What, you don't think she'd let me play out alone?"
"No. I don't." They confirm; and he laughs mockingly. A light flickers overhead but Alex either doesn't notice or doesn't think anything of it because they're too focussed on the prospect of finally ending this. But he, Joseph, does notice. His posture relaxes ever so slightly because now he knows that he's going to be alright. He knows there's a chance that flickering is just a faulty bulb, but probability says it's not.
"Where is she?" Alex repeats.
"Never interested in me, are you? You know, it's so tiring being a supporting character." He replies, with a shrug, lowering his hands now.
"I didn't tell you to move." Alex says. He snorts in response, giggling in a way that's utterly infuriating. "Tell me where she is?"
"I will." He says, unexpectedly. "But can you answer a question, first?"
"What?"
"You didn't say I could move but…can you? Move, I mean?" He asks. Alex's eyes widen, with the realisation that they're frozen to the spot and the even more terrifying realisation of what that means. A well manicured hand comes to rest on Alex's shoulder and, at the bottom of the hill, Joseph claps his hands with glee. "She's here." He says.

The field report confirms that 'Level 3 agent Alex Smith was found dead at 18:08 on the 5th October. The body was recovered from the canal by fellow agents Chris and Amber Smith. They called in a Cleaning crew who were able to quarantine the area and remove the body before the local authorities were informed. An autopsy to discover the cause of death was carried out the following day,' **although the results were never widely released,** 'and the body was destroyed.'

Chapter Two.

And that brings us to the next morning which is the right time to introduce him. That stupid, stupid boy in the idyllic village. Me. Or, sort of. He is a million miles away from who I am now. Do you ever do that? Just look back at a past version of yourself and envy them because they're so innocent. You look back at the stupid things you said and did because you didn't know any better, and because you weren't such a cynic. That Louis is different and it's important that you know that because I want to tell you this story, but it does feel like it happened to someone else.

His part in this begins in that village. Jongleton. It's a place where nothing like what we've just seen ever happens. It's a place where nothing ever happens. He's working as a postman there. He's developed a little bit of a habit of nipping into a local shop to pick up some fresh bread and milk, and a few other things at the end of his rounds. He has a friendly chat with the shop-keeper, as he always does, because he knows him. He asks how his daughter is, she's moved away to University but is adapting to city life well, he hands him a few letters, pays, and leaves.
Louis then continues down the street. The sun is beautiful that day and feels so nice and warm on his skin. It's nice because he knows it won't last much longer; the leaves on the trees are turning brown and winter will take hold soon. He enjoys this little route around the village in the morning. It's given him a chance to get to know lots of people, and really made him feel part of the community. It might be different in winter though, there won't be as many friendly faces in the cold and he might not be as inclined to dawdle. He takes a turn through an open garden gate where an elderly woman looks up at him from her flowers she's been tending to.
"Morning, love." She says, beaming.
"Morning Mrs. McGinty," He politely responds, before handing out the letters and the bag of groceries.
"Oh thanks love," She says, taking off her muddy gloves and taking them. "How much do I owe you?"
"Nothing. It's on me, call it thanks for making me dinner the other night." He replies, practically running back to the gate before she can force money on him.
"At least come in for a cuppa, Owen will be back soon." She says, referring to her Grandson with whom Louis has developed quite the friendship over

the last few months.

"And give you a chance to slip me some cash when I'm not looking? I don't think so!" He says with a somewhat cheeky smile. "Nah, gotta run, post to deliver. Tell Owen I said hey though," He says, as he completes his escape with a wave. He's half way down the street before she can argue.

Louis has been stationed here ever since he graduated from his training at Home Base 25. He'd studied and lived there all his life until then, and so the transition from that place to here was a jarring one at first. It was more than that, it was a lonely one. He'd gone from a place where he was surrounded by tutors and fellow students, people who knew what he did about the world and saw it the same way. He had purpose there and he was part of something. Then it had all stopped. He was ready to go out into the big wide world, but no one had told him how lonely he'd be. He was stationed here, in this village, where no one knew the things he did, where everyone was so distinctly human, and where he had nothing in common with any of them. It took months to get over that. To actually build something resembling a life for himself outside of just sitting and waiting for something to happen. Mrs. McGinty had been the first to reach out to him. She'd noticed he was on his own, about a month after he'd started the job as the postman. She'd taken the time to chat with him when she could, and invited him to stay for tea or join her and her friend for wine one evening. She introduced him to her grandson and helped him properly integrate himself into the community. He'd made friends who were roughly his own age; like Owen, and then Sasha, the shop-keeper's daughter. It had been hard but in the absence of any kind of mission from Home Base and no suspicious activity presenting itself, all he could do was start to build a life for himself. He didn't have anything else.

He'd lied to Mrs McGinty. He'd lied to her many times, actually, but specifically today. She had been his last stop of the day and so from there he made his way home. It wasn't far, because Jongleton was not a large village. He walked peacefully along the street, the sun still shining and a smile still on his face because of how well his day had started. He nipped in through the gate on his small garden and made his way inside the small terraced house. He didn't own this house, but he didn't have to pay rent either. Money wasn't an issue, or at least, not one he had to deal with. His bills were all paid as part of his assignment here. That was part of the deal.

You're given a house and access to funds to live on. Of course, that meant he hadn't really needed to get a job, but it had seemed like a good way to integrate into the local community and build those connections. Obviously that had worked, it had done what he'd wanted it to, and he just donated the extra cash he earned from it straight to a charity. It wasn't much, but it at least made him feel like he was actually doing something helpful with his life. It wasn't his full, proper, purpose; but he got to pick a different charity each month and there was something fun in that. It also eased the guilt he felt about how little impact he was having.

He dumped his bag by the door and made his way inside his home. He headed straight for the kitchen, only briefly glancing into the living room on his way past, and started the kettle boiling. He felt the urge for some strong coffee before he got on with the rest of the day. He paused though, after he'd clicked the kettle on, as something dawned on him. He turned and headed straight back to the living room, popping his head around the door and looking in. There, on a raggedy old arm-chair that he'd inherited with the house, sat a woman. He'd seen her on the way past but she hadn't registered. That was weird. She wore a stern expression that came as a result of having clearly waited longer than she cared to.

"Wha...who are you?" He stammered out, trying to recover from the shock of a stranger in his living room and also buy time to assess how much of a threat she was.

"Good Afternoon, Agent." She said and then, as if she could tell what he was thinking from his face she let out a condescending snort and continued. "Don't you think if I were one of them I'd have already attacked?" She asked, in a rigid and incredibly formal tone. There was no warmth in her voice, or on her face as she spoke. He heard the kettle boiling in the kitchen.

"Can I offer you a drink, umm...?" He asked, rushing the question because of his eagerness to break the tension but faltering when he realised he didn't know her name.

"Rachel," She said, her tone still cold and unwavering. "I'm a Level Four Agent, here on behalf of the Custodians. Your new Level Four Agent, as it happens. You report to me with immediate effect."

"Oh, okay. I never met my last Level Four." Louis explains, a little sheepish.

"Did you ever ask to?" She says, with a raised eyebrow.

"Well, no, but I never really had a reason to."

"Tell me, what have you been doing here?"

"Blending in and waiting." He shrugs. "You know, waiting for something, anything really, to happen."
"Waiting to be told what to do?" The eyebrow is still raised and the tone is almost accusatory.
"Well no but..." He trails off. She makes a small noise of disappointment and drums her fingers on the arm of the chair.
"What do you want, Louis?"
"I'm sorry, I don't think I understand."
"From this." She says, raising her hands and looking around. "From this life. You finished your training and then you've done nothing but sit and wait to be told what to do."
"I want to be able to help. That's the point of us. I want to..." He hesitates.
"You want to what?" She asks, leaning forward.
"...all those stories we were told as kids." He stops, thinking about it. Rachel waits for him to finish. He knows she'll have been told the same stories. They all were. Every single child that was raised to be a Custodian will have been taught the same stories, the ones of triumph, and all the successful battles throughout the years where the Used-to-Bes were held back. "All the Agents who mattered. The ones who saved people. I want to be just like them. I want to be a hero. Isn't that what we all want?"
"Then stop waiting." She says, abruptly. "I've wasted enough time here, and so have you." She stands, brushing the creases from her clothes. "I'm transferring you. You'll have received an email with your train tickets."
"But..." He begins. It's not so much a protest as it is to voice any one of the whirlwind of questions in his mind. She completely ignores his interruption and continues.
"Your new team will be expecting you. The address and details you need are contained within the same email. I will rendezvous with you all there to discuss our strategy moving forward, following some other business I need to attend to." She concludes, starting towards the door.
"Wait. Why now?" He hurries to ask. She stops, visibly considering whether or not to answer and, even as she does, clearly chooses her words carefully.
"There's been...an incident which means I need additional resource, and you are available. Your train is in an hour. That should be enough time to pack your belongings." She turns to leave, making it clear there is no more time for questions or objections. He falls into line, remembering who he's supposed to be.

"Yes ma'am." He replies, with a nod. The door quickly closes behind her and he's left alone. He looks around, kind of sadly. For a long time he's wanted this to happen, something to come along to mean that he can fulfil his purpose in life and actually make a difference in the world but now that it's happened he's realising that it means he'll need to leave his life here in Jongleton behind. He'll need to leave all those people he formed a bond with behind. This chapter of his life, this somewhat boring and mundane chapter, is over and it's on to the next one. He's jolted into action as he realises he has very little time to actually pack and starts frantically collecting things, leaving the boiling water in the kettle unused.

An hour later Louis was on a train for the first time in his life. It was a very strange experience. When he'd first graduated from his training he'd been bundled into the back of a people carrier with some other graduates and driven away. He'd been handed a small envelope with details about the village, his identity there, and the keys to his house. The car had made several stops, quietly dropping off one of his classmates at each, before eventually his time had come. He'd heard from his Level Four supervisor periodically since then, always just by email, but it was the last time he'd had any real contact with anyone from the vast organisation that he was part of. Like the others that day, it was the furthest away from Home Base he had ever been, as far as he could remember. They'd been sheltered within those walls, protected from the world while they learned how to protect it. So, yeah, the feeling of being on a train was weird.

He was standing like a spare part because he didn't have a reserved seat. He'd made the mistake initially of finding one and then having to vacate when a couple came along who'd booked it. He hovered in the aisle like a spare part because he didn't really want to run the risk of another awkward social interaction, of someone else demanding that he move. Eventually the train got busier and he wasn't the only one standing. He also didn't really want to let his luggage out of his sight either. The tattered bag he'd found in a cupboard one day now contained the only belongings he had. Presumably the next occupant of that house would inherit everything he'd left behind, because he assumed that was how it worked. He wondered how long it'd be until another Agent was stepping into his life. There was a pang of sadness at that.

The advantage of standing was that it was better for 'people watching,' and that was something he'd grown to enjoy. He liked to look at the humans around him and try to work out who they were. The couple who had claimed his seat fawned over each other. They were a little older than him but they giggled to each other like children, and he thought that was adorable. There was an older lady, too, who he'd nearly fallen on one time when the train jolted. They chatted for a bit, and he'd told her how he was moving for a new job because that wasn't entirely a lie. She'd wished him luck before she got off at her stop. The email from Rachel had given him some information, but not a lot. He knew he was going to a town called Endsbrough which was the sixth stop that this train made. He also knew that after that he was heading to 11 Brickmere Road which was around a forty minute walk away from the station. But that was it. She'd also referred to a team. He knew in some towns, and certainly in cities, Custodians operated in teams. In Jongleton he'd been alone but nothing had ever happened there and so he suspected there had never been a need for more than one Agent in the area. He didn't know how many people he was going to be working with now, or anything about them, and that scared and excited him. For the last year he'd felt so isolated at times. He'd made friends but he'd always had to hold this piece of himself and his real purpose back, and that had been really hard. He was looking forward to now having people he didn't have to hide from. But, he was also scared because they would all no doubt be more experienced than him and what if they hated him for that? Either way, at least he'd have people he wouldn't need to lie to, and that was something. Eventually, the train reached Endsbrough station and he, and a few others, disembarked and set off walking on his own to find Brickmere Road and everything that awaited him there.

I never got to meet Alex but their death had such an impact on my life. It kick-started this whole thing. That's why we started with Alex's death, because that caused a ripple that brought me to Endsbrough. If it wasn't for that one thing I wouldn't be where I am now, I wouldn't be who I am now. It's just funny to think back, isn't it? To look at something and wonder how that incident could've changed the course of your life. We're going to come across a lot of those and believe me when I tell you I've spent a lot of time in my own head wondering how they could've changed my life. Alex had travelled all around the world, I think I mentioned that earlier, and they had saved so many lives doing it. Was Alex a hero? The definition goes something like 'a person who is admired for their courage, outstanding achievements, or noble qualities.' Humans all strive for admiration, but people like Alex and I have it drummed into us our whole lives that we are created to be heroes, and that we have to be heroic above all else. We are, quite literally, chosen to be the 'good guys.' I'm using inverted commas when I say that because we're not chosen by fate or something else intangible, we're picked by others to do it. People with their own agenda.

I don't know if that makes Alex a hero or somebody else's tool. I don't know how much either of us chose this life or just had it picked for us. I don't think it matters, really, but I wanted to give you some level of context because this isn't a story of heroes and villains and I don't want it to be. I'd hate for you to think that's what I'm trying to tell. This is just a story of people. This is just the story of how that ripple turned me into who I am. Hero, villain, or something else. You can decide. It's all about perspective and you're only going to get mine.

This is just my version of history mixed with a few things I've pulled from reports that were filed or from stories I was told, and memories I inherited. That's how I can tell you about Alex even though I wasn't there, how I can tell you about everything. I spent so long trying to piece it all together and I still don't think I'm fully there. But, let's not talk about where I am, let's talk about where I was. The day after Alex was killed, getting off that train and making my way to the house at Brickmere Road, completely clueless to everything. That person is worlds apart from who I am now, and I really do hate him for it.

Chapter Three.

And in that house on Brickmere Road another kettle has boiled. The water in this one will not go to waste though, because a woman called Lauren happily pours it into four separate cups. She hums to herself as she does, brushing her long, dark, curly hair out of her face and double checking to make sure she's made the drinks correctly. Three milky teas, two with sugar, and one strong black coffee. She collects them all on a tray, with a pack of biscuits she's discovered in the cupboard. She picks up the tray and saunters along the corridor with it, taking her time to approach the room that there are still raised voices coming from. She braces herself before opening the door, and pops a cheery smile back on her face.

"...raid the files. No one's told me not to." Says Amber, quite aggressively to the other two in the room. Her messily tied, bright red dyed, hair is a complete match to her overall demeanour. If there is one colour that describes her personality perfectly, it's red. The room itself, the one they've christened as their War Room, is a mess. It usually is, but today especially so. It's the room they all spend the most time in, especially when there's something to investigate. There are papers strewn over the table in the middle, any snippets of notes they could find without breaking protocol and properly going through Alex's things. They've been trying to piece together exactly what happened all night with one hand tied behind their back because of that protocol. Lauren hands Amber her cup of tea first, hoping it'll distract her from barking at the others.

"I'm telling you not to." Chris replies. He keeps his tone level and his face unmoving. Lauren looks at the two of them, sitting at opposite ends of the table, as she hands Chris his sweet tea and thinks about how in that moment they look like complete opposites. He's dark skinned, tall, and broad. He has incredibly short, shaved hair, and is remaining perfectly composed. She is slim, but muscular, ridiculously pale and masking her fear with anger.

"Nobody with any real authority," She fires back and Lauren knows it's time to intervene.

"I'll take these!" She tells them, interjecting as she grabs their empty cups from the table and places them on her tray. "I brought biscuits this time too. I thought we could all do with a little sustenance." She offers Chris the pack and he shakes his head politely. She does the same with Amber and she grabs one and bites it violently, continuing to glare at Chris as she chomps. Lauren then turns to the third member of their group, swapping his empty cup for the fresh coffee. "Coffee for you Danny." She says, forcing her voice to almost sing-song levels of warmth to counter the other two. Danny, who hasn't been engaging in the argument, barely looks up at her from his laptop screen. Whilst the other two have been arguing about the best way forward he's been scouring the internet. Although they had managed to secure the scene of Alex's death he was obsessively making sure there had been no other witnesses. There was still so much they didn't understand and he hated that.

"Are you sure you don't want tea instead?" She asks, double checking. He rolls his eyes, but does so with a little smirk. She's been trying to get him to switch to tea for months. She knows he won't, but it's her little joke with him. He's always been a little difficult for her to bond with and if she can make him smile by pestering him over his hot beverage choice then that's what she'll keep doing. "Can I get anyone anything else? Any more biscuits or anything?"

"Make him listen to me. Let me go raid the room. The door is open already, just pretend you don't know what's happening. I don't see that being a stretch for you!" Amber snaps, the instant she's finished chewing. Lauren sighs, takes her own cup and sits down, knowing this argument isn't going to end any time soon.

"I've had strict orders from Level Four…" Chris tries to explain. She cuts him off.

"Exactly. You had strict orders. I haven't." She's challenging, and she's pushing it. Amber always pushes it, but usually she's at least vaguely aware of where the line is. Now, it doesn't seem that she is.

"Amber, you're included. You all are." Chris replies, still battling to remain calm.

"Sorry, must've missed that, I'm having problems with my hearing." Maybe she does know where the line is and has just chosen today to be the day she somersaults over it.

"Maybe we need something more substantial than biscuits. Anyone for a sandwich?" Lauren interjects, again trying to diffuse the situation. They ignore her. Clearly it's going to take more than snacks this time.

"Amber!" He snaps, unable to hold his frustration back any longer. "You will listen to me. Those are our orders. Yours and mine. We leave Alex's things alone until Rachel arrives. We do not have the clearance to go investigating…"

"I don't care about clearance! Why are you not worried? If there's something out there that can kill a Level Three then the rest of us are in serious shit."

"I understand Amber, it's just…" He trails off. He doesn't have an end to that sentence, because he knows she's right. The silence between them hangs in the air. They're both glaring, frustrated with each other and with the situation. Frustrated with their own lack of knowledge and with their own helplessness. Danny breaks the silence by slurping his coffee, looking up from his laptop screen at the two of them. The dim screen illuminates his pale but perfect skin wonderfully, almost like he's deliberately angled it that way. Danny is beautiful in the most annoying way, and he probably knows it.

"If you two are done, I've found something." He says, coolly with a soft

smile that contrasts yet compliments his sharp cheekbones.
"Talk to me." Chris says, quickly rushing around so that he can see the screen. Danny, moving at entirely his own pace, hits a few keys and the video he's been looking at appears on a screen on the wall.
"I've been looking at all the surveillance footage near where we found the body. Look, I found one close by where Alex goes past at 17:59. You and Amber go by at 18:06." He explains.
"Okay, so what?" Asks Chris, trying to get Danny to the point. Danny obliges by playing the footage, which shows Jon Hamilton limping desperately away from the scene of Alex's death.
"There's only one other person in that seven minute window. This guy." Danny explains, sitting back triumphantly. "He's our lead."
"So he's one of them? The murderer maybe?" Amber asks.
"No, I don't think so, he looks terrified," Lauren adds.
"Agreed. Obviously human, and the way he's limping I think he got caught in the crossfire." Danny says.
"Or he's one of them and Alex went down fighting." Amber argues.
"Then what was he running from?" Danny asks with a judgemental tut.
"Either way, let's find him and make him tell us what he knows." She replies, looking like she's ready to go there and then.
"No, Amber..." Chris begins, but he's interrupted by the doorbell. "Perfect, this must be her. She can advise how we proceed." He makes his way out into the corridor. Amber takes his place over Danny's shoulder.
"Quick, Dan, gimme a good shot of this guy..." She demands.

Chris tears open the front door eager to catch Rachel up on where they're at so far. He's desperate to tell her about the witness they've just found, and to get her guidance on how to continue. His team are completely out of their depth and he is painfully aware of it. His face drops when he sees a skinny, scruffy looking, mousy haired boy standing there with a dopey smile on his face.
"Hi, I..." Louis begins.
"No, sorry." Chris says, holding up a massive hand to silence him. "I don't have the time."
"What? I was..." Louis continues, his eyes wrinkling in confusion.
"Kid, I said I don't have time. I don't care what you're selling." Chris only has a few years on the boy on the doorstep, but that doesn't matter. He can tell from his face this clueless child doesn't have the first idea what

really goes on in the world.
"Who the hell is this?" Amber demands, sticking her head out of the War Room and into the corridor. She stares at him with impatience that's almost identical to Chris'. It's the most united they've been in quite some time.
"He's nobody." Chris says as he starts to close the door but Amber barks out another question, this time directed at Louis.
"You, who are you?" She strides forward and Chris sighs and moves away, not wanting to waste any more time.
"I'm Louis. I've been assigned here?" He says in a way that's definitely more of a question than a statement. It's enough to make Chris stop in his tracks and whirl around.
"Wait, what?" Amber says.
"Assigned by whom?" Chris demands.
"A Level Four named Rachel." Louis says, his eyes flicking between the two of them in utter confusion. This wasn't the welcome he'd expected at all. "Am I in the right place?"
"Did I hear that right? New team member?!" Lauren says excitedly, bursting through in the hallway and pushing past both Amber and Chris who stand there in a stunned silence glaring at him.
"Umm, yeah?" Louis replies, still thoroughly unsure what's happening or if he's done something terribly wrong.
"Well don't just stand there." She says, beaming at him. "Come on in!" She grabs his bag from the doorstep and ushers him inside, closing the door behind him. "Welcome! What's your name?"
"It's Louis."
"I'm Lauren. We'll put your bag here for now and find somewhere for it later. We'll need to rearrange a few things. I'm sorry we didn't know you were coming or I'd have made sure there was a room ready for you. Nevermind though, we'll sort something out." She babbles at him, mentally wondering how to work the sleeping arrangements. Alex's room is inaccessible to them, and even then, it had been Chris' room previously. He had given it up when Alex had turned up out of the blue a few months ago, saying they were here on a classified mission. He'd practically fallen over himself to give up his room when he realised they were a Level Three Agent, and had been sleeping on the sofa bed ever since. She could put a spare bed in the training room in the loft; but would need to go out and get one later. Amber also wouldn't be particularly happy about that space being invaded, but she'd have to get over it. Lauren leads Louis through

into the War Room where Danny's attention has gone back to his screen.
"Danny this is…" She begins presenting him.
"Agent Louis Smith." Danny replies, his tone cold. His gaze flicks up to the new arrival very briefly, and he seems to look him up and down without actually looking directly at him. He sneers and looks at Chris, who's walked in behind them. "His files just came through. He's got no experience. At all. We don't need this." Louis is completely taken aback by this and just stares, open mouthed, at him. He's not sure what to say but thankfully Lauren is quick to jump to his defence.
"Danny!" She says, chastising him. He shrugs in response.
"It's true. He went straight from training to some tiny village where he's spent over a year doing nothing. He's useless. He's dead weight. We can't afford to carry him." There's no venom in his voice; it's cold and factual, talking as if Louis isn't even there.
"Louis, I'm so sorry. Please, have a seat." She ushers, or forces, him into a seat as he stands staring at Danny, still a little gobsmacked.
"Don't apologise for me. I'm being pragmatic. Chris, will you please weigh in?"
"I agree with Dan, we don't need to be babysitting some newbie. It doesn't sound like he could identify a Used-to-Be if there was one in front of him." Amber says, following them into the room, having taken a quick detour to the fridge to grab some cold meat as a snack.
"Can I take a look at his field reports?" Chris asks, trying to tread delicately. Danny snorts and pushes the laptop across the table towards him.
"Be my guest but there's very little to see." He says, shrugging and sitting back in his chair. He's still not looking at Louis, as if pretending he isn't there will make it so. Chris' face betrays that he doesn't like what he sees on the screen, or rather, he doesn't like that lack of what he sees.
"It's a little scarce but that's just because…" Louis begins to offer, sheepishly. Danny cuts him off with a snort.
"A little scarce" He repeats, mocking him with a laugh.
"Danny." Lauren hisses.
"He's right Lauren. This…" Chris begins. He takes a deep breath, trying his best to be more diplomatic than his team mate. It's not hard to be more diplomatic than Danny. "This must've been a mistake. Agent, who did you say told you to come here?"
"Transfer paperwork was done by Rachel." Danny offers, before Louis has the chance to speak for himself.

"Must've been before last night. It's stupid to bring him here now." Amber interjects.
"You're probably right. We'll straighten this out when she gets here. The circumstances have changed."
"Can I get you a drink at all? Tea? Coffee? Juice?" Lauren asks. She speaks loudly as if that will drown out the others.
"No, don't make him a drink, he's not staying."
"Yep. I'd just go now if I were you. Back to your…" Amber peers at the laptop now and snorts. "…job as the local postman huh? That's brilliant. Back to that!"
"Agent, look, I am sorry. This isn't personal. It's just obviously some kind of admin error. We'll get this straightened out and have you home before nightfall."
"How about that drink?"
Louis looks at them all, open mouthed like a goldfish, in a kind of stunned silence. He doesn't really know what to say as they debate his future without really acknowledging him. Lauren tries to distract him.
"I…" He begins. He's cut off by the sound of the front door opening and shutting. The team tense up and their heads collectively snap towards the door to the hallway. They relax, or rather show tension differently, as Rachel marches briskly in.
"Good, you're all here." She says, her sharp tone showing that she wants to get straight to the point. She tosses her coat to Chris, and stops at the head of the table. She stands with her back towards the window so that her silhouette is illuminated from the late morning sunshine. It makes her look heroic, like she's a metaphorical ray of hope. For Louis she is, because she's shut them all up. Her gaze scans them all one by one, and as she locks on Chris he realises he's still clutching her coat, so he scurries to hang it up. "I can see you've all met your new teammate. Louis, welcome." She nods at him, and he smiles nervously, looking down at his feet.
"Yeah, about that…" Chris begins, hurrying back into the room so that he doesn't miss anything.
"Someone bring me up-to-speed? I expect you have something for us to go on by now." Just like that Chris' objections are silenced and without missing a beat Danny brings the image of Jon Hamilton back onto the screen.
"We want to speak to this guy. Footage shows him fleeing the scene

around the time Alex was killed, we believe he's human, a potential witness."

"Interesting. Let's do it. What of the UTB? Any progress there?" She asks. Chris clears his throat, desperate to take the lead in updating her, and jumps in.

"No, the team and I have been scouring the local surveillance feeds but no one else has been picked up. This man appears to be our best bet of finding the creature that killed Alex."

"Understood. I've had authorisation to view the agent's personal logs, which I hope will provide more information. I'll need you to gather them for me shortly. How do you intend to find out who this human is?"

"I...Danny, any leads?" Chris asks, turning to Danny in a panic. Danny glares at him, noticing how quickly he passed the focus back when he didn't know the answer.

"Not yet, anyone else got any ideas?" He replies flippantly, and he looks at Louis, as if daring him to come up with something. "I was wondering if Louis had any pearls of wisdom to offer from his extensive experience? No? Okay, I've got a clear image, I'll start searching with that. I should have him soon."

"Excellent." Rachel replies, completely ignoring the very thinly veiled hostility. She either didn't pick up on it or didn't care enough to address it, but they all definitely noticed. "What about your police contacts? If he's human and he's seen something he might've contacted the human police."

"Brilliant idea." Chris chimes in, sounding a bit like a child desperate for approval. "Lauren, have you heard anything from your contact?"

"No but I can reach out to him." She says.

"Good." Rachel replies, before Chris can. "Amber, I've not signed off on an inventory of the weapons you hold on site for some time. Perhaps now is a good time to take stock?"

"To...what?"

"You're the combat expert of this team. Surely at a time like this maintenance of weapons and ammunition is paramount?"

"I...guess. I'll get right on that." She says, giving an all too sarcastic thumbs up. Rachel ignores that too as Amber doesn't even try to hide her annoyance at being given an admin task to do.

"Before you do that." Rachel says. She straightens herself up, pushes out her chest, and clears her throat. They all pay attention. "While you're all still here I want to say I understand your frustration. We are all working with

an incomplete story and that can be daunting. One of our own, a Level Three no less, has been lost and we all need to make sense of that. My expectation is that you all give me your very best. I need you all to see beyond your fear and confusion. There's a huge spotlight on us right now, this is a great chance for us to show what we're worth. Get it done. Chris, you're with me." Having been given their assignments they all go to work, except Louis who stands, looking like a spare part. Lauren pats him on the shoulder and gestures for him to follow her out of the room.
"I'm not sure I followed much of that." He admits to her, somewhat sheepishly. She smiles kindly back at him, leading the way to the kitchen. "That's okay sweetie, it sounds like this is still pretty new to you. Tell me which bits you followed and I'll fill in the rest."

Chapter Four.

Exposition time, I suppose. At the beginning of the world there were two opposing forces. You know that story. Of course you do. It's every story, more or less. It's the same story over, and over, and over, and over, and over, and over, and over again. It's ingrained in us all, through folklore, through religion, through life. It's good and evil, it's God and the Devil, it's Yin and Yang.
These two powerful forces coexisted for a time. They worked together, with their powers combined. I don't trust our records on this because they're vague and contradictory, but these two might've even created our world together. They were ancient, even at the beginning.
But after harmony came conflict. Something changed and they disagreed. Their partnership, or relationship, dissolved. Some say it was over you. The human race. The apes that had started to walk on two legs. That would make sense. The Demon, one of the two, didn't think very highly of you. He saw humanity as lesser beings, animals that just weren't worth the life they were given.
It would've happened eventually though. Powerful beings can't coexist forever; and if they were the only two beings in existence it's a miracle they weren't at each other's throats centuries before. Then again, they might've been. It might've been that the human race, who I suppose were akin to their pets, was just the last straw. The records are vague because these beings existed before we even had language to document it. But, it also

doesn't matter what the catalyst was because, like I said, they were Good and Evil. That partnership would've always dissolved.

What came next is even less clear. The Demon left. He was either driven out, or chose to leave. He was either imprisoned or moved on to another world, or another plane. That's not the important bit. The important bit is that although he left he wasn't ever completely gone. There were pieces of him left behind; little tiny bits of demonic energy that ripped through this world like a disease. They infected places, and animals, and people. They twisted and corrupted them. They caused destruction and then moved on and caused more. He didn't need to stay because he poisoned the world he left behind.

That energy still exists and it's everywhere. It's invisible, especially to you, but it's there. It can change people, it can twist things, it can cause chaos, and destruction. It's magic. It's evil. It's everything else that the stories tell you about. The effects will vary because it can combine with any number of things, any number of variables, but all through history there have been people infected by this energy doing awful things. Some you've heard of, others you haven't. Think warlords who embodied the power of the Gods, mysterious killers who disappeared without a trace, or the ones driven to commit genocide. Think about leaders who've abused their power and left nothing but misery in their wake. I'm not saying humans aren't shit all on their own, but they're significantly more shit, and more powerful, once the darkness in them has been amplified and supercharged.

The Demon didn't have to stay, because the pieces of himself could do the damage for him. But, since you know the story you also know what comes next. The other side of the coin. The fighting back. Ever since the infections started there have been people there to fight them off. Knights. Hunters. Warriors. Agents. Custodians. Whatever. Humans, pulled from their lives as children and set on a course for Good. A secret organisation, across the globe, with thousands of us hidden in plain sight, ready to combat any person or thing that's been infected by demonic energy. That's what I am. That's what Alex was. The creature we're now tracking is a person who was infected and empowered by demonic energy. Someone who used to be human. A "Used-to-Be."

"Yeah, that about covers it." Lauren said, encouragingly, once Louis had finished relaying his understanding to her. She then took out her phone and made a call.

At the front desk of Endsbrough Police Station Desk Sergeant Jack Appleby sits leaning back in his chair, with the phone to his ear. With his free hand he's playing a game on his mobile while he listens to the caller. He periodically gives a very bored sounding "uh-huh" to the caller. He looks up as he hears footsteps from down the hall and cranes his neck, creating a bit more space between his chins, to see Detective Chief Inspector Matthew Wade walking down the corridor towards him. Wade is a man of similar age and build to Appleby. That is to say, he's on the wrong side of middle-aged, and out of shape. He still has a good head of hair on his head, even though it's more grey than it is brown now, and the stubble from not being bothered to shave for a few days. They're well acquainted, and Wade greets him with a familiar nod. Appleby holds his finger to his lips in a shushing motion which Wade responds to with an inquisitive scowl.

"Yes, Agent Smith. I will absolutely pass that along and ask him to get in touch with you when he's in." Appleby says to the caller, but locks eyes with Wade so that he knows that is why he was shushed. Wade responds by rolling his eyes and stifling a groan. "Yep, absolutely. Alright then. Yep. Okay. Bye now." Appleby continues, desperate in his attempt to wrap the call up. He slams down the handset with a sigh of relief and locks eyes with Wade.

"Lemme guess, that was 'Counter Terrorism'?" He asks, with an inquisitive but impatient look.

"Aye. Thought she'd never piss off." Appleby answers.

"What did they want this time?"

"I dunno. It was that Lauren. Never tells me out. Just insists on speaking to you. Reckon she's got a crush?" Appleby smirks at him, trying to tease his superior officer. Wade rolls his eyes, clearly very low on patience.

"She's probably just fishing for more cases to take away from us. It's been a few weeks since they nicked one. Cheers for telling her I wasn't around though."

"Ah, of course. I don't want to help them any more than you do."

"Nah, it's not that it's…" He pauses and his forehead wrinkles in thought. "Nevermind. Just keep an eye out. Normally if she can't get hold of me they just turn up."

"I've not seen you all day, Detective Chief Inspector. You're always bloody wandering off." Appleby says as he shrugs, sitting back in his chair and

putting his feet up on the desk.
"Yeah. Cheers." Wade responds, turning around and walking back in the direction he came from. He passes a couple of uniformed officers down the hall and makes sure he's out of earshot of everyone else before he pulls his phone out. The caller on the other end answers but he doesn't even wait for them before he launches, angrily, into a rant. "You'll never guess who's just called fishing for information again. Those bloody Counter Terrorism wankers…"

Meanwhile, in the house on Brickmere Road, Lauren hangs up her phone with a perky smile.
"What a lovely man," She says to Louis, about Appleby, completely oblivious to the fact she's just been lied to and is now being insulted. That's very Lauren, though, she absolutely loves to find the positives in people rather than the negatives and that's very admirable. She takes a large gulp of her tea. "So, where did we get to?"
"You were going to tell me about Alex?" Louis replies.
"Ah, yes! So they turned up here a few months ago and told us very little unfortunately. We worked out they were on the trail of some Used-to-Be they'd tracked, seemingly all over the globe, but that's about as far as we got. Amber and Danny weren't happy about that, which I think already won't be a surprise to you…" Louis shakes his head in response, biting his lip because he's not quite worked out the dynamic of the team's relationships and is scared to say any more. But, he's very sure they didn't like it. He's very sure that Danny doesn't like much. "…but of course that's all part of the job isn't it? Especially with a Level 3. If one of them turns up you pretty much just have to fall in line and do as you're told."
"I wouldn't know really. I don't think I've ever seen one outside of Home Base." He replies.
"That's true. Alex was only the second I've encountered in the field, but you still know the chain of command, regardless?"
"Yeah of course."
"Good, I'm not sure everyone around here does but still, their hearts are in the right place. They may be a little… well, you know. But I always think it's better to just get on with it." She explains.
"A little…?" Danny asks, having been hovering in the kitchen doorway, unbeknownst to them. Lauren, unphased, chuckles to herself and avoids giving an answer. Luckily, Danny doesn't wait long for one either. "If you're

done with storytime I think I've found something."
"I'm about to nip up and check in on Rachel and Chris." She says, gesturing to two cups of tea. "But why don't you talk Louis through it?" Since Louis arrived Danny's face had been wearing a constant expression of dissatisfaction, a seemingly permanent sneer. It was the most unimpressed Louis had ever seen anyone look and, yet, somehow, at that suggestion his face seemed to drop even further. He found new levels of disgust. Levels that no person had ever found before.
"No." He says, simply.
"Danny…"
"He's too dumb to understand."
"I can hear you, you know."
"I'm aware." He says, with an unapologetic shrug. Louis opens his mouth, trying desperately to come up with a reply while trying to shake off the unbelievable rudeness but he doesn't get a chance. Danny turns his attention to Amber, who is walking down the stairs. She also looks unhappy; but that comes more from boredom than anything else.
"Good! Someone I can brag to." Danny says, scarily close to sounding positive about something. He turns and leaves the kitchen, gesturing for her to follow him back into the War Room. Lauren meanwhile picks up the cups of tea and heads to the stairs. She nods for Louis to follow the two of them into the War Room and, even though it's absolutely the last thing he wants to do at that moment, he does. If this is what it takes to force his way into this team, he'll do it.
"Have you got something?" Amber is asking as Louis enters. Danny smirks in response, but it's an annoying smirk. It's the kind of smirk of someone who thinks they're far cleverer than they are.
"Of course I've got something." He says and sits back at his laptop. He pulls the CCTV footage that they found earlier back up onto the screen; it shows the image of Jon Hamilton running away from the scene where Alex died. They, of course, don't currently know that his name is Jon Hamilton, but, obviously, we do because I told you earlier.
"Jon Hamilton." Danny says, bringing the others in on the secret. The image on the screen changes to a clearer image of Jon standing next to a woman. They're both well dressed, obviously at some kind of formal occasion. "Pictured here in a magazine article with his sister Amelia. People care more about her than him, but it helped. Now with a little more technical wizardry…by which I mean I was able to hack into the HR

database for the company he works for...I've got his home address." Danny says, continuing to brag. He stops, clearly waiting for praise.
"That's really clever." Louis offers, a little shyly. Danny pauses, looking over at him and acknowledging that he's in the room for the first time.
"Wow. I'm sorry." He says.
"What for?"
"Am I going too fast? I mean, okay, this is something called a laptop. I know, you're probably not used to seeing them. Just wait, when I've got a little more time I'll tell you about this thing called the internet that'll really blow your mind."
"I know what the internet is. I know what a laptop is. Jongleton wasn't that bad, you know? Yes it was quiet. But it was nice. The people were nice."
"Oh well, as long as the people were nice, who cares about anything else? Who cares about the fact you've got absolutely no field experience, or clue what's happening? Who cares you're so inexperienced you'll probably get yourself or us killed?" He snaps, dropping even the faux pleasantness he had a moment ago. He turns back to Amber before Louis has a chance to reply, not that he really had a retort to any of that, because he knew a lot of it was true. "So what do you say, do you want to take a break from counting your grenades or whatever and go see him?"
"I'm in. I'm so done with paperwork. You coming?" She asks, hiding a snigger at his brutality towards Louis.
"Can't." He puts his hand on top of a closed laptop to the side of him. "They're going through Alex's things. Luckily I'm the only one here who can get into their laptop. If I'm not here to do it now I might not get another chance, and I want to see if there's anything there I can accidentally get a glimpse of."
"Gotcha. Yeah. Remember to share?"
"Of course." He replies. Amber, shockingly, turns to Louis.
"What about you?"
"What about me?" He stutters in response.
"Do you want to come with me?"
"Yes!" He practically shouts, taken aback by the invite. "Wait, really?"
"Yes. Chris will never let me go alone, and I don't want him there. Or Rachel. This human is my best bet of finding out what's going on, assuming he definitely is human, and I want to get all the information I can out of him. You're the least worst option as long as you don't get in my way. Just keep your mouth shut. I'm already finding this perky enthusiasm

annoying. If I wanted that I'd invite Lauren. Got it?" She asks. He opens his mouth to reply but catches himself just in time, says nothing and just nods. She raises her eyebrows, clearly surprised. "Good. Dan, send the address to my phone."
"Already done." He says, shrugging.
"Call me if I miss anything good?" She asks, getting up from her chair. Danny is about to answer when Rachel marches into the room.
"Update me?" She demands, sharply. Chris follows her, and then Lauren.
"I've found the human. Amber and Louis are going to go and question him." Danny says. It's less of a brag this time though, and he doesn't seem to be expecting praise. Rachel clearly takes a moment to think. She looks at Amber, then at Louis, assessing them both. Eventually, she gives a nod of approval.
"Good. But, be cautious. If he's a Used-to-Be call for back-up. If he is a human, as we suspect, then he needs to be quarantined immediately. Don't take time to question him, just get a Cleaning crew to him."
"Yes, of course." Amber says. Louis eyes her with a little confusion because her tone is completely different to how it was before Rachel entered the room. She obviously doesn't intend to quarantine Jon immediately. But Louis' curiosity is also piqued. There's a lot of confusion going on, confusion about who or what killed Alex and what they were investigating and he's not against finding out more. As Danny seems to delight in pointing out, he's not had much experience outside of their training and this seems like the perfect chance to get into something. So, he decides, he won't be objecting too much if Amber decides to ignore Rachel's instructions a little. They both head towards the door as she gives them a nod of dismissal and turns her focus to Danny and the laptop that's filled with secrets.
"How're you getting on?" She asks, placing her hand on it in a gesture that seems a little protective.
"Taking a little more time than I'd like, but I'll get into it…" Danny replies. His tone too is a much more respectful one with Rachel than it is when dealing with anyone else. It's not wholly without his blend of condescension, but it's a lot less obvious.
"Good. I need you to access the files on here, but don't read anything. I have clearance to view the records stored on here but you do not. I need to be very clear on that." She explains, coolly. Louis smiles to himself in the hallway, hearing the exchange, and wondering if Rachel had overheard

them or just suspected that Danny's curiosity could lead to him overstepping.
"Couldn't be any clearer…" Danny replies.
"Liar." Louis mutters to himself and thankfully no one hears.

Chapter Five.

In Endsbrough town centre a large crowd is gathering outside the Eagle Hotel. It's an old hotel that stands at the end of the High Street, right next to the exit to a shopping centre. It's a bulky brown building, late 60s in design, and has been the height of luxury within the town for many years. In front of the hotel, slightly away from the gathered crowd, stands a woman with a tight blonde bun and a bright, attention grabbing, red lipstick. Her name is Kimberly Adams, and she's giving a lot of thought to how she is being framed, as she has done many times before.
"Little to the left, sweetie." She says, not unkindly, to the work experience student she has with her. "I want the sign above the entrance in frame just about my shoulder but we also need to make sure we get a good shot of these cra…" She stops herself. "…passionate fans." Marc, the tall, skinny, awkward-looking 19-year-old Journalism student, shuffles the camera to the left as he's instructed without complaint. She's a perfectionist, but he's grateful to get the chance to learn from her. "Got it?" She checks.
"Yep!" He says brightly. "I think the shot is exactly how you want it."
"Good work," She says, with a wink, taking a large gulp to finish off her coffee. "And thanks again for this," She taps the empty cup before tossing it a few metres into a nearby bin with perfect aim.
"No worries Ms. Adams. Thanks again for letting me come." He says. Her face drops.
"Don't you dare call me Ms. Adams. I am not old enough to be Ms. Adams. You're lucky I let you come along, you should be stuck in the office making tea, like we normally have the work experience kids do." She snaps.
"I'm so sorry!" He stammers, his eyes widening in panic. She bursts out laughing.
"Oh my god your face! I'm kidding, I'm kidding. About the making tea part anyway, I actually would rather you call me Kim."
"Oh thank God I proper thought I'd offended you there." He says, breathing a sigh of relief. She smiles wickedly and raises her eyebrows at him.

"Nah, you need thick skin in this business kid. A thick skin and a lot of caffeine." She explains.

"Do you think...we'll see anyone famous at this thing?" He says, nodding over her shoulder to the crowd gathered just outside the hotel.

"You mean other than the hometown-hero-come-blushing-bride? I think so. A few soap stars, local businessmen and some reality TV rejects, if that's your bag,"

"Sounds more famous than anyone I've met."

"Ha. Don't get too starstruck, especially at this thing. I'll make a massive deal out of when we're on air but this isn't the stuff that matters. This is just the fluff, not why you get into journalism." She pulls out a pair of thick rimmed glasses and pops them on her face, skimming the intro that she's written. "Unless that's your thing, of course. It's perfectly valid journalism and god knows it pays the bills but, and call me idealistic all you want, it's not the celeb stories that make the difference." She finishes, putting her notes back down. She looks up at him over her glasses and he smiles nervously. He's still excited to see c-list celebrities, he just doesn't want to look dumb in front of her. Kim smiles again, more to herself than anything. She can remember what that's like, it wasn't that long ago she was excited to meet anyone she recognised. "Hey, you know who owns the station, right?" Marc's eyes widen, and that's all she needs to see.

"Umm, yeah. I do. Will he be here?" Marc asks, nervously trying to hide his excitement. Alexander Buford, the owner of both SBC News and a whole list of other companies, is very well known. He's a celebrity and a businessman in his own right. Kim has only met him a handful of times but she made absolutely sure to make an impression.

"He is both a local businessman and a c-list celebrity. Though, don't tell him I called him a businessman. I know he's in town for it. If we see him I'll introduce you. See if we can get you something more permanent than two weeks unpaid?"

"Really?" He asks with his eyes lighting up.

"As long as you don't call me Ms. Adams again." She fiddles with her earpiece and positions herself right in the centre of where the camera is pointed, exactly in the shot she wanted. "We ready?"

"Yep!" He says, excitedly, nearly knocking the camera over in his rush to get behind it. She smiles a little bit but maintains her composure as she braces herself for live TV. Mentally, she's listening for her cue from the studio and counting herself in. Her demeanour shifts the second the handover happens and she laughs. It's warm, and not overtly fake, but it's not over the top either. It's the perfect amount of laughter for live TV because Kim Adams is a professional.

"Yes, absolutely. It's a big day here, with many calling it the wedding of the year as local soap-turned-movie-star Amelia Hamilton ties the knot with her fiancée and childhood sweetheart. They'll be married in a small private ceremony but the wedding reception will take place here, at the Eagle Hotel, with all the glitz and glamour you'd expect from a celebrity wedding. As you can see behind me hundreds of fans have gathered to catch a glimpse of the blushing bride and of the many a-listers who've been lucky enough to receive an invite." She says, both to the camera and to the hosts in the studio. She pauses as she listens to their response and laughs again in response. It's another warm and not too fake laugh that she's had a lot of practice perfecting. "No, I think mine must've got lost in the post. I'm not sure who I need to speak to about that but I'm going to ask around." She looks around, as if looking for a specific person, to add a little physical comedy to the act. She then looks back to the camera as she listens to another question from the studio. "Of course Kelly, you know me. I am keeping my eyes peeled. As soon as the guests start to arrive I'll see who'll speak to me – and you never know, I might end up as someone's plus one." She stops, frozen staring into the camera to give enough time to cut back to the studio. As soon as she's clear she becomes a flurry of activity again, directing Marc to follow her into the crowd. "Okay, and we're done. Right, let's start grabbing people now in case no one will speak to us while we're back live. Is there anyone you like the look of?" She gives him another friendly wink before she turns to look at the handful of smartly dressed guests who are arriving behind her from expensive cars which would usually have no right to be in Endsbrough town centre.

Inside the lavish reception of the Eagle Hotel Lisa sits behind the desk. A few guests have started to arrive, but no one she recognises. She's excited; this is the biggest event the hotel has held in the two years she's worked there and she, like Marc outside, is hoping she can catch a glimpse of someone famous. There have been famous people staying at the hotel every so often. It's one of the most luxurious hotels in Endsbrough and so when someone's in town they'll either stay here or at the Hilton. But, just because it's happened before doesn't mean that it's any less exciting. She's been keeping an eye on social media to see who is expected at this. The wedding itself happened at a quiet, intimate little church in the countryside with a few friends and family. It was very exclusive and, as much as she has scoured the tags, there are no photos of the bride and groom online just yet. That'll probably change when they arrive at the hotel of course. Lisa has already spotted several paparazzi and at least one local news crew.

A man clears his throat as he approaches and Lisa looks up and flicks back into smiling receptionist mode. She assesses him. He's tall and skinny, to the point he looks almost unhealthy. He's wearing a gorgeous floral light blue suit and as he gets closer she sees how it makes his blue eyes pop.

"Excuse me," He says, and she tosses her phone out of view. "Which room is the wedding in?" He smiles sweetly and glances around, as if expecting the answer to be right in front of him.

"Are you a guest?" Lisa asks, tentatively. He doesn't look like a wedding crasher, but the staff have all been warned to be vigilant.

"Why yes of course, Amy and I have been friends for years." He says with a friendly chuckle. Lisa's eyes widen at that.

"Really?" She asks, struggling to hide her excitement. A warm smile spreads across his sharp face.

"You know, it's remarkable. I always forget that dear Amelia is a celebrity. We've been friends since school, you see."

"Oh wow, what was that like?"

"Oh it was…" He pauses, just for a second, to think. "…exactly as you'd expect I suppose. In hindsight she always had a flare for acting. I did too of course but, you know, only a small handful of us can get lucky. I do remember going round to her house after school. Her parents were lovely. This is…well…before what happened to her dad. Very sad, of course."

"Wait, what happened to her dad?"

"Look, I don't think this is the right time or place to be discussing family tragedies do you…" He peers down at her name badge, narrowing his eyes. "Lisa?"

"Oh no, of course not." She replies, slightly panicked. "Sorry, I…I didn't mean any offence."

"No, don't be silly, none taken on my behalf." He says with another kind smile. "I'm Joseph, by the way. It's lovely to meet you."

"Oh, yeah." She says, taken aback as he stretches out his hand to shake hers. "You too."

"You're a fan, I take it? Of Amelia's, not mine?" He asks, with a faked chuckle.
"Yeah absolutely."
"Did you see that one film of hers? The one on the plane…?"
"Yes! The Flight of the Lost, I loved it!"
"That's the one. I got to go to the set for that one. I did consider taking a little something…"
"Did you?"
"No, no, I didn't have the guts in the end." He says, with a disarming laugh. "Anyway, enough of me taking up your time. Where am I going for the reception?"
"Ah, yes, it's in our Poseidon suite." She says.
"Perfect, thank you. I'll leave you to it." He says, and begins to walk away. He stops, and turns back to her with a thoughtful look on his face. "Say, Lisa. I've got a crazy idea."
"Yeah?" She says, cautious, but curious.
"What time do you finish?"
"6pm, why?" She says, with yet more caution in her voice.
"Well, I wondered if you'd like to come along as my plus one?"
"What?"
"I know that's a bit weird, and I'm not hitting on you, obviously, I'm rather hoping I can hit it off with one of the groomsmen, but I don't really know anyone besides Amelia. And I've enjoyed our brief chat, so, really, you'd be helping me out?" He explains, a little sheepish. She takes a moment to think about it. It is a crazy idea, but she does desperately want to say yes. She really has no reason not to. She's very aware that she can't be a hotel receptionist for the rest of her life. She has bigger aspirations than that and while she doesn't want to be an actor herself there will be several rich and influential people in that room tonight. It'll be a great opportunity to network. You only live once, she thinks to herself. A thought she'll come to think of as ironic, down the line.
"Yes. Okay. That'd be great." She says, eventually.
"Great. Wonderful. Come join when you get done then." He says. There's a wickedness to his grin that Lisa doesn't really pick up on. "I don't suppose you could show me where this Poseidon suite is?"
"Yes, yes, of course." She says, leaping up excitedly. "This way." She leads the way down a corridor. "Have you visited the set of any of her other films?" She asks as he trails behind her. He's taken out his phone and is

hurriedly typing a message. It's to a contact he has saved as "H" and it reads "Sorry again about last night. I've got something fun that will make up for it xx."

"Ten more seconds and I'm smashing it." Amber declares, glaring at the door.
"You can't just smash his door down?" Louis argues, in a timid way that's really half him asking her.
"Yes I can, who's going to stop me. You?" She responds, with more of a challenge than a question.
"Let me just try knocking again." He says, tapping on the wooden door of Jon Hamilton's home.
"Yeah because that worked so well the first ten times…" She begins, but he holds up a finger to shush her. She looks completely taken aback but does so more out of shock than obedience. He presses his ear to the door.
"I can hear something…" He explains, listening intently. "There's voices inside." He says. "Mr Hamilton? If you can hear us…" Amber elbows him out of the way roughly, pressing her own ear to the door. She nods confirming that she can hear it too and steps back. She reaches into her jacket, pulls out a small tranquilliser pistol and hands it over to him.
"Here. Do you know how to use this?" She asks.
"Yes." He replies, nodding to put extra emphasis on it.
"Are you sure? I can get you a sharp stick if you're more comfortable with it?"
"Amber…I don't think this is the…" He begins, annoyed at her for taking time to insult him. He doesn't get the time to finish though. She pushes against the door. It doesn't look like it's a hard push, but the wooden door splinters and flies from its hinges. She steps over the threshold, brandishing her own pistol and ready to fire. Louis follows her and they do a quick sweep of the house; starting with the hallway and then through into the living room. That is where they find the TV on, with a news reporter talking about a celebrity wedding. Amber drops her weapon and rolls her eyes, glaring at Louis.
"There's your 'voices,' Newbie. Don't think we're going to get much…" She stops, taking in the look on his face. He's pale and his eyes are darting around the floor. He looks manic and jerks suddenly, and moves towards the kitchen. He can feel something. A wave washing over him; something freezing cold and filled with pain and anger. There were people. They're

not here now, but they were. They were here and he doesn't understand how he knows that. It's getting stronger and stronger, this wave, as he moves towards the kitchen and he can't help but be drawn to it. Amber says something else but it's muffled to him now, like the wave has washed over him and he's hearing her from under water. He can hear shouting too, from someone else, they're also muffled and distorted. There are two people, one is scared and in incredible pain and the other is violently angry and also in incredible pain. He's moving towards the voices and the freezing cold pain, it's all in the kitchen and everything is smashed together. It's tearing him apart as much as it's pulling him in. He feels it in the pit of his stomach squeezing and pulling, he feels it stabbing in his heart and he feels a god awful brain shattering pain in his skull. He's dizzy, but he keeps stumbling towards the source of this. It must take only seconds but it feels like hours; like he's walking for miles listening to and feeling this all around him. Finally he gets there and he sees it, the source of some of the pain; Jon Hamilton's dead body, covered in blood from a crack in his skull. It's too much. Louis launches himself through the already open back-door as quickly as he can and vomits the second he's over the threshold.

Meanwhile, across town, the wedding reception of Amelia Hamilton and Carlos Jenkinson is in full swing. The music is playing, the wine is flowing freely, and everyone is in great spirits. Amelia sits for a moment, taking it all in. The speeches are done, the cake has been cut, and all that's left to do is dance. It's been a nearly perfect day. They always say things will go wrong and, of course, they have. The candles in the chapel weren't quite right. The music didn't play properly, partly thanks to Carlos' idiot best man being in charge of it, and her brother completely no-showed the ceremony all together. But, despite all of that, she loved it. Ever since her career really took off it seems so rare she does anything that's for her, something that doesn't come through her agent or publicist. It's a job she loves but sometimes it feels like it's taken over her life and like it's stifling her. It's not like that today though. It's never been like that with Carlos, in fact. He's always been her little bubble of normality. He's always kept her grounded and always made her feel safe, and now he's her husband. She smiles to herself with a little bit of giddy joy at that and gets up. Enough resting. She wants to go dance with her husband some more.

From the bar Joseph watches her go. He's been watching her all night. He checks the time. He's let the party continue this long and that was kind of him, really. But, he also wanted to see what all the fuss was about. A celebrity wedding at a fancy hotel, it's been a while since he's been to a party like this. It's been a disappointment so far. Utterly, utterly dull. Even that frightfully perky receptionist didn't liven it up. It's definitely time for the party to end, he thinks to himself. He finishes the rest of his drink and struts across the room, brushing past Amelia and Carlos on the dancefloor, and straight up to the DJ. Even this guy is apparently famous, some radio host who's a friend of the bride. His music has been shit all night. Maybe he'll be the first one to die.

Chapter Six.

A cigarette. That's the first thing he sees when he looks up. The cigarette she's offering, then her rough dirty boots, and then Amber standing over him.
"I'm good, but, thanks." Louis says, wiping some vomit from around his mouth.
"Suit yourself." She replies, lighting herself one. Louis sits back against the wall of the house, moving away from the plant pot he's vomited in. She shoots him a disgusted look but doesn't say anything.
"Is it always like this?" He asks.
"Filled with dead people? Pretty much." She says with a nonchalant shrug.
"No, that's not what I mean. I mean...don't you feel it?" He takes a breath, struggling to describe it but feeling like it's so important that he does. "Don't you feel that, in there? All the anger and the pain. It's overwhelming."
"I don't." She says, and he sees the moment where her face changes. The moment where her frosty demeanour thaws, ever so slightly, and she looks at him with sympathy. "A little. A tingle of something, maybe. But nothing like you're describing."
"But…" He begins, and then finishes. It doesn't really make any sense to him.
"Okay." She says, sitting down next to him on the ground. She takes a quick look at his makeshift sick bucket and shuffles a little further away.
"You really haven't done anything since we graduated have you?" She asks, screwing up her face in shaking her head. He shrugs in response and hangs his head. "So, alright, I'm not good at this shit. You know like,

when we get our powers? That whole thing?"

"Yeah?" He replies, nodding and trying to cast his mind back to one of the many, many lessons they'd had at Home Base. The basic premise of it was that when they hit the right age each of the students received their powers. It was a mysterious concoction that was administered as part of a coming of age kind of ritual. This ritual was performed by The Superior One, the being who led their organisation in this country. Similar titles were bestowed on several beings around the world and we'll cover the Order of One later in this story, but they're not terribly important at this point. The part that is important is the powers. We all received a basic level of enhancement, strength, speed, and whatever else to allow us to go toe-to-toe with the Used-to-Bes of the world. But on top of that we'd get something extra.

"Okay, so, everyone gets something different, right?" She says, while puffing on her cigarette. Whilst everyone would get the basics it would manifest slightly differently in everyone. While, for example, everyone's speed was enhanced a little there would be some who would become ridiculously quick, able to move in the blink of an eye. There are others who would develop something additional; telekinesis, shock absorption, or even the ability to nullify the powers of a Used-to-Be.

We speculated, of course, where these powers came from. Some of us had dreamed of a specific power, others had just desperately wanted to make sure the process worked and they got any power. "You think this is how mine manifest?" Louis asks. She shrugs.

"Well, did you ever find out what yours were?"

"No because…" He trails off, she knows already. It's because, once again, he has no field experience. No field experience means no real chance to find out how his powers work. For some it was obvious, for some we'd never find out what exactly we could do until we got out into the real world.

"I dunno. Like I said I'm crap at this. I don't really care how it all works. I just know that I'm strong. Way stronger than any of you. Lauren is more than just the self-appointed mother of the group, she heals us when we get hurt. Danny, well, you've seen what he's like with computers. That's gotta be some kinda superpower because he just speaks utter crap to me." Louis laughs at that. "So maybe this is yours. Feelings, or some shit."

"Great." He replies, sarcastically. "That's exactly what we need in a fight, right? Feelings." She snorts too and, for the briefest of seconds, looks like she might actually be warming to him.,

"Leave the fighting to me, trust me, I got it. Do you think you're ready to go back inside? Whatever it is you're sensing, I'm just thinking, maybe it'll give us a lead?"

"Yeah. Okay, I'll give it a go." He says. She stands, and holds out a hand to help him up and he gratefully accepts.

"Yes! I'm brilliant." Danny roars, triumphantly. It's to himself, because he's in an empty room, but he is more than happy to brag to an empty room. It's not the first time and it absolutely won't be the last. After his moment of self congratulations he takes a brief look out of the window. Chris and Rachel are loading books into her car. They've been to Alex's room and pulled out their journals. Rachel is now taking them back to Home Base to see what she can find out from them. That's great, but she's also made it perfectly clear that only she will be allowed to see them, and that annoys him. While he's been less vocal about it, Danny absolutely agrees with Amber. Alex may have been a temporary member of their team but they were a member of their team nonetheless; and whatever it was that was able to take out a Level Three agent might soon become their problem. A Level Three Agent is highly trained and more experienced than any of them, as standard. There's a reason they've got to that level and that's usually that they are the very best. Anything that can kill a Level Three Agent is worth worrying about, especially when you have no idea what or who that thing is. Danny doesn't like not being the smartest person in the room, and part of being the smartest person in the room is being the most well informed person in the room. He simply can't be the most well informed person in the room if he doesn't have access to all the information. That brings us nicely back to the cry of triumph. Alex was, to his viewpoint, a technophobe. They kept far too many paper copies of things. That was evident in the amount of journals Chris and Rachel had been carrying out. But, they also had a laptop, and with how desperately Rachel wanted access there must be something on here too. That's why he'd been trying to bypass the security for the past hour. Okay, no, that's not technically true. He's been holding himself back until a time that he was alone with it. He knew that if Chris and Rachel were in the room when he cracked it he'd never get a chance to lift off some of the files and make sure he was at least partially as informed as Rachel. The second they were out of the room he gave it everything he had, and seconds later the security crumpled, and he had full access to the files stored on here.

So that's what the triumph was. Sledgehammering his way through the security in record time at exactly the right moment. He quickly pops in an external hard drive and begins to copy whatever he can. He puts his hand on it and feels a connection run through him, speaking to the machine and willing it to go faster. They're coming back in now for the rest of the journals and he mutters a small swear word to himself. He rips the hard drive out, with only half the files copied, and tosses it in a drawer a split second before Chris pops his head around the door.
"How's it going?" He asks. Danny raises his eyebrows and plasters a smug smirk on his face. "You're brilliant." Chris says, recognising that look.
"I know."

Once they're back inside the feeling starts over again. It's less intense, but that's because it's less of a surprise. Louis can still feel a whole wave of emotions crashing against him, but overwhelmingly he can feel the fear of death. He can hear a muffled scream, and a distant wet thudding. It takes every ounce of his will to not vomit again, even though he really doesn't know what else he could possibly bring up.
"You're getting something, aren't you?" Amber asks, with the smallest hint of kindness in her voice.
"Yeah but it's nothing I can make sense of." He confirms.
"Okay, well anything we can use would be good." She says, glancing around at the chaos around them. The kitchen is a mess. There's blood everywhere, and Jon's body is in the middle of it. It doesn't look like he was the cleanest person to begin with. There are dirty pans, plates, and glasses piled on nearly every surface; there are cracked egg shells by the sink and an open carton of mango juice. Louis looks around, feeling like there's something specific in the mess that he's missing.
"There is something," He explains. She looks back at him with a raised eyebrow.
"That's pretty vague pal." She says dismissively, as she squats down to Jon's body, inspecting it with a cold clinicism that Louis can't manage. He can barely look at the dead man without picturing the pain he went through. "Looks like he was clubbed with something. Maybe you can use this weird sense to find a murder weapon?" Louis notices that the fridge has been left open, and steps towards it. He takes a look inside. It's relatively empty. There's a pizza box, a few cartons of soup, and a block of cheese. Amber appears looking over his shoulder. "We're looking for

something heavier than cheddar." She reaches over and grabs the pizza box. "I'll take this though." She says, opening it and inspecting what's there. Louis closes his eyes again, trying hard to concentrate on what it was that drew him over here. He tries to drown her out as she complains about the leftover pizza having vegetables on it because he needs to focus on what he's doing, not whether or not she's happy with her stolen snack. He closes the fridge and inspects the front of it, and that's when he sees it. There's a bit of card with a bloody fingerprint on it; and it's a save the date card for the wedding of Amelia Hamilton and Carlos Jenkinson.
"This." He says, turning to Amber who looks at him with a slice of pizza hanging out of her mouth.
"That?" She asks.
"It's an invitation to a wedding." He explains as she chews loudly.
"I don't think that's a murder weapon. I've never seen a papercut that bad." She says, gesturing to Jon's body.
"No. That's not what I mean." He replies, losing his patience a little for her sarcasm. She raises her eyebrows in surprise, but doesn't bite. "The wedding is today."
"Riiiiight." She says, tossing the empty box down on the counter nonchalantly. "So, what, your theory is that it broke in here, killed him, and then decided it still had enough time to catch the…I can't remember what humans do at weddings, but I assume there's some prick with a microphone and some free drinks?"
"Amber, there's something. I can feel something. I can't explain it." He says, almost frantically. It's the truth. This weird sense is completely new to him. It's like he can sense flashes of what the Used-to-Be was thinking about, like it left behind some kind of trace that only he can feel. It's weird, and it's a little bit frightening, but he knows he has to trust it. "Can't you trust me?"
"I barely know you. So, no, sorry." She says, continuing her search now that she's finished her snack. "I want a more concrete clue. But I don't think there's anything here. Let's just call and get a Cleaning crew in."
"Amber…" He says, almost pleading with her. She doesn't respond.

There was blood everywhere and that was so inconvenient. He could've done it cleaner, he supposed, but everyone was being so loud and chaotic. That was understandable, really, but that didn't make it any less of an imposition. Joseph had finished his make-shift speech - which had been

one of the better speeches of the day since he was much more eloquent than half of these fools - and raised a glass to the hope there was an afterlife because he was about to slaughter them all. He didn't really hope there was an afterlife and they didn't believe the second part at first. Some raised their glasses too, chuckling nervously at the strange man that no one really recognised. The penny dropped for the bride first. He saw it on her face the moment she realised something was dreadfully wrong and it was delicious. "And don't even try the doors; thanks to the key I lifted from our darling Lisa, they're locked." He informed them, nodding towards the receptionist. Her eyes widened, but she couldn't tell if he was kidding either. That's when he brought the microphone down with all his strength onto the skull of the "celebrity" DJ. The crack and the squelching echoed through the speakers before it was overpowered by the screams. A lot of them ran towards the doors, despite what he'd just told them. They clearly hadn't listened. A few ran towards him, with a sense of misguided bravery. He emptied his champagne flute, smashed it, and went to work.
Now, here he was, a few minutes later surrounded by dozens of bodies trying to clean some of the blood off him with a table cloth while Lisa, the only survivor, whimpered in the corner.

"...and I just love her so much!" The young girl says, with an excitable glee, as she finishes her answer that's been going on so long Kim can't even remember the question she asked.
"That's perfect, thanks." Kim says, turning to Marc and facing away from the teen in a carefully practised move to make sure she shuts up. "I think we've got everything we need, come on." She walks abruptly away, leaving Marc to grab the camera, smile politely at the girls in thanks, and chase after her. When he catches up she leans into him and whispers. "Think we can use any of that?"
"I dunno, maybe. She talked a lot." He says.
"That's an understatement sweetie." She takes her glasses off and rubs her eyes. "Right, I think we've got everything we need. What do you say we head back and edit this all together for this evening?"
"Yeah, sounds good to me."
"How are you with editing?"
"Yeah, I mean, I'm not the best but we have learned some in my TV workshops."
"Well, stick with me, I'm a pro." She says with a cheeky smile. "I'll have you

up-to-speed in no time." She leads them back to the van.
"Thanks, Ms…I mean…Kim." He says. "I've already learned so much today. I just like, really appreciate your time and everything."
"Oh sweetie, it's all good. You bought me coffee, and coffee to a journalist is everything. That's why I already know you'll go far in this business!" She says, opening the back of the van with "SBC News" boldly printed on the back of it so that he can put the camera equipment away. He smiles gratefully and goes to thank her again, but she waves him off. "Speaking of, I want to stop and get some more on the way. My treat this time though." She opens the door to the driver's side of the van but freezes as she hears something in the distance; the wailing of a police siren, and it's getting closer. "Wait." She snaps, as several cars with flashing blue lights come into view.

"Are you going to get rid of him?" Danny asked, bluntly, keeping an eye out for Rachel who was still out by her car.
"Sorry?" Chris asked, a look of genuine confusion on his face at the sudden topic change. Danny is taking the opportunity while they're both alone and while he's in Chris' good graces.
"The newbie." Danny replied.
"Oh. Danny, I…" He was cut off as Danny groaned and rolled his eyes. Chris shuffles awkwardly. "I know he's inexperienced, but Rachel sent him here herself, deliberately."
"Have you even spoken to her about it?" He asks bluntly.
"No, I haven't. I don't see any reason to…"
"Then maybe I should."
"Danny…"
"Speak to me about what?" Rachel asks, as she enters the room. Chris lets out a surprised yelp and Danny smirks coolly. He'd seen her approaching. She looks between the two of them expectantly.
"I…Danny…the security on the laptop is down. We have full access to the files." Chris explains, scrabbling for anything he can find that isn't challenging her on Louis' assignment to the team.
"Well, that's excellent." She says, and holds her hand out at Danny. He hands her the laptop without hesitation, secretly praying that his file dump provided him with something useful.
"Are you sure we can't see what's on there?" He asks, already knowing the answer. "That's what I wanted to ask." He shoots a quick glance at Chris;

as if telling him that he's welcome for Danny reinforcing his lie.
"I'm certain. As I've said I will share any information that I can, but I'm afraid a lot of Alex's investigations will have to remain classified."
"Hmm. That's what Chris said you'd say." He says, trying to add a false layer of disappointment to his voice.
"Then he was correct." She says, almost sternly.
"Well done though, Dan." Chris adds, evidently grateful that Danny has toed the line on this particular occasion. "For getting into it so quickly. Your talent for this always amazes me." Danny shrugs the praise off, his mind wandering to something else.
"Quite. I'm sure it would've taken days were it not for your support." Rachel adds. Danny doesn't even react to that one. Instead he turns up the volume on one of the screens on the wall which shows the local news.
"What's up?" Chris asks, watching him with curiosity as the reporter's voice starts to boom through the speakers.

There's something they're both missing. Louis doesn't know what it is, he can just feel it. Like there's something huge that he's not seeing and it's really, really annoying. He can see it, but he can't see it. It's like he's looking at a massive gap in the middle of a jigsaw but he has no idea what the picture is supposed to look like. He just knows there's something else that the creature focussed on during his time here. Something other than the wedding invite and his victim and Louis really, really needs to know what it is. He wanders slowly into the living room. There's not really much to see. Jon wasn't tidy, but wasn't all that messy. There are a few glasses and mugs on the coffee table, and the bottom shelf of it is dusty. He doesn't think that's it. He looks around a little more. He can hear Amber in the kitchen calling in a cleaning crew but can't make out what she's saying over the TV.
Louis runs his fingers through the leaves of a plant to see if it's real or fake. It's real. He has a moment of sadness because there will presumably be no one to water it now that Jon is dead. He wonders if he should take it with him or not; and then begins to wonder if there are any particular rules on taking plants from crime scenes. That's something that definitely wasn't covered in training. Surely that would only be an issue if the plant had something to do with the crime. His brain then wanders, weirdly, into whether or not plants could be affected by demonic energy. He didn't remember learning about that; people, yes, places, absolutely, animals,

occasionally, but plants? That one wasn't covered. That's maybe why taking one was never discussed either. He continues looking at the contents of the shelves. There's a picture of Jon and a couple of women, perhaps family members, and a Lego model of a ship that Louis recognises from Star Wars. He spent a lot of time watching TV and movies, and frankly, immersed himself in pop culture as much as he could during the time he spent in Jongleton. It would've been boring if he hadn't. He notices console games too, stacked messily on another shelf and some vinyl records. From what little this tells him about Jon he can't help but feel like they'd have got along. He feels another stab of empathetic pain that this man's life has been snuffed out so soon.

"Louis?" Amber shouts, stepping into the room. He shakes away the cloud of thoughts and focuses on her.

"Sorry, what?"

"I've been shouting you. Cleaners will be here in ten minutes."

"Yeah, I couldn't hear you over the..." He stops as he tunes into something different.

"...wedding day appears to have taken a tragic turn..." The woman on the TV says and suddenly it all falls into place and he can see the full jigsaw at last.

"Shit." He says, as his jaw drops.

Chapter Seven.

"What?" Amber asked, completely obliviously.

"That's the wedding. The one from the invite." Louis explained, with a panic he didn't fully understand slipping into his voice. She raised an eyebrow at him, making it really obvious she still didn't get it. "Amber, he left this on for us to find."

"Oookay." She replied, with the "oh" long and drawn out, because she thought he was talking shit. "Newbie, maybe you should go get some air again?" She said, making it very clear she didn't believe him.

"You don't believe me." He stated, feeling the need to be particularly blunt.

"Do I believe that a murderous creature broke in here to finish off the guy who escaped him and just decided that, since it was going spare, not only was it going to take the spare spot at the wedding, but also leave it out here in case we felt like going too? Not really, no. I get that this is a lot to take in or whatever, that you're not used to dealing with this crap. But that's just not how it works. We're dealing with animals. Now if you just want to get out of the..." She's cut off by her own ringtone. That's probably for the best, Louis thinks. She's wrong. She's completely and utterly wrong but he doesn't know how to tell her that. He doesn't even know how he's so sure of it. But, he is.

"Infections." The teacher declared. "You all know what they are, the remnants of the Demon. This isn't a history lesson." He looked around the class. I don't know when this was or how old I was. It probably didn't happen exactly like this, for the sake of the story I'm probably amalgamating a few lessons together. I don't even remember the teacher's name, he was one of the many retired Agents we had. He seemed old. I remember his face, haggard and scarred, but now I'm not sure he was much older than thirty. "How does an infection affect a human?" He asked, looking around as if the answer was obvious. We all looked around at each other, knowing that it wasn't a simple answer. "Really? None of you?" He asked. I don't think he was actually as grumpy as I remember him. Again, my memories could've made him a combination of many different teachers. If an Agent was injured in the field, too badly injured to continue or to be healed, they were brought in to help train the next generation. That's where the phrase 'those who can do, those who can't teach,' actually comes from. It's one of the many mantras we live by. We fight for as long as we're physically able to, and when we can't any more, we teach.
"It makes them evil?" Said one of the other kids, Reni, holding his hand up.
"Overly simplistic." The teacher replied, quickly. Reni looked disappointed.
"It changes them into a monster." A young girl, Marina, tried.
"Yes, but that's very vague." He replied, with a shrug.
"It brings out the worst in them. All the nasty parts of them, it makes them bigger." Burt, one of my friends, said.
"Getting closer, but still not enough. Not always the case either," the teacher said. "Anyone else?" He looked around. None of us wanted to try. The truth was, we didn't understand, and that was the point he was trying to make. "Okay, good. There isn't a definitive answer. Yes it changes them; yes it makes them evil, and a monster, and everything the demon was. Demonic energy twists and corrupts everything. So, we're going to do an exercise." He picked up a pile of envelopes from his desk. "I'm going to split you into groups and give you a case study. You will be presented with information about the Used-to-Be, and about who they were when they

were alive. I want you to present back to the rest of the class how you think one informed the other." He said, as he began to pass the envelopes around. I was in a group with Burt and Reni, which I was glad about. We were given information about a human who'd died in a fire alongside his family and had spent the next two years incinerating people. My education was a little different to yours, wasn't it?

"Yeah?" She snaps, as she answers the phone. "Yeah, one sec…" She grunts, taking the phone away from her ear and holding it out in front of her. "Okay."
"Right." Danny's voice says, coming out of the handset. "How long until a Cleaning team gets to you?"
"Should only be a few minutes, what's up?" She asks.
"There's a situation developing at the Eagle Hotel downtown. It's linked to the sister of Jon Hamilton. I'm really annoyed with us all for not seeing it earlier."
"Woah, what?"
"You remember that picture I found? With his famous sister? I've been hearing about her wedding all day. It's all over the Human news. One of us should've realised."
"Wedding?" Amber asks, very deliberately not meeting Louis' eye.
"Yeah, wedding, Amber. It's a stupid human tradition. Something about love and owning each other. I don't know. That's not important. The important thing is the event has been attacked and we think it's linked to 4XM. That's the codename we've given this creature, the one that killed Alex." He explains. Louis can hear the clacking of keys in the background, making it really obvious that Danny is furiously multitasking at that moment.
"Right, fine, what did you say the name of the hotel is?" Amber asks, making towards the door.
"No. Wait for your Cleaning crew then come back here. Rachel, Chris and Lauren are arriving at the scene now. We don't have time."
"I'm not just going to sit and…"
"Sorry, you are. Rachel was really clear. There are human hostages too. They're not going to wait for you and Newbie." He says, bluntly.
"Fuck." She replies, looking like she wants to slam her fist into the wall. "So then…"
"I need to go, Rachel needs me." He says. The line goes dead. Amber

looks over at Louis and glares, as if daring him to tell her that he was right. He doesn't say it, but he is tempted,

Danny, meanwhile, switches lines so that he can talk directly to Rachel through her ear-piece.
"I'm online."
"Where are you with the preparations?" She asks, efficiently.
"Got the schematics that you asked for. The best way is through the reception. I can guide you." He explains, looking up at some of the screens on the wall. Although he has left some of them covering the scenes at the Eagle Hotel via local news networks a few have been replaced. One now shows a live feed from a contact lens that Rachel has in, one is tracking his teammates exact locations, and another shows their individual vital signs.
"Visual on the target?"
"No. I've been reviewing security footage but there's nothing in that particular room."
She sighs, as if disappointed. He takes that a little personally because he knows no one else could've done a better job. "Target is definitely male, though. The phone calls to the police that I pulled from the hostages confirm that. They also confirm that there are going to be a lot of dead humans in there."
"Hmm. Okay." She replies, evidently still not impressed. "Anything else?" Clearly she had unrealistic expectations, Danny thought to himself.
"No." He says bluntly.
"I'll call you back when we're ready to go in." With that, she cut the line on him, which annoys him even more.

Lisa is crying. She's trying not to, she's trying to make herself as small and quiet as possible in the hope that he'll forget about her, but she just can't stop no matter what she tries. For a while now Joseph has been dancing around the room on his own; with mid-90s pop songs blasting from the DJ booth. She'd started to wonder if he'd forgotten her. If she'd be able to sneak out, or just blend in amongst the bodies. Never did she imagine that she'd have to think about hiding herself amongst a room full of dead people. That thought alone nearly broke her. But somehow, through the sobs and the terrifying thoughts, she vowed to herself that she'd find a way to get out of this alive.

"Are you enjoying the party?" He asked, appearing in front of her suddenly and sliding down the wall to sit beside her. She didn't look at him. She didn't know what to say or do to appease a murdering psychopath. He stares at her for what feels like hours before tutting and looking at her blood stained blouse. "You're such a mess." Then he looks back at the rest of the room, to the bodies slumped over the tables or collapsed in the middle of the dancefloor. She'd never seen anything like it. Lisa shudders as she remembers him moving between them all, almost too fast to see, slashing with a glass and smacking with his free hand. There were all kinds of weird sounds as blood flew and bones cracked and he danced through it all, seemingly untouchable. She whimpers again now.

"Look, I get it. It's not as lively as either of us were expecting. I mean, I can't believe I'm the only one dancing." He says, elbowing her as if it's a joke and she's supposed to laugh. She still doesn't look at him. "You're really quiet, what's up?" She still doesn't answer; she still wouldn't even know what to say. He rolls his eyes, sighs, and gets up. "I know what's wrong…" He says, with a jovial tone to his voice that really doesn't belong in this situation. He walks away from her, towards the mountain of corpses littering the room. He steps over them, making apologies and asking them to "excuse me," as he goes, until he reaches the body of a woman in a white dress stained crimson. He picks her up and puts an arm over his shoulder so that he can turn back to Lisa. "You're just a little starstruck right?!" He says, warmly. "You don't need to be. Come on over and I'll introduce you!" He's grinning at her and making the corpse of Amelia Hamilton nod as he does.

"Please…" Lisa manages to croak out. Joseph sighs and drops the body which hits the floor with a thud.

"It was a joke Lisa." He looks down at his shirt which has a fresh blood stain on it. "Ugh, this shirt is ruined. Lisa I know she's dead. That's why it was funny. Do you get it? No?" He rolls his eyes again and turns away from her. He begins talking just to himself. "I can't stand people without a sense of humour." He says as he wanders back to the DJ equipment, moving the dead DJ and playing around with song choices to find some kind of entertainment. "She'd have got it, if she was here. That's why these things are never as much fun on your own." He glares back at Lisa and raises his voice to speak to her again. "That's why I invited you. I thought you'd help lighten the mood!" He goes back to talking to himself, only this time he puts on a high pitched voice, mimicking that of a woman. "No

Joseph. We can't attract any more of their attention. You need to stay home and be good and not have any fun." He whines, before returning his voice to normal. "She'll appreciate it in the end though. Once they're all gone, we can just relax. I don't want to have to run again, you know?" His head snaps back to Lisa and his tone is vicious. "Will you stop that irritating whimpering please? You wanted to come to the party and I brought you to the party. I thought you were going to be fun but you've just sat there wailing the whole time and it's really off putting. If you're too miserable to have fun then fine, but keep your mouth shut and stop trying to bring everyone else down with you."

"Please…just…" She begins, trying to find her voice. He cuts her off.
"If you're about to ask me to please just let you go then I swear I will find a way to murder you with what's left of the wedding cake," He says, gesturing to the middle of the dance floor where one of his victims had stumbled into the cake and knocked it to the floor in his last moments. Joseph smiles again, laughing to himself at his own joke, and his tone returns to the earlier friendly one. "Look, Lisa, you're here and you're alive. That's more than can be said for everyone else in this room so how about a little gratitude for that? Not to me, just, to the universe or something. I brought you here because I wanted a little company. So how about a deal; you provide me with company and I'll keep you alive, yeah?" He asked her as if it was a perfectly reasonable request. Like it was just two friends doing each other a favour. She couldn't believe it but she knew she had to answer him.

"Yes." She replies, meekly, nodding to reinforce it.
"Great!" He says, sounding genuinely excited. "Now, what's your favourite song?"

Detective Chief Inspector Matthew Wade was not having a good day. As a self-confessed grumpy old man he rarely did but today seemed particularly annoying. It had started out inoffensive enough. He'd burned his toast and hadn't finished his cup of coffee in enough time before leaving; not much, but it was a sign of things to come. His wife, Kamala, had got up early to go to the gym. That threw his morning routine off. It meant he overslept and, even though he knew it was old fashioned, she usually made his breakfast for him because he was useless in the kitchen.

Once he'd got to work, things didn't get any better. He'd had one of those days where everything seemed like it was at a standstill. Every case he looked at, every file he picked up, just seemed stuck. He was looking at the same reports over and over again and was just at a dead end with everything. He hated days like that, and he especially hated days where he just stuck at a desk.

But then, in a real "be careful what you wish for," moment the call came in that something was going down at the Eagle Hotel. He was due to finish, he knew Kam would have something beautiful on the go for tea, but he also knew this was a big deal and he wanted to be there for it. He needed to be there for it, especially when the scale of it became clear. There had been multiple calls; and they'd all been cut off seconds later. There were either a lot of hostages inside, or a lot of victims.

Then, just when he realised how bad things were. Just when his stomach began rumbling from having eaten only burnt toast and a stale supermarket sandwich all day. Just when he'd received a passive-aggressive "okay" from the wife for being late. Just when he was facing a crisis with potentially dozens of dead bodies right in the eyes of the media. Just when he thought things couldn't get any worse, that's when they turned up. The fucking Counter Terrorism Team. That pack of shits made everything that had happened so far, even the crisis, seem downright pleasant. He finished his cigarette, quietly stubbed it out, and marched over to greet them.

Rachel finished her call with Danny and looked around for her team. She'd instructed Chris and Lauren to make contact with the local police force and could see that they'd done just that. However, she could also see that there was a portly middle-aged Human currently barking at them nearby. Chris was stoically listening to him and Lauren was clearly trying to allay his concerns; but it was evident she would need to be the one to intervene.
"Update me." She ordered, as she marched over to the three of them.
"I'm sorry, who are you?" Asked the man. Rachel could surmise he was a plain clothed officer; perhaps someone with a rank, someone who wasn't too keen on the idea of them coming along and taking over. She didn't much care, and instead of even acknowledging him she turned her head towards Chris and stared.
"We suspect multiple casualties inside, maybe hostages, but can't confirm." He reported.
"Look, this ain't anything to do with you, love, whoever you are." The policeman said.

"Matthew, please, we've been through this." Lauren said, with a soft tone as she tried to calm him.
"It's DCI Wade, thank you very much." He replied, his tone not soft.
"Lauren, can you please…?" Chris begins, indicating he wants her to deal with this man and get him out of the way so that they can speak freely. It makes sense, Lauren is the team-appointed Human Police Liaison. She was by far the team member with the best skill for dealing with people; but it's also clear this man isn't going to respond to the soft touch right now.
"No. She can't 'just,' I've had enough of all this Counter Terrorism bullshit. You lot always think you can just walk in 'ere and take over and I'm done with it." He barks again, and now it's definitely time for Rachel to intervene.
"DCI Wade, correct?" She asks. She pauses, but doesn't give him time to answer. "I'm afraid we don't think we can take over, we know that's the reality of the situation. You can't possibly comprehend the true nature of this, so frankly, you need to get out of my team's way."
"Oh I don't think so…" He starts, his local accent coming through thick, but she cuts him off.
"I'm not overly interested in what you think. I'm in charge here, and you are wasting my time when I should be taking steps to resolve this situation." She finishes and looks back to Chris. That should've been the end of the conversation; but she's always found humans to be particularly egotistical. She can see him, out of the corner of her eye, take a deep breath in and prepare to continue his argument.
"She's right, Matthew." Another voice says, mercifully cutting him off before he can. They all turn to see an older man, tall, with a head of thin grey hair, in a very nice looking suit. She recognises him instantly; not because she knows him, but because he too gives off the authoritative air that she's learned to channel over the years. She gives him a small nod of acknowledgment and he returns it.
"Detective Superintendent Timothy Copper ma'am. I've been told to cede complete control of operations to you; that your team has a special expertise in this matter." He says.
"That's correct." She acknowledges.
"What do you need from us?" He asks. Over his shoulder DCI Wade fumes silently. Lauren looks at him with a warm, sympathetic smile. That's more than he deserves.
"Have you had any contact from inside?"
"Nothing but a few brief and garbled phone calls."

"Anything from the terrorist?" She asks, careful to use the word terrorist, to match the cover that human police are told. It's an effective lie because terrorism is a very broad term; and can often cause so much fear and mystery that it's easy to explain away their involvement in a variety of cases.
"No, ma'am." He says.
"Has anyone from inside made it out?"
"A few staff members from the building, but no one from the room where we believe the incident has occurred."
"Is there anything else you feel I should know, Mr Copper?" The use of "Mr" was an unnecessary power play, but she felt like it was important to show DCI Wade that even his superior was happy to acquiesce to her.
"No. I don't think there is." He tells her.
"We have a firearms team on route, if you're prepared to wait I'm sure they could..." DSI Copper adds. She cuts him off before he can finish.
"Thank you. Leave it to us." She says, and turns away, as if to dismiss him. "Chris, Lauren. We have a floor plan and an entry point. I don't want to wait around." The two human officers seem to pick up the hint, and DSI Copper sidles away, taking his underling with him. "We go in two minutes. Prepare yourselves." Rachel tells the other two.
"Got it." Chris says, walking back to the car to gather some equipment. Lauren sticks around though, and Rachel can tell there's something she wants to say.
"Something on your mind?" She asks her, not unkindly.
"I'm...a bit worried, I suppose." Lauren says, after a moment of hesitation. "I know Amber is loud and a little obnoxious, but I can't get what she's been saying out of my head. We don't know what we're walking into do we?"
"Not entirely, would you rather that we wait?" Rachel asks. Again, there's no unkindness here, more a curiosity. She knows this isn't the time to be authoritative.
"Of course not, I know we need to move, but it just worries me not knowing."
"I agree." Rachel says, smiling kindly at her. This is definitely not a tactic she employs very often; a smile followed by complete honesty. "This is the first time I've been in the field in...months...maybe longer. I was promoted three years ago and I've barely seen a UTB since. I'm not as sharp as I

once was, and I'm concerned. How many years of field experience do you have?"

"Four. Three here, and one further south."

"And what about Chris?" She asks, with a nod towards him as he pulls stab vests from the back of the car. Rachel already knows the answer, of course.

"Five, I think. Over a year here, with me, and some more racked up in a few other locations." Lauren answers.

"I have ten, not counting the last three, and thirty-two captures in that time." It's not a brag, or rather, it's not intended to be, but Lauren's eyes light up with admiration.

"Oh, wow." She exclaims.

"We could wait for Amber and Louis. But if we do that we could miss our chance. There's strength in numbers, I agree. But there's strength in experience too. I deliberately kept you and Chris back, because I wanted the experience with me."

"I am. With you, I mean." She straightens up as she says this, as if trying to allay any doubts of her commitment. Rachel didn't have any, but it's nice to see. She continues with honesty because she knows it's what Lauren needs to hear.

"I am concerned too. There are dozens of reasons to not go in there, or to use caution. But there will always be a risk. We have to weigh that up against the risk of the target getting away. Let's not focus on the information we don't have or the variables we can't control. Let's focus on what we have, and what we can do."

"That sounds good. Thank you." She relaxes, just a little, and becomes more committed.

"You can thank me by doing what we do; by helping me to contain this situation before it gets any worse."

Chapter Eight.

Danny is in his element. He's alone in the War Room and there are no distractions around him. His fingers are primed over his keyboard, the TV news stations are all muted, and there's no one in the room trying to talk at him. This leaves him completely free to focus on only one thing; guiding the team to a successful capture. He can see what Rachel sees through the lenses in her eyes, can track exactly where they are in the building, as

well as each of their individual vital signs. He's also connected to the, very limited, security feed and even to the electrical supply. He's ready.
And inside the Eagle Hotel they're ready too, as Lauren, Rachel and Chris make their way along the eerily quiet corridor that leads from reception. They move in unison, in perfectly practised motion, to ensure that they don't make a sound. They're each wearing body armour and have a standard issue tranquilliser pistol in their hands, and they each have an open communication channel to Danny back in the War Room.
"Keep going, take a right at the end of the corridor and that should lead straight to the Poseidon suite," He instructs, before pausing to listen for something. "Wait, what's that?" He asks.
"Music." Rachel replies, quietly. He recognises the melody from somewhere, though he's not sure where. It's some woman screeching over a soft-rock track, and it's getting louder.
"The rest of the building has been evacuated, so that must be coming from where the target is."
"Seems that way," Chris confirms.
"Okay. Rachel, should I kill the power?" He says, poised ready to do just that.
"No. This helps cover our approach. We're close enough now. " She replies. He places himself on mute; knowing that this means they should maintain radio silence unless he's needed.
The three of them gather around the doors to the Poseidon suite, bracing themselves for a moment. They listen but can only hear the sound of the music inside. It occurs to them that as much as it hides their approach it also gives them no indication of what is going on inside.
In the War Room, Danny is perhaps even more on edge, watching through Rachel's eyes and knowing that despite all the preparation and technical wizardry, he's going to be of no help in the actual fight.
Rachel uses her fingers to count down from three, directly in front of her own face so that Danny can see too, and as she hits one she pushes her weight into one of the doors and bursts into the room. It opens easily, and the three of them quickly scan the room, trying hard not to be distracted by the sight of dead bodies littering the floor. There's a figure standing at the centre of the chaos. It's a woman with dishevelled and messy hair, and makeup is smudged from hours of crying. Her once pristine white blouse, still displaying her hotel name badge, was now spotted with blood and dirt

"He's…" She chokes out, trying to warn them too late. The door, which they've just entered through, slams into Chris and knocks him backwards. They whirl around to see that the target, 4XM, was waiting for them behind it. He shifts his weight, preparing his next move even before the door smashes into Chris. He kicks Lauren in the stomach and whilst her vest absorbs most of the impact she's still knocked off balance and falls backwards. She drops her weapon as she stumbles to catch herself. Rachel manages to react and fires a shot at him; but he's too quick. He grabs Chris, just as he regains his footing, and uses him as a shield. His body armour blocks it, so he's not affected by the drug, but 4XM throws him forward and into Rachel, knocking them both to the ground in a heap. The Used-to-Be pivots again, and gives Lauren a hard smack in the head, pre-empting the attack she was about to launch. Rachel shoves Chris off her and pops back to her feet, aiming her pistol again, but, using the close proximity to his advantage, he's already on her before she can fire. He headbutts her, hard, and snatches the weapon from her hands. He turns it on her and fires into the unprotected skin of her leg. The drug reacts quickly and she collapses backwards.

Back in the War Room Danny's feed is cut off, because only Rachel was wearing the lenses.

"Shit! Chris, Lauren, Rachel is down. What's happening?!" He cries desperately, looking around for any way he can help and coming up short of ideas.

Lauren finally finds her footing and rushes at the target, knocking Rachel's gun from his hand before he has the chance to fire again. It flies through the air and out of sight, and she follows up with strikes to his chest. He stumbles backwards and this gives Chris the chance to get back to his feet. Whilst 4XM is off balance he lurches forward to strike him as well but the creature recovers quicker than expected and catches his arm, using his momentum to throw him into Lauren and regain control of the fight. Even worse, as the two Agents recover, 4XM pulls a sharp kitchen knife from his belt and glides forward. Before either of them can react he drives it into the flesh of Lauren's leg and pulls it horizontally across. She screeches in pain, he headbutts her for good measure, and wrenches it out as she collapses to the floor in a rapidly forming pool of her blood. He slashes at Chris with it now but, though he's still a little dazed, he manages to dodge, then grab his arm and twist it to disarm him. He knocks the knife out of his grasp and kicks it across the floor, away from them. The

Used-to-Be is much stronger than him and pulls, flipping him over it's shoulder, and then, as soon as he connects with the floor, kicking him in the head again and again until he blacks out.
Joseph stops kicking, regains his composure, and brushes himself off. He looks around at the fallen Custodians.
"One...two...three..." He counts, and then looks around as if expecting there to be more. He looks over to Lisa, who's standing there in stunned silence. "There should've been more!" He tells her, irritation evident in his voice. "Wait." He says, fixing his gaze on Rachel. "And I don't recognise her. The other two, yes, but not her." Lauren groans in pain, bleeding from her leg but still conscious, and he zeros in on her. "You!" He practically screeches, bending down and grabbing her by the throat. "Where are the other two?" He demands. She gasps for air as he squeezes, not with his full strength but definitely enough to cut off her breathing. "You were all meant to be here. This doesn't work unless you're all here. Where are they?!" She tries to suck in some air, but she can't. She can neither answer him nor breathe, and he's too lost to blind rage to realise. In a desperate moment to save her own life she grabs at the bloodied knife that Chris kicked over near to her and drives it with as much force as she can muster into his chest. It's enough. He releases his grip, yelps like a wounded animal, and stumbles backwards off her. She sucks in as much air as she can and then rolls over, and climbs to all fours. She knows that even if she can get back to her feet there won't be much more she can do, but she has to try. He tears the knife out of his chest and tosses it aside, whimpering from the pain but not incapacitated by it. Lisa watches the whole thing unfold with wide, terrified, eyes. He screws up his face in rage and charges at Lauren. He kicks her in the head violently, as if it were a football, and she's knocked out instantly. She's lucky. He considered using enough force to separate it from her shoulders entirely.
"That..." He says, regaining his composure again and looking to Lisa, his audience. "...didn't go to plan." He explains before pausing and looking around with curiosity. "Wait, what's that?"

"What's going on?!" Danny snaps, frustrated at his own helplessness. He hates not knowing all the answers and he hates not being in control. Generally, as the most tech savvy member of the team he coordinates their missions which, despite Chris being the official leader, leaves him with a lot of the control over how they go. This current situation has taken away

control and severely restricted his access to the information he needs; and he hates the combination of those two things. "Someone answer me?!" He pleads, desperately. He can see his teammates' vital signs and can tell that they're unconscious but that doesn't stop his desperate hope that the sound of his voice might snap them back into action. "For fucks sake..." He swears in utter, helpless, frustration.
"Hello?" An unfamiliar voice says speaking into Lauren's earpiece. "Is someone there?" Danny's eyes snap back to the screens; though it gives him no extra insight.
"Who are you?" He demands, but really he knows exactly who the voice belongs to, and he knows he needs to tread carefully. Danny shakes his head and bites his lip in frustration.
"Ohh this is fun." 4XM says into the microphone, glee creeping into his tone until it's almost sing-song. "We missed you; your co-workers and I. Is co-workers the right term? I'm sorry, I'm not too familiar. Friends? Family?"
"Danny the Cleaners ha..." Amber says, entering the room, followed by Louis. Danny quickly holds up his hand to stop her, annoyed that he'd not even heard them enter the house. He glares at her too, for good measure. She gets the message too late.
"Ohh, good, the other one is there too! Why aren't you here?" 4XM asks, his sing-song voice echoing through the speakers. Both Amber and Louis shoot Danny an inquisitive look. He quickly mutes their end of the conversation.
"It's him. He's taken the others out. Shut up and let me handle this." He explains, before unmuting himself and addressing the Used-to-Be with fresh determination. There's something about having an audience that's made him feel in control of the situation once more. "What do you want?" He asks coolly. 4XM replies with a sigh so pronounced he must have exaggerated it for impact. Danny rolls his eyes in response.
"You," Is the simple reply. "And the other one. Red hair. Angry looking one. I saw you all the other night when we killed Alex. I thought you'd all be here but you two skipped the party. That's rude. I planned on you all being here. So, if you would be so kind, I'll need you here, quickly. Would you like to know what happens if you don't?" Danny stays quiet for a second, trying to formulate the best response to make sure that he's the one in control. Sadly, not everyone in the room gives it the same thought.
"Oh be careful what you wish for because when I get there I'm going to rip off your head." Amber roars, stepping forward so that she's next to Danny,

as if she can be seen.

"You sound fun!" 4XM says, giggling a little bit to himself. "Let's have fun together."

"Shut your mouth. Come on Danny, we've got to do something!"

"I'm thinking!"

"Ohhh, Danny. That's your name is it? Let me introduce myself properly, I'm Joseph. I'm sure you've got some silly codename for me, your sort always do. Alex did too. Look how well that worked out…" He taunts.

"I've got a few other things I can call you, you…" Amber begins. Joseph's exaggerated laughter blares through the speakers, cutting her off mid-insult.

"You are fun. I hope you turn up. You've got an hour. That's your choice. You turn up in the next hour or I kill them. If you don't burst in, in some daring rescue mission, I'll kill them while they sleep. I might kill Lisa too." Amber and Danny both look at each other as if to question who Lisa is. Amber opens her mouth to ask, but Danny holds up his hand and she actually pays attention and thinks better of it. "Screw it, I'll probably kill Lisa first, just to pass the time. This town is our home now; we don't want you here. So come here so you can all die together and leave us alone. I'm looking forward to meeting you both."

"Oh, I'm going to…"

"Amber. The communicator is offline." He tells her, before she can finish her threat.

"Let's go." Amber declared, simply, with anger fuelled determination. But Danny wasn't so sure. That's where they sat, in a silent stalemate, as precious minutes ticked by. It felt like longer than it was, situations like that always do, I've realised. It felt like the hour would be up before they even continued their discussion, let alone agreed on a solution. It was only minutes, but it felt like hours.

"We can't do this alone." Danny said, finally. "He was ready. He took the three of them out."

"Then let's call in some back-up." Amber demands.

"From where?"

"I dunno, the Cleaners?"

"They're not fighters."

"Well there must be someone."

"There's no guarantee anyone could get here in time. There's another

team nearby but I don't know how to contact them. Home Base is just under an hour away; so by the time they got anyone and got them here…"
"Then just the two of us. I can take him."
"Amber…"
"Three." Louis says, interjecting into the conversation. He's been silent for so long they'd forgotten he was there, and they both look over at him in surprise. Danny's eyes meet his, possibly for the first time, and an understanding flashes between them.
"Yeah, whatever Newbie. You can die too," Amber snaps, not party to their understanding.
"No. I don't mean that. Joseph said two as well."
"He doesn't know about you." Danny says, continuing the thought. "He was watching when we found Alex's body. He saw me, Amber, Lauren and Chris. But you weren't there and neither was Rachel."
"Exactly. You said he was ready. He planned for them to turn up. It's stupid but, maybe we just need to find ways to take him by surprise?"
"Oh great, so the newbie is our secret weapon." Amber says sarcastically.
"No, it's not stupid, you're on to something." Danny says, turning back to his screen and tapping at the keys with a renewed sense of energy. Louis is completely taken aback by even the vaguest praise coming from him. He taps at the keys and pulls up the recording of the footage he has from the failed capture. It begins to play on the screen. "You're right. He was waiting for them."
"Is there another way we could go in? Take him by surprise?"
"I'll surprise him by punching him in the throat." Amber says, sounding like an impatient child.
"Amber!" Danny snaps. "The grown-ups are talking." Both Amber and Louis are visibly taken aback by that, but Danny continues, pulling up the floorplan of the building on screen. "That's the only door. Tactically that room is a really good choice. We could use a window?"
"Maybe. It's better than the door. But…" Louis pauses, looking at the floorplan. His and Danny's eyes meet again and they share an idea. They both turn to look at Amber, who's got over her annoyance at being chastised in favour of Louis.
"Yeah." She says, nodding and grabbing a bit of paper, finally on their wavelength. She points at the handwritten bit of paper, her weapons inventory from earlier. Danny holds back criticising her for not doing an electronic version but thinks it so hard that he hopes she'll get the

message. "I've been wanting to use those for a while. I might have a couple of other ideas too."
"Go get 'em." Danny says, and she doesn't need to be told twice. She rushes out of the room to gather whatever supplies she can.
"That's..." Louis starts, struggling to find the words.
"...a very Amber way to do it." Danny finishes, with a little smile. It fades as quickly as it appeared and Danny stares right into his eyes as he asks the next question. "Are you ready for this?"
"I think so?" Louis replies, not even trying to hide how unsure he is.
"Thinking so isn't good enough. You've seen the footage. I'm worried; and this isn't my first field mission. When we get in there all the surprises in the world won't be able to protect you, we won't be able to protect you."
"I know."
"Do you? You're going straight in at the deep end and if you drown then that's on you."
"Yeah. I understand."
"Okay." Danny says, turning back to his laptop and hammering away at the keys, looking for anything else he can find.
"I'm ready." Louis says. He doesn't believe it, but he tries desperately to make himself believe it. This is what he trained his entire life for, so he has to be ready for it.

Chapter Nine.

This is taking forever. It's been nearly an hour since they heard anything. Some fucking specialists they are, DCI Wade thinks to himself. He checks his watch again and grumbles to himself. There are so many uniformed officers around, the firearms team, and an ever growing group of members of the public and the press. He can see them all getting twitchy, too, because no one has a clue what the hell is going on.
There's a lot of cloak and dagger around this bloody Counter Terrorism team, so he reckons that to a lot of onlookers it looks like everyone's just sat on their arses doing nothing. Even his own officers probably think that. He can't even fathom what the press will make out of this whole mess. As he thinks about the press he looks over to the group of them gathered by the barriers and accidentally catches the eye of someone he recognises.
"Excuse me! DCI Wade!" Kim Adams calls out. He groans again and curses to himself. "What's going on in there?!" He shakes his head and

walks away, pretending that he hasn't heard her because she's the last person he needs right now.
"Do you think he heard you?" Marc, her young cameraman asks.
"Oh he absolutely did." She replies, staring after the Detective with a knowing smile. "Which means there's definitely something going on."
"Well, yeah, we already know that don't we?" He asks, really confused about what she means. It's obvious there's something happening.
"No, I mean other than the obvious Marc. Look around, why aren't the police doing anything? What are they waiting for?" She gestures around her at the officers who are seemingly doing nothing to resolve the situation.
"Oh well, I dunno. Do you reckon he's made some demands? Like, for the hostages to be released I mean."
"Either way, we're going to get nothing standing around here waiting…" She says, turning around and pushing her way back through the crowd. He obediently follows her away.

Wade, meanwhile, has found DSI Copper and hovers around him as he finishes a phone call. The second he's finished, Wade launches a question at him.
"What the bloody hell are we doing?" He says, coming a little closer to a bark than he intends. "We've had no contact. How long do we have to wait?"
"As long as it takes," Copper replies, coolly, not at all phased by his colleague's prickly attitude.
"We could get a team in there now. We're ready to go, let's not leave it to them…"
"Absolutely not. I have had very clear instructions that we're to leave this to them." He says.
"…again." Wade mutters. Copper hears it, and that's okay, because he didn't mean to hide it from him.
"I'm sorry?" He asks.
"This whole Counter Terrorism team. Why is it that any time they show up we just have to bend over for 'em?"
"DCI Wade, that's enough. We've got our orders and we're sticking to them." Copper replies, the authority of his position evident within his tone, trying to end the conversation. It doesn't work. Wade is too frustrated to pick up on it. It's the end of a very, very long day and he lost what little patience he had hours ago.

"But, boss…" He begins before DSI Copper has to cut him off, reaching the end of his tether.
"Enough." He says bluntly. "We're leaving them to it. Look around you. This is too big a thing for you to go rogue. You stick to my orders, or else." He finishes. He braces himself for the inevitable pushback, the 'or else what?' but thankfully Wade keeps his mouth shut. Instead he takes a deep, growling breath in and then out. He wants to argue. He really, really does. But he knows there's no point. He knows, from those many years of working together, that this is simply an argument that he won't win. The key with Tim has always been to pick your battles. The two of them stare at each other for a tense moment, before Wade nods and backs down.
"Fine." He mutters to himself. They both turn as they hear some commotion from the crowd and see three figures pushing their way through to the barricade. Wade recognises two of them. Great, he thinks to himself, that's exactly what this situation needs; more of these Counter Terrorism pricks.

In the Poseidon suite Joseph is pacing up and down as he watches the seconds tick by on the clock. At the head table, where the happy couple sat before their untimely demise, Lisa sits with the unconscious Agents and watches him carefully, worried that he could turn on her at any moment.
"Forty minutes. They've had forty minutes. They should've turned up by now. They will turn up, won't they?" He asks, talking to himself more than her. Lisa braces herself. She's less scared than she was when this ordeal started. Maybe it's because she's started to lose hope she'll get out of here alive. It's like, it doesn't actually matter what she does. If he wants to kill her he will; and if he's going to she'd rather he do it than have this insanity continue.
"When are you going to let me go?" She asks him, bracing for whatever reaction she gets. He stops pacing and stares at her, raising an eyebrow.
"I…don't know." He admits, seemingly honestly. "Half an hour ago, in theory. That was the plan. They all came, I killed them, and then I could just go home and be happy."
"How are you going to do that?" She asks, knowing she's pushing her luck. She knows that sitting quietly is her best chance of survival, but she also knows that's not really got her anywhere so far.
"What?" He asks, sounding a little short but not overly angry.

"I just mean...how're you going to go home? There's got to be armed police outside. Dozens of them. They're not just going to let you walk away?" To her surprise, he laughs. Not the same over-the-top, creepy, intimidating laugh of earlier. This one is genuine. This one is full of surprise; as if she's said something he hadn't thought of and he finds it funny.

"Oh." He replies, simply, before he resumes pacing. "I didn't think of that." He says, and then seemingly goes back to talking to himself. "How did I not think of that? Oh, maybe I should call them?"

"What?" Lisa asks and he looks over at her again.

"You know, play the part. That's what she always says. Should I have called them with some demands? Is that what she'd do next? Maybe that's how I could get away. Demand a getaway car or something. A helicopter would be fun. I can't fly a helicopter. Can you? No, of course you can't..." He says, slowly degenerating into a rambling nonsense as he realises his plans are falling apart.

"Oh shut up Lisa! You wouldn't understand." He says, before she can reply. He lets out a frustrated shout and tips over one of the tables that's littered with dead party guests. "Where are they? I want this over with. I'm bored with this and I don't want to be here any more. Do you think they're actually going to come?" He asks. She's not sure if she should answer. She's not even sure if he's talking to her any more, or if he's talking to himself. He continues to stare at her, though, as if he is expecting an answer from her.

"I don't know?" She says, unsure what she's even giving an answer to any more.

"No, of course you don't. You're useless to me!" He shouts, losing any remaining composure and taking a step towards her. He's on the other side of the room, but she's seen the way he moves; he could be on her in seconds, and she could be dead before she even realised he'd moved.

"I've had enough. Maybe..." He says, taking another step. "...maybe I should just kill you now." His lips curl into a sinister smile; now that he has a plan, even just a temporary one, he seems to have regained his cool. She braces herself, thankful that this whole thing is about to end but sad that it's this way. He takes another step towards her. She closes her eyes and braces for it. She hears a loud bang and feels a rush of heat on her face. She opens her eyes again and sees a large, crumbling hole in the wall, with a space cleared to an adjoining room.

The explosion was controlled, because, worryingly, Amber knows exactly what she's doing with explosives. It was enough to cause a distraction but not much else. They wanted to get his attention, not bring the building down. Joseph stops and stares, wide-eyed, at the crumbling wall. This was unexpected, and before he can react to the first surprise a small device is tossed from the hole and lands at his feet.
"What?" he says. He doesn't really have time to try to work out what it is before it starts emitting a high pitched screeching sound which feels like a thousand nails being driven into his head at once. He clutches his ears, and so does Lisa. He stamps, as hard as he can, on the device and it shatters beneath his foot; but while he's distracted with that two figures burst through the hole. They both fire tranquilliser darts without a second of hesitation and both of them connect. They dig into the fabric of Joseph's suit and he stumbles, collapsing to the floor. It's over.

Amber and Danny move with caution. The target is down; but they don't know he's alone. Amber scans the room while Danny keeps his gaze fixed on the prone form of 4XM. She nudges him and nods at Lisa, who is sitting in a stunned silence next to the unconscious members of their team.
That momentary glance away is a mistake. Joseph launches back to his feet, completely unaffected by the drug loaded rounds. He pulls them out and throws them at Amber, who dodges. He grabs Danny and knocks the weapon out of his hand, then uses him as a shield so that Amber can't fire without hitting him. He punches Danny violently in the face and tosses him aside before throwing himself at Amber. He takes her by surprise and smacks her in the chest with all his strength. If she had been a normal, unarmoured, human, that shot would've shattered her rib cage and probably caused fatal internal damage. Instead, it sends her flying through the air and she lands on a pile of dead party guests, which, grimly, cushions her fall. With a grin Joseph pulls off his light blue floral jacket; revealing a stab vest he stole from another member of the team earlier. That's the reason he was unaffected by the tranquillisers. Amber, clambering back to her feet, is angered by the idea of a Used-to-Be stealing from them and using their equipment to save himself. She silently adds that to the list of things he'll pay for; and vows that next time she'll just shoot him straight in the face. With that added motivation, the second she's back on solid ground, she leaps back at him. It's a superhuman leap

because she uses her strength to propel herself towards him. She connects with him fist first; giving him a taste of his own medicine. He tries to strike back but close combat like this is what she excels at. She initially starts to get the better of him, using her own speed and strength to match his.

She also deliberately pivots, and angles the fight so that Joseph has his back to the hole in the wall. That was always the plan, and Louis takes that as his cue. They were both very, very clear with him. They would handle the Used-to-Be, and he had to get in and handle the hostages the second he had a clear path. He makes a run for it; ducking and dodging between tables so that he's not seen. Amber shifts again, keeping her concentration on blocking and dodging Joseph's blows, but also readjusting so that Louis has a clear path to the table where their team is. He rushes forward again, keeping low. The other woman spots him and he holds up a finger for her to shush. He tries to concentrate on her, to work out who she is. He digs deep to try to tap into whatever power he was able to use at Jon Hamilton's house earlier that day, and to sense if there is any demonic energy within her. He can definitely sense it from Joseph, even from the other side of the room. It calls out to him; like there is someone on the other side of the room screaming to get his attention. He tries to block it out and focus on the task at hand. He can't feel anything coming from her, but he knows he doesn't have enough control over it to be able to rely on that. He'll just have to trust that she's an innocent in this. He looks down at the name badge displayed prominently on her chest.

"You're Lisa, right?" He mouths, remembering 4XM using that name during their call. She nods silently. "We're going to get you out of her, but can you help me with them?" He says, keeping his voice as low as possible. She nods, excitement at the idea of escape appearing suddenly on her face. He gives her a thumbs up and looks across to the rest of the team. Lauren has a nasty looking wound on her leg that has been crudely bandaged. Seeing where he's looking Lisa shrugs in acknowledgement.

"I know some first aid. I did what I could." She explains, in a hushed whisper. He gives her a thankful smile. He glances back over to the fight that's unfolding in the centre of the room. Amber appears to have lost the advantage, and Joseph is managing to counter the majority of her attacks, and land some strikes of his own. He knocks her arms out of the way and grabs her by the throat; but as he does Danny rejoins the fight and smashes him over the head with a discarded silver serving tray until he releases Amber. The second she's free she kicks out at him, creating some distance between them.

Louis realises he's running out of time; but he notices that Lauren is starting to come around. She shakes off the grogginess as quickly as she can, and groans in pain.

"Can you walk?" He asks her the second she's aware of her surroundings.

"I think I'll have to." She answers, looking over at the other two.

"This is Lisa," He says, introducing the two women. "She can help." Lauren smiles sweetly at her and mouths a greeting, Lisa nods eagerly.

"What about those two?" Lauren asks, nodding to Chris and Rachel who are still thoroughly unconscious. Louis reaches into his pocket and pulls out three syringes.

"I brought these." He explains, still careful to keep his voice low, but also thankful that the fight behind them is causing a lot of noise. He wonders if Danny is being deliberately noisy, like with the clanging of the silver tray, so as to increase their chances of a smooth exit. Lauren nods her approval and he jabs the first into Rachel, and then the second into Chris. He holds his breath for a moment, and begins to second guess himself. It was the one's for the antidote to the tranquilliser that he put in his left pocket, wasn't it? He's not just given them a double dose of tranquilliser? But then, he's able to breathe out as Rachel's eyes start to flicker open.

"They'll still be a little groggy; especially Chris, he's probably concussed and I don't have the energy to fix that at the moment." Lauren explains as they both begin to stir. She gestures for Lisa to help her to her feet, which she does. Louis moves quickly but carefully over to the window behind the table. It's been barricaded by Joseph; but he's able to clear that easily and open it.

Behind them Danny tries to smack Joseph with the tray again; but he bats it aside and out of hand, and answers with a punch to the head. Amber charges at him but he catches her with an upper-cut which, because of his super-human strength, sends her into the air and crashing through the already messy buffet table. Unfortunately, that puts Louis and the others right in Joseph's eyeline and as he gets his bearings again he spots them trying to make their escape. He does a somewhat comical looking double take and screws up his face as he stutters an objection.

"No...no! Who are you? What are you doing? You're cheating!" He screeches, like a child losing at a computer game. Danny takes advantage of this and attacks again. He jumps on his back and strikes downwards with his elbow onto Joseph's neck. He lands a couple of hits before he recovers and tosses him off; throwing him into the wall near the hole they made earlier. He crashes head first into it, temporarily incapacitating him. Thankfully, it means Louis has enough time to usher Lisa out of the window, making sure that at the very least the only surviving human hostage is safe. They're only on the ground floor, so thankfully isn't a massive drop, and she now stands by waiting to help the others out. Joseph refocusses, desperate to halt their escape. He scoops up a nearby knife and aims it, ready to throw it straight at Louis. Amber recovers though and uses discarded buffet food as projectiles. They bounce off him, of course, but it's not meant to hurt, just distract him. She can't believe she's resorted to using pastries as projectiles, but here they are. Louis drags Chris to his feet in this extra time and hurries him towards the window as Lauren climbs out, into the waiting arms of Lisa. He gets Chris ready to go next, with the other two on the ground to help him because he's still not fully with it.

Amber, meanwhile, has stopped throwing buffet food and has once again launched herself at Joseph. She tossed a tray full of sandwiches at him and then, as he swatted it away, charged forward, lept onto a table and then at him, kicking him square in the chest and finally causing him to drop the knife. He stumbles backwards but she doesn't let up. She runs at him and jumps into the air again, tackling him shoulder first through the double doors of the room and out into the hallway. They both climb back to their feet and she attacks again, deliberately pushing him backwards and away from the room. As they disappear from Louis' line of sight he can still hear the commotion caused by their fight, by the thudding and clanging as they destroy their surroundings in an effort to do each other as much damage as possible.

Danny stumbles back to his feet and re-joins the fray, chasing them down into the corridor. Louis refocusses on the task at hand and practically drags Rachel to her feet. He ushers her towards the window too, and is just about to help her out when she stops him. They both look outside where there are now several human police officers waiting to help. She stares directly at Louis, ignoring them.

"No." She declares, pulling away from him and steadying herself against the wall. Louis looks over his shoulder to the corridor, and then back at her. She nods. "Go, help them. Give me a minute to pull myself together and I'll join." He doesn't need to be told twice. All fear and hesitation are gone in that moment, because he knows exactly what he should be doing. He runs out of the room and into the corridor, following the trail of destruction but instinctively knowing exactly where they are.

Their battle has spilled into the hotel's kitchen. Amber managed to keep Joseph on the back foot the whole time, deliberately driving him as far away from the others as she could and controlling the flow of the fight to give them space. Now, she doesn't have to worry about that. He's far enough away and she has a room full of new weapons. Now, she thinks to herself, it's time to end this. One of them isn't walking out of here, and she's going to do everything she can to make sure it's him. She attacks again, but he sees it coming and pushes her aside and back into a metal counter. She groans in pain as it smacks against her spine but shakes it off as quickly as possible. She isn't quick enough though; he follows it up with a punch to the face, and another, and another. She hears the crunching of bone under his fist and loses her balance, slumping down to the floor. He doesn't stop though. He keeps hitting her and she can't get her hands up to defend herself.

Danny crashes desperately into the room and tries to tackle him off her. Joseph steps easily out of the way though. Danny is still feeling the after effects of his head wound and can't correct in time; and Joseph adds to his momentum with a shove, sending him into one of the stainless steel counters at the other side. He leaves a person sized dent in it, and Joseph lands a punch to his face too before he can recover.

Amber struggles up to all fours; but Joseph grabs a large pan and cracks her across the face with it to keep her down. They're both showing signs of exhaustion now. They're battered and bleeding; with cracked bones and bruises already showing up, but he isn't. Joseph's power means that he's healing almost as soon as they're damaging him. Yes, his own blood has now mixed in with that of his victims on his clothes, but the wounds that caused that bleeding have long since closed. He gives them another smack each with the pan he's brandishing and smirks because he knows that they won't get a chance to recover now. He can easily keep them both down and finally finish this. Then he'll chase down the others.

That's when Louis charges in. He doesn't really plan his attack, he's not as experienced as the others, and it's been over a year since he even did any real combat training. Instead he just flings himself into the waiting Used-to-Be before he can do anything to react to it. He pushes him desperately, as hard as he can, away from Amber and Danny before he can hurt them any more. Joseph steadies himself quickly and swings the pan at him, but Louis is able to use that momentum to toss him over his shoulder and onto a counter-top. Joseph lands on top of numerous plates of almost-prepared dishes of food that were abandoned earlier when the kitchen was evacuated, and they're sent crashing everywhere, adding to the overall chaos.

Joseph recovers and kicks him away. Louis stumbles back and Joseph clambers back to his feet, with the counter between them. He grabs a discarded knife, left behind by a fleeing chef, and prepares to toss it. Louis quickly kicks out, sending the counter at him. This knocks his aim off and means that Louis can easily dodge the deadly projectile.

Joseph throws the counter aside easily, once again showing superhuman strength that is now fuelled even more by an insane rage. Louis can feel it emanating from him and it's screaming at him. It's enough of a distraction that there's nothing he can do when Joseph grabs him by the head and smacks it off a nearby sink. He pulls a hose from it, wraps it around his throat and pulls, strangling him. Louis pulls at it desperately as his airway is cut off but he just can't get it loose.

Danny stumbles over to intervene but Joseph has no problem swatting him away with only one hand, the other still pulling on the hose, and headbutting him for good measure. He finally has to let go to defend himself from an incoming attack from Amber, but the second she's been tossed aside he pulls on it again, having given Louis barely any time to gasp in some more air. Danny attacks again, and forces him to release his grip, but again Joseph fights him off. Louis pulls the hose from around his throat and lays gasping on the ground.

Now all three of them are broken, exhausted, and more or less defenceless. Joseph, however, still isn't slowing down. That's the nature of a Used-to-Be, and the monstrous power that they possess. He kicks Amber brutally in the stomach, preventing her from climbing back to her feet and sending her into the wall. He picks up the chef's knife again, zeroing in on Danny, who's still down and defenceless. He stalks towards him, raising the knife. Danny sees it. Louis struggles to his feet, he's feeling light-headed and the energy he's picking up from Joseph's bright red anger is making him feel even weaker than the exhaustion from the fight. He tries desperately to shake it off as he watches Joseph bear down on Danny. He reaches into his other pocket, pulls out one of the tranquilliser syringes and throws himself on Joseph's back. Joseph flails around, trying desperately to throw him off. He slashes at the air behind him. Louis' head is spinning from the energy radiating off Joseph. His vision starts to blur and he hears shouting. He's not sure where it's coming from, but he knows it's in his head. He hears people shouting a long time ago and someone being beaten violently. He tries to fight through the dizziness and raises the syringe ready to jab the Used-to-Be with it. He's too slow though, and Joseph knocks it from his hand and it flies across the room. Then, he flings himself backwards and lands on top of Louis. Joseph pops back up, even more angry.

"You little…" Joseph says, staring directly at him and bearing his teeth. He shows every bit of that anger on his face, and raises the knife above his head, ready to land a killing blow. Louis kicks his knee desperately and he stumbles. It only takes him a second to recover his footing; but that one second is enough as two tranquilliser guns fire and two darts dig deep into Joseph's neck. He pauses, his eyes wide as his brain struggles to comprehend what has happened, and he collapses in a heap on the ground, revealing Rachel standing in the doorway brandishing the two formerly discarded weapons.

Amber struggles back to her feet, and Louis helps Danny back to his. The three of them stare at each other in a kind of stunned and relieved silence, unsure what to do next but very grateful that they all survived. It feels like a very long time that they stand there, with no sounds except for their own heavy breathing.

"Well done. All of you." Rachel says, finally breaking the silence. Amber grunts in pain as she pods at her own ribs, wondering just how many are broken. "Amber, Danny, go get yourselves checked out. Lauren's out there, hopefully she feels strong enough to help with your injuries by now." Danny takes a quick look over at Louis, and heads towards the door. Amber, however, delivers a huge kick, with as much strength as she can, to the unconscious form of Joseph. There's a crack and she smiles in satisfaction. She knows it will likely have healed by the time he wakes up, but she feels a lot better for it.

"Happily," She says, with a grin, before she follows Danny out of the room. Rachel, who clearly isn't quite sure what to make of that, watches her leave a little open mouthed.

"What about me?" Louis asks, and her head swiftly snaps back towards him.

"Yes, you will need to be looked at too. There's a Cleaning crew in one of the conference rooms behind reception. If you could get them so that they can secure him. I'll wait here."
"Yeah, of course." He says, making towards the exit.
"You did well, Agent." She says. He stops and turns back to her. "I was right, for what it's worth. You were wasted on your last assignment. We're going to need you here, because I feel like this is far from finished." She stares down at the unconscious form of Joseph. "He's not the end of it." She says, mysteriously. Louis almost doesn't ask. He's not sure if he should. So much was made earlier of what she could and couldn't say; he fully expects that if he does ask he'll be chastised for lack of clearance or something. But, he asks anyway, because he's too exhausted to stop himself.
"What do you mean?" He says. She smiles. It's a warm and honest smile. "I honestly don't know." She says, with a chuckle. She touches him on the shoulder. "Hopefully, the information we recovered from Alex will give me something a little more tangible. But this is a conversation for later." He nods in response, recognising that he's being told that's the end of the conversation and that he's to fetch the Cleaners. He goes to do just that, leaving Rachel alone with the unconscious Used-to-Be.

Chapter Ten.

But Agent Rachel Smith wasn't alone for long.

As Louis left the room she let out a relaxed sigh. She felt like she'd been holding her breath all day; since Danny had first noticed the incident occurring and the links to their target, or even since she'd received the call yesterday evening to tell her a Level Three had been murdered in her area. This wasn't a normal day. A normal day for her lately had been sitting in her office in Home Base looking over field reports, allocating resources, and maybe, once in a while, involving herself in a particularly interesting looking investigation. There was something about this that had called out to her. It was serious. More serious than anything she'd ever come across. It wasn't even just Alex dying. The sad fact was that Custodians were dying all the time, that was the nature of their work and she'd long since accepted that. It wasn't even the fact it was rare to come across a Level Three, especially in the North of England, and even rarer to come across a dead one. There was something else that she couldn't quite put her finger on. A little nagging feeling in the back of her head. One that had perhaps been numbed by being out of the field so long. She lowered her weapons for the first time since entering the room. The target was definitely down and the danger was over, she thought to herself. She placed them down on a nearby kitchen counter but didn't take her eyes off the prone form of 4XM just in case. He was definitely unconscious. She knew that. There would've been no way he could've held back a reaction when Amber kicked him if he wasn't. Rachel knew that wasn't why she'd done it, but she'd already made a mental note to talk about that with her later.

The problem was, that while she thought about that, about the mental notes for later, and all the exhausting sounding clean-up that was still left for the rest of the day she didn't hear the door to the fire escape open ever so gently. That was also the result of being numb from being out of the field for so long too. You always secure the area. If only she'd taken her eyes off 4XM, because she was right in thinking he posed no immediate danger, she would've seen the owner of the perfectly manicured hand that grabbed the meat cleaver hanging nicely on the wall only a few feet away. The woman that the hand belongs to pauses for a second, surveying the carnage and shaking her head in disapproval. If Rachel had turned at that point she might've still stood a chance, but only if she'd decided to run, which she would've never done.

No, unfortunately the first sign Rachel picked up on that she wasn't alone was the sound of high heels making their way across the room towards her. But by then it was deliberate. She could've moved silently if she'd wanted but she wanted her prey to hear her. Rachel grabbed the guns again and swivelled, pointing them at the newcomer who simply whispered to herself.

"Jam." And the guns did. They both clicked as she squeezed the trigger but nothing came out. Her eyes widened as she looked up at the other woman and, in her last seconds she felt the kind of fear she hadn't felt in years. She wouldn't feel it for long though. The meat cleaver landed in the centre of her head and her lifeless body collapsed to the floor.

Hazel Hardcastle reached down, her curled auburn hair falling down to cover that same look of disapproval on her face. She effortlessly picked Joseph up with one hand and tossed him over her shoulder.

"They'll just be…" Louis says, a few minutes later as he wanders back into the room. He feels it even before he sees it; the cold fury. He screams, because it's so strong and so sudden that it's too much for him to handle. He collapses to the ground beside Rachel's body, finding it as hard to breathe now as when he was being strangled earlier, and quickly blacks out.

Agent Rachel Smith, found dead on 6th October at 22:48 by Agent Louis Smith. Her body was recovered by a cleaning crew and destroyed the next day.

Part II: A New Normal

Chapter Eleven.

It's sunrise, a beautiful autumnal sunrise, and Matilda Pearson is very grateful for it. She turned eighty a couple of months ago and you could never be sure how many sunrises you had left when you got to her age. She'd celebrated by sorting through some old photos and giving them out to her kids and grandkids, so that they had something to remember her by once she'd gone. They'd insisted on taking her out for a meal that weekend, but it was that simple task that had meant the world to her. Taking the time to sort through old memories and share them, making sure that she left something behind for her family. Matilda smiles to herself, thinking of those photos and the good times they captured as she arrives, flowers in hand, to the cemetery. She looks down at the other gravestones as she passes. She's been doing this for so long that the names look familiar to her; like she's passing her old friends, albeit ones she's never actually met. She laughs at herself for that thought because she knows how silly it is.
"Morning Archie," She says, as she stops, having arrived at her destination; the grave of her late husband. She reads the inscription, and it's even more familiar to her than all the others. It should be, she chose it. 'Archibald Pearson. 1938 - 2015. Beloved Husband and father. Forever missed.' There's a gap under it for another name. One day, probably soon, someone will add her name to it.
"Yes it's me again," She tells him as she crouches down and picks up the dead flowers that she brought with her last time. She shakes her head, knowing she should've come sooner. It's the turn in the weather, the aching in her bones, it makes her want to just stay inside where it's warm. But then, she can't do that forever. She drives herself mad and would probably end up popping her clogs out of boredom. Still, it's the weather combined with the long journey that's meant that she's not visited him for a couple of weeks and she feels bad about that.
"You can't even get shot of me by dying can you? Just wait till I pop it too. You'll get no peace then!" She says, with a chuckle. She pulls a carrier back from her coat pocket and puts the old flowers in it, before peeling off the plastic wrapper from the new ones and arranging them for him. She smiles to herself once she's happy with the arrangement and struggles back to her feet, using his headstone to help her up.

"Tell you what pet, I'm getting old now. That's the part where you're supposed to say I'm just as beautiful as the day you met me. Ah well, even when you were alive you wouldn't have taken the hint on that one. Good job I love you, ey? Little 'uns coming on a treat. Oh you should see him Archie; he's the spitting image of you. It's such a shame he'll never get to see his Grandad. At least he's got his old Nana though. I spoil him rotten. Of course, I've no idea what to do with boys – raising girls is more my cup of tea. Oh, speaking of which…

She reaches into her handbag and pulls out a flask, and two cups. She sets the cups down on the grass, and, although she struggles a little, she pops open the lid of the flask and pours the tea into each mug. They both steam in the morning air. She moves the cup with the word "Husband" on it closer to the grave and takes a sip from the matching one labelled "Wife" and smiles to herself contently as she thinks back fondly on all their mornings together. They'd had so many good ones over the years. She found her mind wandering as she began reminiscing on a particularly lovely morning on their honeymoon when she was interrupted by the sound of someone else talking. Her ears, even though her hearing wasn't what it once was, prick up and she listens in. She can only hear one voice, which sounds like the voice of a man, and although she can't make out what he's saying it sounds very much like he's alone. She smiled back at the headstone.

"Looks like I'm not the only one mad enough to go around talking to 'emself, ey Arch?" She says, before straightening up and craning her neck to see if she can spot her new companion, but she can't see anyone. Still, it's not fully light and it's a little foggy. "Hello?" She calls out, but finds that, although the mumbling continues, no one calls back. "Everything alright over there?" She asks, a little concerned at the lack of response and she's a little worried it might be someone who's hurt themselves; perhaps someone her age who's had a bad fall visiting the grave of his wife or something. She pops the cuppa down on top of Archie's headstone and begins to walk forward, clutching her mobile phone in case she needs to call an ambulance for him. "Excuse me, are you alright? Shout up if you can hear me?" She says, projecting her voice as best as she can into the freezing morning air. As she hobbles forward, her bad ankle playing up with the cold, she spots a figure hunched over nearby and she cautiously moves towards him. "Do you need an ambulance?" She asks, as she gets closer. She can't tell how old he is because he's not facing her and the bits

of him she can see are absolutely caked in mud. She wondered if he had taken a nasty tumble. "I've got a phone if you do. I can call one?...if I can work out to use this blasted thing anyway…" She offers as she gets closer. He still doesn't react. He must've been through something terrible, she thinks to herself. "Can you understand me?" She asks, placing a hand on his shoulder. His head snaps around to face her suddenly and she bumbles backwards as she sees a crazed look in his eyes. His face, too, is covered in all kinds of muck, but his eyes blaze with a kind of animalistic madness the likes of which she's never seen. She knows instantly she's made a mistake. She notices then he's covered in all kinds of cuts and scrapes too, and that he's sat by an empty grave.
"What happened to me?" He says, almost in a growl.
"I don't know sweetheart." She answers, softly, trying to contain the tremble in her voice. "Whatever it is, it looks like you've been through the wars. Would you like a cup of tea to help get yourself together?" He doesn't answer, he just stares blankly as his mouth starts to quiver, as if he is trying to say something but just can't. His whole body begins to shake slightly, and he gets to his feet, towering over the woman. She steps back again as he advances on her. "Now listen." She says, trying not to sound afraid. "Maybe you should just calm yourself down…" His pace quickens and she can't back away fast enough. She stumbles and falls, as her ankle gives way and she feels a shooting pain in her wrist as she uses it to break her fall. He pounces at her, looking more like an animal than a human now, and bares his teeth as he does. She screams for her life and takes one last look back at her beloved husband's grave, where the cup of tea that she'll never get to finish still sits.

Very few people talked about the death of Matilda Pearson, I'm sad to say. We did, of course, the report came straight through to us the second the police were called to the scene. Danny had some clever technology - he wouldn't elaborate any further - set up to look out for a number of different triggers that could be signs of demonic activity and would be alerted as soon as his system picked something up. He bragged that he'd designed it on his first assignment too. A huge operation in central London. He'd revolutionised it, apparently. He'd go on to tell me he thought that's why he'd been moved here; they wanted him out of the way because he made everyone else feel useless. Danny talked a lot of shit, especially in the beginning. I don't know if he was trying to impress me, condescend me, or

even if it had nothing to do with me whatsoever. But regardless, his ability to speak to technology and bend it to his will was unmatched.
The next day the death of Matilda Pearson was not what everyone was talking about; because she was just some lonely old woman, who died quietly, when the world was still talking about a loud massacre that had claimed the lives of the rich and famous.

Kim Adams stood outside the Eagle Hotel - a location she'd become incredibly familiar with - patiently waiting for her camera man to give her the nod that he'd started recording. The second he does, she leapt into action.
"Nearly a week has passed since the tragic events that took place at the Eagle Hotel, and although we are still no closer to knowing who is responsible for the horrific attack, Amelia Hamilton's fans have been standing together, transforming the now closed hotel into a monument to the fallen star." She'd given him strict instructions around the framing; making sure that he captured both the police tape, and the most visually attractive of the tributes the mourners had left. To match her script she half turns to gesture towards the hundred of bouquets of flowers and photographs that have been placed outside the now abandoned hotel. It had not reopened, and the rumours were that it never would. The hotel had been struggling anyway; securing such a public event could've been its saving grace but given how grisly the wedding had turned out it would likely serve as the final nail in the coffin. Kim finished her piece to camera and gestured for Marc, the student assisting her with the camera work, to cut. She turned to inspect the tributes a little closer.
"Okay," She began, leaning down to a child's drawing that she presumed was meant to be Amelia Hamilton. "Get a few close up shots, I want something to show while I do the voiceover. There's a photo over there with a candle in front of it…" She says, zeroing in on it like a hawk. "That'll be a great one to end on,"
"Yeah, okay." Marc replies, nearly dropping the camera as he fumbles to pick up the tripod. Kim looks back and gives him an encouraging smile. "Get a few options too.."
"Yeah, I will."
"Sorry, I'm being overbearing. I'll leave you to pick what we shoot; get a lot and we can pick together later. This story is huge so we need to make sure we do it justice."

"I know, it's all anyone is talking about at the minute. My gran can't believe I'm covering it." He tells her, with an adorable excitable grin as he leans in to start getting shots of the tributes. She keeps her distance and observes. Kim knows she's a control freak, especially with a story that's getting national coverage, but she's conscious she's been doing a lot of bossing him around and not a lot of letting him make decisions himself. He won't learn that way. She almost jumps in when he starts filming some dull flowers that are already wilting - knowing they won't be a particularly great visual - but stops him because whatever he films she can narrow down when they edit it together. Perhaps she can even think of a way to guide him into realising what a terrible shot it is. "She keeps telling me I have to be careful though...can you believe that? As if whoever did this is going to come back for the journalism student covering it."
"Tell her that while you're with me you'll be just fine, babe." She says, pulling out her phone and checking for any social media updates on the story, partly to distract herself from micromanaging,
"Who do you think did it?" He asks her cautiously; as if he's expecting to be told off for gossiping on the job. "Like, they think it was a crazed fan don't they, the police?" She stops scrolling and looks up at him from her phone screen.
"Supposedly. I don't know if I buy that though. No one really knows where that rumour came from. Besides, it doesn't look to me like the police are actually doing anything."
"Surely they're all over it though? Something as huge as this?"
"Nah, come on, where's that inquisitive journalistic mind? What updates have they actually given us? Everything has been vague, but not in a way like they're holding back information, it's more like they don't have any. There's a massive piece of the puzzle that we aren't seeing, and I'm not sure the police are either." She says, and trails off a little as she sees Marc's blank expression. "Oh ignore me. I just don't like unanswered questions and there are far too many of them flying around this whole thing."
"Do you think...something is being covered up?" He asks, looking over at her with curiosity all over his face. She's definitely distracted him from those dull, wilting, flowers now.
"There's definitely more to find out." She says, smiling mischievously. "But luckily, babe, that's kind of our job." She gives him a playful wink and then claps her hands. "But enough conspiracy theories. Let's get some more

shots and get out of here. I'm sick of the sight of this hotel, and I want this package ready for the lunch time update!"

Across town a car was pulling up at a cemetery. It was a dull and grey day, typical of autumn in the north of England. But, there's something about arriving at a cemetery already filled with human police and cordoned off with their tape that makes it seem even more depressing. People aren't meant to die in cemeteries and yet that was exactly why Louis and Chris had been called there.
Like I said, Danny had picked up the report of a dead body at a cemetery at roughly the same time the police had. The elderly victim had been found by an early morning dog walker, which is frighteningly common. I bet humans don't realise that owning man's best friend comes with such occupational hazards. There were enough contextual clues to flag whatever search Danny had running and he insisted that it be investigated.

A lot had happened in those few days since the Eagle Hotel. First, there was the brief report confirming the death of Rachel Smith, which we knew, and that her body was destroyed. The team had then been invited to a ceremony at the nearby Home Base 25 to discuss the whole situation; and although it had been an invitation, it was absolutely not optional.
The Base itself was the complete antithesis to this current cemetery situation; it was bright, and sunny, and warm. It was always bright and sunny and warm. Hidden away in a rural area, behind all kinds of magical barriers, it was always a place of light and the second those gates opened to reveal the brilliant white structure and sunny fields hidden beyond Louis was struck with a wave of nostalgia. This was the Base he'd grown up at; it was one of the biggest bases in England, and one of only three training facilities in the UK. The grounds that day were filled with young trainees; children as young as five already running fitness drills and starting to learn combat skills. They wouldn't start any serious training until they went through the ceremony to imbue them with their powers, but still, the groundwork was clearly being laid now. Louis had smiled to himself as he fondly remembered those days.
They weren't the only team to be summoned that day, because they weren't the only ones that Rachel looked after. There were three teams in total. One led by Agent Olivia Smith, a strong looking woman who had a

kind smile, and another led by Agent Carter Smith who kept to himself and hadn't interacted much.

The three teams chatted politely outside in the sun before a Level Four Agent came out and demanded their attention. He spoke briefly about working alongside Rachel, and the respect he had for her. He spoke about how she had bravely given her life for the greater good, and done her duty, and how they would all have done the same given the choice. He then announced that there had been long discussions on how to continue and it had been deemed that Olivia's team would now take forward the investigation into 4XM. Amber's face spoke volumes at that point; she was furious, and Louis could understand why. 4XM was their case. It was his very first case and he wanted to see it through to the end, not have it handed off to others. The Level Four Agent, who never properly introduced himself, then announced that given Rachel's death there was a need for a new leader for their three teams and after careful consideration it had been decided that Chris would take her place. Chris beamed, and wasted absolutely no time stepping to the front of the crowd, and accepting his new responsibilities.

That is what had led him and Louis here, to this cemetery. He had wasted absolutely no time in stamping his new authority. He had moved out of the house on Brickmere Road the next day, and had taken Rachel's office and living quarters at Home Base 25, but he was somehow still very present in their lives with video calls every day. He'd demanded that he be made aware of any new cases that came through, and that he be consulted on exactly what action to take in the investigation. Everything was to go through him; and so he had decided, when the call came in about the cemetery, that he would investigate it personally and he wanted Louis to come with him.

"I feel like we got off on the wrong foot, and this is perhaps an opportunity for us to correct that," He'd explained when they got into the car together; and then proceeded to spend the next few minutes telling Louis all about his first few days in his new role, and all the things he was going to do. He spent the whole journey talking about himself in a way that spoke volumes; and yet Louis would grow to think of this as one of their more pleasant earlier interactions.

When they finally arrived, at that murky, grey, cemetery filled with police, Louis was very ready for some interaction with anyone other than Chris;

but his hopes for any friendliness from the human police were quickly dashed. The two of them stepped out of the car and approached the officer stationed on the main entrance to the cemetery, His name was PC John Nelson, and the second he spotted them his face gave everything away.
"They're here." He muttered into his radio, quiet enough that he was trying to hide it from them but loud enough that he was failing. Over his shoulder, a little further beyond the gate, a tent had been erected covering the area where the old lady's body had been found.
"Good morning Constable. What can you tell us about what's going on here?" Chris asked, trying to summon a commanding tone.
"Absolutely nothing." PC Nelson replied
"I'm sorry?" Chris said, clearly unsure what to do with that.
"I've been given very clear instructions that I'm not to tell you anything until…" He begins.
"Until I say so." Roars DCI Wade, bursting from the tent, flanked by another uniformed officer. "Always around you lot, like a bad bloody smell, and just as unwelcome. What're you doing here?" He says, advancing on them, wearing a furious look on his face.
"We were alerted to the situation and thought that we perhaps needed to assess the situation for…" Chris begins.
"Terrorism?" Wade interjects, mockingly. "What the bloody hell do you think some little old lady being killed has to do with terrorism?"
"Ah, so she was murdered?"
"I didn't say that, did I? Looks more like she was mauled by an angry animal to me, but I'm leaving that to the professionals. That's exactly what you should be doing, if you ask me."
"Look, I'd very much appreciate it if you could brief me on what you know so far, in a calm and constructive way…" Chris says, perhaps accidentally sounding incredibly condescending. This only serves to enrage Wade even further and he snorts, like an angry bull about to charge.
"And I'd very much appreciate it if you could kindly piss off for ten minutes and let me do my damn job, rather than popping in to screw everything up…" Wade retorted, clearly throwing all semblance of professionalism away in favour of brutal honesty.
"DCI Wade you're being incredibly unreasonable here. You are well aware that I have the authority to take control of this crime scene…
"Yeah and look what happened last time you had authority over something. That particular cock up still hasn't gone away." He says, with a sneer. This

time it's Chris' turn to lose his cool and snort angrily. Out of the corner of his eye Louis noticed PC Nelson sloping off and, having already had enough of this argument over who exactly was in charge, Louis decided to follow him. As the two angry men's voices begin to fade into the distance PC Nelson stops, leans against a tree, and lights up a cigarette. That's when he notices that Louis has followed him. He gives him a dubious look. "What do you want?" He asks him. Louis tries to give him his best friendly smile.

"Same as you, I think." He says, pointing back over his shoulder to where Chris and Wade are still verbally sparring. "To get out of the blast radius." Nelson lets out a half chuckle, and offers Louis a cigarette but he shakes his head. They stand in silence for a moment, and Louis realises he isn't quite sure what he wanted to achieve by following the human deeper into the cemetery, it just seemed like a better idea than staying put. "We are trying to help, you know." Louis tells him, not entirely sure if he's trying to reassure PC Nelson or himself.

"Yeah, I get it. But you can't really blame him, not after that whole thing at the hotel. Not saying it's your fault but it didn't exactly end well did it?"

"No. I guess not…" Louis agrees with a somewhat defeated shrug.

"And the news has been crucifying us for it all week; talking about how we let the murderer get away. It's been a bit of a nightmare." He adds. Louis nods. He's not sure what else to say. As bad as things were, he knows that things would've been much, much worse had they not been involved. He just doesn't know how to convey that to this human without telling him things he's been sworn to secrecy over. Humans are to be protected from the truth at all costs. That's a pretty important rule. They can't know about the existence of demonic energy; and they can't know the Custodians true purpose. It's better for everyone if they remain ignorant. The police would've never been able to handle the situation with 4XM by themselves. They'd have likely all been slaughtered. But, that's not the most constructive thing to say right now. "What does your department do, exactly?" PC Nelson asks, staring at him curiously.

"What do you mean?" Louis asks, hesitantly. He knows he's going to have to lie here; and he's not sure he'll be very good at it.

"You're always showing up at random scenes and we're just supposed to defer to you, but we've got no idea what you actually do? Like, how does an old lady dying have anything to do with terrorism?"

"It's difficult to define. Like, terrorism can take so many forms. If you think about how terrorism is defined it's just the unlawful use of violence or intimidation, especially against citizens, in the pursuit of political aims." Louis says, before pausing and blinking. He's not quite sure why he thought giving the dictionary definition of terrorism would be helpful, but that's what he'd done. PC Nelson continues to stare and Louis knows he needs to continue but is very worried about what might come out of his mouth next. "So, some of the stuff we look into might seem weird; but…there might be a bigger link…is what I'm trying to explain." He concludes, vaguely managing to rescue it.

"Yeah, weird is probably the right phrase," The officer says, finishing up his cigarette and glancing over Louis' shoulder to see whether there has been any conclusion to the sparring match between Chris and Wade.

"Oh?" Louis asks, spotting an opportunity to get more information.

"Yeah." He nods, clearly wrestling with the internal decision about whether to share any more. "I know he said not to, but…"

"I mean I already know there's a body. We know she didn't die naturally…just fill in a few more blanks?"

"It looks like she was attacked by something. She's a mess. I've seen bodies before but…I don't know…she looks like she was mauled by something. Poor old thing…no person could've done that…" He says, solemnly. It's clearly affected him and he wants to share that with someone. Louis is happy to listen, even if he's not quite sure about using the fact this man is a little traumatised to get information from him. It's also probably not a good idea for him to keep lying.

"You're sort of right, it's probably a human infected by a little piece of Demonic energy. Oh, Demonic energy? Yeah, it's a thing. Has been for YEARS. It's all around you, but no, you can't see it, you just have to kind of know it's there. I can kind of feel it but that's new and I don't really understand it. The others really don't get it." Is what he wants to say. But in this case the truth really wouldn't help. He knows he can't, he knows he's not allowed, and he knows that he'd sound like a mad man and that would severely hamper his attempts to build trust with the human. Instead the best he can come up with is a "that sounds awful," before completely avoiding PC Nelson's eye contact. Unfortunately his wandering eyes land onto something peculiar in the distance and before he can think he's already said "That's…weird," and attracted PC Nelson's attention to it as well.

"What?" He says, craning his neck around the tree and following Louis' eyeline.
"Nothing. Probably." He says, trying to downplay it whilst also taking some cautious steps forward to get a better view. In the distance, completely out of the way, and out of the way of the foot traffic from the police investigation there appears to be an empty grave. But this isn't the kind of empty grave that someone would expect to see in a cemetery; it's not one that's been freshly dug ahead of a funeral that day. This is one where the earth has been disturbed from underneath. This is the kind of grave you'd see in a terrible human horror movie. This is a grave that someone has crawled out of.
PC Nelson sums it up perfectly when he exclaims "What the fuck?" The colour drains from the man's face; and Louis detects a flash of fear. They both take cautious steps towards it in a heavy silence that Louis knows he should be breaking, but just can't find the right words to say to downplay this.
"This is a little more weird than I had in mind." He tries; and instantly regrets it. That was worse than when he tried to define terrorism, but he's a little thrown off by this too.
"This is...this is too much...what the hell happened here?" PC Nelson says, breaking out another cigarette. "Is this it? Are these the kind of things you deal with? There's all kinds of rumours...but I didn't believe them...but now I'm starting to think…" He stammers, clicking desperately at his lighter.
There is no headstone, just a small cross. This shows that it's a fresh grave. Very fresh in fact. The date of death was only a few days earlier.
"Steven Robinson," Louis says, reading the small plaque.
"What?"
"That's the name on there." He says, pointing at it, as if he needs to prove it.
"Maybe it was just a grave robber?" PC Nelson asks, with a little too much hope that he's found the explanation. It takes Louis a second to catch up with that train of thought; but when he does he nods to encourage it.
"Maybe that's it. Maybe it was a grave robber; and the old lady interrupted, so they had to kill her." He says, adding up the various pieces and trying desperately to jam them into something normal. Louis pauses for a moment, and realises it's best to just go with that.
"That's a really good idea. Have there been any other reports of grave robbing?" He asks, thinking so quickly he even surprises himself.

"I don't know…I guess I could check?" Nelson responds.
"Would you be able to do that, when you get back to the station? I need to get someone out here to clean this up." He asks, knowing that'll give him a chance to plant evidence to support the officer's theory. PC Nelson composes himself, getting over the initial shock of seeing the empty grave now that he's managed to find a rational explanation. He switches back to being a, relatively, composed police officer.
"Yes. Or I could call it in now I guess. No sense waiting. Be right back." He says, tossing his half smoked cigarette away and reaching for his radio. He walks away a little bit, to give himself some privacy and the moment he's out of earshot Louis swears, and pulls out his own phone. It rings a couple of times and then is answered and it's like Louis can sense how much he begrudged picking up the call.
"Danny. Can you plant some fake police reports about grave robbing in their system?" He blurts out before he has a chance to say anything.
"Yeah of course I can." He says, dismissively.
"Good, can you do it quickly?"
"Again, yes, if I wanted to. But, why?"
"Because someone is just about the check for them and I need him to find some!" He says, getting a little frustrated.
"Okay but, grave robbing? Why?" Danny asks, completely relaxed. Louis starts to panic; he can see that PC Nelson is talking to someone, and there are only seconds left to back up the story and prevent the policeman asking any more questions.
"Because we are standing at an empty grave, one that looks like someone crawled their way out by the way, and that was the best way to explain it. He jumped to that conclusion and it really, really helps if he now finds evidence to back it up, so hurry?" He says, the frustration bubbling over. Danny sighs, as if this is the biggest imposition he's ever heard of.
"Louis, you call me, making demands when I'm in the middle of something, and what you can't even say please?"
"Please?" Louis says, desperately watching the side of PC Nelson's face for any hint of how his conversation is unfolding. Danny sighs again, one laced with mock exhaustion.
"I dunno if I can be bothered…" He says. PC Nelson has turned around to look at Louis, with an inquisitive look on his face. Louis worries that it's already too late.

"Danny! Please, he's checking right now…" He says, on the verge of pleading, and it elicits a chuckle on the other end of the phone.
"Stop begging. I did it already. I can multitask." He says, cockily.
"Couldn't you have just said that?" He snaps, panic turning into irritation.
"I guess, but I liked the sound of panic in your voice. An empty grave though, really? He asks.
"I've got to go, he's coming back over. Will you have a look into a man called Steve Robinson. He died a few days ago? Thanks."
"I mean, I don't know, I'm really busy with…" Louis hangs up quickly, cutting him off, as PC Nelson makes his way back over.
"Well?"
"Yeah, actually. There have been a few reported lately. I must've missed it. They must be related?" He actually sounds relieved.
"It's definitely worth looking into. You should stay close to that one. Will you let me know what you find out though?" Louis asks, hopefully. He just wants to stay close to it in case PC Nelson stumbles across something else and needs to be guided back to his grave robbing theory.
Chris calls over, having finally resolved things with DCI Wade, who is walking away, looking even angrier.
"Louis, we're taking over here. I've called in a cleaning crew. They'll arrive in five. Constable, you're dismissed. Thank you." With that, Chris goes into the tent, presumably to tell the other officers in there the same. PC Nelson starts to walk away.
"I'm gonna go back to the station and look into this some more. I'll let you know if I find anything." He looks hesitantly at the tent. "Good luck in there, mate."

Chapter Twelve.

Chris wasted absolutely no time handing the crime scene over to the Cleaning crew and practically dragging Louis back to the car as soon as he could. He clearly didn't want to stick around, and so they had begun another awkward journey back to the house on Brickmere Road. After what seemed like hours, but was actually minutes, Chris stopped the car outside and turned to look at Louis.
"I just want to make sure we're 100% clear." He said, pausing for some reason known only to him. "Now that I've been promoted to Level Four; I want everything that happens here to come through me."

"Yes, that is very clear." Louis says, accidentally slipping sarcasm into his tone. It had only been about a week and yet he'd apparently already spent too much time with Amber and Danny.

"I mean it, Louis. I expect you to make sure the others know that, too. I want to keep close to everything that's going on. You get that, right?" He explains.

"I do." He says, a little less sarcastically, because of course he understood why Chris would want to.

"Good. Now, you can tell the others this too, all of your attention goes into this case. Got it? I'll make sure you get the reports from the Cleaners once they're done with the body, though it's pretty obvious how she died. Follow up on that empty grave you told me about. That was a good find, I'm glad we spotted it." He says. Louis' eye twitches a little at the use of the word "we" but he doesn't interrupt. "The most important thing though, is that you all leave the 4XM case alone. Have you got that?"

"Yes." He says, not sure if he means it.

"Good." Chris replies, not giving him enough time to add the 'but why?' that's on the tip of his tongue. "I have Olivia's team working on that; they're more experienced and better equipped to deal with a case this dangerous. I know you've still been looking into it, haven't you?"

"I have, yes, but…" Louis says. Of course he's still been looking at it. It was their case.

"But nothing. That's an order. Drop it. Anything relating to 4XM goes straight to the other team. Got it?"

"Yes." Louis agrees, begrudgingly. Chris nods, indicating he's dismissed. He doesn't need any further cues, he's happy to open the door and get out. Clearly, Chris shares that sentiment because the car is already moving before he's fully closed the door. As he watches him leave he pauses for a moment and composes himself by leaning against the fence. He chuckles to himself; thinking about the empty grave of Steven Robinson. It's not that it's funny that someone has been infected. No, he feels bad for Steven Robinson, whoever he was when he was alive. It's funny, and utterly ridiculous, that it's his second case and he's already dealing with something that sounds so like the work of a terrible fiction writer. Rarely, very rarely, it happens; if the infection is particularly slow moving, and the family insists on a quick funeral, but on the whole people crawling out of their own grave doesn't generally happen. It's just typical that it would happen for him.

Still part amused and part exasperated by that thought Louis eventually makes his way inside the house. He hangs up his coat and takes a left into the War Room where he knows the rest of the team will be. Straight away he spots Danny, silently and moodily researching on his laptop, and Lauren who is next to him waiting for a chance to be helpful.
"Hey," Louis says, greeting them both. Lauren perks up and smiles at his arrival, but Danny doesn't even acknowledge him.
"Hi sweetie." She says warmly, getting up from the chair. "How was it? Can I get you anything…?"
"No, thank you," Louis says, taking a seat on the other side of Danny.
"Oh, are you sure?" She says, looking a little disappointed.
"Will you stop running around after him?" Danny snaps, annoyed that his concentration is being broken. "Of the very few things he's capable of, it seems like he can at least manage to get himself food and drink." Louis is becoming used to this now. Danny is prickly, moody, and takes every opportunity he can to throw a veiled insult his way. He's trying very hard to just ignore it, because he's worried it'll only get worse if he doesn't. Whatever reason Danny dislikes him, he's not going to be able to change that by arguing with him. They're interrupted before Louis can decide exactly how it's best to respond by Amber thundering down the stairs and bursting into the room.
"You! Good. I thought I heard you." She says, pointing at Louis like she's accusing him of something.
"Me?" He says, surprised. She hasn't exactly warmed to him over the last week either.
"Yes. You. You said you wanted to brush up on close combat. So c'mon, let's go."
"Now?"
"Yes. The sooner the better." She snaps. "You want my help don't you?"
"Well, yeah, but.."
"Then enough questions; because right now I'm torn between disliking you and knowing that I might need you to be able to fight to keep one of us alive. So let's go." She says, and leaves the room as abruptly as she enters. Louis looks across at the other two, not quite sure what he's looking for, and very unclear on whether this is a good idea or not. Lauren gives him an encouraging look and he takes this to mean that she thinks it's a good idea, so he gets up and follows Amber out of the room and to the top floor of the house where their training room is. As soon as she's

confident he's out of earshot Lauren rounds on Danny, summoning the best stern look that she can muster. He's unphased.
"Why are you so hard on him?" She demands.
"I just don't like him. He's really annoying. Amber thinks so too." He says, with an apathetic shrug.
"At least she's trying." She argues.
"Please, she's only doing it so she can punch him. I'd be nicer too if it meant I could do that." Lauren huffs in response to this. He remains unphased.

It was the noise. That's the thing that really stood out to him. The noise everywhere. The ticking of clocks, the hum of electricals, the movement of the pipes, and everything else. The street outside, the people walking past, the birds in the sky, the rustling of trees. He could hear everything, everywhere, and it was driving him crazy. He was disorientated. He couldn't remember how he got home or how long it had been and everything was so overwhelming. Why did he feel like this? What had happened to him? There were so many questions that it seemed impossible to focus on any of them. Then came a thudding; loud, and obnoxious, and it took over everything.

He knocked gently at the front door. He'd seen it when he returned home from the supermarket. He'd just been to get a few bits in. It was midweek, and he usually did his big shop with his wife on the weekend, but the milk had been turning far too quickly and they needed some onions for the stew he wanted to make for tea. That's when he spotted their door was slightly ajar and had taken a mental note. Vincent wasn't a nosy neighbour, or he tried not to be anyway, but he knew with everything going on with that family they needed someone looking out for them. He'd left it half an hour, peeking out of the window every now and again after settling down with a cuppa and a custard slice, but there were no signs of movement so he'd decided to go in for a closer look.
"Cheryl?" He called out when there was no response from the knock. He was certain he'd heard a little movement though. He did so hope he wasn't about to walk in on a burglary. "Is that you?" He said, cautiously stepping inside. He gave a quick scan of the living room and concluded it was utter chaos. The problem was, from what he could tell, Steve hadn't been a particularly tidy man and so Vincent couldn't really tell whether the chaos

was from a burglary or from his general state of living. There was mess everywhere, but soon the scales started to tip more into burglary related chaos as he started to mentally catalogue several things that had been broken. This didn't seem good, Vincent thought to himself. There was a clock on the wall that, whilst still ticking, had been smashed. There was one of those electric photo frames, frozen on a picture of their little girl, that had been thrown against one of the walls. This wasn't just a man living in a pig sty, he concluded, and reached for his phone. "Is anyone here?" There was a loud thud and movement from the kitchen and Vincent jumped. "If someone's there you'd better come out now. I'm calling the police!" He says, raising his voice, trying to sound threatening, and moving cautiously towards the kitchen and the sounds of movement. He dials 999 and the operator answers. "Yes, I'd like the police please, I think my neighbours house has been..." He makes it to the kitchen doorway and breathes a sigh of relief as he finds the room seemingly empty. "...broken into. There seems to be..."
He screams and drops the phone.

Louis hits the ground hard. It's not the first time, either. This isn't going well for him, and Amber once again stands over him with a smirk on her face, having dropped him effortlessly. They're in the training room, which is the converted attic of the house. The floor is solid wood and there are only thin mats covering it, so he's definitely starting to feel it.
"This is easy." She says, backing off to give him room to climb gingerly to his feet. "Not that I mind, it's just, it's so obvious you don't have a clue what you're doing beyond a very, very basic level." Louis clambers up and tries to shake it off. He realises she's not even trying to goad him; she is just unpleasant, and unfortunately, she's right. He tries to attack, lurching forward, but she sees it coming, fends him off, and knocks him to the ground again. "If this was real you'd be dead by now. Really dead." She says, with a little too much glee, as she strolls away to take a sip of water. She's clearly not working up a sweat, so taking time to hydrate just seems pointed. He picks himself back up again, rubbing his shoulder as he does. "You're not actually giving me any advice though; you're just throwing me around and laughing about it."
"You asked for help, this is me helping." She says placing her bottle down next to her and lurching suddenly. It takes him by surprise but he avoids a strike by, not entirely gracefully, stumbling backwards. He tries to hit her

but she ducks, and kicks him, knocking him further backwards but not off his feet.

"But if you're not going to help me improve then why are we doing this?"

"I was bored. I hate sitting around waiting for the next thing to happen. This is taking my mind off that." She says, lunging forward at him. He dodges it, barely. "And I am teaching you a lesson."

"No you're not!" He whines, trying for a clumsy strike which she easily steps out of the way of. "I get you don't like me, but I don't understand why?" He says, letting the frustration get to him once he's recovered his footing. This is all it's been for the last half an hour. No pointers, no tips, just her taking a perverse pleasure in hitting him.

"I don't really like anyone. Maybe Danny, but only sometimes."

"Why?"

"Why what?"

"Why're you such a dick?" He asks, suddenly. That shocks her, and it was meant to. He figured the only way to catch her off guard physically would be to say something suddenly that would surprise her. He takes advantage of this and jabs her right in the face. She stumbles backwards and smirks to herself. He pushes his luck by attempting another strike but she grabs his arm before he can connect, flipping him over her to the ground and twists his arm painfully.

"Because you're rushing." She tells him, continuing to twist. "You're inexperienced and clearly out of practice, and that will get you killed. Worse, that might get me killed." She releases him and lets out a noise that's somewhere between a sigh and a growl. "I can see it in that dumb look you wear on your face 90% of the time. This is still new and fun to you. But it's real. You should care more about whether you can keep yourself alive than whether I like you." She looks like she's about to attack him again as he lays nursing his arm, but backs off for more water. "You're rushing at me. I'm not really having to do anything except react and that's making it really easy for me. I rush into a fight, but I'm always in control when I'm in one. You need to slow down and let them lead. You said something about how 4XM felt angry, right?"

"I did?" He says.

"Yeah. Your weird sense thing, when we were at that guy's house. You said how you could feel how angry he was."

"Oh. Yeah." He says, not really wanting to think too much about that feeling, or even about that day. None of them had spoken about it much since. They'd all quietly got on with it, seemingly silently agreeing that they needed to find the person responsible for Rachel's death, but they'd not really talked it through together. It wasn't so much sensing 4XM's feelings that he didn't want to talk about; it was the other one. As he'd stumbled across Rachel's body the feelings had been so intense and so overwhelming he didn't even want to revisit what it felt like. He was scared to. Whoever it was that had driven the clever into Rachel's skull was so deeply infected with demonic energy, and with an intense level of emotion and pain, that even trying to go back to that place made his head spin a little.

"That's how they always are. Angry, emotional, and stupid." Amber said, bringing his focus back to the moment. "I can relate," She adds, which seems to stray as close as she's willing to get to an apology. "But that's the advantage over them. They rush you, like you keep trying to do with me. Breath. Let them come to you. They're always going to be stronger than you; so you have to be in control of as much as you can. Yes, I get pissed off easily. Yes I am a dick. I get so frustrated sitting around chasing shitty leads that go nowhere. I guess things make sense to me when I'm fighting. It's the one time I feel like I'm in control." She says, and in that moment Louis feels like he's a little bit closer to understanding her. He can see it on her face, as it drops slightly as she finishes talking, because it's like she's suddenly a little less guarded. All the bravado and bluster is gone. Fighting is what makes sense to her. It's the one thing she knows she's good at; it's the one time she feels like she can impact the outcome. Not in the tracking, or the investigation, or the waiting around. She's in control when she's fighting for her life, and it's the one time she's not afraid. There's a subtle cough at the doorway and they both turn to see Danny standing there, watching them.

"As much as I don't want to interrupt before there's any real injuries…" He says, nodding at Louis who has a split lip from an earlier blow. "That name you gave me. From the cemetery. The police have just had a report of a break-in at his house. I thought you might want to check it out."

"Absolutely. Thanks!" He says, with a level of enthusiasm that almost sounds juvenile. He looks around at Amber, who has her usual demeanour fully back in place. "Want to come?"

"Not really. I think I've done my turn babysitting you." She snipes, before focusing on Danny. "Tag, you're it."

"Oh thanks." He says, making Louis regret thanking him.

"Just give me the address...I'll go by myself."
"Nah I'll come. If you got yourself killed it'd be unbearable...Lauren would never let it go." He replies, with a smirk.
"Fine, come on then." Louis says, grabbing his things and leaving the room without another word. Amber and Danny catch each other's eye and exchange a smile.

Church Street was usually so quiet. It was a little cul-de-sac that was a pleasant mix of old residents who'd lived there for years, and young families looking for a place to settle. There was never any trouble and people knew each other because this was the kind of place you settled for life. Or it was, until today. Everyone had heard the scream, you see, and it wasn't the kind of thing that anyone would forget.
Sarah, from number 42, had thought this would be where she'd live for a long time. She'd called it her 'forever home' when she and her husband Rakesh had bought it two years ago, just after they'd adopted their daughter Erica. It was the kind of place that she could see herself raising a full family in. They'd adopt more children, and one day Erica and the others would come to visit with their own children. She'd thought her and Rakesh would be happy here for a long, long time. But that changed mere minutes after she'd seen her neighbour, Vincent, crossing the street to number 45, where the Robinsons lived.
Sarah liked Vincent. He was a good neighbour. When they'd first moved in he'd wasted no time in coming over to introduce himself. He'd lived at number 44 all his life, he'd told them. He'd grown up there with his parents, both of whom had passed on now, and his two sisters. He was a florist by trade, and he'd brought them a bouquet of pink lilies and roses as a housewarming gift and in return they'd fed his cat when he'd gone away once. He'd invited them round for dinner to say thank you, and they'd meant to take him up on it but hadn't had the chance. They never would be able to now.
She'd waved at him through the window as he'd headed across the street, but he hadn't seen her. She couldn't help but wonder if things would've been different if he had; if maybe she'd have caught his attention and invited him to come over for a cup of tea. It wasn't something she'd ever done, but it was the kind of thing she'd always wanted to do, and today would've been the perfect day to start it. She hadn't though, and she would think about that decision a lot over the coming years.

She'd checked her phone next, spending a couple of minutes scrolling pointlessly through her social media. That was when she'd heard it. The scream. The shriek. The cry. For the briefest of moments she'd thought it had come from her phone, but quickly realised it had come from outside the house. Her attention snapped back to the window, and she wasn't the only one. Sarah saw Grace, from number 47, poking her head out from behind her blinds. Their gazes met, and they had one of those weird silent conversations where they both asked each other if they'd really heard that and if there was anything they should do.
She went to the front door and opened it cautiously, looking up and down the street for any signs of commotion; for some teenagers messing around, maybe. But there was nothing. She looked across the street to number 45 and somehow she just knew. It was Vincent. Something had happened to her lovely neighbour. This was confirmed moments later when the sound of police sirens thundered through their quiet street and all hell broke loose. She'd been looking at pictures of her friends living happily on Instagram while a man died just across the street; and while everyone would tell her there was nothing she could've done she'd never really be able to get over the strange feeling of guilt over that. Six months later she'd tell Rakesh she wanted to put the house up for sale, and they'd move to Dorset, where her Grandparents lived and could help raise Erica. They would not adopt another.

There were already two police cars, an ambulance, and far too many bystanders. That was very much not a good sign, which Louis and Danny conveyed to each other silently before stepping out of the car and into the crowd. Danny wore a look of utter disdain for the gathered human crowd as they battled through them to the front where PC Dean Nadin stood at the garden gate.
"I'm sorry, you can't…" He began, but Danny cut him off by flashing a badge. They were slightly exaggerated credentials, of course, one which complimented their usual Counter Terrorism cover story. In that moment Louis did begin to wonder just how much scrutiny they would hold up to, but thankfully that was irrelevant in that moment. Although PC Nadin didn't exactly look happy about it, he waved them through and they entered the Robinson family home.
As they did they were watched curiously by an on-looker. Kim Adams had been standing in the crowd taking in the scene. She'd been on her way

home, calling it a day early for a change, when she'd got wind of something happening on Church Street. Something that was both newsworthy and involved the police, and given that she was leading the charge in the criticism of their handling of the Eagle Hotel incident she knew she had to check it out. She wasn't disappointed she had. It was obvious to everyone there was a body inside, they just weren't announcing that. That was standard enough, but her interest was definitely piqued by these two boys who'd just turned up in their incredibly cliched unmarked black car and waltzed straight in with just the flash of a badge. She follows their lead and pushes her way to the front of the crowd and, before PC Nadin can open his mouth, flashes her press pass. He snorts.
"Nice try, but absolutely not." He says, making no effort to hide the hint of contempt in his voice. She hadn't really expected it to work, but it got her a little bit closer.
"It worked for them." She says, trying to get a sneaky look over his shoulder.
"They showed me something a little more…commanding." He says, lowering his eyebrows into a scowl. She responds with her sweetest possible smile.
"And what was that exactly? They seemed very young to hold any kind of position of authority, especially over you Dean," She asks, doing her best to sound conversational and complimentary. She can see he almost takes the bait, but stops himself at the last moment.
"I'm not in a position to disclose that at this time."
"And what about what's going on here? This seems like a lot of fuss…"
"Again, this is an active investigation Ms Adams. If you're looking for an official statement I'd refer you to…"
"C'mon Dean, just a little something. Completely off the record?" She says, dialling up the sweet smile to an almost sickly level and blinking innocently. He doesn't bite to that either, sadly.
"Absolutely not."
"Hmm, but there are so many police in such a quiet area, it seems…" She begins, but it quickly becomes apparent she's pushed her luck too far.
"Are you stupid?" He snaps. "After the way you've been slating us in your little reports do you really think I'm giving you anything? If you don't get out of here now I'll…" She whips her phone out and presses record, shoving it right in his face and dropping her sweet expression to one that's far more stoic and almost challenging.

"You'll ...?"

"No comment, Miss Adams. Now move along please." He says, calming his tone back down. She lets out a sigh of frustration and stops recording him, turning her focus to trying to see what is going on inside, as she sees some paramedics leaving.

Inside, it took only seconds for DCI Wade's gaze to fall upon Danny and Louis, and for his face to drop to the familiar one of annoyance and disdain. He was in the kitchen, with a group of Scene of Crime Officers, around a dead body.

"Hi Detective." Louis says, adopting a friendly tone to preemptively compensate for whatever Danny is about to say.

"Hold up lads, the experts are here." Wade replies, his response filled to the brim with sarcasm.

"I'm glad you recognise that." Danny says, ignoring the sarcasm and starting to inspect the scene. Louis mentally scrambles for what to say next to at least try to diffuse the situation a little.

"What happened here?" He stutters. In response Wade looks him up and down and seems to come close to snarling.

"Ain't really had time to work that out yet. We got a call from the victim, who you will currently find all over the kitchen." He gestures behind him to the body. It's a gruesome sight. It looks like the man was torn apart by something. "He said there'd been a break in. Signs of forced entry too, so it fits. But he must've got attacked while he were on the phone and, well, you can see the results. I recognised the address from a case I've been looking at and, since I ain't had much to do after your mate lightened my workload this morning, I thought I'd stop by. I assume history is about to repeat itself?" He asks, bitterness evident in his gruff voice.

"Do you know who he is?" Louis asks, hoping that if he doesn't rise to it and stays pleasant he'll be able to win him over. Who knows why he thought this, he wasn't exactly doing the best job of winning people over so far.

"Vincent Pape." He says, curtly. "He lives across the street. Not had chance to tell his family yet. Don't suppose you fancy taking that bit of the job too?" He asks. Louis is a little taken aback and can't quite form words quick enough. Instead he just kind of stands mouthing like a goldfish and trying to think about whether that's something he even should do. Wade quickly puts him out of his misery. "Nah, thought not." He says, shaking his

head. Louis was briefly grateful when Danny approached, having clearly finished his inspection of the living room. The gratitude soon ceased though, when Danny opened his mouth. Louis saw it coming, too, but was powerless to stop it. The second he walked into the kitchen and laid his eyes on the Scene of Crime Officers he clapped loudly to get their attention as if he was addressing animals.
"Stop. Now." He commanded abruptly. They all looked at him, and then over at Wade for further instruction. Danny glared at them and shook his head. "Are you all deaf? Stop. Leave. Get out. You're done." Wade finally nods his approval, rolling his eyes as he does, and they begin to gather their things and leave, mumbling between them as they do. Danny swoops in for a closer look at the victim like some kind of vulture.
"Oh wow. He's a mess. The Cleaners are going to have their work cut out here." He says, to no one in particular.
"Cleaners?" Wade asks Louis, his tone curious, which is a nice change.
"Yeah it's our version of your Scene of Crime Officers."
"Cleaners…that's…"
"Simple?" Louis offers. "So you said you recognised the address from another case?" He follows up, hoping to use the exchange of information to attempt to build a relationship.
"Yeah." He replies, simply. That didn't work, then, Louis thought to himself.
"What happened?"
"Home owner was murdered at work." Wade offers, attempting to walk a fine line between not being helpful, but not being obstructive either.
"Okay?" He asks, hoping that'll prompt the Human to share more. It doesn't. "Can you tell me any more?" He adds, when it doesn't.
"Not much more to tell right now."
"Have you actually been investigating it or are you just hoping we'll come along and take over that one too?" Danny pipes up, quickly shattering any hope of building up good will. DCI Wade lets out a very sarcastic laugh.
"Yeah, because you guys did such a great job at the hotel, didn't ya?" He roars.
"You wouldn't have done any better." Danny fires back coolly.
"Whatever you say, kid. You go around saying you're some kinda specialists, but the two of you look about twelve. I bet you're barely experts in wiping your own arses. If you care that much I'll have someone send over the file and you can try your luck. Don't call me when you screw it up

though." He says, and starts to head for the door, clearly very keen to get this conversation over with.

"Can someone send it to me now?" Danny asks. He's been way too rude to expect Wade to do anything even vaguely helpful but, for some reason, the man stops, thinks about it, and nods.

"Yeah wait there." He says, pulling his phone out before continuing forward to find somewhere private he can make the call. Louis wonders whether he'd just concluded it was better to get it over with than drag it out.

"We'll let the Cleaners deal with this. It's a mess." Danny explains standing up and walking out of the kitchen. He speaks in Louis' direction, but not quite to Louis.

"Was it a Used-to-Be?" Louis asks him.

"Probably. You can see what I can. Can't you, I dunno, sense something or whatever?" His tone is incredibly condescending, like he's making fun of him, so Louis takes a deep breath and closes his eyes. When it happened at the hotel, and even before that, it hadn't been anything he'd done. It was more something that had hit him. But he concentrates on what's around him. He's determined, but his motivation is more to prove Danny wrong than because he thinks it'll help discover what happened. He can only imagine the conversations he and Amber have been having about it, and how much ridicule was involved.

"I just...I feel a sense of dread, but maybe that's just me." He says, trying to separate his own feelings from what he might be able to feel in the air. "A little confusion. I felt that at the cemetery too, so maybe..."

"Confusion is definitely you." Danny says, unhelpfully.

"I'm not really getting anything strong. Before it was like...flashes of something. It was kinda like I could...see?" He says, trying to explain what it feels like when he doesn't really understand himself. He opens his eyes to see Danny with a smug smirk on his face and everything else he might've been able to feel is replaced with his own sense of irritation.

"Enough." Danny says, cutting him off with an eye roll. "It's a dead body at the house of someone who's empty grave you found. I think it's someone who's newly infected. I don't need to sense anything to tell you that, just my big brain. I'd say he crawled his way out, he was probably confused but that's obvious so no points, made his way back home and said hello to his neighbour." Danny explains, clearly trying to demonstrate how clever he is. "We've got to find him."

"Oh, look at you. Full of great ideas. Where do we start?" He replies, blinking and shooting him another infuriatingly smug look. Louis, sadly, doesn't have an answer for him. "Exactly. I need to see what the police have got. There might be something in that. It might take me a little while though."

"Why? He said he was sending the file over now. I thought you were some kind of genius?" Louis snaps, somewhat accidentally.

"I am, thank you." Danny says, completely ignoring the sarcasm. "He doesn't like helping us though so I don't trust that he'll give us everything. I just need to work out why…" As if on cue Wade walks back over to them, hanging up the phone.

"Apparently we're having problems with our e-mails, so I'm going to have copies of the physical file brought to you. Same address as usual?" He says.

"Yes, please." Danny says, with an uncharacteristically sweet and amicable tone. The look he shoots at Louis says 'I told you so,' though.

"It'll be with you this afternoon." Wade tells them, and Danny nods. They both stare at each other for a second. Louis begins to wonder which one is going to break the staring contest first, but he's distracted when he spots something. The living room is in complete disarray, which is perhaps why it wasn't obvious at first. There seems to have been a lot of things that were smashed; and it's not really clear if that was in the struggle with Vincent or from something else. There is, afterall, a little blood on the carpet near the door to the kitchen which suggests there was at least some attempt made to escape. But it's not the blood on the floor that's caught Louis' eye; it's the bloody fingerprints on what appears to be a digital photo frame. It's been damaged, and it's laying on the floor as if discarded or thrown, but it's still cycling through photos of a seemingly happy family. There's something that draws Louis to it. A feeling he can't quite put his finger on. He walks over to it, to have a closer look, and inspects the smudged bloody fingerprints a little closer.

"Did the man who lived here have a family?" He shouts over his shoulder to Wade, feeling like he already knows the answer.

"He did." He replies, still not breaking eye contact with Danny, who's still smiling at him.

"A wife?"

"Yeah. They were separated though; and yes before you ask, questioning her was pretty much the first thing we did."

"...and where is she?" Louis asks, making Wade finally look over at him.
"Well she'd already moved out." He explains. "Poor guy. She took their kid with her too. Made me feel bad for him. First his wife up and leaves him and then...well, you'll see when I get the file over to you anyway." He says. Louis glances over at Danny, and he can tell that he's reached a similar conclusion, though he would never admit that Louis got there first.
"Where does she live?" Danny asks, his cocky smile gone now.
"I can't remember the address, but like I said, it's in the file." Wade tells them, visibly confused as to why they're so insistent on this.
"I think I need to go see her now. Could you find it?" Louis explains, adding a little urgency to his ask which attracts Wade's curiosity.
"I can call the station again and see if they can. Why?"
"It's a theory. I might be wrong, but..." He says, trailing off as he looks into the kitchen at Vincent Pape's mangled body. "...humour me? Please?" Wade tilts his head, indicating he's listening. "What if the same person who did this goes after her, too?" Louis finishes, obviously not wanting to give everything away but swaying as close to the truth as he can. Wade is clearly willing to listen a little, but he'd likely switch off the second Louis started talking about dead husbands and empty graves.
"You don't think this was a random break in, do you?" Wade asks, after a moment of thought.
"I do not." Louis tells him.
"Okay. I think I can remember where it is, let's go." Wade says, turning towards the door.
"But..." Louis begins to protest.
"No, I'm coming. You want my help, so I'm coming with you." He tells him, making it clear he's not going to budge on this. Louis looks across to Danny for help but, unsurprisingly, finds none.
"Great. You two go. I'll stay here and wait for the Cleaners, then hopefully I can start working on that file. Have fun boys," He says, dismissively, before pausing and letting out a large sigh as if he's being inconvenienced. "Wait." He says, gesturing Louis over. He leans in close so that Wade can't overhear him. He's uncomfortably close; closer than Louis has any desire for him to be. "Be careful." He whispers, but in a tone that sounds more like he's being told off. "Don't be an idiot, and don't die. I don't trust him." He leans back and speaks a little further back. "I probably should come with you, but I really don't want to, so you two are on your own. Have fun and watch your back." With that he backs off entirely, not waiting for a

response, and goes for another look at the body. Louis hesitates. He's reluctant to go with Wade. Taking the Human with him could put him in unnecessary danger. He's also a little wary about what Danny said. He doesn't really think Wade means any harm, but he could be wrong. He also can't see any other way, and Steven Robinson's wife could be in danger from her recently infected husband, especially if the state of their neighbour was anything to go by. He nods for Wade to lead the way and begins to follow him out of the door; but just before he leaves Danny calls for him. "Louis? I mean it. Don't die." He says, repeating himself before grinning and pulling out his phone to make a call to the Cleaning team.

Chapter Thirteen.

This was Cheryl's favourite part of the day because it belonged entirely to them. It always had. Ever since Jasmine was three weeks old she'd made sure to read to her every night. It was strange. People always said how quickly kids grew up and she never felt that more than during these times. She knew there were only a finite amount of nights left that she would read to her daughter; and every story brought her one closer to that day when she'd stop reading to her. Whether it was because she'd outgrow being read a bedtime story or, even worse, because Cheryl was no longer able to do it. She'd been thinking more like that for the past week, ever since Jasmine's father had been found dead at work. Like everything had been brought suddenly into focus, like the best parts of her life could all be brought to a half suddenly. While her estranged husband wasn't exactly Cheryl's favourite person, she'd always known he was a good man, and he hadn't deserved that. Still, everyone dies, and one day she too would leave their daughter behind. For now though, she finished the story, kissed her daughter on the forehead, and tucked her in.
"Goodnight, my darling." She said gently.
"'Night mummy," Jasmine replied. Cheryl took a quick look around the room with a sense of pride. They'd only moved in a few weeks ago and while the rest of the house was still a mess, Jas' room looked great. Although she'd definitely felt the strain of living on a budget now that she was a one income household, she had done what she could. She wanted to make sure that her little girl, who was already unsettled by the move, had a place that felt like a home, even if it wasn't the one she was used to.

She blew her daughter a kiss, which she returned with a giggle and cheeky smile, and turned the light out.
Cheryl then made her way slowly downstairs. The hallway was bare, and that wouldn't be changing any time soon. First Jas' room, then the kitchen, then the living room, then her room, and then finally the hallway. She had considered moving back to Church Street now that Steven was dead, but that felt a little disrespectful. She hadn't wanted to live there with him so it felt wrong to move back in there when he was barely cold. No, she'd sell that house, clear the mortgage, and maybe put the money away somewhere for Jasmine's future. Her thoughts are interrupted by a banging that makes her jump midway down the stairs. She gets down to the bottom and heads into the living room, to the source of the banging, and finds her brother Cain hammering a nail into the wall.
"You'll have to stop that now, I've got Jas settled." She instructs him, with a grateful smile. Her twin brother has barely left her side for the last week; ever since they found out the news about Steven. It's like he's hanging around waiting for her to crash, and honestly, she doesn't really know how she hasn't yet.
"She got off okay?" He asks her gently, laying the hammer down and throwing himself down on the sofa.
"I give her ten minutes before she's down asking for something else; but let's not give her any more excuses by hammering." She says, sitting next to him.
"I had to do something Chez, you've lived here nearly a month and barely decorated. Can you imagine when mum comes to visit?"
"God, can you imagine? It'll be another reason I shouldn't have left Steve..." She says, trailing off and pausing sadly after she mentions his name out loud and realising she might be closer to breaking than she thought.
"Nope! We're not doing that. I'm here to cheer you up. So you stay there..." He says, popping back up from the sofa with a mischievous grin on his face "...and I'm going to grab a couple of those cans I spotted in the fridge..." He says, making a beeline for the kitchen.
"...I'm surprised it's taken you till now to sniff those out..."
"...while you get on your phone and find us a half decent Chinese."
"Haven't you got work tomorrow?" She asks with a raised eyebrow, knowing that it won't just be one can, there's at least eight in the fridge and he's probably spotted the bottle of vodka she's got in the freezer too.

"Yeah but sod it, it's worth it for my favourite sister." He says with a chuckle, coming out of the kitchen and handing her a can. She rolls her eyes. She's his only sister.

"You're an arse." She replies. He's about to reply when there's a loud thud from upstairs. They both stop and look up, as Cheryl furrows her brow and shouts up to her daughter. "Jas, you okay up there honey?" She waits, but there's no answer, so she puts down the can on top of a box that'll soon be an assembled coffee table, and gets herself up off the sofa. "I'll go check on her, you take a look for that Chinese." She quickly makes her way out of the room and he swipes open his phone to find something to eat as she thunders up the stairs.

He's looking through options when the half hammered nail catches his eye. He gets back up, gives it another whack with the hammer and then grabs the picture frame that's propped up against the wall waiting to be given a home. He hangs it and stands back to admire his handiwork. That's when Cheryl screams.

"Oh my God! Cain, help!" She cries; and he doesn't need to be called twice. Hammer still in hand he bolts up the stairs to his niece's bedroom and finds his sister frozen in terror in the doorway. He looks over her shoulder, and sees what she's looking at; there's a man sitting at the foot of the child's bed. He pushes past his sister, puffing out his chest and making himself look as big as possible.

"Who the fuck are you?" He roars at the figure; but there's no response. "Answer me or I'll…"

"It's Daddy!" Jasmine says with a giggle, as if laughing at how silly her uncle is being.

"What the f…No, Jas honey, it can't be…" He replies, looking back at Cheryl who's still frozen, eyes wide in shock. The figure still hasn't moved; he's sitting, staring at the child. Cain moves forward, he knows he has to get her out of here and so he reaches over and grabs her, pulling her roughly out of the bed. "Jas, go with your mum…" But as he moves the child away the figure reacts, shooting to his feet with a guttural growl and grabbing hold of his arm with a filthy, muddy, hand. Cain headbutts him in the nose, and practically flings the little girl behind him. He still has the hammer in his hand and he raises it above his head and the figure stumbles back from the shock of the headbutt. "I'm warning you." He says, brandishing the weapon. "Chez, get her out of here." He commands. But his sister is still frozen. The figure darts forward. He tries to swing the hammer but the blow is knocked away as the man lunges and grabs him. For a brief second the light from the hallway catches his face and Cain realises he does look an awful lot like his brother-in-law. He's thrown through the air by the figure, as if he weighs nothing, and sent crashing into a wardrobe he'd built only days earlier. There's a crunching and as he hits the floor his brain tries to work out if it was the wood or his bones; and even before the wardrobe tumbles down on top of him he realises there's nothing else he can do to help his sister.

As soon as Cain hit the floor this man, whoever he was, charged at her. He grabbed her painfully by the arm but it was this that finally snapped her out of her stunned silence and she smacked him across the face.
"Get off me," She roared, reaching behind her to lay one hand on her cowering daughter's shoulder. The man stares at her, stunned more by the fact that she struck him than by the force of it. She stares back, equally stunned at just how close his features look to that of her dead husband in the light. She pushes those thoughts to the back of her mind. She can work out what the hell is going on later. She stares straight into his dark eyes, trying not to show how terrified she is. His eyes are way darker than Steven's ever were, and he has a kind of vacant expression on his face, like he's not quite sure what's going on either. He reaches to grab her again, ripping her away from Jasmine, and tossing her out of his way. She's winded but she knows she needs to get back up as she hears her daughter scream and sees the man advance on her.
There's a crash from downstairs…

…because the banging hadn't been enough, but the screams were. Louis takes a leaf out of Amber's book and throws all of his weight at the front door. Although he's not as strong, as graceful, or as well practised in smashing open a door as she is, it pops open very easily. As he charges up the stairs he wonders if he should've pretended to make more of an effort for Wade's sake, because of course he's second guessing himself as he charges towards potential danger. He gets to the top of the stairs, Wade bumbling along just behind him, and takes in the scene before him. It's clearly the little girl, Steven Robinson's daughter perhaps, that's screaming as a dirty, pale, scary looking man advances on her. Her father, perhaps? Louis doesn't know for sure but he quickly grabs at his jacket pocket for his tranquilliser pistol and points it.

"Stop!" He cries. He's not really sure of the protocol here. Should he have warned him? Maybe, maybe not. He's not even sure if this is a Used-to-Be that he's pointing the gun at, or just a very ill human. He definitely hadn't expected to actually find the Used-to-Be here. That seemed way too easy. He keeps the weapon aimed; deciding this likely is the target and that he should definitely assume he is until he knows otherwise. The hesitation to reach that decision is enough time for the man's attention to whip around onto him. He starts to charge with some horrific, animalistic, screech. Yep, that's definitely the Used-to-Be then, he concludes. Louis fires but his aim is off, probably because he spent too much time thinking and not enough aiming, and he misses. The creature throws itself into him; sending him crashing backwards into Wade, and them both crumpling into the wall. He pops quickly back to his feet, untangling himself from the older man, but Steven Robinson has already hurtled down the stairs and is shooting out of the door and into the street. Louis considers giving chase but decides against it as the girl's mother starts shouting about her brother needing help. The priority is definitely making sure everyone is okay here, and maybe getting a Cleaning team here. For the briefest moment, Louis actually wishes Danny had come too. Or, actually, Amber.

Across town Danny is arriving back at the house on Brickmere Road, having left the Cleaners to their tasks, because there was no need for him to waste any more time there. He would shortly receive a report confirming that all evidence had been removed, and that the body had been destroyed in case of infection and that was all that needed to be done now. He heads straight to the War Room, pulls out his laptop, and gets to work. He mutters to himself as he hammers away on the keys, because he absolutely does not have the patience to wait for Wade and the human police to do something as ridiculous as send him over paper copies of their case. He's going to hack straight into their system, with relative ease, and take what he needs himself.

"Oh, hi." Lauren says, popping her head around the door to see who it is. He vaguely nods at her in recognition, but never takes his eyes away from his screen. She takes that small gesture as an invitation to join him and pulls up a chair at the table. "What're you working on? Can I help?"
"No." He says.
"There must be something I can do…" She says, taking no offence at his bluntness. Perhaps because she's used to Danny's overall demeanour, or

perhaps because she simply won't be deterred from finding something to keep her occupied. She isn't fully healed from the wounds she suffered at the hands of 4XM and so has been feeling a little useless, especially with him and Louis out investigating this afternoon.

"Fine." He says, knowing it's easier to accept the help. He hits a few keys and something prints off over the other side of the room. "Go over that, find me the cause of death. I'm going to see how far into the investigation they got." She hobbles over to the printer and retrieves the reports, grateful to have something to do.

"Investigation? Are you going to catch me up?"

"Yes. That empty grave this morning, the break-in we've just been to. It's all linked to a murder victim from last week. I think the victim was infected. I want to find a cause of death so we can start to work out what effect it's had on him. I have a suspicion…"

"Oh, okay. Where's Louis?" She asks, with a little excitement as she flicks through the pages.

"Mm?" He says, looking up in confusion as if he's completely forgotten who Louis is, before he seems to remember. "Oh I don't know, he went off to speak to the dead guys' wife."

"And you let him go alone?" She asks. He peers up at her with a look that's somewhere between confusion and indignation.

"Lauren, he's not a child, I don't actually need to babysit him."

"You can be so pig-headed sometimes Daniel, we're supposed to be a team; none of us should be going off alone at the moment." She tells him, her voice bordering on the tone of a parent.

"Ah, he's not, I left him with the idiot policeman. Although, I'm not sure he can be trusted right now."

"Do you mean Matthew?" She asks him, and he kind of waves his hand in a nonchalant way, indicating that he doesn't really care what the man's name is.

"Yeah, yeah. Whatever it is, the one who's been hiding stuff from us." He explains, pulling the conversation back to their investigation to avoid any more talk of Louis.

"I'm sure that wasn't deliberate." Lauren says, and Danny rolls his eyes at her blind naivety.

"These reports say it was pretty gruesome. That's exactly the kind of thing that he should be telling us about. He knows that by now. I just can't believe it didn't turn up in any of the auto-search filters I have set up…"

"Danny, look at the date. We had other things to be dealing with. Which is a perfect reminder of why we should be looking out for each other..." She says, with a slight shake of her head. The date on the report shows that Steven Robinson died the same night as the incident at the Eagle Hotel.
"I still wouldn't have missed it" He insists stubbornly. "I think it's been kept from us deliberately. Okay. He was murdered while he was working at the shop he worked at...there must be CCTV..." He continues, glossing over what she said about looking out for each other. She peers at the report too.
"It looks like they had some trouble identifying the cause of death. He was pretty badly beaten. Lots of lacerations, broken bones. Oh dear."
"The in-store equipment was destroyed and they couldn't retrieve any of the footage. Urgh. Okay, so, there must've been some kind of backup. DJ&G Security. Okay I'm on their website now..".
"Oh, he lost a lot of blood. This poor, poor man. He must've suffered."
"It says they can set it up so that the footage is regularly backed up to your cloud account. Why couldn't the police do this? It's not hard, just needs a little..."
"He bled out. What an awful way to go, just being left to bleed out, all alone. What must he have been thinking?"
"Okay I've got his account. Now all I need to do is a little...and I've got it. Humans really don't have an ounce of common sense. Okay...now just to find the date...and...."
The footage begins to play and as soon as Lauren sees the change in his expression on his face she knows something is wrong. He's found something he really doesn't like.

Louis takes a slow walk out of the house, deep in his own thoughts and processing what has happened so far tonight. He froze, however briefly, when coming face-to-face with Steven Robinson and he can't help but dwell on that. Things could've been different if he'd reacted quicker, if he had fired faster or been better at anticipating the hit. If any of the others had been in his position, this might be over now.
Arthur and David, two of the human paramedics that Wade insisted on calling to the scene, rush past him and into the house to assist their colleagues with Cain. He's survived, for now, though when Louis left him he was bleeding heavily and no doubt had some internal injuries from being crushed by the wardrobe. The street was quiet when he and Wade arrived and now it's in chaos, just like Church Street was, with additional

police cars and ambulances on the scene. There are men in uniform everywhere.

"What the hell did we just walk in on?" Wade says in a low growl. Louis jumps because he hadn't realised the man had followed him out of the house. Louis doesn't answer. He just keeps staring absently at the lights that are still flashing on top of the ambulance. Wade, meanwhile, stares awkwardly at the young man's face, as if he's expecting to find answers in it. "Are you alright?" He adds, finally and a little hesitantly.

"Yeah…I just…" Louis begins, but trails off because he's not sure where the sentence will end. "I'm still not…" He says, again not quite able to finish the sentence as he looks down at his hands. They're covered in blood from trying to help Cain. It's dried and flaky, and crumbles off as he moves his fingers. He can't help but stare at it and get lost again in thoughts of what he could've done better. Could he have been faster getting here? Maybe if he'd realised what the photo frame meant sooner? He could've picked up on it much quicker, surely. Or should he have insisted that Danny come too?

"You're still new to this." Wade says, with an uncharacteristically kind tone to his voice. Louis isn't sure if it's a question or a statement and so he answers anyway.

"I am." He says, and Wade nods.

"Yeah. There's summit different about you. Not quite like the others. Not as smug, for starters. Definitely not as much of a dick as that Danny lad. But you seem younger than all of 'em. You're all dead young. Too young, if you ask me. But you seem…I dunno, just different to them." He explains.

"Like they all know what they're doing?"

"No, like they're all numb to it. Like they've already seen too much. I see it with the guys at the station too. Ones what've been doing it longer than you've been alive. You see a change in their eyes over the years. It's good in a way, practical, even. But I've never been able to do it."

"I froze." Louis blurts out before he can stop himself. "Just for a second. If I hadn't, we could've stopped him."

"What happened has happened." Wade tells him, with a shrug. "Can't change it now. But if we hadn't been here, what do you think would've happened?

"I…don't know." Louis says, with hesitation. He does know, and Wade does too. "I guess it would've been worse."

"Exactly." He says, tentatively clapping a comforting hand on Louis' shoulder. "So I'd say this is still a win, wouldn't you?" He asks, but there's no time to answer. Their attention is diverted to the paramedics rushing out of the house with Cain on a stretcher. He's not conscious, and Cheryl stands at the doorway to the house, hysterical with fear and confusion.
"...needs surgery immediately. We're going to do everything we can." Arthur, the paramedic, explains to her. For a moment she stands frozen as they load her brother into the back of the ambulance but as her gaze flicks across to Louis and Wade her expression changes dramatically and it's as if she comes to life again, like a machine rebooting.
"You." She shouts at them, voice laced with anger that even she doesn't fully understand. "You need to find him."
"Okay, calm down. We do need to speak to you, but maybe here isn't the right place." Wade explains, and Louis is happy to let him take the lead.
"No, let's get this done. I want him found." She says, with a clear determination that falters only when she glances beyond them to the waiting ambulance. "But can you take me to the hospital when we're done?"
"Of course." Wade tells her. Louis notices that he didn't even take time to think about it, he just agreed. There is something, Louis decides, inherently trustworthy about that. This woman is in pain, in crisis, and he's supporting her as best he can. Cheryl meanwhile nods to the paramedic, who has been looking over to see if she wants to ride in the ambulance or not. With that confirmation he climbs into the back of the ambulance and seconds later they set off, lights flashing and siren wailing. Cheryl turns back to Wade and Louis and is about to open her mouth to say something when she notices that Jasmine has appeared at the door behind her, the young girl's face wet with tears. She composes herself before squatting down to her daughter's level.
"Listen, Jas, sweetie, Uncle Cain is going to be okay. I need you to go inside and get yourself a toy to take to see him at the hospital while I talk to these nice policemen. Okay?" She explains, softly. Jasmine nods in response and rushes off inside.
"My name is Detective..." Wade begins, but Louis suddenly finds himself jumping in and talking over him. It's a terrible habit, and one that, in hindsight, he probably picked up from Danny.
"Can you tell us what happened?" He asks.

"Yes. No. I'm not sure. Someone was in my daughter's room. He looked…" She begins, but trails off because she doesn't believe it herself. "You're going to think I'm crazy but it looked like my dead husband. I know. I know it can't be. This makes no sense." She concludes.
"Can you think of anyone else that would want to harm you or your daughter?" Wade asks; trying to ignore the whole part about a man being back from the dead and looking for a rational explanation. That really doesn't help, Louis thinks to himself.
"No, of course not. Do you think it's him? Is he…is he haunting me? No, that's so stupid." She says, shaken and trying to rationalise what she's seen.
"We're not going to rule anything out. If it was your husband, do you know where else he might go? Does he have any family nearby or…" Louis says, before Wade can answer. He's keen to keep the conversation on the track he needs it on despite the side eye he's getting from the human policeman.
"No. His mum died last year. He had no other family. Probably just that bloody shop. He was always there. Look, for all his faults Steve wasn't a violent man. Whoever that was…that wasn't him. Please, just find whoever it is?" She explains. She looks genuinely rattled, and with good reason. She doesn't understand what's happening, and she's hoping that the two men in front of her can give her answers that make some kind of sense of the apparent resurrection of her estranged husband.
"Look, I don't think this is too helpful right now. Why don't you grab some things and then I can take you and your daughter to the hospital?" Wade tells her, gently taking back control. She opens her mouth to protest but he continues, adding a little authoring to his words. "You took a nasty fall too, so we need to get you looked over too. Just in case." Louis wonders if that's the story Wade has concocted in his head to explain the woman's version of events, If he's just written it off as someone confused after a head injury, seeing something that can't possibly be possible. It'd probably be better, in the long run, to leave him to think that.
That's the thing with doing this "job," it involved so much secrecy and lying when I first started out. So much misdirection that just got in the way of everything. It was one of the very first things that was drilled into us. There was so much that went into maintaining the secrecy surrounding us and the Used-to-Bes. To shrouding our war in secrecy; because humanity couldn't possibly know that the very things they feared actually existed.

Every single bit of folklore or fairytale has some kind of basis in the real world. Everything that someone's ever seen that they weren't supposed to see has been explained away as either hysteria or some made-up story, the details of which have been twisted and diluted until they're barely true. Every monster you can think of is real. BigFoot, for example, was an actual thing; I've read the report from 1958. Even some of the monsters you know are real have demonic origin, and even though it's not always clear how, most major instances of tragedy for humanity can be traced back to a Used-to-Be. I've often wondered what humanity would be without them, without the residual demonic energy twisting and amplifying everything that's wicked in the world. Would they be peaceful; getting along beautifully and quietly, or would there be another catalyst for their abhorrent behaviour?

"My colleague here will start the search for the person responsible for this," Wade says, gesturing to Louis. That comes as a huge surprise because it feels like an endorsement of sorts. Up until now Wade had been very clear about his disdain for the group, and yet here he was referring to Louis as some kind of equal. That was a very odd and very puzzling turnaround, but Louis was certainly not going to argue.

"Yeah, okay. Thank you. Give me two minutes." Cheryl says, somewhat reluctantly. Despite her need for a resolution she clearly knows that on some level Wade is right; and it's for the best that she goes to the hospital. He watches until she's back in the house and then rounds on Louis.

"I don't get it." He says, with that camaraderie dropped from his voice.

"Get what?" Louis replies, trying not to be too taken aback.

"She's there talking about a dead man trying to kidnap her daughter and you don't even flinch?"

"Well, people say all sorts when they're in shock." Louis says, in a blatant scramble for a lie.

"So why were you asking about the murder back at the house?" He says and internally Louis curses.

"Just like, exploring all the avenues. Trying to get the full picture. His death, the neighbour, and now this, I dunno there's obviously some kind of connection." He says, a little desperately. Wade pauses for a very long moment.

"Hmm. Agreed. I still feel like you're keeping something from me though." Well, he's not exactly wrong there, Louis was keeping an awful lot from him. A whole world of things that would blow his mind. "I was there, you know."

"What do you mean?" Louis asks, genuinely not following the train of thought.

"I was there after they found him. It was brutal. There's no way they could've faked that. I saw his body. He's definitely dead."

"Ah, okay. He's definitely dead then. Agreed." He replies, maybe a little too quickly.

"There was something off about it though…"

"Oh?"

"Good. The whole thing looked like a robbery gone wrong, but nothing was really taken. We couldn't get our hands on any CCTV footage and the investigation was just closed down. It felt off to me, but I couldn't put my finger on why."

"Well, that's one of the things we'll look at; why he died." …and that, thankfully, wasn't a lie. Louis was certain Steven Robinson was dead. He and Wade agreed on that, he had died that day. But as you know, being up, walking around, and breaking and entering are not the traditional actions of a dead man. So perhaps it was more their definitions of dead that they disagreed on.

Though, truth be told, this was unusual. As much as I talked earlier about creatures from horror and fairytales being based in genuine cases of Used-to-Bes the idea of a deadman stalking his former family just wasn't something we'd expected. I'd expected Used-to-Bes to be pure agents of chaos. More like vicious, roaming, animals than anything else. When I look back now I realise our training was distinctly lacking in analysis of Used-to-Be behaviour, particularly the why they do what they do. If I could fill in a feedback form for my education that's what I would say. Because that was the question here; if Steven Robinson was up and walking around then why was he doing what he was doing? What was driving him to eviscerate his neighbour, assault his brother-in-law, and terrify his estranged wife. That's what Louis was trying to add up in that moment, all while trying to keep Wade off that scent, because there were a lot of things he didn't understand yet and even though he desperately wanted the Detective to like him, he couldn't involve him in the answers to some of the questions. Louis needed to understand why Steven Robinson had died, and that was the truth, but he also needed to understand why he hadn't stayed dead and that was a question Wade couldn't possibly comprehend at this stage without writing him off as a lunatic.

Wade narrows his eyes and grunts, seemingly resigning himself to the face he's not going to get any answers. "This whole Counter Terrorism thing is bollocks isn't it? A cover for summit else." He asks, with some of his usual gruffness back, but not all of it. It's clear that Louis has made some progress, at least. Cheryl comes out of the house before Louis has a chance to come up with a suitable answer; but the look on Wade's face tells him that he wasn't expecting one. She has Jasmine in tow and Wade tries his best to greet them with a comforting smile. He might be gruff and grumpy; but Louis admires how well he's switched to make these two feel at ease. "I'm parked just over here…" He tells them, showing them to the old, dirty car that he and Louis arrived in. He turns back to Louis as the two of them climb into the back. "I'll stay with them tonight and make sure they're safe. Keep me updated?"

"I'll…" He begins, with his brain already racing about what he might be able to share and what he can't.

"Please?" Wade asks, and that throws him completely.

"Yes, of course." Louis replies, before he can control the words coming out of his mouth and then mentally kicking himself for making a promise he might not be able to keep.

"Thank you," Wade says, flashing him a genuinely grateful smile as he clambers into the driver's seat of his car. Louis waits a moment, watching Cheryl, who looks confused and frazzled, and her young daughter who looks tired and scared, as Wade starts the car and drives away. He lets the looks on their faces sit with him for a moment, realising he needs to do everything he can to fix this situation for them, and then pulls out his phone to call Danny.

"We're definitely dealing with a Used-to-Be" He tells him, not giving him a chance to speak when he answers the phone because he knows it'll annoy him, and he wants to have at least a small victory here.

"We know," Danny says, the condescension rife in his tone. "I've found something. Get back here now, you need to see it." He continues, and this time a little concern slips into his voice. Louis picks up on that and knows he needs to get back as soon as he can.

"Okay, I'm not far."

"Good." He says, and hangs up, a little curtly. Louis takes a deep breath and tries to wipe some of the dried blood off his hands onto his black jeans. He looks around and catches the attention of one of the uniformed police officers that Wade stationed by the door.

"Hi." Louis says, trying to be politer than most of his peers would be. "Can you do something for me?" He asks. The policeman nods. "Great. I'm going to send some of my…kind of like Scene of Crime Officers over. A specialist team. Sort of. That doesn't matter. Can you just stay here until they arrive and keep anyone else out?"

"Yes." PC Morris replies, also somewhat curtly. Louis begins to wonder if he should take that personally, but knows there are far more important issues at hand.

"Cool. Thanks. They should be here soon but I need to go." He explains, wondering if this will draw any more from the tall, stoic, pale man before him. PC Morris vaguely nods and twitches his ginger moustache, and Louis knows that's the best he's going to get. He gives him a polite and thankful smile before turning to get his bearings and heading off in the direction of home.

What he doesn't realise, but what he might've been able to if he'd had a better control of his power at this point, is that in the distance, beyond the police cars, and the crowd of nosy neighbours, there's a sinister figure in the shadows. It's Steven. His dark, sickly grey coloured, face is obscured by the shadows of overgrown shrubbery. He's been watching the whole thing unfold and piecing it together slowly. His brain is still foggy, and things aren't fully clear to him. There's a lot of feelings and intense emotions he really doesn't understand. But, one thing he did make sense of in all of that; he quite clearly heard and understood exactly where the one thing he wants is going.

Chapter Fourteen.

A week earlier things were dramatically different for Steven Robinson. One major difference, for example, is that a week ago he was up late drinking himself into a stupor and watching terrible action movies at home, rather than creeping around in his wife's neighbour's bushes. And oh boy, did he regret drinking himself into that stupor when his alarm screeched early the next morning. He sat up, rubbing his head at the eye-watering headache that hit him straight away. Then he steadied himself, fighting the urge to vomit back up the half a pizza he smashed into his face before passing out, fully clothed, on the sofa. He didn't even have the wherewithal to turn

the TV off and now it'd gone from whatever late night film he was watching to the local breakfast news, and a reporter standing in front of a hotel. He takes no notice of it though.
He drags himself to his feet and glances at what's left of the pizza on the mess of a coffee table. He considers it, briefly, and then grabs a slice for breakfast, hoping it'll help the queasy feeling in his stomach. He switches off the TV and takes a proper look at his phone, which was the source of the annoying screeching moments ago. It shows a text from Cheryl; "Stop calling me wen ur pissed and get on with ur life" it reads. He grunts to himself, admonishing his drunken self for being so stupid, again, and pockets the device. The battery is so shockingly low, because in his drunken stupor he didn't bother to charge it, that he's lucky his alarm went off at all. He takes himself off to the bathroom, has a piss, splashes water on his face and gargles with mouthwash, and then leaves the house still wearing the clothes from the night before. He doesn't have the time or the energy to get changed.

A few hours passed, a hell of a lot slower than he would've liked, but that's always the way when you're hanging and stuck in a job you hate. He's leaning against the counter, in the small, empty, depressing corner shop he works in. He's got some old school rock music on to perk him up a bit while he's not being disturbed by customers. It's been a ridiculously quiet day, and he's not seen another person for well over an hour now. He's not necessarily sad about that, but a customer every now and again does help to pass the time. There's some big event happening in the town and so everyone is busy with that. It's been all over the news today and he's had to stop looking at it because it was annoying him. Some wedding or something. That's the last thing you want shoved in your face when your wife left you a few weeks ago.
Before he knows it, it's dark and the day has completely crept by. Of course, it's winter, so even though it's dark there are still too many hours until closing. At least there's been a few people coming in on their way home from work, and that's made things go a little faster. He's helped himself to a few snacks along the way. A beef pasty and a bag of crisps. That's helped to pass the time. He's also sneakily opened up one of the little bottles of super cheap vodka and slipped it in a bottle of lemonade. That little bit of Dutch, or Russian, courage is all he needs to try to get hold of Cheryl again. See, despite what she's said, despite her packing up her

things and leaving with his daughter, he knows they can still work it out. That hope is waning but it is still very far from being dead. Unlike him; unfortunately, because he's very close to being dead.

"Listen, Chez, I'm sorry about last night." He explains to her voicemail. "You're right I shouldn't have called you after a drink but look I miss you, that's all. I miss Jas too. I'm just so angry at you for leaving. And I guess I'm angry at me too for not being the man you need. It's all just going to shit and I can't…" He's cut off as his phone battery dies. "Ah for fucks sake." He roars and tosses the phone across the shop in frustration. Then he angrily pushes a display over, breathing heavily and on the verge of angry tears. He sinks into a chair behind the counter with his head in his hands.

That's when a little bell dings as a customer comes in. Steven barely looks up as the dishevelled and upset looking man stumbles into the shop. He's stumbling because he's still suffering the after effects of a round of tranquiliser darts that were fired into him a couple of hours earlier. He's been ripped back to consciousness but the drugs are still very much in his system. He's a little woozy, and has been told he shouldn't be outside, but if you were to ask him he'd say he kind of likes the feeling. It's like he's not quite in control in the most beautiful way. It's a bit of a thrill ride. He knocks a few tins of soup off a shelf, I don't know whether it was deliberate or not, and staggers over to the till with a little giggle. Steven hasn't even looked up at him yet, so he hasn't seen the state that his last ever customer is in. While he was clearly well dressed, as we saw earlier, his expensive clothes are covered in the blood of his victims from the massacre at the hotel. Joseph straightens himself up as he gets to the counter and looks down at Steve, who still has his head in his hands.

"Ooooh. You look terrible." He tells him.

"Look mate I'm not in the mood." Steven retorts, finally looking up at him. His jaw drops a little as he takes him in.

"What abhorrent customer service." Joseph says, in a bit of a sing-song voice. He looks down as he notices the shop-keeper taking in his outfit. "Oh. Yes. Got a little messy at work. Nevermind. Pour me a drink would you? On the house of course, to make up for your attitude."

"The fuck are you on about Loony Tunes? This ain't a bar, so just get out, I can't be arsed with this." Steven tells him, standing and coming around the counter. He approaches the man to usher him out but Joseph doesn't even flinch. Instead he looks him dead in the eye.

"You smell terrible. Keep away from me you filthy little man." He tells him.
"I dunno what's wrong with you but you need to get out." Steven tells him, rolling his eyes and grabbing his arm. That, obviously, was a mistake.
"I told you not to touch me!" Joseph says, with a bit of a screech in his voice.
"And I told you to get out!" Steven roars back, attempting to drag him to the door. Steven isn't a terribly large or strong man. He would never have been compared to any towering Greek gods. But he's not small either. He's tall, with pretty large shoulders, and a wide chest, and he has a little bit of middle-aged podge around his stomach. So while he's not a tall man he towers over the incredibly skinny Joseph. He should be able to tear him from where he stands and toss him out of the door with ease. And yet; Joseph doesn't move. Not even a muscle. Instead a chillingly cold smile spreads across his face and he looks the man up and down.
"You're very angry. You're a very, very angry little man. Ohh. I can feel it. Look at you. I didn't catch it at first, under that smell of stale booze and sweat. But it's delicious." He explains, and then grabs the wrist of the arm that's trying to drag him towards the door. There's a crunch, as he squeezes down and crushes the bones in it. Steven yelps and tries to pull away, but Joseph keeps hold of his shattered wrist and swings the man around with ease. He sends him careening through the air and smashing into the shelves of spirits behind the counter. He's no longer dazed and stumbling; he's been invigorated by the smell of this man's rage. "I've known so many men like you." He explains, sliding gracefully over the counter and crunching the broken glass under his feet. Steven groans and moans, rolling around in an expanding puddle of booze, blood, and broken glass. "It adds a little something to you, you know? A little bit of spice." The last word is a low, threatening hiss, like a snake coiled and ready to attack. Joseph runs his finger along the blood on the man's back, which was lacerated as it smashed into the bottles on the shelves. He licks it clean and moans to himself, before grinning and swooping down on his prey. There's the sound of tearing flesh, screams of agony, and a disgusting slurping sound, none of which are well hidden by the blaring rock music. Joseph pops back up, standing up straight and stretching. Like he's just woken up from a restful sleep.
"Mmmm. That was exactly what I needed. Thank you." He explains looking down at his victim who is in his final stages of bleeding to death. "You know." He says, pausing to think about it. "I don't normally do this kind of

thing, especially when it's not planned, but screw it. If any night is the night to be spontaneous and break the rules…" He picks up a discarded piece of glass and studies it before a moment, before slicing it along his arm, bending down, and letting his own blood fall into the open wounds of the dying man below him. Steven lets out another gasp as a fresh wave of pain washes over him and, when he's satisfied it's done the trick, Joseph stands back up straight and wipes the excess blood on his already stained shirt. He tosses the glass aside and then scoops up a bottle of vodka he spies that survived the fall from the shelves. "Why don't you see if you can use that delicious anger of yours to cause a little chaos?" He says, with a giggle, on his way out of the door.

Chapter Fifteen.

That description did not do the footage justice. It was brutal. Louis and Amber, who have just seen it for the first time, are both left a little speechless. One looks horrified and the other looks furious. No prizes for guessing which way around.
"…he was murdered by 4XM." Louis says, at last. Danny shoots him a look that says he wants to respond with some cutting sarcasm about his perceptiveness, but he keeps his mouth shut for a change.
"Because we didn't stop him." Amber adds.
"Well now, let's not do that…" Lauren says, jumping in to try to reassure them both.
"No, she's right." Louis says, echoing her but instantly regretting the snappy tone he's directed at Lauren. He didn't mean it, of course, she's the only one who's actually nice to him. He's just incredibly frustrated and he doesn't want her to try to make any of them feel better about their failure. "He'd still be alive if we hadn't let 4XM get away." He explains, a little softer
"Yep. There's one more of those things in the world now because we screwed up." Amber adds. They catch each other's eyes, both realising how odd it is that they're agreeing.
"I think we should all just take a moment and breathe." Lauren says, getting up from her chair on the cusp of offering them refreshments.
"No, we need to find them both." Louis says, firmly. "Let's start with Steven Robinson."
"Oh and where do you propose we start?" Danny finally snaps, unable to bite back his cutting sarcasm any longer.

"I...don't know." Louis says, drawing an exasperated sigh from Danny.
"Maybe we can take a few things from the footage then" Lauren offers.
"We can." Danny says, with an irritating know-it-all tone to his voice. "For starters, we now know more about how he was infected and what kind we're dealing with."
"Blood to blood infection." Louis offers. "That's how. Which means he might have some element of blood lust too?"
"One point to the newbie!" Danny says, with mock enthusiasm. "You do know things after all! A quick glance over his medical history already told me he has a bit of an addictive personality so this is bound to impact his behaviour. So what else do we know?" He says, opening up a fresh page on his laptop screen, which is mirrored on the wall screen.
"Well for the first few days after blood to blood they're a little chaotic." Amber adds. "Like, even more animalistic than usual." She explains further, and Danny adds that to the screen.
"That definitely goes some way to explaining that whole scene at the cemetery." Lauren explains. "That poor human woman."
"Yep. He ripped her apart just to satisfy his urges." Danny explains, to no one in particular.
"Surely it gives us an insight into 4XM too?" Louis says; somewhere between a question and a statement. "Don't they have to have been infected through blood-to-blood to be able to infect others that way? You know, like vampires. That's where all those stories come from?" He says. Danny stares at him blankly, before his gaze flicks over to Amber who rolls her eyes in response.
"I'm taking back that point. There's no such thing as vampires." He says, looking over his laptop screen and raising an eyebrow. "You know that, don't you? We're not about to load up on pieces of wood and religious symbols or whatever?"
"Yes I know." Louis snaps back. "I just mean...It's human folklore isn't it. That's where the whole vampire thing started, because of Used-to-Bes who feed on blood and infect each other through it."
"Why is this relevant, and in what way is it helpful?" Danny retorts; making a point of moving his hand away from the laptop, because he knows he won't need to record anything Louis says.
"I just mean we now know that's how 4XM was infected too!" Louis says, getting frustrated, and knowing that he kind of has lost his point by waffling about human culture. But hey, it's good exposition for you, right?

"Let's just focus on this target for now." Lauren says kindly. "What else can we take away from this?"
"I'm not sure there's anything else productive to add." Danny says. "We know our target. I bet if you all leave me alone for twenty minutes I can find him." He turns the screen on the wall off so they can no longer see what's in front of him.
"What about his family?" Louis asks.
"What about them?" Amber says.
"Well. Look at one he's done so far. We know he's confused and acting impulsively. We also know he has unresolved issues with his ex-wife."
"...yeah you should see his phone records. I lost count of the amount of calls in the few days before he died..." Danny adds, more to display his own knowledge than to support Louis' point.
"Exactly. He's confused. He died confused. That's even worse now. So...I think he'll keep trying to track his family down. They're what make sense to him. You know? If we stick with them then it's only a matter of time until he finds us." Louis explains. He's certain he's right, so he doesn't quite know why his voice isn't reflecting that.
"That's a stupid idea. Let's find him, not wait for him to find us, and probably kill dozens of people in the meantime." Danny says, shooting his idea down without even thinking about it in favour of his own.
"But he's bound to go after them again..."
"No. It's a stupid plan and I'm not doing it." Danny snaps. "Amber, what do you think?" He asks, thinking he can rely on her backup.
"Honestly? I don't care." She says standing up. "You two sort it out between you. I'm going to get changed and ready to move out. Point me in a direction, I don't care which, and I'll take him down." She quickly leaves the room, showing little interest in arguing with either of them.
"How about we compromise?" Lauren offers. "Louis you and I can go with the family.; and Danny you keep looking for him here."
"That's a waste of time. I'll have found him by the time you get to the hospital. It'll be even sooner if you'll both shut up. He's early in his transformation, we're still within the first forty-eight hours of the body waking back up, he's not going to be particularly skilled at hide-and-seek." He snaps, hammering on the keys in frustration at having to explain himself. "He's probably gone back to his shop. Or circling in that area. It'll be familiar. I'm searching footage in that area using his image..."

"Okay, but, in the meantime maybe…" Louis begins, still pushing his idea, but very cautiously.

"Fine." Danny growls. "If only because it'll get rid of you. But Lauren, you stay here, you're no use to anyone with that leg, which is lucky because the stuff I need help with Amber would be no use with. I need the cleaning crews to wrap up; and I need to make sure there's no press. I'm still blocking all mentions of today on social media, just to make sure the stupid human police aren't planning on putting out a press release or anything. The last thing we need is a story about a local shop owner eating people. Louis, take your phone and make sure to pay attention to it. As soon as I find him I'll call you." He says; taking the time to slow down for the last two sentences as if Louis is a moron. But Louis is too happy he got him to agree to care.

"Great." He says enthusiastically. "I'll give Wade a call on the way and…"

"Oh for…" Danny cries, exasperated. "Keep him away from this. I told you, I don't trust him. He's either hiding something or he's an idiot. I don't have the patience for either. Not when I'm already having to deal with you."

Louis rolls his eyes at that; but he doesn't see the need to continue to argue. He's kind of got his way and gleefully tells Amber that much as she comes back down the stairs.

"C'mon, we're going to the hospital?" He tells her.

"Oh? You won then…" She says with a casual shrug, and follows him out of the door with no argument.

Across town in North River Hospital, Ward 20, on the fourth floor, Wade and Cheryl are sitting in silence. Jasmine is curled up on a chair, with her head resting in her mother's lap. Cheryl seems to be staring off into space, as if in a trance. They haven't spoken in some time, having quickly run out of hospital appropriate small talk, and it's been even longer since the doctors provided an update on Cain's condition. He was in surgery; but they were hopeful it'd be successful and he'd make a full recovery. At first Wade had considered suggesting he take Cheryl home, but something about that option didn't feel right when he knew so little about who her attacker was, and so he decided that, for now, this was the safest option. He had reluctantly concluded that he just needed to buy Louis and the others a little time. Their silence was interrupted by his phone vibrating. This snapped Cheryl out of her trance and she shot him a glare, worried it

would wake Jasmine. He offered a hushed apology and rushed off to a stairwell before answering it.
"Yeah?" He said, gruffly.
"It's me.., Louis. Are you still at the hospital?"
"Yeah we are."
"Good. How's things?"
"They're doing all they can for the brother. They sound hopeful but I dunno. I'm gonna call a couple of officers to come sit with Mrs Robinson in a bit so I can get home…"
"I'm on my way."
"What? Why?"
"Can I just explain when I get there?" Louis asks. He sounds a little desperate and so, strangely, Wade decides to trust him for now and not push.
"I guess so." He tells him.
"Great just…stick close to her until we get there?" He says, and that pushes the boundaries of this tenuous trust. Several questions shoot through Wade's mind; why? Who's 'we'? Did that mean he was bringing one of the others, and if so which one? Was there immediate danger or was this just caution? But, before he had a chance to ask any of them Louis hung up, which Wade found suitably infuriating. Maybe he was like the others after all. He gave a bemused look at his phone and decided he should chase his officers and see where they were, but before he could redial he heard footsteps coming up the stairs. He freezes as the source of the noise comes into view. His stomach sinks, as he recognises the person instantly, and he's filled with a unique sense of dread.
"Oh come on, don't give me that look." Kim Adams says, as she reaches the top of the stairs. She brushes her blonde hair coolly out of her face and gives him an innocent smile.
"What are you doing here Kimmy?" He growls, making sure to be very clear on the point that he isn't happy to see her.
"Well you weren't answering my calls; and your charming desk sergeant told me this is where I could find you, so I decided to try my luck." She says with a chuckle that he doesn't need to be a detective to spot as fake.
"You went to the station? Very brave. You ain't the most popular person there at the moment."

"Mmm." She says, in agreement. "I could tell. I think I got frostbite from the glares I got. You all know that none of this is personal right? I'm a journalist and I take that very seriously…"
"Yeah, you always have." He interrupts.
"…and that means I have to get to the truth of what's going on, no matter who I upset along the way." She finishes, undeterred. "There's a killer on the loose Matthew, and the public need to know what's being done to protect them."
"…yeah, there's a few of those on the go at the minute…" He says with an eye roll, instantly regretting it when he sees her eyebrows raise.
"Ah; so Church Street earlier today is being treated as suspicious?" She says.
"Talk to the press office." He grunts back at her, dismissively.
"Oh come on Matthew! I already did and they wouldn't tell me anything."
"Hmm, well then Kimmy, maybe there's nothing to tell."
"I hate it when you call me Kimmy. Is it related to the Hamilton investigation?" She asks. He stays silent, and so she takes a different approach. "Okay so why are you here? At the station they said you were here with a witness…"
"They shouldn't have told you that."
"No, but they did anyway. So is it related? Who is it?"
"It's none of your business who she is,"
"She?"
"Kimmy…" He says, and there's a warning behind it.
"Don't Kimmy me! You're hiding something."
"That is police business." He tells her, throwing some authority into it. She huffs, finally showing a little frustration of her own at being stonewalled. "I think it's time you left, don't you?" He says, just as his phone begins to ring again. He glances at the screen and it shows him it's PC Nadin, who he'd been about to call when Kim turned up anyway.
"Hmph. Fine." She agrees. "I'll just nip and use the little girls room and then I'll be on my way," She says, brushing past him and through the door into the fourth floor corridor. He looks after her and considers following her to make sure she does, but decides that might be a little too far and answers his phone instead.
Once she's through the door she takes a quick look around the corridor, which is deserted apart from a nurse wandering around. She knows he won't really have fallen for the toilet lie but was just too awkward to

challenge her on it, and she knows she has a limited time if she's going to find anything out. She looks left and right, and then picks a direction. Left. Always try left first. It's a system that's based on absolutely nothing but it's one she employs when there's no other way to decide. She peers around the corner to see if there is anyone that way and spots Cheryl and Jasmine, and shrugs to herself, wondering if her 'go left' system really has helped her stumble on this mystery witness. "Let's give this a go." She says quietly to herself.
As she rounds the corner her demeanour changes; and instead of walking with her usual air of confidence she does a marvellous job of acting like she's lost. She wanders down the corridor towards Cheryl, seemingly looking confused and searching for a sign to direct her. As she gets closer to Cheryl, who's still staring into space, she clears her throat.
"Excuse me, sweetie. Is this the maternity ward? I feel like I got turned around somewhere." She asks, her voice overly sweet. Cheryl looks up at her, struggling to take her in at first. Kim notices her bloodshot eyes straight away. She's tired and has recently been crying.
"No, no. It's one floor up, I think." She answers, looking like a deer in headlights.
"Thanks so much! Sorry to disturb." Kim says with a little too much enthusiasm. She makes a mental note to tone it down. Her gaze hones in on Jasmine, still fast asleep on her mother's lap. That's her way in, she thinks. "What a little cutie." She exclaims, before making up some more details about her cover story on the spot. "I'm visiting a friend who's just had a baby. I need to rescue her from her overbearing mother. You know how it is…" She explains, taking a gamble on the mother thing. That's only got a fifty percent chance of success. If this woman's mother is dead or, even worse, perfectly lovely, she's blown it. Luckily, she takes a deep breath stifling tears. "Oh, gosh, I'm sorry, I didn't mean…" She adds, secretly thinking that, as sad as it is she's hit on something traumatic, she might've also hit the jackpot in terms of fishing for answers.
"Oh, no. It's okay. I just realised I'm going to have to call my overbearing mother…that's what Cain always calls her too…and I've not got a clue what I'm going to tell her." She tries to force a smile, wiping away a tear. Kim looks at her inquisitively, baiting her into continuing. "Cain's my brother. He's why I'm…well, no, I'm why he's here I think."
"Oh?" The reporter asks, continuing to fish.

"Yeah. Sorry, sorry. I bet you wish you'd asked someone else now. I should probably let you go…"
"No, no, Jane'll keep for a bit. I'm sure she's got plenty of people fussing around her anyway; and you look like you could use a friend a bit more." She says, having no idea where she plucked the name Jane from. Everyone knows a 'Jane' though, so she must've met one at some point. She sits down in the empty seat, not waiting for an invitation, and shooting a casual glance over her shoulder to make sure that Wade isn't coming back yet. "The name's Lois." She says. This one at least, she's prepared. Always keep a fake name on hand in case of awkward encounters with men in bars or doing things you don't want your real name associated with. "Lois Ridley."
"Cheryl Robinson."
"Lovely to meet you, Cheryl. So what's this about your brother being here because of you?" She asks, and her new friend lets out a big sigh.
"I've been sat here for the past few hours trying to make sense of it. He was attacked by someone who…this is insane…but the more I think about it the more I'm certain it was my husband." She says. That's not that strange, Kim thinks to herself.
"Well why did your husband attack your brother?" She asks.
"No, it can't have been. I must just think it's my husband but it can't have been him."
"Why not?"
"Because he died a week ago. It looked so much like him. I know it was him but I know it can't have been, you know? And now I have to call my Mam and let her know that Cain's in here and it's totally my fault." She says, clearly showing the emotional toll that whatever has happened today has taken on her.
"Wow. Erm…okay…" Kim stutters, suddenly lost for words. She can't help but be phased by that odd journey; and even worse she can hear footsteps behind her. She's absolutely stayed here too long, and clearly all she's got to show for it is nonsense. "I should really be going." She says, dramatically jumping to her feet and preparing to rush off in the opposite direction. She hesitates though, knowing she can't be quite that much of a bitch to this stranger who's clearly struggling. "But look. It doesn't sound like any of this is your fault. Call your mum and just tell her the bits that make sense to you. And make sure the police catch your husband. Or whoever." She says, before rushing off and scrambling around a corner

before Wade can get close enough to realise it's her. She doesn't even register the strange man in the hoodie hovering in the corridor, and she darts through a door and into another stairwell. She's pulling out her phone to see what else she can find out about Cheryl Robinson and her maybe-deceased-maybe-not-husband before she's even down the first flight.

Meanwhile, the man loitering in the hallway peaks around the corner. The brain fog is getting a little clearer, for the moment; but the fluorescent lights hurt his eyes as he peers down the corridor at his wife and daughter, and the policeman who's helping to keep them from him.
"Who was that?" Wade asks, taking up his seat again.
"Someone who probably thinks I'm crazy now." Cheryl responds, before resigning herself to the fact she's about to sound crazy once again. "Look, Detective. I know you won't believe me, but the more I think about it the more I know it was Steven at the house. I don't know how. But it was. I'm sure of it." She says, almost pleading with him to validate what she saw. "And I'm scared. You have to find him."
"You're safe here." Wade explains, side-stepping the question of the dead husband. "Whoever it is. I've got more officers on the way. We'll keep you safe."
"Whatever you say…" She says, not even hiding that she doesn't believe him.

On the ground floor the hospital is much busier; and there are a lot of patients wandering, either trying to find A&E or the correct department to see them. It's a hive of activity; with lost looking members of the public and overworked staff. Amber casually leans against the wall, a little unhelpfully, while Louis searches a map on the wall to work out where they are and where they need to be.
"I'm sure it's this way." He mutters to himself.
"You should've asked your 'friend' what floor they were on." She mocks. Clearly she's not keen on DCI Wade either.
"Got it!" He says, ignoring her. "Fourth floor. Ward 20." He leads her off to a door to the stairs, and as they approach Kim Adams walks out, finishing up a phone call.
"Just do what you can. I'm going to stick around. Call me back if you get anything juicy. Yep. Bye!" She says to the person on the other end of it,

and gives Louis a nod of thanks as he holds the door open for her. Amber storms through it, practically barging her out of the way and, were it not for that, she might not have given it any more thought. But she does, realising she recognises Louis and trying to place his face. He looks at her apologetically.
"Sorry, she's a little tense. We're visiting a friend who…broke something. More than a friend to her, really. She's…tense!" He stammers, clearly really needing to work on coming up with lies at pace.
"Yeah. No problem." She says furrowing her brow at him, but trying not to look like she's suspicious. He dashes through the door after Amber and she watches him go. She looks down at the time on her phone. It's 21:49. She leans over and asks a man behind a desk the question that's on her mind. "Sorry to be a pain. I've got a friend who's in because she was in a bad car accident. She's okay, just a few broken bones but she's being kept in for observation. Am I okay to nip up and see her for ten minutes?" The man, without looking up, replies abruptly.
"Sorry, visiting hours are only till 9."
"Yeah. That's what I thought." She says.

Louis catches up to Amber on the stairs. She barely acknowledges him, focussing instead on powering up to the right floor, but she at least offers to toss a tranquilliser pistol back to him.
"Got one thanks." He says. She shrugs and pops the spare back in her pocket.
"Well just remember these only carry one shot; so try to make it count. I'm trying to get some better ones but Chris keeps giving me some shit about budget…" She tells him.
"Okay." He replies.
"If you see the target, put a round in it as quickly as you can. If we're lucky it's still confused and groggy and will go down easy. It won't be used to it's own strength yet so we need to be fast."
"Okay," he says again. "But…?" He begins to ask.
"Oh, what?" She cuts off, leaping straight in with frustration.
"Well. His family is here. I just…don't think they should see us burst in and shoot him full of darts. Not if there's another way."
"Is this a joke?" She asks, stopping dead so that he almost collides with her. "We're dealing with a vicious animal. We just have to stop it. It's that simple. Something we failed to do with 4XM."

131

"But…" he begins.

"But nothing." She replies, very firmly, and carries on walking. Louis looks after her a moment, shaking his head in a dejected kind of frustration before continuing after her.

…and one floor above DCI Wade and Cheryl are still sitting side-by-side stuck in the same loop they have been for the past-however long. She sits with her head in her hands and he anxiously checks his phone every few minutes, only to see he has not received any more news from Louis or his officers. He's getting increasingly annoyed that he's kept in the dark; not really sure whether he's in danger or what to expect. Then, to make matters worse, he was bloody starving. His stomach grumbled, and then he grumbled too, thinking back to the bacon sandwich he'd grabbed on the way out of the house. He'd considered grabbing something from the stupidly overpriced vending machine but he knew a packet of crisps and a chocolate bar wouldn't satisfy him. It'd been a long day and he needed to throw something substantial down his neck. When he eventually got out of here he only hoped his wife, who he'd thankfully remembered to text this time at least, had left some leftovers for him to reheat. She usually did, she was good like that. That's if he even made it home. There was a twenty-four hour McDonalds nearby he might have to stop at instead. He checks his phone again, and once again tuts and sighs at the lack of updates, shaking his head. Next to him Jasmine stirs and begins to sit up from her mother's lap. Wade is just beginning to wonder whether he'll now need to add children's entertainment to his duties for the evening when Cheryl's head shoots up too.

"Daddy?" Jasmine says, clearly in that confused state of not being fully awake and aware.

"No sweetie, Daddy isn't here." Cheryl says without a second thought, sounding almost as if she's on autopilot; and Wade wonders just how many times in the past few weeks the confused girl has woken up asking about her father. But, that's when he sees movement out of the corner of his eye and follows the kid's eyeline to the figure her gaze has landed on. He too spots the figure standing there, just beginning to move forward into the offensively bright hospital light. He looks dishevelled. His clothes and skin are covered in muck, all kinds of dirt and grime, and mud and blood. He growls a word that sounds only a little like his daughter's name and his pace picks up now that he's been fully discovered.

"Oh no." Wade groans, hopping to his feet as well as any tired, out of shape, middle aged man can expect to. He pulls an extendible baton from his jacket. "Stop!" He roars, putting every ounce of police authority he can muster behind the instruction.
"Steve!" Cheryl shouts out at the same time, staring at her husband in shock and fear, and moving their daughter behind her. He keeps marching forward, eyes locked on the two of them and completely ignoring Wade.
"I said stop." Wade roars again; moving himself in front of Cheryl now. "I'm warning…" He begins, pulling the baton back ready to swing it. The other man still doesn't pay any attention and Wade takes his shot. He catches it and swings it around to send Wade bouncing off a wall and onto the floor with a grunt. He doesn't have any time to cover before Steven is bearing down on him…

Chapter Sixteen.

…just as they reached the top of the stairs they heard a loud thud and voices crying out, and that more than Amber needed to spring into action. She barrels through the door out of the stairwell and charges ahead, and she's already rounding the corner towards the commotion as Louis struggles to keep up.
The Used-to-Be is towering over a downed DCI Wade, snarling and squeezing the man's skull as he squeals in pain and thrashes to try to shake him off. Louis finds himself blown away by how quickly Amber reacts; she has her weapon raised and is firing almost the second she sees the threat. Her aim is perfect and it would've all been over then had the UTB not reacted even quicker and twisted to use DCI Wade as a shield. The dart, meant to resolve this, burrows into his back and he loses consciousness almost instantly.
"Shit!" She shouts; and the infected human is charging at them before she can reload. Louis manages to fire off a round, but he dodges, scaling the wall to avoid it, while continuing to advance upon them. Amber plants her feet and braces for impact, and as he attacks she rolls backwards and flips him, letting his momentum carry him over her and into the floor with a thud. She follows him and plants herself on top of him, punching him several times in the head as Louis scrambles to reload his gun. The Used-to-Be recovers from the initial shock and, using all his strength, pushes her off him and launches her up into the ceiling. He scrambles, like some

panicked animal, back to his feet and takes stock of the situation. Louis is aiming again, Amber is getting back to her feet for another assault, and Cheryl is brandishing one of the hospital's plastic chairs as a weapon to shield her daughter. He runs at his wife, shoving Amber again before she can properly regain her footing, and then dodging a swing from Cheryl, before bolting past her and further down the corridor, out of sight. Amber is after him again in a flash, grabbing Wade's discarded baton, and giving chase.

"Wait!" Louis calls after her. "We need to get them out of here." He says, not at all keeping his cool. She stops for a second and looks back at him. "You do it. I'm not letting him get away." She says, ignoring any option that doesn't involve hunting down her target.

"You can't go after him alone!" Louis tells her. He hopes that it'll make her wait for back-up and consider something that isn't her single-handedly and somewhat pig-headedly chasing down a strong, vicious, and scared Used-to-Be. It doesn't. She has no interest in continuing the conversation, and continues her chase.

"Can. Am." She shouts over her shoulder dismissively. He mutters in frustration to himself, annoyed that she ignored him, and worried that it'll cost her. He tries for composure and turns to Cheryl, knowing he needs to prioritise keeping her safe.

"Are you okay?" He asks. She nods, clearly still shell-shocked. "We need to get you both out of here."

"What about him?" She asks, nodding to Wade who's out cold on the floor. Louis stares at him, considering it and weighing his options. Wade had been hit with a tranquiliser that, while Louis was no medic, was far too strong for him. That probably wasn't good; but there was nothing he could do about it right this second. Cheryl was also the target. Cheryl and Jasmine. Everyone else so far had just been in the way; and Wade being laid unconscious in the middle of a hospital corridor didn't seem all that in the way. Not for this, anyway. Tactically, too, he knew it was better to leave Wade behind in case the Used-to-Be came back. He wasn't sure how well he could carry Wade and protect Cheryl and her daughter. But still, he wasn't sure if he could take that risk because if he was wrong then Wade's blood was on his hands.

"I'll carry him." He says at last. Chery gives him a look to say she doesn't quite believe him. He could understand why. Wade was a middle-aged and rather large man. Louis, in comparison, probably looked quite scrawny.

Tall, but skinny looking. But if she was shocked when he effortlessly pulled Wade to his feet and supported him at his side with only one arm and no sign of strain she didn't really show it. This wasn't the time to be coy with his strength. She squats down to her daughter, who's been in a stunned silence since her father left.

"Jas, sweetie, are you okay?" She asks first, and the little girl just continues looking at her with big, almost doe-like eyes. "I need you to be really good for me, we've got to go with this nice man," She explains, quickly but calmly, before looking back at Louis.

"Louis." He offers, hoping that's what she was looking at him for.

"Yeah. We've got to go with Louis." She finishes.

"What about Daddy?" She asks, so quietly Louis almost doesn't hear it. Cheryl stares back at her. She's trying her best but she's clearly confused and scared and there's only so far her maternal instinct can carry her. Louis knows he needs to step in, Louis, who as we discussed earlier, isn't the best at coming up with convincing lies on the spot.

"My...friend Amber..." He starts, only pausing briefly to consider what her reaction would be to being described as his friend but knowing that colleague wouldn't particularly help in this situation. "She's gone to find your father. He's ill. We're going to get you two and the nice policeman here..." He jostles Wade in the same way that people in something reminiscent of that kind of a comedy scene where he might as well have thrown his voice too, "...out safely. Then I'll come back in and help. But we need to get you all out first." He was quite proud of himself for that. It wasn't the worst he'd done.

"Yes. Exactly." Cheryl agrees, seemingly tagging back into the conversation. "So we need to get out quickly so that Louis and his friend can properly help Daddy." Jasmine seems to nod in agreement, so seemingly she bought it and as she stands back up straight Louis nods to Cheryl to indicate that they should get moving.

"Okay, come on then." He says, and she and the girl lead the way. Tactically, maybe not the best choice, he thinks to himself as he starts to carry his new comedy sidekick down the corridor. He stops mid-way and, having a stupid idea, smashes a fire alarm.

"What are you doing?" She asks, shepherding Jasmine towards the stairwell.

"I need to get everyone else out too." He says, reaching into his pocket with his freehand and pulling out an earpiece that he realises he should've

put in by now. It connects instantly to Danny, who is back at Brickmere Road, no doubt with a look of indignation on his face.
"I need your help, he's here." He explains, before Danny can speak.
"Okay, where's Amber?" He replies, with a welcome lack of snark.
"She's gone after him; I'm getting the family out."
"Of course she has." He sighs and Louis hears a clattering of a keyboard. "I've got your location. The stairs around the corner on your next left are the quickest way out and why is there an alarm ringing?"
"I thought it was best to get everyone else out?" He answers.
"And you want the fire brigade there to do what exactly? Are you going to blast them all out with a really long hose pipe? Or maybe you think that this Used-to-Be is particularly afraid of big ladders?"
"Danny…this isn't helping." Louis snaps.
"I'm multitasking. I've diverted them, while calling you dumb. I've probably bought you five minutes." There's a small beep on the line as Amber joins the channel. "Got her," Danny continues. "Amber, Louis is escorting the family out. He's just reaching the stairs. I'm tracking your location as well."
"Fine." She says, confirming her understanding but clearly not taking her focus away from her hunt.
"Wait." Cheryl says, stopping suddenly as she reaches the door to the stairs, pulling Louis away from the conversation in his ear. "What about my brother?" She asks, looking across at him with scared eyes.
"Louis no. The brother is dead weight, and I can see you're already carrying one sack of potatoes. He's inconsequential anyway; they've got all kinds of fire doors that they're currently closing." Danny interjects before Louis can even think of an answer, though thankfully not loud enough for her to hear.
"He'll be fine. They'll think it's a real fire, they'll keep him safe." He says, relaying the message with several filters applied. She nods in understanding and continues through the door. "How did you know that I…?" He begins, to Danny, before spotting a camera on the wall.
"Exactly." Danny replies, smugly. "Well done for working that one out."
"Amber, any sign of him?" Louis asks, diverting the conversation.
"No, and now there's a bunch of panicking people in my way. Thanks for that. I was right behind him. Danny, give me a clue?"
"I'm searching but I don't have anything, yet."
"The second you have him let me know." She growls, clearly hungry to fight. Cheryl catches Louis' eye as he starts to carry Wade down the stairs.

"Do you want some help?" She asks. "I've had plenty of friends in worse states."
"I'm okay, thanks." He says, cautiously taking a look over the railings. They're four floors up. It's not far, but the lights are dimmer here and he suddenly feels a pang of anxiety in his stomach. He reaches into his pocket to pull out his tranquilliser pistol again and brace himself for an attack.
"You really should've left him behind." Danny lectures; and Louis chooses not to rise to the bait offered by the annoying voice in his ear. Instead, he tries to focus on the sounds around him. Someone from the next floor up gallops down the stairs, nearly crashing into them, which initially panics him. It's not the Used-to-Be though. They struggle down one floor.
"I've swept at least half this floor and there's no sign of him. Danny, anything?" Amber barks, and there's another rattling of keys.
"Nothing yet. The humans are sweeping the floors too, to get everyone out. If any of them question you, just…"
"Danny, I know." She says, and there's silence. Louis' group continues down the next flight of stairs. They stop half way between the second and third floor as Jasmine pulls on her mother's arm.
"Mummy, I'm scared." She says. Cheryl squats down to her level again.
"I know. It's okay, you just need to be brave for me for a few more minutes until we're outside. Okay?" She asks, and the child nods. Louis looks at her, trying his best to look patient, but feeling more and more that they should pick up the pace.
"Louis, Amber, I went back through the footage. He's not still on the fourth floor; he bolted straight out of the door and onto the…"

And with that, as if he'd been listening in on them, Steven pounced. He sprang down from the gap in the stairwell to the floor above, and launched himself at Louis and his unconscious passenger before he had time to react. They both tumble to the ground in a mass tangle of limbs. He drops his weapon and it falls through the gap in the railings and clatters onto the floor below.
The creature is on top of him in no time; and bangs his head off the cold concrete floor, then smacks him across the face. His head is starting to get fuzzy; and the Used-to-Be doesn't show any signs of relenting and he strikes him again and again. Cheryl stands frozen, shielding Jasmine from the violence, and Wade lies still unconscious on the floor next to him.

There's no one to help him. Finally, Louis somehow manages to raise his arm to block another attack, and returns fire with an elbow to the man's head which knocks him back and gives him a split second of breathing room.

"He's here!" He shouts, to Danny and Amber.

"Amber?" Danny replies, with a vague hint of panic.

"On it!" She replies, her footsteps thundering through the receiver on her end.

Louis manages to scramble back to his feet, but the UTB is on him again, attacking him from behind and sending him sternum first into the bannister railings. He fights back with a desperate flailing of defensive punches and kicks; they're just enough to briefly hold his attacker off but he's no match for him really. Whilst all Custodians have an element of enhanced strength it rarely matches that of a Used-to-Be who are generally overflowing with demonic power. Louis can feel that right now, too, and it doesn't feel good. Rage and confusion are positively leaking from Steven Robinson as he attacks again and again. Louis can feel it all in one messy blur inside his already fuzzy head, and it hurts. He can feel the agony this man has endured; and is now experiencing echoes of that mixed with the pain that man is causing him. It bleeds together. The fight becomes increasingly one-sided as Louis is overwhelmed and he's down on the ground being beaten.

"What the hell happened to you?" Cheryl screams and it cuts through the storm of everything else. The rage stops and Steven hears her. And the flood of pain lessens slightly at her voice. He turns, finally giving Louis some space, to the woman his human self had loved and there's hesitation as he moves slowly towards her. She shakes her head and backs up, pushing Jasmine along too. "No!" She says, raising her arms. "You stay away from us you…you 're a monster!" He continues to approach the two of them, almost stalking forward as the rage inside him builds up again. Louis drags himself to his feet and throws himself into him, intercepting and tumbling to the ground on top of him.

"Run!" He tells Cheryl, and she picks up the young girl and bolts down the stairs. Louis had felt it; there had been some recognition and a brief pause in Steven's mind, but it hadn't lasted long. As he'd stalked towards Cheryl he'd felt the intention, clear as day, to kill her for keeping his daughter from him. There would be no reasoning with the beast inside his head. Louis gets in a couple of shots, knowing he can't win this but hoping he can buy a little time. It turns again; the Used-to-Be is stronger and a lot more vicious, and overpowers him in no time. It picks him up and tosses him over the railings; he lands with a thud and a crack right in front of Cheryl blocking her path. She screams in fright and surprise and stops; giving Steven enough time to pounce down and land in front of her.

"Jasmine." He growls, in a way that can only be described as animalistic. "No!" Cheryl answers, firmly, putting the young girl, who's sobbing in fear, down behind her. Louis can't get up, however desperate he is to. He's in pain everywhere and it's a fight to simply remain conscious. "I've had enough!" Cheryl shouts at him. "Leave us alone!" She charges towards him, taking a swing with a balled up fist and cracking him in the jaw. He's shocked, not hurt, and when she tries for a second he grabs her, picks her up and tosses her out of his way. She flies through the air, straight over the railing, and plummets the two floors and head-first into the tiled floor at the bottom.

He's killed the woman he loved, and it doesn't even register in his mind as he advances on the scared little girl she died trying to protect. Jasmine screams and cries and he doesn't stop. Louis tries to pull himself up, sensing that he won't be any kinder to her than he was to her mother, but it's Amber who gets there first. She comes flying down the stairs, still brandishing Wade's discarded baton, and strikes him in the face. She hits him again, and again, and again. She gives him no chance to react or to fight back. She kicks him hard in the chest knocking him down a flight of stairs and follows him, not letting up, He tries to strike, but she dodges. She's so quick, Louis realises as he watches. Finally he's able to summon the strength to limp back to his feet again. He's about to go and join her when the door at the bottom of the stairs is flung open and four figures in body armour burst in. It's a team of Custodians, led by Chris. They make their way around Cheryl's lifeless body and move swiftly to the skirmish between Amber and the target. He turns to assess the new threat; but before he can even take them in fully two of them have fired several rounds of darts into his chest and he drops to the floor instantly.

"Target secured. Cleaners proceed." Chris orders. And instantly a team of Cleaners follow the same path in through the door at the bottom of the stairs. Two of them stop at Cheryl's lifeless body and the others make their way up to them. Chris makes his way up the flight of stairs to where Louis stands protectively before Jasmine, who's a crumpled, scared, weeping heap on the floor.

"Chris, I..." He begins, but is cut off as Chris bursts into a furious rant. "What the fuck was this? I told you to keep me informed; so why did I not hear about this from you? Why was I only informed about an attempted capture when it was mid-way through descending into chaos?"
"I..." Louis tries, the second there's a gap.
"No!" He screams, a little spit flying out of his mouth. He turns to one of the Cleaners that have followed him up the stairs. "Check her, then get her to quarantine. There's a potential infection here." He says, not bothering to calm his tone at all. Louis opens his mouth to try again, but Chris won't even let him speak. "I said no. I don't care. Get out of here, I'll sort this mess out." Louis hesitates. He wants to tell them about Wade, still lying unconscious on the third floor, but Chris' eyes are getting wider and wider with every second he's standing there not obeying him.
"There's an unconscious policeman on the..." He says, as quickly as he possibly can, as he pulls himself along the railings.
"Go!" Chris demands, and Louis does. He doesn't really have any other option. He limps away as quickly as he can. He sees the Cleaners, strange figures with blank eyes who are all clad in grey uniforms, securing the unconscious Used-to-Be onto a stretcher with metal restraints. Amber is giving one of the others a run down of what happened, and doesn't even acknowledge him as he passes. He reaches the bottom of the stairs, where Cheryl's body is being tended to, and then leaves via the fire exit the others came in through. As the cold air hits him he once again finds himself leaving a scene of utter chaos and knowing he should've been better. If he'd have been quicker, or cleverer, or stronger, or just done something differently then Cheryl could still be alive to raise her daughter. Or, if he'd stopped 4XM in the first place then Cheryl and Steven could raise their daughter together. Now, because of him, Jasmine didn't have any living parents and he didn't have a clue what would happen to her next. Her life was in tatters, and he was to blame. Against the darkness of the night he found himself nearly blinded by the flashing lights of sirens of the fire brigade that had turned up following Danny's distraction, as well as several police cars that were just arriving too. Several of the officers, quite rightly, looked at the figure of a bedraggled, blood soaked, twenty-year-old leaving the hospital with suspicion. Danny's voice suddenly cuts through it all; coming through the ear-piece that is miraculously still in.
"Are you alright?" He asks.

Chapter Seventeen.

A few hours later, across town, there's a room filled with expectant journalists waiting for a press conference. Kim Adams is, of course, amongst them. There's a buzz of chatter and anticipation; because they've been told they'll receive an update on the case of the Hamilton Massacre, as it's now being called. They fall silent as DSI Tim Copper walks into the room, flanked by a few uniformed officers. He strides to the front of the room, and seats himself in the middle of a table bearing the logo of Endsbrough Police. He gives a quick glance across the room, and very, very briefly locks eyes with Chris, who stands at the back of the crowd with his arms folded. He already knows the update the officer will give, of course he does, he had Danny write it. Copper takes a last look down at the sheet of paper in front of him, clears his throat, and begins.
"Good evening. I want to bring you up to date on our activity earlier this evening and to reassure the public of our on-going determination to trace and apprehend those responsible for the incident that occurred at the Eagle Hotel just one week ago. I want to thank the people of Endsborough for their support and cooperation in what was, and remains, a challenging time for that community. Tonight we have made a key breakthrough as we have arrested a 32-year-old male who we believe to be responsible for the attack, as well as further incidents that occurred earlier today. This was a critical time for our investigation; but I would like to stress that public safety was, and always will be, a priority…"

"Okay, that's the press conference done." Danny says, closing his laptop and looking across the table to where Lauren is still fussing over Louis' wounds. "I'll release the name in a few days time, then plant a story in a few months about him killing himself in prison." He explains. "A great idea really, it all matches up nicely and now the poor little humans can sleep soundly in their beds knowing that a killer has been caught." The idea that he's describing was his, apparently. He'd seen the opportunity to pin the crimes of 4XM on Steven Robinson, as well as his own. With that particularly Used-to-Be now in custody he had seemed like a great scapegoat to take some of the attention away from the situation at the Eagle Hotel, stop people asking questions about what had happened, and shut down any lingering Human Police involvement in it.

"Right. That's that." Lauren says, seemingly finally satisfied with the work she's done in patching him up. She packs away her first aid kit, which she'd used on some of the more minor injuries, as she'd explained that she needed to focus her energy on the bigger stuff, like the broken bones he'd received.
"Thanks." He mumbled to her, grateful but still a little embarrassed that he'd needed it. He hadn't said much since returning home from the hospital. Instead he'd sat back as the others went into overdrive, with Lauren fussing over him and his wounds, and Danny managing the crisis on his screen. The incident at the hospital had attracted a lot of attention, so Louis could definitely see the logic in marrying that incident to the one at the Eagle Hotel. Danny's press release should stop the attention around both incidents so that behind the scenes Olivia's team could continue the hunt for 4XM.
"My pleasure. The lingering cuts and scrapes are all clean, and should heal on their own fairly quickly." Lauren explains. "Now, I'm going to go check on Amber and then get some rest. That really took it out of me..."
"Sorry." He says, still a little sheepish.
"Oh don't be silly." She tells him, heading to the door. "Just let's all try to stay out of trouble for the next few weeks." She leaves, and Danny and Louis sit on opposite sides of the table awkwardly. They hadn't spoken since Louis had returned; and now they were alone he expected to be called an idiot once more.
"What will happen to the girl?" Louis asks him, ending the awkward quiet.
"What girl?" Danny asks, a genuine look of confusion across his face.
"The daughter. Jasmine."
"Oh. I don't know." He says, a little dismissively.
"Know or care?" Louis fires back, without really thinking.
"Pick one." he replies, with a shrug. He opens his laptop back up, and Louis wonders if it's in an effort to distract from the conversation. He's not going to let that happen, though. He's not sure if it's guilt over his part in the situation, or just anger at the lack of compassion that Danny shows absolutely everything, but he decides to push it further.
"How can you not care? It's because of us she's left with no parents!" He snaps, feeling so angry at the other man and the stupid smug look on his face. Danny's gaze shoots up from his laptop.
"What do you mean? I wasn't there. And why are you so bothered about an inconsequential Human Child? Used-to-Be apprehended, job done as

far as I'm concerned." He says with a stomach churning amount of nonchalance. Louis can't stand it.

"But it all happened because of 4XM. Because we didn't stop him. Both of her parents would still be alive if we'd just..." He stops, trailing off before he finishes. He's not really angry with Danny. Sure, he's irritating and unsympathetic, but it's not his fault. It's all guilt. He feels so bad at how the day turned out. It was a mess.

"Stop being so self involved." Danny tells him, and it almost makes his jaw drop. It's less shocking though, than what comes next. "Look. It happens. We're not perfect. I'm close, but you're not. I'm frustrated too. But I'm not going to sit around and whine and obsess over things that have already happened. Make a difference next time instead." He says, stunning Louis into silence. "As for the girl, I don't know. But she's alive. That's better than it could've gone."

"You told Chris, didn't you? Was that just to get me into trouble?" Louis asks, knowing it's the most logical explanation for how Chris knew to turn up at the hospital and why he was so angry at being kept out of the loop. Louis has calmed a little. It comes out as more of a question than would've only moments ago.

"Did you consider maybe I did it because you were in trouble?" He retorts, his eyes narrowing and a smirk returning to his face. "Then again, maybe I did it just to be a dick. Who knows?"

"Chris is furious at me. He even knows about the link to 4XM, and that I didn't tell him immediately..."

"Yep."

"But that was your idea! We're meant to be on the same team. I know you don't like me, but isn't this better if we at least try to work together?"

"Yes, and that means not running off by yourself to get killed, I wanted to teach you that now before it gets out of hand." He has such arrogance in his voice that Louis wants to throw something at his face.

"What do you mean?" Louis asks, trying to fight that urge.

"I'm saying you were going to run off to that hospital tonight no matter what I said, and it nearly got you killed."

"Because you wouldn't listen to me; and I was right!" Louis yells.

"That's fair." He says, with a dismissive shrug, still looking unphased. "I've been far from welcoming to you, but that doesn't mean I want you dead. I don't want anyone else to die. Something is changing. The whole thing with 4XM, and now this. I feel like being in a state of crisis is the new

normal for us. I know I made a big thing about your lack of experience but…" He says, looking away as if he's about to admit some big secret. "I'm not used to this either. We're used to a mild case a month and now we're dealing with a brutal one a week? So yes, we're a team. Let's try and act like one. You can't run off and do your own thing. You need my help."
"Then you need to stop treating me like I don't belong here."
"Fine. Deal. You want to keep looking for 4XM, don't you?" Danny says; locking eyes with him again at last, and looking as if he has a proposal. Louis thinks about it, about whether he can trust him, but there's something in Danny's deep brown eyes that seems to be begging for him to say yes in a way that his lips never would.
"I do. Chris told us not to, but, he's the cause of all this and I just…"
"Chris doesn't need to know everything." Danny says. "We just need to be careful and controlled about what we tell him and when. He cares about the big stuff, the things he can take credit for. We give him enough of that and we'll keep him happy."
"So, we're going to keep investigating, together?" Louis asks, his stomach lurching a little with excitement.
"I'm just trying to stop you getting killed," He says, with another nonchalant shrug. But Louis swears he can see a hint of gratitude in those eyes.
"So, yes then?" He asks him, now with a cocky smile of his own. Danny tosses a file across the table to him.
"Get started on that."
"What is it?"
"It's everything the police had on Steven Robinson."
"But…"
"Yes, but I still want to go through what they've sent us." He explained, like it's the most obvious thing in the world and he's talking to a toddler. Louis doesn't let that phase him though; because he's pretty safe in the knowledge that maybe, just maybe, Danny doesn't hate him quite as much as he thought. He can even forgive him for getting him in trouble with Chris, because he's pretty sure it was, in his own way, to help keep him safe. He takes a look in the folder; there's copies of a bunch of reports and a USB drive.
"I'm guessing this is the CCTV footage?" He asks, looking over at Danny.
"Ah yeah. The one they didn't have." His reply is laced with sarcasm as he slides his laptop towards Louis. They've already seen it, of course, but Louis doesn't question it. He only assumes that Danny wants to check to

make sure it matches. He's suspicious of Wade and the Human Police in general. He said as much earlier. Maybe he wants to make sure they've not cut anything out of it that would help them to identify 4XM as the killer. He inserts the drive into the laptop and a video opens automatically. It appears on the screens on the wall too, because of the existing connection. The video shows the silhouette of a woman; but she's lit in a way that none of her features are visible except for her frame and her long hazel coloured wavy hair.
"This is a warning. Consider it your only warning. I will not be pursued. I will not have my associate pursued. Two of your kind have discovered this already, and you will follow. I'm giving you a choice. Leave us alone, or incur my full wrath. Leave us alone, or die."
The screen cuts out and the drive starts to fizzle and spark. Danny lurches forward to pull it from the laptop before it causes serious damage and tosses it across the room. They both stare at each other, wondering the same thing. Who the hell was that?

"But how do you expect me to just let someone else take the credit for it?" Joseph screeches down the phone. He's alone in an expensive hotel suite. The very best that this particular hotel has to offer. On the screen in front of him is a twenty-four hour news channel that shows the reports of Steven's supposed arrest and links to the "Hamilton Massacre." There's a half empty glass of red wine that's been abandoned in favour of the screaming argument with whoever is on the other end of the phone. Laid in his luxury robe Joseph had been having such a lovely evening until the news had broken; the news that someone else was being credited with his work. "It was me!" He proclaims. "It was all me; and it's like you always say…"
She cuts him off. It's the same voice Louis and Danny just heard. "Enough already." She says, with so very little patience for this mood he's in. "Just stop. I can't protect you forever."
"…but…" He tries to protect feebly, wanting to stand his ground but not push his luck.
"But nothing. Joseph, darling. Please. You will stay in that hotel until my return. I will not hear any more of your escapades. Are we clear on that?" Her tone is crisp and cool; but it's not unkind.
"I…yes, okay. I'm sorry." He replies; sticking out his bottom lip and pulling a face like a petulant child.

"Then I will see you when I get back." She says; and disconnects the call. He screams in frustration and tosses the handset out of the balcony doors in a dramatic rage.
"Bitch."

Part III: Hunting 4XM

Chapter Eighteen.

Reading, November 1999
Billy Mason enters his apartment after a long day at his telesales job. The young man takes a cautious look around his dark apartment before placing some shopping bags down on the kitchen counter and throwing on all the lights. He returns to the front door, fastening several bolts and chains to make sure it's locked. He's jittery; but that isn't unusual. He looks tired, too, and skinny. If his mother could see him she'd tell him he's not looking after himself properly, and she'd absolutely be right. If he thought about it he wouldn't be able to tell you the last time he slept properly. But he won't think about it, which means he won't tell you about it, because he desperately wants to ignore it and hope that it leaves him alone. He begins to put away the few things he grabbed in his brief trip to Safeway and notices that his answering machine is flashing with a message. That's unusual, and it makes his stomach lurch with a pang of fear. He shuffles over to it and presses the button cautiously, then holds his breath before the beep and the message playing.
"Hey Billy, it's me." The voice of his co-worker, Maria, comes through the little speaker, and he relaxes a little. "Just one last try, we've all gone to…" He presses the button to stop the message, and deletes it. He doesn't want to join them for drinks, no matter how persistent Maria has been. Well, it's not that he doesn't want to. He'd love to join them. Maria's quite hot, actually, and she's definitely got the hots for him. But he doesn't want to risk it. He grabs a cold bottle of beer from the fridge, knowing that will have to do, but when there's a sudden bang from upstairs he jumps in fright and drops it. The bottle smashes all over the floor and he loudly swears to himself. He shakes his head, annoyed with himself and squats down to pick up the pieces of glass.
"Be careful you don't cut yourself." A sing-song voice calls, stepping into sight from God-knows-where. Billy knows the voice instantly. It's the voice that's been haunting him for months. His eyes widen in terror and he slips backwards into the pool of glass and beer.
"No!" He calls out, and scrambles to get back to his feet. He winces as he cuts one of his palms on the glass in a panic as the gaunt and pale figure of Joseph stalks him across the apartment. "I'm sorry!" He begs, skittering back to his feet and backing away. He's cornered in the kitchen, and all he can do is cower like trapped prey facing a predator. That's exactly what he

is. "I never meant to…mmmph!" Joseph reaches out and slaps his hand over his mouth.

"I don't care how sorry you are," He spits, tossing the other man back to the ground with ease. Billy scrambles to try to get away, but there's still no escape. Joseph has deliberately tossed him further away from the front door, which is the only viable exit. "And I don't care how far you run, or how many times you change your name…" He's on him again, and with a powerful grip hoists him back to his feet. "…you're going to die Zachary. Scared and in pain." He takes a moment and the other man weeps and looks at him with pleading eyes, then he tosses him backwards, through the window, and watches as he plummets to the hard ground below. "Just like me," He finishes, sadly, and to himself.

Present Day, well, as far as storytelling goes. It's actually about five years ago if you want to be completely accurate. But we'll say present day. It's a few days after Part Two. Flashbacks within what is essentially a big flashback are complicated, sorry.
Inside Technicolour Bar Hugo Davies is sneakily watching news coverage on his phone. Kim Adams is reporting on the events that happened a few nights ago at Endsbrough hospital. He's been gripped to her coverage of the whole Hamilton Massacre and, even though he's working, he can't tear himself away from this latest development.

"…can be laid to rest knowing that their killer has been found, whilst the rest of us are left to speculate on exactly what his motive was for such a heinous and…" She explains; looking straight into the camera with a stern and sober, but dependable, level of grace. Hugo's focus is broken as one of the customers hovers awkwardly at the bar.

"Hey man, can I get the same again?" Ben asks, with what he hopes is a charming smile, as he finishes sending a message on his phone.

"Sure." Hugo replies, tearing himself away from the coverage to get the drinks. It's not hard to remember what he and his friend were drinking; it's a Tuesday night so the bar isn't exactly filled to the brim.

"Oh I love this song; it's a classic!" Ben says; as an early 2010s pop song starts to play. Hugo, at a glance, is probably about 20-years older than this kid, and definitely disagrees on his definition of a classic. "Not a fan then?" He adds.

"£7.20 please." Hugo tells him, slapping a couple of rum and cokes down on the bar. Ben tries a friendly smile again, but Hugo doesn't return it.

"Well, I'm definitely a fan of happy hour prices!" He says, presenting his card to the reader to pay. Hugo doesn't reply, he just turns his back to him, and Ben grabs his drinks. He carries them back to the table where his friend Emily is waiting. "He was not a fan of my charming small talk." He tells her with a laugh. She pulls her drink toward her and takes a sip before raising her eyebrows.
"Since when were you charming?"
"Since when were you funny?"
"Ha! Don't it personally; he was the same when I went up, He had his head buried in his phone watching the coverage about that guy who…" She stops herself suddenly, catching the words in her mouth. "Shit." She finishes. Ben laughs it off with a toothy grin. He'd briefly considered milking it but decided not to.
"It's fine babe I didn't know her." He tells her.
"Bit weird isn't it? I had my 18th at that hotel!"
"Yeah I remember…ish…"
"You were a dick that night."
"So changing the subject; I believe we were talking about your new job?" He says, trying hard to pivot away from any stories about drunk Ben.
"We were! Oh god I love it so much. It already feels like home. It's properly my dream job. But, like, how are things for you on the job front?" She asks, reigning her happiness in for fear of rubbing his nose in it.,
"Ah, same old. I'm a bit stuck. I don't really know what I want to do. Except I know I can't work in a call centre too much longer." He explains, trying not to let her see the smile on his face slip.
"Well what do you want to do? Like if you woke up tomorrow and all your dreams had come true, or whatever that question is?"
"I kinda feel like all my dreams are dead." He says, with briefly sobering clarity, before bursting out laughing "Okay that was ridiculously depressing. There's just not much out there, you know?"
"Well, I blame the Government for that because…"
"Emmy! No. No politics tonight!" He says, looking down at his phone as it pings with a distinctive noise only one app makes. He tries to slyly check in but she raises a quizzical eyebrow at him which tells him he's failed. "Do you…think you'd be alright by yourself for a few minutes?" He asks, sheepishly.
"Nope! I know that look Benjamin…" She says.

"He's only like, just passing. I swear a quick hello and I'll come straight back…"

"You can't say hello with a di…"

"Emily Louise Morgan, how dare you!" He says, and they both laugh. "I promise; I'll be gone fifteen minutes at most. Then when I'm back you can rant and rave about the Tory Government as much as you like."

"Fine. But you get the next round too."

"Deal." He says with a grin, hopping up from his seat and already making his way to the door. She rolls her eyes after him and pulls his glass towards her too, having implemented a rule with him many years ago that if he left a drink with her to go chase after some man, she'd likely finish it for him.

As soon as Ben gets outside he ducks to the left and down an alleyway by the side of the bar that he's seen many a drunk man use as a makeshift toilet on a night. There's a figure there waiting for him; one that he recognises.

"Finally," Says Joseph, the man Ben has rushed to meet.

"Sorry, sorry." He says, "I can only stay for a few but I just wanted to say…" He kisses him suddenly, a little messily, and Joseph is a little taken by surprise. He smirks though as Ben pulls away. "Hi."

"You're way cuter in person." Joseph tells him, biting his lip and staring at Ben like he's hungry. "Before we start…" He begins, and his eyes dart away for a very brief moment. "You seem sweet. So, I'm sorry…"

Kamala Wade knew her husband; they'd been married for twenty-five years and he wasn't an overly complicated man, so she ought to. So when he came downstairs that morning and she looked up from emptying the dishwasher to see him fully dressed for work she was not at all surprised.

"I thought today would be the day." She said, with a knowing smile.

"I've gotta. I'm climbing the walls here." He replied, sheepishly.

"And I supposed I'd be wasting my breath to remind you what the doctor said?"

"Aye. probably." He says, rummaging through the cupboards. That was good. At least he intended to eat before he left. "Besides, I feel fine love, I've had plenty of bumps to the head in my time."

"…and not enough of them from me." She says, shaking her head and reaching for a thermos she's already filled with coffee for him. "There's soup in the fridge too. I'm surprised you made it this long." He smiles

warmly back at her, grabbing a sugary cereal from the cupboard like the big kid he is, and she smiles back. He's an idiot, she thinks to herself, but he's an idiot who's a good man.
"I bloody love you." He says.
"As well you should." She declares, kissing him on the cheek and grabbing her handbag from the kitchen table. "Just take it easy, don't do any more damage to yourself, and sort the washing out before you go." She orders, before heading to the door, and to work herself.
"Will do, see you tonight," He calls after her as she grabs her car keys from the little silver bowl by the front door.
"Sure. I'll expect you promptly at six shall I?"
"Oh as always." He says with a chuckle. It's their regular joke. It might seem odd to some people, joking about how you can never rely on your husband to be home at the time he says he will. But in a twenty-five year relationship you need to learn what you can and can't expect from your partner, and Kam had learned years ago that it just wasn't something he could guarantee. Matty was very passionate about his job; and if that meant working long day after long day to feel like he was doing some good in the world then that was just something she would have to concede. Besides, she was a teacher, so it wasn't like she didn't ever bring work home with it. He just wasn't necessarily around to see her work her way through piles of marking with a cup of tea on an evening. She shot him one last smile and closed the door, leaving him to tuck into his child's breakfast.

"Do I need to help you pack?" Danny asked, without a hint of genuine concern, the second Louis walked back into the War Room. That, bizarrely, made him smile. A week ago he hadn't thought it possible that Danny, of all people, could say something to cheer him up but it had been a very long day and it was only 10am.
The call he'd been dreading for the last couple of days had come through yesterday; after leaving him to stew, Chris finally wanted to speak to him. Louis had never really been in trouble before. Even growing up, he didn't remember a time when he'd been anything other than a studious and quiet child. There were around seventy "Home Bases" scattered around the UK - and they'd been called that long before the home improvement store had been founded in 1979 - which were the central hubs for all Custodian activity in the area. They all varied in size and only three were large enough to contain training facilities. The nearest one, where Chris now

resides, was located within a National Park in North Yorkshire. It was also where Louis had grown up; so going back there this morning to be told off like the naughty child he never was had been a very strange experience. Chris had ranted and raved about the chain of command and about following orders, all while not even giving Louis a chance to speak. He'd threatened him, saying he should have him relocated, or even worse retrained. He'd once again questioned Rachel's judgement in assigning him here. Chris had made him feel tiny, and if this was what being in trouble was like he was glad he'd been well behaved as a child. Part of him had considered whether he would be better off being moved again. Things in Endsbrough hadn't exactly got off to the best start. There had been 4XM, there had been the Robinson family, and there was the fact that two thirds of his current team made it very obvious that they weren't keen on him. Faced with that, maybe he should've jumped in and volunteered to be moved. Chris wouldn't have really put up a fight to keep him; he'd have been glad to send him somewhere that wasn't under his authority. Somewhere far away. Down South perhaps? Or even Scotland? They both seemed like great options, he had thought, as Chris continued to rant and rave about how he should follow instructions to the letter and run every decision by him, rather than running off and thinking for himself (he'd not said that last part, but it was heavily implied.) There was a definite irony in the fact that Louis' mind was wandering whilst Chris was ranting about not being listened to.

"If I said yes, would you?" Louis asked, sitting down in the chair at the opposite side of the table.

"It really depends on how much stuff you have. Do I need to?" Danny asked, and Louis wondered for a second if he heard a little trepidation in his voice. But, he figured, that was likely just because they'd worked together quite well on the 4XM investigation over the last few days.

"Well, no. Sorry. He threatened it, but I'm staying put for now." He told him; and it was the truth. After shouting, and ranting, and threatening, Chris had ultimately concluded that Louis should stay put for now. That was good, too, because despite this not being the best start in a new location he felt determined to make it work. He knew he could do some good, he could help stop 4XM, and he might even be able to win over Danny if they kept working together. Quite why he wanted to win Danny over, he didn't know, but he'd always been a bit of a people pleaser.

"Good," Danny said, nodding and looking away.

"Good?" Louis repeated.

"Yes. We've got work to do. You're not leaving all this on me."

"Ah. About that."

"You're not?"

"No. No, definitely not." Louis said, with a little too much enthusiasm. "We need to find 4XM. It's just that Chris was very, very insistent that we shouldn't, so we need to be careful." Danny sighed; but it didn't seem to be directed at Louis which was a nice change.

"Yeah. That's why it needs to stay just between us, for now. Lauren won't like hiding it from him, and Amber's not familiar with the word 'subtle.'" He says, and Louis snorts with laughter at the last part, but he's still worried. Worried about what will happen if Chris finds out they're continuing the investigation without him, and maybe even a little worried about what will happen if they find 4XM; especially if the others aren't around when they do.

"Why is he so insistent that we leave it alone?" He asks; hoping Danny will offer something other than sarcasm.

"Glory, probably. He'll be worried we'll work it out before he does."

"That's stupid? The more people looking at this, the better the chance of stopping him before he kills someone else. That's the important thing."

"To you, yeah. To Chris? Maybe not." Danny explained with a cynical laugh; and Louis decided he didn't really want to push any further on that topic. The idea that someone would care more about their own self interest than saving lives was a worrying one. He wasn't totally naive, he knew that happened all the time. He knew that people, even Custodians, could be inherently selfish, but he didn't like the idea of having to take orders from someone like that. Instead, he broached an equally worrying subject; the other warning they'd received.

"Speaking of us solving this; are you any closer to knowing who that message came from?" He asked, tentatively. They hadn't really discussed the woman's warning much. They had been focussed on going through what they had on 4XM, which was actually very little, in case they'd missed something. Danny had said he'd look into it, and he'd been blunt enough that Louis had decided to leave him to it and pretty much do what he was told. Odd how he didn't really have any problems following instructions from Danny.

"I still think your police friend. It was in the evidence he sent."

"No, I don't think it is. Besides, he was with Cheryl Robinson pretty much the whole time."

"Just because he didn't send it himself doesn't mean he didn't have someone do it. There's still something not right with him; he's either an idiot or he's hiding something. So just, don't go over-sharing with him, either."

"Okay. I won't. What do we do next though? We've been through everything we have."

"Not everything." Danny says, looking up at him. His deep brown eyes look directly at him, almost through him. His gaze lingers and he looks deep in thought. It gives Louis a weird feeling in the very pit of his stomach; like he should be scared by whatever is going to come next. "Can I trust you?" He asks at last.

"Yes." Louis replied instantly, without even thinking about it and Danny lets out a deep breath.

"Really though, I mean. I know I got you into trouble but I don't want to…" He hesitates, trying to pick his words carefully which seems very unusual for him. "If Chris finds out what I'm about to tell you I'll be sent for retraining for sure; and I'll make sure you go down with me." He says, not taking his eyes away from Louis'.

"You don't have to threaten me." Louis tells him. "Whatever it is, yes. You can trust me. I wouldn't…you know…I'm enjoying us working together. I don't want to ruin it." At this Danny pulls a face which was equal parts confusion and disgust.

"Okay, settle down. We're not best friends; I still can't stand you, I just don't want to do this alone." He said; and honestly, even though he was only reverting back to the way he normally was, it stung a little bit. Louis knew it wasn't wholly true, but the words still cut because he'd thought they were making progress. "When Chris and Rachel had me break into Alex's laptop." Danny continued, and Louis did his best to not let his face betray the hurt. "There were some files. Classified ones. Rachel would've never shared them with us; and Chris definitely won't." He paused again at this point, and hesitated. "I kept copies. What I could get, anyway."

"And Alex was investigating 4XM!" Louis states, with a little too much enthusiasm. Danny tilted his head and told him that yes, obviously, with only a look. "Have you got anything from them?" Louis asks; excited to know about their new lead.

"I've not had a chance. They're a mess. Alex's record keeping system was…interesting. They're all scans and photos from journals, and weird articles from newspapers. The majority of it is handwritten. I don't know if you even know the word technophobe, having lived in the village that time forgot, but Alex was definitely that. So we start by going through them together and trying to make them make sense."

"Okay, great idea." Louis gets up and walks over to get a look at Danny's screen, desperate to get going.

"Yes, obviously. It was my idea, they're always good." Danny replies, rolling his eyes and accessing his stolen files.

SBC News is one of the UK's leading providers of news coverage, owned by media mogul Alexander Buford. He's one of the richest men in the country; and his news service is one of the reasons why he's so influential and respected. Kim had met him a few times and he'd even called her personally after the Hamilton Wedding. He'd been on the guestlist, he'd explained, but had needed to take a flight to the US at the last moment for a business deal. That was a relief, honestly, there hadn't been a single survivor and Buford seemed like a good man. She wouldn't have wanted him added to the extensive list of the dead. But that's why it was so peculiar to her that everyone had outright accepted this seemingly half baked explanation about Steven Robinson being behind the murder. It just didn't add up. She couldn't explain why exactly; but after more than twenty years she was allowed to cite her journalistic instinct as a reason and for that to be enough. She'd started with an internship at a newspaper when she was nineteen and had quickly found that it was her passion. This job had been her constant; whether it was hard news, or the softer celebrity stuff. She'd done print, radio, TV, online, and everything in-between. She'd worked for national newspapers, and even done a stint with the BBC, but had settled with SBC News ten years ago as one of their senior northern reporters. So here she was, sitting at her desk, having driven an hour and a half at the crack of dawn to get to their regional offices, pouring over all the footage she had captured before the wedding. She'd been here for hours, hidden away in the corner because she didn't want anyone to know what she was doing until she had something concrete. Slowly the office had got busier and busier, the team had been and gone to do the morning bulletin, and yet she still sat here obsessively going over every tiny detail of the hours and hours of footage they'd captured because she just knew there was something to find.

She didn't see Mr Robinson anywhere in it; but she hadn't expected to. She did, however, finally, about 10am, see someone else she recognised. Initially Kim had started her search to look at the guests who'd gone in; thinking that might lead to some clue she'd not really considered, but she ended up going far beyond that and having a spark of recognition for someone who'd come out. Now that she thought about it she remembered the moment vividly. The sudden commotion, hours after the apparent siege had started, as people started to leave. Not the guests, obviously, and not quite the police either. They were a bloodied and battered team of apparent specialists who'd gone in to try to resolve the situation.The details of who they were had been incredibly vague, and her cameraman had only just caught a glimpse of them coming out of a side door, helping one of their own to walk, before they'd been obscured from view. It was brief, and it was in the middle of so much chaos and confusion that she'd forgotten about it until now. There had been so many people in and out at that time. But the thing that made this particularly unique was this wasn't the last time she'd seen a couple of these people. They were all young and slim. One was a woman with bright dyed red hair, the other was tall with a look of arrogance plastered on his face, and they were supporting another pale boy with very messed up, dirty blonde hair. She recognised the red one and the pale one from the hospital only a few nights ago, when Steven Robinson had supposedly been arrested. That was very interesting and her mind started to race with dozens of questions about their identities.

A sudden hand on her shoulder made her jump; she quickly pulled out her headphone and turned to glare at the source of it. Marc, the work experience student, stared at her with wide, apologetic eyes.

"I'm sorry Ms Adams I didn't mean to…I tried calling you…" He explained sheepishly backing up. She was annoyed at being interrupted, but she knew he meant well so she settled her expression down and forced a smile as she stared at him over her glasses.

"No, no, it's fine. You just startled me babe. Everything okay?" She says, like she's calming a skittish animal.

"Yeah, absolutely. I just saw you over here and wanted to see what you're working on and if I could help?" He said, with a clear sense of nervous hesitation, that she found kind of adorable.

"Ahhh." She replies, because she understands exactly what he means. "You're bored aren't you? I told you, work experience kids don't get much around here beyond the chance to make cups of tea and coffee." She told him with a chuckle, moving aside and motioning for him to look at the screen.
"The Hamilton Massacre?" He asked straight away, already sounding excited. She was cautious about sharing her theories with him; but she knew it'd help to talk them through with someone, and this kid seemed way more fun than half the people around the office, so she nodded to let him know he's right. "But why? They arrested the guy?"
"So they say. But I'm just not buying it," She says with a raised eyebrow. That definitely piqued his interest; and now she knew telling him was the right thing. Taking this kid along to investigate her crazy little theory would be fun and educational for him. Way more so than getting coffee for Suzanne Shepherd, the anchor who hadn't stepped foot in the real world in about ten years. "My nose for journalism smells a cover up; whoever Steven Robinson is, I don't even think he was at that wedding. But this little merry gang here." She points at the three, Red, Messy, and Arrogant, she's mentally named them. "They don't look like police and yet they were at both the wedding, and the hospital the other night. They're part of it, whatever it is." She then sighs, and minimises the footage. "But you probably don't want to hear my crackpot conspiracy theories. I'm sure you'll have another drinks run to do for Suzanne and Duncan before long…"
"No! Please let me help!" He says, a little desperately. It worked like a charm; she's got him hooked.
"I was hoping you'd say that." She said, with a devilish smile. "One thing first though?"
"Sure, anything?"
"I'd love another coffee…"

Chapter Nineteen.

It was unusual these days, Detective Superintendent Tim Copper understood, to have an office to yourself. There was something about being amongst your officers, about leading from the front; and yes he could see the appeal of that but he was a lover of tradition. Honestly, a quick look at him would've told you that, because he was exactly what you'd expect from a middle class, white, cisgender middle-aged man working in the police force. He had a bald spot he tried, badly, to hide, although hadn't quite gone to the effort of getting a toupe. He had a large desk filled with a few personal items that were neatly arranged, a grey jacket hanging over the back of the brown leather chair he'd bought himself, and he was sitting writing some notes with an expensive fountain pen that had been given to him as a gift. Timothy Copper was a man who valued tradition, rules, and institution; and that's what had made him a perfect fit for the police force. He believed that his office was a reflection of his standing and that it would inspire respect. Luckily for him, Endsbrough police station was an old building too, that hadn't been renovated in decades, and so it was perfectly set up for him to have his own space. He looked up as there was a knock at the door. That was another benefit of having your own office, you could choose to not be disturbed.

"Come in." He said, after clearing his throat and placing his pen down neatly at his side. DCI Matthew Wade shuffles in, a little awkwardly. "Ah, Matthew." He gestures for him to take a seat.

"Sir." He replies, with a respectful nod, which Copper does appreciate.

"I thought you were going to take a few more days, at least."

"Nah, I'm feeling fine. Besides, you know I don't do well being stuck at home." He says, with a little chuckle. Copper responds with a small eyebrow raise, and takes a moment to really take his colleague in. The two of them have worked together for more years than he cares to remember; long before Tim was promoted to his superior. They've always got along, they could even consider each other friends, but they're also very, very different. Where Tim is tall and svelte, Matthew is short and squat. Where Tim's clothes are perfectly ironed and he's always clean shaved, Wade's always seem to be creased and he's perennially sporting at least a day's worth of stubble. One takes care of himself; and one doesn't. A few years ago Tim asked Matthew to do the Great North Run with him for Police Care UK and his reaction was a laugh that soon turned into a hacking cough. But one thing that has always tied them together, that they've always agreed on, is work ethic. It's why it was no surprise then that Detective Chief Inspector Matthew Wade was already back at work; and why Copper hoped he would never have to be without the man.

"So what can I do for you?" He asked him.

"How's your better half?" Wade asks him, catching sight of a picture of his wife Rebecca on the desk and clearly deflecting.

"She's well," He responds, humouring him slightly. "We don't get enough time together, of course, you know how it is."
"Yeah Kam's the same; at least until the last few days, now I think she'll be glad I'm back. I was just getting in her way."
"Well, I don't imagine she's used to spending quite so much time with you."
"Heh, ain't that the truth? I'm alright though. I've had plenty of bumps to the noggin' over the years. Anyway, I've not come to chat about our lasses." He says, still holding back from whatever it is he actually wants to talk about and looking around the office for any more ways to delay the subject.
"I had guessed as much, so what's on your mind?" Tim asks, directly. He has all the time in the world for his old friend, but he'd really rather not waste that time dancing around a topic.
"Counter Terrorism." Wade says, looking directly at him as he clearly commits to the awkward topic he wants to discuss.
"Generally, or…" Tim replies, being a little guilty himself of dancing around the topic. He absolutely doesn't want to have to shoot this conversation down again.
"No. I want to talk about that team."
"Matthew…"
"Tim."
"I understand you have concerns, but…" He begins, trying to navigate this politely, but Wade interrupts.
"It's more than just concerns, they're interfering more and more, and there's something not right about 'em."
"I'm sorry you feel that way." Tim tells him; and it was perhaps not the right choice of words to calm the situation.
"Don't gimme that bollocks." Wade replies, as usual throwing professionalism out of the window the second he gets annoyed. "They're constantly getting in the way of real police work, they just make everything worse, and if you ask me they're just a pack of…"
"I didn't ask you." Tim says sternly, cutting him off before he can go too far. He's had enough of this. They've had this conversation too many times for his liking; and Wade knows that nothing is going to change. The Counter Terrorism team have friends in high places and there is nothing either of them can do about it. He's explained that, multiple times. More times than he would to anyone else. "What exactly are you hoping to achieve with this tirade?"

"I dunno Tim. You and me, we've worked together donkey's years. We trust each other, and that's important in what we do. I don't trust them. I dunno why you just let them run roughshod over everything."
"Look," Tim begins, rubbing his temples in exasperation. Matthew has been giving him headaches for years. "You said you trust me?"
"Yes."
"There's nothing I can do. If they want to take over I don't have the authority to stop them; and I'm not even sure I'd want to. If the last few weeks show us anything it's that we want no part of their cases. Can I ask you to trust me when I tell you that, and drop this?" He knew he was getting a little too close to emotional blackmail, but he really couldn't keep having this conversation. Whatever his personal feelings about them, and he definitely had some, the Counter Terrorism team were here to stay for now. Wade let out a noise that was somewhere between a grunt and a growl, which he chose to interpret as acceptance, followed by a very reluctant nod. "Why don't you take an extra few days? See if you can get Kamala to agree to go away for a long weekend somewhere?"
"You gonna give me a pay rise with that?" Wade replies, with a warm smile that shows off all the lines on his face. They really have known each for too long.
"You'd only accuse me of giving you hush money." Tim replies. He tries to return the smile; but it comes across as a little muted in comparison.
"Too right." Wade says with a laugh, getting to his feet. At least the conversation seems to have ended well. "Wouldn't turn it down though."
"If I did, would you promise to use the money to buy a clean shirt?" Tim asks and Wade snorts in response.
"Nowt wrong with this." He says, ignoring the obvious coffee stain and the fact that it looks like it's not been white in a number of years.
"Well, we'll have to agree to disagree on that." Time says, standing up and offering a respectful handshake as a farewell. "But do think about that time off, won't you?"
"Aye, I'll give it some thought. No promises though." He says, shaking his hand and heading for the door. As Tim sits back in his chair, and the leather creaks, he knows he'll never take it.

In just a few short hours Louis and Danny had already made a mess of the War Room. Quite how they'd have explained it if Amber or Lauren had walked in, Louis didn't know, because they'd printed out the majority of the stolen documents and spread them out across the large table to try to make sense of them. They'd been through several cups of coffee, which had been a risk itself as Lauren had appeared whenever Louis had entered the kitchen and offered to take over. There were also brightly coloured sticky notes scattered amongst the printouts to help them remember what was what; which had been Louis' idea. Danny had scoffed initially, but agreed.

"This is a mess." Louis says with an exasperated groan as he drains the last of another coffee. "Where are you?"

"France, last year. You?" Danny replies without looking up from the piece of paper he's clutching.

"Disgustingly gruesome police report from a murder in 1998. We've been at this for hours and it still makes no sense." He says, looking at the table. There were still hundreds of bits of paper there. So many different reports and resources, and none of it had been in any kind of logical order. Louis had assumed that Danny was just being overly critical of whatever filing system Alex had in place, but he'd now come to agree with him. It was more like that files had just been dumped in any old order. He placed down the paper and walked over to the board on the wall where they had created a digital record to help them keep track. There were names and dates scattered all over it; names of victims that had been pulled from police reports, or articles that Alex had sourced, and a bunch of dates. "I just want to find the one page that's like "oh for anyone reading this here's a summary of what I found," instead, we've got some weird diary of Alex's tour of Europe over the last three years, mixed with police reports and news articles for murders that go back as far as, what, 1996?" Louis asks, turning back to Danny who was still engrossed in whatever account from France he was reading.

"Sorry, what, all I heard there was a load of whining?" He mocks as he looks up with that infuriating smirk of his. Louis rolls his eyes and considers throwing something at his stupid face.

"Have you seen anything before that murder I found from late '96?" He asked, instead.

"No, not yet. I think I saw a picture of him though, the guy that was killed." He says, scanning the table. "It was definitely linked to that one anyway. I wish I'd got more of the files. Maybe there would be one that'd make this make sense. Like one that's a summary of everything that was found?"

"Oh, yeah, that'd be great." Louis replies, sarcastically and genuinely not sure if Danny is repeating what he'd just said to infuriate him or because he actually hadn't listened.

"This is useless." Danny huffs, throwing down the paper he's been staring at. Louis was a little taken aback by this. He might've only known him a short time but Louis got the impression Danny had never met a problem that he didn't think, and loudly tell everyone, he could solve.

"Maybe not." Louis says, scrambling to get them back on track by turning to the board and desperately willing the list of names to make sense.

"Really? You know what's going on, do you? Suddenly worked it all out?" Danny scoffs, clearly lashing out in frustration. He really didn't like it when he didn't understand something, it seemed.

"I think there's a pattern in all of this. We just can't see it." Louis tells him, continuing to stare hard at the summary of what they'd gathered so far. "He killed a brother and sister. I don't think that's a coincidence. And I saw somewhere…" He reaches down and grabs a bit of paper; it's a letter addressed to Jonathan Hamilton, offering him a job a year ago, "This! Alex was tracking Jonathan Hamilton before he died. I think she knew 4XM would target him. Would target them."

"Them, Alex was non-binary." Danny corrects. Uncharacteristic for Danny to care how someone wanted to be referred to, but very in character to correct.

"Sorry, I think they knew 4XM would target him." Louis amends.

"And what about our shop-keeper? How does he fit into the pattern?"

"I…don't know. I told you I can't see it yet."

"You're looking for something that isn't there. Used-to-Bes don't plan murders, they just murder."

"Alex was clearly looking at…" Louis begins; but there's a ping with an alert on Danny's laptop and he stops.

"Oh what now?" Danny sighs, making his way to the keyboard and hitting a few keys. He stands back up straight, and makes his way to the door.

"Where are you going?" Louis asks him; unsure if he should follow or not.

"One of my programmes just caught a police call about a body being found outside a bar in town. If we're quick we can beat the humans to it, and I think we need to get some air anyway. This is making you crazy." He said, before looking back at Louis like he was an idiot for not moving yet. "Come on!"

As Wade came out into the waiting area at the police station he was met with a very unwelcome sight. Kim Adams, smiling at him sweetly with two takeaway coffees in hand. He let out an exasperated sigh and suddenly regretted his decision to come back to work.

"Well, that's more or less the greeting I expected." She says, as she stands and holds one of the coffees out to him.

"What's this?" He says, suspiciously eyeing it. With Kim everything came with strings.

"It's coffee…and a peace offering." She explains, with obvious contrition. Perhaps he was cynical, but it seemed a little too obvious. Almost as if it wasn't genuine. He accepts it, however cautiously, it was still coffee and it was still one of his many vices.

"You gonna buy coffee for everyone here then? The way you spent the last few weeks slating us, I'd say that's the least you can do."

"And I'm very sorry if I've upset any of these fine men and women." She tells him, with an accepting nod. "But, it is also my job, and I know you understand that."

"Hmm." He says, with a scowl. She's right. Journalists were always sticking their nose in and telling them how they could do their job better, but as annoying as that was there were plenty of times when they'd been just as helpful. There were plenty in that industry who were blood sucking leeches, as far as he was concerned, only chasing glory, and willing to make stuff up as it suited them. But, that wasn't Kim. No matter how annoying she could be at times, Kim Adams had integrity. She always wanted the truth and that was why they'd always had a bit of an understanding. "I get it." He acknowledges, very reluctantly. She'd been very vocal of her criticism of the Endsbrough police force ever since that bloody wedding, but, in actual fact, her viewpoint wasn't all that different to his own. It was a monumental balls up, it just wasn't one the force were actually responsible for. She could sense there was something fishy about it, and he agreed. The only difference was that he knew about this supposed Counter Terrorism team and she didn't.

"I know you do. But that's also why I didn't like the idea you were mad at me." She said, with an affectionate slap on the arm. "Normally we can do our whole nosy journalist and grumpy policeman dance and still be friends after; but you were not at all my friend when I saw you at the hospital," She said. He had a fuzzy recollection of seeing her but he couldn't quite remember what they'd spoken about, or even if they definitely had. There was still so much about that night that didn't seem right, so much insanity, and in the middle of that there were some real gaps in his memory. The head injury hadn't helped, he supposed. "How're you feeling, anyway?" She asks, and he could tell the look of concern she gave him was a genuine one.

"Oh you know me Kimmy. Got a thick skull."

"And we're all very grateful for it. Speaking of which, how about an interview with the brave officer responsible for bringing to justice the monster behind the Hamilton Massacre?" She asked. There it was, just as he'd stopped suspecting it was coming, the string attached to the apology coffee. He shook his head and rolled his eyes.

"You know the answer to that already." Throughout the years he'd been happy to point her in the right direction, give her the odd tip every now and again, and maybe, just maybe, a quote or two. But he certainly didn't want to be the focus of some heroic puff piece, and she damn well knew that.

"I know, I know. But you can't blame a girl for trying."

"Besides," He said, trying to put some authoritative police presence into his tone. "There's nowt more to say than what was in the press conference, right now it's still an active investigation." She raised her eyebrows knowingly, and took a quick look around to make sure no one else was listening.

"Active investigation or not I think we both know there's way more going on that the public are being told."

"No comment, Ms Adams." He told her, sternly. "And this coffee tastes like crap."

"Hey! That's from one of my favourite little independent coffee houses; and it wasn't cheap."

"Ah, well, when you've sold your soul to Alexander Buford you should at least be able to afford decent coffee, right?"

"Exactly," She retorts with a devilish smile. "Don't think that's distracted me. Who were those people at the hospital with you?"

"At this time we're not in a position to release the names of…"

"Oh stop it. A couple of them were at the Eagle Hotel too."

"Who?" He asks, genuinely confused. He'd assumed that she'd meant Jasmine and Cheryl.

"You know. Young. One of them is pale, skinny and a bit messy looking. He's cute too; but in that can't-quite-grow-facial-hair kind of way. He was

with a red head who looked like she was ready to kill someone. They were trying a little too hard to look like they fit in and it had the opposite effect."
"Oh. Them." He couldn't hide the contempt from his voice, and her eyes lit up when she heard it. He knew showing Kim a weakness like that was a recipe for disaster and maybe, just maybe, he'd done it deliberately. She'd know for sure she was on to something now, and that might not be a bad thing. After all, they both wanted the same thing. They both wanted answers and he wasn't going to get them alone. He took a quick look around. The station was quiet. Only Desk Sergeant Appleby was around, and he was well out of earshot. "You're right," He told her. "There's something not right with them. And yeah, they've been involved in everything."
"Tell me more…" She said, in an excitable whisper, leaning in close.
"I can't, they're…" He began, but he was interrupted as Appleby called over to them.
"Sorry to interrupt. But there's a call come in, there's…" He pauses, and looks over at Kim. He clearly wants to be cautious about what he says in front of her.
"It's fine. She'll behave." Wade tells him with a nod to continue.
"There seems to have been a bit of confusion over it, I dunno why but there was a delay with it getting through. Got lost in the system or something. But there's been a body found downtown. Technicolor bar? You know, the…" The older policeman hesitates again, but this time it's not for fear of Kim, it's because he's reluctant to say the word. Wade has to fight the urge to roll his eyes at him.
"I know the one you mean Jack. The gay bar."
"Aye. That one. A young lad. Looks like foul play but you never know, d'ya? Anyway, PC Nadin is on route but I figured you'd probably wanna check it out."
"I'm barely even through the door. But yeah. Tell him I'm on the way." With that, Appleby sits back down and Wade gives his full attention back to Kim.
"So. Looks like I'm heading into town if you'd like a lift? We can finish this catch-up on the way, if you promise to behave yourself when we get there?"
"Oh babe." She says, practically purring. "I always behave myself."

Chapter Twenty.

The look on PC Nadin's face as they arrived at the alley told him all he needed to know. The Counter Terrorism team beat him here. On a normal day that would normally infuriate him, but today, it helped. Kim was still with him, and he'd shared a lot of his frustrations on the drive over here. He couldn't tell her everything, he wasn't going to throw all the rules out of the window, but he'd told her enough. So, now seemed like the perfect time for her to introduce herself to them and see what she thought.
"Welcome back." Nadin grunted with a nod. "They're already here."
"'Course they are." Wade replied, with a sideways smile to Kim. Nadin shoots her a look too, but it's not a pleasant one. He doesn't like her, like most of the lads at the station, but instead of saying anything he just looks back at Wade for an answer. He gives him a quick nod back to try to tell him that it's okay, she's fine to be there, and the bulky uniformed officer moves out the way to let them pass. He gets a proper look at the scene and the two very familiar figures within. It's a dark and sad little alley, littered with overflowing bins that have spewed rubbish all over the floor. It's been raining this morning too, so everything is damp and even more miserable looking. It's a terrible place to stand, but it's an even worse place to die, and Wade spares a thought for the poor sod who's last moments were spent here. Behind one of the large bins there's a foot sticking out, wearing a dirty trainer. That was the victim; dead, wet, and surrounded by rubbish. Poor kid. Danny looks up and spots them first.
"You're too late." He tells him, quickly and dismissively with a wave of his hand. That makes Louis turn too, and as he spots him his face lights up with a smile. It's odd that the kid seems happy to see him, because the feeling isn't mutual. It wasn't unpleasant working together a few days ago, and maybe he could grow to like him in different circumstances, but right now all that's on Wade's mind is finding out what secrets they're keeping from him. He's determined to find out what's really going on, and he doesn't see a day when he'll be happy to see any of them until that happens.
"Alright?" Wade grunts, giving Louis a polite nod because it's the most he can muster.

"How are you?" Louis asked. He was glad to see Wade. He'd not really heard from him since the night at the hospital and he'd been a little worried about the human. He'd been a little distracted by both the investigation with Danny, and with being on Chris' naughty list. He'd been assured that Wade was fine, but it was good to have it confirmed. He'd started to quite like the grumpy human policeman and he could've sworn he, in turn, was warming up to him.

"Yeah. What's the situation here?" Wade asked, side-stepping his question. That's when Louis noticed that Kim Adams was with him. He recognised her; he'd watched enough news over the last few weeks, but it was a surprise to see her here.

"The situation is you're too late." Danny answered and Louis couldn't help but cringe a little bit and jump in to try to cover for his rudeness.

"We've got the body of a human male. Young adult. Early 20s. Member of staff found him; and your man over there took a statement, which he's helpfully handed over." Louis explained, hoping to compensate for Danny's bluntness.

"But that's where your involvement ends." Danny said, in turn trying to compensate for Louis' politeness. "Sorry, who are you?" He asked, tilting his head as he looked at Kim. He knows who she is, Louis thought to himself, he was just trying extra hard to be rude. Or maybe he wasn't even trying. He did seem to be a natural, after all.

"Kim Adams, reporter for SBC News." She said, looking a little too happy with herself. That wasn't a good sign. She extended a hand to shake but Danny just stared at her blankly.

"I'm Louis, this is Danny, it's nice to meet you, Ms Adams." Louis said.

"Why?" Danny asked him, quickly.

"Why what?"

"Why's it nice to meet her?" He asked; and Louis honestly wasn't sure what to make of that. He didn't know if this was just another attempt to be rude or if Danny genuinely didn't understand the need for pleasantries. It really could've been either.

"Louis." Kim said, locking her eyes on him. "I'm sure I recognise you from somewhere. Where are you from?"

"Oh, I'm new in town." He said, trying to deflect. He was well aware he'd run into her at the hospital; but even he knew it was probably best to avoid disclosing that. The less this woman knew about what was going on the better.

"Still, you look familiar." She said, with a thoughtfulness that did seem a little threatening. Her face changed suddenly and she shrugged, as if

decided it didn't matter. She painted a huge grin on her face. "So what do you boys do? Matthew was just giving me a feel for what his average day is like, I'm doing a piece on him you see, and he said something about counter terrorism? Surely this has nothing to do with terrorism?"
"Oh, well..." Louis began. She was definitely trying to size him up, and that panicked him a little bit. As we know, he's still not particularly well versed at coming up with a cover story on the spot; and Danny really didn't care enough about it to be of any use. "Well. We don't know yet. That's what we're trying to...um...work out...because this could be...something like..." He mentally searching for some kind of explanation.
"It's nothing to do with you." Danny said, somewhat helpfully jumping in and saving him from himself. "Either of you. Whatever he's trying to show you by bringing you here, you're wasting everyone's time. It's our investigation. Please leave."
"Actually, you'll get no argument from me today." Wade said, with a surprisingly nonchalant shrug. "But can I have a quick word in private, Louis?"
"Umm, yeah, sure." Louis replied and Danny shot him a glare that told him that was absolutely not a good idea, but he'd already agreed to it.

As Wade and Louis wander off to somewhere a little quieter, where they can't be overheard, Kim smirks mischievously to herself and hovers closer to Danny as he returns to trying to look for something around the crime scene. She can sense she's irritating him and that's exactly what her aim is.
"What?" He snaps, glaring at her.
"I'm just curious." She replies, with a friendly smile and a tilt of her head. For a brief moment she wonders if flirting will get her anywhere; but she doubts it. The better move is to try to annoy him to the point he slips up and spills something.
"What about?" He demands to know.
"You." She says; with a tone that veers a little too close to the flirting plan. "This. All of this. About what happened here, and what's been happening all over town, and how it's all linked. I'm a journalist, it's my job to be curious." He shakes his head, and she can see the moment where he makes the decision to not engage. That won't do. "Tell me about yourself Danny?" She asks, trying to keep his attention and maybe bordering on

flirting again. It's amazing how fine the line between flirting with someone and annoying them is. .
"No." He says, intent on going back to his search. "I don't want to do this. This small talk thing. I want to do my job and you're in my way." She takes a dramatic step back and raises her arms, with a friendly chuckle.
"Well then please, carry on. Just pretend I'm not here." She tells him. He looks back at her, but decides to only retort by making a vague 'ugh' sound and going back to his search.

Meanwhile, Wade and Louis have taken a short walk past PC Nadin, and up the street to where they're certain they won't be overheard. Wade then takes the opportunity to pounce and get whatever info he can from Louis.
"I need to know what happened at the hospital. It was definitely the husband, wasn't it?" He asks, and that's an easy one for Louis to answer. After all, Danny had Endsbrough Police issue a press release confirming it.
"Yes." He says, and Wade nods. He looks like he had been desperately hoping there would be some other plot twist that would explain it.
"How the hell is that possible?" He asks next; and this was a less easy one because he couldn't tell the truth. "Don't spin no bullshit here." Wade says, as if reading Louis' mind. "I want the truth."
"I...can't." He says, after a moment of hesitation and rapid thought. "I'm sorry." At that, Wade let out a frustrated sigh.
"At least tell me what happened to the little girl? Is she safe?" His question causes a pang of guilt to hit Louis. He'd been asking the same question straight after the incident but, somewhere in the last few days, it had gone completely from his mind. He could kick himself for that. Jasmine, poor, poor Jasmine had lost both of her parents and been taken away by a group of strangers who would run further tests to see if she'd been in any way infected. Even in the best possible scenario, her life was dramatically different from now on, and he'd forgotten about her almost the second Danny had dangled the carrot of investigating 4XM together.
"I...I think so." He says at last. That's not enough to placate Wade, or even himself. The man lets out an irritated grunt.
"You think so?" He asks.
"Yes." Louis tells him, avoiding his gaze. "She was taken into the care of one of our teams and...I don't really get given any updates after that."
"Oh what kind of bullshit is that?" Wade replies, raising his voice and causing Louis to back up a little.

"I know. I'm sorry." He says.
"Can you at least try to find her?" He asks.
"Yes, I can try." He replies, hoping that'll be good enough to please Wade and keep at bay his rising sense of shame over not knowing what actually happened to the poor little girl. The noise Wade makes suggests it is, and also that he's done with the conversation. He turns away without another word and walks back towards Danny and Kim. Louis follows.

"Shouldn't you be examining the body, or something?" Kim asks, now leaning nonchalantly against a wall.
"Already done, he's dead." Danny says, moving a few bags around in the bin as he continues his search.
"And you've found the victim's phone, right?" She asks, taking a guess at what he might be looking for. He stops his search and turns to look at her again. That got his attention, she thinks. "The victim's phone," She repeats casually, and points under the bin he's currently rummaging through. "I think that's it under there. Assumed you knew." She has to try very hard not to laugh to herself, triumphantly, as she sees the look of irritation that crosses his face. He scoops down to pick it up.

"How about you answer some of my questions as a thank you?" Louis hears Kim ask as they get close. Danny glares; not at her but at him, and raises the phone they've been looking for over at him.
"We should probably get going Kimmy." Wade says, and she turns to walk over to him looking very pleased with herself.
"Of course. Let's leave these experts to it." She says, with a little wink to Louis as she passes.
"Let me know if you find anything out." Wade says to him, and then, without waiting for a response, turns and begins to walk away.
"Oh, yeah, I will." Louis tells him, sounding a little too desperate for approval. They're quickly out of sight and Danny wanders over and shoves the phone under his nose.
"You said you looked under that bin." He says.
"No, I said I looked in the bin." Louis argues, not at all surprised that this is his fault.
"You didn't." He says. Luckily, the phone still works perfectly and still has some battery life left. The screen lights up with a picture of the victim, who they've been able to identify as Benjamin Bailey from the ID he had in his

pocket. There are several notifications, including 5 missed calls, 2 voicemails, and a number of texts from someone saved as 'Emmy.' "What did the human want?" Danny asks, his curiosity taking Louis by surprise a little.

"He was asking about the other night at the hospital. He asked about the little girl, too, the daughter. Is there any way we can find out what happened to her?"

"Doubt it. Why's he asking?"

"I think he cares?" Louis suggests, as if it's obvious.

"It must be something else. He's fishing for information. I don't trust him. He's connected to 4XM. He must be. Those files he sent…" Danny says. He's shared this theory multiple times now; and he's obviously not going to drop it anytime soon. Louis really hopes he's wrong. Wade doesn't seem like a bad man.

"Speaking of…" Louis tells him with a sudden subject change, because there's something more important to talk about right now. "It was him." He confirms. It takes Danny a second to catch up.

"What was?" Danny asks. Louis nods towards the foot of the body sticking out from behind the bin, and Danny connects the dots. "Oh. Your weird feeling thing?" He asks.

"Yes." Louis confirms. It's a huge oversimplification; it's way more than a weird feeling. But he's not even sure if he can describe what it is or how it feels. He can sense some of the feelings from the time of the murder; like some of the demonic energy that was expended has been left behind and lingers in the air. It tastes like anger, and it feels like it did at Jonathan Hamilton's house, and at the wedding. It's not quite as painfully, blindingly, strong here. He can't really see what happened. But he can definitely tell, without any doubt, who was responsible. He realises Danny is looking at him, awaiting some further explanation. "It's not as raw here. I dunno, I don't think I can explain it without feeling dumb." He tells him.

"I think a lot of the things you say are dumb, just tell me." Danny retorts.

"It's like he leaves a trace and that's what I can sense. They all do. It happened with Steven Robinson, too. Maybe it's faded here, or he wasn't quite as emotional, or brutal. This looks like it was quick. I'm not "seeing" anything like I have other times. But I know it's him."

"Okay, but you don't know that." Danny says, and Louis blinks at him in confusion.

"No, I…" He begins, trying to argue, but Danny holds up a hand.

"No. Listen. I believe you, really. But in terms of concrete facts, we don't know 4XM is involved in this case, right?"

"I don't understand?"

"No, of course you don't." He says with a sigh. "Chris said anything where 4XM was involved, we should stop investigating and hand it to him."

"Oh. I don't know, Danny, do you think we should…?" Louis asks, a little baffled. Danny sighs in frustration and rolls his eyes.

"A feeling isn't evidence. We have no evidence that 4XM is involved." He says, slowly, and now it's Louis' turn to catch-up.

"Oh." He says. "Yep. Thinking about it, that feeling could be anything, really."

"Exactly. So let's play dumb. Well, I'll play dumb, you just be yourself. But there's no reason to involve anyone else in this particular case right now. Agree?" He asks.

"Agree," Louis replies with a grin. "So," He says, holding up the victim's phone. "Someone was obviously keen to get hold of him. Maybe that's where we start? If you could just…" He holds the phone out to Danny. It's locked, and that's not a problem he can deal with. But the technical wizard of the team loves an excuse to show how brilliant he is. Danny opens something up on his own phone, holds them close together, and the other unlocks. He finds the number for "Emmy" and searches for it using his browser.

"It looks like we're off to see Emily Morgan, at 32 Bagnell Road." Danny says, triumphantly.

Chapter Twenty-One.

A few minutes later Wade and Kim find themselves in a small, run down cafe. Wade nods to greet the waitress with an odd familiarity and Kim smiles to herself because this place, with it's beige walls, greasy smell, and tables that look like they should've been replaced a hundred times over is so obviously him

"Two coffees please Jan." He tells the dumpy woman with a messy grey ponytail before taking a seat at one of the tables. Kim hesitates. It's not that she's a snob; it's just that, you know when you can just tell a surface is going to be sticky? That's how she feels looking at the table. Eventually she sits, and of course she was right, but this is Wade's place, and if she wants him to spill all the answers then he's got to be comfortable. She knows that. She's never been able to get anything out of Detective Chief Inspector Matthew Wade unless he wanted to give her it.

"It's after eleven, I'd have thought you'd have wanted something stronger?" She says, trying to lighten his mood with a teasing smile. It works and he chuckles back.

"I don't think this place has a licence." He replies.

"No but Jan looks like the kinda girl who's got a gin bottle stashed under that apron. Could always ask her if she'd share?"

"Maybe not on my first day back." He says, as over at the counter Jan pours them two filter coffees and brings them over.

"Here you go sweetheart." She says, with a growl in her voice that suggests her wages go almost entirely on cigarettes, as she practically drops the cups on the table.

"How much do I owe you?" He asks her with a friendly smile. This is definitely his regular haunt.

"Nah these ones are on me. Heard about what happened last week." She says, stomping away from the table before he can protest. He shakes his head and switches his focus back to Kim. It's adorable how much he hates the praise being lavished on him. It's all she can do to not tease him by telling him that heroes shouldn't have to pay for their coffee.

"So. That's them. Your Counter Terrorism team?" She says, striking.

"Yep. That's them. What did you think of 'em?"

"Fake." She says, with a shrug before braving a sip of the coffee. "I've been kicked out of enough crime scenes to know how they're supposed to look; and those two were absolute amateurs. No gloves, no thought of protecting evidence, nothing. It was a mess." She concluded.

"Yep." He says, leaning back in the chair. "Little things like that made me suspicious at first too. The cases they pick are always slightly weird, and they've been a lot more active in the past few weeks."

"Do their credentials, or whatever, check out? What's happened when you've asked about them?" She asks, leaning in closer. She has so many questions and she feels like she's finally on the cusp of getting some answers.

"They do. Whoever they actually are, they got influence, that's for sure. Copper bows to 'em too. He knows more but he won't share. I dunno." He says, and the more he speaks the more she can see he's exasperated with the situation.

"So why're you telling me?"

"I've felt like I'm banging my head against a wall for weeks."
"When did it start?" She asked.
"They've been around for ages now, but I'd rarely see 'em. Then they had this one, Alex, turned up a few months ago, proper bossy, would storm into crime scenes and just start barking questions like they were looking for summit specific. Occasionally they'd take over but nine times outta ten they'd leave me to it. But now. Well, they took over at the Eagle, then again a few days later, and then the whole Robinson fiasco. Now today. God knows how this one is gonna spiral. I dunno Kimmy..." He says, taking a long sip of the coffee and clearly thinking. "I don't even know why I'm telling you all this. I'm just hoping maybe you can get further than I can. Freedom of the press and all that. I'm at a dead end."
"I'm not really sure what I'm investigating though. On the face of it, it's just a department with way too much influence who are a bit useless. Welcome to the world." She says, with a shrug. She's not going as far as to deliberately antagonise him, but she is pushing for more info.
"Well you asked about 'em. I'm sharing what I know."
"And there's nothing else?"
"Other than telling you who they are. You met Louis and Danny. Then there's that Amber who you saw at the hospital. There's Lauren who's the only nice one of the bunch, and then a black guy called Chris, who might be the worst one of the lot because he seems to be in charge and he bloody lets that go to his head."
"Are you going to work with me on it? Keep me in the loop with what they're up to, and the cases they have?"
"I can't Kimmy. I shouldn't even be telling you all this..."
"There's something else, isn't there? What did you ask Louis about?" She says; and she knows instantly she's pushed him too far. She's got too keen and got too over excited, and it's pushed him away.
"That's just..." He says, looking agitated. "That's nothing. Look. I've told you all I can. I need to go." He says, and he's so desperate to escape he gets up there and then, and makes for the door before she can even react.
"Wait, no, Matthew..." She calls after him, but he's already marching towards the exit and, even though she considers it, she knows giving chase isn't the best idea. She reaches into her pocket and stops the recording on her phone. At least she knows more than she did this morning, she thinks to herself.

Louis and Danny knocked on the door of a small suburban home; and after a little banging a young, slightly shy looking, blonde human girl answered. "Are you Emily Morgan?" Danny demanded of her almost instantly.
"Um, yeah?" She replied, peering around the door with a quizzical look.
"Good. Can we come in?" he asks, flashing a fake badge to her.
"Yeah of course, what's this about?" She asks, stepping out of the way as Danny lurches forward to get inside. He made it very clear on the way over here that he didn't like this bit. He called it 'talking to the dumb humans.' In truth, Louis wasn't too keen on the thought of it either but for different reasons. They were going to have to question this girl but also tell her someone that she cared about was dead. Louis wondered if the two of them had been romantically linked. That felt like it would make it worse somehow, if they were about to tell her someone she was in love with was dead. The idea of love was a weird one. He'd never experienced it but he knew it made everything messy and difficult. He knew that much from all the movies he'd watched. But, whatever the case, it was going to be down to Louis to approach the situation with sensitivity as Danny definitely wouldn't, and he knew the more difficult this got the less he'd be able to rely on him.
"We need to talk to you about someone we think you know." He tells her in a soft tone as she leads them into a living room and sits down in a chair. She gestured for them to do the same on the sofa.
"Benjamin Bailey." Danny offers, before she asks, obviously wanting to speed this process along.
"Ben, yeah. What's happened?" She asks, a look of concern already spreading over her face.
"You tried ringing him a few times last night?" Louis asks, sitting down and practically pulling Danny down to sit next to him.
"Yeah, we were out together. He…went to meet someone and didn't come back so I got worried. Has…" She swallows, as if she doesn't want to ask. "Has something happened?"
"He's dead." Danny says quickly and her jaw drops. "Murdered." He adds.
"What?!"
"Yeah we found his body dumped in an alley outside a bar called Technicolour. Is that where you were?" Danny asks without even giving the poor girl time to process what he's told her. Louis flights the overwhelming urge to punch him in the arm. She nods quietly; her mouth still open in shock. "What time did he leave? Who was he going to meet? Did he…"

"Danny, shut up a second." Louis says, finally. Emily is just staring. She's not listening to his questions, and anyone that isn't Danny would realise that she needed a moment or two to process what she was being told. "Are you okay?" He asks, leaning forward as Danny rolls his eyes.

"I…" She begins, and it's obvious she's fighting back tears. "I knew something was wrong. Oh God and he always…" She makes a whimpering sound, and tries to maintain her composure. "He always said…" She groans and breathes in deeply as tears start to form in her eyes.

"It's okay. Take your time." Louis assures her. He gives Danny a quick glance that he hopes will be enough to get him to keep his mouth shut. "What can you tell us?"

"I don't know." She whimpers, but she's clearly got something on the tip of her tongue. This time Danny does interject, but it's oddly not that insensitive.

"Tell us what you know and we can get out of here…and leave you to…" He clearly pauses, probably to think of a word that isn't insulting, but it's short enough that only Louis notices. "…process this. And then we can catch what…who…the person who did this."

"He always…" She begins again with a deep and sad sigh. "…this sounds so dumb that I never took him seriously. Oh shit why didn't I listen to him? He always said he was going to die young. He said that his family was…oh god I can't, I can't believe I'm talking about this." She says, shaking her head and having to look away from them.

"Please." Louis says. "I promise we won't think it's dumb; and it might help."

"He said his family was cursed." She says with a sad chuckle. "It wasn't just him; his mum said it too. They had this theory. It started with his uncle or something. Then his Grandad. His brother died really young too and…look are you sure it's him?" She says, slipping into a blissful denial. She clearly really cared about him, whoever he was to her.

"Yes." Danny tells her bluntly.

"Unfortunately, yes, we've ID'd him." Louis adds, keeping his tone soft and sympathetic. It pained him to see this total stranger in so much pain. "And he had his phone. That's how we found you, and…"

"His phone!" She says suddenly. "That'll tell you who did it! He was messaging…he was using that stupid hook-up app, Meetr." Not romantically involved, then, Louis realises.

"What?" Danny asks, pulling a face of confusion.
"He left to meet someone he was talking to on that." She explained; somewhere between grief and excitement at having worked out a way to catch her friend's killer. There was probably some vague hope this was all a misunderstanding that could be solved through further investigation too. Denial was a weird thing, Louis knew. "I waited about an hour and…fuck…" She said, deflating again. "I can't believe I just left him. I should've looked for him. Oh god. What if I could've helped or stopped it, or…"
"You couldn't have stopped it." Danny says suddenly and Louis is a little taken aback. "You'd just both be dead." One step forward, two steps back.
"And it was over quickly." Louis offers suddenly. "You shouldn't blame yourself. At all. We will find whoever actually is responsible though. Can you tell us anything else about the man he was going to meet? Did you see a picture?"
"I dunno. He was good looking I guess. But skinny. Dark hair. I dunno, I'm sorry." She brings her face to her palms now and begins to breathe heavily, Louis knows they won't get much else out of her and it'd be cruel to try. Besides, if they're lucky, they'll be able to get the information from his phone. "I'm sorry." She says again, as her emotions get the better of her.
"It's okay." Louis says, and slowly stands. "What you've given us is helpful. We'll leave you to…"
"Can I see him?" She asks, looking up at him with red eyes.
"Oh, no, we don't do that bit." Says Danny, he too is already on his feet.
"It's not possible right now." Louis says, trying once again to soften the harshness of Danny's delivery. "We've had to take him for some of our experts to examine properly. We can't let anyone see him yet." He says. He doesn't sound entirely confident in that answer, as it's only a half-truth, but she doesn't seem to pick up on it.
"God, what about his mother?" She whimpers.
"Still alive." Danny offers.
"She's not been contacted yet; but someone will speak to her shortly." Louis blurts out, once again having to curtail the urge to smack some tact into Danny. They need to get out of there now before Danny says anything else insensitive and before Louis makes any other promises to try to help with this poor woman's grief.

"I should call her. She's my...oh god he was my best friend. Please find out who did this..." She says, and finally can't hold the tears back any longer. She weeps.
"Yep. We will. In fact that's what we're going to go and do right now." Danny says, making a beeline for the door.
"Thank you. You've been really helpful." Louis offers, as he quickly follows him. "Oh sorry for your loss!" He adds as he closes her front door behind him. Clearly, they were both terrible at this in equally stupid ways.
"That could've gone better." Louis said, as soon as they were outside.
"We got what we needed." Danny replied, clearly ignorant to how badly they'd handled that conversation.
"Yeah but..." Louis stares after him, completely baffled. "You don't do well with sensitivity, do you?" He says; and Danny turns back to him.
"I can be sensitive." There's a hint of irritation in his voice that is all too familiar by now. "I just didn't see a reason to be. Surely it was better for everyone to get that over with as quickly as possible. Time spent dancing around someone's emotions is time I could be using to properly crack open this phone and get us what we need." He explains; and then continues his journey back to the car. Louis shakes his head, and realises this conversation is hopeless. It continues to annoy him just how ignorant Danny is to other people around him.
"Fine. Let's go." He says, and follows him to the car.

Chapter Twenty-Two.

Back at Brickmere Road Lauren has had a fairly uneventful day so far. She is sitting on the sofa flicking through the local news site on a tablet when Amber stomps into the room, still high from her energetic morning workout. She throws herself down in the chair at the other side of the room and huffs.
"I am bored." She states, simply, and Lauren looks over at her and considers it before answering.
"Yeah. Me too." She says at last.
"There's nothing to do."
"Agree. I've cleaned, I've restocked the food. I even considered taking up gardening, but it's autumn so there's really no point. I'm out of things to do."

"And I've done way more fun things; like strength training and some cardio." Amber retorts.

"I'm still taking it easy." Lauren says with a smile in her direction to explain why she's not been excessively up in the training room. The truth is she wouldn't have been anyway. She and Amber have different interests, and that's okay. "The leg is better, but I'm just trying not to push myself." That was true. The leg injury she'd sustained in their fight with 4XM at the hotel was healing nicely. "You're right though. I've grown used to crisis I think. It feels odd that things aren't manic."

"I don't like it." Amber says, echoing her feelings in a much more succinct way.

"No." Lauren concedes. "Me neither. I wanted to be positive at first and think it was good for us to have a chance to regroup and rest, and then maybe I could be ready to go back into the field by the time of our next case. But now I feel like I can't quite relax. I feel..." She trails off, searching for the right word. It's not quite fear, but it's something close.

"Anxious?" Amber offers.

"I don't know. It's just a feeling in my chest, like I'm waiting for something to happen and like I should be doing something about it but I don't know what." She explains, thinking it through as she does.

"Yeah. Anxious. I feel that all the time." Amber says, with a shrug, as if that feeling is as familiar to her as breathing.

"Well what do you do about it?" Lauren asks her.

"Easy." She replies, with a smile. "Punching bag. C'mon." With that she excitedly hops to her feet; clearly happy at the prospect of having some form of sparring partner.

"Oh I don't know Amber, maybe later..." She says, unsure what her hesitation is. Maybe it's that her leg isn't fully healed. Maybe it's that she doesn't want to tire herself out on a punching bag in case she is needed with something any moment.

"There is a case, by the way." Amber says, as if she's suddenly remembered, "Danny text a little while ago."

"I did wonder where the boys were." Lauren offers.

"Well, apparently we're not needed. Just a two person case." Amber says obviously she's baiting her.

"Well it's nice those two are getting along at last; maybe that should be what we focus on."

"Really?"

"Yes, it'll be so much nicer if they get along, it'll make things around here a lot less…" She stops herself, and finally gives in. "Oh fine, let's go and hit something."
"Yes!" Amber says, gleefully rushing to the door. "Wait until we really get going, I'm going to smash right through that sunny-everything-is-wonderful attitude of yours and drag you down to my level." She tells her, with a worrying sense of pride.
"Amber…" Lauren says, tutting and following her to the stairs. She's on the very first step up when Danny and Louis crash through the door; clearly mid debate. "Oh hey guys!" She offers with a welcoming smile…and they ignore her completely.
"Why are you still talking at me?" Danny groans, clearly very frustrated with whatever debate they're having.
"Because, it's just that you miss any element of actually being human." Louis explains, and she can tell he's equally frustrated.
"And?" Danny replies; heading straight to the War Room on the left.
"That's not a good thing!" Louis calls out, and follows him in. Lauren and Amber, who's stopped a few steps up, exchange a knowing glance.
"Well, what're we waiting for?" Lauren asks, and ushers for her to continue up. They're clearly still not needed; and whatever is going on she'd rather just leave them to it.

"Right, what's this thing she was talking about then?" Danny asks, sitting down in his usual chair and dropping Ben's phone down on the table. He looks at Louis as if he should know exactly what he means and yet he's left feeling like he's been brought in half way through a conversation.
Louis, "What thing?"
Danny, "Hook-up app. What is it?"
Louis, "What do you mean?"
Danny, "I mean what's it for?"
"You don't know what a hook-up app is?" Louis clarifies, unable to hide a smirk at the idea Danny doesn't know something.
"No?" He snaps back, annoyed that Louis knows something he doesn't.
"It's an app that Humans use to arrange to…meet up with others for sex."
"Oh," Danny says, taking a second to ponder it. "That's efficient. I didn't know they had apps for that." He continues.
"You baffle me." Louis tells him with a chuckle.

"Thanks." Danny says, with a trademark cocky smile, and grabs the phone again. Louis sighs in exasperation. It wasn't a compliment but of course Danny had taken it as one.
"I just mean that…it's weird that for someone so smart you have no idea about people, do you?" He asks, and Danny doesn't answer. Instead he's busying himself trying to get into Ben's phone and access the app so that they can get a look at the man he was speaking to and confirm if Louis' suspicions were correct. "It's like you didn't even go to Human Behaviour Class." Louis says.
"It wasn't my favourite." He mutters, in response. He knew the answer would be something snarky like that, but Louis still finds it annoying. Their entire purpose is to protect people.
"Don't you think that we need to understand people though? We're out there protecting them; we have to understand things about them, and how their world works. Like, that's why we call Used-to-Bes what we call them; they used to be human. They're driven by similar things. I just…don't think you can go through your life with no empathy, especially when it comes to the people you're trying to help."
"Well, maybe that's why you're here." Danny replies, and it's so nonchalant and dismissive that it takes Louis a second to realise that it veered close to a compliment.
"What?" He asks; and Danny rolls his eyes.
"You're right. It's not my biggest strength." He explains, looking back up from his work again. "Maybe we…maybe I…" He pauses, obviously picking his words carefully. That's not a good sign, Louis thinks to himself. "Okay. Yes. I need help with that part. That's where you fit in." He admits and Louis is stunned. His stomach leaps at the idea that Danny just admitted that he fits into the team in any way; and he panics about how to respond because he doesn't want to ruin this moment.
"Oh," is the best he can muster.
"So what do you think we should do next?" Danny asks; and that is even more shocking to him. First he admits that Louis has a skill he doesn't and now he's actually asking for his opinion. This isn't like Danny at all!
"Umm." Louis began, his mind working at a million miles an hour through the different options laid before them. It was important he got this right. If he was starting to gain Danny's trust enough that he was actually asking for his opinion, which again didn't seem in keeping with what he knew about Danny's character, then it was important he knock this out of the

park. Whatever that phrase meant. "We need to get onto that app. It'll show us who he was talking to and who he went to meet, even though I think we already know."

"4XM." Danny stated, simply. Louis nodded.

"So maybe we don't need to get onto Ben's account. Maybe, actually, it's better that we don't, because if he sees Ben's profile active again he'll know that it's someone else."

"Right?"

"Maybe one of us downloads and creates a profile."

"Sorry; you want to download this hook-up app and, what, meet men for sex?" Danny asks, narrowing his eyes inquisitively. He clearly wasn't following and Louis couldn't help but laugh.

"No!" He says, giggling as he does. "No. We use it to catfish him, and we set a trap."

"Cat…fish?" Danny asks, still not following. Mentally Louis searched for where he'd even learned that phrase.

"Sorry, yeah. I learned that from watching too much TV I think. It's where you pretend to be someone you're not online."

"Why?"

"I don't know." Louis says. "Other than this exact reason!" He says, curbing his urge to discuss his theories about other reasons people would catfish; from the nefarious to the relatively harmless reasons relating to body image. "We arrange to meet him; and then we've got him!" He finishes, excited that he's been able to come up with what sounds like a pretty serviceable plan.

"That idea could be worse." Danny says, after briefly thinking about it, and shamefully this makes Louis grin. "But how do we know he'll go for it?" He looks around at all their research. "You said there was a pattern. Is there anything in that we can use?" He asks and Louis fears they're going to be thrown back into the loop of theorising how on earth the victims are linked. They'd not landed on anything concrete yet and there was clearly so much more to Alex's research than they had.

"Can I borrow?" He asks, and Danny hesitates.

"Don't blow it up." He says at last, pushing it towards him. Louis chooses to ignore that comment, because he's had an idea.

"I can't get what Ben's friend said out of my head." He explains; and Danny looks back at him blankly. Of course he does. He didn't listen to a word she said. "About the family being cursed."

"Right?" He says.
"It's a shot in the dark, but what if…" He hammers away at the keys, like he's seen Danny do a hundred times. His jaw drops because he's right, and it was so much easier than he thought. "Shit. Hang on…" He says, trying to catch up with himself before he explains it.
"I'm hanging?" Danny says, clearly getting a little impatient that something is being kept from him.
"Benjamin Bailey, born on 31.05.1999. But, that's not his birth name." He says, reading from the screen in front of him and watching for the moment Danny connects the dots. He's really savouring being one step ahead for a change. "He was born Benjamin Hamilton. He and his mother, born Margaret Young, changed to Bailey, she remarried in 2015 following the death of his father, Michael. That surname isn't a coincidence, either. Ben is Amelia's cousin." He finishes and looks triumphant. Danny doesn't seem too convinced, though.
"That's a connection, but a curse?" He says.
"No but what if 4XM is the curse?"
"Hmm. But why?"
"Well, let's work out when it starts?" Louis has to admit, he's enjoying this. It's not the best of circumstances, investigating some pretty horrific murders, but this feels exhilarating. They're solving a puzzle; and he and Danny bouncing ideas and questions off each other like this is really helping to give the pieces of that puzzle shape.
"Didn't she say something about the uncle?" Danny asks.
"Oh, you were listening then?" Louis teases.
"A little." Danny says; and pulls the laptop back to him, clearly deciding that he should take over now. "Let me. Like you said, I'm cleverer than you."
"No, I said…" Louis begins, but sees Danny smirking at him and knows there's no point debating because he's goading him.
"Okay. He has two uncles on his father's side. I'm assuming, because of the Hamilton link, that's the one we're looking at. William Hamilton, father of Amelia and Jonathan, who died in 2010. Then we have Jason who…was brutally murdered in 1996. Okay."
"I feel like I've seen that. It was an article." He says trying to remember it and consulting their board. "Fuck. Yes. Jason Hamilton. How did we miss that?! A group of guys were attacked on their way home in October 1996. One was killed, the others sustained serious injuries. Wow…" He says,

reading the details of it. Danny meanwhile, continues his search of the family tree on the laptop.

"There's no suspicious deaths in the family before that, that I can see, so for now we can assume that's the one that started it." He tells Louis, squinting at his screen as he looks through causes of deaths for the Hamilton family through the generations. "But the year after Jason's father was killed. Then his mother two years after that. He even had a son who died in 2008; and Ben had a brother who died in 2001. Wow. Yeah. The only surviving relatives are now Victoria Hamilton, Amelia and Jonathan's mother, and Margaret Bailey, who is Ben's."

"So he's targeting that family." Louis says, staring at their summary of Alex's research so far. "But it's not just that family. There's so many more. Why?"

"You're the one who's all about understanding Used-to-Bes, you tell me." Danny says, a little dismissively. Louis continues to stare; determined that this is on the cusp of making sense. "While we're on that topic though, help me 'empathise' with something." Danny continues, and breaks Louis' concentration.

"Sure?" He asks, curious.

"Why is 4XM so important? You don't seem like someone who's well versed in breaking any kind of rule, we're past the point where we can really deny that we think this is him, so we should stop and hand it to Chris. But we're not."

"No, we're not."

"And that's right. I just don't understand why you're not. I don't like when I don't have all the answers. I'm clever, and yes, a smart arse. You're not the rebellious type so I don't understand why you don't want to stop. Help me empathise, or whatever.

"You'll make fun of it."

"Yes, probably, but tell me anyway.

"The stuff you said before was right, about me having no experience."

"I know, but...?"

"Let me finish." Louis says, deliberately taking his time. "I'm getting to it. This just isn't how I pictured it. We grew up being taught that we're superheroes, basically. That we're the ones that stop these things. Then, I graduate, and it's an anti-climax. I end up in this quiet little town where I'm not doing anything, I'm not helping anyone. I was lonely and I was bored, and I felt useless." At this Danny opens his mouth, clearly instinctively, to

make a joke but then stops himself and just listens. Louis continues; "It's not like I could go and make friends because...how do you explain to people where you come from? I mean, there were some but it was like, I could never be myself, not fully anyway. Oh yeah, you have parents, but I was raised by a super secretive order of...are they even people? Beings? A super secretive order of beings who trained me for eighteen years to hunt creatures infected with demonic energy. Creatures that you don't think exist. It's not like I'll be able to find common ground that way. That's before mentioning magical powers which, for me, apparently includes migraines." He stops and sighs, and Danny nods silently, trying to tell Louis he understands. "Anyway, after a while I found ways to build connections. I formed bonds and it was really nice. And then people started to talk to me about films, and books, and TV, and art, and I found they were a fun way to fill my time. Storytelling is really powerful, and being able to lose yourself in a story is really nice – and then you can talk to other people about it, and about what that story has made you feel and it's so great to be a part of that. I know you're still waiting for my point." He says, as Danny's expression betrays his confusion. "So many great and compelling stories are about someone making a difference. This is the part where you're going to laugh, but superheroes. I really got into comic books and comic book films and TV series. It's a big thing for humans. It's really cool, or uncool. Apparently I'm a geek. I don't know. But, I know that we are kind of like real life superheroes. The stuff in stories like that is all about saving people and doing the right thing. It's what we were raised to do. Humans spend their lives dreaming about being extraordinary and we are."
"Okay, Superboy, but I'm still not sure I get what this has to do with 4XM?" Danny says, unable to stop himself from interrupting at last. Louis smirks in response.
"You're not completely ignorant to Human culture then?" He says, oddly satisfied.
"I pay some attention." Danny says with a dismissive shrug.
"Well. After all that time losing myself in stories I got to come here. I got the chance to come here and be a hero myself, finally. But so far? I've failed, haven't I? I'm still pretty useless. Rachel died. 4XM got away. He's killed at least three people since then. Until we catch 4XM everyone he kills is on me because I'm meant to be able to..." He hesitates, self conscious because Danny hasn't made fun of him yet but he's still scared it's coming. "...be a superhero. I'm meant to be able to stop him. To stop people from

dying. But, I'm failing and I guess that's just not the way I want my story to go…" He finishes and sighs, a little sadly. It felt good to share that but equally it upset him to speak it out loud, and he feels on edge as he waits for Danny's reaction.

"You baffle me." He says at last and it makes Louis laugh, and that feels good.

"Thank you," He says in response, deliberately echoing Danny's own reaction from earlier.

"Let's find this pattern then." Danny says.

Chapter Twenty-Three

Oldham, Manchester, 5th February 1997
It's a dark, miserable, cold night. It's been raining all day and Thomas Marshall is just so fed up with it. It's pretty much been this way since New Year; just wet and dreary. He's had a shit day at work, too. It might be the middle of the week but he's determined to cheer himself up tonight. He's rented himself a video, and he's just leaving his favourite pizza shop with a large meat feast all to himself. He's just gonna sit, and chill out, and not think about anything. It'll be perfect. Or, it would've been. But as he turned a corner and headed down a quiet street, filled with small terraced houses that were tightly packed together, his peace was interrupted suddenly and violently with the swinging of a pipe. He dropped the pizza and it flew forward, out of the box, and splattered against the pavement. That would be pretty much the last thing that Thomas would ever be aware of; the sight of his meat feast sailing through the air. Joseph swung the pipe again, and again, and again, until he was satisfied that the damage was done. Then he dropped it on the floor and the clanging of the blood soaked weapon thundered through the quiet street.

"That'll fucking show you," He hissed; looking down at his victim as he drew in his last few breaths. He spat at him, before turning and walking away quickly and quietly. Several of the residents began to look out of their windows and see the lifeless form of Thomas Marshall laying in a rapidly growing pool of blood, being soaked by the heavy rain, and even though some would rush out to help they would be too late. He was dead before the ambulance arrived, and the police would never catch his attacker.

Present-ish Day, again.
They're still pouring over the research and it still feels like they're not really getting anywhere. There's so much of it, and there's just scattered bits of paper strewn across the table. Danny had said he only got a portion of what he could recover; but now that they've been over and over it Louis isn't sure that more would've helped. On the one hand they would be trying to do a puzzle with all the pieces, but on the other it already feels like they have way too many pieces. They're frustrated, they're tired, and they've been at this nearly all night.
"Fine." Danny says, biting his lip in frustration and glaring at their board of names and dates. He doesn't want to admit defeat, and Louis gets that, but it's time. It's time they asked for help.
"Are you sure?" Louis checks. He suggested this hours ago but had let Danny's stubbornness win out.
"Yes." He says quietly. He clearly really doesn't like that they can't do it without help. Louis doesn't wait any longer; he walks to the door and opens it. He knows they're both still awake. Custodians need very little sleep to get by, particularly when none of them have been active, and he's heard them both moving around. He takes a deep breath and calls them.
"Lauren, Amber, can you both come here?" He hears movement, and almost at the same time Amber comes stomping down the stairs and Lauren moves swiftly from the living room.
"What?" Amber demands, and Louis motions for them to follow him into the room. They oblige. He takes a seat next to Danny and gives them a second to take in the chaotic mess before them. Lauren sits herself down calmly and waits for more of an explanation and Amber stares blankly at the board. "What the hell is this?" She asks, scrunching her face up as she reads through it.
"It's a lot of information, and we thought you'd like to help us sort through it." Danny explains.
"And we need your help," Louis says, jumping in to clarify in what was already becoming too practised a motion.
"Oh, so suddenly that case from earlier that was 'just me and Louis' has become a group activity?" She mocks, revelling a little in it. Louis can't really blame her either. It's exactly what Danny would do, if the situation was reversed. "I don't know. This doesn't really look like my thing."
"What is it boys?" Lauren says, with an exasperated huff at Amber's teasing. "Start from the beginning and tell us what's happening."

"It's everything we've found out so far about 4XM." Louis tells them, and the words are met by an anxious silence as they take that in. Part of the debate he and Danny had over the last few hours was just how they'd react to this; and if they'd be willing to go along with the plan of keeping this exclusively to their group while they made sense of it.
"I'm listening." Amber says at last, and takes a seat.
"I'm not sure I should," Lauren explains.
"Chris was very clear about this, and I don't want to..."
"Please." Louis says, cutting her off and feeling bad about it. "Just hear us out. We are going to tell Chris. We just need to...figure some things out first." He says. That's the truth. They agreed they would tell him; but they wanted to have the full story before they did, so they at least knew why this was happening.
"Okay." Lauren says after a terrifying period of contemplation, and gives him a nod to continue. She obviously has reservations, but she's at least willing to listen. He can tell she wants to be supportive of them, as much as that conflicts with her desire to follow Chris' orders.
"Do you wanna...?" Louis asks Danny; but he's met with a shrug and an indication that he should be the one. He chooses to take that as a sign of faith, rather than nonchalance on Danny's part. "4XM killed again." He tells them, with an accidental sense of drama as he points towards a picture of Ben they've added to their wall board. "This is Benjamin Bailey. He used an app to meet up with 4XM...for sex." He looks towards Lauren, strangely worried about saying that in front of her because of the maternal role she's taken on in the group. He's suddenly worried about offending her. She looks unbothered by it. Instead it's Amber that shouts out in surprise.
"What the fuck? Since when do...what?" She says. He's not sure which bit she's confused about, because it could be any number of things.
"Go on Louis." Lauren tells him.
"I've downloaded the same app." He says; and is met with the exact confused stares he knew he would be. "Our plan is to use it to lure him to a meeting point so that we can capture him."
"Why do you think that'll work?" Lauren asks, looking interested. He's glad she's taking the time to consider their plan properly.
"I'm not going to be talking as 'me.' We'll create a different profile. We have Ben's phone, and we have the conversation he had with him. Danny jumped through all kinds of hoops to retrieve that." He says, with a nod to his teammate. The praise is met with an apathetic shrug.

"Less hoops, more expertly hacking a company's records." He explains. It was true, too. They couldn't find the profile on Ben's own app, which would've meant he'd be blocked by 4XM's profile and so that, and the conversation, had disappeared. Obviously that would stop a normal person; but not Danny.
"Yeah. So thanks to that we know which his profile is. We just need to create a profile that we're sure he'll want to meet." Louis continues.
"So your whole plan is to ask a Used-to-Be on a date?" Amber says.
"I mean…yeah." Louis tells her. It's an oversimplification, but it's not untrue.
"Sorry, I'm still now following how you can guarantee he'll want to meet though? You seem certain he will." Lauren asks.
"Yes! I hope so, anyway. If we can find the right person. There's a reason he killed Ben…"
"This sounds dumb." Amber interrupts, just as he's about to get to the good bit. "I don't ever remember standard capture strategies that involved dating a UTB, and I still don't think that much thought goes into who they kill…"
"Wait for it." Danny tells her. "Newbie, carry on…" That stings a little, and it throws him. He's not called him that in days and it feels like a bit of a gut punch. He's not quite sure why, particularly because Danny was defending him at the same time. But, he doesn't like it.
"Umm, yeah, we realised that Ben Bailey was connected to the Hamilton killings. He's Amelia's and Jonathan's cousin!" He stands and moves across to their board, recapturing the excitement after the momentary lapse. He's actually quite proud of the work they've done together so far.
"These names. They're all from the same family, and it goes back to 1996."
"Oh, wow. Okay. So what about all the others?" Lauren asks.
"We're still trying to work that out. There's a lot of information to sift through," He explains, gesturing at the table at the sheets and sheets of printouts they have. Lauren eyes it cautiously.
"Where has this come from?" She asks; and he's worried this will be the deal breaker. He looks over at Danny, unsure if he should go on or not.
"Alex's case files. I kept a copy." He admits, but without any hint of contrition.
"You did what?" Lauren asks, gobsmacked. Amber, meanwhile, reaches over the table to offer him a celebratory high five, impressed at his boldness. He doesn't respond and keeps his eyes on Lauren. Clearly Danny knows this could be a step too far for her too and even he knows not to go as far as to outright celebrate it.

"Danny, this is…if Chris finds out…I can't even imagine what he'll do…" " She says, shaking her head. Her face looks as if she wants to get up, leave, and forget all of this. But she doesn't. She stays in her seat thinking it all over.

"Surely nothing is more important than stopping him." Danny says. He quickly glances at Louis but won't fully meet his eye. "Not Chris' rules, not the trouble we'll all be in, but correcting our mistake. We were supposed to stop him. There are humans who are dead now who wouldn't be if we'd stopped him that night. We stop him and then we stop whoever he's working with." He says, and not for the first time Louis is hit with a confusing wave of emotion. Danny's words veered very close to the feelings he'd expressed earlier, and he was unsure what to make of that. Was it that Danny felt that feeling or failure too, or was it just that he thought echoing what Louis had said would be particularly persuasive to the others? Why was it so important to Danny; there had to be more to it than just his dislike of not knowing the answers? He'd begun to see beneath Danny's spikey disposition in the last few days, little by little. There was something more there, he cared about this. He cared about getting the answers and saving lives. No matter what he said this wasn't just a chance to show off. Louis didn't fully understand him yet but he really, really wanted to. Perhaps even more than he wanted to find and stop 4XM.

"Well, I'm in." Amber declared, and whipped her head around to face Lauren. She was the one they were waiting on now. There was a tense pause that felt like it went on forever. If she decided to tell Chris what they'd been up to, rather than help, it'd all be over. They'd never know what was going on, and Louis would definitely be sent somewhere else. Possibly even retrained. He held his breath.

"Okay." She said at last. "But we do need to tell Chris as soon as we properly work it out."

"We will. Definitely." Louis says, and Danny quickly begins dishing out some pages for them all to look through.

"It's messy and unfocussed. It's part newspaper clippings, part diary. It's all over the place and I think I've only got half of it. I think there's more names to go up. But…"

"We can do it." Lauren tells them.

"Yeah, we can." Louis says, and he can't fight back a smile. The team is all about to work together, properly, and it feels amazing. He finally feels like he's one of them.
"Yeah. We need a timeline of Alex's investigation – then we can work out what links his victims, and once we know what he's going for…we know how to trap him." Danny says, taking control as he starts on his own pile.
"…I better get to punch someone if I have to do paperwork…." Amber mutters; but has already started reading. Lauren rolls her eyes at her, and they all get to work.

Chapter Twenty-Four

Central Manchester, 10th October 1996
It had been a little intimidating seeing him like this again; drunk and lairy. It brought back unpleasant flashbacks, but Joseph knew he'd push through it because things were very different this time around. Jason didn't even recognise him and that was the worst thing about it. Even if he'd have had doubts, seeing him here, drunk and surrounded by a different feral pack of mates, then the fact he was able to walk straight past him without an ounce of recognition would've made his blood boil to the point where those doubts were erased. Now, there's just the part of the blood boiling, and oh how it boiled. He'd thought about this moment so much; and thought about what he'd say, what he'd do, and even if he'd have the strength to do it. He needn't have bothered thinking about it, because at that moment all rational thought evacuated his brain. The moment Jason and his ugly group of friends had stumbled past him nonchalantly he'd lost the ability to even think clearly. He'd stood for a moment, blinded by the indignation of someone who's face was burned into his memory not even acknowledging him, and then he'd snapped and screamed.
One moment they were joking about something "Jase" had said to another lad, and shoving each other, like fucking monkies, and the next it was all blind rage and Joseph was charging. The other three dove out of the way initially as the skinny, pale, screeching boy charged towards their beefy, meat-headed leader. He shouldn't have been able to take him down, but oh he did, and Jason landed headfirst with a crack against the concrete. That's when the meat-head's monkeys leapt into action. They tore him off the bigger man, as he thrashed and scratched, and even bit them. He would not be deterred; not from this and not now. Monkey number one was

pushed backwards with such rage fuelled strength that the collision with a lamppost nearly snapped him in half. Monkey number two was swatted away like a fly that didn't have the sense to dodge and flew into the side of a parked car. The car, like the lamppost, won that battle and he shattered an assortment of bones. Joseph heard the sound of them snapping. It was beautiful. Monkey number three stood as the last obstacle, and if he'd had any sense he would've run. But he didn't. He wouldn't have been hanging around with Jason fucking Hamilton if he'd have had any sense. So Joseph did the kindest thing he could. He grabbed either side of his head and dug his thumbs into his eyeballs so that he wouldn't have to see what was about to become of his friend. The monkey screamed, and then was tossed aside. Jason, bleeding from his head wound, was trying to scramble away. There was no way he was going to let that happen. Not after all this time.

"This is all your fault!" Joseph roars, finally managing to form words from within the red mist that had descended. He throws himself down on top of him again, scratching and clawing at the man that's haunted his thoughts for weeks.

"Please! I'm sorry!" Jason begs, pathetically, and Joseph doesn't even stop to wonder if it's because he recognises him or not, if he knows what he's apologising for or he's just gambling on the idea that he's done something to be sorry for. He just keeps hitting him; striking, and clawing, and punching with everything he has. Jason's dead now. He doesn't even know how long he's been dead for, or how long he's been hitting him. He just knows his hands are absolutely covered in blood and gore and mush. Behind him, a woman approaches. It's her. There's an irony to that, and it's not lost on him. She lays a hand on his shoulder and he stops hitting the empty shell of the man that caused him so much pain.

"Do you feel any better?" She asks him, and he looks up at her with tears in his eyes. She already knows the answer. She told him as much.

"No." He tells her; and then he weeps, grabbing her hand with his bloodied one and collapsing into a sobbing heap at her side.

...and back again...

And finally it felt like they'd cracked it; and that feeling was indescribable. Louis stood in front of the board that was now populated with a lot more information. There were names circled in three different colours, denoting three separate patterns.

"I think..." He begins, taking it in for a second and stopping because he doesn't quite want to vocalise his hope.
"Have we got it?" Amber asks, eagerly. For someone who said she wasn't particularly interested she managed to get very into this puzzle in the last few hours.
"I think so." Louis says; and takes a look at the full picture of what they have. "So red are all related to Zach Thompson."
"Killed 19th November 1998." Lauren adds, from the little notepad she has in front of her.
"Yep." Louis says, tracing the victims that followed with his finger. His dad Robert, then his brother-in-law two years later, and so on.
"Living relatives are sparse." Danny says, jumping in to add the part that he's researching. "I'm having to go out to second cousins to find one."
"Okay. So those in green are related to Jason Hamilton."
"10th October 1996." Lauren adds again.
"Then his parents in 1997 and 1998; all the way through to his niece and nephew Amelia and Jonathan, and his other nephew Ben."
"Some sister-in-laws left; plus Victoria Hamilton and Margaret Bailey. And they're not really suitable." Danny explains. He's right. They need a male. Louis' mind wanders for a second, wondering if there's a reason he's wiping more men out than women. He's sure there are a thousand; but maybe it's that, for whatever reason, it all started with these three men.
"Okay, so then in blue we have the family of Thomas Marshall."
"5th February 1997,"
"Then his sister Louise in 1999, their parents Donald and Joan in 2002..."
"His brother survived until 2012; and he was married and had three kids. One of them, Richard, had two sons of his own. There's Jacob, 2000, and Ethan, 2006. Both living. Jacob could be who we need." Danny explains, tapping away at his laptop.
"There's a lot of names up there." Lauren says, and that hasn't escaped Louis' notice either. By human standards 4XM would be classified as a serial killer, but some of these deaths hadn't even been investigated by police, and none of them had found the true killer. There continued to be victims outside of those three families mentioned, of course, names like the Robinson family. Other people who were just in the wrong place at the wrong time rather than deliberate targets, presumably. But it was very clear that for whatever reason 4XM had taken it upon himself to prune these three family trees. The only link that they could find was that the boys it all

started with were friends. There was no rhyme or reason beyond that, and that really bothered Louis.

"Why these three families?" He asks, turning to the others even though he knows they won't have an answer.

"It doesn't matter." Amber says dismissively. It does, he thinks. "We've got our pattern, who cares why. We got what you wanted so let's get him." She says, cracking her knuckles symbolically. I'd still like to understand, Louis thinks to himself.

"Amber's right," Danny interjects, and Louis knows that any protests and suggestions to dig deeper will ultimately be dismissed. "We've got what we need. But if you really want to know, maybe you'll get a chance to ask him." He says, and with a characteristically cocky flourish he pulls up Jacob's social media for them all to see. "I've got everything we need here to create a fake profile." He says, and Louis doesn't react. Instead he stares at that list of names. There's so many of them, and why? Why would someone go to the trouble of tracking down and murdering all these people? It felt important. It felt like there was still a piece of the puzzle missing right at the centre. Nothing would make it okay, nothing would make these deaths okay, but it still mattered why they'd happened. And who was the other person involved in it? They knew there was someone, they'd had that warning from her and yet there was no evidence in all of this of someone else. "Louis!" Danny calls, pulling him out of that particularly thought spiral. He turns away from the names and the other three are all staring at him, waiting for him to answer.

"Yeah." He says, with a reluctant nod. "You get the info and photos, and I'll create the profile." He confirms.

"And I'll call Chris." Lauren says, standing, as if she needs to leave before she's talked out of it. "It's time. We can't let this go any further, and we certainly can't make a move to capture, without telling him." And there's no room for argument because she's right. At the moment they can still salvage this, and that was their plan. Danny was convinced that if they went to Chris with a fully formed and easy plan, when it was still possible for him to be involved enough to take credit, then it would cancel out his rage at the work they'd done behind his back. Louis silently prayed to whoever was listening that he was right.

It didn't take him long. Night had long since crept into morning as they'd sat there going over and over the files and assigning meaning to the

cryptic logs of meaningless deaths. It should've taken an hour for Chris to get from his office at Home Base to Brickmere Road but it felt like it took him half of that, and the second he walked through the door he launched into a rant that felt like it lasted double that. He was standing, and had made them all sit, as he started a tirade of how irresponsible they had all been. Danny and Louis would agree later that he was mostly just pissed because they'd done what he couldn't. That was a feeling he'd get used to, eventually.
"…completely…stupid!" He finished, somewhat running out of steam. He had been huffing and puffing for quite some time. "…with just absolutely no regard for your…" he continued. Louis had kind of zoned out by this point. He was hitting very similar notes to the ones he'd thrown around when they were one on one. It included them endangering lives, their own and other people's, and a few other things too. They sat for as long as it took to get it out of his system. That was the plan. To let him rant and rave until he was satisfied. "…and I think it'll work." He finishes, very begrudgingly. "I'm not happy about it, but it will." The team do their best to look surprised; but Danny and Louis can't help smirking at each other. This was exactly how they had wanted it to go. It was exactly what they'd been gambling on. "I can't believe you all went behind my back with this, but, it's a good plan. If we can pull this off then I'll forget about the fact you disobeyed my orders, just this once. But only if it works. Louis, do you have everything you need?"
"Yes." Louis confirmed quickly. "I've created the profile; it's very clearly identifiable…" He explains
"But not so much that it's obvious. I've backed it up by hacking the real Human's social media. I've added some posts about being in Endsbrough visiting Uni friends, and then locked him out. It's only for 24 hours but it'll be enough." Danny adds.
"And I found 4XM's profile, and I'm ready to make first contact. We knew it'd be best to speak with you first though, before we did anything." He said, and it took so much to stop himself there. It was sorely tempting to add something sarcastic about how they'd not needed him for any other stage of the plan but this, this was the absolutely crucial stage that needed his sign off. He'd clearly been spending too much time in Danny's company already, but then, he was starting to find Chris' whole demeanour infuriating. He'd have to get used to that.

"Right, well, go ahead." Chris says, giving them the permission that they shouldn't really need to execute the plan he had nothing to do with.
"Yeah?" Lauren clarifies; making absolutely sure they have that approval.
"Yes. Go ahead and make contact with the target," He confirms, and Louis doesn't hesitate a second longer. He pulls open Meetr and sends a quick 'hey' with a winking emoji.
"Done." He tells them, as the others all stare at him. He puts his phone back on the table and, for a moment, they all stare and wait for a reply.
"We've agreed on a location?" Chris asks, breaking their focus.
"We have, we'll invite him to a bar downtown." Danny explains as he pulls up a map of their chosen location on the electronic board. It shows 'Vanity Bar' and the surrounding area.
"I'll speak to DCI Wade and ask if we can have the police clear it. It'll attract less attention than us." Louis adds. They made sure to plan this thoroughly, so that there was no room for criticism.
"Okay. I'll speak to Olivia and we can have her team ready to go. They can be inside."
"We'll be ready too." Amber adds.
"Yes, be ready. This is a good plan." He starts, begrudgingly admitting it, and Louis has a terrible feeling that there's a 'but' coming just before it lands. "But, I'm going to make a couple of tactical changes. Amber, you'll be with me and Olivia's team inside the bar. Lauren, Louis, and Danny, you can support from across the street and be ready to support." He explains and points to a street on the map. "That provides good tactical cover, in case he gets away, but it should be close enough that the location on your phone won't raise any alarm bells."
"Wait, we're back-up?" Danny snaps.
"Yes." Chris tells him, simply.
"This is our plan?" Louis says, not disguising the anger and earning himself a glare from Chris.
"And I've said it's a good one. But you kept investigating after I told you not to. If this isn't a success…" He trails off, and clearly loses himself for a moment in thoughts of what the consequences of failure will be. He also clearly decides not to share those thoughts with the group. "This needs to be a success."
"It will be." Louis says, firmly, though he knows he has a different motive for wanting it to go well. Louis wants to succeed so that no one else dies at

4XM's hands; and yet Chris' fear of failure probably comes from a much more self-serving place.

"Indeed. But it's important that it all runs smoothly. It's important that I have people with me who are able to follow my orders."

"That's a load of…" Amber begins, but Chris, raising his voice now, interrupts her.

"You can be back-up too? Or, if you all feel this emotional about it, then I can handle this with only Olivia's team?" He asks, puffing his chest out and looking down at them all. His gaze looms over them as if they're all misbehaving school children and he's just waiting for the next one to step out of line. "Good." He says, when none of them do. "Louis, please make the call to sort the location out. I'll get the team ready. Keep the conversation with the target going and keep me informed. Let me know when you've agreed to meet." He stops, and stares at Louis until he gets a response.

"Yes…" He says reluctantly. Chris continues to stare; and Louis knows exactly what he wants. He did it during the conversation in his office too. The word sticks in his throat, Chris only wants it to assert his power in this situation, but he relents because he doesn't have any other choice. "Sir." He adds at last. Chris nods, and smiles. He's satisfied and his posture relaxes a little.

"Ok. Good work. I'm disappointed by how this came about but…this gives us an opportunity to capture 4XM. That'll be…it'll be good. Thank you." He says, before giving them all one last annoyed glance, and leaving. They wait in silence until the front door closes behind him and they see him through the window approaching his car.

"This is absolute bullshit. I can't believe he's keeping you on the side lines." Amber growls. Danny groans and shakes his head. He gives Louis a look which borders on a look of concern. It's like he's silently trying to check he's okay. But before Louis can really work out if that's what it is Danny's brown eyes have flicked away from him.

"He just wants the glory. It doesn't matter, as long as we get 4XM, right?" Danny says.

"Am I the only one who wanted to punch him?" Amber says, with a pointed look out of the window as if she's considering chasing him down to do just that.

"No, but…" Danny says.

"It could've gone worse." Louis sighs. "I was a little worried we'd all be sent for re-training, just because he could. But Danny is right. We get to end this, and as long as it goes well, it sounds like we'll be punishment free."
"Oh shut it Newbie." Amber snaps, clearly needing a focus for her irritation. "We'll rely on Lauren for the sunny bright-side shit. She's got that covered without your help." Louis is about to bite back at her when his phone pings and all of their eyes widen in a mixture of surprise and fear. They've had a reply.

Wade's toast lets out a satisfying crunch as he bites into it. It's only got the faintest scraping of margarine on it, because that low-fat stuff Kam's been buying doesn't add any flavour anyway, so it's basically just a piece of nearly-burnt bread on its own. But that's pretty much how he likes it. Dry, crunchy, bread and a strong coffee. He's taking his time this morning. Everyone at work seems to want him to slow down a little, so he's going to do just that. He's going to sit and have a moment to himself and a decent breakfast before he starts his day properly. He's leafing through the pages of the newspaper when Kamala marches into the room, the complete opposite to him. She's a whirlwind of activity as she breezes past him and grabs her lunch out of the fridge, ready to set off. She's also fully dressed and looking immaculate, whereas he is still in his dressing gown and slippers.

"That's yesterday's," She tells him, nodding to the paper.
"I know. But I didn't get chance to read it yesterday." He retorts with a sly smile.
"Well, I'll be sure not to throw away today's then." She says with a chuckle.
"Aye, I'd appreciate that." He retorts.
"I love you very much you silly man," She tells him, planting a quick kiss on his cheek. "What time should I expect you home tonight, before or after midnight?"
"Oh I think I fancy being home for dinner tonight." He says and this elicits a gasp of surprise. It was a genuine one too, not one for dramatic effect. "I think I'll even sort it, if you like?"
"Did you take another bump to the head?" She asks and stops to take the time to sit down opposite him. The truth is, that made him feel even worse than he had been already. There was something Tim had said the day before that had resonated with him. When he'd floated the idea of taking more time off and going on a trip with Kam he'd realised that it'd been so long since he'd done that. He was a workaholic and he had been for years.

She knew that when she married him, of course, but it didn't excuse neglecting their marriage for the sake of a job where he'd never feel like he'd done enough. It didn't feel good; the idea that you'd been neglecting the woman you love for years. "Talk to me?" She half asked, half demanded of him.

"I'm just fine." He groans back at her, doing his best to sound convincing. "It's just this job. Maybe I could do with slowing down a bit. Tim told me to take a few more days off and I'm inclined to do just that." Kamala raises her eyebrows and takes a moment to size him up. He knows that look very well. She's a very intelligent woman, that wife of his, and she's currently looking for bullshit. "Don't gimme that look." He tells her.

"Hmm." She says, thoughtfully. "I don't think you're telling me everything Matthew Wade. But luckily for you…" She begins, standing up and grabbing her bag. "…I don't really have the time to dig any deeper." She leans over and pecks him on the cheek "…until tonight anyway. You can tell me then." She stops for a second in the kitchen doorway. "Have you walked the dog though?"

"Yes of course I've walked the bastard dog. I don't get no peace until I do!" He tells her. She laughs and heads for the door. He smiles too. More time off with her wouldn't be the worst thing in the world, not at all. That's when his phone rings, with a private number, which is never a good sign.

"Wade." He says, answering it somewhat hesitantly.

"Hi, it's me." Louis says, making him wish he'd not bothered to pick up. "It's Louis." He clarifies nervously, in response to the silence he's been met with.

"Yes," Wade says simply.

"I need your help with something."

"Go on?"

"Well, we need a bar in town cleared out. I thought it'd be a little smoother if some of your uniformed officers did it maybe?" He asks.

"Right, and can I ask why?" Wade responds. Louis takes a pause, and it's like Wade can hear the cogs turning as he assesses his options.

"We have a suspect for the victim yesterday. We're luring him to a meeting and we need that space." He tells him.

"That was unusually informative." Wade says, unable to hold that particular thought back. "Which bar?"

"Vanity." Louis tells him.

"Right. I'll see what I can do. I'll call you back in ten." Wade tells him, and ends the call abruptly. He will help, and maybe he'll come to regret it, but this seems like an opportunity to fit another piece into the vastly confusing puzzle of what the hell the Counter Terrorism team actually do. He realises that he desperately wants to complete that puzzle; and that there's no way he can walk away from it, and unfortunately that means more time off with Kam would have to wait. He knows he can't do it alone though. Thankfully, he thinks, he knows someone who is infuriatingly good at puzzles. He dials another number as soon as he's ended the call to Louis.
"It's me. I seem to remember you were rather close with the owner of Vanity Bar, once upon a time. I have a small favour to ask…"

Chapter Twenty-Five.

A few hours later Chris stands inside Vanity Bar, as they planned. There are only a few other people in the bar, which is normal for a weekday afternoon, but what's not normal is that they're all Custodians disguised as patrons.
"The others are here. Are you in position?" Chris asks into his phone. He's on edge.
"Yes." Danny confirms from the car that's parked a little down the road. "We've got a clear view of the bar, and I can see the feed for all the cameras around here, so I should see him coming." He confirms. They're all there, speaking to Chris on Lauren's phone which is connected to the car. She sits in the driver's seat with Amber next to her, and Danny and Louis are in the back.
"One of Olivia's team had already done that, so we have eyes on the camera here." Chris tells him, and Danny's face beautifully gives away how unhappy he is with that information. Louis has to hold back a smirk at the look of indignation he gives. He really doesn't like not being able to show off his intelligence; and it's hilarious to see him usurped as the tech-expert like that. Louis makes a mental note to meet this person from Olivia's team, and ask them to do this again, as regularly as possible. "Amber, please make your way to us." Chris' voice orders through the car. She grunts in response and opens the passenger door to climb out. She's already in a bad mood because she feels uncomfortable. Her and Chris are the biggest risks to this plan; because 4XM has already seen them. Danny had needed to talk her into wearing an outfit that didn't look

completely out of place in a bar, rather than her usual loose fitting black joggers and jumper, so that she'd blend in better. She had insisted that she still kept the flexibility to 'kick someone in the face,' so they'd agreed in the end on a loose skirt that would still give her that freedom, though it now looked very odd. The biggest battle was getting her to cover up her bright red hair with a blonde wig so that she wasn't so distinctive. They'd all had to take part in that one, convincing her that it might blow their cover before she was in a position to capture him. "I'm ripping it off the second I have eyes on him." She'd told them sternly, agreeing at last.

"I'll see you lot soon." She tells them, as she steps fully out of the car and stands up straight. Danny nods to her and activates the camera feed in the contact lenses she's wearing so that he can have a clear view of what's going on. Louis leans in to watch on his tablet as she approaches and enters, meeting Chris at the bar. He looks stone faced as he nods at her in greeting.

"Louis, any update on the target?" He asks. It's a confusing over stimulation for the briefest moment, as his lips move on the screen but his voice booms through the car's speakers.

"No. Last message was that he was leaving and he'd be there for the agreed time. Should I send another?"

"Okay. Yes. We've got five minutes till the agreed time so everyone be on their guard. I'm ending this call. I'll activate my earpiece but I want radio silence unless there's a problem." There's a click as Chris' line disconnects. The car radio kicks back in but Lauren stops it quickly and they sit in silence. Louis unlocks his phone and opens up the "Meetr" app as the other two watch him anxiously. He goes straight for the chat with 4XM and types "I'm here. Drink?", then sends it quickly. They all stare at his phone, waiting for a response.

"I'm still not sure how you can do that." Says Lauren, with a little tut, breaking the silence.

"Do what?"

"Well, the whole…flirting thing. Especially with a Used-to-Be." She explains. She doesn't sound like she's being judgmental or unkind, just that she's genuinely puzzled by it.

"It's just…playing a role I suppose. I'm not me, I'm Jacob. It's easier because if you think about it, he's doing it too," He explains with a shrug. Whoever 4XM was being, it wasn't himself. From the conversation so far he was apparently a 20-year-old called Liam who worked in insurance.

That definitely wasn't who they'd met at the Eagle Hotel . "We're probably both just saying what we think we should say."
"I'm still just a little uncomfortable with the whole thing." She explains, shaking her head a little. "I just wouldn't be able to." The truth is, this isn't Louis' first time flirting. It's not something they were taught, obviously, but he'd spent a long time on his own in Jongleton.
"You should see some of the other messages I got." He replies with a cheeky grin, and instantly regrets it.
"What do you mean?" She asks, and he blushes. That's not something he wants to tell her about. Thankfully, Amber interjects to save him via their earpieces.
"Lauren, get over it. Humans over complicate sex, like they do everything else. It's just enjoyment. I'm not recommending Newbie does *that* with a Used-to-Be, but maybe we should find you someone to get on. Enjoy yourself, it's just basic pleasure fulfilment and it's a great stress relief." She explains, and Lauren looks utterly horrified at the idea of it. Her mouth moves as she tries to form a response but nothing comes out. Louis wishes that they could see Amber right now, so he could try to work out whether that was her goal or not.
"I said radio silence, please. Besides, this really isn't an appropriate conversation…" Chris interjects, chastising them.
"Oh shut up, it's not like you haven't done it. I know you've done it. It's just sex!" Amber continues, and now, thanks to Danny's tablet, Louis can see it's Chris' turn to blush. He's got a wig too, and is wearing glasses, to try to disguise himself. Behind him two of the other agents chuckle to themselves because they can all hear what's being said through the earpieces.
"Amber…" Chris says, trying to shut her up.
"What? There's no rule against us having sex!" She says, loudly.
"No, it's just…" He says, gesturing around them.
"Chris, we're in a bar. We should be making conversation. Humans talk about this stuff in bars. You don't think it'll look weird if It walks in here and we're standing in silence?" At the table to her right Olivia, the senior agent of the other team, smirks and nods in agreement. Amber catches that and it encourages her. "See?" She says, gesturing towards her.
"Yes. Okay. Fine." He agrees, very begrudgingly and getting a little flustered. "Maybe just don't have a conversation with people who aren't here?" He offers instead.

"Then you and me can talk." She replies, and while Louis can't see the scary grin on her face through the tablet he's certain it's there. "Vodka, neat." She says, turning to the agent who's undercover as a bartender. He looks unsure and looks to Chris for approval; he wasn't expecting to actually serve a drink. Chris nods, reluctantly. "You not having one?" Amber asks, grabbing the glass as soon as it's put in front of her and raising it to Chris. She's having far too much fun, Louis thinks, but it's quite entertaining when it's not at his expense.

"No, Amber, I'm not drinking while we're…you know…" Chris says.

"While we're on a date?" She offers and it causes the dark skin on his face to turn red in embarrassment. "It's okay, you can say it. Don't be shy! Honestly though, it's not going well. You seem a bit uptight, so maybe it'd help."

"Amber, sorry, really important question; do you mean vodka or sex?" Danny chimes in and she laughs and gets a little closer, rubbing Chris' arm playfully, and making him very uncomfortable in the process.

"Well, happy to try either if it loosens him up…"

"Enough!" He snaps, taking control of the situation back and pulling away from Amber. "Both of you." He says.

"Both of who? Are you talking to people who aren't here?" Amber asks, infuriating him further. Louis and Danny smile at each other in the car; they're quite enjoying it.

"Louis, any reply?" Chris asks, obviously now ignoring his own rule for the sake of refocusing Amber's attention.

"No, he is online though." As soon as those words have left his mouth there's a ping as a reply comes through from 4XM's profile. "Oh, wait. No. 'How about a shot?'" He says, reading the message out to them.

"I could go for a tequila." Amber says, catching the fake bartender's eye again.

"Okay." Louis says, typing out a message that reads; 'okay what about tequila?' He hits send and almost instantly another reply comes through. It reads 'Didn't mean that kind Louis.' His stomach lurches as his brain makes sense of what he's read. "Wha…" He begins, but he's cut off by the loud bang of a gunshot piercing through the otherwise quiet street. The glass window in the bar shatters, and there's shouting from inside.

Part IV: Finding Joseph

Chapter Twenty-Six.

It's 1996. I can't quite tell when. It's not like the other deaths, because it's not recorded anywhere, but it definitely came before them. That'll be obvious. I'd say not long before the death of Jason Hamilton which was on the 10th October. A few weeks before that maybe. I could work it out, I'm sure, but the date isn't an important part of the story.

There's a man, or a boy, laying in bed. He's in his late teens. By bed, I mean just a mattress on the floor. The so-called bedroom is definitely not lavish, it doesn't even border on nice. It just is. The paint is peeling, there's spots of damp, and it looks like the window won't close properly. The few belongings he owns are strewn across the room, which is understandable because why would you make an effort to keep things tidy when it's going to be a bit of a shithole no matter what you do?

The boy rolls over, in a tangle of sheets that don't match and looks over at his alarm clock.

"Oh shit!" Joseph says, because he's drastically overslept. Yes, the boy is Joseph and at this point he's still human. He's not a monster, he's not a murderer, he's just a teenager, living in a terrible apartment because it's all he can afford, who's late for work. See, I told you it'd be obvious that this came before the deaths of Jason, Thomas, and Zach. Joseph bursts out of bed, just wearing a pair of loose fitting boxers, and scrambles around on the floor to try to find some clothes that are clean enough to be able to rewear them. He has milky skin and is very skinny, not through any kind of conscious exercise or strength, more through a lack of eating. He kind of looks like a stork, with knobbly, spindly legs, but he has no sense of bird-like grace as he rushes out into the hallway and nearly smashing into his flatmate Heather on the way. "I'm late! Why didn't you wake me?" He whines at her as he darts into the bathroom.

"You're at work this afternoon? My bad, I didn't realise, sorry Joey!" She says with a grimace.

"No, no, it's fine!" He says, a little frantic as he starts the shower and grabs at his tooth brush. "My boss will just freak out on me if I'm late again."

…and about fifteen minutes later when he rushes into the bar he works at, looking red faced and dishevelled having run all the way there, that's exactly what happens. There's an older, fat, balding man waiting for him. He's called Pat and he's just red faced because that's how Pat looks.

"You're late." He grunts at him.

"I know, sorry, sorry, It's only a minute though!" Joseph pleads, practically leaping behind the bar and throwing off a coat so that he's ready to serve the customers that haven't even materialised yet.
"I'm not cutting you any more slack. I mean it Joe. I already took a risk hiring someone like you…one more late and you're done here. You got it?" Pat tells him. The phrase 'someone like you,' hits Joseph like a slap, and you can see that. But he endures it because he has to.
"Yes, sorry, I swear, no more being late. I really appreciate this job. I'm sorry." He says, and it's bordering on grovelling. Pat doesn't respond with words immediately, he just lets his harsh glare linger on him for a moment and then goes about his business, which is a stack of forms laid on the bar.
"Well, you can show it then, 'cause you were late I want you to stay behind tonight to lock up. Fred was supposed to close but he called in sick." He explains.
"Lucky Fred…" Joseph mumbles, and Pat grunts. Who knows if it was actually in response, or if Pat is just the kind of man who grunts a lot. He does look an awful lot like a warthog, so the grunting probably wouldn't be out of character. "It's not like I had plans anyway…" Joseph says, which elicits another grunt from the warthog-made-human. Pat then scoops up his paperwork and takes it to a table at the back of the bar, looking as if he's irritated that his employee has continued to talk and break his concentration. Joseph lets out a sigh and fiddles around with the sound system. He puts some music on and then leans against the bar and waits for his first customer.

"Present" (or close enough)
They've been sitting in silence for what feels like forever; and it's taking everything she has to hold back and not push him for more info. Kim is a pro. She knows when to push and when to leave space; and if she doesn't play this one just right then she'll see DCI Wade running out of the door again.
But, although she knows when to be patient, she's never been all that great at it. The curious part of her brain is screaming at her and it has been ever since he messaged her asking to meet.
She tries to focus on the coffee instead and the pattern in the foam. It's not a deliberate one, nothing artsy or overly kitsch, it's the way the foam landed in her overly large mug. She cups her hands around it. It's big enough for both of them, and that's exactly how she likes it. Journalism

and excessive caffeine consumption go hand in hand. When she was a little younger, just starting out, she'd happily pull all-nighters, surviving on coffee and sugar alone, to be the first to break a story. When Whitney Housten died in 2012 she'd worked through the night to make sure the channel she worked for had an obituary package ready to go. It was frustrating, actually, because it was standard practice to have one ready to go for most celebrities, but for some reason they'd missed Whitney. She managed to throw one together using old clips and interviews, and still have it ready to go hours before they went on air. All that and she was still in the studio looking sprightly the next day. That was all thanks to coffee.
"Why are we here?" She asked, finally letting her curiosity get the better of her. It came out a little blunter than she meant it to, but there was nothing she could do to take it back now. The coffee shop was busy and noisy, at just the right level so that they wouldn't be overheard because it was too loud for their conversation to carry, but quiet enough that they could sit at a table away from everyone else.
"I want it on the record that I'm still…conflicted." Wade replied, finally.
"Then that is what the record shall state." She assures him.
"And I want the final say before you publish anything." He says; and this makes her pause and contemplate. In theory agreeing to that is a terrible idea. It's something that, if she stuck to, could cause her some real problems further down the line. Especially if he backs out. She knows there's a story with this phoney Counter Terrorism Team. Something going on below the surface, something being hidden that she wants to dig up, and to properly expose that she needs to be able to share whatever the truth is uninhibited by Wade changing his mind.
"Okay. We have to agree it together before I publish," She says, knowing full well that might turn out to be a lie. "What made you reconsider?"
"There's too many unanswered questions. I just can't leave it alone." He explains, and lord knows she can relate to that.
"Okay, so…I feel like there was something you weren't telling me yesterday." She says, still trying to proceed a little cautiously with him. Her and Wade have always had a good working relationship; but this seems different. He's never shared anything like this with her before and has instead been very good at keeping a professional line. He's hesitant to tell her, she can see that much, but there's more to it than just not wanting to spill secrets. There's something else in the expression on his face.

"The guy we got for the Hamilton killings. I was investigating his murder at the same time." He says at last, and his words hang there for a moment because she can't really make sense of them.

"What?" She asks, still not properly able to make the sentence fit.

"He was dead, and then he wasn't and I can't work it out." He offers, as if that goes any way to explaining it. Kim takes a deep breath and looks down at her cup on the table in front of her, clasping her hands around it again and enjoying the warmth. She tries to take in his words as she stares into what's left of the foam. "Yeah." He continues. "I figured you'd think I'd lost it."

"It's not that." She says quickly, whipping her head back up to meet his gaze. "I'm just processing. Besides, his wife said something similar when I spoke to her…" She deliberately dropped that in there. It's better to tell him she'd slipped by him to speak to her, after he'd clearly told her to leave. It was best all out in the open, and all that. He opens his mouth to respond, probably to chastise her, but she jumps in with a question. "Do you think he faked it?" She asks him quickly, to divert his attention. It works like a charm.

"I don't know." He says thoughtfully. "I dunno what to think, in all honesty. That's not all. Their daughter disappeared and they won't tell me where she is. The Counter Terrorism People. They took her, I think. They just keep saying something about keeping her safe. But safe from who? It don't make sense. It's just too much cloak and dagger rubbish."

"So we have resurrections and disappearances. What the hell are we dealing with?" She asks and all Wade can really do is chuckle.

"If I knew that…" He says gruffly. "…you're a pain in the arse Kimmy. You always have been. But I know you've got a good heart and you're the best at uncovering a mystery." She takes another sip from her giant mug of coffee, appreciating the compliment but not entirely sure she deserves it.

"What the hell are we dealing with here?" She asks him, again in disbelief and unable to stop herself from laughing a little at the ridiculousness of it all. He returns it with a chuckle and a tired smile.

"God knows. But you're my best bet of finding out what the hell is going on. Hopefully together we can get somewhere."

"Last chance to back out on me." She says, quite seriously. "Whatever this is, it's something you've been told to leave alone. There's risks and…I don't want to face Kamala's wrath if you lose your job or something."

"No, me neither. We need to be really careful. You need to promise me you'll be careful, too. No more sneaking around hospitals. Not without me, anyway."
"Matthew, you don't need to protect me." She tells him sternly, a little annoyed at the idea of it but also conscious that he means well.
"No, but, if you got hurt I'd feel responsible." He says.
"It won't come to that. So where do we even start?" No sooner had she asked than her question was answered; the sound of gunfire roared through the street outside and a window in the bar over the street shattered.

Chris crumples to the ground and his blood sprays everywhere. Amber reacts instinctively and is covering him before she fully realises he's been shot. Another bang and another agent goes down. He falls behind a table, so she can't see what state he's in. Another shot thunders through the air and it skims past her head and into the wooden bar. It was only centimetres from connecting, and it was something she wouldn't have survived. The others, including the agent behind the bar, all scramble for cover. Amber scans the area but she can't see their attacker. Olivia and Noel, who was the agent sitting with her, dive over to help her with Chris. Olivia flips a table and uses it to block them all from view; but a bullet splinters through it seconds later, narrowly missing them all. Amber rips off her wig.
"We need to move him." Olivia tells her as Chris groans in pain below them. He's still alive, for now at least. He's bleeding profusely from the hole in his chest, and even Amber's limited medical knowledge tells her that he needs help soon if he's going to survive. The three of them pull him, not so gently, across the floor and further into the building, hoping it's enough to keep them safe.
"Danny!" Amber roars desperately into her earpiece. Across the street he's already furiously flicking through the surveillance feeds, desperate to find something helpful.
"He could be anywhere." He says, unhelpfully. Lauren stares at the building as another shot rings out through the air and shatters another window.
"What's going on?" She asks. Her tone is slow and calm; but Louis can see the effort on her face as she tries to keep it that way.
"Chris has been hit. Another agent too." Amber says; and through the screen they see her gaze flick to the other side of the bar where the other

victim being tended to. From that distance it looks like he's alive too. "Other guy looks okay. But Chris…" Her gaze flicks back to him and Lauren grabs the tablet from Danny's hand for a better look. "He's bleeding a lot. Dan, is there a back way out?" Amber asks,

"It'll bring you out on the same street. We picked it for that reason, so until we can figure out where he's firing from…" Danny tells her. The location that they picked for its tactical advantages had come back to bite them spectacularly.

"Fuck!" Amber groans, knowing she's trapped with no hope of fighting her way out. Another shot is fired and it splinters the floor near them. Now their attacker is just firing to keep them pinned down. Amber growls in frustration again, like a wild animal trapped and ready to rip the face off the first person it can get it's teeth into. "Get me a way out of here." She demands and in the car the three of them look between each other.

"We need to get me in there." Lauren says to the other two, not taking her eyes off the live feed from Amber's eyes. "He needs help, soon." There's a ping suddenly and it cuts through the chaos as Louis realises what it means. He's got another message. This one comes with a pin showing a location; a block of flats a few kilometres away. The message reads 'I know it's a little quick, but let's take this back to my place. Number 434.' He tilts the phone and shows it to Danny, and they meet each other's gaze and nod.

"It's a set up." Louis tells him.

"One-hundred percent." Danny agrees.

"And only the two of us can go?" Louis asks.

"Yep. It's just me and you." Danny replies.

"But we have to." Louis says, a little solemnly.

"We don't have a choice." Danny agrees. Lauren, who hasn't seen the message, looks up at the two of them, a little lost. Danny pulls the tablet from her grip, closing it and leaning over to put it in the glove compartment. "Lauren, get out and take cover. The second it's safe, get in there." He explains to her.

"Bu…" She begins; and Louis shakes his head at her.

"You said it yourself; we need you in there." He says.

"Whatever you're doing, hurry." Amber says and the hint of quiet desperation in her voice forces Lauren into action. She nods and gets out of the car; and Danny climbs forward and into the driver's seat. She hands him the keys before she closes the door behind her, then darts across the street ducking for cover. All around her there are humans, and they're all confused and scared by what's going on. Danny starts the car and they speed away.

Chapter Twenty-Seven.

You would think, really, that it'd be the police officer who was on his feet and running towards the gunfire first. It should be, realistically. He's the one with some kind of training to be in these situations. But it was Kim who nearly knocked over the table as she leapt to her feet and charged towards the door before she even properly realised what was going on. There's fight or flight, and then there's Kim's instinct to run as fast as possible towards any sign of danger.
"Come on!" She shouted back to him. Wade tried to call for her to stop, or to slow down, and give him some kind of chance to assess the situation, but she was already out of the door and into the street before he could protest.
Another shot had already sounded by the time he'd pulled himself up and followed her. He fights his way through some of the other patrons who've gathered to try to get a view of what is going on but haven't quite been brave, or stupid, enough to leave the safety of the coffee shop. The sound of gunfire is very foreign to English people, and there are so many of them questioning whether it was that at all. Wade knows it, but he'd wager none of them have heard it in real life before. He barks for them to move, telling them he's a police officer, and they do, most looking grateful that there's some kind of law enforcement on hand so they don't have to feel bad about not doing anyway.
He tears the door open and there's another shot. The first one had stopped the crowd. It was the middle of the day, right in the middle of the town centre, and suddenly everyone was standing as if they were frozen. It was like they were a collective group of deer in headlights, just waiting to see what happened next and all looking at each other for confirmation that was actually what they thought it was. But the next shot was enough to unleash a panic that breaks through the stunned silence like the first one broke the glass window.
Wade catches up with Kim, who has paused in the middle of the stampede and is trying to take the scene in, just as the third shot rings out. He grabs her by the arm and drags her to a place where they're better covered.

Thankfully, she doesn't protest too much. It would appear she ran out into the street with no real plan to follow up.

"Why would you run towards the place that's being shot at?" He snaps at her as he fumbles for his phone.

"Where's it coming from? Can you tell?" She asks him as her eyes flick around trying to find the shooter.

"No. It's sniper fire, it could be anywhere. I need to call this in." He says, as he finally slides his phone out of his pocket and dials. He too keeps his head on a swivel and scans the scenes before him as if he'll be able to pick out the gunman. "Appleby, it's me." He says, the second the call is picked up.

"Alr…" The other man begins, but Wade ploughs on. There is no time to lose.

"Shots fired downtown. Vanity bar. Possible sniper. Get armed response here immediately." He orders. He sees customers from the shops across the street, the same side as the bar, starting to cautiously step out onto the street to see what's happening. He drops the call and grabs his badge, flashing it at them to get their attention. "Get back inside." He shouts over the general sounds of panic. "Take cover. I'm a police officer. Stay inside until I say it's safe." Thankfully they do, retreating back inside like turtles going into their shells. Another shot punches through the air, which helps to punctuate his point. Kim taps him on the arm for attention and nods towards a black car, which she is already recording on her phone, as it speeds away up the street. Just as it did a woman jumped out, one he recognises. He knew they were here. He was the one who'd made the arrangements for them, following Louis' call, to clear out Vanity Bar. It was no coincidence that he and Kim had met at a coffee shop only a few metres away. But it's not until he sees Lauren standing there on the side of the road that his brain properly puts it together. Of course this is something else they're at the centre of.

"Is that one of them?" Kim asks, gesturing towards Lauren as she crouches behind cover to avoid gunfire. Wade nods and Kim, without missing a beat, bolts towards her and dives for cover right next to her. Lauren's gaze swivels to inspect them and assess if she's a threat, but as she sees him following she goes back to staring intently at the bar that is still under fire. "My name's Kim Adams. I'm working with DCI Wade." Kim explains, holding out a hand. Lauren glances back at her as she speaks, but then goes back to peering at the bar. She's tense and poised, as if she's ready to run inside at any moment. In his experience with the team Lauren has always been one of the more pleasant members; and so it's jarring to see her make very little effort at greeting them. Something must be very wrong.

"What's going on?" He asks her.

"You shouldn't really be here, it's not the best time." She tells them, with a stern but polite tone. It's nice that she hasn't lost that.

"What's going on?" He repeats. There's something, whether it's her body language or her tone, but it tells him that she's very worried and she needs help. Wade dislikes the Counter Terrorism Team, on the whole. Danny, Chris, Amber are arseholes. He's undecided on Louis. But Lauren, she's the most tolerable one. She's never been anything but polite to him, despite the flack he can often throw her way just by being associated with the others, and so whatever this is that's got her so worried, he wants to help.

"We have people inside under fire." She says, after a considered pause. "Several have been hit. I need to get inside before…" She stops and shakes her head. She doesn't want to add 'before it's too late.'

"Let me make a call and get paramedics here."

"No!" She says, snapping her head towards him. "No. I can treat our people, I just need to get inside."

"Are you sure, I…" He begins, and she cuts him off.

"Yes." She says, simply and firmly. "I just need to get in there." She looks around nervously, peering out into a set of buildings in the distance, and as if she's expecting something to happen. That could well be where the shots are coming from, Wade thinks to himself.

"Who was in the car?" Kim asks her. Lauren looks at her with a wild expression on her face, and then over to him. He can see the worry in her eyes and it's only growing with each passing second. He desperately wants to do something to help.

"Danny and Louis. They've gone after the shooter." She explains. He opens his mouth, ready to offer them support too, but she shakes her head as if she knows what he's going to say. "You two shouldn't be here." She says again.

"Well we are, and it looks like you could use our help." Wade says. He's not backing down this time; and it doesn't really look like she has the will to fight him on it anyway. "Do you really value whatever you're covering up more than your people's lives? Just let us help. I'm first aid trained and I can…"

"It's not a case of valuing secrets. It's about safety. Everyone's safety. You shouldn't be here because you have no idea what you're involved in." She says, rounding on him and stopping him mid sentence. He obviously misjudged her will to fight and he's a little caught off guard by it, and makes him feel a little like he's being told off by a teacher. "I'm waiting for their signal. Once I get it, then we go. You can help inside. But nobody else." She says,

"I've got an armed response…" He begins, in protest.

"No. Absolutely not. I'm sorry, I know you don't understand it. I know you're frustrated. It's my friends that are in there so, frankly, it's my call. Your men turning up with guns will do nothing except attract us even more unwanted attention."

"You're getting shot at in the middle of town, how much more unwanted attention can you get?" He says, and the look on her face tells him there will be no more debate and he sighs and nods in agreement. Somehow this small, fiery woman terrifies him and it takes him a moment to connect the dots. She's usually the polite and friendly one of the group, the one he'd rather deal with if he absolutely had to deal with any one of them, but right now she's someone who's family is under threat. He pulls his phone back out, and ponders just how he can explain away an armed response team and she goes back to waiting patiently for her signal.

Chapter Twenty-Eight

The speed and the skill with which Danny drives are admirable and terrifying in equal measure; and within a few minutes they stop abruptly outside of the Abbeygate apartment block. It's a towering, grey building, just outside the city centre that looks like it's only a few years old. Louis and Danny bolt for the door, with their tranquilliser guns already out and ready. They have no idea what they're walking into, but they know they're expected, and so they need to be prepared. The entrance to the building requires an electronic key fob for entry and for a moment Louis thinks that will block them; but without missing a beat Danny pulls out his phone, opens an app and holds it close to the scanner. There's a buzz and the door unlocks, allowing them to race inside. They run past a puzzled looking resident collecting some post in the lobby and make a break for the stairs. They get to the second floor, and as they do they hear another gunshot ring out. Without saying anything they both quicken their already urgent pace. They hit the fourth floor and sprint through the hallway, counting down the door numbers as they go. There are several confused residents looking out into the corridor; either just peeking out from the safety of their apartment, or fully out in the corridor with their doors flung wide open as if they can be the ones to stop the roar of gunfire. They all stare at the young men racing past.

The two of them come to a halt outside of the door marked 434 and take a second to check in with each other. Danny mouths to Louis, silently asking if he's ready and Louis nods in response. He doesn't really feel ready, but they can't afford to wait until he does. Instead of waiting for any further collaboration Louis throws his weight at the door and he stumbles forward as it crashes open. He struggles to find his footing but before he can Danny throws himself forward and tackles him to the ground. Another shot thunders through the air and a bullet hits the wall in the corridor behind them. If it wasn't for Danny it would've gone straight through Louis' chest. They lay for a second in a crumpled heap on the floor; and Danny, who's body weight presses down on top of him, looks up and scans the apartment. Louis' brain takes a moment to catch up as he struggles to process the tumble, and the near death experience, as well as having Danny's body, which seems to be radiating heat, on top of him. They lay there for a moment before Danny squirms and scrambles back to his feet and Louis follows him. There is no sign of 4XM in the apartment, which is lucky because they'd have been very vulnerable to attack. Instead the shot had been fired because the door had been booby trapped. There's a string leading from it to the rifle by the window, which had been repositioned to face the door. Danny moves to examine it while Louis takes in the rest of their surroundings.

It's a small one-bedroom apartment. Louis feels a wave of pain coming from the back corner, and it feels so red. It doesn't take him long to work out why. The former occupant lays dead and slumped on the floor with his head twisted around at an unnatural angle. He hears whispers of the violence that took place. It was quick and it was impersonal, and it feels that. It was jarring and hasty, because this man was just in the way of a bigger goal. Louis stares at the body, distracted by the frantic energy that surrounds him. He's caught up in what 4XM was feeling again. Frantic yet focussed; angry yet excited, red with tinges of gold.

"Another one." Louis says at last, because this is another person who's lost their life because they've been unable to stop 4XM. There was Steven, who then killed Matilda Pearson and Cheryl, and Ben, and now this man who's name they didn't even know. Five people. That was five too many. Danny looks over, spotting the body for the first time and realises what he means.
"He can't be far. We only just heard another shot!" He says, looking out of the window again as if he'll suddenly see their target. "Lauren, you're clear. Go" He snaps into his earpiece.
"I can't believe we lost him, again." Louis says. It seemed like they were so close to ending it, to making sure he couldn't add any more names to the list, but here they are again with nothing to show for it. He's so annoyed.
"He can't have left the way we came in." Danny says, pointing to the rifle that's hooked up to the door. He's right. He'd have had to leave a different way to set that trap. That must mean the window, then. But then he could be anywhere; has he just climbed to another apartment? Or has he left this building completely? There's a ping. It's another message on Meetr. This time it's a voice note. Louis jabs at his phone to play it.
"Did I get you?" The voice asks, and it's taunting him. "I really hope I got at least one of you. That would be fun. Was it you or your little friend? Whichever one it was, then I bet that rifle tore right through him. Oh I hope it got messy and I wish I could've seen it. I wonder how many of your friends in that bar are dead? Stop trying to catch me. I'm so much smarter than you." The voice-note cuts out. Danny snatches the phone, desperate to find some kind of clue. The profile disappears as the account blocks them. Danny throws the phone across the room in frustration, and Louis doesn't bother to go after it. They've got all they're going to from the app.
"I can't let him outsmart us again." He practically growls. This is the most genuinely frustrated Louis has seen him and he remembers just how much Danny hates losing. "He thinks he's cleverer than us, but we just need to work out where he went."
He stares out of the window and then his head snaps back to Louis as he has a sudden idea. "What about your stupid visions? Are you seeing anything?"
"No. No, I just feel a bit sick." Louis says lethargically. "I can't really picture anything. I just…" He retches a little bit. The feeling of red is beginning to get overwhelming, and there's a serious risk he's going to vomit again.
"Try harder." Danny tells him, bluntly.

"That's not how it works." He replies, meekly.
"Oh, well that's convenient." Danny says with an eye roll.
"What?"
"I just mean you can never seem to do it when it might actually be helpful."
"Danny, I can't…"
"Control it? Oh, I know. Need someone to pass out and let the target escape. Louis' your man. Need to stop that same target from escaping and killing anyone else, and suddenly, nah not interested, going to choose not to bother and feel all the self pity later." He says and the sick feeling starts to dissipate, replaced by just feeling really fucking angry.
"Not interested?" He says, straightening himself to his full height.
"Yeah, clearly your hero complex will only carry us so far." He retorts; and it's so flippant that it makes it cut even deeper. I knew the moment I met him that I'd end up hitting Danny in the face one day. Right from the beginning he was obnoxious, insulting, and incredibly self-centred. In some ways he was the worst person I'd ever met. This was very nearly the day.
"What the fuck is wrong with you?" Louis shouts, stepping towards him, and Danny answers with a tilt of his head and a cocky smile. "Are you genuinely that ignorant to how other people feel or do you just not care? If I could use it then I would. God, I thought I was actually getting somewhere with you but you're always just going to treat me like…" He stops because of the red, because of the anger and the energy. Danny steps aside suddenly, giving Louis a clear view out of the window and there's a spike of clarity all of a sudden. There's a flash of 4XM staring out of the same window and it falls into place. It's not just his own anger he's feeling. He's tapped into the flow of red and he's ridden it. "Oh." He finishes.
"Always going to treat you like oh?" Danny asks, that stupid smile still on his face.
"No, I…" He points out of the window, just waiting for the flashes to settle as he pieces together the path their target took. "Just over there, behind that building is. That's where the Eagle hotel is."
"Yeah, I think so."
"That's where he's gone. It's still closed, too, so it'll be so easy for him." Louis explains and Danny's infuriating smile widens even further. He looks pleased with himself.
"Knew you could do it." He says, triumphantly. "You just needed the right motivation. More self-pitying and blaming yourself wasn't going to do it. Anger was much more useful. You're welcome."

"You mean, you…"
"Do you want to tell me again how I don't get people? Or, shall we just go?" He says, and the fucking arsehole winks as he does. He'd goaded him, successfully, into revealing the way and now he had the nerve to wink at him. All Louis can do is shake his head because he's lost for words.
"You're welcome." Danny tells him again, casually, as he leads the way out of the door.

"Go," Lauren repeats to the other two the second she is given Danny's cue, and then she is gone, hurtling across the street and throwing herself through the door to Vanity Bar. Kim and Wade follow, but can't match her speed.
"Amber!?" She roars when she's inside.
"Here!" The red headed woman calls, peeking her head out from behind cover. Lauren makes a beeline for her and once she clears her way through finds Amber and Olivia crouched over Chris. He is bleeding heavily from a bullet wound in his chest. Amber has been trying her best to tend to the wound, and she's now coated in his blood too. Wade raises his head to look over at it. He's not a medic by any stretch of the imagination, but he wouldn't give him great odds at surviving right now. He looks across to Kim who is taking in the scene but also, incredibly, appears to still be filming on her phone.
"Kim," He tries to say, quietly and through gritted teeth. Unfortunately, he doesn't quite manage it quietly enough and it attracts Amber's attention as Lauren shoos her back from Chris so that she can have full access to his wound. She spots the phone, realises immediately what's going on, and explodes.
"What the fuck?" She roars, clambering to her feet.
"We're just…" Wade begins, stepping in front of Kim. Amber looks crazed; dishevelled, furious, blood-soaked, and like she's dying for an excuse to tear someone's head off.
"I don't care what you're doing, back the hell up before I…"
"Shh. I need to focus." Lauren says, laying her hands over Chris' wound and directing Olivia to shuffle to the side. This means that what she's doing is no longer visible to Wade, Kim, or perhaps most importantly, the camera. He can't help but feel that was a deliberate effort to obscure whatever it is she's doing. Amber doesn't move, but her fists are curled into bloody balls as if she's ready to strike any moment.

"Humans, there's someone else over there who took a bullet to the shoulder. You wanna help? Go over there" She growls.
"Sure, c'mon Kim." Wade says, as he herds Kim over in the direction Amber gestured. He subtly puts his hand over the phone and lowers it.

Amber glares after the two humans; still furious that the reporter woman was recording and torn over whether she should follow them and smash the stupid thing. By 'thing' she means the reporter.
"It doesn't look like anything major has been hit. He's lost a lot of blood, but I can fix this. Chris, can you hear me?" Lauren asks, and Amber looks over Olivia's shoulder to see him weakly nod and she's able to breathe a sigh of relief. Her adrenaline is racing, and her heart is thumping blood around her body ridiculously quickly. It felt like hours since Chris went down and all she could focus on was keeping him alive. Now, she wants to focus on what she does next with all this excess energy and anger. Ironically, her and Kim have a lot in common because Amber's fight or flight response never even treats flight as an option; and in that moment she badly wanted to be able to fight something. She can see Lauren breathing in a steady and controlled way as she focuses on healing Chris' wound, she braces for the coming pain as she lets energy flow between the two of them. Amber has seen her do this kind of thing a few times before, and she knows that there's nothing that she can do to help now. So, that frees her up to find that thing to fight.
"Where are Danny and Louis?" She asks Lauren, even though breaking her concentration is a risk.
"Amber…please…" She says, straining through gritted teeth.
"They went after the shooter." Wade interjects, midway through bandaging the Custodian from Olivia's team while the reporter watches. He'll be fine. Whoever it was with the rifle, she suspects 4XM, was a crappy shot. She kicks an overturned chair hard and it sails across the room. Everyone stares at her but she doesn't care. This fucking Used-to-Be opened fire on them with a sniper rifle and didn't even have the skill to do it properly. She wanted to find that rifle and wrap it around his head. But now Danny and the Newbie had gone chasing after him by themselves. She takes a quick look around the floor, scanning through the commotion for her earpiece that she lost in the blind panic of taking cover. Once she spots it she scoops it up off the floor and fixes it back in place.

"Danny! What's your situation?" She asks, hopeful that the connection is still open on the other end. After a brief, heart stopping moment, he responds.
"He's gone...but we think we know where." He says.
"Where?" She demands.
"Eagle Hotel. We're on our way there." He tells her, and there's relief, she's not too late to join them.
"Pick me up."
"No, it'll take longer to come back and get you. We need to move if we've got any chance." He explains, and she knows he's right. She cries out in frustration and tosses her earpiece across the room in the same direction the chair went. Lauren half-collapses, fatigued from healing Chris. Amber is straight back down to the floor to help her, practically shoving Olivia out of the way.
"Are you...?" She asks, snapping straight back into being worried.
"I'm okay. He will be too." Lauren tells her. Chris has passed out, but the wound in his chest is closed now.
"They're back at the Eagle Hotel. I'm going. Have you got this?" She asks both Lauren and Olivia. They both nod, and without saying anything else she makes her decision. She leaps to her feet, throws one last glare at the humans, and starts a desperate sprint out of the door.

Chapter Twenty-Nine.

1996, in Pat's Bar.
It's later on that same day; an hour or two later. It's the middle of the day and Joseph hasn't been rushed off his feet. There's a handful of older men day-drinking and Pat has long since abandoned his quest to do the accounts, or learn to read, or whatever it was he was trying to do. Joseph is still alone, leaning against the bar, and daydreaming. So he's very grateful when Dionne strolls in through the front door. His face lights up with a grin at the sight of her. Her entrance to the building couldn't be any more different to his. While he ran in, frantic and dishevelled, she strolls, relaxed and poised. Where his hair was still a wet mess, hers is blow dried and styled to perfection. They're opposites in nearly every way; he's meek and frighteningly pale, and she's beautifully dark and bold. He came in apologetically; and she walked in like she owned the damn place.

"'Sup?" She asks him as she makes her way behind the bar and hangs her coat up.
"Where the hell have you been?" He asks her.
"What?" She says, looking around. "It's dead."
"Yeah, and I've been so bored." He whines.
"Uh-huh. Well take a chill pill, I'm here now." She says, and pulls him into a huge hug.
"Thank God." He tells her. "It's just been pretty much Billy and Greg or whatever you call 'em so far." He says, as he gestures at the two older men in the corner. Dionne catches their eye and waves. They don't respond.
"Fred and Gerry." She corrects.
"Miserable bastards," He recorrects.
"Well, enjoy the quiet now. It'll be all football hooligans and stag parties this afternoon." She tells him.
"Why is it never anyone with any class?" He asks, and she lets out a deep laugh at that which makes Fred and Gerry look over.
"Because look at this place. Old man Pat hasn't redecorated since the 70s. But, that's why we here. Class it up. And since there's no one else around we can catch-up. I've been dying to know, what's the 411 on that guy you been…." She starts but he scrunches up his face and shakes his head, and that's all the answer she needs. "Oh. So it's like that."
"Yeah. It's like that. Plus, this…definitely isn't the place for it. Fat Pat was already all like "I took a risk hiring someone like you" I don't wanna give him any more reason to fire me by getting my gayness all over the bar or something."
"As if!" She says, outraged, before stopping and narrowing her eyes at him. "Wait, were you late again?"
"By like a minute!" He protests.
"Yeah but he wigs out whenever anyone is late." She says, giving him a light slap on the arm. "You know that. He never comes at me with that shit 'cause I'm always early; and because if he came at me with that "someone like you" I'd smack him straight in the mouth."
"It's not like I did it on purpose!" Joseph tells her.
"Yeah but you're so unorganised. It's gonna keep happening unless you get yourself organised." She tells him; and she's not being cruel, or chastising him. She's trying to help, because she obviously doesn't want to see her friend fired.

"I've heard that before…" He mumbles.

"Yeah, from me. Over and over…and over."

"Okay!" He says, holding his hands up in defence. "Okay. I get it. Less about me, what's with you? How's Russell?" He asks, badly wanting to change the subject before being told off any more for being late. She nods over his shoulder.

"Customer first. Then I'll tell you why I'm mad at him." She tells him, and he turns to see a woman perched at the bar. He's taken aback because he was too caught up in his discussion with Dionne that he didn't even hear her come in. She's a brunette with pale skin and dark eyes. Not pale in the same ghastly way his is, but more like porcelain. A precious and flawless kind of pale. She looks like the kind of woman who would've stood out even if the bar was crowded; she's poised and graceful, cool and glamorous, and clearly very much in the wrong place. He bounds over to her like an excitable child at the sight of someone so out of the ordinary.

"What can I get for you?" He asks, and she surveys him with her cold gaze. She looks through him, assessing the choice of drinks, and she somehow looks disgusted without really moving her face.

"I'm not sure you can get me anything." She says. Her accent matches her exactly; it's perfectly put together and paced, with impeccable pronunciation. It's not her natural accent, but rather a speech pattern that's been formed over time, like she's stepped straight out of an old movie where everyone had to speak properly. He's completely awestruck by her.

"Are you capable of making a cocktail? A martini, perhaps?" She asks.

"Yeah!" He practically squeals. "Gin or vodka?" She vaguely raises a perfectly shaped eyebrow at the question. "Gin! Got it." He says, words tumbling out of his mouth in excitement. "I'll just see if we have the right glasses!...and that they're clean…" He scurries off to begin his hunt and she rolls her eyes and pulls out a cigarette.

"Need a light, beautiful?" Says another new patron, a wide man in a business suit, as he sidles up to her. He looks greasy, with his hair slicked back. He orders a drink from Dionne as the woman ignores him and lights her own cigarette. "How're y…"

"The man stops talking." She says, not even looking at him, and he does. She takes a deep Inhale from the cigarette and then finally turns her gaze onto him and quite clearly assesses him. He stands there, leaning on the bar with a smarmy smirk on his face but a far away look in his eyes. He doesn't attempt to talk again. "Do you have a…" She begins to ask, and

shows a little frustration as she can't quite think of the word. "One of those…it's small and it beeps…" She clicks as it comes back to her. "A pager." She looks at him, expecting an answer that he doesn't provide because he doesn't really think to. "You may answer." She tells him.
"Yeah darling, I d…"
"That's enough." She says, and nods. There's a sudden beeping sound from his pocket. He looks down, takes out his pager and mutters something to himself before rushing out of the bar. "Having received an urgent communication from his wife the man is filled with an overwhelming sense of guilt. He leaves at once, and returns   home, vowing to give up his terrible habit of frequenting bars and bothering women who have absolutely no interest in him." She narrates, to no one in particular, as Dionne calls after him holding the drink she'd just made. She slams it down on the bar and the woman lets out a tiny smirk before taking another drag of the cigarette. "That last part will never stick, but you gotta try." She says to herself, just as Joseph comes out proudly carrying a martini.
"Here you go!" He tells her, placing it down in front of her like some kind of prize. She glances at it and then takes a tentative sip. Her flawless face doesn't betray a lot of emotion; but she doesn't look unimpressed.
"Well done." She says simply, placing her credit card on the bar.
"First one's on the house." He says, glowing with pride at the compliment. "I never get the chance to make cocktails, plus I hate my boss so…" Her mouth curves into the tiniest of smiles and she tilts her head, properly considering him.
"Then you may as well get started on the next." She tells him, not picking her credit card back.
"Coming right up!"

Chapter Thirty.

The almost-present
Danny and Louis make it to the hotel in what has to be some kind of record. As the car lurches to a halt outside Louis can briefly relax; because for several moments during the very short trip he was worried they were going to crash. Though, he can only relax until the reality of what comes next sets in. He looks across to Danny and they share a moment of hesitation. This is stupid. Going after a target that is clearly dangerous by themselves is not a good idea. They've been swept up in the adrenaline of

the chase, and the stress-inducing car journey, and now it's like they both realise at the same time that it isn't the smartest idea.
"Ready?" Danny asks him, ignoring that feeling.
"No." He replies, honestly. "But, I know we can't wait." He says, knowing Danny was about to say something similar.
"To be fair, we don't even know he's definitely in there. You're probably wrong, he's probably long gone." Danny says with a shrug, in a very transparent attempt to comfort him. That makes him smile.
"You're probably right." He agrees. "That's if he was even here to begin with."
"True. Let's just get going, and then, when he's not there, I'll just endlessly make fun of you for it." He says. There's a tiny, almost imperceptible, moment where he readies himself and then opens the car door and steps out. Louis takes a much more noticeable pause and follows him. They lock eyes again and silently try to give each other some reassurance; before moving forward.

The eery, abandoned reception area of the hotel isn't hard to access. There are no signs they're not the first ones to do so, but that more than likely just means he entered another way. They move through the entrance silently and in complete darkness. The only light at all is that which is coming through semi-boarded up windows. The darkness, coupled with the fact that nothing has been moved or really cleaned up since the day of the wedding, creates an almost ghostly atmosphere and just adds to how on edge Louis feels. They really need to get this over with, he thinks to himself.
They move silently through the corridors and into the room where the wedding reception was held. This is somehow even more unnerving because, unlike the other areas of the hotel so far, this is now spotless. There are absolutely no signs of the struggle; and even the hole they blew in the wall has been repaired. This really throws him, because it seems so strange that this part of the day would be completely erased and yet the rest just left in exactly the state it was left. He focuses on the task at hand, and it doesn't take them long to be sure this room is empty. They move across the hallway to the kitchen, where their fight had spilled next. They have to use torches for this because there is no natural light from outside; and when they do light up the dark room they see that this too has been cleaned flawlessly. Even when they'd entered it during the fight it had been

a mess; with half prepared meals abandoned in a panic. But now it looks like it's ready for a brand new day. Again, it's an odd contrast to the rest of the hotel that was abandoned in the middle of the day and not returned to. As they enter Louis looks straight down at the spot where Rachel's body was discovered, fixating on it slightly. He sees flashes of what happened to her. He sees flashes of discovering the body and it starts to overwhelm him. His head is spinning as that same thing he felt at the time washes over him, the rage and the taste of death, and he stumbles. Danny grips his shoulder to steady him and squeezes.
"Get it together." He hisses. "I need you, Louis." He says, a little gentler. Louis shakes his head to try to clear it and tries to stay in the present, not leaning into that sense that's just hovering at the edge of his consciousness.
"Yeah. I'm okay. Sorry." He says to Danny, who nods to acknowledge it and continue his search. Louis takes one last look down at the floor where Rachel had been. "I'm sorry." He says again, and this time it's not to Danny. There is a huge crash from below them; a rattling boom that sounds like it's come from the basement and makes them both jump. They look at each other, with wide eyes silently communicating, and bolt towards the stairs.

The dust has settled, as it were, in Vanity Bar and Wade and Kim are standing a little further back from the others, silently taking a moment to take it all in. One of the first things Wade had picked up on in the chaos was that there were more of them than he'd realised. They had called in reinforcements for this seemingly failed operation. This whole thing was getting bigger. Lauren was now tending to the shoulder wound of the guy named Phil, meanwhile the still unconscious Chris was being watched over by newcomers Olivia and Noel. It makes sense that it's even bigger than they thought. He always knew it was more than just the five he dealt with, that it had to be. He knew it went up further than his boss, and so it couldn't just be the five of them. But how big was this? And more importantly, what was it? There were still frustratingly more answers appearing by the day.
"What is going on?" Kim whispers to him.
"I wish I knew." He told her, and that was underselling it. He was starting to be desperate to find out.

"Did they get the shooter? Where did the angry one run off to?" She says, just as eager to find out. He shakes his head, not really having any extra answers for her, and thinking this probably isn't the best time for them to have a full debrief. "C'mon Matthew, you must've heard something?" She says, pushing him "We can't walk out of this with nothing." It wasn't quite nothing, he thinks. They helped out and maybe, just maybe, built a little trust with Lauren.

"Kimmy, let's just…wait." He tells her. "I heard them say the Eagle Hotel, but…" He stops as Lauren finishes tending to Phil and makes her way over to them. It's odd; maybe it's just that he's sitting over the other side of the bar to them, but Wade could've sworn his bullet wound was now completely gone. "How's he doing?" He asks her.

"Oh, absolutely fine. It's healing up nicely. Thank you for all your help." She says, back to her more usual friendly, less fraught, demeanour.

"And what about him…" Kim says, with a somewhat suspicious nod to Chris. He too seems to be healing very well. Much better than he had any right to after a straight bullet wound to the chest with no real medical intervention.

"Yes, don't worry, he'll be alright too. No permanent damage done." She says. "He got very lucky." She adds, catching Wade's eyes narrowing suspiciously. He knows he shouldn't. He knows it'd be best to not rock the boat and just take the good will that's come from what little help they offered today in the hope that it might eventually build enough trust for them to be honest. But he really can't help himself, and if he didn't ask, then Kim probably would.

"Healing up nicely? He was shot in the bloody chest, he should be in a hospital. What's going on here?"

"Oh, things got a little out of hand, but it's quite alright, thankfully. Now, if I can ask, what are you doing here?" She asks, that stern, almost school teacher tone that she had earlier making a reappearance.

"Well, we were in the area." He says, bluntly.

"Yes. In the area of the bar that I believe Louis specifically asked for your help to clear out?" She says, raising her eyebrow and giving him a knowing smile.

"Yeah, I guess I might as well be honest. I was curious what you were up to. Thought maybe I should come check it out for myself, and frankly, I'm glad I did. It's not often we get sniper fire in the middle of Endsbrough High

Street." He grumbles back, not really appreciating the feeling that he's being told off.

"Have your people caught him?" Kim chimes in, making Wade glad he wasn't the only bull in this particular china shop.

"We've got the situation under control." Lauren tells them, calmly.

"Don't look like it." He mutters, not being able to hold it in.

"Sorry to interrupt," Olivia says, joining them. "The Cleaners are here, and Chris is starting to come round so you should probably…" She tells Lauren, gesturing towards them but not really acknowledging them.

"Yes, thank you." She responds, with a nod. "It's time the two of you left. Thank you for all your help."

"Cleaners?" Kim asks, ignoring her.

"I've heard of them before." Wade says, remembering something from a few days ago "Your scene of crime officers, right?"

"If you like. But it really is time the two of you left." Lauren repeats. He opens his mouth to protest and she holds up hand to cut him off. "I insist." She tells them, and glances back over her shoulder as three, tall, thin, pale figures enter. They're all gaunt, pale, bald, and just plain weird looking. They're not identical but they look eerily similar to one another, they all look like they don't get out much, and they're all wearing the same grey uniform. They take direction from Olivia as Lauren ushers Kim and Wade to the back door before they can really get a good look at the Cleaners, or they at them. "Thank you again, but you must leave." She says, to really hammer the point home, as she practically forces them out of the door and into the alleyway that leads back to the street at the front before they can protest or question it at all. Before the door closes behind them Wade notices Olivia looking over at them and Lauren with a slight look of disapproval before they're quite literally shut out of whatever is going on once more.

They rush down the stairs and frantically try to locate the location of the sound. They're looking for whatever is directly below the kitchen. They rush past a conference room, knowing that's not it, and further into the basement level floor. The gym is the closest room to the location they need, not quite directly underneath the kitchen but almost. Looking through the small window in the door it looks like it's in total darkness too, and so they can't see anything that's waiting for them inside or identify the source of the crash.

Danny gives Louis a quick glance to check on him, and then nods. He prepares himself and concentrates. There's a panel for a keycard by the door and he grabs hold of it tightly. Danny concentrates and Louis watches as he lets his power flow through it and seep into the mechanics behind it. He's communicating with it, and it's fascinating to watch. He's seen this regularly with computers and other things and, much like the apartment entrance earlier, he can often use other devices to help make the process quicker, but it's spectacular to think that with enough focus he can just convince an electronic lock to open. That's exactly what happens, and it beeps to signify it's given them access.

Danny tries the door but it's blocked by something. Louis helps, and between them they're able to force a large enough gap for them to get through. They look around, using the light of their torches. The small room is well equipped with gym equipment. One of the machines had been pushed over to barricade the door, and as there doesn't appear to be another way in, then the person responsible must still be in the room. Their tranquilliser guns are poised and ready, and they're on edge for the slightest hint of 4XM. They're completely thrown, then, when they spot the shape of a woman quietly sobbing in the corner.

"Hello?" Louis calls out, as they approach. "Are you alright?" The weeping only intensifies and as they get closer they begin to make out more details. She's wearing a dirty, formerly pristine white shirt with a logo and a name badge. The uniform of the hotel. She looks up and Louis recognises her. It's Lisa, the woman who was taken hostage alongside their team by 4XM. He stops dead and shoots Danny a sideways glance to see if he recognises her too. He doesn't get time to work it out though. She opens her mouth and she screams. It's not a normal scream though; it's a loud and ear-piercing shriek, but it's more than that. It's powered by demonic energy. It's a shockwave. It tears forward and propels the two of them backwards and into the wall. Louis tries to shake it off and looks up. 4XM has entered the room behind them, and is pointing a handgun at them with a smug smile on his face.

"Will you kids keep it down?" He asks, with a cackle.

Chapter Thirty-One.

Back in 1996
"Who is she?" Dionne asks, with a look of admiration at the women at the bar, as Joseph makes the third martini.
"I don't know but she's fascinating! Look at her." he whispers.
"You sure you're gay? You're way too fascinated by a glamorous woman."
"Have you met a gay man before? We love glamorous women! Besides, when was the last time we even saw a glamorous woman around here?"
"Erm…Hello?!" She says, gesturing to herself.
"Other than you,"
"I didn't quite buy that save but I'll take it." She says, preening a little. Another customer comes in and she goes to take his order while Joseph returns to the glamorous woman, drink in hand.
"Thank you." She says simply, still working her way through the second drink. He turns and is about to walk away when he stops and turns back to her. He summons up a little courage because just her presence is making him a little nervous. Everything about her oozes a kind of intimidating and unattainable quality. It's a bit like there's a Goddess sitting at the bar.
"What're you in the…you don't sound like you're from here?" He asks.
"Is being local a prerequisite to drinking here?" She retorts, taking an impatient sip from her glass.
"No! No," He says in a flustered panic. "I don't mean it like that. I'm just curious. You don't seem…like our usual crowd. Better, I mean." He explains, and she remains stoic. "Are you…you've got an air like you're an actress or something." Her stoicism breaks and she flashes a devilish grin.
"Not any more. But you're right, I am big. It's the pictures that got small." She says, adding an element of grandeur, as if she's delivering that line to the whole room. She laughs to herself, but he looks confused.
"What?" He asks, and she rolls her eyes..
"I used to be, but I got too old."
"Too old? What? You really don't look it." He says, and she laughs again, locking her gaze on him.
"You're a terrible flirt." She says, and waggles her eyebrows slightly.
"What?" He says, panicking. "No, I wasn't! I'm…" He begins, but she smiles again and shakes her head.
"I know, darling. I can tell. You don't fit in here either." She says.

230

"That's one way to put it." He says, and looks down, sadly, because there's a lot more to that story. She understands that. She can relate to that. She reaches across the bar to place one hand on his in a brief display of kinship before pulling it back and pulling another cigarette out. She offers him one but he shakes his head. He doesn't smoke. She shrugs, puts the packet away, and looks around the bar.
"This place used to be a lot nicer, you know." She explains to him.
"You've been here before?"
"Long before you worked here."
"Yeah, I've only had this job a couple of months." He says, nodding. She smiles again, in a way that says he completely missed her meaning,
"Well, you're a natural. This martini is berries to me."
"Berries?" He asks, confused.
"Ha, forget it. I forgot where I was for a second." She says. She laughs, but this time there is a tinge of sadness in it, and of longing.
"So, where are you from?" He asks, and she shakes her head and looks away from him.
"Not from around here. I'll let you know when I need another." She says, and it's very clear that is meant to dismiss him. He looks taken aback but then, as instructed, walks away, worried he's said something to upset her.

Sorry, this jumping around is irritating, Let's get back to the Eagle Hotel:

…where the modern day Joseph looks incredibly pleased with himself as he points the gun between Louis and Danny.
"Well, thanks for coming, Jacob," He says, referencing the identity he'd used on Meetr. It really should've been the least of his concerns at that moment but Louis was a little annoyed he'd worked it out, especially because he couldn't work out what had given him away. He thought he'd done a great job of playing Jacob. How did he know? "Sorry about the last minute change. I just didn't feel like going to a bar tonight. Thought we could go straight to getting a hotel together." He says, continuing the act. Louis and Danny get slowly, cautiously, to their feet and he allows it. His eyes dart between the two of them. "I didn't realise you were bringing a third though…or is this a jealous boyfriend?" He says, gesturing the weapon at Danny.

"Straight to a hotel seems a little full on though." Louis interjects, not sure if playing along will have any benefit but instinctively wanting to direct the Used-to-Bes attention back to him. "Maybe we should slow things down?"
"Oh you're fun!" Joseph says, as Danny glares over at him, quite obviously vexed about him engaging in seemingly casual conversation with their target. It's really baffling how someone so intelligent can be so ignorant at times. It's then that Lisa moves forward, standing next to Joseph, and Louis gets a proper look at her. She looks awful; she's coated in blood, and dust, and she looks ill, like she's spent the last few days going through hell. She probably has. "Second date though!" Joseph coos, with false excitement. "Must be doing something right; you just can't leave me alone."
"Well, we keep finding your victims. It makes it hard to leave you alone." Louis retorts. He's not sure what he's trying to achieve, beyond the simple fact that if he's talking he's not shooting, and that will at least buy them a little time.
"Ah, I thought poor little Benjamin might attract your attention. Don't worry, it was completely justified, morally, I mean."
"Justified?" Louis splutters, because of all the things he expected to hear that wasn't one of them. How could killing an innocent young man be justified?
"Absolutely. There's a whole rotten family tree situation. It'd take too long to explain." Joseph says.
"What did those three families do to you?" Louis asks; and it's pointed. It's meant to be pointed. It works, too. The gun lowers a little.
"You are clever, aren't you?" Joseph says, with a smile that shows every single one of his teeth.
"Why them?" Louis asks, hoping that he's right and continuing to dig is their way out of this. To his left Danny narrows his eyes in a scowl, still confused about what he's doing.
"Now that…is a complicated question. I spent a long time asking myself that. Why me? Why them? Why any of this? After a while I just stopped. The answers don't matter. Anyway, enough about that. I thought since you brought a friend I would too. Double date! You remember Lisa?" He walks over to her and rests his arm casually on her shoulder. She doesn't really react, just continues to blankly stare at the two of them. There's something in her deep dark eyes that's broken. He broke her. "Weirdly, she doesn't remember you. She didn't remember me, either." He stares at her, with a mock expression of sadness."You see," He continues to explain to them.

"She had no idea what happened at the party. No idea she was even here. Her memory of that night was completely gone. How do you suppose that happened?" He says, as he throws an accusatory glare their way. They know the answer. The Cleaners. They'll have wiped part of Lisa's memory so that she couldn't remember the horrors she'd seen that day; and so that she didn't remember that monsters were very real, and that she'd met one. "That's you people all over isn't it. Make her forget like it fixes anything. Erasure. That's the idea isn't it? Erase everything you don't like. But I helped her. It took days. Days and days of little painful reminders. Days of screaming and whining. But we got there…and the best part is she knows exactly who's to blame. Isn't that right Lisa?" He says, and together they both stare over at Louis and Danny as she nods with an expression that's stuck somewhere between timid and sinister. "I'm hoping she'll talk a bit more as she gets older. But for now, thanks to me all she can do is scream…" He explains, and on cue she takes a deep breath and lets out another scream. Danny is ready; he throws himself into Louis and the two of them crash out of the way. The shockwave she creates damages the wall behind them, causing it to tremble and crack, weakening it. They land in front of a row of treadmills, obscuring Joseph's view just enough so that he can't fire at them. Desperate to be able to shoot at them he jumps up onto one of the treadmills to get a better shot. Danny, in sheer blind panic, thinks fast and uses his power to start all of the treadmills. Joseph loses his footing just before he can fire. Danny leaps back to his feet, smacks Joseph's head into the machine, and wrestles the gun away from him. He throws it across the room, as far away as he can. Joseph curses but recovers and throws himself at Danny, slamming him into the already damaged wall. Lisa meanwhile charges forward, clawing and scratching at Louis in a bizarre frenzy. "Stop!" He says, trying to appeal to whatever is left of the poor, sweet, human receptionist. It's no use though. She doesn't exist any more. As she claws at him he feels the demonic energy seeping out of her and knows she can't be reasoned with. She's angry and terrified, and he can feel it. He sees flashes of the torture she's endured at the hands of Joseph. He hears her screaming in the darkness. It overwhelms him a little bit, but he tries to fight her off, kicking her in the stomach and shoving her backwards to try to give himself some space.

Danny is fighting with Joseph. The Used-to-Be has him pinned to the wall and he's trying to strangle him. Danny scrambles desperately to fight him off but Joseph is too strong and manages to wrap his hands around his neck.

Louis rushes to try to help him but Lisa hits him with another screech that throws him through the air and tumbling into a rack full of weights, which crash down on top of him. She advances forward quickly. She picks up a barbell effortlessly and uses it to push down on his throat before he can recover and get back to his feet.

Danny, seeing this, intensifies his fight back against Joseph. In desperation he jabs him in the eye with a finger, then punches him in the side of the head. It's enough to get him to release his grip and Danny gasps for air. But then Joseph is right back at him, smacking him in the side of the head. Meanwhile, Louis desperately struggles to breathe as Lisa pushes down on his throat, he sees more flashes of the torture she endured, locked in a dark room in the basement of a hotel. It overwhelms him. Her screams echo in his head as he slips closer and closer to unconsciousness. Overwhelmed, he lets a frustrated shout. A shout that, like her scream, becomes a physical thing. It smacks her in the face. There's very little force behind it, because he didn't even intend to do it, but it's enough to make her stumble backwards and give him a brief reprieve before she's back on him. Danny and Louis desperately lock eyes; with one being strangled by sheer force and the other having his windpipe crushed by a weighted metal pole. Neither can get out, no matter how much they flail, and they don't have long left. Maybe this was an even worse idea than they thought. They reach desperately out for the other; each wanting to help their teammate before it's too late.

There's an almighty crash as the door, which had locked behind Joseph, is smashed open by the brute force of Amber's arrival. She pauses for a split second to assess the situation, and then darts for Louis and Lisa. She grabs the Used-to-Be by the shoulders and throws her at Joseph. He panics and reacts just in time; ducking out of the way and releasing the pressure on Danny's throat. He swears loudly as Lisa collides with, and goes through, the wall. The mixture of the earlier damage and the strength that Amber put behind the toss clearly had unexpectedly dramatic results. The look of rage on her face is replaced by a proud grin at having thrown someone through a wall into the next room. Joseph, realising he's outnumbered again, runs towards the door and disappears into the hallway. Danny, without a second thought, charges after him. Amber grabs Louis' hand and pulls him back to his feet.

"What are you waiting for? Go on!" She says, gesturing for him to go after them. He glances over at the crumbling hole in the wall.
"What about…?" He says, meaning Lisa, who will no doubt recover from that.
"Obviously I've got it." She says, craning her neck to see where Lisa, who is staggering back to her feet, landed. "Wait, she is on his side right?" She checks.
"Yes."
"Good. Go!" She demands. He hesitates for a moment; but adding it up he's way more worried about Danny and Joseph than he is about Amber. He follows the other two out of the room, pausing only to scoop up Joseph's discarded weapon.
Amber advances on Lisa, climbing through the rubble. It turns out the room that she broke them into was the abandoned hotel swimming pool. Lisa has pulled herself back to her full height, but her arm now sticks out at an odd angle, as if it's broken. She screams again and Amber is knocked off her feet, yelling "fuck," as she falls. Lisa draws in a bigger breath as she advances on her, knowing that the closer she is the more damage it'll do. Amber responds by tossing a piece of rubble at her, which knocks her on the head just as she's about to unleash. It doesn't buy her long; but it buys her enough time to charge at the Used-to-Be and tackle her into the swimming pool.

The Bronze Duck, that was a few minutes walk away from Vanity Bar, was much more Wade's cup of tea. It's funny, isn't it, the relationship between a person and a bar. Vanity Bar was a gay bar, which now that Kim thought about it might've been important. But it was also definitely not the place for straight, long-since married Matthew Wade. She knew he wasn't homophobic, which needs to be said when he's a straight, white, policeman of a certain age. It's just that the kind of place where you could guarantee the musical stylings for Kylie Minogue and a drag queen after a certain hour didn't really gel with who Wade was. Likewise, she much preferred the quiet cocktail bar around the corner with limited seating and charcuterie platter options. The Bronze Duck was neither of those things. It was a grotty old man pub, that served drinks out of a dirty pint glass or wine from a tap, a choice of burgers, and was always busy on match days. It was no surprise when Wade had steered them towards it, but she didn't protest, it was close and she desperately wanted to analyse everything they'd just seen.

"Alright Eddie? I'll take a pint, and…?" Wade says to the skeletal looking bartender before looking over to her for her drinks order.

"Pinot. Large." She says. Eddie nods and goes about quietly making the drinks. She takes a look around. It's 6pm on a Wednesday, and she's the youngest one here by far. Wade places second. The skeleton behind the bar hands them their drinks, Wade hands over £10, gets his change, and the entire interaction goes by without a single word being said.

"Sooo." She says, after taking a large sip of very cheap wine.

"Yeah…" He says. They don't really know where to start.

"Let's take a minute to assess and work out exactly what we saw." She tells him, trying to tackle this constructively.

"Where do we start?" He asks, and that's a good question. The sniper fire? The weird 'Cleaners' that looked dead behind the eyes? The wounds that seemed to heal way faster than they had any right to? Before she can open her mouth Wade's phone rings. He takes a quick look at the screen and shows it to her. It's his boss, DSI Copper. He gestures and they step away to a table far away from the bar, in a quiet corner, which isn't hard to find, and puts the call on speaker.

"Hello?"

"Wade! What's going on? There's all kinds of reports of sniper fire downtown; and you called off an armed response team? Are you even supposed to be working right now? What is going on?" Says Copper through the phone. She can hear his struggle to remain calm.

"Alright, calm down. It's summit to do with that Counter Terrorism team you're so fond of."

"Oh." He says, starting to sound a little more on edge. "What happened?"

"Well, that bar I told you they wanted closing down. It got shot up with some of them inside."

"Did they get him?" He asked. "The shooter?"

"Not yet. From the sounds of it they've tracked him down to the Eagle. Looks like we're gonna end up with another standoff there. But don't worry I'm gonna keep far away from it."

"Oh. Oh dear. I certainly hope this doesn't turn out like last time. We don't need that kind of attention right now. I need to go, see what else I can find out about what's going on." He says, sounding even more worried now.

"Good lu…" Wade says, but Copper has already hung up. "Charming." He says with a shrug.
"I think we should go, too." Kim says, making a decision.
"Yeah, Kam will be expecting me home, but gimme a minute to finish my drink…" He says, taking a large gulp of the lager and completely missing her point.
"No." She says, and locks eyes with him. "I mean to the hotel."
"Kimmy…." He begins, but she cuts him off because she's already pretty sure she knows what he's going to say.
"We've already been in the firing line once today, and I don't know about you babes but I want answers more than ever. Sounds like your boss was pretty worried too from the way he dropped your call just now. Something big is going to go down at the hotel and I don't want to miss out." He sighs and gulps down more of his lager. She can read the expression on his face perfectly and knows it's coming even before he says it.
"Oh fuck it," He says, and makes for the door. She takes another mouthful of the god-awful wine and follows him.

Chapter Thirty-Two.

Louis thunders up the stairs. He can hear the running ahead of him and so he knows he's going the right way. Up, and up, and up, until he bursts out on the top floor and finds Danny waiting and staring cautiously down the corridor.
"Where did he go?" Louis asks.
"I don't know…" Danny whispers
"Should we…?"
"Shhh!" He says, and slowly proceeds. They pass room after room in this deathly silent hallway.
"Are you sure he…"
"Yes." Danny snaps, cutting him off because he doesn't want to give their position away. They creep down the corridor as best they can, squinting out into the darkness that surrounds them. Much like the basement, the lights are off and there's a worry that any shape could be the Used-to-Be disguising himself. There's no natural light and dozens of rooms he could've ducked into. They try to look for clues to where he went; a broken handle, a splintered frame or even a scuffed carpet, but it's nearly impossible to make anything out. Danny leans in and whispers to Louis.

"Do you feel anything?" It takes him aback at first but as his brain ticks over the weird question he realises he's asking if he can sense any energy Joseph is giving off. He shakes his head in response.
"I don't think..." He begins, and he's cut off as Joseph comes tearing out of one of the rooms to their left and throws himself into Danny, pushing him through a door and into another of the hotel rooms. He and Danny crash into the room and Louis quickly follows. They tussle, and Danny gets in a couple of good shots, but Joseph quickly gets the better of him. Joseph picks Danny up and smashes him down onto the floor. He pulls out a knife and raises it over his head.

1996, still in Pat's Bar, still that same day.
A group of three drunken men walk into a bar. It's not the start of a joke, sadly, it's quite the opposite. They're all laughing and joking, and shoving each other playfully. It's Jason Hamilton and his friends Zach and Thomas. They're all wearing football shirts, because that's where they've spent their day, watching their favourite team and drinking. They stumble up to the bar, partly because of the alcohol and partly because of the shoving, and try to catch Dionne's attention. She's serving someone else, because Pat's is starting to get quite busy now, so it's Joseph that approaches to take their order.
"What can I get you?" He asks, with a tired smile.
"Three pints mate." Jason tells him. Joseph nods and grabs the empty glasses from behind the bar. They're not paying attention to him really, they're continuing to stare over at Dionne, and the second she glances over at them Zach winks. She doesn't even acknowledge it.
"£4.23 please." Joseph asks, putting the three full pints down. The lads all look at each other and Jason shrugs.
"Don't look at me, I got the last ones." Thomas protests
"Your round mate." Zach tells Jason, who begrudgingly digs through his pockets.
"Ey, how do you work with her all day?" Thomas asks Joseph. "Bet you've got a constant stiffy ey?" He says with a laugh. Joseph tries to hold back a grimace and just gives him a really obviously uncomfortable smile. It was probably the word stiffy. It'll do that to anyone.
"Wait a sec, do I know you?" Thomas asks him, focussing to try to get a good look at him. Jason, meanwhile, hands over the money and waits for his change while Thomas contemplates his own question. "Yeah!" He says

finally. "You were in our year at school. Do you remember guys? Joe something or other." He says, nudging the other two.
"Sorry, no." Joseph replies, uncomfortable. Probably because he knows what's coming next. He tries to serve the next customer but Thomas' next words stop him dead.
"Didn't your mother kick you out for being a dirty fag?" He stops. Silent. Jason and Zach laugh.
"Not sure we want these pints then. They're probably riddled with AIDS." Zach says.
"Yeah. Go get her to pour us some fresh ones, you dirty queer." Jason adds, jumping in on the action. They all laugh. Joseph shuffles uncomfortably. He blinks and stares, a little too intently, at the customer next to them, who won't meet his gaze.
"What can I get you?" He asks him, determined to move on.
"Erm…a glass of white and a pint of bitter please." The man says.
"Ey, don't ignore us gay boy. Tell your fit mate she needs to make us fresh drinks." Thomas interjects, so loudly that a lot of people heard. Everyone at the bar looks at each other uncomfortably, everyone except the glamorous woman who quietly sips her martini, staring intently at the situation as it unfolds.
"That's enough." Snaps Dionne, coming over and protectively moving Joseph behind her. "'She' is not doing anything, except kicking the three of you out." She says, pointing aggressively at them.
"Steady on flower, we was just joking around. That's right, innit Tommy?" Jason tells her, trying to laugh it off.
"Yeah, just having a little fun with our old friend Joe Gayboy here." Thomas agrees. She stares at them with fire in her eyes and shakes her head.
"I said enough." She tells them, and looks to the entrance where it's now late enough that there is now a bouncer on the door. "Get out." She tells them, making sure that he can hear her too. He does and he starts to make his way over, parting the crowd as he does because he's a six-foot mountain of a man. "Georgie, these boys are leaving." She tells him, and turns away, because she'll entertain no more discussion on the matter.
"Right, come on lads." Georgie tells him, also making it clear that there'll be no more discussion on it. She shoots Joseph a quick look and he gives her a timid smile, whispering his thanks as he does.
"For fuck sake! Stupid bitch." Jason shouts. Georgie grabs him by the collar and practically drags him out of the bar. The other two follow,

amazingly not looking ashamed. Joseph goes back to serving the man who wanted the wine and the pint of bitter, and Dionne gives him a friendly and reassuring pat on the arm before going back to work too. The glamorous woman continues to watch silently.

"Stop!" Louis roars; pointing the gun at Joseph. He freezes with a smirk and lowers his knife slowly.
"Well, look at you!" He laughs, wiping a little blood from his nose. "Put it down. You're not going to use it." He taunts.
"Back away from him." Louis orders him. Joseph rolls his eyes and does what he's told. Louis helps Danny up from the ground.
"Are you going to shoot me? Go on. I dare you."
"Why those families?" Louis asks. There's no tactical reason for this now; he just needs to know.
"I'm so bored with these questions." He says, and he takes one challenging step forward. Louis flinches, just a tiny bit, but it's not from the movement. He can feel the red hot rage building in Joseph. "They. Deserved. It." He says with a snarl, punctuating every word with a clap of his hands. "I don't know why you people can't just leave it alone. If you'd just let me do that…if you'd just leave me to kill the ones who deserve it…" He steps closer again, and the feeling emanating from him intensifies. Louis feels sick. "…but you show up with all this…misguided righteous energy. I know what I am. What they turned me into but you…look at you…you're clueless." Another step.
"Stop." Louis says, but this time it's less of an order, it's got less authority behind it because he's trembling. "Stop moving…I…" He loses concentration for just a moment, pained now by flashes of Joseph's past. Joseph grins and pounces. He knocks the gun from his grip, and tries to stab him. Danny intercepts him and they both crash through a glass coffee table. Joseph flips so that he's on top and starts wrapping his hands around his throat again, determined that this time he'll choke the life out of him.
Louis tries to shake it off and forces himself back into the fray, kicking Joseph in the face, and making him release his grip. He pops quickly back to his feet though, and fights right back, striking quickly and using every ounce of his demonic strength and anger. Danny gets up and tries to interject, but Joseph keeps him at bay with an elbow to the face. They attack together, but even then they don't get the advantage. His attacks

are swift, visceral, and violent. Their skill is no match for his superhuman strength combined with his overwhelming anger. The three of them crash violently through the hotel room, destroying furniture and tearing hangings from the wall, and every time it looks like it's going their way he pulls it back. He knocks Louis against the wall and aims a fist at his head. Louis ducks and Joseph leaves a severe dent. This gives them an opening, and Louis manages to smack him twice in the face. Joseph pulls his fist back to retaliate, but from behind Danny clings onto his arm. Louis makes a dive for his discarded gun, and Joseph swings his arm and throws Danny at him to stop him getting it. Once again the two agents end up as a crumpled heap on the floor. Joseph smiles, clearly nowhere near as exhausted as they are. He pounces forward again, grabbing Danny from on top of Louis and throwing him up through a door and into the bathroom. Louis scrambles to get back up, but a swift kick to the head keeps him down. Joseph follows Danny into the bathroom. He stops him from getting up with a couple more brutal punches to the head. He cracks his head violently off the porcelain toilet, again, and again, and again. Danny tries to crawl away, but Joseph violently beats him down some more. He pauses. The smile is long gone from his face.
"This'll fucking show you." He spits, in an angry whisper.
He kicks him again. Louis finally drags himself back up and charges into the room. He throws his bodyweight at Joseph in an act of sheer desperation. He knocks him away from Danny and the two of them crash into the bathtub. The back of Joseph's head cracks violently against the wall, leaving a bloodied splatter on the tiles, and he lays limp and unmoving.
Louis rolls back out of the bath, with a thud, and desperately tries to check on Danny who is a bloodied heap on the cold tiled floor. He's still alive, but he doesn't look good. A groan comes from Joseph's body as he swims back to consciousness and with a roar of frustration he drags himself back to his feet. Louis pulls himself up too, and braces to continue the fight. He knows he's alone now, because it doesn't look like Danny will be getting up any time soon. Joseph pushes him with all of his strength and it throws him back, out of the bathroom and smashing into a TV on the wall. The Used-to-Be steps over Danny, who's just barely moving, and swoops down on him. Louis' head is swimming. The mixture of the beating and the red wave of emotion is overwhelming. It washes over him in a bloody haze and he can see flashes of Joseph's past as if they were his own. He can hear

the cracking of bones and he doesn't know if they're his or Joseph's. His ability to sense meshes perfectly with Joseph's anger and it engulfs him in a sea of crimson, fiery, painful emotion. Joseph screams both in the memories and in the present. Louis sees one chance, one last chance, a tiny little window of opportunity to save his life and he takes it. He pulls a syringe from his pocket, as fists continue to rain down on him in the present and on Joseph in the past. He stops fighting, he stops trying to block, and he just jams it into the first bit of flesh he can find. The screaming stops. The fight stops. Joseph stumbles back. Louis struggles, using the furniture and the wall to help him stand.
"What…" Joseph asks; completely lost. He pulls the empty syringe out and stares at it, horrified. Tears are streaming down his face. "No. This isn't how it's supposed to…no!" He stumbles, because the drug is taking hold, and with his last burst of energy he charges. But now the red has settled, it's been numbed, and Louis has time to breathe. Joseph is slow and sluggish, stumbling towards him, and Louis' head is clear. He pauses and he waits and at just the right moment he drops backward and uses Joseph's momentum against him. He launches him over his head and, inadvertently, through the window.

DCI Matthew Wade and Kim Adams are close to the Eagle Hotel. They're approaching slowly and cautiously as they look out for any sign of what it is the Counter Terrorism team have come to confront. They don't have to wait long because, at that moment, there is a loud smash and they look up in time to see a body fly through a fifth story window.
"What the…?" Wade shouts and they look at each other, wide-eyed. They didn't see where the body landed, or even who it was but they silently agree to start running towards the hotel. Two black cars and a van pass them at speed and pull up outside, blocking their view from across the street. They see Chris hurtle out of the car, seemingly fully recovered from his earlier injuries. He doesn't see them because he's too busy barking orders as several other figures get out of their vehicles.
"Secure the scene!" They hear him roar, as Olivia and Lauren get out of the car too. Cleaners start to pour from the van.
"I think we need to go…" Chris tells Kim, stopping dead.

And there, on the floor, with his body broken, Joseph swims out of consciousness as sirens wail in the distance and the damn Custodians swarm around him.

Danny drags himself out of the bathroom, responding to the sound of the broken window and thinking the worst. He's visibly relieved when he sees Louis standing there, wounded but alive. They hobble towards each other, both breathing heavily and utterly exhausted, and practically prop each other up as they silently congratulate themselves on surviving.

Chapter Thirty-Four.

A little while later Danny stands just outside the hotel watching several Cleaners load a restrained and unconscious 4XM into the back of their unmarked white van. He's badly injured from the fall but he'll heal, way faster than Louis and Danny would without Lauren's help.
"You look terrible." Amber says as she joins him. Her still wet hair is scraped back so that it's out of her face and her clothes are still drying, but she's right, she looks a lot better than he does right now. She jabs him in the ribs.
"Ow!" He cries. "Maybe if you'd spent less time swimming we could've wrapped it up a little sooner." He retorts.
"Yeah. Maybe." She agrees with a laugh. Danny nods towards Chris who's still ordering people around in the distance, trying to take control of the carnage. "He survived then." He says.
"Yep. Healed up in enough time to at least try to take the glory for this."
"Good. He's going to be so annoyed we did it without him. I'd hate for him to have missed it." Danny says, with a playful grin at the thought of Chris scrambling to explain how this was all his doing.
"I'm annoyed I missed it!" She protests, "But, you did good."
"Thanks." Danny says, and he looks past the group of people directly in front of them to one lone figure who's sitting on a bench on his own across the street. Amber follows his gaze to Louis. "It was...some of it, anyway. He wasn't totally useless is what I'm saying."
"Maybe we have been too hard on him." She says, and they share a mischievous look.
"Or maybe we just inspired him to be better." Danny offers and she laughs again.

"Yes. That's the one." She confirms.
"We did it though, and this was an important one. But…" he says, and he's hesitant to continue. There's something else on his mind. The one bit of information they'd held back from the others. "He wasn't alone. We got a message…last week…after what happened at the hospital. A warning."
"What?" She snaps, furious that he's kept that back.
"It was a woman. Said she was the one who killed Alex, and Rachel." He explains.
"Why're you just telling me this now?" She demands.
"I don't know. I'm sorry." He says, and she jabs him in the ribs again and he winces.
"You and me, we don't keep stuff from each other. What did it say?"
"It said…it was a threat to leave them alone. And…this…is the opposite of leaving them alone." He tells her. He's right. Hunting and capturing 4XM was definitely not doing what the mysterious woman had told them to do.
"To the next one, then…" Amber says.
"Run a little bit faster next time?" he asks.
"Don't start without me next time!" She demands.
"Deal."
"I'm glad you're okay." She tells her friend.
"Yeah. Me too." He says. And she rests her head on his shoulder affectionately as the two of them watch the van leave, hoping they're able to put this behind them and return to normality. Unfortunately, as they'd soon realise, this was nowhere near the end.

1996, for the last time.
It's finally closing time at Pat's, and for Joseph it's been a fucking long day. You can see he's exhausted and he's over it. He's stacking glasses while Dionne wipes the bar down. She's stayed late to help him close up, and there's been no sign of the warthog since that morning. The glamorous woman slipped out quietly, and thankfully the rest of the shift was relatively uneventful.
"I'm gonna bounce. You good to finish up?" Dionna asks him, and for a second he looks like he's too far away to hear her.
"Yeah. Yeah, I'm good." He confirms with a small smile as he comes back to reality, but he still looks a little troubled.
"Cool." She says, and starts to get her coat on.
"Dee?" He asks, hesitantly.

"'Sup?"
"Thanks again for earlier." His fake smile is gone and he looks sad. The whole thing with those guys is still weighing heavy on him.
"It's cool." She says, turning to face him and reading his look instantly. "You know I got you." He nods and looks as if he wants to say more, but doesn't. "You working tomorrow?" She asks.
"Yeah."
"Then I'll see you then!" She says, brightly. "Another day of bringing glamour to this place!" He laughs at this, and suddenly he's the same bright, happy, slightly messy boy that he was at the start of the day.
"Give Russ my love." He says as she hugs him and then heads to the door.
"I'm doing no such thing; he doesn't deserve it and I've not even told you why!" She tells him.
"Tomorrow?"
"Absolutely!" She goes to leave. Her hand is on the door. But something stops her. Something that still needs to be said. "Joe?" She says, turning back to him.
"Yeah?"
"Don't let those fuckers get to you, yeah? You're amazing." He nods, but doesn't say anything. "I'm glad you're okay." With that, she waves one last time, and leaves.

A few minutes later he has finished up, he turns the lights out, grabs his jacket and leaves, locking up behind him. It's late now, after 1am. Pat's is just outside the city centre so after a certain time there aren't many people out on the streets. It's dark and it's cold, and it's drizzling a little bit. He passes a couple of harmless drunks as he walks down the street and they stumble out of his way, giggling to themselves. He gives them a smile but quickens his pace because he's keen to get back to his mattress-bed, where it's at least a little warmer than being out on the street and he can sleep. But his thoughts of a nice warm sleep are interrupted suddenly by the thump, thump, thump of footsteps on the pavement running up behind him. Before he can turn he's smacked in the back of the head by a large fist. He falls forwards, smacking his head on the concrete. He skitters back to his feet, his instinct screaming at him to run from the unseen attacker. His head is bleeding and he hasn't quite had the chance to process what's happening, but he rushes forward as quickly as he can in the desperate hope that he can escape. Run, his brain is telling him. Just run. Nothing else matters, just running. It's clumsy and desperate and he lurches to the

right. off the street and into an alleyway that he usually cuts through, and the footsteps are just behind him.
"Somebody he…" He calls out, but the call for help is cut off by a thump as he receives another blow to the head, and this time it's metal, rather than a fist. that connects with the back of his skull.
"Shut the fuck up, you fucking queer." Jason snarls at him. He's dazed and confused, and he's lying there on the ground. He can't make his body work to get back up, even though his brain is still screaming to run. The three men descend and they kick and punch and bash him. "This'll fucking show you." Jason tells him, spitting the words that will stick with him forever. He starts screaming and begging for help but the more they hit him the more the screams turn into shrieks, and then the shrieks turn into whines, and then the whines turn into gurgles, and still they continue to beat him. Finally, it's Zach that backs off first.
"I think…I think that's enough." He says, taking in exactly what it is that they've done.
"No, not yet." Jason says, and he swings the pipe again. It crashes down with a wet, meaty, thump. "We've got to teach him a lesson."
They don't know it but they're being watched and they have been this entire time. There's been someone trying to decide exactly what she should do and whether or not she should intervene. It wouldn't be something she'd usually do, but for some reason this feels different. She's conflicted but after another crack of the pipe onto bone, the glamorous woman steps forward.
"Stop." She says, simply and calmly, but commandingly. Her voice projects through the alley and the men round on her in unison.
"Fuck off bitch." Jason says, brandishing the bloody pipe threateningly and making it clear he's not afraid to use it on her. It's meant to scare her. But it doesn't. They're the ones who should be afraid. She narrows her eyes and tilts her head, as if she's perplexed by him.
"No." She says simply. He's drunk, he's angry, he's violent, and his adrenaline is surging. He doesn't really think, he just lurches forward at her, swinging the bloody pipe.
"I said fu…" He roars, mid swing. The words die in his mouth as she catches it, halting his momentum and causing him to stumble. She looks completely unfazed by him. The dim light in the alleyway flickers and the ground under their feet seems to thrum, and everything around them shudders. She crushes the pipe in her hand and shakes her head.

"You asked for this." She says. She rips the pipe easily from his grasp and tosses it behind her. He tries to swing a big stupid fist at her and she steps easily out of the way. Then, she hits him in the chest and he is thrown backwards like he was hit by a truck. He is sent careening the length of the alleyway and the other two stare at her, wide eyed. Lightning cracks overhead, even though there was no storm only a moment ago, and it's enough of a message. Thomas and Zach run for their lives, picking up Jason on the way and getting the hell out of there as quickly as they can. For a moment she considers going after them. There are a hundred different ways to murder them running through her brain. But she doesn't, she looks down at Joseph, bleeding and gurgling, and barely clinging to life, and she feels like she has to stay. He sees her and he tries to say something. She kneels down at his side and smiles kindly. "I am sorry. It might've been kinder to just let them finish." She says and she takes his hand, which is covered in his own blood. "You were kind to me earlier. I…haven't always depended on the kindness of strangers…so it was unexpected. It was nice, thank you." She tells him.
"Please…" He manages to say.
"There's nothing I can do, my dear. It's…there's no time." She explains, and it's true. He doesn't have long left.
"Stay…?" He begs and the words are barely audible. He's cold and in pain, and dying, and he doesn't want to be alone. She puts her hand on his cheek, getting his blood on her in the process.
"Stay with you 'till the end?" She asks him. "Oh my sweet child. I can do that." Her voice is the same as it was in the bar earlier; poised and measured, but it does crack a little bit and she lets some emotion dramatically enter her tone. She takes her hand from his face to a necklace she's wearing. He'd not seen it earlier, not properly, but it's a vial with a few drops of crimson in it. She smears his blood onto the glass as she touches it. "Or, I could save you. I don't know if that would be any kinder." She runs her fingers up and down the bloody vial as she considers it. She knows this is a major turning point in her story; and she has the power to determine whether it's the end of his. "And here it is. The convenient plot device that I've been saving, just in case. The drops of Infected blood I kept all those years ago. Just in case." She hesitates and pulls away from him. "But, you wouldn't be you. You wouldn't be kind." She explains to him, looking down and wondering about the bright-eyed, enthusiastic human who had served her a martini earlier. The one who'd

taken a genuine interest in who she was for the first time in decades. She gently removes her necklace and pops open the vial. The decision has been made. "But then, look at what this world does to kindness." She empties it into one of his open wounds and the tiny droplets of red mingle with his own and within seconds it starts to burn him, like she has poured fire into his bloodstream. She straightens herself up, dusts herself off, and waits.
"And here we go." She says, to the audience in her head.

It's finished, isn't it? That's the question that's running around in Louis' head as he sits across the street from the chaos unfolding outside the Eagle Hotel, just taking a moment for himself. He can see Amber and Danny, who have now been joined by Lauren, and he feels a warm sense of affection for them. They're his team and now, after this, it's starting to feel like he belongs. The van that contains 4XM, or Joseph, is gone. After having such a vivid look into the man's history it feels wrong to think of him by anything but his actual name. He doesn't know everything. But now he knows how those families he was hunting were the relatives of the men who killed him. It's knowledge that was somehow absorbed into his brain through being in close proximity; he understands Joseph now. That's not to say that he in any way agrees with his actions, just that he can understand where all of it came from. He's getting a better grip on this power of his. It's not stable, and it's still so painful and so tiring, but he's starting to understand it more. He can feel their demonic energy and how it's tied to who they are. He saw and felt the moment that Joseph, as he is now, was created. He can't remember all the details of it, but he remembered all the feelings and all the pain, and how that warped and twisted him into the creature they've fought today. He knows that Joseph was brutally murdered and then spent the next few decades desperately seeking revenge on anyone even vaguely related to his killers in the hope that it would make him feel whole again. It didn't. It never would've, and now, he'll be taken to a secure facility and won't be able to finish that mission. So, it's over, isn't it?
He got everything he wanted. He's starting to feel properly part of the team and Joseph has been stopped. So why did it feel like there was still something there, some little detail that still eluded him. Something sitting just on the outside of what he can see. He's so tired, he thinks to himself. Maybe there was something, or maybe it's just that he knew this was just

his first real victory and there will be many, many more battles to come. Whatever it is, he can work it out after he's slept.

"I take it you're the one…the hero who saved the day…?" A woman asks suddenly, making him jump as she sits down next to him on the bench and joins him in watching the activity across the street.

"I wouldn't say that…but…" He says. He feels like he recognises her but he can't tell where from; she's well dressed, wearing a stylish suit and sunglasses. She exudes elegance and glamour.

"It all sounds like it was terrifying. Gunshots and people falling out of windows." She continues; speaking in a melodic way that makes what she's saying sound even more dramatic. He's reminded of old movies he used to watch during his time in Jongleton.

"I guess so," He says, peering at her and trying to place where he knows her from.

"Good." She says, simply.

"Good?" He asks, more than a little puzzled. She breathes deeply, and takes a thoughtful pause before nodding, sadly.

"Yes. I'm glad he went out with a bang. He deserved a wonderful finale." She tells him, and it starts to become clear. The last piece is falling into place.

"I'm…" He begins, but for some reason he can't fully understand he stops. As if he wasn't meant to be speaking.

"Shhh. You're stepping on my lines." She tells him, and somehow that makes sense too. She's supposed to be speaking right now, not him. This is a monologue. "I never wanted this. It's really important you know that. I wanted to live peacefully. It's important because, well, you should know that what comes next is all your fault."

"Who are y…" He begins again and he stops when she raises her hand. He did it again, he thinks, it wasn't his time to speak.

"You will not interrupt me again." She tells him; and he knows he won't. She takes a deep breath and her posture shifts. She removes the sunglasses and the sky darkens a little bit, as if it's switching to reflect the place she's going to. There's a chill in the air and he could swear it's coming from her. He shivers.

"I am who you've cast me as. I warned you to stop and you didn't. You hunted him like rabid dogs, so I'm going to put you down." She turns to face him and she sneers.

"...and I'm going to find pleasure in playing this role. I'm going to tear you and your friends apart and I'm going to relish every single second of it." She leans in close; putting a hand on his neck, and she whispers. He can't shake her off because that's not what he's supposed to do. She stares across the street at his team.

"I could do it now. I could snap your neck, and then walk over there and cut through them. They're nothing. How far do you think I'd get? I think they'd be dead before they even realised what was happening. There'd be so many in the crossfire, too. Blood, and guts, and bone, and death. Oh it'd be such a show. It's been a long-time since I've gone to that place...but you never forget how...you just need the right motivation." She releases him and she leans back.

"But, not today. Not now...because I don't want it to be quick. I want it to hurt, the way that you taking him away hurts. You've given me all the motivation I need to play the villain you so badly want."

She stands, and brushes the creases out of her suit. She puts her sunglasses back on, but not before another quick, threatening look across the street, and a wink at him. The last piece is in place and he knows that this is far from finished.

"My name is Hazel...and I'll see you again soon."

Part V: Who Are These People?

Chapter Thirty-Five

Louis is exactly where she left him; and even from across the street the others can see something isn't right. He's hunched over, breathing heavily, and clutching the bench for stability because the world is spinning. He's lost because once again everything around him feels so loud and overwhelming. They see this and they know, even from across the street, that he needs them. Lauren is first, followed very closely by Danny, and tailed by Amber.
"Louis, what's wrong?" Lauren asks, stern but concerned, as she gets down in front of him. "Breathe. Focus on your breath." She tells him.
"What's wrong with him?" Danny asks her, with impatience, but with concern bursting through too. He grabs Louis' shoulder and squeezes.
"Some kind of panic attack." She explains, partly to answer his question, but also to explain it to Louis. "Focus on your breath and on the things around you. Think about what you can hear, what you can see, what you can touch." She tells him, staying calm.
"I..." He begins, but he can't get any more words out. He's fighting against his own body because it's just so overwhelmed by everything else. Hazel and all her power, and her rage and everything she has left behind, that's still sitting there next to him. Stuff he can't understand because it just all feels too much to process. Decades of emotional and demonic trauma encircling him like smog.
"Come on. Snap out of it." Danny orders, and he's there, like a beacon in the dark.
"She was here." He finally gets out.
"Who? Lauren asks, confused. But he looks up at Danny and he can tell he knows who he means.
"The woman from the video?" He asks, and Louis nods.
"What?" Lauren asks, completely left behind. "What woman? What video?"
Danny starts wildly scanning the nearby area, his head whipping back and forth as if he'd have any idea what this woman looked like. Amber, clearly catching on, starts to do the same.
"Which way?" She demands, stepping forward.
"I don't know." Louis croaks out, his whole body drooping as his panic response starts to calm.
"Are you hurt?" Danny asks.
"Where did she go?!" Amber snaps.

"What woman?" Lauren still wants to know.
"What happened?" Danny says.
"Stop. All of you." Louis whispers, in a whimper.
"Tell me which way she went!" Amber continues.
"Stop!" He shouts, finally finding the strength. They aren't helping. They're just adding to the noise. "She's gone. It was just a warning. She said her name was Hazel and that she's going to kill us all for taking him away."
"She's welcome to come and say that to my face."
"Amber! She was really powerful. So much more so than…I could feel it. I couldn't move because she told me not to."
"What do you mean you couldn't move?"
"What did she look like?"
"Are you alright?"
He lets his head fall into his hands and tries to compose himself as the other three all talk over each other and continue to bark questions at him. They bleed into the background and just become white noise. He doesn't have the answers they want. He feels so damn tired and I remember thinking just how fucking unfair it was. We barely even got a minute. Stopping Joseph had nearly killed us and that was my first big victory. I should've been allowed to enjoy it, we should've been allowed to enjoy it. Instead, it felt like a huge deal one moment and then like absolutely nothing the next. Stopping Joseph was a tiny, tiny little step because there was still so much further to go and in that moment I started to understand that. I didn't know quite how much further, but Hazel certainly made me realise we'd not really accomplished anything. Joseph, really, was just chapter one. I'm glad you've stuck with me this long. I really hope there's time to finish all of this, but we've definitely come to a part in the story when you need a little more background and to tell you a little more about who the Custodians are.

But before we get to that there were some humans wondering the same thing, and what they'd seen of Joseph's capture had only heightened that curiosity. Wade knocked Kim's front door, clutching two takeaway cups. It was 7.30am on the dot, precisely the time they'd agreed upon. He'd grabbed them some coffees from her favourite shop because he couldn't be arsed with the moaning about it if he'd brought any other kind. They'd planned for a long day when they'd discussed it. A whole day of just knuckling down and solving this thing. He knew they'd need caffeine for that. But, he'd also been running ridiculously early and a trip fifteen minutes out of his way to the nearest coffee chain was a good way to kill time. He'd been up all night thinking about this, and needed to get started. He couldn't sleep because he needed answers, and because he couldn't sleep he needed coffee to help him make sense of the questions. It was all a bit of a vicious jumble and at the centre of it all was the desire to know what the bloody hell was going on. Kim opened the door with a friendly, but tired, smile and ushered him inside.

"Figured you'd need this." He said, handing her the cup.

"Yes!" She said, excitedly, accepting the cup gratefully. He steps inside and takes a look around. It's a small, but chic, open plan one bedroom apartment. There's a coffee table right in the centre of the living room area and it's absolutely covered in clippings, and notes, and other scattered bits of paper and clutter. One look at it tells him that she too has been up ridiculously early and has been scouring for all the tidbits of information she could find. He'd been tempted to see if she was up in the middle of the night; and seeing this he wishes he had. Then again, Kam might just raise an eyebrow at the idea of him sneaking out in the middle of the night to meet another woman, and he wasn't quite ready to explain to her what they were up to. It didn't even make sense to him so it was best to keep that headache from her, for now. Kim sees him looking at the paperwork and clearly feels the need to explain.

"Yeah that's everything I've found so far. I couldn't really sleep." She says.

"I know that feeling." He says, leaning down and peering at what she's gathered. She's got pictures of them all that she's clearly managed to pull from footage she's filmed. Some of it's from the Eagle Hotel, some is from Endsbrough hospital, and a few photos she took at Vanity Bar when no one was looking.

"I'm just gathering as much as I can." She explains, obviously trying to make sense of the current scattergun approach to information gathering. "The more pieces of whatever puzzle this is we can see, the better."

"Spoken like a true detective." He says, with a little admiration, knowing that sharing this with her was the right thing to do. He smirks to himself as he sees the names 'Red,' 'Messy,' and 'Arrogant,' attached to the pictures of Amber, Louis and Danny.

"Do you want their actual names or are you happy with those?" He asks.

"Are you sure you even have their real names?" She retorts, and he realises she's right. He can't be sure anything these people have told him is the truth. "What're you doing about work?" She asks.

"I said I'd take one more day. That I'm not quite ready to be back, and being part of a shoot out made me realise that." He says, leaving out that Tim was very happy to hear that. It felt too easy to take more time off.

"I think this'll take more than one." She says, raising her eyebrows. She's not wrong, but he'd much rather take it one day at a time than commit to taking a lengthy period of absence. There's obviously something deep rooted here, and yes, he's determined to get to the bottom of it, but he's not quite sure yet that he's prepared for where it leads. Whatever this little Counter Terrorism team are up to, it's dangerous. He doesn't want innocent people to get caught in the cross-fire and he's not sure yet whether exposing what's really going on will minimise or exaggerate the likelihood of that. Essentially, he's still keeping one eye on the door of their little project, just in case.

"Well, this'll help." He says, pulling a file from the plastic carrier bag he's brought with him. It's got a little battered in transit. She grabs it and starts to leaf through it. "It's everything I had on Steven Robinson, or at least what I could get without being asked questions." She stops perusing the file, and puts it down on the table with everything else.

"Matthew?" She asks, and there's a change in her demeanour.

"Yeah?"

"There's something really sticking in my head about yesterday. It's something that, well, sounds a little…" She trails off. There's a lot about this that sounds a little…

"What is it?" He asks, trying to sound encouraging.

"Humans." She says simply.

"Eh?" He grunts back at her in confusion.

"That's what they called us. More than once, too. First 'Arrogant,' then 'Red' later on. They both referred to the two of us as Humans. That seems like a really weird thing to call someone unless you're, well, not human."

"It is weird but…you're not suggesting…?" He says. She shakes her head and shrugs.

"I'm not suggesting anything, necessarily. Just that, if they're referring to us as humans, then it means they at least think they're not." She goes back to the Steven Robinson file and starts to pull out bits of paperwork. She pauses and her gaze lingers on an image of the team pulled from outside of the Eagle Hotel. She shakes her head. "Who are these people?"

Their car pulled up by the side of an old country road, and the four of them got out. It was less than twenty-four hours removed from the capture of Joseph and Chris had wasted no time in summoning them back to Home Base for an urgent meeting.

The Custodians, and those responsible for them, were well embedded in the world. That shouldn't be a surprise, like I said back in Chapter Six this isn't a new thing, it's something that has existed for a long, long time. That means that they have been there for the formation of Governments, of Monarchies and of religions. They've accumulated wealth and influence because it's easy to be an integral part of society if you were there when it formed. Humans are obsessed with the idea of the Illuminati and that's really funny to me now because, yes the Illuminati are real by the way, the beings at the core of the Custodians are infinitely more influential and powerful and yet no one ever talks about them.

Louis, Amber, Lauren and Danny were all Level Five Custodians. That was pretty much the lowest on the ladder. The basic pawns stationed all over the world in groups to wage the war on the front line. Then you had the Level Fours, like Chris and Rachel before him. They were the team leaders, responsible for groups of Level Fives but still pretty low in terms of rank. Chris had three teams, ours, Olivias, and Carters. Above them you would have Level Threes, like Alex. They were the Agents who would travel all over the world as needed. They would be given specific assignments and track specific targets. They were experienced. Then there were the Twos, who were the equivalent of some kind of special forces. They were raised differently because they never needed to fit in. They just had to get into a situation and resolve it. The Level Ones were completely secret. We never knew how many of them they were but they would be deep, deep undercover. Some of them are in the very heart of a country's Government, giving orders and running things from afar.

Above all of us you had the Sevens. Seven Superior beings. One on each continent. Our fathers. Our Superiors. Yeah, it's weird, isn't it? 'Superior One' was the name of the one I was familiar with. The one who'd been a presence throughout my entire childhood, and who was the closest thing any of us had known to a parent. Custodians all grew up in a Home Base. It just so happens I grew up in the one that was closest to us. The one we'd been summoned to now.

It was late afternoon, and there was already another car parked up when they got out.

"Looks like Chris' favourites are already here. Of course they got here early. I wonder if they brought him a gift too." Amber said, her tone positively dripping with both sarcasm and contempt for Olivia's team.

"Good, get this all now so that you can be polite when we're in there." Lauren tells her.

"Is not going at all an option?" Amber asked, as they started to make their way up a path and away from the road. The Home Base was located in North Yorkshire, hidden away in an area of countryside protected by the Human's National Trust. Again, National Heritage sites given extra protections are no coincidence.

"If it's an option I'd like to not go, too?" Danny chimes in.

"It's not an option." Lauren confirms, with a scowl.

"Why? We're clearly the B team here. He won't even notice." Amber argues

"Because Chris specifically said he wanted all of us here." Lauren tells her

"Why? We've never had to do a debrief before. It sounds really boring." Amber whines. As they walk deeper into a wooded area, along a path that's overgrown from years of neglect, Danny drops back slightly to leave Lauren and Amber leading the way so that he can speak to Louis.

"Are you alright?" He asks; and Louis is still a little taken aback by the concern. He nods quietly in response, but that's clearly not enough. "No, but really?" He follows up.

"I can't stop thinking about yesterday. About Hazel." Louis explains to him.

"Oh god I'm getting deja vu." He teases with an eye roll, which was much more in character but not entirely convincing.

"No, it's not like Jos…4XM. I wanted to find him. I needed to, even." He explains, and Danny nods, understanding, as they walk side by side. "With her it's more…that it feels like we're totally out of our depth. Please don't make fun of me, but I'm scared." He tells him, and braces for his reaction.

"We're not out of our depth." He says, simply and calmly.

"What makes you so sure?" Louis asks him.

"I feel like I'm channelling you, of all people, but look at what we did with 4XM. We got him. You and me. My brain and your…" He pauses, vaguely gesturing as if that's enough. Louis waits until it's obvious he's not going to finish that thought. He doesn't intend to let him get away with that, though.

"My...?" He prompts. Danny looks past him, off to Amber and Lauren who are deep in conversation and too focussed on that to be listening in to them.
"Obsessive nature?" He offers, before realising himself that's not quite a compliment. "Bizarre Hero complex? Weird optimism? Whatever it is; it works for you."
"Thanks?" Louis says, raising an eyebrow and giving him a look that even someone as oblivious as Danny can read.
"You're good." He continues, practically whispering the words to make sure he's not overheard.
"Thank you." Louis says, preening a little.
"So, once we're done here we can start work." Danny says, moving on quickly from the discomfort of actually being nice. That was probably for the best, Louis wasn't fully comfortable with it either. "We'll list everything we know about her. We'll go back through Alex's journals and case files. We'll take another look at all the 4XM murders we know about. We'll come up with a plan and we'll find her." He says, and when he laid it out like that it did seem a little comforting. But, Louis wasn't convinced they'd have that time.
"I think I'm more worried about her finding us..." He told him quietly.
"Danny, is anyone around?" Lauren called back to them, before the conversation could continue. They had stopped in front of an old rusty gate which led to an empty, overgrown and unkept field. The sky above it looked grey and miserable, and the field itself was filled with so many weeds and nettles and brambles; and even they looked like they were barely clinging on to life. Everything in his mind told Louis to look away, to keep walking, and that this wasn't a nice place. It's like it was being whispered into his ear to keep going and pay no attention to it. He could see the field beyond the gate but he knew with every fibre of his being that it wasn't a place he wanted to be and he had to fight every instinct he had to keep walking towards the old gate.
"Nope, nobody but us." Danny confirms, after doing a scan of the area on his smart-watch.
"Okay." Lauren says. She braces herself and takes a step forward, until she's right at the gate. She too feels the urge to just ignore it and move on, but she fights it. There's a small beep as she presses a hidden button on the gate. This opens a pad on the post, and she places her hand on it. It takes a fingerprint and a quick blood sample and pauses for a moment to

analyse it. There's another beep and now a light flashes, scanning the four of them and analysing them. Once it's satisfied, there's another beep and that feeling of "walk away" and "ignore" quickly fades. The gate, and the scene behind it, part straight down the middle and they're bathed in a warm glow of sunlight.

A huge gateway opens; revealing that the unwelcoming field was nothing but an illusion. Instead, the grounds beyond are beautifully green and vibrant, and the sun shines down upon a huge white, stone building right in the centre. It's a stark contrast; from uninviting and unwelcoming to a place that instantly makes you feel relaxed and welcome. The Home Base stands tall in the light and is surrounded by the richness of nature, hidden and untouched by the Human world, existing in a little bubble of protected perfection. It feels like home; and Louis can feel his fears about Hazel melting away as he catches a glance at future Custodians training in the distance. This was where he grew up, it's where he spent the first eighteen years of his life, and suddenly everything feels like it's going to be okay again.

There were around 70 Home Bases around the UK and a lot more around the world. Some were purely designed to act as an operational management facility, some were for UTB detainment, and others were just training facilities, Home Base 25, this one, was all three of those things. At that particular moment it will have housed a number of active Custodians, as well as preparing a large number of trainees of all different ages.

The group reached the building and, with a pneumatic hiss, the fifteen-foot-high double doors opened before them giving way to an enormous foyer. It was a huge, brilliant, white, airy, open space that was filled with activity. There were large marble pillars and a floor that was constantly impossibly shiny. As the four of them make their way through the lobby they're surrounded by others; by Level 3s and 4s who've taken up residence to use this as a base of operations, there are teens who're between lessons, and there are Cleaners. It's busy, but the constant activity doesn't feel overwhelming. The warmth of being back home and surrounded by their own kind brings a smile to each of their faces, though Amber and Danny try to conceal it.

A young girl, Sophie, is sitting behind a reception desk of sorts. She's a student. This was one of the many possible tasks on the extensive list of chores they needed to complete around the base. Lauren approaches her and she looks up.

"Hi, we're here to meet with…"
"You're Chris' second group, right?" She replies, with a bright smile.
"Yep. B-Team, reporting for duty." Amber says, with a mocking, sing-song brightness to it.
"Great, he's upstairs with the others right now. He left a message for you to meet him in the small library on the ground floor." Sophie tells them.
"Thank you," Lauren says with a polite smile.
"Do you remember the way?" Sophie asks, and Lauren nods. Of course she does. Louis does too. They head off through the crowd, and into one of the corridors that takes them deeper into the base.

"Where did it start?" Kim asked. They were sitting around her coffee table. She'd sat down on the floor, cross-legged, to get a little closer and had her thick rimmed glasses on her face. Wade stuck to the sofa because if he got down on the floor he wouldn't get back up again. It was much later in the morning now and it was clear they weren't getting anywhere fast.
"Well, they've been around a couple of years. Didn't pop up much. At most once every few months. They'd turn up, have a look at what we had, and usually disappear again. Sometimes they'd take over, but mostly they wouldn't. It's been the last few weeks they've been so interested in everything going on." He explained.
"What kind of cases?"
"It's never been anything straight forward. It is like they watch out for the weird ones and swoop in."
"But weird how?"
"I dunno. Like that old lady the other week. Found mauled by something in a cemetery. Poor old bird was a mess. They couldn't grab hold of that one quick enough." He said, realising he'd completely lost track of that with all the drama about Steven Robinson crawling out of his own grave. He couldn't even remember the old dear's name.
"I didn't see anything about that?" Kim said curiously.
"No, you wouldn't. It was the same day as that shitshow at the hospital, but the cases they take don't usually get that much attention. They just kind of disappear. That was one of the first things that drove me mad but, I dunno, it feels like I'm alone in that." He said, and even he could hear the bitterness in his tone. He let out a deep sigh. This was exhausting. This was all exhausting.

"What do you mean?" She asked him, tilting her head like some curious animal. He didn't know how much more straightforward he could be. No one else seemed to give a shit.

"First time they showed up and took one. I dunno if you remember, Andy Parkinson?" He asked, and she shook her head. That was exactly what he expected, but he'd known Andy. "I knew him from years back. He was running for Mayor. Looked like he was gonna get it, too, until his body turned up one day. It looked like a suicide but it just felt a bit off."

"Off how?"

"I don't know Kimmy." He snapped, accidentally. He was frustrated at the memory of it, not at her. He remembered knowing something was wrong about it but he'd been cut off at the knees. There was no way Andy would've just committed suicide like that. He knew that was the point of suicide sometimes, you never saw it coming with some people, but this felt different. This was different. "I never got chance to look into it properly before I had two of 'em on my case. Come to think of it, Tim was fuming about it at first. This was before his big promotion, so he was just one of the boys. Ever since then though, whenever they've come around, it's like he cares more about an easy life than the job." He sighs and leans back, staring at the pile of papers sadly.

"We're not getting anywhere here Kimmy." He said, feeling defeated. Just like he had when that investigation had been taken away from him.

"Oh will you stop it." She said, rolling her eyes and standing up.

"I know, it's just, the more we dig the more questions there are and the deeper this seems to go. I dunno if I've got the same fight in me that you have. I'm a little too long in the tooth for it." She ignores him completely, and goes over to the window to give her eyes a break from staring at bits of paper.

"No. We just need to start getting answers. Let's just take it one thing at a time." She says, coming back to the table like she's had a sudden brainwave. "Our way in. That's all we need." She grabs the folder on Steven Robinson. "Let's dig a little deeper into these weird cases they take on. This one feels like it was the key to it because it's the one we know the best. A dead man getting back up and murdering his wife. Where is he being held while he waits for trial?" She asks, and that makes him pause and furrow his brow.

"I dunno, actually." He sits forward and reaches out for the file. She hands it to him and he starts to flick through it. That should've been one of the

things in here but he's not sure he ever saw it. "It's not anywhere. I don't remember ever seeing it. That's weird."
"Okay," She says, moving on to a different idea. "So the wife had a brother didn't she? He was in the hospital. Any updates there?"
"Yeah, he was fine in the end. Released the next day, I believe."
"Has anyone spoken to him? Does he know anything? That sounds like a starting point. I'll start looking to see if that boy from the other day had any family. Anyone that can shed any light on this for us…" She asks, and he can't help but chuckle to himself. Maybe he is a little too long in the tooth, and a little too defeatist about this whole thing. He's a tired old policeman who's a little sick of being told no at every turn but Kim, well, she's a breath of fresh air and she's never been one to take no for an answer.
"I guess I'll go speak to the brother then…" He says, dragging himself up off the sofa.

Chapter Thirty-Six

"It's always a little strange coming back here, don't you think?" Lauren says to him as they lead the others through the corridors deep in the heart of Home Base. Amber and Danny are whispering together behind them, as Louis and Lauren wander through the corridor with wide-eyed looks of nostalgia that are almost a mirror image of each other.
"Yeah, it's weird, it's like I never left." He tells her, unable to believe how long it had actually been and how much had happened, and yet how little seemed to have changed here. It made sense, of course, Home Base existed in a perfect little bubble safe from the rest of the world. It was only Custodians that knew where it was, and it was only them that could access it, so it remained protected whilst everything else changed.
Lauren stops at the door to the library and scans her access card. It's linked to her so that only she can use it, and if anyone else ever tried it would be rejected. That was one of the many security measures in place to make sure the Base remained safe from anyone who wasn't a Custodian. They step inside and Louis is hit with another fresh wave of nostalgia. It's a huge room that looks tiny because it's so filled with shelves and shelves of books. Books of all different topics and ages; covering everything from all areas of human history. This was one of the smaller ones, there's a bigger one upstairs, and some of the libraries at the Home Bases further down south are legendary.

"Well, while we sit in Chris' waiting room we might as well make a start on finding this Hazel." Danny said, sitting himself down at a small table and pulling his laptop from his bag. He hadn't grown up here, so maybe he wasn't feeling quite as nostalgic as they were.

"I'm sure he won't keep us waiting long," Lauren offered, trying to reassure him. Louis smirked to himself; he didn't think Danny needed reassurance about that. He'd probably be a lot happier if Chris had forgotten about them. They all would, even if Lauren wasn't quite ready to admit that outloud.

"Why're we here anyway?" Amber asked her. It was a fair question, but mostly a rhetorical one, because Lauren had been given the same vague invite they had. Chris wanted to debrief about the 4XM incident. That wasn't particularly usual practice, and so Louis and Danny had suspected that it was some veiled excuse to chastise them for their handling of it, despite the overall positive results. "Has he organised some kind of celebration in his honour?" Amber offered. It was laced with sarcasm but, equally, it did seem like a realistic option.

"We're probably about to hear some grand speech about his single-handed capture of 4XM." Danny offered. That sounded even more likely.

"I heard the creature threw itself out of the window because it was so scared of Chris." Amber chimed in, building on the story.

"Face an eight story fall or death by boredom? I know which I'd pick." Danny added.

"Oh stop it both of you!" Lauren said, tutting like a disapproving parent. Amber and Danny exchanged smiles like naughty children. He'd noticed this quite a lot. The two of them would bounce off each other mischievously until Lauren stepped in, and he found himself wondering if it was something they planned in advance. If they got together to conspire about how to frustrate Lauren that day, and for a second he felt a little pang of jealousy at the idea of being left out of that. He certainly wasn't Chris' biggest fan either, and knew that would likely get worse, but he didn't necessarily want to deliberately annoy Lauren. She was the one who'd been kind to him from the beginning. Amber and Danny had gotten better; but there was still a long way to go. He supposed that was it. He wanted to feel included by them, but not necessarily in the activity of pushing Lauren's buttons. "I'm not sure why we're here either. I'm glad we are though. I'm feeling very nostalgic. I spent hours in this library pouring over some of these books." She runs her finger along the shelves. Amber raises

her eyebrow and pulls a mocking expression, which Lauren catches. "And how did you like to spend your time Amber?"
"Clubs." She says with a simple shrug. "Wrestling was a good one, because I kicked everyone's arse. I was a top competitor. I still remember the first time I broke someone's arm." She says proudly; and even Danny gives her a quizzical look at that. "What?" She asks, obliviously.
"I think we're just all glad you're on our side." Danny tells her.
"For now." She says with a smirk. "What about you, Newbie?" She asks, passing the attention over to him. Before he can answer, Danny jumps in. "No, let me guess. You spent more time in the bigger library upstairs. The one with all the sections on human history?" He asks, and Louis scowls, sucks his teeth, and considers whether to answer that honestly. Danny waggles his eyebrows at him because he knows he's right. "I knew it!" He laughs and Louis shakes his head. Amber gives the two of them a peculiar look.
"Yes. Reading and learning as much as I could. Demonic infections and the influence they've had throughout history. The way they exist just on the cusp,   but still playing a part, both on the events that've happened and just how they've become part of the culture over the years. So much fiction has been…" He stops as he looks at their expressions.
"We're very different people…" Amber tells him.
"Yeah, I noticed." He says, and quickly offers up a subject change "Where did you all end up, after you graduated?" Amber looks visibly uncomfortable about the question, and kind of grumbles an answer. Lauren spots her reaction and quickly jumps in to answer, which seems confusing because cutting someone else off was out of character for her.
"I should start. I think I graduated before all of you! I did two years down south, near Brighton to start."
"Wow, that's really far." Louis says, stating the absolute obvious.
"Yeah, I liked it there. You probably would too. After that I transferred here. The team was totally different then too. Completely different people." She told them, with a sweet smile as she thought about all the other team members she'd known over the years.
"Different like you preferred them?" Danny asked, feigning a look of hurt.
"Different personalities, that's all. You come from further down south too, don't you?"
"Yeah. There's a huge operations centre that covers all of London. It was much better organised there, so obviously they had me doing a lot more

tech support and a lot less field work." He closes his laptop, becoming more engrossed in the conversation. It's one of the first times Louis had seen him do that. Choose social interaction over burying his head in technology. "I led on loads of cases but, actually, I don't think I really saw a Used-to-Be until I arrived here. Not face-to-face anyway."
"I hadn't really. One or two. Which was your first...?" Lauren asks, and a smirk spreads across Danny's face at the memory.
"Do you remember the musician? He got electrocuted at his gig and..."
"Yes, and she nearly killed herself kicking him in the face?" Lauren finishes, with a chuckle as she points at Amber.
"That's the one!" Danny confirms,
"Think you'll find it worked." Amber grunts at them.
"It did. I still feel like there was a better way to get there, though..." Danny tells her. She shrugs in response, and Danny's brown eyes dart over to Louis inquisitively.
"So, what was it really like in that little village of yours?" He asks, and surprisingly there was no hint of mockery.
"It was honestly nice. Did you guys not feel a little bit lost when you first graduated? We spent like 18 years here, it was weird to just be kicked out into the big wide world. That little village though, it was a nice little community. It felt like a home. I said hi to the same people every morning, picked up shopping for one of my elderly neighbours, and made a few friends I could hang out with. I miss it."
"Doesn't the house with us feel like home?" Lauren asked.
"Not really." He answered, before he could stop himself. It was true but he still shuffled uncomfortably and avoided Danny's gaze, because he was part of the reason why.
"Was 4XM your first then?" Danny asked.
"No, actually."
"But I thought...?" Danny was getting that look he got when he didn't have the answer to something. A look that Louis already recognised; which really should've revealed he wasn't anywhere near as clever as he thought. He was confused because Louis had never filed a report during his time in Jongleton village and Danny had seen that within minutes of him arriving. That didn't mean he'd never seen a Used-to-Be in person though.
"Nothing happened in that little village, that's true. It was long before that. It was here, actually..."

265

"Here?" Danny asked;
"Yep." He said, with the sudden urge to draw this out because of the look on Danny's face. "So, obviously, this is where the Cleaners bring them after capture and…" He stops as Danny raises his eyebrows. This is clearly new information to him too. "Didn't you know that?" Louis asks. Danny scowls, and Louis feels brilliantly smug for a moment.

So back in Chapter Four, well done for sticking with me by the way, I explained how the Used-to-Bes came to exist. The traces of Demon that were left behind in the world that infected and twisted Humans. Humans like Joseph. We saw that, thanks to me seeing it when we captured him. But it was here, within these walls of Home Base, that I learned all about it. I don't even remember when I was first told it, it's just something I've always known. The story of the Demon being driven out of the world. At first it was just a story. Like how you tell your kids about Santa or the Easter Bunny – stories that might actually have demonic links by the way, but let's cover that later – I was told about the Demon and the Used-to-Bes. The difference though is when your kids see Santa it's just a man in a fake beard, if they're lucky, but the first time I saw a Used-to-Be there was nothing fake about it.

I actually looked up the field report a few years ago, out of curiosity and to see how much of it my memory had embellished.
3rd July. Subject 3KG, captured by Agent Evan Smith escaped custody in Home Base 25 and was recaptured by Agent Evan Smith.
It was deep in the corridors of Home Base because Louis, who was about eight years old at the time, was just looking for somewhere quiet and peaceful to read. He'd found a corridor that just led to a dead end, and he liked to come here to be away from everyone else because everywhere in the Base was constantly active. The libraries always had other students or real, fully grown, Custodians in them. The dormitories were full of noise. The grounds always had people engaging in some kind of fitness or combat training. This was the one place where no one else was. Just a silly, pointless little corridor that didn't go anywhere. That was all he wanted, just somewhere he could sit and lose himself in a book without anything distracting him. That's what the stupid little boy with messy brown hair thought he'd found. But, that peace wouldn't last long because his focus was broken by the sounds of clanking metal and thudding footsteps

as people hurried through a corridor nearby.

Young-Louis looks up from his book wondering what the strange sounds are as a group of figures burst around the corner.

It's really unusual to accompany the Cleaners back to the detainment facility. That's why Danny didn't even know it was here. Once the targets are handed over to the Cleaners that's our job done. But for some reason, Agent Evan Smith had decided to that day. It had been a particularly messy capture, from what I read, with several human casualties and so maybe he just wanted that added security. Whatever his reasoning, I'm very grateful for that decision.

He's the one who leads the group round the corner. He's tall and muscular, with dark skin and dark hair. He looks dishevelled and messy, and his clothes have holes that look like they were caused by a fire, but it's still very apparent he's in charge. He leads three Cleaners, and they all rush along with a medical stretcher with a Used-to-Be strapped to it. Their captive is starting to wake, as the drugs wear off, and is struggling against the restraints.

"Sedatives are wearing off, hurry." Evan orders; cool under the obvious time pressure. "Move." He orders as he looks down the corridor and spots the tiny, messy haired child in his way. Louis obeys instantly, pressing himself as flat as he can against the wall as the group rush towards the dead-end of the corridor. One of the Cleaners pushes a button on a remote in his hand and a set of lift doors appear and open. Young-Louis stares, wide-eyed.

"Wow!" He proclaims. But, as this happens, the Cleaner who opened the door gets a little too close to the Used-to-Be. 3KG grabs the Cleaner by the wrist, and there is sudden roar of fire as the Cleaner combusts. The remote is destroyed; and in turn the metal restraints holding the creature in place pop open and he is released.

"No!" Evan shouts. He was already in the lift and spins to meet the chaos. The Used-to-Be is still a little groggy, but is fast enough to grab another of the Cleaners as it gets up. That one catches fire too. Evan bellows for the remaining Cleaner to run as he tries to fight his way to the other side of the gurney. Young-Louis stands, transfixed. The Used-to-Be drops the immolated remains it's clutching and hurls a fireball at the last fleeing Cleaner. It hits them and they let out a screech. Then, the Used-to-Be turns it's attention to Louis who is frozen in place and staring wide-eyed. Evan dives towards the boy as the Used-to-Be stumbles forward. Evan is

able to generate a kind of protective bubble around the two of them just in time to prevent the Used-to-Be from reaching him. It hammers down on the bubble, generating more flames as it does, but doesn't manage to penetrate it. Young-Louis looks terrified, screaming and covering his face. Evan tries to reassure him whilst focussing his energy on maintaining their protection.
"It's okay. I've got this!" He tells him, trying to hide the strain in his voice. The hammering continues. For Louis it feels like this goes on forever. The thudding and the roaring, as he hides his face. The Used-to-Be isn't tiring, if anything it's getting stronger and more ferocious. Evan pushes harder to maintain his concentration against the onslaught, and just when he's beginning to reach the very edge of his capability a group of five figures appear at the end of the corridor. They open fire without blinking; 3KG, now sedated once again, drops limply to the floor. Evan finally lets go of his protective bubble and collapses too, exhausted from the effort.
"I'm fine, I'm fine. Let's get this thing downstairs." He tells the other Agents as they check on him. Louis, meanwhile, runs straight for the older looking man who had led the charge. The Agents pick up the unconscious Used-to-Be and place it back on the stretcher, and continue the journey towards the lift. A fresh batch of Cleaners round the corner too, and shoo them away so that they can get the work.
"Fear not, it's over now." Superior One tells Louis, lowering himself to the child's level and putting an arm around him. The being's face was unfathomably wrinkled and showed so many of his years. I never knew how old he actually was; but I knew his lifespan was a lot longer than that of an average human. The Seven Superior beings had always looked after the Custodians but there was never really a straight answer as to whether they were the same Seven, or whether the roles were inherited. I always knew that one and he always looked ancient. It wouldn't have surprised me if I found out he was as old as the world itself. But, despite looking as old as time, he had a strength to him. He looked old but he never looked frail. He always walked tall and spoke with authority. He was always in charge of every situation and no one ever had the inclination to question that. "Are you harmed?" He asked that child, so very long ago, with a kind smile and a soft tone. "You're very brave. This was your first encounter..." He told the boy, before shooting a look right past him to the lift doors as the Cleaners and the Used-to-Be disappear behind them. Once they're gone he turns his attention back to his young charge. "And it's not one you're likely to

forget are you?" The young Louis shakes his head and wipes away some tears. "Good, and nor should you. Remember this day Louis. Remember what you feel now and use it. Remember it'll one day be your job to protect people as Evan protected you today. Next time you face one of these creatures you'll be much better prepared, won't you?" He asks, and Louis nods. "Excellent. You'll be a wonderful Agent one day Louis, I just know it. Remember today and use that to focus you in your learning. Prepare yourself for the next time…"

"Ah, good, you're here." Chris says, interrupting Louis' story as he enters the library.
"Hi Chris," Lauren says, greeting him with a smile that the others don't copy. "The girl on reception told us to wai…"
"Follow me. The others are already upstairs. I've been waiting to start." He says, cutting her off impatiently. He turns, without another word, and leads them out of the room.

Chapter Thirty-Seven.

Wade hesitates before he knocks. He's got to play this very carefully. Being a policeman does come with a certain authority, everyone knows that, and it's usually an authority he can use quite well. The difference here is that he doesn't really have any authority because he isn't asking about any investigation he's officially involved in. Therefore, what he's doing is no better than Joe Public knocking on someone's door and claiming to be a policeman. He can't let on that he has no real authority here; and he certainly can't let it get back to anyone that he's been asking around about a case that he shouldn't have anything to do with any more. Still, none of that is going to stop him. He sighs and hammers on the door, a little harder than he means to. He waits and it's a little while until anything happens. He's at that point where he's about to pack it in and go back to Kim when the door slowly opens a crack and a man peers out at him. It's Cain, Cheryl Robinson's brother. He looks like a frightened animal, poised to flee.
"Mr. Hague? Detective Chief Inspector Wade, I'm not sure if you remember me from…" He tails off, deliberately, hoping it'll be obvious. Cain shakes his head.
"From when? I'm sorry, I don't remember you…" He says, still looking very cautious.

"From the night you were attacked." He says.
"Oh." He replies, his eyes wide with the realisation.
"Could I come in, I'd like to have a chat with you about that night?" Wade asks, hoping that if he can just get inside and get the man sat down he'll loosen up a bit. That idea quickly goes out of the window though.
"I'm sorry, no. And I won't be able to be any help." He says, which was more abrupt than Wade was expecting.
"It won't take long!" He says quickly, like a desperate door-to-door salesman. "I just need to follow up on a couple of things."
"It doesn't matter how long you say it'll take." Cain explains, with a sad laugh as he shakes his head and opens the door just an inch winder. "You can't come in, and I can't help you."
"Why not…if you don't mind me asking?" Wade asks, remembering he needs a softer approach.
"Haven't you already got the man who killed my sister?" He replies, straight to the point.
"Well, yes, but…" This is where it starts getting a little sticky and where he's probably going to have to dance around the truth.
"Then how can I be of any help?" Cain asks bluntly.
"Just need a couple of details from that night clarifying, if it's all the same to you." Wade snaps back at him. Probably not the best strategy, granted, but he's getting a little annoyed now. There's reluctant and then there's obstructive and this guy is leaning more towards the latter.
"Good luck. I don't remember anything!" Cain tells him finally and that stops Wade in his tracks. "Yep. Nothing." He says, clearly reading the look on his face. "There's a huge chunk of my memory missing. Days worth. So there you go, how do you propose I'll be any help? I don't remember anything from that day. Or from the day before. I don't remember being in the hospital. They said it's the trauma, or something else…but long story short I can't help you. I can't remember the last day I spent with my sister and my niece." He tells him, and the poor guy is on the verge of tears by the end of it. Wade's heart breaks for him a little bit. "Now is there anything else, detective?"
"No. No, I'm sorry…call into the station and ask for me if you remember anything?" He stutters, desperately.
"Whatever." He says, as he shuts the door abruptly. Well, there goes that lead then.

The meeting room is as bright and airy as the rest of the building; and there's a huge window displaying the beautiful green fields of the Home Base grounds. Chris, who has silently led the way through the halls and up to the second floor, strides straight to the front of the room and turns to face them. He indicates for them to take a seat. There are two rectangular tables set up; and Olivia, with her team members Rich, Noel, and Phil have already claimed one.

"Now that you're here we can make a start." He says. It's meant to sound warm and inviting but his tone is very forced, like he's saying it how he thinks he should say it. They all take a seat nonetheless.

"Nice to see you all again." Olivia says, trying to bridge the very obvious and very awkward gap between the two sides.

"Yes, you too." Lauren offers, silently elected as the spokesperson for their group. "Are we missing a couple of your people?" She asks curiously, but pleasantly.

"Oh, yeah. Brian and Josh. We were mid-way through a case, and I didn't want to tear them away from it." She explains. Danny mumbles something about wishing he could've used that excuse. Lauren gives him a nudge under the table. Lauren's gaze moves to Brian.

"How's the...?" She asks, gesturing to his shoulder. The shoulder that she helped to heal after he was hit by Joseph's sniper fire.

"Yeah, fully healed. Thanks again." He replies. Lauren will have known that already, but she'll have no doubt just wanted to double check. Chris clears his throat and gestures stiffly off to the side, where there's a selection of buffet food spread across a table.

"Please, help yourselves to something to eat." He says, with that forced tone once again.

"Fantastic, I'm starving." Amber cries, with way more enthusiasm than she's shown about anything to do with the day so far. She grabs herself a plate and goes in to inspect. "Oh, good selection." He stares at her. It's obvious to everyone, her included, that he didn't mean to get food immediately, but it's too late. It's also obvious that he's waiting for her to be done loading her plate before he starts. She knows that, but she's not at all phased by it.

"Please, start without me!" She says, waving him on with one hand and grabbing at sandwiches with the other.

"Erm...ok. So, I suppose I wanted to get you all together today for a bit of a well done, of sorts. The capture of 4XM was just a wonderful achievement and I'm very proud of what we achieved." He says stiffly, sounding like he's rehearsed it.

"Oh yeah, we all did a great job." Amber says, adding extra emphasis on the word 'we.' She finally returns to their table and loudly places her plate down with a thud, before proceeding to pull apart one of her sandwiches and take out the lettuce. "Not a fan of anything green." She explains to the room, who are all staring at her. "But sorry, I interrupted. Go on. We did well…" At this Lauren gives her a discreet kick under the table too. She's clearly been silently elected as peacekeeper of the group too.

"Lauren, you just kicked me." Amber cries, innocently.

"Oh…yeah, sorry. Accident." She says, genuinely looking embarrassed that it's been pointed out. Louis spots Olivia and Noel chuckling to themselves. This isn't subtle at all; and Amber knows exactly what she's doing.

"It's fine, don't worry about it pal." She says, waving it off and starting to chew on a chicken drumstick. Chris is visibly irritated by the disruption, but he continues.

"Yes, a great effort from everyone. It's unfortunate I wasn't able to fully play my part due to being injured in the field, but you executed my plan to the best of your ability and we were able to capture a high profile Used-to-Be responsible for a number of deaths. Well done. Our efforts have been highly praised all round." At this Amber coughs loudly and disruptively, and it was definitely done on purpose.

"Sorry…nearly choked." She says, with a grin.

"Yes, sure. Try not to be careful," Chris says, with a glare.

"So what's next?" Louis asks, cutting to it. He found himself asking this a little out of pity for Chris, but mostly because he genuinely wanted to know. They'd let Chris know all about Hazel - it didn't seem like there was any sense in keeping more secrets - so he was keen to know what he actually wanted to do to find and deal with that threat.

"Good question," He said, and Louis couldn't hear it any way other than condescendingly. "4XM has been captured and contained. He won't be a problem for us any more but it does seem there has been a spike in demonic activity in the region recently. Between us I'd like to come up with a plan of how your two teams will work together a little better to address that… "

"I meant, what about Hazel?" He asked; because that was what they needed to come up with a plan for.

"Ah. Yes, I read your summary of the incident that happened after 4XM's capture...I'm not sure there is too much to worry about with this Hazel, there's no conclusive evidence to suggest that..."

"Sorry, what?" This time it's Danny that interrupts. He's gone from smirking at Amber's antics to looking irritated very quickly.

"Well, Used-to-Bes...from what I've seen...they don't usually form social circles." Chris explains, looking uncomfortable at the challenge.

"Oh come on. They're animals. Animals are all about packs." Amber chimes in, through a mouthful of sandwich.

"Yes, yes, and still I'm going to look into it. But, whoever she was, I don't imagine she'll be bothering us again. Even if she and 4XM were working together she'd be foolish to openly attack us."

"Haven't you..." Louis begins. But he hesitates. He feels like his concerns are just being dismissed, and it feels like that's coming from arrogance on Chris' part. He knows that Hazel is a threat. He could tell just from that brief time with her; but it feels like because it's coming from him Chris isn't taking it seriously. He doesn't want to over step because he's scared it'll make things even worse, and his position here is far from stable after everything so far. But ultimately, he's too annoyed and too worried to not say it. "...you're just recovering from a Used-to-Be openly attacking us."

"Louis...that's..." Chris begins. He's flustered. For whatever reason he's trying to stay calm and just move past the whole Hazel thing, and pretend that Joseph's capture went perfectly. He doesn't quite know how to brush that one away. Olivia jumps in.

"Don't worry. I've been taking a look into it. We've got a case file open on her. Chris asked us to after the report you filed following the incident at the hotel when 4XM first popped up, and we've been working it through since. We've catalogued some of Agent Alex Smith's case files, the ones that we have clearance for obviously, and we're combing them for any mention of an associate. We've not seen anything so far, but we're all over it." She tells them.

"Yeah, exactly. If we find anything you guys will be the first to know." Noel adds, and Chris clears his throat. "After Chris, obviously." He clarifies. So that makes a little more sense. He's not totally trying to brush the thing with Hazel away; he just wants to keep Louis, Danny and the others away from this the same way he wanted to keep them away from the whole Joseph thing. That made no sense. They were the ones who'd found the pattern, who'd realised that Joseph was going after those three families and who'd been able to use that. Yes, it hadn't gone brilliantly. Yes, they still weren't sure how he'd worked out that Louis was using Meetr to lure him to that bar. But, it worked. They'd had far more success with this investigation than Olivia's team and yet, Amber was right, they were being treated like a B team.

"Good." Chris says, clearly very keen to move on.

"I just wanna say as well guys, the pattern that you found with 4XM and those families, I was really impressed. I've been staring at those journals for weeks and I didn't piece it together." Noel blurts out before he can stop himself. "Am I right in thinking that was you, Louis?" Louis blushes at that, and the compliment momentarily derails his frustration.

"Well, it was kinda a team effort, yeah." He says, a little sheepishly.

"I helped a lot." Amber adds boldly, still chewing.

"Can we help at all, with the investigation into Hazel? Surely we have access to the same resources you do." Louis asks, determined to just push a little bit more. They should be involved. From what she said they'll be the ones who are targeted and he wants to know all he can about her.

"Well, not any more." Chris says, desperate to take control of the conversation back before it gets any further into this topic. "Danny informs me he's destroyed the copies of Alex's journals that you did have. I also wouldn't make it widely known that you had them at all. I'm willing to turn a blind eye to this once, but it's absolutely not a practice I want to encourage." He says sternly. Danny catches Louis' eye, and when he's sure only he will see it, winks. Of course he hasn't destroyed the journals. That's something at least. It looks like they're once again going to continue investigating without Chris knowing. Louis never ever thought he'd be so liberally disobeying orders from his Level Four. He wouldn't have even dreamed about doing it two months ago. But, there are so many things different from two months ago. His life wasn't in danger, he wasn't surrounded by this team, and he didn't have a Level Four who was as annoying and distrustful of him as Chris. He wasn't sure which factor played the strongest role in his comfort with disobedience; but he knew they all complimented each other perfectly to get to this outcome.

"But, as I was saying, you all did well with 4XM." Chris continues, fully snatching back control of the conversation. "I do want to look to the future though, to our next successes, and perhaps look at a little more cross team collaboration. Since I took over from Rachel I've been thinking it would be good to get us all together and talk about what we want our objectives to be." He explains, going back to his overly rehearsed lines that Louis now realises are on notes in front of him. That at least explains the unnatural delivery. "I thought perhaps we could start with a game to get to know each other. It's something I've come up with called two truths and a lie."

"Ah, a game. How marvellous." Says a soft but warm and comforting voice from behind them all. Louis recognises it instantly; but their heads all whip around in excitement and it's like all the fear and frustration he was feeling melts away and is replaced by a sense of peace and calm. There, in the open doorway, stands the Superior One. He has his wrinkled hands clapped together and a bright smile on his face. He wears a perfectly white and gold suit, which almost glows, and matches the overall Home Base aesthetic. It's almost like he's part of the building himself. They all shuffle a little nervously in their chairs at the sight of him and Chris stammers at the unexpected interruption. The old man, or being, stands tall and beams at them; he looks simultaneously ancient and youthful and even though it made no sense it was just something they all accepted.

"I…I…didn't realise you'd be joining us, sir." Chris says, tripping over his words nervously.

"Oh I was simply passing and thought I would share in congratulating your teams on their recent capture. I wondered if I may have a moment alone with you, too, Louis?" Superior One asks. Louis' eyes widen and it takes a moment to realise he's not talking to someone else who's also called Louis and sitting directly behind him. He quickly looks behind him, just to double check. "Won't you join me for a walk?"

He nods silently and gets clumsily to his feet, and follows his mentor out of the room. Louis looks a little nervous and Chris stares after them with jealousy and contempt blazing in his eyes. Lauren, ever the peacemaker, tries to bring his attention back to the moment at hand.

"So, what's this game?" She asks.

"Oh. Yes." He says, returning to his notes."You tell three things about yourself, and the rest of the room has to guess which two are true and which is the lie. Who would like to go first?" He asks. Danny and Amber flash each other a look of disgust, silently communicating that they both hate the sounds of it but, as ever, are willing to exploit it to make things a little awkward.

"I will." Danny says, so eagerly that everyone else should've seen the next words coming. "I'm more intelligent than everyone else in the room, I absolutely hate being here, and my hair is blue." He says, running his hand through his short dark brown hair playfully. Amber bursts out laughing, Lauren shakes her head with a tut, and Chris' eyes narrow.

Chapter Thirty-Eight.

Kim had lost a certain amount of motivation once Matthew had left to go talk to the witness. She couldn't keep staring at the same bits of paper and the same images that she'd been looking over all morning and all night. It was all just blurring into the same big mess. She regretted not going with him, if only just to get away from the piles of nonsense they'd amassed on her table. That's why she'd called Marc. He had hours and hours of footage saved from the stories they'd covered together, and his youthful enthusiasm was a little infectious. He came straight over, bringing his laptop with him. His work experience placement had ended but that didn't stop him being keen to get involved, and he simply ate up the details she had to share with him.
"…in the background there." He said, pausing the footage they were looking through.
"Yep! Got 'em" She said. "I knew I'd seen them before." She's talking about the figures on screen. They're all wearing identical grey jumpsuits, they all have the same boring shaved head, and they all have a sickly pale look to them. They're the ones that these Counter Terrorism people called 'Cleaners.'
"They give me the creeps a little bit. Who are they?" Marc says, visibly intrigued. She can't help but agree. They all have the same weird dead behind the eyes look about them, and because of the face masks they wear that's the only bit of their face you can really see. That makes it even worse.
"Not sure yet but we'll work it out. I think whatever is being covered up they're the ones that're doing it." She confirms. That was another reason to invite him over; she'd gone down a bit of a rabbit hole about the cover up and realised that these people were involved too. She'd seen it for herself at Vanity Bar.
"This is mental Kim. This feels like proper spy-thriller style stuff." He says, with that exact youthful excitement that she invited him for. There's a knock at the door and he jumps, and looks at her with a little panic, as if he sort of expects it'll be the Cleaners here to silence them. She's mostly sure it's

not, so she gets up from the sofa and crosses the room to open the door. She's a little more relieved than she expected when it's just Wade.

"Kim." He says with a nod, and she stands aside to show him in. Well, more just gets out of his way, because he's already halfway through the door by the time she steps aside. He's clearly in a hurry to tell her how his chat went.

"So I spoke to the brother." He confirms.

"Great, anything useful?" She asks, scared that she already knows what he's going to say.

"No. He remembers absolutely nothing from that night, or from days before." He tells her, making his way over to the sofa. He stops, spotting Marc who still has his head buried in his laptop. She nods to tell him he's fine but doesn't bother to introduce the two of them.

"Another dead end then." She says, somehow not surprised.

"Yeah. Maybe I've listened to a couple too many of your conspiracy theories but this seems a bit too wrong. Days worth of amnesia from a stabbing and maybe a mild head wound. I'm no doctor but…"

"Spy thriller stuff!" Marc chimes in. "Memory erasure. It's gotta be."

"What?" Wade growls, and Kim smirks to herself. There's a little too much youthful enthusiasm to Marc's excitement and Wade is the perfect anthesis. She doesn't think she's seen Matthew show excitement over something in the entire time she's known him.

"Marc…" She says, trying to temper his eagerness.

"What? You're the one who said these people aren't actually…people! And that there's some mysterious "cleaning" crew that follow them around. Now someone who can't remember anything. Is memory erasure really that far-fetched?" He says, babbling a little but actually speaking some sense.

"I see your point." She admits. Wade doesn't look as convinced. "Whatever this is we're dealing with we probably need to expand our definition of far-fetched."

"I'm gonna need a lot more convincing before I get on board with that…You must be the work experience kid, though?" Wade says, extending a rough hand to the boy.

"Well, work placement. And not any more. But yeah, I'm Marc." He says, standing up to shake his hand.

"DCI Wade," is what the gruff older man gives in response. Not ready to be informal, then. Clearly it'll take Matthew a little time to warm up to her new apprentice. She's not quite sure when he became that, but she likes him,

and he's pretty good. Maybe, this is her little team. The eager apprentice, the no-nonsense detective, and the stubborn journalist. That sounds pretty good to her.
"Nice to meet you, sir." Marc coos, like an excitable bird. The sir will probably help with the warming up, she thinks.
"We're getting close. I can feel it. We've been back over some old footage. I knew our team were in it, but I wanted to see if these Cleaners were." She explains.
"And?" Wade asks.
"Always. Hotel. Hospital. Everywhere. Any case they've taken from you the Cleaners have been there. I just wish we could talk to one of them."
"Is that what's next?" Marc asks, but she shakes her head.
"Actually, I had another idea." She says, and they both snap to attention at that. "I want to speak to other people who knew the victims though and see what they know, and now, see if they have any memory gaps. I've reached out to Amelia Hamilton's mother for an interview, I'll see if she accepts. Same with Benjamin Bailey's   mother. Did you know those two were related?" She explains, smugly, betting that he doesn't.
"Who?" Wade asks, puzzled.
"Ben Bailey and Amelia Hamilton. Cousins."
"Is that relevant?" Marc asks.
"Well, it's a pattern between two murder victims." Wade confirms, thinking the same way she is.
"But, Amelia Hamilton and her husband were murdered by Steven Robinson, who was already in custody by the time Ben Bailey was killed?" Marc questions, naively.
"He was…but the more I think about it, the less sense that makes. Especially now that I know they were related. I don't think Stephen Robinson killed anyone except his wife." Wade says. Again, mirroring her thinking.
"Agreed. For whatever reason, they pinned the massacre at the hotel on him. I just wish we knew where he was being held."
"There's absolutely no record of him after that night. I made a call to the station on my way back."
"Very cloak and dagger!" Marc says with a grin.
"Ok. So we have numerous murder victims and now one disappearance."
"Two. Jasmine Robinson, his daughter. She's recorded as being killed that night too. Her uncle even believes it. But Louis told me that isn't the case.

The more we tug the more it's unravelling." Wade explains to them both. She can see he's warming to Marc a little. His excitement is even infectious for an old grump like Matthew Wade.

"We need to keep tugging then. Various murders, two disappearances, and one mysterious memory loss." She says. She knows they're close to at least some of this falling into place. It doesn't make any sense right now but they're on the cusp of finding something. They just need to keep going.

"Okay I'm going to need some more coffee."

"I'll make it," Marc says, practically jumping to the kitchen. Bless him, he's very happy to be involved.

"Oh god, no. I'm going to go and buy some. I could do with some air anyway. Anyone want one?" She says. She needs a break; it'll help her process everything. Marc asks for a latte and Wade shrugs off the offer politely, but she decides she'll just get him one anyway. She grabs her keys, has a quick check in the mirror to make sure she looks presentable, and leaves them to it. Wade will either love or hate Marc by the time she's back, and she's honestly not prepared to bet on which.

Chapter Thirty-Nine.

The second floor of Home Base seems ridiculously quiet, and it makes Louis' footsteps feel even clunkier and out of place as they echo through the corridor. The Superior One, in contrast, seems to glide along effortlessly and silently, and that just seems to represent the two of them perfectly. Louis is loud and clumsy, and Superior One is effortless and graceful.

"Wha…what did you want to speak to me about?" Louis asks, after summoning up the courage to break the silence. Instead of answering immediately Superior One pauses at a large window. The Base is so airy, and open, and filled with windows to look out onto the beautiful grounds that surround it. He thoughtfully watches the group of children who are training out in the sunny fields.

"The next generation. That class is due to be imbued with their powers tonight." He explains, answering a question that's different to the one Louis actually asked.

"I don't remember how it happens." Louis says, realising himself that he doesn't have that particular memory. The children outside are young, around the same age he was when he saw that Used-to-Be. He has memories from that age. He remembers a time without any kind of powers and that he was given them at some point. But, he doesn't remember how that happened or even really when. It's like there's a bit of a gap and he'd not realised before. The Superior One flashes him a warm smile. That trademark comforting smile that every one of them has come to know so well. "Well, it was a very long time ago for you." He explains, before gesturing to a door at the end of the corridor and smoothly moving towards it and entering.

Once they're through the door Louis realises that the room is the Superior One's living quarters. Although he does regularly travel around the continent, Home Base 25 is one of the biggest in the country, so he will often stay here for weeks at a time. There's a large marble table and chairs, framed by another huge window. There's an imposing stone bookcase, which is filled with many ancient books, and next to that bookcase there is a curtained doorway that leads to the sleeping quarters. Upon the desk there is an open case that is filled with vials filled with a luminous white liquid. The Superior One smoothly but swiftly moves to it and closes it, before placing it back in a cabinet.

"My apologies. I was preparing those for the ceremony this afternoon and neglected to clear them away." He explains, and then sits down at his desk, inviting Louis to do the same. The silence hangs. It's not uncomfortable, though it is a little awkward because Louis doesn't really know why he's there. Finally, the other man speaks again, "I sense, perhaps, you would like the opportunity to talk. Chris tells me you're settling in well with your new team..."

"I'm not so sure, sir." Louis says, interrupting without really meaning to. Superior One raises his eyebrows inquisitively.

"Oh? I'm right in thinking you aided in the capture of a high-profile target, am I not?"

"I did." Louis confirms. There's no chance he'll be able to keep anything from this man, this man who has been present in his life since he was a child, but that doesn't stop him from keeping the answer brief and hoping that's the end of it. He knows he's not exactly been the ideal agent, collaborating with Danny behind his Level Four's back. It felt like it was the only way but despite the overall positive result he's scared to mention his rule breaking. He's worried about disappointing the closest person he's ever had to a parent. That's not the only thing on his mind either. He got very, very lucky with Joseph. It was that luck, more than any kind of talent or control over his powers, that saved his and Danny's lives.

"And yet, you're troubled?" Superior One asks, staring a hole through him. Louis tries his best to avoid both his gaze, and giving an answer.

"I'm okay." He replies, and it's an answer that would convince no one.

"Louis, my child, share with me. Please." He says, doing his best to coax the answer out of him. Louis sighs. Somewhere in the last few minutes he's realised how much there is on his mind. There's something about being here, where life was so much simpler, that has made him realise how complicated and hard everything is now. Chris' unwillingness to listen, Hazel and her threats, and above all else his powers and his own feeling of inadequacy and inexperience. It's all just swimming around in his head in a big tangled ball and he can't see a way through any of it.

"I don't remember what it was like receiving these powers but I remember what it was like to be their age. It was so different." He says, trying to start to express all the thoughts running around in his head. The Superior One listens, tilting his head ever so slightly. "Being back here is a reminder I suppose, of what I'm supposed to be. Not that I could ever forget, but..." He trails off.

"And what are you meant to be?"

"A protector. A..." He pauses again. The idea of that seems too far removed from where he's actually at. "We captured 4XM, barely and way too late, and now I'm scared that we've made things worse in the end anyway."

"Ah, yes this mysterious 'Hazel.' Chris mentioned another creature had been sighted."

"Yes. Chris seems to think..." He begins, but he's not sure he should continue that thought. He's not sure directly criticising Chris' decisions will lead anywhere good. But it's too late, because he's already picked up on it.

"Go on, please." The man opposite asks, encouragingly with that warm and welcoming smile making another experience to help coax the answer out of him.

"Well Chris doesn't think it's anything to worry about, but he wasn't there. He says we won't see her again but I know we will. She meant her threats. I could feel it."

"Ah yes, your ability to feel the emotion of the Used-to-Bes. A powerful tool indeed."

"I'm not so sure." He admits, and just like that they've accidentally landed on the real issue here, the part Louise wanted to avoid.

"What gives you cause for doubt?" Superior One asks him and Louis realises that somehow, he already knows. Whether through Chris or through something else, this man already knew about his fears.

"When I was fighting with 4XM…it nearly went very differently. It's happened a few times, but I could see images of him and his past in my head and it was overwhelming. I nearly couldn't fight back because of his pain. I nearly died because I couldn't control whatever this power is that I have. I'm just so scared that I can't control this, and that it's going to do more harm than good. I see the others around me…" He pauses again. He sees how much better the others are. Amber with her strength, Lauren with her healing, and Danny with his control over technology. They all make it so effortless; and yet he's just there getting headaches and being overwhelmed by flashes of images in his mind.

"You see how their gifts have manifested differently, and you're, dare I say it, a little envious of your brothers and sisters?" The Superior One says; taking exactly how he feels but phrasing it that little bit better.

"I guess. Yes. Strength, and healing, and everything else…seems a bit more useful than headaches." He says, hearing the teasing he's received from Amber and Danny coming out of his own mouth. Superior One leans back in his chair and takes a moment to consider this.

"I'm a firm believer that all my children receive the gifts they can make the best use of." He says, at last.

"I just…don't know if I can do it. I don't know if I'm at the same level as everyone else. When I was young it seemed like it would be so much easier. I thought I'd go out into the world and it'd all make sense. But I feel like I'm in over my head. The others all know exactly what they're doing and I don't even understand what it is I can do." He says, looking down at the floor rather than at the being who gave him these powers. He feels like he's letting him down, too.

"You are not the first to sit before me and express that feeling. Louis. Later today I shall lead the ceremony to imbue those children with their powers, and they will gain the same burden of responsibility that you feel. Or, some of them will. The sad reality is that not all are cut out for this life, for this path, and for some of those children their journey will end today. Fate will decide who will become one of our Custodians and who will not. If you were not able to shoulder this burden then your journey would've ended many years ago. You must believe in yourself, as I believe in you." He says; and now Louis feels even more embarrassed. He can feel his cheeks turning red. "I am very old. I have seen many, many things. Above all, I have come to believe that you are rarely given that which you can't handle. You, Chris, and the others will find your way through this next threat. Speaking of, I should really leave you to go back to your team. I'd hate to take any more time away from whatever Chris has planned..." He stands, suddenly, and it's obvious the conversation is over. Before Louis can even process it he has stood up too, and he's being ushered towards the door. It's very abrupt and leaves his head spinning a little.

"Thank you, sir." He's able to say, before he's stepping back out into the corridor and the door is being closed behind him. He wanders back to the meeting room slowly, trying to make sense of exactly what had just been said to him and to take as much time as possible. There was encouragement in those words, but it didn't get him any closer to knowing how to control it. He knew that he had to work it out though, and now that he'd properly spoken his insecurities out loud he was determined to find a way to get his shit together, to control his weird abilities, and to be a useful member of the team. He was the one who'd worked out Joseph's plan; and he could also be the one to help stop Hazel before she enacted whatever revenge she had planned. But first, he had to get back to this tedious meeting of Chris'.

Chapter Forty.

Of course she travelled the extra ten minutes to her favourite coffee shop. She likes what she likes, and this one gets it just right. It's strong but smooth. It doesn't hurt that, occasionally, there's a rather attractive barista working there too. He also looks like he's strong but smooth. She's already ordered from him, and given him her best flirty smile when he remembered her name. Now she's standing waiting for her order as she scrolls through her social media feeds on her phone, giving him a quick glance every now and again.

That is precisely when the trip suddenly becomes very worthwhile, no just for the excuse to flirt with Nathan, but because Detective Superintendent Tim Copper is standing in the queue ready to order. She mulls it over for a moment, considering whether it would cause more trouble than it's worth, but she decides to approach him because in reality she can never pass up an opportunity to cause trouble or to push for more details. It just wouldn't feel right.

"Hi." She says to him, simply, and takes great pleasure in the confused look she knew she'd cause. It puts him on the back foot straight away. It's always a slightly uncomfortable start to a conversation when someone clearly remembers you, and you don't recognise them. "I'm not sure if you remember me? Kim Adams, SBC News." She explains, and she sees his face quite obviously change at that as it dawns on him. It's beautiful to see his expression change, and very telling.

"Of course, Ms. Adams." He says, politely but with a grimace.

"Good. I'm really curious about something, I was hoping you could help…"

"I'm not entirely sure that…" He begins, but she cuts him off.

"As you're aware I reported on the killings at the Eagle Hotel."

"I believe that case is closed, perhaps I can refer you to my briefing from a few weeks ago…" He says, trying to fob her off. He really shouldn't have expected that to work.

"Yes, I saw that. Very well done, great air of authority. You'd be a great politician." She says, intentionally slipping in a back-handed compliment because, again, she can't help herself. "My question is more around the murderer though. Steven Robinson. Where's he being held?"

"I…" He says, and he's visibly flustered. That's her intention. She doesn't expect him to answer her questions deliberately but if she's clever, and she likes to think she is, he'll give something away. "Ms. Adams I feel it might be best if I referred you to the proper channels for press enquiries…" He says, gathering himself.

"Sure. Will do. But can you at least tell me when his trial is?" She asks, pushing further. His phone rings suddenly, and he's not quite quick enough to hide the relief on his face. Damn, she thinks.

"I'm sorry, I really need to take this." He explains, with a smile.

"Saved by the bell?" She says, cheerily.

"Quite." He mutters, before leaving the queue and heading to the door.

"Hello. Yes, just give me a moment…" He explains to the caller, and then he's out of earshot. She rattled him, at least, and that's something. Men with nothing to hide don't get rattled.

"Vanilla Latte with coconut milk and two regular lattes, for Kim?" Nathan calls out and she turns to him, trots back to the counter, and grabs the coffees with a quick wink.

"Thanks babe." She says, before following Copper out of the door. Naturally he's completely out of sight. She didn't expect she'd be able to eavesdrop, but it was worth a look. Instead though, she spots something else quite curious. She looks across the street to Vanity Bar, and then, biting her lip, wanders over for a closer look. The window that was shot through has been replaced. She takes a look inside, and it's open for business as normal and filled with customers. She opens her phone and googles it, searching for any news coverage of the shooting and there's absolutely nothing. That makes absolutely no sense. A shooting in broad daylight in the middle of the town centre, a bar damaged, and it's like nothing happened. So, she decided to go in and ask a few questions.

Chapter Forty-One.

In the meeting room at Home Base 25 Chris' session is in full swing. He's mixed the two teams up . Amber, Brian, Olivia and Rich occupy one table, whilst Lauren, Danny and Noel occupy another.
Chris has given them whiteboards and a task to talk through. List everything they think is important for teamwork. On one table Brian, Olivia and Rich seem to be scribbling down a lot of answers; whilst Amber leans back in her chair, working her way through a second plate of food.
As Louis enters the room, Chris abruptly directs him to join the other team where Lauren has taken charge of writing their answers down.
"Yes, I like that one." She says, praising Noel for an answer he's just given.
"Oh, good, you're back. We're looking for the essentials of teamwork." She explains as Louis joins them at the table. Noel reaches out to offer an enthusiastic handshake.
"Hey. I realised I've not introduced myself. I'm Noel. You're Louis, right?" He says with a smile.
"Oh. Yeah. Hi." Louis says, returning the smile.
"Good to meet you properly. Just want to say again I was really impressed with what you did with 4XM. We'd been pouring over it for weeks and couldn't find a pattern. And that capture…well done!"
"Thanks." Louis says with a nervous, slightly embarrassed, laugh. Noel is a welcome breath of fresh air and seems genuinely excited to talk to him.
"It's because he listened to me." Danny interjects with a sigh. "You should put that one down. Listening to Danny."
"Maybe just listening to each other…" Noel offers politely.

"Yes. Agree." Lauren says, scribbling it down.
"Why?" Danny asks. He feigns confusion and Louis laughs to himself about it. He then panics a little because he's starting to find Danny funny, and that doesn't feel like it leads to anything good.
"Because…we're talking about how to effectively work together as a team." Lauren explains, because she can't quite tell that he understands exactly what he's doing. Danny shrugs it off and Louis catches his eye.
"Not been listening to the task?" He jokes. .
"Why do you suddenly think you're funny?" Danny bites back. .
"Can you think of anything else Louis? It looks like the other team has loads…" Noel asks. Danny huffs and rolls his eyes. He clearly thinks the task is stupid and is frustrated with the other group for taking it seriously.
"Of course they have…" He mutters, and Louis knows he needs to jump in with an answer before Danny insults Noel's whole team.
"Umm…supporting each other?" He blurts.
"That's a good one!" Noel says, and Lauren writes it down.
"Encouraging each other, too." She adds.
"Okay, that's your five minutes done. Let's feed back what we've got. Team one, let's start with you." Chris says, towering over them like a teacher at the front of the room.
"We got a few, we got accountabil…" Olivia begins, reading from their list. She's interrupted by a loud ping from Danny's phone. Everyone glares at him.
"Oh! That's an alert from my facial recognition software." He says, with uncharacteristic excitement.,
"Thank God. What is it? Something we need to look into right now?" Amber says, putting her plate down.
"Hang on, let me check it." He says, and, Danny being Danny doesn't miss out on an opportunity to multitask by belittling someone as he does something clever. He looks over at Noel and gives a very pointed explanation for what he's doing. "I set up some facial recognition software linked to the database of all known active Used-to-Bes. That way if any from an active case enter the area I know about it instantly. Pretty clever right?"
"Okay?" Noel says, confused at getting an answer to a question he didn't ask.

"Thanks." Danny says, not listening to his reply but assuming it was one of praise. "Amber, I've identified a link to one of your old ones." He explains, looking at his phone screen with a little confusion.

"What?" She says, screwing up her face. He nods and gets up to walk to the front of the room, where Chris is standing. He nudges him out of the way so that he can turn on the screen on the wall. He connects his phone to it so that they mirror each other, and he can show everyone the image. It's a grainy image from a CCTV camera by the river. It shows a large, muscular man who looks to be in his early 40s. He has a large ugly looking scar over the right side of his bald head.

"Look familiar?" Danny asks her. Her eyes widen and her jaw drops, and there's a moment of scary silence before she answers where all the colour drains from her face.

"What the fuck?" She says in a whisper.

"I'll take that as a yes…?" Danny says, a little taken aback.

"Fuck, fuck." Her chair scrapes as she gets to her feet and marches for the door. "No. I'm out of here." She says as she reaches it and, with that, she's gone.

"Amber!" Chris shouts after her, looking like he's about to malfunction.

"That was…" Danny says, not really sure what that was. None of them are.

"Chris, one of us should…?" Lauren says, and she sounds worried. Her and Chris exchange a look that's difficult to read, a look that carries a lot that's unsaid.

"Danny, send me over the reference for that case immediately." Chris orders, following a brief moment of silent communication, and for once Danny agrees with no argument or snark.

"I'll meet you both back at the car!" Lauren blurts out as she too disappears out of the door, giving chase to Amber with a manic urgency.

"I think perhaps sadly, we should probably cut this short…it looks like there's something a little more pressing…I'll reschedule our meeting." Chris explains to the others; once again scrambling to regain control. He too looks a little shaken.

"Well, that's terrible news. Louis, shall we…?" Danny asks, glaring at him and willing him to move right that second.

"Actually, if it's okay I'd just like a minute with you Louis?" Chris says.

"Sure?" He replies, knowing he doesn't have a choice,

"Also, Olivia, perhaps this case provides a good opportunity to build a few bridges between the two teams – it'll make sure the objective of this isn't completely lost." Chris adds, nodding to her.
"Yeah, that sounds like a great idea." She replies calmly, and stands.
"I'm in!" Noel blurts out.
"Ok. I don't think it needs all of us though; how about we take Rich and Phil home and then join you at your place?" She says. Danny wanders out of the room without responding. He's either decided to ignore the question because he hopes that ignoring them will make them go away, or he got bored and wanted to go after Amber, or a mixture of both. Louis answers on their behalf.
"Yes, ok. That's a good idea. I'll let the others know you're joining us." He says.
"Great, we'll see you there soon. C'mon guys." Olivia replies, and with that her team all get up and follow her out of the room efficiently. That just leaves him and Chris, unfortunately, alone.
"I...wanted to apologise." Chris says, and Louis can't hide shock at that.
"It seems you and I are not starting off on the best of terms. I perhaps have not given you the best first impression."
"I agree. I mean, yes, not the best start." He says, because his mouth started before his brain engaged. He does a good enough job of rescuing it though because Chris seems placated and nods in response.
"Well, it's been a very unusual time for all of us. It's been unsettling. I'm still trying to find my feet as the Level 4 for this area. I'm sure you and I can work well together and I'd hate for you to do anything to...disrupt that."
"What do you mean?" Louis asks.
"I mean your private conversation with our Superior One. I'd hate for you to have done anything to undermine me."
"What? No, it wasn't like that..." Louis stammers out.
"Hmm. Well. I guess what I'm trying to say is that you and I can work well together. You're obviously passionate, if a little rough around the edges. I can teach you a lot." Chris says, in a low and almost threatening tone. His face is blank and stony.
"Thank you?" Louis says, really confused about what this conversation is and where it's heading. It doesn't really feel like an apology.
"You're welcome. I can help you with all of that. But you have to follow my lead. No more running off and starting your own investigations, no more

challenging my decisions, especially not in front of everyone, and no more trying to go behind my back."

"No, honestly, it wasn't that it was…" He scrambles, trying to explain that it's not what Chris has assumed.

"I could make things incredibly difficult for you Louis. Please don't make me do that. I'm a few years older than you, and far more experienced, so I understand your enthusiasm but I know best. Got it?"

"Yeah. Okay." Louis mutters. He's confused by the whole thing; but he's especially left reeling at how this started with an apology from Chris and has ended up as a threat.

"Good. Then I'm sure we can have a much better working relationship going forward, yeah? I'd like you to take ownership of updating me on this old case of Amber's. I'm going to refamiliarise myself with it now, but you should get back home, find out the background, come up with a plan and then you and I can discuss it before you do anything. Got it?" He instructs.

"Absolutely." Louis agrees, just wanting nothing more than to get out of there as soon as possible because he's confused and uncomfortable.

"Wonderful. I'll leave you to get on with it then." Chris says , and walks past him and out of the room in a clear display that their conversation is over. He genuinely looks happy; like he feels better for getting all that off his chest, and leaves Louis standing there baffled and a little annoyed.

Chapter Forty-Two.

Kim rushes back into her apartment excitedly and is met by a weird awkward silence. The coffees went cold, so she binned them. Well, no, she drank hers and binned the other two. It doesn't matter though because what she's brought is even better. Marc and Wade are sat at almost opposite ends of the room, going about completely different tasks. Wade settled on disliking him then.

"I've just been to Vanity." She tells them.

"What?" Wade asks, with a touch of confusion. It's fine. He'll catch up soon.

"The bar! Fixed window, no damage, and no one has a clue about any shooting. There was nothing in the news, either. It's like it never happened."

"Another cover up?" Marc asks, catching on first and mirroring her excitement.

"It must be! C'mon, a shooting in the middle of town and there's nothing in the news?" She says, and Wade lets out a low groan.
"I don't like this." He says, simply, and shakes his head. He looks really tired, and she can't blame him, they've been at this all day now.
"This is definitely a cover up." Marc adds. "I was surprised when you told me about it; I'd not heard anything about a shooting but I thought I'd just missed it."
"How do you even contain something like that?" Kim asked, which was the question she'd been asking herself all the way home. "Oh, and, I bumped into your boss!" She says, directing it at Wade. He narrows his eyes and shakes his head. He's well versed in what her 'bumping into' someone means.
"And?" He asks, cautiously.
"Well, I asked him about Steven Robinson, where he's being held, court dates, and he didn't have anything to say for himself. Clearly a little rattled too. He knows way more than he's letting on."
"Kimmy, you shouldn't have done that." He tells her, the policeman slipping back into his voice all of a sudden.
"I thought you wanted answers?" She says, sitting herself down next to Marc at the kitchen counter.
"I do, but...forget it." He says, with a heavy sigh, and stands up. "I need to be going. I feel like we're hitting a wall here anyway."
"What? No. We're getting somewhere!" She argues, hoping she's not about to have to deal with him getting cold feet again. She absolutely does not regret cornering Tim Copper.
"I don't think a bar having a window replaced is answering many of our questions. But, the Mrs. will be expecting me home anyway." He says. She knows it's not just that, but she knows there's no arguing with him either. She rolls her eyes at him and he heads towards the door. "How about I meet you at Jan's tomorrow morning before work?" He asks, and that's the best she's going to get from him right now.
"Okay, deal." She agrees, and with a quick nod of acknowledgement to Marc, he leaves. They can carry on without him, she decides. The plucky reporter and her eager apprentice. What a team.

Earlier that morning, around the time Wade was arriving at Kim's apartment and long before the team got to Home Base there were two more people meeting. The sun was just coming up, and this was exactly where the CCTV image Danny was alerted to was taken. It's a quiet path, down next to the river and just at the cusp of an old, run down, industrial estate. The two men are standing together, leaning on the railings, and staring out at the water. One of them, Andy, is a weedy, thin, but well dressed human. The other towers over him. He's a tall, wide, muscular man who looks like he's in his mid-40s. His name is Brick, and he is the one that the facial recognition software picked up. He has a large, deep, ugly scar over the back of his bald head. It looks fresh but old all at the same time. It's as if it healed when his body wasn't sure it should and it's been left a deep purple colour. He and Andy share a quiet familiarity as they look out at the river. They've spent a lot of time together in many different places just like this.

"It's all here and accounted for. I've got the guys packaging it up now, it'll be ready to go by the time the driver gets here." Andy tells him, finally breaking the comfortable silence between them.

"Good." Says Brick. He's still deep in thought, like he's only really half there.

"Brick...?" Andy asks him, a little timidly.

"What's up?" He asks, dropping fully back into the conversation and away from his own thoughts.

"I know it's probably none of my business but..."

"Why're we branching out into this shitty town?" Brick says, finishing his friend's thought with a chuckle. It's a fair question, he knows. He'd be wondering the same if the situation was reversed.

"Well...yes." Andy confirms.

"Ha. Always lookin' out for me. That's why I like having you around. There's definitely money to be made, don't you worry." He says, patting his associate on the back so hard he stumbles a little.

"That's good. We barely got anything out of that last delivery and, well, it's not that I mind it's just..." Brick laughs and puts a massive arm around him, it's both warm and threatening at the same time.

"Don't worry. There's plenty of people here looking for their next fix. I've got dealers lined up. I'll make sure you're looked after, I always do. Now go on, get yourself back to it. I'm sure there's a million and one things on that clipboard of yours to tick off." He tells him with another chuckle.

"Yes, of course." He says. He's about to scurry off obediently, but he pauses, hoping he's not about to push his luck too far. "But Brick...?"

"Yeah?"

"It's not just the money this time, is it? There's something else isn't there? I just need to know if there's anything I need to be ready for." He asks, practically in a whisper. Brick smiles. A gesture that, again, appears both reassuring and also terrifying.

"I am expecting a few old friends will drop by, yeah." He says. There's no chuckle this time.

"Your old friends are…" He asks, digging that little more.

"I get it Andy. It's your job to worry. I pay you very well to worry so that I don't have to. I'll just say be ready for anything. Now go on…" He tells him. Andy nods, knowing he's pushed his luck as far as he can, and got as much information he'll receive as Brick is willing to share. He walks away and back to work. Brick pulls out his phone and opens the web browser. There's an open page on his screen already; and it's a news report from the night of the attack at the hospital when Steven Robinson was captured. It's paused on an article from Kim Adams who is standing in front of Endsbrough hospital. In the background, though, Amber and Louis can be seen clearly.

Part VI: How I Used-To-Be

Chapter Forty-Three.

Under the cover of dusk a truck cautiously pulls into an old, rundown, and seemingly empty warehouse. The only light when it pulls inside comes from the truck's headlights and the illumination they bring doesn't exactly convince the drivers they're in the right place, because everything they see is an abandoned mess. The two men, George and Terry, climb out and leave the engine running. They're both heavy set and balding men who's years have obviously not been kind to them.
"It's us." Terry grunts into the darkness, hoping there's someone to hear him.
"'Ello? Anyone?" George tries, as they continue to be met with no sound except the humming of their engine. There's still nothing and they look over at each other cautiously. "This even the right place?" George asks.
"I thought so but maybe Sat Nav got it wrong" Terry answers with a shrug, as he turns back to the van. The lights in the warehouse suddenly come to life and show they're now surrounded. It's crowded, filled with boxes, shipping containers, and armed men who've snuck up on them in the dark. Terry and George both put their hands up, wide-eyed and like a couple of scared looking pigs. Andy, the weedy man in the suit from earlier that day, pushes his way through the crowd and Terry, then George, relax at the sight of him.
"How was the drive?" He asks, though it's very clear from his tone he's not at all interested.
"Yeah it was alright." Terry tells him. "Nice and quiet."
"Great." He says, and moves on swiftly now that the pleasantries are out of the way. "The lads will get you stocked up. You know where you're going." He says, looking down at the clipboard in his hand. In the background a few of the men have started to grab some boxes and load them into the back of the truck. George scurries around to open it for them.
"'Course they do," comes a thundering voice and Brick comes into view. There's a tiny shift in the room as everyone becomes a little more tense. He towers over the other men and is so much more intimidating, even though he's not armed. His large ugly scar is very visible under the bright warehouse lighting, but everyone does their best to avert their gaze from it.
"Old pro at this aren't ya Tez?" He says, with a nod towards Terry.
"Yeah of course. We got this Brick." He blurts out. There's a tremble in voice, even though he tries to hide it. Brick smiles and walks over to him.

He throws an arm around him. For most people this would be a friendly gesture, but there's a not-so-subtle threat here. Terry is a tall and wide man, but he looks tiny next to the muscular, towering frame of Brick. He stands at over seven feet tall and his chest seems like it's wider than the front of the truck they arrived in.

"See Andy. Told ya. It's all good." Brick continues, pulling Terry in close. "Andy were worried, ya see." He explains as Andy pushes his glasses up and disengages from this interaction. He's seen hundreds of men like this. He's more concerned with making sure they get the right amount of boxes to shift. He knows exactly how Brick is about to 'set expectations,' because he's seen his boss do it a hundred times before. "And this guy looks like he knows the score." Brick says, pointing to George who's still standing at the back of the truck, seemingly in awe of the man mountain before him. "A good one ey? Not like the guy you were working with last time. What was his name again?" He asks with a friendly chuckle.

"Ethan...his name was Ethan." Terry stutters.

"That was the one." Brick says, with a nod over to Andy. "You remember Ethan. The small mouthy one?" He asks.

"I do." Andy replies, coldly, uninterested but playing his part.

"And what did he do again Terry boy?" Brick asks.

"He...stole from you." Terry answers, dipping his head.

"That was it. And what happened next?" Brick asks, as if he can't remember himself.

"You...smashed his skull." Terry says, seemingly as quietly as he possibly can.

"I did! Caved it right in. I remember feelin' his brains on my knuckles." Brick laughs, and his laughter seems to ring out through the warehouse. It's a sound that sends a chill down the spine of every man in there. He points at George. "So I assume you trust this one?" He asks, no longer laughing. George's eyes widen in terror and once again he has that scared little pig look.

"Yes. Yes. He's my brother-in-law." Terry says, trying to reassure Brick.

"Smart." Brick replies, finally removing his arm from around Terry and giving him a little space. "Stick to the family. You know what the good news is though Terry?"

"Wh...what?" He stammers.

"If he fucks up, you won't need to explain to your sister...sorry, that was rude...I assume it's your sister?" Brick asks, and Terry nods. "Good. You

won't need to explain to your sister why he's disappeared. Do you know why?" He says, with a wicked smile and his gaze fixed on George.
"He...he won't fuck it up...I promise." Terry utters, meekly.
"Still. Speakin' hypothetically. Do you know why you won't need to tell her she's a widow?" Brick asks again.
"W...w...why?" Terry asks, and honestly, he looks like he'd like nothing more than to just curl into a ball right there.
"'Cause I'll rip your fucking jaw off and beat you to death with it if there's a single fucking gram of my stock missing. Got it?" Brick says, and his tone is no longer jovial. He looks like a bear ready to rip his prey apart.
"Yes, of course Brick." Terry says, blurting the words out as quickly as he can.
"Good. And what about you Georgie boy?" He growls at the other man.
"Oh. Yeah. Definitely!" George mutters.
"Excellent. Glad we're all on the same..." Brick starts but he stops when the lights suddenly go back out and, with even the headlights of the truck gone, they're engulfed in complete darkness.
"Boys!" Andy shouts, quickly taking charge. There's so much commotion around them as dozens of clumsy human men all fumble around in the darkness to find their weapons, or their torches, or both, in blind panic. In amongst the crashing and the grunting there's the loud clipping sound that they vaguely recognise as the sound of high heels on the hard concrete floor. They all round on the sound, trying to find the source of it, and when some of them finally get their torches out and on they see the figure of a woman standing in front of the truck. There's murmuring and grunting and they all point their guns at her. She slowly raises her right hand and clicks; and the lights all come back on.
Hazel stands, with a threatening smirk on her face and cold stare that passes over every single one of them. It's as if she's daring one of them to fire. She stands, elegantly dressed with a thick and stylish coat draped over her shoulders, utterly unphased by the dozens of guns pointed at her. Brick chuckles to himself.
"Always gotta make an entrance." He says, with a sigh, and she raises an eyebrow and shrugs.
"Are you going to tell your staff to lower their firearms or would you like me to make them?" She asks him.
"Boys. You heard the lady. Guns down. She's not a threat." He orders "Not yet, anyway.".They cautiously obey. She winks at one of them.

"Pieces away, boys." She says, gleefully taunting them. "I don't know why you still surround yourself with these animals, Brickolas."

"This feels like it should be a private conversation, H." Her arrival caused an odd shift in the atmosphere. He had his men exactly where he wanted them, hanging on his every word in fear, and now they're all staring at this new arrival. She's upstaged him and he needs to get her away and get back to the status quo. "I've got an office set up back here. C'mon."

"Lead the way." She says.

"Boys, as you were." He roars, beginning to escort her further into the warehouse. She calmly follows him, the sound of her heeled boots echoing through the nearly silent warehouse. Just as he's nearly out of sight Brick calls back to the men who are still watching after them both in a stunned silence "I said as you were!"

"That's right boys." She calls too, with a ridiculous, flirtatious giggle. He storms into his office, waits for Hazel to slink inside, and then slams the door behind her. She saunters over to the old desk, clearly left over from the previous occupants of the warehouse, and sits herself atop it casually.

"What the fuck is with the theatrics?" He demands of her.

"You'd be mindful to remember who you're speaking to. I wanted to show you how it was done. I caught the back of your testosterone fuelled head crushing speech and, well, if you're going to give people a show, give 'em a show." She says, raising her arms and posing, as if there's an audience there applauding her.

"Yeah, whatever. I think a little violence gets people a lot more scared than switching the lights on and off." He grunts, because he's got no time for this woman's nonsense right now.

"Oh Brickleton. You and I both know I'm plenty capable of violence." She tells him, with a sinister smile.

"What do you want, H?" He snarls, already tired of her.

"Well, for starters you've still not answered my previous enquiry regarding your continued employment of Humans, doing your dirty work for you?" She asks again, actually wagging a finger at him.

"But what d'ya really want?"

"It's swell to see you again, Bricky, really it is." She says, with a friendly chuckle that rivals his own from earlier.

"There's a but comin'" He grunts, and she rolls her eyes and sighs. Her faux friendliness drops, as he knew it would.

"But I want to know what the hell you're doing here?" She tells him, leaning forward with a stone cold glare.
"I don't think that's any of your business." He says bluntly.
"Well you've never been one to think, don't start now." She snaps back.
"What can I say, I like it up north. I saw an opportunity to branch out, and I've got an old friend to see." He says. It's not untrue, but he's not giving her all the details either.
"I don't begrudge you making a few pennies from heaven, even though I object to the nature of your business, but just not here." She tells him, and he chuckles, because she's not going to push him around. "I've got a good set-up here. I've got big plans, powerful allies, and a whole host of people who I owe a great deal of pain to. I can't allow you to peddle your dirty dope here. It's a wrinkle I don't want. Pack up, quietly, and leave. Don't cause me any trouble." She instructs.
"Listen, H. It's good to see you again too. I heard about Joseph getting himself caught, so you're obviously feeling emotional, and so I'll forgive this outburst." She glares at him at that, which was exactly what he was hoping for. He has a lot of respect for this woman, but he's not going to let her show up and kick him out. Not when he's got some unfinished business on his mind. "But you don't scare me. If I'm inclined to stick around and cause a little trouble I ain't gonna stop myself 'cause you flicked a light switch on and off. It's tough to scare me when nothin' can touch me. Maybe, in your emotional state, you forgot that." He says; and for a brief moment she stares a hole right through him. He wonders if she might actually get up from that desk and start something and, deep down, he's not actually sure if he could take her. But then she smiles, with a grin that shows every single one of her pearly white teeth.
"Brickory, darling, I think it's you who's having the lapse in memory. Remember who you're dealing with. I've more tricks in my carpet bag than just a lighting change." She says, laughing again. Now he gets that same chill that he gave everyone else earlier.
"Are we done 'ere?" He asks, not backing down. He knows not to. No matter what.
"I believe we are. I'll leave the traditional way." She coos, sliding back to her feet and brushing past him to the door. She reaches for the handle and looks back at him. "It's lovely to see you, Brichard. Really. But please think about what I said. I have enough battles to fight without adding you to the list, old friend." And before he can respond, she leaves, slinking her way

back out onto the warehouse floor, smirking to herself. She winks at Andy, who's hovering around the office, and shows herself out.

Chapter Forty-Four.

Louis hasn't really been a part of many car journeys. It's a weird thing, I know. Being in a car is something so inherently part of human life that you probably can't remember the first time you were in a car. The Custodians were given many choices of subjects during training and learning to drive was one of them, but it was not something he'd picked. No, for Louis, the first time in a car that he could remember was when he left Home Base 25 to move to Jongleton at eighteen. Since then, it's only really been the ones in the last few weeks. So, it doesn't mean all that much to say this was the most awkward car ride of his life, but this was indeed the most awkward car ride of his life. Lauren is driving and Amber is in the front. She's silently seething, looking out of the window restlessly, and not wanting to talk to any of them about what's wrong. He's not known her for long, but Amber doesn't seem like the type to be quiet when pissed about something. She's normally, frighteningly, vocal about what's annoying her. He and Danny are sitting together in the back, and Danny is shuffling uncomfortably because he too is clearly unnerved. He looks like he wants to say something but is thinking better of it, which is also out of character and adds to the overall discomfort of the situation, because Danny thinking before he speaks is weird. Finally, after way too long in this loaded silence, it's Lauren that attempts to break it.
"Do we want the radio on? That seems like it'd be a good idea. Right?" She asks, very softly. She glances at the others for some kind of approval. Danny and Louis look to Amber for the answer.
"Yeah, whatever." She snaps, aware all eyes are on her.
"Okay, perfect." Lauren says, her tone the most cheery it has ever been. She switches it on. It fills the silence. Danny decides to start tapping away on his phone but keeps glancing at the back of Amber's head, still clearly struggling to find something to say. Finally he seems to settle on something and Louis spots that he braces himself before opening his mouth.
"You should've seen Chris' face when you left. It was priceless." He says, but he doesn't get a reaction. "I'm glad you did it. Whatever he was intending to get from that teamwork exercise…all I was getting was how stupid Noel is."

"I liked him." Louis says, jumping in to help Danny with this one-sided conversation.
"Well, stupid sticks together." Danny says, dismissively. "How was your group Amber? Bet it was great being stuck with most of the A team." She shrugs in response to this, still not giving him the engagement he wants.
"And I can't believe you invited them to help us out."
"I didn't, they offered and I…" Louis mutters, and Danny cuts him off.
"Didn't say no, therefore inviting them." He says, smugly.
"It wasn't…" Louis begins.
"Please stop." Lauren says. And that's it. That ends the conversation and they have another ten minutes worth of silence, though, at least, it's now filled by the very quiet music coming from the radio.
Finally the car comes to a stop outside the house, and the second it does, Amber bolts out and makes a beeline inside the house. Danny is quickly after her, but halts as she bolts up the stairs. Lauren and Louis enter the house behind them. Danny considers following her, but Lauren puts a hand gently on his shoulder and shakes her head. She gestures for them to follow her into the War Room, and they do, hoping that she can help this make sense.
"Have a seat boys." She says with a sigh, closing the door behind them. She takes a seat too and braces herself, looking very uneasy.
"What is going on?" Danny demands. She nods, sadly, at him, and begins to explain.
"I've been stationed here longer than all of you. I've seen so many people come and go. I've had the pleasure of seeing you all arrive. Danny, I was here when you turned up all fresh faced and excitable, desperate to overhaul all of this technology and show us all how brilliantly clever you are. Before that, I was here the day Chris turned up, he was an ambitious high flyer who was getting lost in the shuffle in the large big city team he was part of. He was so eager to make his mark. And I was here the night Rachel brought a timid broken girl here, because she was the sole survivor of her team following the failed attempt to catch a Used-to-Be." She says, and pauses, remembering it. "Oh, I should probably make a pot of tea for this…" She says, starting to get up.
"Come on Lauren." Danny snaps at her, impatiently.
"It's probably better if you just tell us…" Louis says, trying to encourage her softly to counteract Danny. She nods and lowers herself back to her chair.

"It was just me and Chris back then. Well, no, there was a charming young man called Simon, and a lovely girl called Caroline. She went on to bigger and better things. I think she's moved up to being a Level 3 Agent now. No idea where she's stationed, but I just know she'll be making a success of it. I saw big things in her from the start and I was so proud of her when she moved on."

"Lauren!" Danny says through gritted teeth. It's odd to see him annoyed, too. Normally he's cold and sarcastic, and insulting, but there's a desperation to this. Louis realises how much he genuinely cares about Amber and it's like seeing a different side to him, something underneath the frosty exterior.

"Yes, sorry." She says, and braces herself to continue. "I believe the creature they were tracking was involved in drug trading or dealing or whatever it is that humans do. There'd been an element of Amber having to go under cover within the organisation. They weren't fully sure of his status or how deep it ran. I think he was heading it up but surrounding himself with Humans so his status as a Used-to-Be never stood out. There was just something a little different about him that had alerted them to the police investigation. It didn't take long to confirm those suspicions, and they moved to capture him. What she'd not managed to gather was just how the infection had manifested itself in him. It turned out the Used-to-Be had armoured skin of some kind, he was invulnerable to their attacks, and so, the takedown went badly, three other agents lost their lives. She was lucky to escape with hers."

"How do you know all this?" Danny asks, his impatience fading now.

"I recognised the picture straight away. I told you, the poor girl was a wreck but…you know how these things are. There was still a report to be filed. I helped her do it. A couple of weeks went by and she settled in. Eventually, I saw her go from timid and mild to…well…our Amber."

"Tell me more about the armoured skin thing?" Louis asks, looking across to Danny who's thinking the same; they need to understand it so they can find a way around it.

"I'm not sure I can. I managed to get enough to make the report passable but…I think their tranquilliser darts bounced straight off him, and none of their physical attacks did any good." She explains.

"Well I need to know more, we need some kind of plan." Danny says; but before Lauren can answer Amber bursts back into the room and dumps a holdall full of weapons onto the table.

"I've got a plan." She roars. "We kill him. Whatever it takes."
"Amber, I…" Danny begins; and she cuts him off instead slamming her hand on the table. It cracks the wood.
"Whatever it is, I don't wanna hear it. Lauren's right. His skin is tough. They called him Brick. I think that's why. Or one of the reasons. I don't know. I just know that tranqs won't work so I say we try bullets and bombs and whatever else we can get our hands on. No capture this time. He's an animal so we put him down." She tells them, looking as if she'll rip the head off the first one who argues with her.
"I'm not sure that's…" Lauren begins, kindly.
"Not sure it's what?" She responds, with a glare.
"Well, we need authorisation for lethal force. I'm not sure Chris will sign that off…"
"Don't care. I'm going. You guys can come with or I'll do it alone." She tells them. She's determined and hot headed and she means every word of it. Louis' mind is whirring, wondering what on earth he can say to dissuade her and he's sure the other two are doing the same.
"Slow down. Give us…" Danny begins.
"No." She snaps. He takes a breath, but continues.
"Give us a chance to find him first." He says, reasoning with her a little.
"You need to know where he is before you run off on this little suicide kick."
"The photo you showed earlier. It's down by the river. I'll start there." She says, simply.
"That was hours ago! He could be anywhere now." Danny says, almost pleading with her.
"Can we just…we want to help. We really do and we can…but just tell us a bit more about what we're walking into…" Louis says. Her head snaps towards him and he is genuinely worried she's going to throw something but, instead, she angrily shakes her head and sits down.
"Fine." She says, begrudgingly.
"So, he's a drug dealer?" Louis clarifies. In truth he's not sure why he's asking that, he's just scrambling for some kind of follow up to keep her talking and not rushing out of the door.
"Yes. He's a supplier. He moves into an area and starts distributing his product. He laces it with something special, I couldn't find out what. It makes it unique though. That's what he said. People are clamouring for it because there's nothing else like it. This is all just the shit he sprouts off but it seemed to work. There were a few deaths linked to it and that's what

caught our attention." She says, and the more she talks the more her desire to run out of the door seems to diminish slightly.
"He works with humans, too?" Louis asks, to keep the details flowing, but also because he has an idea.
"Yeah, a load of hired thugs with no idea what he is." She confirms. Louis nods at Danny, who catches on to his thought and starts tapping on his laptop. "What?" She snaps, annoyed at being left out of their silent plan..
"Well, that means he behaves like a Human criminal, too." Louis explains
"And Humans are way better at catching human criminals than they are at Used-to-Bes," Danny continues.
"Right?" She says, not catching on.
"So maybe their investigation continued after yours. It's a good idea…and of course with a little technical brilliance…" Danny says; and Louis smiles a little to see his cocky demeanour back. Amber, however, is less thrilled.
"Danny I don't want 72 reasons you're a fucking genius right now." She says with her arms crossed.
"Marcel "Brick" Green. That's our guy. Police have never been able to get enough evidence for an arrest but they're very interested in him. There's a whole list of known associates. Instead of searching for him we could get one of them to do the hard work. They can lead us to him." Danny explains.
"So then we just need a plan for how to incapacitate him." Lauren chimes in.
"Yep." Louis confirms.
"I've covered that one." Amber says, pointing at her big bag of weapons.
"Let me speak to Chris." Louis offers, to try to placate her.
"You?" Danny huffs, as if it's ridiculous.
"Yeah. He specifically asked me to keep him updated once we had a plan…so…" He explains. He's unsure of the words even as they leave his mouth. Chris clearly hates him, so he's really not confident he'll be able to get him to sign off on any kind of lethal force, but he's willing to try. "I'll give it a go at least." He tells them with a shrug.

When Matthew Wade returns home that evening he's quite surprised to find Kamala sitting at the kitchen table with a large glass of red wine. That's very unusual for his wife. Something is very wrong.
"Wine on a Tuesday?" He asks her, raising an eyebrow. She sighs, gives him a forced smile and nods. He pulls out a chair and sits opposite her.

"It's Wednesday, and you look like you could do it yourself." She says, with a chuckle. She's not wrong, he's not caught sight of himself in the mirror in a little while but he can tell he looks like shit.
"I'm alright for now, cheers." He says. They both know he'd prefer a beer anyway.
"Were you back at work today?" She asks, with a concerned look.
"Nah. Been working on a story with Kim actually." He says. He's exhausted and he can't be arsed to think about whether he should be telling her about this or not.
"Oh. And how is she?" Kam asks. She's known Kim nearly as long as he has.
"As persistent and pig-headed as ever." He says.
"That's our Kim. We should have her round soon." She says, and takes another large swig from her glass. She looks tense but he can't tell why. He hopes it's nothing he's done. "What's the story?" She asks. He feels like she's skirting around something, which must be how she feels a lot of the time with him. He's been keeping his suspicions about the Counter Terrorism team from her, mostly. But right now he can't be bothered to skirt around it. She's his wife, the person he trusts the most in the world, and actually, she's the most balanced and pragmatic person he knows. He's having all kinds of doubts about whether to continue down this bloody rabbit hole and so she might be the best person to talk to.
"A complicated one." He tells her. "Remember that Counter Terrorism team I told you about before? Last few weeks they've been everywhere I look. Really started to piss me off. Kim and I both think there's something more going on…" He pauses, wondering how to continue without sounding crazy. She picks up on it anyway.
"So what's the plan, get Kim to write some kind of expose?" Her tone is laced with a harmless kind of mockery, and he laughs to himself hearing it come out of her mouth and hearing the ridicule.
"Something like that, yeah. I think I got a bit carried away. Thing is, there's summit weird going on with them and I just can't…"
"I lost my job today." She says, interrupting him. That stops him dead, and he stares at her, open mouthed. "My thoughts exactly. Budget cuts, apparently. So, we can't afford for you to be fired just cause some kids have annoyed you. You've not been happy at work for a while though, have you?" She asks, and she's right. It's probably not even just them, they're just the symptom of a bigger problem.

"No love, I don't think I have. I just wanna be able to do something worthwhile." He says, honestly. Kamala reaches over and grabs his hand. "The thing is Matthew, when we're not happy then everything can be annoying. Maybe it's time we look at a fresh start? We've been talking for years about getting out of this town. I've got nothing keeping me here now, and I don't want you in a job that makes you unhappy. So, maybe it's time. Before we really are too old." She says, and it makes sense. They've been talking about moving somewhere a little quieter for a long time, some rural getaway where things aren't so busy, or so grubby as they are in Endsbrough. The place really is a shithole and it's just getting worse every day. He nods and gets up, heading to the fridge for a beer.
"Aye maybe. Time to think about something to eat first though, I'm starving. Have you eaten yet?" He asks, cracking a can open.
"No, I'm waiting for you to buy me a takeaway. I just lost my job." She says, with a cheeky smile.
"Best get me debit card then…" He says, fumbling around in his pocket to work out where he left the bloody thing.

Chapter Forty-Five.

Brick hadn't left his office since that woman, whoever she was, had slinked out of here. Andy had never seen her before and that was unsettling. He knew everyone Brick did business with. He certainly wasn't going to let it throw him off track though. The sooner he got everything set up properly, the sooner they could be out of this town, because this town was unsettling him more than some mystery woman.
It had been only a few days ago when Brick had announced that they'd be packing up and travelling north. Brick was usually prone to spur of the moment ideas; but this seemed different somehow. Even when his ideas came from nowhere Andy could usually see the logic in them. But not here there was nothing. No explanation and no room for questions. He was Brick's right hand though, and like a good right hand man he fell in line. He'd found this old abandoned factory warehouse, he'd arranged travel and stock, and he'd reached out to their contacts in the area. Now, he'd make sure the job was done, no matter what unexpected hurdles came up.
"We only need a couple more and we should be done." He tells the men loading up the truck. Then he looks towards George and Terry, who are watching and waiting. Terry is puffing on a cigarette. The sooner these two

are out of his hair and on the road the better. Then, maybe, he'll check in on Brick and see if there's anything else that needs doing. "You two definitely know where you're going? Last thing we need is something going wrong tonight." He asks.
"Yep, we've got the list, it's all good." George says with a friendly and irritating chuckle.
"Ok. Check in after every one and let me know. I wanna make sure all of our dealers have what they asked for. Brick is pretty insistent we get this stuff out there as quick as possible. And let me know the second you run into trouble. Brick has history with some of the people operating in this area. Some of them would love to cost him some money." He tells them, because these two are obviously idiots and he feels like he needs to be very clear with them.
"We've got it, don't worry." Terry says, with a nonchalant wave of his hand. Andy glares at him because that nonchalance doesn't offer reassurance.
"Easy for you to say. I'm the one who'll have to calm him down if something goes wrong." He snaps, but then, with a shrug, reconsiders. "But then, it'll be you he'll wanna get his hands on, so swings on roundabouts I guess."
"Isn't it...?" George begins but Terry shakes his head to shut him up. Just as Andy is beginning to think that Terry is smarter than he gave him credit for, he speaks.
"Who was that earlier anyway, the woman?"
"None of your business, mate." He says, though obviously he's wondering the same thing. "You're fully loaded. Best get on your way." He says, checking his watch. "If he comes back out here and sees you've not set off he won't be happy." That's a lie. Brick has no idea about the schedule. He leaves it all to him. But they don't need to know that.
"We'll be off then." Terry says, tossing his cigarette away and struggling back up into the driver's seat.
"Remember. Regular check-ins. And we know exactly how much you're carrying. Any of it goes missing..." He reminds them.
"I know, I know." Terry says, waving him off and shutting the door. He starts the engine, and reverses out of the warehouse and Andy goes on to his next task. One step closer to being out of here.
"That was a lot more intense than I expected." George says to his brother-in-law, once they're back on the road.
"Oh yeah, your other drug deals more relaxed?" He replies.
"Fuck off that's not what I meant. I just didn't think..."

"Yeah I know what you mean mate. Look, let's just get this done and we'll make a load off it." Terry explains, trying to reassure him. It'll be worth it when they're done.
"Where do you know this guy from?" George asks.
"Met him a couple of years ago when I worked down south. Didn't think he remembered me until I got his call, so clearly he does. Not sure if I should be flattered or scared."
"What's with the...?" He asks, pointing to his own head to indicate Brick's scar.
"I dunno." Terry says. "There's all kindsa stories about him. Got himself in too deep a few years ago and got his head bashed in seems to be the most common. Also heard he got dumped in the Mersey River, smacked his head off something on the bottom. Chucked out of a window and smashed his head on the ground. Either way, he lived, and he's been an angry, violent fucker ever since."
"Sounds like exactly the kinda guy I wanna work for." George mutters.
"You didn't have to take the job mate. And like I said. It's a one and done; and he always pays well. He might be a violent bastard but he'll look after ya if you don't cross him. Says he's already made enough to set himself up for life. Think he just does this to piss everyone off now."
"So he's like Robin Hood?" George laughs.
"What?"
"Taking from the rich, givin' to us." He explains.
"I don't think that was about criminals and drug dealers though George."
"No but the same principles apply, that's all I'm saying." It makes absolutely no sense, but Terry can't help but laugh. Maybe it's a nervous laugh now that he can actually relax and he's not gonna get his jaw ripped off for saying the wrong thing.
"Wouldn't wanna see him in tights though would ya?" He asks with a smile, as they approach their first stop.

Chapter Forty-Six.

Louis, who's taken himself off to the living room, is mid-way through explaining the situation to a tablet he's video calling Chris on.
"...once we've tracked him that way we'll move in. But with everything we know we'd like the option to use lethal force." He finishes. Chris takes a long pause. He's sitting at his desk in Home Base 25, and he leans back in

his chair, making a show of mulling the request over. He lets out a long breath, enjoying the power of this moment far too much.

"I need this written up as a proposal, so that I can have proper time to think about this and how it fits with our policies and procedures." He says, at last. Out of sight of the tablet's camera Louis clenches his fist and digs his nails into the palm of his hand in frustration to stop his face giving away what he's thinking.

"I think it's important that we do this quickly." He pushes, with as much tact as he can muster. He needs Chris to agree to this. Amber is obviously going to do it anyway.

"Yes, I agree, but there's lots to consider. What's your current supply of ammunition like? When were the weapons you have on site tested? Do you even know they'll work on him?" Chris replies with an edge of condescension. He's right, he's right about all of it. Louis doesn't have a clue and there's no sense hiding that, because he already knows Louis doesn't know and that's why he's asking.

"No, I don't know any of that." He tells him.

"This is the kind of thing I need to know to authorise the use of lethal force with a UTB. It's a very serious matter and it needs to be given all due consideration." Chris explains, not even bothering to hide the superior tone in his voice. It's so obvious how much he's enjoying this.

"But…" Louis begins, and then he stops himself before he says anything else. This won't get him anywhere. Arguing with Chris isn't the right tactic and he knows it. His Level Four is set on doing things his way, and his way just happens to be as obstructive as possible. Their conversation earlier made it really clear that Chris doesn't trust him. There's no way he's going to authorise this because someone he neither likes nor trusts argues with him about it. "Okay. Sure." He agrees, admitting defeat and starting to plan another way to placate Amber. "Are Olivia and Noel on site yet?" Chris asks.

"They arrived a few minutes ago." Louis confirms. They'd turned up just as he took himself off to make the call and, frankly, a call with Chris seemed more pleasant than sitting in the War Room whilst Amber and Danny were outright hostile to their temporary teammates. Chris takes another long and considered pause. He sucks his teeth.

"Okay." He says, quietly, and Louis doesn't quite catch on to his meaning at first. "As long as you provide all the necessary paperwork retrospectively, and have them review everything you're using, then I'm

okay to sign it off on this occasion. You need to make sure to follow the correct process next time though." He continues and Louis' eyes widen in surprise when his shocked brain finally processes the words.
"Thank you." He stutters, scared to say anything else in case it changes Chris' mind.
"It's only for the UTB too. I want no human casualties, and have a Cleaningcrew standing by ready for when you're done." He continues.
"Yeah, definitely." He confirms.
"Okay. Well get yourselves ready, let me know when you have a lead, and we'll go from there." Chris tells him.
"Yes. Thank you." Louis says, meaning it because he's actually really grateful that Chris has given him permission for this. It would make things with Amber much, much easier, not to mention the Used-to-Be. They currently had no way to incapacitate it and had to work one out. Working out a non-lethal one felt like it was an even more insurmountable task. This would at least give them a few more options.
"I'll speak to you then." Chris says and ends the call. Louis lets out a huge sigh of relief, because he really hadn't expected it to end that positively. He heads out into the hallway, leaving the tablet behind just on the off chance Chris is about to call back and say he was kidding.

"Oh, hey. I'm making tea. Give me a hand?" Lauren says, appearing as soon as he's through the door. He's pretty sure it was more coincidence than her waiting for him; but he wouldn't have blamed her if she had been. She'll have been anxious to hear the outcome too.
"Yeah, sure." He says, following her through into the kitchen, relieved to not have to walk straight back into whatever messy situation will currently be going on in the War Room.
Lauren goes about her usual routine of filling the kettle, and laying out various cups once they're in the kitchen. He'd already seen her do this so many times.
"How did that go?" She asks, hesitantly. Lauren, as the most level headed of the team by far, undoubtedly understood the importance of getting this signed off by Chris. Amber was going to do what she wanted regardless; and they really couldn't afford to annoy him any more than they already had. Given the conversation they'd had back at Home Base, it was pretty obvious that Chris would hold Louis responsible for anything that went wrong. That was ridiculous of course, because he couldn't influence

Amber, or Danny, to do anything they didn't want to, or even stop them from doing something they did.

"Better than I thought it would, actually." He confirms; and she looks as relieved as he feels.

"Yeah?" She asks, with cautious optimism.

"I have a lot of paperwork in my future, but he's authorised it. I think it's more because Olivia is here than anything else, but it's still a win right?"

"Of course! Oh well done Louis. I don't necessarily like the idea of going for the kill but I know having the option on the table will mean a lot to Amber." She says, over the sound of the kettle boiling. "I know she won't show it." She continues, still a little hesitantly. It seems like she's kept Amber's past to herself for a while and it must be a little strange to finally be able to share it. "Hopefully you can understand her a little more now." She says, and it's true, to an extent. A lot of the things she's done or said do make more sense when looked at again with this fresh knowledge about how she came to be here and what happened to her previous team. Though it wouldn't be in the same way, he was sure that he'd be completely different if the last team he'd been with - if he'd been with a team - had been murdered in front of him. Even the idea of that kind of harm coming to this team was tough to think about; and he'd only known them a few weeks.

"I do, yeah." Louis told her with a thoughtful nod.

"And how're you?" She says, pivoting from the subject of Amber.

"I'm good." He replied, without really thinking about it in the way that everyone does.

"No, I mean really?" She pushed. "Ever since the other day you've seemed quiet. And then at the Home Base you seemed…Is it this Hazel thing that's bothering you?" She asks, very intuitively.

"Yes…and no." He explains, taking a seat as she hands him a coffee. His mind went straight back to his conversation with the Superior One, and on how that had helped him make sense of the things he was feeling a little. Talking out loud had helped him to understand some of the things that were swirling around in his head, and he knew that the best thing here would be to share them with Lauren too. Of all the people he currently knew she was undoubtedly the kindest. "She definitely worries me…but I'm also worried about my powers. Being able to pick up on Demonic energy and sense things…I can see how it could be useful but it can be really overpowering too. I lost control during the fight with Joseph. There was a point where it completely overwhelmed me."

"The first time I tried to heal someone I blacked out and spent a week in bed." She told him, without hesitating. "For about the first year I would get a migraine or a nosebleed every time I tried. Sometimes both." That already made him feel better. She was brilliant; he'd seen some of the things she could do and she'd made it look virtually effortless. "This house has seen so many disasters." She continued, and pointed over to the splintered door frame. "The kitchen doesn't have a door because Amber ripped it off one day when she meant to open it." She said, chuckling at the memory.

"I did wonder about that." He said, quietly.

"Yep. There was no fixing it. Everyone goes through this, it's okay. It's a bit like the muscles in your body, you need to exercise it. If you don't then the first time you use it then it'll hurt like hell, but if you work it out regularly you'll get stronger and be much better at using it. Does the analogy work?"

"It makes perfect sense, yeah." He says with a nod, because it does. This was something brand new he was discovering. A power he had never used before, because he'd never really been in a situation to. He needed to exercise it, to practise, and to get stronger. "...I'm not sure how to practise using it though, outside of being in the field?"

"There may be a few things you can practise though. Meditation and breathing exercises have helped me. That's why I told you to breathe, remember? It helped me to learn how to focus when I needed to. You can also just try sensing, whatever it is you sense, in objects? There's so much demonic energy out there that you're bound to be able to pick up on something, somewhere?" She tried, and that too was helpful. The way she explained it made so much sense, and mentally he berated himself for not thinking of it. He'd been too busy feeling overwhelmed, and a little sorry for himself, that he'd not really considered the idea of just breaking it down. Demonic energy was everywhere, not just in Used-to-Bes. If he tried sensing it in smaller, less intense forms, then maybe he could build up to the bigger ones without being so overwhelmed by what he felt.

"Thank you." He said, with an embarrassed smile, silently worrying that Lauren would think him an idiot for not thinking of it all too. Somehow, he knew she wouldn't though. The others might've, but not her.

"My pleasure. I'm always here for you. I know the others aren't the easiest to talk to but...you're not alone. Talk to me. Whatever it is, I've probably been through it or seen someone go through it. And I won't judge." She said, and Louis couldn't help but grin appreciatively. He wasn't alone, and

that still felt really new. He'd had to spend so long dealing with this all on his own and keeping so much locked up inside. He'd spent so long surrounded by humans who knew nothing about Custodians and Used-to-Bes, and he had to make sure it stayed that way. Then when he'd come here it had all been so crazy and so intense that he'd not really had the time to process that he was part of a team now. Sure, he and Danny had worked pretty well together, but he'd still not really added it all up. He wasn't alone; and that really meant something.
"Grab me the biscuits?" She asks, putting the other cups on a tray.
"Sure." He said, getting back up, grabbing a pack from the cupboard, and following her out of the room and, finally, towards the War Room and whatever chaos was unfolding in there.

…and that's exactly what they walked into seconds later. Utter chaos.
"I've got tea!...oh and a coffee for you Danny." Lauren announced loudly, trying to cut through the noise as the others all debated what their next move would be. "Where are we up to?" She asked, elevating her tone to be incredibly cheery in that way she did when the others were bickering.
"We've got a lead. There's an old industrial estate, not far from where the target was spotted. It's mostly abandoned. There are a couple of businesses operational but most of them have gone bust. We spotted this guy…" Danny explains, quickly and before any of the others can interject. He flicks the screen on and a mugshot of Terry appears. "Terrance Church. Arrested a couple of times for assault. Believed Human." He continues. "He's had links with the target going back about five years, we got a hit on his van in the area, and then it's been all over town afterwards. Logic says he's making drop offs and one of those abandoned buildings is his pick-up point. It might be worth flagging to the police; they can bring him in while we capture the Used-to-Be." Noel says, with a friendly smile. Louis spots that Danny is quietly glaring at him; and knows it's because he's incensed at being interrupted when he's busy demonstrating how clever he is.
"What are you doing?" He practically barks and poor Noel clearly doesn't know what to make of it. You really have to put the work in to understand Danny, and learn when to just let him talk.
"So we're going to comb the area." Olivia begins, sensing that she needs to step in. "We think there are a total of five buildings to check. Danny, can you bring the map up please?" She asks. He obliges, silently. The map of the industrial estate replaces the mugshot. "I think two teams. One starts

here at the South East corner. The second starts North West. I'll run one team. Louis, since Chris asked you to lead on this, can you run the other?"
"Oh, umm, yeah. Sure." Louis says, completely taken aback by the idea of him leading and suddenly very nervous about it.
"Cool. Noel, can you go with him?" She asks, nodding to her teammate.
"Yeah, great idea" He replies, with a wide grin.
"And me." Danny says, jumping in with a scowl.
"Okay." Olivia says, nodding towards the remaining two who will make up her team. "Then ladies, that leaves us together."
"Right. But what about weapons?" Asks Amber; who has been sitting quietly with her feet up on the table and uninterested in the conversation since Louis and Lauren entered the room.
"Chris said yes." Louis blurts out. "To the lethal force, I mean." He clarifies, as if he could've meant anything else..
"Really?" Amber asks, with a genuine intrigue on her face.
"Yeah. He had some reservations but, Olivia, I think you being here helped." Louis tells the room. "So, thanks."
"Happy to help." Olivia says, and it's clear that she means it. He'd been worried, and no doubt the others were too, that she'd been sent to supervise them or to report back in some way. But actually, right now, it seemed like she and Noel just genuinely want to support them. There are multiple levels to this whole team thing, Louis quietly thinks to himself.
"Then why're we still sat here? Let's go." Amber says, standing. The others all look at each other and nod in agreement.
"Louis, you good?" Olivia asks.
"Yep. Let's go…" He confirms, nodding as well.

Chapter Forty-Seven.

The van comes to a quiet stop on a dark street and George looks over to Terry, list in hand.
"Alright so we only got a couple to go." He tells him as he reads from the paper.
"No, there's three ain't there?" Terry asks.
"Yeah a couple." George confirms, nodding.
"It's one more than a couple." Terry disagrees.

"Oh either way I'm starving." George says, waving him off.
"You're always fucking hungry, ya gannet." Terry says, because he never stops shoving food in his face.
"Yeah well c'mon lets get this done. Maybe then we can go to that drive thru on Woodrow Road." George says, because he's already planned it and he's been looking forward to that early morning burger since they started.
"Yeah alright, let's see what time we get done though. It's already getting late." Terry says, and opens the door, clambers down, and grabs one of the packages from the back of the van.
"It's 24 hours Tez, it don't matter." He explains, being very familiar with said drive-thru. "What is that stuff anyway?" George asks as he leans in for a closer look at the package. .
"I dunno, some designer drug." He mutters back
"You what? What's that even mean."
"It's just a phrase for a posh drug int it?" Terry tells him, beginning to wonder if his chatty brother-in-law was actually the best person to bring.
"Why's it look weird though?" He asks.
"What d'ya mean?" Terry replies, freezing in panic. George has seen it and it shouldn't have because it's all in sealed packages.. "Why've you been looking in the packages?" He demands.
"Calm down. I didn't do nothing. I just saw it when the last bloke opened it. Said he wanted to sample it and I caught a glimpse. It's like a bright red powder. I've not seen out like it." George explains, as Terry lugs the box out of the van and across the road towards the door of a building without any help from his companion.
"Alright, I'm just a bit jumpy is all." He asks him.
"Oh I imagine you've got a very good reason to be nervous." Says a well dressed gentleman looking sort in front of them. Terry could've sworn he wasn't there a minute ago.
"Who are you?" George grunts, hoping he's who they're meeting. .
"I'm your worst nightmare." The gentleman replies; and he flashes a badge at them.
"Shit!" They cry out in unison. Terry chucks the box at him and they start to run.
"Get after them!" Detective Superintendent Tim Copper instructs, calmly, as PC Nadin and PC Nelson dart out to chase down their two targets. Nelson

is on Terry before he can get far; knocking him to the ground with surprising strength.

"Terrance Church you're under arrest on suspicion of possession with intent to supply. You do not have to say anything but it may harm your defence if you do not mention when questioned something you later rely on in court. Anything you do say may be given in evidence." He explains, as he slaps the handcuffs on him. Terry struggles; but it's no use. DSI Copper, who had gracefully caught the box that had been thrown at him, opens it up and then begins to dig through and open one of the packages inside of it. Red powder spills out and, looking up from the ground, Terry realises that George was right. It does look weird. Copper takes a little on his finger, sniffs it, and recoils. He sighs, looking disappointed.

"Is it...?" PC Nelson asks him, and Copper nods.

"Yeah it is. We've got a big problem. Who else have you delivered these packages to?" Copper asks, striding closer to Terry who is face down and cuffed on the wet pavement.

"I dunno what you mean." He growls, shaking his head as much as he's able to. PC Nadin strolls back towards them, effortlessly dragging a handcuffed George with him.

"Honestly gentleman, this will be much neater if you are liberal with the information I need." Copper explains to them.

"Fuck off we've done nothing, I'm saying nothing." George roars defiantly.

"Let's check the van." Copper says to his two officers, and strolls methodically over to their vehicle. He carefully opens the unlocked back doors and shakes his head and tuts as he sees a few more of the boxes identical to the one that was thrown at him. He walks around to the front, snaps on a latex glove, then cautiously pokes around in the messy interior of the cabin of the van. He digs through the various food wrappers, because George has been snacking all night, and pulls out a list of handwritten addresses.

"Looks like we've got our list of customers gentlemen. PC Nadin I'd like you to get a few more officers together and see if we can't recover some of these packages. I'd rather keep this monstrosity off the streets." He instructs, handing the list over. In the meantime PC Nelson has pulled Terry upright and sat George down next to him. DSI Copper turns to the two of them.

"Now, for the two of you..." He says, focussing his dark eyes on them.

In his dank little makeshift office in the old factory warehouse by the river Brick was having a rare moment of quiet and serenity. He never likes to sit still for long. People in his line of work can rarely afford to do that. He's rolling a pair of dice around in his palm, toying with them as he ponders the situation he's found himself in.

He and Andy had been harmlessly going about their business down south, near Plymouth, when he'd received a link to some little local news story anonymously. Naturally, it had piqued his curiosity so he gave it a watch. That's when he'd seen her lurking in the background behind the reporter. The bitch that got away. It had taken him a moment to place her, at first. He knew he recognised her straight away; but this was a completely different woman to the last time he'd seen her. Back then she'd been brown haired and mousey looking. Now she had red hair and was fierce. He was really looking forward to introducing himself to this new version of her.

It was about ten years ago when Brick had been left for dead by some people he'd thought of as friends. Well, not so much left for dead as left dead. But, by betraying him they'd actually done him a favour. Oh boy, had they done him a favour. He still wore the scar of that day, of the head wound that should've been fatal. That was the last time anyone had managed to hurt him. He picked himself back up, tore through the fuckers who thought they could stab him in the back, and stepped into a whole new world that was beyond his imagination. He'd thought he'd known power before his 'death,' he'd seen many men who thought themselves untouchable, but now he actually was. And that high he felt? Well, like all good things, he knew there was a way to market it. It had taken him a few years, a lot of money, and the use of minds much cleverer than him, but he'd found a way to distil a tiny bit of demonic energy into a hallucinogenic drug that would give people the trip of a lifetime. It was like nothing else on the market and people were willing to pay very highly for an exclusive product. That's when the cash started to roll in, the kind of money he'd dreamed about having as a lad. He was set for the rest of his life, however the fuck that worked now.

But a few years after that was when he'd first discovered the Custodians. He'd been warned by others of his kind that he'd bumped into along the way; if you're too loud, if you're too obvious, they'll come for you. But, no fucker could hurt him, so he'd never been that scared. They'd found him though. They'd burst in one day and done some serious damage to his set-up and he'd paid them back in kind. He'd met them head on and ripped the fuckers apart. All but one. And now he'd found himself travelling all the way to this shithole town to right that particular wrong. He'd finally get to kill the bitch that got away. He knew it still wasn't the cleverest move. These people, these Custodians, they scared people. Hell, even Hazel seemed to steer clear of them. Invulnerable or not it wasn't a good idea to goad the boogeyman. But he'd hated the idea that they'd cost him and gotten away with it. He hated that anyone was able to do that. So, it was worth the risk. His serenity was interrupted, as he knew it would be eventually, by a quiet knock at the door. It was Andy. He knew it before it even opened; partly because he was familiar with the man's knock and because he was probably the only one brave enough to interrupt him.

"How's it going?" He says in greeting as Andy lets himself in.

"All the deliveries are on schedule so far. It's looking good." He confirms quietly.

"Ha, see, that's what I like to hear. I told you so, didn't I?" He says with a chuckle. He had, too. Endsbrough might be a shithole but shitholes were very good for his particular business. The shittier the place, the more people there were wanting to escape their problems.

"Yes, you were right. We're moving a lot. It'll make the trip worthwhile." Andy says,

"It will that." Brick tells him. He reaches into the drawer of his temporary desk and tosses an envelope of cash at his pal. "There's your cut." He tells him. As the other man reaches out for it Brick pulls it back towards him, flashing his best cheeky smile. "Unless you fancy playing double or nothing again?" He asks, rattling the dice in his hand. Andy quickly shakes his head.

"Never again." He says quickly, and Brick chuckles again. It was a simple enough game. You rolled the dice and if you got a double you got your cut doubled. If you didn't, you got fuck all. Poor Andy had gambled away his cut once and had stubbornly refused ever since.

"Ahh, you'll never get anywhere if you don't take a risk every now and again. That's how I got where I am." He tells him. Risks and invulnerability, that's actually how.

"I've seen it when those risks didn't pay off." Andy says, not budging.

"Point taken." Brick says, letting him take the money. He and Andy had been friends since Brick was alive. He didn't know the full extent of what had happened to him. It'd taken Brick long enough to understand it. But he'd always been there by his side, and that would probably be what got

him killed one day. Andy's phone rings and he answers it quickly. Thing is, they've been together so long that he can read Andy like a book and the first thing he notices is a little panic. This is obviously an unscheduled call. Andy likes everything to be done in a particular order and so something happening out of that order isn't a good sign.
"I see. Okay. Thank you." He says to the caller, shaking his head ever so slightly but trying to hide it. That's another bad sign. He hangs up and looks across at Brick with trepidation. Despite being by his side for so long Andy is still scared of him. That's the right decision. He's not afraid to cut someone out, no matter how long they've been around.
"Spit it out. I know that look is never followed by good news." Brick tells him, lacking any kind of patience.
"The carriers have been picked up by the police, and they're starting to raid locations they've already delivered to." He replies, quietly. To Andy's surprise, he chuckles.
"Oh that sneaky bitch. I should've seen that coming. C'mon." He says, and without any explanation he stands, shoves the desk out of his way, and makes straight for the door. He marches with purpose out onto the factory floor. He clears his throat but the dozen or so men are too busy to hear him, so, as he's not in a patient mood, he slams his fist into the wall next to him. The sound of concrete shattering attracts their attention, and they all freeze and shut up. "Gentleman. Now that I have your attention. Brace yourselves because we're going to have incoming. It might be the police, it might be someone else. You can leave now. But, if you stay I'll double your pay for every person you kill. Shoot now, ask questions later. Andy, shift as much stuff as you can out of here. Everyone else, make sure you're alert, locked and loaded. Stop gawping at me and get to work!" He orders and then turns and heads back to his office to get himself ready too. It's time for a fight.

Chapter Forty-Eight.

And not too far away Brick has reason to be worried; the Custodians have arrived. Olivia, as Chris' unofficial second in command, has taken control of the operation and unsurprisingly it's only really Amber and Danny that have an issue with that.
They've split into the two teams and arrived at two different sides of the industrial estate, ready to sweep through and, hopefully, find evidence of

the Used-to-Be's operation as quickly as possible. Amber, Lauren and Olivia arrived in one car, and Louis, Danny, and Noel in another. They're now grouped around those cars discussing strategy between the six of them via their comms devices.

"So, we have five potential buildings." Olivia begins explaining to the two teams. They've all seen a map and are clear on which ones are which. There are two at each end, and one further in. "Team One will take building one and two, Team Two you start with building four and five. We'll converge on number three if we've not found anything. Four and three have recently been leased, so be on particularly high alert for those, but any could be serving as a potential base. At this time there shouldn't be anyone around with a legitimate reason, but just be careful. We don't want any more exposure to humans than we have to." She continued. Danny had quickly matched the warehouses to existing businesses and at this time of the night they should all be closed and empty. That should make it very easy because in theory the only one that was active would be the one that Brick was using for his base of operations. "I'd ask everyone to silence their comms channel unless we need support. We don't need to be in constant contact. Everyone clear?"

"Yep. Got it." Noel said quickly.

"Clear." Louis confirmed.

"Sure." Lauren followed

"Silencing comms now." Olivia said as she muted herself. The line would remain open; the other team just wouldn't be able to hear anything until she unmuted herself. The others all follow her lead. "So which team do you think will find something first?" She asked Amber and Lauren cheerily and in a completely transparent way.

"Us. I don't need any team competition bullshit to motivate me, so save it." Amber snapped quickly, bringing the mood crashing back down.

"Okay. Noted." Olivia says. Lauren shoots her an apologetic look but she shakes her head. "It's fine, my ego isn't that fragile." She tells her.

"Amber, are you sure..." Lauren begins; and Amber knows where it's heading. It's a question they've all been dancing around and however well intentioned, Lauren should know better than to ask her whether or not she was 'up to this.' Amber knew she was. She knew that what she felt was a kind of determination like nothing she'd ever felt. She would either stop Brick once and for all or she'd die trying. That was it. Those were the two options. Success, or death. There was no sitting this one out because she

'didn't feel up to it.' That was bullshit, as far as she was concerned, and Lauren should've known there wasn't a force on this earth that would stop her fighting this fight.
"Lauren, don't. Let's just get this over with." Amber replied in what was, by her standards, actually quite polite.
"Okay." Lauren said with a nod, because ultimately, she understood. Probably better than everyone else. "Perhaps we should just…is the first one this way?"
"Yes. Everyone ready?" Olivia asked, which was a ridiculous question. Amber decided to answer it by simply striding forward towards the first warehouse on their map. Lauren caught Olivia's eye and smiled before the two of them followed her.

Team two, having just silenced their comms too, made their way to the first building assigned to them. Danny was lagging behind the other two, watching the pair of them as they walked side by side chatting.
"So you're relatively new here, aren't you?" Noel asks Louis.
"Umm, yeah." Louis replied, cautiously. He'd become sensitive to being 'new.'
"Cool," Noel replied, with surprising brightness. "How're you finding it so far?"
"It's been intense." He said, careful to not sound like he's incapable of handling it.
"Ha, yeah I've heard." Noel said, responding with a warm laugh that put Louis that little more at ease.
"Seriously though. I graduated and moved to a tiny town where nothing happened. Now I'm here and every other day we're…" He looked around and gestured, struggling to even describe the chaos the last few weeks had brought.
"Searching abandoned warehouses for a drug dealing Used-to-Be surrounded by an army of potentially gun wielding humans?" Noel offered.
"Not always that scenario…but that kind of area, yes."
"Yeah man I get it. I moved to a two person team in Wales right after graduation. We had two cases in the 9 months I was stationed there. I moved here about 6 months ago and, up until a few weeks ago, cases were sparse.
"Oh, so I caused it then?" Louis asked, with mock outrage.

"Yeah I think you might've." Noel said, chuckling again, as they came to a stop in front of their first warehouse. Louis takes a moment to inspect the doors at the front and they are padlocked shut. He gives it a try, but it's locked tight.
"How do we…" He asks, pausing to consider whether any of them are strong enough to break the padlock. Amber would be, but she's on the other team.
"There's another door around the back. I looked up the floor plan while you two were…" Danny interjects and waves his hand dismissively at the two of them.
"Ah, yeah good idea." Noel says. Louis wonders whether he should tell Noel there's no point in trying to be friendly here. It's Danny.
"I know." He replies, accepting the praise nonchalantly. "This is why it was a waste to have both tech experts on one team. You need one on each."
"You volunteered for this team after me, so it was your idea?" Noel offers, with confusion evident on his face. That's another thing he needs to learn; Danny never has a bad idea. True to form, he doesn't even acknowledge that, he just walks away to find the other door.

Chapter Forty-Nine.

Team One has found their way around the side of their first assigned warehouse.
"I must say, it's very nice to get a chance for our teams to work together properly" Lauren tells Olivia as Amber investigates the side door. She tries the handle and it's locked.
"I agree." Olivia replies, with a smile to show that she means it. "I'm honestly happy we've had the chance to help." There may be some bitterness towards her team, particularly from Amber and Danny, but it's clear that's not reciprocated.
"Shut up." Amber snaps, pressing her ear against the door. "I can hear something." She explains. They both look at her. This is one of the warehouses that, according to their records, isn't currently leased. The three of them are all aware then what it means that there are voices inside. Whoever is in there probably shouldn't be. It could be human kids messing around, or humans who don't have an actual home to go to, or it could be Brick and his gang. Before they get a chance to discuss what to do Amber makes the decision for them and snaps the door handle and the lock,

using the strength Louis was wishing for earlier. She pulls the door open and enters.

The other two follow her lead.

They enter and have a choice of going straight into the factory floor or up a set of stairs. They silently communicate with each other and take the stairs to the first level, knowing it's a better place to assess what's going on.

They begin their search, keeping low, and moving cautiously but quickly through the upper levels of the building. The warehouse is dirty and disused, it's rundown and in a state of disrepair, but there are signs of fresh activity; boxes that aren't covered in dust, and things have been moved recently. Even more revealing though, is that they can all hear the sounds of activity coming from deeper within the building. They quickly move through an upstairs corridor with a few empty and abandoned rooms that appear, at most, to be used as storage and get closer and closer to above where the factory floor is.

They proceed, with the same silent efficiency, to get a better view of what's going on, and move onto a walkway above the factory floor. It gives them a birds eye view of what's going on, and strongly suggests that they're in the right place as they see men loading some of the remaining boxes into another van. Amber scans through the crowd, frantically looking for any sign of Brick, but she can't see him anywhere.

"I don't see him." She mutters to the others.

"Is this definitely the place?" Lauren asks cautiously, both because she's still worried for Amber and because she doesn't want to launch and attack some Humans who aren't caught up in demonic activity.

"It's meant to be abandoned. So I'd say it's very likely." Olivia confirms, also scanning the floor. Unbeknownst to the three Custodians there are a number of guards patrolling the building and searching for intruders. Brick ordered it because he guessed that either the Custodians or the Police would be on their way. One of the armed guards, at that moment, finds himself walking through the very same door that the three of them walked through not long ago and out onto the same walkway they're on now.

"They're here!" He shouts, as he sees the three of them. He raises his gun and he fires.

Danny had stormed ahead; straight into the middle of what was, thankfully, an abandoned warehouse. It was cluttered with old, rusted machines and debris. He has his weapon drawn and does proceed with some ounce of

caution; but overall it looks more like he just wants to get this over with. Louis and Noel hang back, sticking together and keeping their voices low as Danny marches ahead to continue the search.
"He doesn't seem to like me very much." Noel says, clearly approaching the topic with some caution. Louis can't really see why he'd feel the need to be cautious. It's clear to everyone who's ever met Danny that he's a bit of a dick, he's certainly not going to defend him.
"Don't take it personally." he tells him. "He's a bit…like that with everyone."
"I dunno, it seems like it's a little more than that." Noel continues, and Louis is lost. As far as he knows Danny has nothing against him, beyond his general dislike of everyone that's not himself. Maybe it's just him picking up on a dislike of that team because of their proximity to Chris. Noel looks ahead to see if Danny is listening. "From what I hear the two of you made a really good team with that last investigation?" He asks, and now Louis really is lost. They did, but that doesn't mean he has the key to understanding him.
"I guess, yeah." Louis says with a shrug. "But he didn't like me that much before then. Even now, I don't think he actually likes me, he just is a little more tolerant of me being around."
"I think he does." Noel says, with a snort of laughter.
"You two!" Danny snaps, having stopped in front and rounded on them. "Pointless talking isn't stealthy." He says. Louis opens his mouth to argue but he's interrupted by a loud and sudden clattering from the upper levels; like something smacking against the metal struts on the ceiling.
"Did you just hear what I just heard?" Danny says, quickly. Louis does a double take as he looks at him because his tone sounds off. It sounds uncharacteristically jumpy.
"It might just be a bird?" Noel replies. Something sounds off with him too; his tone is almost melodic.
"That noise doesn't come from an ordinary bird." Danny replies and, strangely, throughout the warehouse a haunting music starts to play. It's out of place and yet, somehow, seems to make total sense. They brace themselves, weapons raised, searching up to the ceiling of the warehouse.
"Who's there?" Noel asks, and disturbingly, he receives an answer.
"Who's that hiding…in the treetops…" Begins the voice; replying in a cheerful, manic sort of sing-song way that fits with the music. It echoes throughout the warehouse. "It's that rascal…" It continues; and Louis' head snaps away from the ceiling. It's not coming from there. Whoever it is, is on

323

the ground floor with them. "The jitterbug." Hazel says, as she steps out, with a flourish, from behind a pile of old machinery. She raises her arms, poses, and cackles to herself. She's wearing a flowing black gown, adorned with excessive gold and emerald jewellery. She lowers her arms, the smile fades from her face and it's replaced by a snarl. The music lowers and stops, as if it somehow reacting to her cue. Louis' eyes widen in terror. He'd worked it out, the second he'd heard the voice he'd known, he just didn't want to admit it. Danny sees the look on his face and realises what's going on; he fires multiple shots without so much as a warning. Hazel disappears suddenly in a cloud of emerald green smoke and the bullets ping off something metal.
"Where did she go?" Noel asks, panicking. Another loud cackle rips through the warehouse, as if she's now high above them.
"Sleeeeeeeep. Now you'll sleep." She whispers. Louis turns and sees that she's suddenly behind Noel; waving her hand and somehow causing a fine powder to fall from the air and onto him.
"What's happening…what is it…I'm so…" He says and falls to the ground.
"Hello, my pretties." She says, with another wicked smirk towards the two of them. Louis is too stunned to do anything. "There's no room for superfluous characters in this show right now." She explains, looking down to Noel. "Best to keep him around though, he might be useful later." Danny, also reeling from her sudden appearance, raises his gun again and Louis follows his lead and grasps at his. She clicks her fingers and music starts again. This time it's much more upbeat and lively; but it thunders through the air and unbearably through Louis' head. He can feel the beat deep down inside him. Danny tries to fire but he can't pull the trigger. He drops the gun and starts to sway in time to the music. His eyes widen in terror as he loses control of his own body. Louis does the same, unable to fight the feeling of the music tearing through him and demanding that he move his feet. They both look at each other; scared, and uncomfortable, and pained as their limbs move without them having any say in it. Hazel grins, and returns to her earlier sing-song voice. "Just be careful of that rascal, keep away from…the jitterbug!"
She rockets forward and joins them in the dance, swaying in time to the music and moving lightly between them. She twirls and flaps her dress dramatically. She looks utterly joyful, and it's evident she's having a great time. Her whole expression, her whole mood, matches the upbeat music perfectly. Danny and Louis strain desperately against it but they can't help

themselves. They simply have to join in, they're compelled somehow by the music and by their bodies understanding the part of the story that has somehow skipped their brains. They're unwilling players in her demented musical number; and she's using them to give a performance out to an unseen audience. She dances and they follow. They're her backing dancers and they have absolutely no choice, and it's both painful and terrifying all at the same time because their bodies are not their own. Eventually, she slows and pivots to face them. The music slows and fades to something less upbeat and their dancing slows to match. They turn to face each other, and they're suddenly face to face. Danny throws an arm around Louis' waist, and he responds with one over Danny's shoulder. He's never danced before in his life and he has no idea what he's doing but somehow his body does. Danny pulls him in close and his face looks so pained and his eyes look so scared. They begin to slow dance together in time to the new tune and they're led around the limited warehouse space by a force that neither of them understands. It feels both intimate and comfortable; but like they're somehow being horrifically violated because this is not their own doing. They're simply Hazel's puppets.
She watches them, smiling with a creepy kind of enjoyment as she forces them to dance for her entertainment with their bodies so intertwined. She clicks again suddenly, and the music stops and they freeze. The two of them remain locked in position. She lowers her voice to a sinister and chilling whisper, taking the jovial tone away completely as she moves in close to the frozen pair.

"I told you I'd play a villain. Thought I'd start with a wicked tribute to one of my favourites." She says, getting very close to Louis. He can't look at her because his head remains locked forward and staring straight into Danny's terror-filled brown eyes. "There's something here, isn't there?" She says as she gestures at the space between the two of them. She pauses and contemplates it, and Louis, who's brain is firing a million panicked thoughts a second, can't make sense of what she means. She gestures at the narrow space between the two of them. "Or maybe that's just the dancing. Either way, I'll remember it." She tells him. Louis strains desperately to talk, to say something, to scream at her or to cry for help but the most he can muster is an inaudible mumble. "What's that my dear? I'm guessing something like 'what do you want?' or some other heroic cliche. Let me tell you. I'm here to send you a message, Louis. Oh, that's right, I know your name. I know all about the two of you, the two who schemed and plotted to

take my Joseph away from me. The two who'll pay dearly for it. My two dead doves." She says and Louis' stomach leaps. There is nothing they can do to defend themselves. "But not today. No, I'll bide my time." The last few words come out a lot deeper; almost a growl. She lets the threat hang for a moment, before she grins to herself, turns, and walks a few steps away from them. Her tone shifts again and she's back to being more upbeat and jovial; like she's chatting to two friends rather than people she's planning to kill. She sits herself down delicately on a nearby crate.
"I've got my own plans and schemes and, if you die today then they go to waste. So, this is a warning of a different kind. A horse of a different colour, if you will. Be careful." She reaches behind her, running her fingertips poignantly over an exposed brick wall. "Everyone has a weakness. Even a brick can be easily cracked if you know where to look." She says slowly, and pointedly. She enunciates to emphasise the word 'look' and raises her eyebrows as she does. She chuckles to herself and pops back to her feet. "That's all you get. But don't worry, I'll see…you later." She turns and walks away from them, deeper into the warehouse where she first stood. They're still frozen in place but they have a perfect view of her exit. "Oh." She says, swinging back around to face them with a gleeful expression on her face. "And just try to stay out of my way….just try!" She cackles; there's another puff of smoke and she's gone, leaving her laughter hanging in the air. Louis and Danny finally release each other and collapse to the floor; gasping in pain.

Chapter Fifty.

Amber, Olivia, and Lauren all spin towards the shout of the guard just as he shoots. The promise of cash per kill seems to make him extra trigger-happy and he fires his weapon repeatedly. The bullets stream through the air and at this close range it would've been impossible for him to miss. They head towards the three women with deadly accuracy. He's shooting to kill. Therefore, it's quite lucky that Olivia reacts as quickly as she does. She steps forward, throws her hands up and reaches out using her power. In her it manifested as a kind of telekinesis. She throws it all forward and knocks the bullets off their deadly trajectory. One clips her in the shoulder, and she cries out in pain, but she sends the armed man flying from the walkway and tumbling through the top of an old wooden, rotted, crate in retaliation.

The noise is more than enough to attract the attention of the others below, and they open fire without hesitation. Amber rushes the three of them quickly off the walkway and back through the door to find cover from the gunfire. She's very aware that the respite will only be temporary though; because now around a dozen armed Humans know their position. They need a plan quickly. Olivia groans in pain as she leans against a wall.
"Move your hand, let me see." Lauren delicately orders her,
"It's fine, I'll be ok." Olivia stubbornly replies.
"Oh just move your hand and let me at it." Lauren tuts; using a sterner tone that Amber is very familiar with. She complies, and Lauren inspects the wound. "It's fine, it didn't hit anything major. I can take care of this now. Amber could you…" She begins to ask; and Amber knows where the question is heading.
"On it." She says and pulls a handgun from a holster on her hip. She leans out of the doorway and empties the gun's clip by firing down below. She's not aiming for anyone in particular, she's just trying to buy them a little more time while Lauren goes to work.
Behind her, Lauren lays her hands over Olivia's bullet wounds, one on the front and one on the back. She closes her eyes, takes a few deep breaths, and concentrates on helping the body to heal itself. She straightens her posture, loosens her shoulders, and lets out a small groan as energy flows through her and heals the bullet wound. She removes her hands and it's gone.
"There. Good as new. It'll smart for a few days, but I fixed most of the damage." She explains.
"Thanks, you didn't need to…" Olivia begins, but Lauren shakes her head.
"Oh I think I did. We're in a little bit of trouble, we probably need you at full strength if we're going to stand a chance." Meanwhile, Amber fires off a few more shots onto the factory floor to keep the humans at bay.
"I see him." She says, as she suddenly stops firing. Right at the opposite side of the warehouse, in the corridor that leads to his makeshift office, Brick has come out to inspect the commotion. He stands tall, hand on his hips, looking up to their position. It takes everything she has to fight the urge to throw herself off the side of the walkway and make a dash for him. She wonders if she could make it through all the armed humans and get to him. She plants her feet, considering springing over the railing. Lauren lays a hand on her shoulder and her shoulders droop, and she suddenly

realises how tense her whole body has become. She relaxes it, just a little, and allows herself to be pulled back onto the other side of the doorway.
"I'll radio the others. We need a plan though, and quickly." Lauren says; making a clear conscious effort to keep her tone as calm as she can. She turns her earpiece off silent to call the others.
"Louis…Louis do you read me? Danny? Anyone?" She asks, but she doesn't get a reply. She looks at the others and Olivia shares her look of concern. "I'm worried." She tells her.
"We need to worry about ourselves first. What are our options here?" Olivia asks, trying to stay focussed on their current problem. She's right, of course, but Lauren can't fully take her mind off the others.
"We could retreat. Go find the others and come back…?" She says, though she knows that's not really an option for Amber.
"No! That gives him time to get away." She snaps, confirming that suspicion.
Amber peers through the doorway again, back out to the floor, and glares directly at Brick. One of the humans shoots; and it just misses her, catching the doorframe right next to her head.
"Amber, we're severely outnumbered…" Lauren tries, as if that argument will carry any weight.
"We can take them. We need to get downstairs, there's more cover there. We can pick them off one by one and then make a move on him. They're only humans. They'll go down easy." Amber explains with a surprising calmness. After the initial urge to vault over the balcony and throw herself head first into the fight had passed, she started working on a little less suicidal strategy. She was still fighting the desire to just charge, to an extent, but she was more intent on finding something that would work.
"I don't know…" Lauren says. She's torn because she wants to make sure the others are okay but she knows Amber won't agree to leave.
"Let's do it." Olivia concludes, and that's enough for Lauren to be persuaded. "Lead the way." She tells Amber, who doesn't need a second invitation. She charges forward, down the stairs and back the way they came. Two of the men have been silently making their way up to their position. She rounds the corner and, even though she's surprised, she acts quickly and decisively. In the enclosed space she's able to take them out easily, throwing herself viciously down the stairs to land on top of one, and then slamming the second into the wall before he can shoot. She incapacitates them quickly and efficiently, knocking them out.

"See, two down already." She says, looking back to Lauren. "Only another…did anyone count them?" She asks. They both shake their heads. Amber shrugs and looks to the doorway out onto the warehouse floor. "Then there's only one way to find out." She says, and reaches into her rucksack to pull out a pair of smoke grenades. She has a more concrete plan forming now. "Let's split. I'll go right, you two go left. The target is at the back, we can circle round and take him from either side. Remember, shoot to kill and don't let that fucker get anywhere near you." She explains to the other two. If Olivia, who had assumed the role of leader, has any issues with this she doesn't voice them.
"But, remember, no human casualties." She reminds them both. Amber shrugs again and Lauren shoots her a look of warning.
"Yes, fine. No human casualties. As long as we stop him then I don't care. Are you both ready?" She asks. They both nod but she's already tossing the grenades. She waits a moment, and then dashes forward, covered by the smoke, and they follow her lead.

His whole body is sore because every muscle has been fighting with itself and it takes a moment to recover from that. He and Danny are in a heap on the floor but he wills himself to clamber slowly back to his feet, still feeling a little disoriented by everything that just happened. He shakes his head to clear it and recover his senses. He offers Danny a hand and pulls him back to his feet. He stumbles and falls forward and they linger for a moment, pressed up against each other again, before they both separate and deliberately create a large physical distance between them.
"Are you okay?" Louis asks Danny, struggling to read the expression on his face.
"I…yeah. Fine. You?" Danny says, his voice shaking with uncertainty.
"Yeah. I think so." Louis replies. They stare at each other and struggle to find the right words; either to process what the hell just happened, or to try to plan what to do next, or even just to break the tension. "That was her." Louis offers, just because it's the only thing he can really think to say.
"Yes. I worked that out, thanks." Danny retorts, and Louis almost welcomes the hint of his usual condescending tone.
"What did she do to us?" Louis asks. Danny shakes his head, because he doesn't even know where to begin with answering that. Instead he nods down at Noel.
"Is he alive?" He asks, with very little concern. Louis has a pang of guilt

because he'd forgotten all about him, and rushes quickly to his side. He's breathing peacefully.
"Yes." He confirms as Noel groans and his eyes start to flicker open as he wakes up from a deep, deep sleep.
"What happened?" He mutters, looking up at him.
"We don't have time." Danny interjects before Louis can even comprehend how to explain.
"Yeah, you're right. The others." Louis agrees. He'd heard Lauren calling for them in the midst of the…whatever it was but he was unable to even register it at the time because of the compulsion to move. He shakes his head again, wanting to focus on the task at hand. He unmutes his microphone. "Lauren? We're here. Sorry…what's going on?"

Chapter Fifty-One

Amber is, for lack of a better term, a demon in the smoke. She uses it as cover to get the drop on another human and launches herself from behind cover so that she can tackle him. She smashes his head through a wooden shipping crate and punches him again until she's sure he's knocked out. She pulls the punch slightly, being sure to not cave his skull in, but uses a little more force than was strictly necessary. Then she ducks back into the smoke and moves forward until she's able to surprise another. She uses a hip throw to ground him, and then violently snaps his arm. He screams, attracting the attention of the others and giving away her position. She dives out of sight as a few of them whirl around to fire and is well hidden before they can.
The other two have taken cover as a pair of the humans have them pinned down with gun fire. Olivia is firing back; being as loud and obvious as possible to draw attention to her and away from Amber. Lauren, meanwhile, communicates their location to Louis now that he's finally replied.
At the back of the warehouse Brick is smirking to himself as he sees the silhouettes of his five remaining men fumbling around trying to stop the assault, and thinks to himself what useless bastards they all are. Andy is at his side, with a distinctly less amused look on his face.
"What should we do?" He stammers.
"Heh, don't worry, I don't rely on you for your brawn, get out of here. There's a back door that way," He says, gesturing over his shoulder. "This

lot are going down, but I can handle this by myself." He tells him, rolling his shoulders and getting ready for the fight that's coming. It's true, too, they both know Andy is there to help with the business. When it comes to the violence he's no use and Brick has never needed help with that. It's better that he's out of the way so he doesn't get caught in the cross-fire here. Andy clearly pauses and carefully considers this for a moment, wondering if he actually can abandon his boss, but ultimately he knows Brick is right. He'll be absolutely no use here. He turns and runs.
Brick doesn't take his gaze away from the floor, peering through the smoke to try to catch a glimpse of Amber. "She's making you look like idiots, lads." He calls out to them. "Then again, you've learnt a thing or two since last time I saw you, haven't you sweetheart?" He roars, with a chuckle, hoping that'll draw her out.
Lauren pops up from cover and shoots one of the men in the shoulder. Olivia uses her power to throw some debris into another, distracting him long enough for Amber to take him down. There are now three left. Brick sighs, and shakes his head, bemused as they take out another. He leans against the wall, casually, and waits for the inevitability of the last two men going down. They sure as hell won't be getting paid for this.
"What should we do?" One of them asks, turning to him in a panic.
"I woulda tried shooting 'em myself." He retorts and strides forward to where the grunt is. The man's demeanour brightens for a second, hoping that Brick is about to do something to save him, but instead he raises his hand high and brings it crashing down onto his head to incapacitate him.
"C'mon, get it over with. I'll give you that one for free." He shouts over to Amber, wherever she is. The last remaining man spins around to face his boss, stunned that he's turned on his own men.
"What the hell?" He asks, just before Amber springs up behind him, wraps her arms around his neck, and chokes him into unconsciousness. She pulls her gun out and aims it at Brick.
"Nice to…" He begins; and the sound of gunfire cuts him off mid-sentence. She fires again and again, rapidly and repetitively. She empties the gun at him but none of the bullets pierce his skin. He stands and lets them hit him like it's nothing. "That's no way to greet your old pal." He tells her with a shrug. She throws the gun at him in frustration. It bounces off too. She lets out a guttural growl and scoops a led pipe up from the floor. She charges at him and smacks him across the head with it. It bends from the impact and the force behind it, but it doesn't do any damage to him. He responds

by backhanding her across the face and launching her backwards. "I like this new you." He says with another infuriating smirk. "You're feisty. Can't wait to beat that outta you." He says, and strides forward to where she's picking herself back up.

Olivia and Lauren charge forward to intervene and repeatedly fire at him too. It does no damage but it does attract his attention and he charges at them like some kind of unstoppable bull, looking to charge right through Olivia. They both jump out of the way and he stops himself just before he collides with the wall. The three of them take a second to regroup as he stares them down.

"The bullets aren't piercing his skin. What do we do?" Lauren asks Olivia.

"I'm not sure." She replies.

"Find something else to hit him with!" Amber snaps, stepping in front of the two of them and fixing her eyes on him.

"I should be pissed off at ya. Getting my boys arrested earlier in the night. But honestly, I'm just happy to see you. You're like the one that got away. Glad we get to finish that tonight. It's nice you've brought some new friends for me to meet too. Funny idea of a girls night though, coming to die together." He tells her, trying to goad her into another attack. It works and she grabs the weapon of one of the henchmen she took out earlier, an automatic rifle, and empties it at him. The bullets thump into his chest and do no damage and he starts to stalk towards them. Olivia and Lauren rush forward to meet him before Amber can, with a flurry of strikes that he simply bats aside. Amber rushes at him too, she ducks under an attempt at a punch, climbs up his back and wraps her arms around his neck. Using all her strength she tries to squeeze down on the flesh but it won't budge; she can't constrict it and he tosses her off easily. She rolls as she hits the ground, pops back to her feet and is back on the attack. She punches and kicks and flails at him with everything she has but none of it has an impact. The other two join in, but even combined they can't do any damage. They're quick, and they're able to avoid his attempts to fight them off for a while, but they still can't do any damage. He catches Lauren with a vicious backhander and knocks her away. He then grabs hold of Olivia, throwing her back on top of Lauren. Amber keeps fighting, using every ounce of anger she has stored up at this violent, evil, bastard of a Used-to-Be to fuel her as she pounds away at him. Her knuckles are bleeding and still it's not even scratching him. He reaches out and grabs her by the throat. She

scrabbles, still fighting and flailing and attacking to try to get him to release his grip.
"You're doing more damage to you than you are to me." He says, taunting her. She knees him in the groin with everything she can because, when in doubt, go low. But even that doesn't phase him.
"Why won't you fucking die?" She chokes out at him.
"Like all your friends did?" He asks her with a sickening smile. She spits in his eye, and he drops her in surprise. She goes right back to punching him, angrily pounding at his chest and he retaliates, punching her so hard she's launched halfway across the factory floor. She collides with some old machinery and, even though it hurts her like hell she stubbornly starts to drag herself back to her feet almost instantly. He walks towards Lauren and Olivia who are also struggling to get up. "How about I kill a couple more and then we can have the place to ourselves?" He asks over his shoulder as he moves towards them like a hunter. They scramble up, ready to continue the fight. Olivia tries to use her powers to push him backwards, but he's heavy and she's not strong enough to do anything other than slow his approach down a little to give them some breathing room. He doubles down, planting his feet and continuing to walk towards them as if he's just being held back by a heavy wind.
Louis and Danny charge in through the front of the building and join Amber just as she's finished dragging herself up. "About time." Amber barks.
"Yeah, we got held up with…I'll tell you about it later. You look like shit." Danny tells her. She wipes a little blood from her face.
"Bullets don't work. We need to try something else." She explains.
"I've got an idea." Louis says. Once they'd heard the call from Lauren saying that they'd found Brick they knew they had to get over there as soon as possible. Danny and Louis had once again silently communicated and ran, as quickly as they could, towards the warehouse she'd indicated. They'd left Noel behind because he still wasn't fully with it and they couldn't afford to slow down. But on that short and desperate run over here his brain had been firing through all kinds of options to defeat a man who's skin couldn't be pierced; and that was when he remembered something he'd heard very recently. It was such a deliberately placed clue he wasn't sure if it would work, and if it did what Hazel would gain from it. But right now it was worth a try. He pulled out a syringe full of tranquilliser. "What if we go for his e…" He began.

"Yes. I just worked that out too." Amber said, cutting him off, because she'd just realised how she'd got him to stop choking her. She snatches the syringe from him. "Distract him?" She asks the two of them. They both nod quickly. They'll do whatever she wants them to right now.
Brick has now made it to Olivia and Lauren and they're again trying to fight him off. They're slower now because they're in pain and it's not long before he catches them again. He cracks Olivia across the face, breaking her nose and knocking her to the floor with a yelp. Lauren instinctively tries to reach out to help her and he smacks her with a heavy punch to the jaw. He takes a moment to stare down at them, considering exactly how to finish them off. A small bag of red powder smashes into his shoulder and explodes everywhere.
"...the fuck?" He asks; realising that it's from his remaining supply of drugs. Behind him Danny and Louis have invaded the half loaded van, which would've been their last one of the day, and are throwing around his product. Louis throws another one directly at him; and that's enough to make him charge at them. "I'm going to fucking rip your heads off." He roars. Expecting it, they both roll out of the way as he comes charging at them. Danny drops another one of the smoke grenades, and they disappear into the cover it provides. Brick grumbles and looks around, trying to see out of the smoke screen and coughing as he inhales it. Louis leaps out and throws his entire body weight into Bricks back. It doesn't do any damage but he does stumble, slightly, because he didn't quite have his feet planted. Louis rushes past him and into the smoke, but Brick follows. He chases Louis, who's much smaller than he is, out of the front of the warehouse and the night air helps to clear the smoke so that he can see him perfectly. He catches him and wraps his massive arms around his throat. Danny appears and cracks a plank of wood over the back of Brick's head. This causes an irritation rather than pain, but that's the plan and he drops Louis to try to grab at Danny. He dodges out of the way, and Louis pulls back, dropping something as he does. They both run off in opposite directions and Brick hesitates while he decides which one to chase and that's just enough time for the flash grenade Louis dropped to go off. It explodes right at his feet and the bright light blinds him momentarily. He stumbles, swearing and swaying around to try to get his bearings. He hears the roar of an engine from directly in front of him as he blinks and tries to recover; and just too late he's able to see a pair of blurry headlights heading straight at him.

The distance they managed to lure him away gives Amber just enough acceleration room to gather some good speed in the would-be delivery van. She rolls out of it just before impact and it collides with him, crushing the front of the van but knocking him over and trapping his legs underneath it.
She's back on her feet almost instantly, despite the pain she's in, because this is her chance. He will get back up if she gives him the chance, she knows that, and she can't let him. She dives at him and jams the syringe straight into his eye as she hits the ground beside him. He lets out a satisfying shriek as he feels pain for the first time in years, and she injects the drug. He opens his mouth to shout abuse at her but it quickly takes hold and he passes out. She picks herself up one final time and dusts herself off. Danny and Louis are at her side quickly, looking between him and her to make sure she's okay and that he's definitely down. She grabs the holstered gun from Louis' hip and points it right into Brick's face. If a needle can pierce his eye then she's sure that a bullet can do the same and she contemplates that for a moment. She could empty the whole thing into the bastard's eyes and end him for good. But she lowers it, and hands it back to Louis, because she's done enough. She could kill him. She should kill him. But, she has stopped him and That's enough.
"Better call the Cleaners. This place is a fucking mess." She says simply.

Chapter Fifty-Two.

Several hours later, after the Cleaners and after the clean-up, after the talking and the healing, and after making sure that Brick was taken away, and that the Humans would all have their memories wiped. After all that, Amber was finally alone in the War Room back at the house on Brickmere Road. She was exhausted and badly needed to sleep, but there was something she needed to do first. She'd taken Danny's laptop and dug back through her old case files and there, buried amongst the brutal details of their deaths, was a picture of her old team. She exhales deeply and nods to herself as she stares at it. She never thought she'd be able to do anything to make it easier and so she buried the pain and the feeling of guilt. She always thought that if Brick ever found her again there would be nothing she could do. She never, even for a second, truly contemplated that she might be able to bring some form of justice to the creature that had taken everything from the people she cared about. She never

considered it and yet it feels so satisfying to have finally achieved it.
"Sorry...I..." Louis says, opening the door and sees her sitting there in silence.
"It's ok." She says. "I was done anyway. Just...it doesn't matter." She shakes her head. Louis sits down at the table opposite her and just lets the silence hang there. "Stop it." She tells him.
"What?" He asks.
"This like...sympathetic silence. It's bollocks. This is why..." She trails off again and sighs in irritation. "This is why I don't talk about...you know..."
"Feelings?" He offers, with a little smile and it makes her laugh.
"Yes. Feelings. I didn't want you looking at me like I'm some kind of victim."
"I'm not." He says, quickly.
"I can see it." She insists, with a look of warning. He shakes his head again, because that's not what he's thinking.
"No. That's not what it is. I feel like I know you a little better now." He explains.
"Is that right?" She says, with an eyebrow raised.
"There's one bit I still don't understand though..." he begins, hesitantly, because he's still not really sure how far he can push. She gives him a look that he chooses to take as encouragement to continue. "Why didn't you kill him?" He asks. At first she just shrugs it off, but he keeps looking at her and waiting for an answer and eventually she relents.
"I dunno. I'll regret it, I bet. But I've spent so long scared about what would happen when he found me again. About how I wouldn't be able to stop it from happening again. I guess I wanted a little payback. I wanted him to wake up in, wherever the fuck it is we send these monsters, and know that I beat him...and to know that I can do it again. I wanted him to be scared of me." She says, sounding absolutely terrifying.
"I'm a little bit scared of you." He tells her and she laughs at that. A proper, hearty laugh that feels good. It's like she releases a lot of emotion in that laugh and she looks genuinely relieved.
"Good. I'd rather that than pity." She says.
"I'll keep being scared of you, then." He says with a smile.
"Thank you. I'm just glad I don't have to do the paperwork this time around." She says, getting to her feet and looking, for the first time since he arrived, like she's actually relaxed. "I'm off to bed. You have fun." She tells him as she leaves. She crosses paths with Lauren at the door, who gives her a gentle little tap on the arm as she passes and continues up the

stairs to bed. Lauren places a black coffee down in front of Louis.
"Here you go, sweetheart." She says.
"Thanks." He says with a grateful smile as he pulls the laptop across the table to him so that he can make a start on all this paperwork.
"I checked in with Olivia, she and Noel are back home and fully recovered. How're you feeling?" She asks,
"Yeah, I'm fine." He replies; having missed most of the actual fighting.
"Even with Hazel making another appearance?" She asks, and his stomach does some kind of sickening lurch at the mention of her name.
"I think I'll take a page from Amber's book because I'd rather not talk about that right now." He answers honestly. She's coming, he knows she's coming. But she also helped them. He's tired because it's been a long night and he has an unknown amount of report writing ahead of him too, so he really doesn't have the brain space to unpack everything about that interaction with Hazel. It's very much a tomorrow problem. "Besides, Chris made it very clear that this field report needed to be done…well, already."
"Would you like some help?" She offers.
"I think I'm okay with it. I've already made a start. You could call DCI Wade for me though?" He asks.
"Sure, what for?" She asks brightly.
"The drugs that weren't recovered at the warehouse, I want to see if they have any leads on where they might be. We're waiting to hear back what they were but…I think it's best we try to recover them." He explains, wanting to tie up all the loose ends with this case as quickly as possible.
"Oh! They probably do have them. Brick said that they had arrested his men."
"They did?" Louis asks. "How did they even know? We didn't call them?" He asks, and then kicks himself a little. That makes it sound like he thinks the human police are incompetent and that's not what he means. It's just that they discussed whether to get them involved when they used his associate's records to help identify his hideout.
"No, no, we didn't in the end." She confirms.
"Weird." He says, "I'll have to ask Danny to see if he can find any arrest reports. I need to speak to him anyway. Things felt awkward after the Hazel thing." He says, without really thinking. Again, he's tired, and so he hadn't really thought through what he was saying before it came out of his mouth.

"Awkward? What do you mean awkward?" She says, looking intrigued. He's not really sure, honestly. It was another part of the whole Hazel situation that he was avoiding thinking about. But she continues to stare at him, eyebrows raised, in a similar way to how he had with Amber only a few minutes ago.

"I don't know," He begins, still struggling to find what he really means. "I just, the way she made us dance together and stuff, I don't know it felt really weird. Being together like that I…" He trails off and she looks at him thoughtfully.

"Hmm. Yeah, I think you should talk to him." She says, pretty firmly.

"No." Louis groans. "Not about that anyway. I don't know." He honestly doesn't know what he's trying to say and what he feels here. Danny has been weird with him all day, even before that. He seems to have been extra prickly; and poking at some weird nonconsensual dance routine won't exactly make him any friendlier. "But I guess I do need his help."

"I think he's up in his room." She tells him, and it feels like more of an instruction than her helpfully sharing information. He nods, reluctantly.

"Okay. Sure." He says, a little flustered and wondering if he knows how to pull a police report without him. He doesn't, and he doesn't have time to work it out, and so he leaves the room and climbs the stairs.

He spends at least an awkward minute just hovering outside Danny's bedroom, laptop in hand, trying to work up the courage to knock. He's not even sure why. He'll knock, Danny will be a dick, but eventually will help. He knows how it'll go but for some reason he feels really nervous about it. He braces himself and knocks on the door. There's a shuffling sound on the other side and, after what feels like the longest thirty seconds of his entire life, Danny opens the door. He stands there with his hair wet and a towel wrapped around his waist, because he's clearly just got out of the shower and Louis' brain malfunctions. He doesn't know where to look or what to say and his jaw drops a little bit.

"What do you want?" Danny snaps.

"Oh." Louis says, remembering that he needs to speak but not quite being able to. It's like he's lost control of his body all over again and it feels unbearable. He's completely embarrassed and scared to say anything.

"I…erm…sorry…need your help with…" He stutters trying to look at anything but Danny.

"With what? What do you want, I'm busy. Can it wait?" He snaps.

"I didn't know, sorry. Yeah." He says and practically runs away, back down the stairs. Danny glares after him and then slams the door.

Chapter Fifty-Three.

It is ridiculously, stupidly, early. The sun isn't even up yet. Tim Copper hasn't been to sleep yet. But that's okay. He doesn't actually need much sleep. He hasn't for the last few years. Ever since the infection. He sits on a bench in Endsbrough park, mid-way through his first meeting of the day. This one isn't the sort he adds to the shared calendar, though.
"We picked up the last batch of his vile narcotics at 3am. They've all been destroyed." He tells her, and looks across, as if waiting for praise. "Off the record, of course." He adds. Hazel eyes him over her sunglasses, because even though the sun isn't up she's still wearing sunglasses and a large hat which serve absolutely no practical purpose.
"Good. I don't appreciate that dirty habit anyway, and I certainly don't condone his marketing of that beastly concoction." She dramatically shudders at the thought. "The good news is that his right hand man sang like a canary. Particularly when I threatened to pluck him like one. He spilled all his secrets. Even the ones he didn't realise he knew." She says with glee as she remembers the violent interrogation process she performed when she grabbed Andy as he fled from the warehouse.
"It feels a shame...to let one of our own get captured. Normally I try everything I can to avoid it." Copper adds.
"A necessary evil my dear. That was the point of us engineering his arrival. I did give him the chance to leave quietly, just to ease my own conscience but he refused. Brick isn't really one of us anyway. We look after each other, you and I. He's never understood that. He's always just chased profit. Peddling those drugs laced with...eww." She says, pulling a face. "It's nasty. I've never agreed with it. But the way he does it. Ohh that is something to be coveted."
"Is there a body I need to take care of?" Copper asks her
"What's that dear?" She asks; having got lost in her own thoughts.
"The 'canary.'"
"Ah, yes, if you don't mind. I don't want them finding the body. Let's keep their attention elsewhere to avoid giving them spoilers. It's nearly time. They just need to be misdirected a little longer before my grand finale..." She says, adding some dramatic flare to her words.

"I wish you'd reconsider." He asks her sadly. He spends a lot of his time and resources trying to avoid any kind of conflict with the Custodians, and here she is inviting it. He'll never argue with her about it, that's not his place, but he's been desperately trying to get her to not go to war with them.

"I can't." She says sombrely. "It's not just about Joseph. Not really…" She tails off, looking sad for a moment. She allows herself that. One moment. Then, she catches herself, and returns to a more upbeat and performative tone. "You said the reporter was asking questions?" She asks.

"Yeah, cornered me in a coffee shop earlier today." He explains.

"Well. Maybe it's time we give her some answers." Hazel tells him with a smirk and glides gracefully to her feet. She adjusts her hat, stands, and grabs her bag from under the bench. She starts to walk away and then looks back at him, wistfully.

"It'll soon be time. I need to know you'll play your part?" She asks.

"I will. Of course, I will." He says eagerly. He may not agree with her course of action, but he is loyal to her no matter what.

"Good. Good. Timothy…I'm curious, and I can't believe I've never asked. What is your favourite movie?" She asks him.

"The Green Mile…why?"

"Ah, an excellent and, thankfully, fitting choice." She says, before straightening her shoulders and preparing to leave him with one last message. "We each owe a death. There are no exceptions. But, oh God, sometimes the Green Mile seems so long." She says, and nods, as if that made complete sense. She turns on her heels and strides away, leaving him alone on the bench in the early morning, thinking about what's to come.

Part VII: And That's Why I Hate You

Chapter Fifty-Four.

"Puddles!" Hannah called out across the field. It's been a long, shitty, Autumn day, and the last thing she needs is her dog running off into the muddy and damp field and getting herself covered in all kinds of filth. But it looks like that is exactly what is about to happen. The deep and defeated sigh that comes from her fiancee beside her says that he's equally as resigned to their fate of having to bathe the Border Terrier when they get home. Still, at least that gives them something to do other than fall asleep on the sofa after the beef ragu that's been in the slow cooker all day. The couple, in their mid-30s, have been in a bit of a rut lately because Autumn, frankly, is depressing. It's getting to the point of the year where the sun is down early and no matter whether it's rained or not it's still damp. There's no freshness in the air, just a chill, and their post work-walk with Puddles is the only time they can really make for each other through the week.
"Nooo!" Paul groans as the dog, having ignored Hannah's call, starts to roll around in something. They're definitely giving her that bath then.
But, that's when they hear the hammering of feet suddenly from behind them; and a stranger charges straight through them and knocks Hannah over into the mud. She shouts in surprise and Paul stands watching after the figure and wondering if he should give chase. Puddles charges back towards them, yapping as she does.
"Watch where you're going!" Paul shouts after the stranger, who is already a considerable distance away, charging across the field and away from the tiny little damp dog who never got close enough to offer a real threat.
"Help me up!" Hannah cries meekly.
"Oh, sorry." Paul says, apologetically and reaches down to help pull her up to her feet. They laugh to each other as another figure thunders through the entrance to the park, giving chase to the first. Paul rounds on him to get some answers but before he can open his mouth Danny is already barking an order at him.
"Move!" He shouts, but they don't have time to react and this time it's Paul that's shoved out of the way and into the mud. Hannah bursts out laughing, seeing the funny side of the whole messy situation, and because he looks like even more of a mess than she does, but Paul's jaw drops in fury. She offers him a hand, still laughing, but he struggles to his feet himself while shaking his head and staring off in the direction of the two figures.
There's a third set of footsteps, and this time a woman enters through the

gate, struggling to keep pace with the others.

"Oi, you! What's going on?" Paul shouts at her.

"Ooh, I really can't stop!" Lauren explains, dodging politely around them and briefly petting Puddles, who has finally returned to her owners, as she does. She really has no desire to stop and chat to two muddy looking humans.

"Lauren, hurry up!" Danny's voice orders through her earpiece, and she quickens her pace again. Up ahead he dives into a patch of bushes that the target had thrown itself into in an attempt to escape them.

"I'm coming!" Lauren responds, as he battles his way through the foliage, getting scraped and scratched as he does. He feels some particularly aggressive greenery scratch at his cheek and wonders why the Used-To-Be couldn't have stuck to the path. Fighting his way through bushes is not how he had wanted to spend this evening.

"He's getting away." He snaps into his earpiece as he bursts through the other side, scratched, scraped, and unpleasantly damp from the residual rainwater on the leaves he'd pushed through. The target is gaining more of a lead and is now more than halfway across the football pitch on this side of the park with no hint he's slowing down. There's no sign of Lauren behind him and he doesn't know where the other two are. He sets off again, swearing to himself about the lack of backup.

"Oh shut up, we're coming." Amber says over the comms channel. Ahead of him the Used-to-Be reaches the end of the pitch and runs up a hill, towards a patch of trees with a busy road on the other side. If he makes it there's a good chance he'll escape; because he could duck down any number of side streets.

"Where are yo…?" Danny begins to snap back; but his question is cut off before he can finish asking it. As the Used-to-Be reaches the tree line Louis steps out suddenly, having used the trees for cover, and smacks him in the stomach with a thick, broken branch. The Used-to-Be stumbles back, confused and angry. Louis swings again, but the creature, which they've codenamed 5DG, jumps backwards to avoid it and flings himself forward. Louis ducks and rolls, sending him crashing into a tree. 5DG stumbles back to his feet and considers charging at Louis again. He'll never admit it, but Danny is actually a little impressed and Louis has slowed the target down enough for him to catch up. 5DG, a scruffy looking beardy man in torn dark clothes, looks between the two of them as they stand side by side and clearly decides the odds are not in his favour. He

takes off again but this time it's Amber that meets him. She launches herself from one of the trees and drop-kicks him square in the chest; sending him skidding across the mud and back to their feet. Louis, as if they've planned it, tosses her a syringe over and she catches it before diving down and jamming it in 5DG's neck. He quickly loses consciousness, she stands up tall and then, of all things, Louis and Amber high-five and Danny stands staring at them in awe.
"Cute." He says, tilting his head and scowling.
"We took a shortcut." Amber says with a shrug.
"She means we doubled back, jumped in the car, and drove around to the other side." Louis says, gesturing over his shoulder to the edge of the park where the car has been left abandoned on the path.
"Well we obviously weren't going to catch up to him." Amber says dismissively.
"Great, well thanks for wasting my time." Danny bites back, finding himself really annoyed by being left out of the plan. Not that he'd have gone for it if he'd have known. There's no way he'd have been the one chasing the target across a muddy field if there was an option of just jumping back in the car.
"It wasn't a waste, you directed him to us." She says, with a playful punch in the arm. He glares and she gives him the most deliberately sweet smile.
"It was Louis' idea anyway. Blame him." Danny glares over at him too, but Louis completely avoids his gaze. Danny opens his mouth to say something, something insulting no doubt, but he's interrupted by the arrival of Lauren who is being tailed by two very muddy humans and their dog.
"Lauren, who are your friends?" Amber asks, as Puddles yips at the group and Paul surveys the group angrily.
"Who are you people!?" He demands. Lauren gives them all an apologetic look, indicating that she couldn't get rid of them.
"Clear for Cleaners." Danny instructs the team they have nearby, hoping that he can avoid whatever ridiculous Human dramatic outburst is about to occur. He's tired and damp and can't really be bothered with this.
"You're the one who shoved me over!" Paul says, shattering that particular hope.
"You were in my way." Danny tells him coolly.
"What happened to him?" Hannah asks as she catches sight of the scruffy looking man lying flat on the floor at their feet. Amber, Louis and Lauren all look at each other in a panic as they try to come up with a convincing

explanation. Sadly, it's Louis that opens his mouth first.
"Erm...narcolepsy?" He blurts out and all of them, even the dog, stare at him in awe.
"What?" Hannah asks.
"Narcolepsy?" Amber repeats, laughing. Louis can only shrug. In the distance a van has pulled up next to their abandoned car and three Cleaners start to approach through the patch of trees. They look a little like ghosts, and if you didn't know what was happening it would definitely look spooky; three nearly identical figures descending from the woods in the dead of night. Or, from a small patch of trees in the evening. Either way, the two humans look at each other nervously, and Louis, for some reason, decides that it's time to start talking again.
"Okay, so..." He starts, fumbling around in his pocket for a badge that he flashes at them. "We're with the police. This man is a criminal that we've apprehended, these men are here to help take him into custody."
"What kinda police officers?" Paul asks, distrustfully.
"Why's he unconscious then?" Hannah asks. At least it distracted them from the Cleaners. Amber crosses her arms, leaving Louis hanging with no help. Danny exits the conversation and starts directing the Cleaners.
"Well, he's very dangerous. We really had no choice but to sedate him." Lauren jumps in, seemingly the only one unable to leave Louis to flounder.
"What's he done?" Paul demands. Louis glances over to Amber but all she does is shake her head.
"Murder. Lots of murder." He blurts out. Even Danny turns back to gawp at that. He takes a moment to shake his head and stare, thinking about how even after all these weeks Louis is still totally hopeless. He then directs one of Cleaners to talk to the two Humans, before it's too late. Lauren jumps in to explain this as well, because he didn't have the patience to try.
"This gentleman will take a statement from you both for what you saw; he can provide you with the right contacts to get your cleaning bill taken care of." She says to the two of them.
"Just the last hour will do it." Danny tells the Cleaner, who confirms their understanding with a subtle nod.
"...the last...what?" Paul asks.
"Not talking to you." Danny says.
"Our colleague will explain everything." Lauren tells them and, with only a little trepidation, they allow the Cleaner to lead them off a little way, away from the other two who are securing 5DG. Once they're out of earshot

Amber whispers to the others.
"Memory wipe?" She asks.
"It was easier." Danny says, with an eye roll.
"Probably best. Not sure they fell for the Narcoleptic Serial Killer bit." Amber laughs.
"Yeah. Maybe narcolepsy wasn't the best way to start." Louis admits. "I think I could've saved it though?"
"No, you were floundering. It was like watching a puppy drown." She tells him.
"We found out his identity because he fell asleep at the wrong time, and one of his victims escaped. The survivor was able to give us a perfect description and, being the wonderful detective team we are, we tracked him down immediately. He was our chief suspect anyway. We'd just already written him off, because of, ironically, the narcolepsy." He continues, with a laugh.
"You're an idiot. You're making it worse." Amber says, joining in on the laughter.
"I think it could be a great film." Louis offers up.
"I'd probably watch it, actually…" Lauren adds, and they begin to walk back to the car, expanding on the joke that Danny refuses to acknowledge. Their job is done and he can't wait to get his wet, muddy, shoes off.

Chapter Fifty-Five.

"I want food." Amber says the very second they're through the front door; and marches straight for the kitchen.
"I'll come help." Lauren says, following her with the intention of just doing it for her. "Boys, want anything?" She shouts back over her shoulder.
"No I'm okay, thanks." Louis says.
"Yeah, same." Danny says, fighting off his soggy trainers. As the two women disappear off into the kitchen, with Amber listing off all the things she wants to eat, it leaves the two of them standing together in an awkward silence.
It's been a week since Brick's capture and, for two people who live in the same house, they've done a really good job of avoiding each other for almost the whole time. It's been a lot of leaving rooms as the other entered, or making sure that there was at least one of the others there at all times. It had helped that their Narcoleptic Serial Killer, who was actually

neither, had been the first hint of demonic activity since Brick. It made it easier to not interact because they had no case to talk about. This is the first time they've been alone since Danny opened his bedroom door shirtless and Louis inexplicably lost the ability to function. Then, of course, there was the weird, Hazel-induced, dance routine that they'd still not spoken about. There was a lot that had been left unsaid. Or that had been avoided. Whichever.

"Well, I think I'm going to…" Louis begins, already heading for the stairs before he even finishes explaining that he's going to bed.

"Wait." Danny says and Louis stops dead; but still avoids turning to actually look at him. "I thought maybe we could start looking at this Hazel thing?" He offers.

"No. Not tonight." Louis says, still not turning around to actually face his teammate.

"Why?"

"I'm tired." He says. It's not a total lie.

"In the morning?" Danny asks.

"Maybe." Louis replies coldly, and continues the march up the stairs before Danny can force any more conversation from him. The truth is it has been mostly Louis avoiding Danny. The truth is Danny is probably completely ignorant of the things that aren't being said between the two of them, because Danny is ignorant about everything. But Louis isn't. For someone who labels himself as intelligent Danny is someone who doesn't think an awful lot; especially when it comes to other people. Louis though? He's a complete over-thinker and whilst right now he should probably be obsessing over Hazel and her vendetta against them, he's been spending the last week trying very hard not to think about everything that's being left unsaid between them because he's finally starting to work it out. He's avoided Danny and distracted himself with everything except Danny, but yet all he's really thought about is Danny. That's why he just can't look at him. Danny, meanwhile, shrugs off his teammate's weirdness and heads into the War Room without giving it another thought.

Elsewhere in Endsbrough someone else has spent the last few days avoiding thinking about something. Kim is alone in her apartment; it's clean now, and all of her research and clutter has been thrown in the bin.

The day after their investigation had really kicked off Matthew had met her for breakfast at Jan's and told her it was over. He'd been a reluctant

partner all along, but this was very different. He'd explained how he couldn't risk his job on a wild goose chase, and that he was going to take some time to focus on his life outside of the police force rather than obsessing over this. She'd tried to talk him out of it. She'd tried everything she had in her arsenal, dangled every little tidbit, but he was more stubborn and determined than he'd ever been. So, instead, and she wasn't proud of this, she stormed out of the little cafe insisting she wasn't going to drink any more shitty coffee and calling him a coward. They were so close to getting somewhere with this little mystery and she couldn't believe he was ditching her. It felt like he'd dangled this tantalising puzzle in front of her and then tried to tear it away just after he'd started putting it together. Kim and Marc had continued trying to research the story for the next few days but without Wade they were just meeting dead end after dead end; and without that man on the inside to help pull up case files that the Counter Terrorism Team had been involved in they really were lacking a lot of the tools they needed. Begrudgingly, they had given up a couple of days later. She'd sent Marc back to University and she'd thrown her research and days worth of empty food containers and takeaway coffee cups away. She loved a good story to obsess over but the clean-up was always a bit of a bitch afterwards; when you really get your head stuck in something then everything else goes out of the window. So her apartment is clean now, and that's the sign that it's truly, properly over. But, as she towel dries her wet hair ready to go to the station that morning, her phone rings.
"Hello? Yes! Hi. That's amazing. Thank you. Okay. Yes, just text me the address, and whatever time works for you and I'll be there." She says, and hangs up looking a lot more hopeful because, actually, the story isn't as dead as she thought.

Chapter Fifty-Six.

It is cold in the morning, because again, this is taking place in late Autumn. But there's something Louis quite enjoys about sitting at the little metal table in the tiny back garden of the house in the chilly morning air.
It probably doesn't need to be specified, but the only one of them with any kind of green fingers was Lauren; and she'd clearly spent a lot of time out here making use of what little space they had. There was a small patio area, with a little wall surrounding it and on the other side all kinds of lucious and well cared for plants. It was the perfect little escape from the

madness that was seemingly always happening inside and that's exactly what he's been using it for.

He takes a long inhale, filling his nose with both the crisp morning air and the smell of his black coffee, and then slowly and mindfully breathes out. He keeps his neck and back perfectly straight, with his shoulders back, and just pays attention to what he can hear. There's the sound of the next door neighbour's garden chimes in the gentle breeze, the odd bird chirping, and the distant hum of traffic from the nearby main road as humans commute to their jobs. It's nice because it's a reminder that there is so much of the world around him; and so much outside of his problems with Hazel, and Danny, and everything else.

He takes another deep breath in and reaches out into the world around him, doing what Lauren said and using his power to reach out and find what he can. He'd felt things last night, with 5DG, he'd seen flashes of the man he was before. He had been another one that had been identified by Danny's surveillance system from an open case in Wales. His system wouldn't be able to pick up everything, he had explained, but would be able to search case files that were shared widely throughout the Custodian network. That was often the practice if a Used-to-Be had escaped capture and was believed to have fled the area. It wouldn't be done for the more high profile ones; like the file that no doubt existed on Hazel, or even the one on Joseph. Information on those kinds of high profile Used-to-Bes would be kept on a need-to-know basis. Those are the kind of files that would be taken on only by Level Three and above. The ones that were widely shared though, the creatures that had evaded capture through some fluke rather than the really dangerous ones. But still, when confronting 5DG last night he had been able to feel him. The same way he had with Joseph. He'd been able to see flashes of the man he'd been all those years ago. But this time it didn't overwhelm him. This time he'd kept his calm and let it flow through him. He'd breathed through it. Sure, 5DG, or Aethan as Louis had learned he'd once been called, was a lot less filled with rage than Joseph had been. He'd not been brutally murdered and he'd not had decades to stew on it and let his anger grow from it. But it was an achievement nonetheless. It was a sign that, as Lauren had said, with time and practice Louis might be able to control this and actually use it properly. Use it to learn about the Used-to-Bes they faced, to understand why they act the way they do and maybe even to track them or anticipate what they'll do next. He didn't know the true limits of it; but after Brick and now

Aethan being successfully captured he was hopeful that he could learn. He just hoped it would be before Hazel made her next move.

So he reached out to see if he could feel anything, anything at all in the nearby area. Demonic energy was everywhere in the world, it was constantly spreading like a disease across the globe and infecting humans and objects every day. There must be some nearby.

…but he was interrupted by an incoming video call from his phone on the table in front of him. It was Chris. He did think about just ignoring it, and was very, very tempted by that idea. But he knew it wouldn't do any good in the long run. He put down his cup, still with half a coffee in it, and rested the phone against it before sliding the screen to answer it. Chris appears on screen, sitting at his desk, in his office, in Home Base.

"Ah, Louis. Good morning." He says.

"Hi." Louis replies, a little meekly.

"Sorry to call you early, just had a few things I wanted to go through with you. I finally got around to reading your report about the incident a few days ago. I've been too busy. But I got to it this morning." He says, gesturing to a print out of the report in front of him. Louis had submitted it the day they'd captured Brick and that had been over a week ago. Chris had been very insistent that it was done immediately and yet, had taken a week to actually look at it. Louis wants to question that. He'd stayed up for hours, tired and aching and desperate for some rest but knowing he had to finish the report. Instead, he just asks:

"Yeah, the one about Brick?"

"Yes, but again I'd rather you address them by their code names. 3SP." Chris replies, and begins reading from a list he's made that's in front of him. "I'm concerned there are still several loose ends. I can see most of his men were detained, which is good. The Cleaners were able to test them, clear parts of their memory, and release them…but I notice there are still a few unaccounted for. My primary concern is with the Human Terrance Church and the man who was with him. I'm a little disappointed you've not tracked them down already. Why haven't you done this? Unless this is incomplete and you've taken further action?"

"The human police supposedly arrested them; but there's been no record of that." Louis confirms.

"So where are they?" Chris asks.

"I don't know." Louis says hesitantly. It was a question that had been bothering him, too, but with his insistence on avoiding Danny it wasn't one

he really had the tools to look into.
"Exactly." Chris says, with a heavy sigh. "You should."
"Yes, ok." Louis admits, because although it pains him to agree with Chris, he's right. "I'm sorry. Did the tests come back on the drug he was selling?"
"That's not important. Finding these men is." Chris says, shutting down his curiosity.
"Okay, well what about the part of the report about Hazel? Did you read that?" He asks, finding it odd that wasn't the first bit that Chris was drawn to. He'd covered extensively their encounter with her, the power she'd had over them, and even how she appeared to have helped him in identifying Brick's weakness.
"I did," Chris says with an impatient tut. "And that seems unimportant too."
"But what are we going to do about her?" Louis asks, even though he knows he shouldn't. Chris doesn't seem to have any interest in Hazel. Just in tying up this particular case.
"Look, Louis. I've been thinking about this quite a bit…and I think I'm going to look at transferring you back to your old post." He says, and it's like all the air suddenly leaves Louis' lungs.
"What? Why?" He asks; and that just antagonises Chris further. He's clearly displeased with being asked to justify himself, and he furrows his brow before snapping his response.
"That, for a start." He begins. "But that's not all. From everything I've seen so far I just don't think you're ready to be here. You have no respect for the chain of command, your report writing skills are subpar, and you are too easily distracted. First your obsession with 4XM and now this. I just don't think you belong in that team right now. You're not seasoned enough, you're not experienced enough, and frankly, I'm not sure you're a good enough Agent." He says, and that last part hurts. It makes his stomach lurch like he's suddenly been turned upside down. "I held off out of respect for Rachel. Bringing you here was the last decision she made, after all, but I think it was a poor one. Frankly, you're lucky I'm not sending you to be retrained." he says, with one final jab.
"I don't want to go back…" Louis says quietly, and, if he's honest, a little pathetically. It's true. He doesn't. Jongleton had felt like home for so long but so much had changed in the weeks since he arrived here. He couldn't go back to that quiet life of nothing.
"I'll think on it a little more. It really feels like the best option for you, though." Chris says, and it's very obvious he's already made up his mind.

He wants Louis out of the way and that's been clear for a while now.
"But…" Louis begins to protest. Chris cuts him off like a parent scolding a child.
"I said I'll think a bit more. In the meantime focus on the task at hand – and find out where those humans are. We can speak more about this later, I've not really got time for it now. Bye." And with that he ends the call, leaving no more room for discussion. Louis is left a little stunned by the whole thing. He sinks in the chair, no longer sitting up straight, and lets out a low, sad, groan of frustration as he shakes his head. After a minute of quiet sulking he jumps as he feels a hand on his shoulder.
"Sorry! Didn't mean to startle you." Lauren says, moving around and taking a seat opposite him.
"Did you overhear any of that?" He asks, cautious and embarrassed.
"Any of what?" She replies, in a sweet tone. He's not sure whether she genuinely didn't, or she's lying out of kindness.
"Just a conversation with Chris. It doesn't matter," He says, brushing it off because, whichever it is, he doesn't want to talk about it anyway.
"Ah, I just assumed you were out here trying to meditate." She told him, with a kind smile. She'd definitely overheard some of it, then. He could tell by the smile. But, it was well-intentioned and he knew that.
"I was until Chris called. Neither went particularly well, honestly." He said, rolling his eyes.
"You just need a little patience." She tells him, giving him a look that said that covered both things. He didn't see how patience would help with Chris.
"Not sure I've got time to be patient." He replied, and that also covered both. He really would need to pick a lane for this conversation eventually.
"Ah." She said, with a nod. "As far as this Hazel goes, we'll work it out." She said; picking the conversational lane for him. "Danny's already up and pouring over the evidence. I assumed you'd be joining him. Or…are you still avoiding him?" She asked, with a knowing little smile. Now he was beginning to question her intention.
"I'm not…I'm…" He snapped. Though, he didn't finish that thought, he couldn't, really, because she was right. So he just glared at her like some kind of petulant child because he was annoyed she was right.
"Anyway…" She said, standing up. "I just came to see if you wanted any breakfast. I'm making bacon and eggs?" And in that moment he let go of any bubbling resentment because all he'd had so far this morning was

coffee; and his stomach wasn't particularly happy about it.
"Yes, please." He said, cracking a little apologetic smile.
"Lovely." She replies, cheerfully clapping her hands together. "I'll bring yours and Danny's through together since you'll be off to help him." And with that she turns and goes back inside, before he has the chance to argue.

"Hi." Danny said, with an extremely smug smile as Louis crept into the War Room a few minutes later. Danny didn't even look at him at first, and that was welcome for a change.
"Hi." Louis repeated. As Louis awkwardly shuffled further in and took a seat opposite him Danny's eyes darted away from the screen and peered directly at him over the top of his glasses. Louis was fairly certain he only wore them to look clever.
"Decided to stop avoiding me, then?" He asks him, as his deep brown eyes fixed on him. Louis was stunned into silence for a second as their eyes met and he felt a jolt of queasiness.
"I haven't been." He argues, but struggles to regain his composure.
"Oh, really?" He says, with a cruel little eyebrow raise. Louis could feel sweat on his brow and he wasn't really sure why. This wasn't good. Danny just kept staring at him, as if waiting for an answer. Louis decided the only way to deal with it was to stubbornly stare back and it works, because eventually Danny relents. Probably through boredom. "Either way, you can make yourself useful."
"What do you need me to do?" He asks reluctantly. He doesn't want to slip back into this. It feels like too big a risk. Like he'll be drawn into something he's not sure he wants to be part of, even though he's not quite sure what it is. Danny's face seems to light up a little when he agrees to help; and Louis' stomach lurches again.
"Okay, so, I remember when I worked out the 4XM thing it was the link between the victims." He says.
"When you...?" He repeats, laughing in amazement.
"Yeah, when I single-handedly worked out the pattern with 4XM's murders and used it to capture him, because I'm incredibly clever." Danny replies, with another grin. He's such an arsehole; but this isn't the same kind of being an arsehole it was all those weeks ago when Louis had first arrived. This seems way more playful, and that seems even worse, somehow.
"Yes, I remember now. Clearly I forgot because I wasn't there." Louis

replies, unable to stop himself grinning back at him as he plays along. "So when I did that…it was revealing that pattern that helped piece everything together. We need to find whatever that is for Hazel." Danny explains, with excitement creeping into his voice.
"How do we do that?"
"Not sure. Was hoping you'd have some ideas for a change." And just like that they seem to have slipped back into being a team. Here Danny was, however subtly, asking for his help. That definitely wouldn't have happened a few weeks ago either. It was obvious that the way Danny felt about him had changed, too. This was getting even more dangerous.
"Well, we could start by giving Olivia and Noel a call, they said they were investigating already…" Louis suggests, and it's mostly because he's desperate to avoid the dynamic of it being just the two of them.
"Absolutely not. Noel's an idiot. Olivia's not much better." Danny says dismissively. So much for that idea then. "Let's just not bring them into it. We did just fine together before." And there it is again. That little jolt in his stomach.
"We? I thought it was all you?" Louis says, with a laugh.
"Okay, fine, you vaguely helped. Just as a sounding board, really. Someone to bounce ideas off."
"Ah yes, of course. So bounce away then."
"We just need the one thing that makes everything else make sense. Let's work through the questions we already have." Danny says; and there's clearly no escaping this now. They're in it together. But then Louis has a little pang of guilt. Chris seemed pretty determined that he would be sending Louis back to Jongleton, so chances are he won't be here to see this through. That's especially true if he continues down this rabbit hole with Danny, because Chris was pretty clear they should leave the Hazel thing alone. Then again, that wasn't going to stop Danny, and Chris seemed to have already made up his mind already, so he might as well dive in for what little time he had left here. He might as well spend as much time on this, with Danny, as he could.
"I guess the big one is why she helped us with Brick?" Louis asks, committing.
"Yes! I guess because she wanted us alive?" Danny wonders.
"Maybe but I'm not sure."
"Okay, what else?"
"We don't know who she was, before she was infected." Louis says,

thoughtfully.

"Okay. And that's important..." Danny says, narrowing his eyes slightly and sounding like he's asking a question. Louis laughs at him and nods. He finds it a little endearing; again, the Danny of a few weeks ago wouldn't have even considered acknowledging that who a Used-to-Be was before they were infected was important. Maybe he had learned a few things from him too. Maybe, he'd even softened him slightly. If that was the case, at least Louis would be able to head back to Jongleton knowing he'd accomplished something.

"It is." He confirmed. "If you think about all the success we...you had with Joseph. It was linked to those killings. They were motivated by what had happened to him while he was human."

"Well, I'm glad you were paying attention."

"Of course. We've got a few questions left about the Brick case while we're at it, and I think maybe they're linked." Louis continues, thinking it through as he talks. There really is more to Hazel's involvement with Brick than simply wanting to keep them alive for her own twisted game. There has to be.

"Oh. Shit." Danny says, looking like he's having his own epiphany. "Links!" He says, as if that's supposed to make sense. Louis looks at him blankly, silently asking him to elaborate. "I read your report. On Brick. I didn't hate it. Your best one yet." He continues. That's backhanded because Danny knows that's the first time Louis has written one, but it still makes him smile a little too much. But it doesn't actually explain anything about his train of thought. "You said about the arrests of those two humans, but there's no record of them right?"

"Yeah?"

"Well, I think we can assume that Hazel was the one behind that exploding warning we got?" He says. Louis still isn't caught up. "You remember!" Danny tells him. "The whole 'I will not be pursued thing,' when you broke my laptop?!" He explains. And it does ring a bell. It was so long ago; but it was the warning they'd received the night of Steven Robinson's capture (in part two, chapter seventeen).

"Oh! Yes!" Louis says, and his eyes widen as he realises what Danny means.

"...and it was delivered..."

"...by the human police..."

"...so maybe..."
"...someone in the Human Police..."
"...has a link to Hazel!" Danny finishes; with a look of pride like he's just solved the whole thing. "It's Wade. Obviously." He adds.
"What?" Louis protests.
"It makes sense. He was at the Hotel. Could've tipped her off. He was the one you called to help clear out that bar we were supposed to meet Joseph at. You're a bad actor but I don't even think you're bad enough to give it away over message. He had to have been tipped off!" He explains and, actually, it makes sense. But Louis still doesn't believe it.
"Okay, okay. It's worth looking into. But where do we start?" Louis asks and, as if she's been waiting for her cue, Lauren bursts into the room carrying a tray full of food and two fresh coffees.
"You start by eating." She says, announcing her arrival. She places the plates down in front of them. "Scrambled eggs, bacon, and two black coffees..." She says, before adding; "Are you sure you don't want tea? No? Fine suit yourselves. Right. And while you eat you bring me up-to-speed too. I want to help. And I'm sure when Amber drags herself from her pit she will too. We all know how she'd feel if she missed an excuse to punch something." She tells them, matter of factly. And it's nice. There's absolutely no hesitation about what Chris will think, or about defying him. She's just ready to be part of their little team. Louis explains to her where they've got to so far, how they're trying to build the bigger picture of Hazel and who she is, and how they suspect that there's someone within the Human police that is working with her.
"Danny?" She asks, when he finishes.
"Yeah?" He says.
"Didn't you identify those two humans by tracking their van?" She asks; and again Louis wants to kick himself for not thinking of that sooner.
"Yes!" Danny says, catching on too and beginning to tap the keys on his laptop excitedly. They were tracking the van so surely they can find out where it was actually stopped that night. If they can do that...
"And in the meantime. Chris made a point of saying you'd destroyed all of Alex's records..." She begins hesitantly, knowing she probably doesn't want to ask the question because she already knows the answer. Danny reaches into a draw behind him, without moving his eyes away from the laptop, and pulls out a stack of paperwork. He drops it on the table in front of her. "Yes. I thought so." She says as she calmly picks it up and begins to

leaf through it. "I'll also reach out to Olivia and see if she has anything at all she can share."

"Great idea!" Louis says before Danny can object. He gets glared at for that; but it doesn't last long because his attention is pulled back to his search.

"Oh! I've got it." He says. "Obviously, because I'm amazing." He adds. With a quick tap of the keys the footage appears on screen of Terrance Church and his accomplice being arrested by three officers. Louis recognises one of the uniformed officers; but he can't place the man in charge at all. He's relieved that none of them are Wade, though. Not that this exonerates him. But it's a good start.

"That's DCI Wade's superior." Lauren says quickly.

"Hmm." Danny says, as if that backs up his idea that Wade is behind it all.

"I don't remember seeing him before?" Louis says.

"He was at the Hotel when Chris, Rachel and I arrived." Lauren explains, and Louis and Danny eye each other suspiciously.

"Maybe I should go speak to DCI Wade, and see if he can help us at all. Even if it's just to find some information about the arrests. This could still be perfectly innocent."

"Well yeah. They're either deliberately covering it up or they're just morons." Danny says. "I'm not sure which is more likely."

"And that is exactly why you shouldn't come with me." Louis says with a smile.

"Yeah. I'll just stay and have it all solved by the time you get back." Danny retorts. "But, be careful." He adds, with a flash of genuine concern across his face that makes Louis' stomach lurch one more time.

Chapter Fifty-Seven.

A few weeks ago not hearing from Kim would've been no big deal. But that was before. That was before they'd spent so much time together researching and digging; and it was before he'd severely pissed her off by telling her he was out. Wade had met her for breakfast the day after Kamala had broken the news about her job, and in turn broke the bad news to Kim that he was out because his family had to come first for once. To say she wasn't happy was an understatement. He'd tried to get her to kill the story all-together without him there to offer at least some level of protection, but she'd refused and stormed out of Jan's and that was the last he'd heard from her. It was properly winding him up too, because she wasn't answering his calls or returning his messages and he wanted to make sure she wasn't doing anything stupid. He was giving serious thought to the idea of just going over there to make sure she hadn't gotten herself killed.

And then, to make his mood even better, when he arrived at the station that morning Louis was already standing there waiting for him.

"Oh fantastic start to the day. What do you want?"

"Is there somewhere else we can go?" Louis asked him, looking around suspiciously.

A few minutes later Wade had led the way out of the police station. There were plenty of people around making their way to work, because Endsbrough police station was right at the edge of the town centre, and so they'd taken a walk across the bridge, the busy road filled with morning commuters, and to the path that was down by the river. It wasn't all that private; but it was a lot quieter than anywhere else.

"This is better." Louis says, taking a quick look around to make sure there's no one else from the station there. He's not planning to tell Wade the full story; but he definitely doesn't want to be overheard.

"This ain't where I'd usually talk shop." DCI Wade tells him. "Bit nippy out here too, so maybe we should make this quick?"

"Sure. I just thought it was a good idea to make sure we weren't overheard." Louis explains.

"That seems a little suspicious if you ask me." Wade says, impatiently. He waits, as if he's expecting Louis to disagree, so when he doesn't he continues. "Just spit it out. What is it this time?" He asks.

"There were arrests made a few nights ago, a couple of men transporting drugs. Terrance Church and someone else. I need information about it."

"Can't help you, even if I wanted to." He says, with a shrug. "I've heard nothing about no drug arrests. You must've got the wrong end of the stick."

It's painfully obvious he's not willing to help, and Louis doesn't really blame him. He's been clashing with Chris because of being cut out of investigations and not being able to do his job; and that's exactly what they do to Wade. It's difficult, of course, because it would require a lot of explanation and breaking one of the fundamental rules of the Custodians. Part of their whole purpose was to make sure that humans didn't know about the things that hunted them. But he's not going to get anywhere unless he gives a little, and even then he doesn't know how much he should give because Danny's distrust of the human policeman could still be justified. Just because he doesn't get a particularly bad feeling about Wade, doesn't necessarily mean Danny is wrong. He can't sense anything though. There's nothing demonic about Wade. There's a trace of something, but it's not strong and he can't tell what it is. He's not even sure if it's demonic; he could just be picking up on Wade's dislike of him and the rest of the team. He decides to continue cautiously.

"Ok. Yeah. So, we saw some CCTV footage of a couple of men being arrested." He pulls out his phone and shows Wade the footage Danny found. He gives him a moment to watch it, before pressing further. "I think that's DSI Copper? Your boss? There's no record of anything about this and…"

"Let me stop you right there." Wade growls, defensively. "Tim Copper is an incredibly meticulous man. I'm certain there will be a very good reason there's no record of the arrests, and I don't see how it's any of your business anyway. What does an arrest for possession of drugs have to do with terrorism?"

"It wasn't possession, I think they were supplying them…" Louis clarifies, but it doesn't help.

"Question still stands." He snaps. He lights up a cigarette and sits himself down on a nearby bench, quite clearly trying to get his temper under control. Louis gives him a moment because he doesn't want to push too hard and not get any help. "You lot. You just pop-up making demands with no real rhyme or reason. I don't get it. Nothing about it makes any sense and you're not a great liar. I want to understand, I want to believe you lot are doing something good. You seem like a good kid, I'm not so sold on some of the others, but you seem alright. Tell me what this is all about and I might be able to help. Tell me what you're covering up. What was the deal with Steven Robinson? What happened to his daughter? And what was that fucking shoot out all about? I'm not helping you until I understand what you're doing. Get me in trouble over it if you want. Go over my head. I don't care any more. There, I said it." He says, letting it all out. Louis sits down next to him. He quickly gets a face full of second-hand smoke and regrets it. He stands back up and moves away, leaning against the railing in front of the water, staring at Wade, and considering his next words very carefully.

"I can't tell you a lot." He says.

"Bullshit." Wade laughs.
"No, really, I can't." Louis says, with a nervous laugh. "You probably wouldn't even believe most of it, and one of the very first things I learnt growing up was not to share what we're doing with…" He tails off, catching himself just in time but his eyes widen as Wade fills in the blank.
"With us Humans?" He says.
"…what?" He says, panicking.
"That's what you were gonna say, wasn't it? Kim heard it. The other week. When that young lad was killed. Your friend Danny called us it. Humans." Wade says, staring a hole right through him. This is going very badly, Louis realises.
"I…" He starts. But, he's stumped. "I'm…" He tries again but he's still not sure what to say. He considers whether he should just leave, just getting up and walking away to avoid it. He can't though, he'll never get anything from Wade if he does. But then, if he handles this badly and gives away too much then he'll definitely be sent for retraining.
"Does that mean you're not? Human, I mean. She was right…" Wade says, jumping in and taking Louis' silence as all the answer he needs.
"I don't know, actually." Louis says with a shrug, realising that it's the truth.
"The fuck do you mean you don't know?" Wade says, sounding annoyed by it.
"I've not…thought about it." Louis explains, realising that he hasn't. He's never actually questioned what he is. He knows he started as a human but he's not entirely human any more. "I think I'm mostly Human. Human…plus?"
"Plus what?" Wade asks with another puff on his cigarette.
"I don't know. I've never asked." Louis says, laughing to himself a little because it's kind of funny. How has he never really thought about this? He's given so much thought to who he is and what he's supposed to be but he's never actually asked himself this question. He just always accepted that he was gifted these powers but never how it all worked, because he's never had to explain it to someone else. At that moment he felt like a complete fool.
"Asked who?" Wade says, and he's softening because he can see that Louis is as confused as he is.
"Long story. Look, I can't even…it'd take me about five years to explain it. This isn't…I didn't mean to…please don't tell anyone I said all of this."
"You've still not really said anything. Just a bunch of crazy gibberish, and

it's makin' me even less inclined to help you."
"I get that." Louis says, leaning on the railing and facing out towards the river. In the distance he can see the industrial estate where they fought with Brick and where Hazel appeared to them. It gives him an odd little pang of emotion as he remembers being forced to dance for her with his body pressed against Danny. He knows he needs to say something to get Wade to help because this is tied to her somehow and they need to stop her.
"I can't tell you everything." He confirms, turning back to Wade with a little more resolve. "But, I do need your help. The hotel massacre, and Steven Robinson and his family, and the shooting and probably a lot more…the same person was behind all of that. We stopped him, and I thought that'd be it but now there's someone even more dangerous. Someone…really powerful…and I'm supposed to be able to stop her too…but I'm terrified of the thought of even seeing her again. We're supposed to be the ones who…I don't know…I have all these stupid ideas in my head like I can make any kind of difference in the world…and this woman…it's like she's made me realise just how stupid they are…and how powerless I am. I'm dreading what she's going to do next and I don't know   how to stop her. I need your help because I'm scared. I'm not meant to be scared. But I am. And I think Chris is right. I'm terrible at this. Shit. I'm sorry. I didn't mean to…" He looks down at the floor. He didn't mean for all of that to come out but he's desperate. He's desperate to stop Hazel. But not for himself. He's scared of what she's going to do to the others. He lets out a sigh because he's just admitted things to Wade he's not admitted to anyone else; and he's definitely starting to realise something he's not quite ready to face.
"It's alright. That's the most honest any of ya have been with me." Wade says, and he takes a long pause to consider it. "What can I do?"
"I need to know why those people were arrested. How your boss knew to arrest them, I mean. Was there a tip off? And what happened to the men, because there's no record of them."
"I'll see what I can dig up." He says with a nod. "Steven Robinson's daughter. What happened to her?"
"I don't know." He says, honestly. "She's safe, I think. Her dad was very sick…and there's a chance that she got sick too. When we captured him…they'll have taken her too. To make sure that she's not sick. If she's not then, I think, she'll be given a new life."
"What if she is?" He asks.

"Then she'll be in the right place." Louis tells him with a nod, because that's all he can say. If the tests they ran showed she was infected then he doesn't think he'll ever know; but she'll already be in custody so she won't be able to hurt anyone the way her father did.
"I dunno what that means…but it's the best I'm gonna get isn't it?"
"It's all I know." Louis says with an apologetic look. "Minus the bits you'll say are crazy. I tried to find out more but…I can't. I'm sorry." Wade tosses his cigarette and gets up, then brushes himself off from the dirty bench.
"It'll have to be enough then. I'll see what I can dig up about these arrests for you. I'm not making no promises but I appreciate the honesty…it still don't really make sense to me. But…I can see you're not lying to me and that's enough for now." He says, and he gives him a look that borders on kind. Louis appreciates that more than he'll ever know.
"Please don't…" He begins to ask, and Wade raises a hand to stop him.
"I won't."
"Thank you." he says. "For listening, too." They wait in an awkward silence for a moment. Neither really sure what to do next. Louis catches a glimpse of a human couple walking past and his eyes follow them and it gives him a little pang of sadness. Wade gives him a little nod and turns to walk back to the police station. Louis takes a deep breath, building up to something, because there is more he has to say. "Wait. One more thing…"

Chapter Fifty-Eight.

Kim arrives at the street of the address she's been given bursting with excitement. She's thrown a tight and light blue skirt and blazer combo on; doing her best to look the part of a professional journalist. She's well aware of the impression clothes can make and right now she wants to make the best possible impression. She needs to be accepted by, and to be trusted to tell the story of, the woman she's going to meet. She has a coffee in one hand and her tripod in the other. No Marc or any other help today. Again, the goal is to get her interviewee to open up and the best way to do that is for it to be as intimate as possible. She stops at number 12, takes a moment to get her game face on, and then knocks gently on the door. All while not spilling a drop of her latte, obviously. It opens almost immediately, because she's exactly at the time they agreed, and she's greeted by a predictably messy woman.
"Margaret Bailey?" She asks, already knowing the answer. The woman's

messy greying brown hair is sloppily tied up and she's wearing a huge thick pair of glasses that make her look like some sort of insect. She wears an old, worn out house coat that covers her entire figure and makes her look frumpy and out of proportion. She looks very much like someone who recently lost her son. "It's Kim. We spoke on the phone?"

"Oh. Yes." The timid woman says, and opens the door wider to show her inside. "Please, come in." She says, and as Kim does she seems to nervously check outside to make sure there is no one else.

"Don't worry, it's just me." Kim says, in an effort to put her at ease. She knows she needs to tread really gently here. Margaret nods and closes the door behind her.

"Am I okay to set up in here?" Kim says brightly, pointing through to what looks like the living room. Ms. Bailey hesitates, and then nods.

"Yes. That…probably makes sense." She says.

"Great. I'll get the camera ready." Kim replies. She still keeps her tone deliberately bright and friendly, but the other woman's eyes widen in a panic. It's a look that's only heightened by the large glasses she has on.

"Oh, I didn't realise we'd be recording. I've not got my face on. Do you…do you mind if we don't? I'm still happy to answer your questions but…I'm afraid I'm a little camera shy." Kim is disappointed, but she does her best to not let that show on her face. She's so keen for answers that this will still be incredibly useful. This woman, the mother of one of the victims - Benjamin Bailey who's crime scene Kim was at (part three, chapter twenty) - is bound to be able to provide another piece of the puzzle.

"No problem. Can I still record the sound on my phone though? Makes it easier to type up later."

"Yes, yes, that'll be fine. Please, have a seat." Margaret says, ushering her into the living room and onto one of the sofas. The house is covered with a thin layer of dust, like it's been left to sit and fester for a little while. That makes sense though, Kim thinks to herself as she tries not to notice it, this woman has lost her son so housework has probably been the last thing on her mind. She shouldn't be judging herself for it, not when her apartment quite often looks like this for no good reason. She places her phone down on the table in front of her and pulls her notepad from her handbag. "Can I get you anything before we start?" Margaret asks her, hovering.

"No, no, I'm all set thanks." Kim says, holding up her coffee cup.

"Okay, well I'm going to make myself a quick cuppa." The other woman replies, making a hasty exit and leaving Kim alone.

Kim proudly wore the label of being nosy when she decided to go into journalism. Yes, she'd always enjoyed writing and that was a massive contributing factor. It was a much more practical choice than the hope of being a successful author. But it was her desperate desire to know everyone else's business that had really led her to start interning at a newspaper all those years ago. It was no surprise then that in the very short window she has left alone she can't fight the urge to snoop a little and is quickly on her feet cataloguing the contents of the room. It's filled with all sorts of eclectic nick-nacks and Kim focussed in quickly on a photo of Margaret's son Ben. It, like everything else, is covered in a layer of dust that she doesn't want to disturb but it's definitely him. Mrs. Bailey breezes back into the room and practically throws herself down on the sofa opposite Kim with an exasperated sigh.
"Oh, I hope you don't mind..." Kim says, having been caught red handed. Kim eyes her awkwardly, and straight away notices the lack of tea. Unsure whether she just changed her mind, or came back because she realised Kim was snooping, she continues her mission to tread carefully. "I'm sorry for your loss." She says.
"Thank you, dear. My boy was beautiful. My world is...a much darker place without him." Margaret tells her, with an odd new found energy to her. Kim nods, sympathetically.
"I'm sure. Do you have any photos of the two of you together?" She asks, unable to stop herself from mentioning the lack of them.
"They're around here somewhere. They've been a little painful to look at though..." She explains, somewhat dismissively. Kim doesn't push, she just sits down and grabs her notebook. It's at that moment her phone starts to ring. It's Wade. He can wait. She switches it to 'do not disturb' and hits record.
"Why don't you tell me about him?"

Determined to get to what's actually going on, both for his own sanity and because he actually wants to help Louis, Wade goes to work as soon as he gets back to the station. He tried calling Kim on the walk back, but isn't surprised she didn't answer. He heads straight to the front desk, which is empty, and helps himself to the stack of unfiled paperwork that's there. He flicks through it looking for anything to do with the arrests.
"Everything okay?" The desk sergeant, Jack Appleby, asks him as he returns from wherever he's been. He's eyeing Wade suspiciously.

"Yeah. Yeah. Just looking for something." He mutters dismissively, knowing that won't be enough to dismiss the nosy old bastard.

"Anything I can help with mate?" Appleby asks him, stepping in front of the computer as Wade turns towards it.

"Maybe, yeah. Are we holding anyone on drugs charges? Or have we brought anyone in recently that's been involved?"

"Not that I know of. Erm…I can double check if you like." He offers.

"Nah it's alright." He says, because he wants to look by himself. If Tim has cocked up, or worse, then he wants to be the first to know about it. Besides, Jack is alright to go for a pint with, as they've done many times over the years, but he's not the most efficient.

"Is this…because of that kid from the Counter Terrorism Unit?" Appleby asks, having obviously seen Louis when he first arrived.

"Yeah. He's got some mad theory that, well, it's probably bullshit."

"Yeah. Thought murders were more their bag?" He laughs. A lot of the lads on the force dislike them for the same reason Matthew does; and Jack Appleby is definitely in that club.

"Me too. Like I said, it don't make a right lot of sense." He says, reconsidering his want to help. But that's when he spots something really suspicious. A small post-it note on the desk with two names written on it. The two names of the men who were arrested; and it's in Jack's handwriting. "What's that?"

"Oh nothing." He says with a wave of his hand, sitting himself down. "Woman trying to report her husband and brother as missing."

"Right? And?"

"Well, didn't seem like a priority if I'm honest. They've both got a criminal record. They probably just got themselves mixed up in summit dodgy." Wade raises his eyebrows at him, giving him a look that says it all. Appleby hunches like a kid who's just been caught by the teacher. "I can probably get someone to pop round and speak to her later…"

"Yeah probably should…" Wade orders; eyeing his colleague suspiciously. Appleby smiles and tries to laugh it off. He always does. Laughing along about how useless he is with the other lads. It's a running joke, how useless Jack Appleby is. But Wade can't help but wonder if there's more to it than just a little laziness. It's a pretty big coincidence.

"Probably turn out they're just a couple of puffs who've ran off together! …not that there's anything wrong with that these days…I just…" Jack says, trying to diffuse with a really shitty joke. Wade shakes his head at him and

turns to walk away.
"Just send someone out to speak to her." He says over his shoulder "I'm off out for a cig."
He pulls out his phone as he heads to the door, because now he really needs to speak to Kim. She's going to have to get over how mad she is at him; because she's one of the few people he can trust to help him make sense of this. It goes straight to voicemail.
"Kim, gimme a call. I need your help with something."

Chapter Fifty-Nine.

"Oh Ms. Adams I'm not sure exactly what you're looking for here." Margaret says, eyeing her in a peculiar way through her smudged glasses.
"I just want to hear what you have to say." Kim prompts, gently. She hasn't even answered the first question yet, so this really isn't going well. Kim is determined though.
"What is it you really want to know?" She asks. "Because I don't think you're here for the biography of my dear, dear son." The same meek woman she met moments ago is coming alive in front of her eyes. Perhaps she's getting a glimpse of who Margaret Bailey was before her son was murdered. Kim sighs and hesitates for a moment. Of course she's not here for a biography. She's here because she thinks this woman will be able to provide some insight into the Counter Terrorism team. Even if that is just another mysterious memory lapse. But it's obvious that her initial tactic of kind charm isn't going to be a winner here. She decides that she'll try something a little closer to the truth, something a little less gentle.
"There's been nothing reported about your son's killer. The police don't seem able to find him. I thought maybe, if we spoke, I could help." She says, careful to skirt the line between a lie and the whole truth.
"Help catch a killer?" Margaret says with a strange smirk.
"Something like that. I'm sorry, this must be so difficult for you. But, I promise, I do want to help. Why don't you tell me about him?" Kim says, trying the soft and kind approach once more.
"I can see you do." Margaret says. She stops for a moment then. A dramatic pause, almost. She gets a faraway look in her eyes, as if she is delving deep into her memories. "He was special." She says at last, with an affectionate little smile on her face. "You know when someone comes into your life at just the right time? That. He popped up at just the right

moment and he lit the place up, and now that he's gone I'm just left with so much anger. Just pure white-hot rage at the people who took him from me."

"The people?" Kim asks excitedly before she can even think about it. She's a little ashamed because she's not sure it was the right response; but her stomach had lurched at 'people' and the idea that her suspicions could be leading somewhere here.

"Yes." Margaret says, simply and coldly.

"Do you know who killed your son?" Kim asks.

"I know who's responsible, yes."

"Have you told the police?"

"Oh no, dear, the people who took him away are above the law."

"What makes you say that?" Kim asks. She's aware that she's probing a grieving mother for information and that feels like it comes with all kinds of moral complications; but she also feels like she's on the cusp of something that will help this all make sense. And, as it turned out, she was.

"Because they've been doing it for years and they've always got away with it. Just hiding there, picking us off. I should probably be afraid that I'm next." Margaret says; and Kim can't stop her eyes widening at that.

"There's a link isn't there? Your son's death and the massacre at the Eagle Hotel. They're related." She asks, again a little too quickly.

"You could say that. It sounds like you've got it all worked out."

"Not quite. I can see pieces of it but the whole story, I can't see that yet. Please, help me fill in the blanks. What really happened to Ben?"

"He was born into the wrong family." Margaret says with a strangely nonchalant shrug that Kim is too excited to really process in that moment.

"What...what is it about your family? Who's targeting you?" She says, eagerly. Margaret takes a long pause, with her head in her hands, to collect her thoughts. She takes off her thick glasses and sets them down on the table; and it's only then that Kim notices her perfectly manicured red nails which contrast completely with the rest of her appearance.

"Oh you're asking all the wrong questions." She says.

"What do you mean?" Kim replies, and Margaret stands up, slowly, but with a grace that she didn't have before. She sighs deeply and walks over to the mantlepiece to look at the photos there.

"You're here to quiz me about my dead son...there's an expectation there you'll leave all sense of tact and decorum at the door. If you want to ask me something just ask it." She tells her.

"Okay." Kim says, before double checking that her phone is recording and bracing herself because, this is it. "There's a group of people. They work under the guise of being some kind of Counter Terrorism Unit but it's paper thin. It's clear they're involved in something else. Were they involved in the death of your son?"
"Yes." Margaret says without taking a single moment to pause. But what Kim doesn't realise is that she's not speaking to Margaret Bailey, the grieving mother of a son who was taken too soon. No, she's speaking to someone who's been playing that role, and who is fast growing impatient with it. She turns to face Kim, who has absolutely no idea how much danger she's in.

Just as Louis gets through the front door, taking off his coat as he does, Danny happens to be coming out of the War Room to grab his own.
"Oh, good, you're alive." Danny says.
"Yep." He replies. "Where are you going?"
"I've got a plan." Danny says, grabbing his jacket, like that answers it.
"A plan?" Louis questions.
"Yep. So don't worry. You just sit yourself down here and chill. I've got this." He says, cockily. Louis smirks because he's so irritating and it's so strangely endearing.
"What's the plan?" He asks.
"I suppose I've got time to explain it." Danny says, grinning at him and pretending to check the watch he isn't wearing. "The drug Brick was selling has been analysed by the Cleaners. There's a record of it; but it's one I can't access."
"Right?"
"Or rather, I can't access it here. If I go back to Home Base I'm inside the network and it should be a lot easier." He explains.
"Should I come?" Louis asks, because it sounds like it could easily go wrong.
"No, no. You stay. You'll be no help." He says, casually. Louis' face drops at that; and Danny actually notices. "No, I didn't actually mean it like that. I just mean it should be easy. Once I'm inside and on their network the security is a little friendlier. And if I really need to I'll just ask Chris' computer."
"Danny that sounds…" He begins cautiously. Danny waves him away.
"It'll be fine." He says, confidently. "I was thinking though, do you want to

do something later?"
"Huh?"
"I'm bored, honestly." He says. "The only time I get out of the house at the moment is to work a case. Why don't we just go do something Human? We can still talk about Hazel and Brick's drugs, and whatever else, but let's do it somewhere else. You were waffling on about movies before, why don't we go see one? Or, I don't want to be shot at, but how about a bar?" He asks, tilting his head towards him in the most peculiar way, his deep brown eyes burrowing into him. Louis gets that feeling in his stomach again; and he's so confused by it. It seems very unlike Danny to be offering something that sounds so friendly. But, he cautiously leans into it.
"Okay. Sure. If you want…" He says, hesitantly in case it's a joke.
"Good. Okay. That one we went to the other week, that first kid that was killed? In the alley outside?" Danny suggests, and it's obvious he's given this some thought.
"Technicolor?" He says, remembering the scene.
"Yes, that one. I'll have this all wrapped up by like five. I'll meet you there, then?" He asks; and again Louis is still waiting for the catch.
"Umm, yeah, okay." He says, narrowing his eyes at him.
"Good. I can tell you what I find – and you can debrief me on whatever boring nuggets you got from Wade." Danny says, turning away from him and to the door.
"Well, actually he…" Louis begins.
"No, save all this boring shit for later." He says; and then he's gone before Louis can protest. He rolls his eyes and walks into the War Room, where he finds Amber. She grins with excitement as he enters.
"You're back! Good…" She says with a smile that inspires only terror.

Chapter Sixty.

"How do you know they're involved?" Kim asks, not even thinking to try to hide the excitement in her voice because this feels like everything she's been waiting for.
"You're still not asking the right questions." The other woman says; and her tone has completely changed now, because she's dropping the act. "C'mon Kimberly. I'm not enjoying this."
"Not enjoying what?" Kim says, quickly catching on to the fact that something isn't quite right.

"This conversation. I thought I'd want to keep it up longer. But playing the role of a grieving mother I guess it just hit too close to home. Plus, you're not an ideal scene partner. I'm having to carry you." She explains, frustration seeping into her voice and she drums her nails on the dusty mantlepiece.

"What're you talking about?" Kim says, and her heart is sinking because now she knows this isn't what it seems.

"You came close to blowing the whole thing early on." 'Margaret' explains, adding a layer of exposition to the proceedings. She grabs a picture from the mantel-piece and tosses it over to Kim. She catches it and takes a look. It shows Ben and his mother Margaret. The woman in that photo looks nothing like the woman in front of her. Kim looks between her and the photo, her eyes widening as she does the maths.

"Who are you?" She asks, just as Hazel removes the greying wig and tosses it aside. She takes off the wig cap and lets her wild brown hair loose.

"Not Margaret Bailey, obviously." She explains, as she tosses the old house coat aside too. She stretches and her posture alters completely too. She looks far more poised. She turns back towards Kim and smiles, looking like a completely different woman. "I'm an actress, darling." She says with a laugh.

"Where is Margaret Bailey?"

"Dead." Hazel says with a shrug. "Maybe. I don't know. I don't care. The house has been empty for weeks. Maybe she ran. Maybe she was taken. It's really not my problem."

"Taken by who?" That question elicits a playful wink from Hazel and that's enough to make Kim lean forward to stop the recording in frustration. This is all useless now that she's realised she's talking to some lunatic, rather than the grieving mother she came to meet.

"Oh I wouldn't." Hazel says. You see we're only just getting started. All that stuff I said, those wonderful lines about my son and the white-hot rage. That wasn't just gold; it was true. So I'm not Margaret Bailey, but this team of yours did take away the closest thing I've ever had to a darling son." She explains, sitting herself back down on the sofa.

"I'm listening." Kim says after a moment of hesitation. Even if this woman is a lunatic, she's an intriguing lunatic. She leans back and lets this mad woman, and the recording, continue.

"Good." She replies, sitting back and crossing her legs gracefully. "Really this all started in the 1940s..."

Louis slams face first into the floor and lets out a pathetic little 'ow' as he does. Amber steps back, clearly happy with her handiwork.
"You're getting better," She tells him. He clambers back to his feet, massaging his jaw where she struck him. They've been sparring since Danny left. She had demanded that she was bored, that he needed practice, and so had dragged him upstairs.
"That's not that comforting when you said I was terrible five minutes ago."
"Well, you're getting less terrible. Let's go again." She says, squaring her shoulders.
"This isn't all that fair when you're like five times stronger than me." He tells her, bracing himself too.
"I'm holding back." She scoffs.
"You've still got super-strength." He protests.
"So have you!" She retorts, and then, considering it adds; "Just...less of it. And so have they. What you gonna do crybaby, stop and ask the next Used-to-Be you face to give you a fair fight? Stop whining and hit me." She demands. So he does. Right in the face and she doesn't block it. She smiles as he pulls back. "There we go." She says proudly, and then she lunges at him. He ducks out of the way, narrowly evading her. She tries again, and he manages to dodge again. They continue like this. Sometimes he dodgers, sometimes she connects. She seems genuinely pleased every time he manages to block or dodge her; but equally she seems to take a perverse pleasure every time he doesn't. She's constantly the attacker, and he's on the defence the whole time.
"Did I hear Danny talking about going out later?" She asks while lunging. It throws him off, but not quite enough for her to connect.
"Oh yeah. He was just saying he wanted to get out. I wouldn't have thought a bar full of people would be Danny's thing, or anywhere involving people for that matter. Do you wanna come?" He asks, and she smirks to herself.
"You're so dumb." She says, and lunges again. This time she punches him in the mouth. He stumbles backwards but doesn't fall.
"Ow." He protests.
"Seriously though. Dumb. No, I don't wanna come." She says, firmly.
"Yeah. Same issue as Danny isn't it? Other people not your thing?" He says with a smile. She laughs and he uses that as an opening to strike her in the jaw. He connects.

"Nice" She says, surprised. "But seriously?"
"Seriously what?" He asks, not following her. She throws a punch, he dodges it. She smirks to herself.
"I don't actually mind a bar when I'm not being shot at. Not today though." She tries to kick him. He ducks, and charges at her, taking advantage of her lack of footing to tackle her to the ground. She fights back, punching him and rolling him off her. They both pop back to their feet. "Even less terrible!" She says with approval. They're interrupted by a knock at the door, and then Lauren enters, tightly clutching a laptop, like she's scared she might drop it. .
"I think I might've found something…" She says. Amber takes a quick second to smack Louis in the face as he turns to look at her. He yelps in pain and she bursts into a fit of laughter.
"Shit, I thought you'd duck!" She says, through chuckles. "Something else you didn't see coming…"
"Listen!" Lauren scolds
"Sorry, go on." Amber tells her, still holding back laughter.
"I just got off the telephone with Olivia." Lauren continues, doing her best to ignore them. "She and I have been working together on Alex's logs. We probably shouldn't be, I know. But she had a brilliant little theory."
She presses a few buttons, and a screen on the wall, similar to the one downstairs, lights up. "Oh, good that worked. Now, if I can just…how do we…" She taps a few keys, tuts, and then taps a few more. On screen there are pages from Alex's journals, where there are some words circled.
"What's this?" Louis asks, peering at it.
"We struggled before when we were looking for references to 4XM because there was so much of it. The investigation had been going on for years, it was garbled, a little all over the place. Chunks of it were even written in code."
"Yeah, I remember. Have you got somewhere?" He replies.
"Olivia has." She confirms. "They've been going over them for weeks; she noticed that Alex made references to 'the actress,' a lot of them actually." She tells them
"The actress?" Amber says, screwing her face up a little.
"Yes! We saw all of the research on 4XM, all the notes on his murders, and those articles. It was only part of the story. We've only got bits and pieces. Even now, between the two teams, we don't have the full set of journals. But, what we have is enough that we've realised he was never the target;

Alex was tracking 'the actress.' That's why it never made sense. It was never really about him. There's even a documented encounter as recently as last year in Edinburgh which is just before Alex turned up here. There's still a lot of the story missing but we're seeing what we can decipher."

"Lauren! You're amazing." Louis exclaims, really excited because this is the first concrete information they've had. "This can help us work out who she is."

"Well, it was much more of a team effort than anything else. Olivia had already noticed it. I was just able to help by providing the entries that we had that she didn't." She says, blushing a little with modesty. The complete opposite of when Danny reveals information he's found.

"It's great! We're actually making progress. Thank you." He says again, and she waves him off.

"Oh. Well. It's my pleasure. We might know more soon. Noel is searching for anything related to actresses called Hazel, any suspicious disappearances, or murders, or anything like that. Hopefully that'll bring us even closer." She says.

"Amazing. I can't wait to tell Danny!" He blurts.

"I wonder why that is…" Amber mutters, but not quite quietly enough for it to go unnoticed.

"It'll motivate him. He'll want to find it before Noel does." He explains. It's true. Nothing motivates Danny like the ability to rub his intelligence and skill in someone else's face.

"Sure." She says. "Speaking of which, shouldn't you go clean yourself up before…?" Louis wipes a little blood from his face. He's got a split lip from Amber's last punch.

"Oh, yeah!" He says, taking a quick look at the time on the wall. It's 16:03. "Good point. Lauren, thanks again." He bounds out of the room excitedly and Lauren stares after him with an eyebrow raised.

"Where's he going?" She asks Amber after he's passed her. Amber grins, keen to share what she knows.

"Alright, enough." Kim says, when Hazel takes a pause in her story. "I don't know who you are but I'm not gullible enough to believe you're some…hundred-year-old actress who developed some kind of crazy magic because she was left dead in a ditch. Someone obviously put you up to this, but I'm not wasting any more time here. I'm done." She stops her phone recording and stands up, ending this ridiculous charade. Her money

is on the idea that someone associated with the Counter Terrorism team paid this woman to feed her this crazy story to throw her off what's really going on. "Oh, and if this is meant to scare me off whatever is actually going on here, you have no idea who I am." She says, irritated that anyone would try such a stupid trick. Like she was just some newly published hack who'd be too grateful for a big story to properly give it any thought. The woman opposite her, Hazel, lets a small grin spread across her face, maybe because she knows she's been rumbled.
"If I wanted to scare you, Kimberely..." She says, eerily. Kim rolls her eyes at her; refusing to be intimidated by someone who believes herself to be some kind of witch. She grabs her things and makes for the door and, thankfully, this woman does nothing to try to stop her. But when she grabs the handle and pulls the door doesn't budge.
"Alright, let me out of here." She demands, rattling the handle.
"You could just ask nicely." Hazel says, still from her seat. She waves her hand and the door pops open. Kim steps back in surprise.
"How did you do that?" She asks, searching for some kind of mechanism to explain it.
"Crazy magic." Hazel says with a cackle and, seeing no kind of mechanics within the frame, Kim turns to look at her again with interest. Hazel waggles her eyebrows because she knows she's got her back on the hook. "To put it incredibly simply, my powers are based in theatrics." The door slams shut again and Kim jumps. "I can add a level of drama to any situation I please." She stands back up and walks back over to the mantlepiece, hovering around some of the ornaments. "Lighting..." She says, and the lights respond to her cue "...or sound..." She says and from nowhere music begins to play. It sounds like jazz music and she begins to sway to it, dancing around the living room a little and thoroughly enjoying herself. There are no lyrics to it but Kim recognises the tune. "Benny Goodman, In a Sentimental Mood." Hazel tells her with a wink before she stops swaying and returns to the mantlepiece. "...and then of course, we have props..." She says and blows the dust of one of the ornaments. It's a small statue of two dancers. She waves her hand and they come alive; they too are now dancing to the music.
"This can't be real..." Kim mutters, trying to reassure herself. Hazel sighs and the music, the dancers, and the lights all stop and return to normal.
"I assure you it is. I always had a flare for the dramatic and now I am life imitating art. If I've seen it on the silver screen I can make it happen in the

real world. What's your favourite movie, Kimberly?"
"What does that have to do with anything?" She asks the question with a tone of indignation. She's still desperately searching for another explanation to this. This woman simply can't be who she says she is; but her curiosity is definitely back and she can't hide that. Hazel stares at her, waiting for an answer, and so she relents. "It's Moulin Rouge."
"Oh, a fabulous choice." She says with a gleeful clap of her hands. "Do you see yourself as Satine? Wait, no. You're a storyteller, of course, you're more of a Christian." She says, but Kim refuses to be distracted by being drawn into being analysed based on her choice of movie.
"This seems like a stupid question at this point…but what do you want?"
"No, no. That's exactly the question this script calls for. Tonight's a special night for me. Your 'Counter Terrorism' people. They're the people who've hunted me my whole life. They despise my very existence and the feeling is entirely mutual." And that's it. That's the point where Kim is fully sold. She walks back into the room, still somewhat cautiously, starts her phone recording again, and takes a seat.
"Tell me more."
"My kind have always been around. Poor little twists of fate, chewed up and spat back out. It can happen to anyone, anywhere…."
"The "infection"?" She asks, because Hazel had mentioned that bit in her story earlier.
"Yes. It's always there, circling like a dark cloud and the second you're at your most vulnerable it strikes. And it hurts Kimberly." She explains; and all the joy drains from her face as she casts her mind back to that time in her life. Her tone is solemn. "I'll never forget it. It was like something being stuffed down into my lungs, and expanding, and it felt like I was going to burst. I couldn't breath and I couldn't move and I couldn't stop it and all I wanted to do was die. And then it was like my entire body was burning, like instead of blood pumping through my veins it was fire. Scolding and melting away who I was." She breathes out, and her tone changes back to a more relaxed one. "I walked away from it, obviously. I was a whole new woman, and that fire stayed in my veins. I'll admit, I wasn't the most pleasant person to be around. But they'd have hunted me no matter what. This self-righteous bunch who've taken it upon themselves to police the world. They've no right. They've no right to just cart people away because they don't like who we are."
"You…mentioned your son?" Kim asks, tentatively.

"My beautiful Joseph. I rescued him. Horrid hateful humans killed him because they didn't like who he was. It struck a nerve. He's the killer you're looking for, from that hotel." She says, casually, and Kim's eyes widen in surprise. "Oh don't give me that look. He couldn't help it. He was obsessed with the men who tried to end his story. He let it consume him. He murdered them and it wasn't enough, so he worked his way through their families. Wiping them all out. He murdered this woman's boy. He was so damaged. But, they would've hunted him regardless because they fundamentally don't think we should be allowed to exist."
"Have you ever killed anyone?" Kim asks, trying to keep her tone level. The question doesn't come from fear, or judgement. She can tell Hazel doesn't want her dead. She seems to just want to tell her story.
"Oh god yes, of course I have." She says with a laugh, like it was the most ridiculous and obvious question in the world. In truth, it kind of was, Kim knew that would be the answer but she wanted it confirmed. It still doesn't make her afraid though. "Everything my sweet boy did he learned from me. Everyone I killed had it coming, and I was trying to stop. Okay, I put a cleaver through one of their heads and drowned another…but you're missing the point. Do you know what it's like to be constantly hunted like an animal? You're hung up with who's a killer and who isn't. I've got news for you Kimberly. We're all killers. Christian kills Satine. I'm hunted because I'm a killer but I'm only a killer because they hunt me. Oh but I'm getting too far off script." She says, sounding a little frustrated with herself. She shakes her head in what appears to be an attempt to compose herself. "Ask me again, what I want."
"What…what do you want?" Kim asks, hesitantly obliging.
"Tell our story, Kimberly, that way I'll always be with you." She says, dramatically, and with a chuckle.
"How would you have got to that if I'd not said Moulin Rouge?" Kim asks; but again, she knows the answer. Hazel just winks at her.
"Tonight is my big night. Tonight is my grand finale. I've been typecast as a villain and tonight I'm going to give them exactly what they want…a performance that'll knock 'em dead. Tonight I am going to war and I am ending this." She explains, and pauses, dramatically. "There have been tyrants and murderers and for a time they can seem invincible, but in the end they always fall. Think of it. Always." She says.
"Did you…did you just quote Gandhi?" Kim asks, unable to stop herself laughing at the ridiculousness of it.

"No, I quoted the film, Gandhi."
"But that's still…"
"Frankly my dear, I don't give a damn." She shouts, cutting her off. She stands and smiles, as if Kim should be impressed with how she arrived at another movie quote, or as if she should be applauding the performance. When she receives no such reaction, she continues. "In showbiz…you've always gotta have a backup plan. That's you. If I don't win then I'll disappear forever. I've spent so long obsessed with other people's stories and I want someone to tell mine. That's you, my darling. No catch. You wanted answers and I've given you them, or, close enough for you to fill in any blanks. Go ahead and look me up. Write your article. Solve the mystery of my disappearance, the Tragedy of Hazel Hardcastle, for anyone who still cares."
"I don't know if…anyone will believe me." Kim says.
"They will if you play your role with conviction. Set that camera up if you want. Now I'm not playing the role of Margaret Bailey I'm…"
"Ready for your close up?"
"Now you're getting it." She says with a wink, and sits herself back down.

Chapter Sixty-One.

He'd left it another hour and just ended up pacing around and not really getting a right lot done, because he couldn't think of anything else. So Wade had gone out for another cig, and tried Kim again. It went straight to voicemail, again. At this point leaving her another message would be ridiculous. He'd probably end up having to charge himself for harassment. But he wished she'd just call him back because she's the one he wants to speak to. He still doesn't fully trust Louis; and now he's starting to doubt whether he can trust people within the station. He doesn't want to be involved in this, he wanted to step away and stop digging like he told her he was going to, but clearly that's not going to happen. He considers ringing Kamala and talking it through with her. She'd be able to help him make sense of it, or just talk him into resigning with a big fuck you to everyone. But she's also got enough on her plate with the mess going on at her work and it doesn't feel fair to load this on her too. He grumpily sighs to himself and takes a drag of his cigarette.
"Fucks sake." He mutters to himself.
"Matthew." Tim Copper says as a greeting, as he walks out of the station

suddenly.

"Sir." Wade says, making at least some effort to compose himself. "Didn't realise you were here today."

"It's a fleeting visit. I just needed to check in on something." He explains, before peering at his old colleague with an obvious look of concern. "Is everything alright?"

"Aye, never better." Wade says, tossing his cigarette away. "As you're here anyway, I've got something I wanted to ask you about." He says, deciding he might as well go straight to the horse's mouth.

"Of course, what can I help you with?" Tim asks.

"Were you involved in any arrests a couple of nights ago? A couple of lads in who were arrested for transporting drugs, but there don't appear to be any record of it. Names were George Green and Terry Church. Ring any bells?" He asks, and braces himself, watching Tim's face for any sign of a reaction.

"Oh." He replies, and his face seems to fall a little. "May I ask the reason behind this sudden curiosity?"

"Well, the Counter Terrorism guys came round asking about it, to be completely honest." He says, because there's no reason for him to lie.

"I see." Tim nods.

"...and then I noticed someone had tried to file a missing persons report for them. Seemed like a bit too much of a coincidence."

"Yes, yes it rather does." He answers, still not giving a straight answer. He continues to watch him to try to read his face.

"Does that mean you do know something?" Wade prompts.

"I'm afraid not, no. Matthew...are you alright?" He says. Wade isn't sure whether this is expert deflection or it's genuine concern. It's worrying that he can't tell any more. He used to trust this man completely, and now he's questioning him like this. It all seems so wrong. He saw that arrest with his own eyes. Yes, the Tim Copper he used to work side-by-side with wouldn't have lied to him; but this Tim Copper just did because he was involved and he does know something.

"Like I said, never better." He replies, trying to push his feelings of betrayal down and just look at this as objectively as possible.

"Really? You've seemed very distracted of late. I know it's related to the involvement of the Counter Terrorism Team. You're troubled by them, but I didn't think that would lead to you becoming suspicious of me." He says, and there's accusation laced within it. There's no backing out now, it would seem.

"Well, there's been a few things you've not been upfront about, hasn't there?"

"What exactly are you referring to?" Tim says, and his tone is sharp and warning him not to go any further. Wade won't heed that warning, of course.

"I don't feel like you're being totally honest with me, Tim. You're different. I thought it was since that team popped up more, but now I'm thinking it goes back further than that. You've been different for a while."

"And what do you mean by different?"

"A lot more bloody secretive."

"I'm not being secretive." Tim says, his face still difficult to read.

"Where was Steven Robinson held while he awaits trial?" Wade says with a glare.

"Excuse me? I'm sorry, I don't know that offhand and you certainly shouldn't perceive that as some kind of secret keeping." He scoffs.

"Hmmm. And yet you gave a whole press conference on him."

"Look, Matthew. I'm sorry I can't give you your answers. Please, I'm worried about you. You seem to be putting yourself under a lot of pressure." He reaches into his jacket pocket, takes out a couple of tickets and hands them to Wade.

"Here. It's a couple of tickets to the theatre tonight. It's just a small, local production. I was going to take Rebecca, but we can't make it now. You and Kamala should go. I think you need some escapism." He tells him; and again Wade can't quite read his tone. Is it concern, or condescension? He looks at the outstretched olive branch, and gently takes them. He's not keen on the idea, he's not keen on the theatre at the best of times, but he doesn't want to be completely rude.

"Yeah, cheers." He grunts. Tim pats him gently on the shoulder.

"Let's speak again soon." He says with a broad smile, before walking past him and over to his car. Wade watches him the whole way. Once he's gone he turns around and swiftly walks back inside; because he knows exactly where to go with this next.

"Have you sent anyone over to take a statement about those two missing persons yet?" He says, as he marches over to Appleby's desk.

"Oh. Erm. No, not yet. Sorry. Not got round to it." He says, stumbling over his words in panic.

"It's fine. Give me the address I'll call in on her. I've got a bit of free time."

"Yeah, give me a minute, I'll dig it out." Appleby replies.
"Cheers. I'll just nip to the loo while you get it then." He tells him with a determined and commanding nod; just to make it really clear he doesn't have time to fuck around.

It's already 17:12 and Louis is sitting alone at a table in Technicolor bar. He'd arrived early anyway, because he was oddly nervous and it made sense to get there first, and so he has been quietly nursing his drink and patiently waiting for Danny to arrive. He's distracted himself from that odd feeling in his stomach by taking a bit of enjoyment in watching the humans around him. There are groups of them laughing and drinking together and, although he feels completely disconnected from them, it feels really nice to be in that atmosphere. He checks the time and then quietly takes another sip from his glass. He feels self-conscious as he catches one of the humans looking over at him. He hunches over to try to make himself a little more inconspicuous. His phone rings and he feels a shot of relief as he sees on the screen that it's Danny.
"Hello?" He says, probably a little too eagerly.
"Hey. Update. Finally managed to get hold of the chemical analysis, a bit more difficult than I thought but obviously I got there in the end because I'm amazing. I'll be home in about ten minutes. You around and I can share what I found?" He asks, launching straight into babbling. Louis' stomach drops, and so does his face.
"Home? I thought…didn't you, erm…you want to go out somewhere?" He asks, feeling a little stupid.
"Oh, yeah. I forgot about that. But, it was a dumb idea anyway. Everyone gets one, right? Let's just forget it." Danny says, clearly oblivious.
"Oh. Yeah okay."
"Wait. You're not there already are you?" He says, his supposed superior intellect obviously catching up.
"No, no." Louis lies. "I was just about to. I thought I'd have another chat with Wade to see if…yeah if he got anywhere. I'd better go…he's just bringing me a file now to have a look at." He feels even more embarrassed; like everyone in the bar is looking at him as he realises the person he was excited to see doesn't even care enough to turn up. He knows he completely misread this situation, and that's on him. He should've never expected anything else from Danny.
"Okay, well, we'll catch up la…" Louis hangs up, cutting him off. It feels

petty, but he just doesn't want to hear him any more. He puts the phone down on the table then puts his head in his hands.

"I am...so dumb." He laughs to himself and takes a large gulp from his glass.

"Now I know that look." Says an older woman with short grey hair as she sits down at his table. She's just walked over from one of the groups he'd been watching. "It's the sad look of a little gay boy who's been stood up." She says with a sympathetic smile; and he's completely taken aback by both her sudden presence and the directness of what she's saying.

"What?" He laughs, nervously.

"Okay, and I overheard you too." She explains. "Girls and I thought I should come check on you." She says, gesturing over her shoulder to a bunch of men and women, who all look away and try to act like they're deep in conversation when Louis glances in their direction.

"Oh...I..." He stutters.

"What's your name sweetheart?" She asks.

"Louis." He says, after a brief pause to internally debate whether to tell her or not.

"Well Louis. I'm Sarah. I'm a 52-year-old dyke and I'm here to tell you, it's nothing to be ashamed of. We've all had dates stand us up. What was his excuse?" Sarah tells him.

"He...forgot." Louis says, with another laugh at himself. "Plus ...it's not like that. I don't think he...We're just..." He struggles, fumbling over his words and feeling really uncomfortable trying to explain something he doesn't understand himself. Something he's been avoiding even trying to understand.

"It's complicated?" She offers.

"Yeah. Exactly."

"It always is, my love, no matter who they are. So what's complicated about it?" She asks him, and there's something about her that he likes. It could just be that she's someone completely outside of the situation, someone so much simpler to talk to than it would be to Lauren or Amber. Now that he's over the shock of her forwardness, he's suddenly quite glad she sat down.

"There's...a lot!" He says, feeling oddly relieved to be able to talk to someone about this. "I think I just...misunderstood what this was supposed to be. I don't think I even realised what I thought this was until I was here."

"Oh, I've been there. Many a time."

"Plus, there's this whole…" He pauses and takes another gulp of his drink while he thinks about how to delicately phrase this. It's been a whole day of opening up to humans, but he knows he still needs to be cautious. Plus, it's genuinely difficult to explain his situation with Danny. "…family thing. Like, I guess put simply my family wouldn't approve."
"Ahh I see." She says, sounding like she genuinely does know exactly what he's talking about. "Well do you know what, it can take time. Took my dad nearly 20 years. But, even if they don't accept you for being gay…I say fuck 'em."
"No! That's not what I mean. I am…I guess." He says, though he's never really thought about it like that. He stops to think it through himself. "I am attracted to men. I've just never put that label on it. I've never thought about it because it felt like I shouldn't. My family is weird. I know you all say that. But, growing up there were so many expectations on the life I'm going to lead. Romance with men, or otherwise, it wasn't even part of the conversation. In fact, if anything, it was discouraged. It was always just 'grow up and do your job,' and there was never any talk of anything else, and I didn't even really realise that was something I wanted until…until really recently…and now it's just something else that I'm getting wrong. And, I've just realised I'm waffling to a complete stranger. I'm so sorry." He says; having just started babbling at her without really meaning to. It was like there was something about this woman and this situation that had just made this all come out.
"Oh I don't care. I've been drinking since lunchtime love." She says with a deep laugh. "And anyway, I'm not a stranger no more. That feeling you're describing, trying to ignore a part of you because you're not who you're told you're supposed to be? Well, everyone in here has felt it. That's what brings us all together. No one's family should be against 'em falling in love, for any reason. No one should want to stop you from being your whole self. I've been coming here for years and I've seen so many people who've spent a good chunk of time being unhappy because they hid who they were and what they wanted, and all it does is hold you back. You'll never be able to "get it right" if you're holding back a piece of yourself. If you wanna fall in love then you fall in love with whoever, because no proper family would want to deny you that."
"Oh god, it's not love." He says, with another laugh at how ridiculous that would be. "I don't even think I like him. But, I think I came here because I was hoping it would be something. I think I've been hoping for that for a

little while and I didn't realise it. It's a really weird situation."
"Well either way he's a bastard for standing you up, whoever he is." She says, quite bluntly. That really makes him laugh because it sums Danny up perfectly.
"Oh yeah, he is. Complete dick." He confirms.
"Send him my way, I'll tell him that." She says as she leans back in the chair, cracks her knuckles, and winks at him. He can't explain it, but he feels such a wild swell of affection for this Human. "What d'ya say you come and join us for a drink?" She asks.
"Absolutely." He says with a genuine grin.

Wade returns from the bathroom and marches straight up to the front desk, hoping that Appleby has done what he's told because he doesn't have the patience for any more diversions. As he approaches Appleby hangs up the phone and turns to face him.
"You got it then?" He asks; but he tries to make it very clear it's not a request.
"I'm afraid I haven't, no." He says.
"Well, out the way I'll find it myself." Wade snaps, moving around the desk and almost shoving him out of the way.
"No, it's not that." He starts to explain, while looking apologetic. "You were right, alright. I should've taken this seriously earlier."
"What's happened?" He asks; sensing this will be another of the diversions he's run out of patience for.
"A body's been found in an old warehouse. Fits the description of one of 'em. Probably not the best idea for you to go asking questions until we know…" Appleby explains.
"Yeah, yeah, you're right." He agrees begrudgingly. If this is a distraction, it's a good one.
"Good. Shouldn't you be finishing soon?" He asks him.
"Course not." Wade says, patting him on the shoulder. "Not if there's a murder investigation going on. Gimme the address where the body was found and I'll head there now…"
"But I thought…?" Appleby says, because that's clearly not the answer he was expecting. Wade shoots him an impatient glare, and he relents. Appleby reluctantly scribbles the address down on a post-it note and hands it to him.
"Cheers." He says, and swiftly marches out from behind the desk and out

of the police station. He's determined to get some answers. Appleby watches after him, shaking his head.

Louis feels so much more relaxed now that he's joined Sarah and her group of friends. They were warm and inviting, and they included him in the conversation from the very start. He knew he didn't belong with them, they were human and he was something human adjacent. But he'd had friends before, in Jongleton, and this reminded him a little of that. People to laugh and joke with, people who didn't really have the stress of demon-infected-former-people trying to kill them. They're people who just got to live their lives. Louis wanted to live up to everything he was supposed to be, to be someone who made a difference and saved people from Used-to-Bes. He knew he could never, would never, have a life like Sarah and her friends, and he didn't really want that, but it was nice to be in their group even for a little bit. Plus he'd had another drink or two, and that helped.

One of them, a balding man with a beard called Paul is nearing the end of a story as the others listen intently.

"And well, the chocolate bar was there, and I was hungry and it's not like I was having the time of my life so I just grabbed it and started eating it…"

He gives a deliberately overdramatised awkward facial expression to punctuate his story.

"What so you just…had a snack mid-way…through?" Louis clarifies, laughing at the ridiculous image in his head.

"Yes darling. Yes I did. A lady like me can multitask." Paul says, sweetly patting Louis on the leg.

"I hope he kicked you out. I woulda done." Sarah says, rolling her eyes.

"He wouldn't have dared!" Paul tells her with mock outrage. "Besides, I promised to buy him another one. Never did though. Didn't see him again after that." He shrugs and turns his focus fully to Louis. "So, what about you, any wild stories you want to share with the group?"

"Nah, this one's brand new to dating from the sounds of it." Sarah interjects with a playful nudge.

"Oh honey, I wasn't asking about dating." He says, waggling his eyebrows. Louis blushes.

"Well…not like brand new…" He says. "There was one guy I met on Meetr…but…"

He pauses, awkwardly thinking back to the time he'd actually properly

used the app back in Jongleton and he awkwardly struggles for the next words. His phone pings loudly.
"Oh, saved by the bell. Is that *him*?" Paul asks.
"No. No," Louis says, looking down at the screen. "But it does mean I have to go. It's a work thing." He explains, and Sarah raises a questioning eyebrow at him. "This has been…really nice though. Thank you." He says, and he genuinely means that. Just getting to be normal for a few hours has been so refreshing. She stands up when he does and throws her arms around him in a surprising, but not unwelcome, hug.
"Remember what I said. And we're always here." She says.
"She means it literally. She doesn't go home." Paul adds, and the group laughs.
"Shut up you old queen." She tells him, and punches him in the arm.
"Ow!" He objects. Louis grins. It's really amazing how quickly he's felt like part of their friendship group. His phone pings again, and his smile fades because he realises he needs to go. He's enjoyed a brief hiatus from a life of Used-to-Bes and demonic infections; but now it's definitely over.
"I really need to go. But thank you. Hopefully I'll see you again!?" He says, finishing off his drink and rushing to the door. Then, with one last wave, he's gone and it's back to work.

Chapter Sixty-Two.

Wade's car rolls to a stop outside the address he's been given. It's an old factory warehouse down by the river. Exactly the kind of place he'd expect a body or two to be found. It's quiet though, which isn't what he'd expect. If this is a crime scene then it should look like one. For starters there should be uniformed officers around but he can't see another soul. That doesn't feel right. But, he's too far into this now. He peers into the old warehouse and there's no real signs of disturbance, though it seems oddly clean. There's some old machinery around, and some old wooden crates, but it still just doesn't feel right. It's not as filthy as a place like this should be. It's abandoned and unlocked; it should be a magnet for all kinds of stuff, from homeless people, to wild animals, to criminals looking for somewhere quiet for a drug deal, but this place looks like it's just had the maids in. He shrugs it off, and looks over his shoulder to make sure there aren't any other cars approaching before he fully commits himself to entering.
"Hello?" He calls out, and it echos. "Anyone here?" He asks again, moving

slowly inside. Everything about this feels off. This doesn't look like an active crime scene. Why is he the only one here? "Guess not." He mutters to himself and after another scan of the factory floor he begins to wonder whether he's even been given the right address. What's more, if not, he wonders whether that was an accident or not. "What're you playing at, Appleby?" He asks himself, patting his pocket and grabbing his phone with the intention of tearing Jack a new one.

"He was a little premature." Tim Copper says, stepping out from behind one of the pillars and startling Wade as he spins around to face him and furrows his brow. "Apologies, that was a little dramatic. I imagine it's the company I keep rubbing off on me. I think Jack perhaps got a little ahead of himself." He explains, a solemn look on his face. "There's no body. Yet."
"What're you waffling about?" Wade asks him, but deep down he's worried he already knows. On some level, it's exactly what he was expecting to find here.

"You just couldn't stop yourself, could you?" Tim asks, as he shakes his head. "Just accepted the theatre tickets and let the problem solve itself?"
"Theatre ain't my thing. Neither is leaving well enough alone." Wade says, with a shrug. His eyes dart around nervously to see if there is anyone else lurking, because he really doesn't like this. "So what's goin' on?" Copper groans, like he's tired.

"I'm so sick of that question from you." He says, pacing a little closer. Wade stands his ground, even as his footsteps echo threateningly through the building. "The same thing that's been going on for years. And I made it work. I let the occasional case slip through, just to give them something so they didn't get suspicious. But it was a balancing act. I had to give them enough, but not so many that you and the others would start asking questions." He stops and stares a hole through him at that point. "When did you start to notice?"

"Notice what mate?" He asks him, realising that he doesn't recognise the man in front of him at all.

"Was it the tiresome reporter?" Tim continues, ignoring his question. "Or was it that ridiculous child. Louis, is it? He's caused so many problems. I can't wait until he's dead." He sighs and he looks so very tired. He gently takes off his jacket, folds it, and places it neatly on top of a box. "I am sorry, old friend," He says, and Wade can tell it's genuine. He doesn't like where this is heading at all, but he can at least tell that his old friend is sorry about what's coming next. "I think I was too preoccupied. I thought I was doing enough to make sure this wouldn't happen." He says, and begins to roll up the sleeves of his shirt. "I hope you know I didn't want it to come to this. I don't want to have to do it."

"Again, what are you wafflin' on about?" Wade grunts. "Whatever it is Tim, I'm sure we can fix it. There was a time when me and you could've worked anything out." He says, because it's true. He knows deep down Tim Copper is a good man, or, he thought he did. He wants him to stop so they can sort this, together, before it's too late.

"It will be fixed." He says. "You just won't be around to see it." He finishes. Wade nods.

"I figured that's what you were building up to." He says. "What is so important you'd kill me to protect it?" Copper takes another step towards him, and finally Wade breaks and takes a step back.

"You honestly wouldn't understand." Tim laughs. "I did consider sharing it with you. Countless times. So many of the others got it. But you've always had such high moral standards, you'd never…"

"Try me?" Wade interrupts, with another step back. He wants to keep him talking.

"I'm afraid not. This has gone on a little too long, and I have plans tonight."

"What plans?" He asks, just trying to string it out that little bit longer. His old friend might be about to try to kill him; but right now he's getting answers he's waited years for. Copper shakes his head, and begins to advance much faster. It's very clear that he's not willing to chat any more, and Wade can see in his eyes that their friendship is gone. The once warm look in his old friend's eyes has been replaced with something much scarier. Wade braces himself and squares his shoulders. He's determined to fight back. He gets in the first shot and punches him in the jaw, but Copper doesn't even falter, he just grabs out at him, snatching his hand and squeezing.

"No, really though. What plans?" Louis asks, and they both turn to see him standing in a doorway.

"Where did you come from?" Tim groans, releasing his grip.

"Took your bloody time." Wade adds.

Earlier that day…

"Wait. One more thing." Louis said, breathing out. Wade stopped, paused, and turned back to face him.

"Yeah?" He grunted. Louis wanted to tell him everything. He really, really did. He knew he couldn't but that didn't stop it. But as much as he couldn't

tell him everything, he also hadn't told him enough. He knew deep down that he could trust Wade. He just hoped that he could do the same.
"The guy behind the desk, in the station?" He asked, and Wade nodded.
"When I first got there, he seemed like he was a little too intent on listening to our conversation."
"Yeah, well, Appleby's always been a bit of a nosy prick. What of it?" Wade mutters.
"It's not just that." Louis tries. He can't explain it fully. Not to Wade anyway. But he felt it instantly. Appleby is infected with demonic energy. He's either a Used-to-Be himself, or has spent a lot of time around one. "Look, this is going to sound crazy, but just don't trust him?"
"Why not?" Wade asks, and Louis can't blame him for that. It's not a lot to go on.
"Just a feeling I get, call it a little bit of intuition." He offers, and it quite obviously doesn't have the desired effect.
"So, you want me to have blind faith in you when you barely share anything with me?" He asks, rolling his eyes.
"…yes." Louis shrugs. "Look. Something is going on. Your boss is involved, that footage shows it. I can see you know it. The arrests of these guys are being covered up. So it can't possibly just be him that's involved. I need your help but be careful, please, and if there's anything suspicious, just call me. That's all I'm asking. Especially if it involves this Appleby guy. I'll be there to back you up. Just me, if that's what it takes. I won't bring the others."
"Alright, fine." He sighs. "I'll keep my guard up…and I'll call you." And with that he turns and heads back to the station.

And back again
"There's a back door, came in that way." Louis explains, pointing over his shoulder, with maybe a little too much of a grin on his face. He's kind of proud this worked. "Oh, Matthew. What've you done?" Copper asks, his disapproval apparent. "Everyone's been lying to me recently. I chose to side with the one who was being the most honest about lying." Copper looks between the two of them, weighing up his options. Wade takes out an extendable baton. "Looks like I made the right choice too. He's not the one threatening to kill me."
"So what were you saying about your plans?" Louis asks, quite boldly. He has had a few drinks and he realises that is tempering his usual inhibitions

a little.

"She's going to be so annoyed when I kill you little Custodian…"

"I knew she was involved!" He blurts excitedly, because he's talking about Hazel. Of course he's talking about Hazel. Copper lunges at him; but thankfully he's not had so much to drink he can't see it coming and he manages to duck out of the way. He takes a second to mentally thank Amber for that refresher earlier, before Copper lunges again striking out at his face. He's too slow, and Louis dodges and takes him down. He lands a couple of punches and quickly rolls away before he can recover. He's adapting his fighting style, and using what Amber had taught him earlier, and he's consciously staying out of reach because he doesn't know the extent of Copper's powers.

Copper gets back to his feet and tries to attack again, and Louis continues to duck and dodge until eventually he mistimes it and Copper smacks him across the face and knocks him to the floor. Wade rushes forward to intervene before he can recover.

"No!" Louis calls, because as well intentioned as Wade is he's no match for a Used-to-Be. Truthfully, Louis isn't, but at least he's a lot closer to a match. It's too late though; Wade charges forward but is taken by surprise by Copper's strength. He swats him aside like it's nothing and Wade is knocked through the air and lands hard on the concrete floor with a crunch. His baton flies in another direction; and rolls to a stop at Louis' feet as he pulls himself back up. Copper draws a knife and swoops on the defenceless Wade, Louis scoops up the baton and charges to intercept. He strikes quickly, before Copper can plunge the knife down into his defenceless former friend. Louis smacks him in the knee, then slams into his wrist to dislodge the knife and kicks it away across the warehouse and out of sight. He smacks Copper in the face with all the strength he can muster; and pauses to help Wade back up and make sure he's not harmed. He hands the baton back to him and the two of them stare down Copper as he staggers back up, glaring at them.

"What happened to the two men you arrested?" Louis demands.

"Those two filthy drug peddling humans? The same thing that's going to happen to you. They're dead; and no one will miss them." He spits back. He grabs a heavy old wooden crate and launches it at the two of them. Louis dodgers and pulls Wade out of the way too. It misses them but it was just a distraction, and Copper scrambles away to escape through the back door.

Louis bolts after him; rushing through the corridor, and past what was Brick's office, but he's a step too slow. By the time he crashes out through the door and to the cold autumn air, Copper is already in his car. He runs at the vehicle, hoping he can stop him, but it's already accelerating by the time he gets to it. Copper makes his escape as Wade too thunders out of the warehouse trying to catch his breath.
"What the hell just happened?" He demands of Louis as they watch the car speed away, and that's a very good question. The enormity of it hits Louis like he's just collided with a brick wall. Nothing good just happened. Yes, he exposed Copper. Yes, he kept Wade safe and alive in the short term. But this is very not good. Copper is exposed and clearly dangerous; he has power and influence and there are clearly others within the police force that are either infected or at least loyal to him. It's not just Hazel, she potentially has an army. And Wade might be safe for now, but it's obvious Copper will kill to keep his secret.
"Right, quick." Louis says, thinking fast and turning on him. "Family members. You've got a wife, yeah?"
"Erm, yeah?"
"Is she home?" He asks.
"No, no. Said she was gonna go see her friend after work. Why?" Wade says, clearly still in too much of a state of shock to properly connect the dots here.
"Call her. Tell her to stay there. I don't know what the hell we do but…she shouldn't go home and neither should you."
"Right. Okay. But then you need to tell me what's going on. I think I deserve some answers now…" He says and pulls out his phone. It comes out of his pocket in pieces; having been smashed in the fight. Louis quickly hands him his instead.
"Do you know her number?"
"Yeah…yeah I think so."
"Then call her, now." Louis says, and the commanding tone in his voice surprises them both.
"Please?" Wade asks him. "If I'm in danger, if she is, then I just need to know." All the anger, all the irritation, and all the contempt is gone. Louis can see it. When he first met Wade he was unwelcome, he and the others were an inconvenience. Now there's a change. Louis has just saved his life and, even though he was partly responsible for him being there, it seems like Wade has started to trust him. He's no longer demanding answers,

he's asking for them. Somewhere between that, the adrenaline, and the alcohol, Louis decides it's time to give him them.

"Fine." He says. "The really simplified version, your boss and at least one of your colleagues are infected with demonic energy. I know that sounds crazy. Evil exists. You can believe that, or you can not. But that's why he was so strong."

"So Tim's…not in control of himself? A demon is?"

"Not quite. It's still him; it's just all the worst of him, that tiny little part of you that is usually balanced out just given all the control. And again, it's not even that, it's always amplified by something else, fear, or pain, or…I don't know. Does that make any sense?" Louis asks, desperately trying to tamper his urge to launch into a lengthy explanation because they don't have the time.

"Yes. I mean…" He sighs, pulling together the pieces in his mind. "He's not been the same bloke I knew for a long time, when I look back at it."

"Everything you've been asking about; the whole thing at the hotel, the shooting, every case we've been involved in. It's all been demonic infection. It might be hard to believe but it's everywhere, and part of what we have to do is cover it up, and so I could never tell you because that goes against everything I've ever been taught, and…"

"Okay." Wade says, holding up a hand. "I get it. I think that's enough for now. I mean, I've got a hundred more questions. But…"

"You should call your wife." Louis reiterates; so grateful that Wade understands. Wade takes a few steps away for a modicum of privacy, and Louis' brain begins to race, working out what comes next. Chris was pissed at him before, and this will probably solidify his decision that Louis should be sent away and back to Jongleton. But if that's the case then it's okay. Wade deserved the truth.

Chapter Sixty-Three.

Hazel reaches the end of her story and there's a genuine sadness to her. Kim stops the recording and she's struck by what happened; by how this woman's life was forever changed by violence.

"You know, even with this people will probably still claim it's a hoax." Kim tells her, cautiously.

"Then, like I said, play your role convincingly." She replies and the mask and the theatrics seem like they're gone. There's no dramatic inflection. It's just her.

"I'm not even sure I can get this published." She replies, shaking her head sadly because she really, really wants to be able to do what's being asked of her.

"I am." Hazel replies, with steely certainty. She glances up at the clock on the wall and nods to herself. "I'm afraid that's a wrap for our time together."

"Look, I can tell you're set on whatever it is you're going to do tonight but, I need to say this. You could stop it all. This violence. I know someone. A policeman. He's a good man. He could help, and could offer you protection…"

"Stop." She says coldly, holding up a hand, and Kim does. "I've enjoyed our afternoon together. Really, I have. But don't ruin it by trying to save me."

"It's not just you" Kim starts, and it's the truth. She wants to help this woman but she wants to stop more people getting hurt too. "Whatever it is you're planning, it sounds like people are going to die needlessly…

"I wouldn't say needlessly." Hazel shrugs "You and I have shared a little connection, that's true, but don't think you know me. You've seen only what I've chosen to show you. Just do what I've asked and play your role as the diligent little writer." And the mask is back. Kim can see it. Whatever glimpse she has had under it, she won't get any more.

"Fine. I can do that. I'll tell your story. Thank you, if nothing else, this has been…well you're sort of terrifying but you're fascinating."

"It's time to leave." Hazel nods, a little sadly. "And It's time for me to get into character…and believe me you don't want to be here to see it…" She says, baring her teeth a little. The door flies open, with a dramatic gust of wind. Kim blinks, weighing her options. There's so much more she wants to say to this fascinating woman. But, she knows she can't push, and, frankly, she daren't. Hazel has given her her task, and that's where their relationship ends. She holds her tongue, she collects her things, and leaves without another word spoken between the two. Once outside she returns Wade's call because she so badly wants to tell him everything that has happened here. It goes to voicemail.

"Matthew, call me back. I've got something crazy to tell you."

"Oh finally, I've got so much to tell you…" Danny says as Louis walks into the War Room. He's sitting there with Amber and Lauren, and they're obviously strategising. Louis takes a deep breath. He doesn't know how they're going to react to this at all, and he's scared.

"Yeah. Me too." He says nervously, as DCI Wade shuffles in next to him. Danny's face, which is the one he's fixed on, drops and his eyes widen.

"Wait, what is he doing here?!" He asks. Louis ignores him.

"Take a seat," He tells Wade, gesturing to the table.

"...should I...?" Lauren begins, and he shakes his head.

"Let me get this out, first." Louis says, just wanting this to be over with.

"I went to the police station earlier, like we discussed. When I got there I felt something from one of the other officers. I think he was infected. I should've told you all then but, well, I thought..." He shakes his head. He was planning to tell Danny when they met. He wanted to tell him first because it felt like they were a partnership. Or he thought they could be. But it doesn't matter what he thought now. "...well, it doesn't matter. Wade started asking questions and...

"You can call me Matthew." He interjects. "I think we're on first name terms now that I know what it is you all do." He says, and Louis badly wishes he hadn't because all of their faces react, and they all start a hole right through him.

"Yeah. Well. That." Louis confirms. "We suspected that there was something not right. That there might be someone working with Hazel..."

"Yeah, him." Danny snaps.

"No. Not him. There's a guy called Appleby, and his boss who we saw in the footage you found. There's at least two of them and I think it goes deeper than that..."

"Louis...I..." Lauren begins, looking between both him and Matthew. She looks really worried, and he hates it.

"I had to tell him everything." Louis says. "He started asking questions, for me, and when he did..."

"They tried to kill me." Wade says, matter of factly.

"What?!" Lauren gasps. Danny continues to eye him suspiciously. Amber just scowls.

"Turns out I was getting a little too close, and my old mate Tim decided he'd had enough." Wade explains. "If it wasn't for Louis turning up when he did, he'd have stopped me asking questions for good."

"Wait." Amber says, looking directly at him. "You fought off a Used-to-Be solo? Proud!" She looks so excited at that prospect that she reaches over to high-five him. Louis doesn't deliberately ignore her, he's just too intently

focussed on Danny, who refuses to meet his gaze. She quietly rescinds it.
"Yep. I'd be dead if it weren't for him." Matthew adds.
"It makes sense." Danny says, considering it. "Brick's drugs contained small traces of demonic energy. Very small. Not enough to infect anyone but he'd somehow found a way to channel demonic energy. It's not like anything we've ever seen. Even the Cleaners are stumped. It's not something that we knew was possible. So it makes sense they'd want to cover that up."
"What the…" Louis says, his jaw dropping. The implications of that blow his mind as his brain fires off so many different possibilities. Deliberate infections are possible where the Used-to-Be has been infected with blood-to-blood transmission, like with Joseph, but that's rare and has very limited results. Most of the time it's based on a series of random factors all converging; trauma, and violence, and someone who's susceptible to it. That's why Used-to-Bes exist in secret; because there aren't enough of them. If Brick had a way to channel demonic energy into a substance, then it stands to reason that it's possible to deliberately infect people without the need for blood. And that's a terrifying concept.
"It's not enough to infect. But it has one hell of an impact on the human brain." Danny continues, still not meeting his eye.
"Okay." Louis says. "One problem at a time. Matthew isn't safe. The Used-to-Be got away from me, and who knows how many others there are. Until we do we need to…"
"I can't believe you…" Danny snaps, interrupting him and looking at him at last. His brown eyes are filled with fire. "I knew you were stupid, but this. Going off on your own, bringing him here…this isn't some shelter. He shouldn't be here. He shouldn't be hearing this."
"I didn't feel like I had a choice."
"You had hundreds of options, you just picked the shit one." He roars; and everyone else looks on awkwardly.
"How about you just shut and help me?" Louis shouts back, because he's had enough of this. He's had enough of Danny.
"Maybe you should've asked me for help before you fucked this up." Danny snaps back, folding his arms and shaking his head.
"And maybe I could've if you'd turned up when you were supposed to." Louis says, before he can really think.
"What?" Danny asks, screwing up his face in such an annoying display of ignorance that Louis wants to throw something at him.

"I think…" Lauren interjects, and Louis is very grateful for it because he doesn't want to say anything else to the utterly unpleasant person sitting directly across from him. They just stare at each other while she continues. "I don't think you'll like this. But we have to call Chris." She finishes.
"I know." Louis says, because he does. He's done the absolute best he can, and even though it's all gone a little wrong he doesn't regret it. He doesn't regret saving Wade's life or finally telling him what's going on. But he also knows that'll be the thing that makes up Chris' mind about transferring him back to Jongleton; and actually, now, he thinks that might be okay. Everything here is so messy and he's clearly not cut out for it. He also wants to be as far from Danny as he can possibly get right now. "And I agree." He says. "Can you call him? I need to get some air." He says, and leaves the room before she has a chance to answer.

Chapter Sixty-Four.

The familiar tune of old jazz music floats its way through the suite as she prepares herself. This lavish penthouse, one the best hotels in town, has been her home for months now and there are so many trinkets and memories scattered throughout it. There are many of Joseph's too. She's perched at a dressing table in front of a huge mirror, powdering her face and humming along to the tune as she puts the final touches on her appearance. She can do it a much quicker way, of course, but Hazel prefers the old school approach of applying make-up by hand while she gets herself into character for that evening. It's almost a ritual. Her hair is pinned up and her make-up is dark, but simple. She finishes it off with a bright red lipstick and blows herself a little kiss in the mirror. She lingers, just for a moment, staring at herself thoughtfully. Then she completes the look by taking a brimmed boater hat from a nearby stand. It's black with some simple flowers adorning it. She grabs a large vintage handbag and an umbrella with a crook handle. She smiles to herself; but there's still a melancholy to it, which she takes one last moment to embrace as she looks down at a photograph on her dressing table. It's her and Joseph in New York, in the summer of 2019. He'd insisted on going to celebrate what would've been her hundredth birthday and they had a glorious time, celebrating and laughing, and drinking, and taking in shows. For the shortest time there had been no being hunted and no death, and they had just lived. He'd had the photo printed as a gift for her to commemorate it.

Well, a gift and an apology after he'd attracted a little too much attention on their trip to San Francisco a few months later. She reaches down and runs her fingers over the picture.
"Waiting in place where the lost things go." She whispers to herself, sadly. And then it's over. She stares back at the mirror and her face changes to one of steely resolve. Her transformation is complete; and she is ready. She spins on her heel and marches towards the lift.
And in reception, much to the curiosity of the hotel staff, half a dozen uniformed police officers await her. They include PC Nadin, and Jack Appleby. DSI Tim Copper stands at the head of them, waiting patiently to greet her.
"Timothy, you made it. Gentlemen." She says, with a wicked grin and a tip of her hat.
"I nearly didn't. I met your friend Louis." He tells her.
"How unfortunate. I hope he lived to tell the tale?" She says, reaching to caress his face in both a caring and threatening gesture.
"Yes, ma'am." He confirms.
"Excellent." She says, pulling away from him. "Then worry not. These fine gentlemen and I shall take care of everything else."
"I'll see you when it's done?" He asks, and there's something to it. A hint of worry, almost. She doesn't answer, not directly at least, she just winks at him and turns her attention to the other. She bangs the tip of the umbrella on the floor and it echos.
"Come along boys. Spit spot. It's showtime." She says, and marches forward, leading them out onto the street.

Everything feels like it's gone wrong. Not quite in a 'this is the end of the world' way, but definitely in a hugely fucked up, lots of mistakes were made, and now there's really no coming back from this kind of way. Louis is sitting at that same table in the back garden where his day had started. The morning coffee and the meditation were wonderful, but it went downhill with Chris' phone call and despite a couple of times where it looked like it would, it never really got back on track. He's been here just under a month and the whole thing has just been one mess after the other. There's a strong and cooling wind that makes the neighbours' trees rustle and in the distance there's a sound of a wailing siren. There are ominous looking grey clouds above and he pulls his hoodie tightly around him as the wind really picks up. He feels stupid, and like he should've been able to do more, and what's more he knows he's just feeling sorry for himself but he just can't seem to pull himself out of the bad mood that's been lingering for most of the day. He knows his time here has come to an end and he's been grappling with it for the last few hours. He can't help but feel that Chris is right, and that all the negative things Danny has said are true. In only a few weeks he's nearly been killed several times, revealed the truth about Used-to-Bes to a human, and attracted the attention of someone incredibly scary that he has seemingly no hope of stopping. It's a good thing this has come to an end before he made it any worse.

He looks up at the dusky sky and takes a deep breath in. And then there's the feelings he's developed towards Danny. The one's he's not meant to have. The sky flashes with lightning as a storm makes its way slowly across; and he jumps as the wind rattles a fence panel nearby. That's when he spots him, just out of the corner of his eye, Danny standing in the doorway watching him.

"What?" Louis snaps, partly because he took him by surprise.

"I didn't want to...you looked..." He rolls his eyes and groans awkwardly. He steps forward and approaches the table. Louis doesn't invite him to sit down, but obviously he doesn't get the hint and sits down anyway.

"Did you want something? I was hoping for a bit of space before Chris arrives and sends me packing."

"I wanted to see if you were..." He begins, and then shakes his head and rolls his eyes again, apparently at himself. "He won't send you anywhere."

"That's not what he said this morning, and that was before everything today. I think that'll seal the deal." Louis explains, his tone softening but his anger remaining.

"What?" Danny says, his eyes widening. "Why didn't you tell me?"

"Will you make up your mind?" Louis laughs, and Danny looks confused. There's part of him that enjoys that.

"What?" He asks, scowling.

"Nevermind." Louis scoffs.

"You should've told me." Danny says again. "Just like you should've told me what you'd found at the police station. You could've been killed and we're meant to be a team. That was the deal." He sounds oddly concerned, and Louis doesn't know what to say. This doesn't sound like Danny at all. There's no harsh edge or insult lingering. This is the person that Louis keeps getting glimpses of when his walls are down. But Louis still wants to scream at him that he would've told him if he'd turned up when he was supposed to. "And, about what I said…" He continues, shuffling awkwardly in his chair. "I didn't mean it. Louis, this is hard. You know me, you know this is hard. I don't normally apologise if I hurt someone's feelings but…I guess I'm sorry." No sooner have the words left his mouth than there's a huge crack of thunder overhead and Louis can't help but let out a genuine laugh. It feels good.

"That was appropriately dramatic timing to go with you apologising." He says, his anger fading away. "It doesn't matter though. You were probably right. I've fucked this all up, and…" He trails off, smiling, because it doesn't matter now.

"I always am." Danny says, "But…you're…so different." He says, sighing as he struggles with the words. "We should go in." He says, as the rain finally starts.

"What do you want, Danny?" Louis asks, ignoring it.

"To not get wet?" Danny says, either through ignorance or deflection.

"You either hate me or you don't?" Louis asks, staring so deeply into his eyes he thinks he might get lost in them. Danny shakes his head and lets out a sound that resembles a whimper.

"Why can't it be both?" He says, definitely deflecting.

"Let's go in." Louis says, frustrated and resigning himself to the fact that he might never know. He gets up and turns towards the door, but Danny stays seated.

"I do." He says, and Louis' heart skips. "I hate you, and yet I don't think I do." He says, the mask and the walls firmly gone. The heavens open at that, the weather once again having ridiculously appropriate timing, and rain comes pouring down on them. They rush inside, with Danny pushing Louis aside so that he can get in first, and laughing as he does. Louis slams the door behind him, and turns to insult him, but his breath is taken away as Danny pounces and kisses him. It's hungry and it's wet and his stomach does somersaults as he presses him back against the door. There's tongues everywhere and it's messy and it's perfect. It's what he's wanted since the moment he saw him, and there, for the briefest of moments they're just two normal boys who like each other. Danny pulls back first, but his hands remain on Louis' waist.

"And that's why I hate you." He says, his voice cracking. "You annoy me so much and yet every time I look at you I just…" He groans in frustration because he can't find the words and Louis smirks at him. "Stop looking at me like that!" Danny demands, but doesn't pull his hands away. They both

just stand quietly, staring at each other, completely lost. "I really don't know what we do now." Danny says, laughing and shaking his head.
"Me neither." Louis replies. "But…" He's interrupted by a knock at the front door.
"Thank God. For once Chris arriving is welcome…" Danny sighs, and finally pulls away.
"…Danny…" Louis mumbles, his eyes going wide as he watches him move into the hallway and towards the door. Louis' body gives chase before his mind can catch-up, but he feels it…

…seconds before it happens, it reaches out and smacks him in the face. "Stop!" He cries; but Danny doesn't react in time. He tears open the door, expecting it to be Chris, but finds himself face-to-face with Hazel.
"Good to see you again boys." She coos, with a smile plastered across her face. She strikes Danny in the chest before he can react and sends him hurtling through the air and into Louis, they tumble to the ground, a mass of wet limbs. She takes her umbrella down and steps confidently inside the house. Danny is the first one back to his feet and he charges at her. Louis scrambles to grab him and to stop him because he knows they can't take her on, but he slips out of his grip. She smacks him with her umbrella and tosses him with one hand through the wooden spindles on the stairs with a horrific crash. Louis charges too, but she outstretches her arm and catches him by the throat. She squeezes and lifts him easily off his feet, then smashes him into the mirror hanging on the wall and pins him there. There's shards of glass sticking into his back and she squeezes even harder but all he can focus on is the crumpled heap of Danny on the stairs.
"Shhh, don't worry. It's still not your time. But it's drifting ever closer." She whispers in his ear as he struggles and claws at her. Amber and Lauren rush out from the War Room, alerted by the sounds of the carnage. She drops Louis, he thumps to the floor and she wields her umbrella as a weapon to bash at them both. She's ridiculously quick and in the confined space they don't have enough room to dodge. She forces them to retreat with quick, vicious strikes, and they move backwards through the doorway. She opens the umbrella and uses it to force them back inside the room and keep them there while she puts her hands on either side of the doorframe and seemingly makes it disappear. They're both trapped in the room with no way out and there's the sound of swearing from Amber on the other side.

"What're you waiting for? He's the one." Hazel tells the two policemen who are hovering at the door. They crash into the house and make their way halfway up the stairs, to where Danny is. She swoops down and grabs Louis, once again picking him up by the throat and making him watch as one of the men grabs Danny by a handful of his hair and drags him down the stairs. He thuds to the bottom and they proceed to punch and kick and beat him to make sure he's unconscious. She lets out a chuckle as Louis tries to croak out a protest. One of them picks Danny up and throws him over his shoulder, and they carry him out. Hazel's gaze snaps back to Louis. They're practically nose to nose and there is just so much hatred emanating from her, and with that combined with the pain Louis' head is swimming and he's having to fight to stay conscious.

"Remember what I told you? You cast me in this role, and I'm going to play it." She hisses at him, squeezing a little harder. "So here is your role, hero." She starts to explain as spots appear in his vision. "I will kill him by sunrise. You have a choice. You can launch a daring rescue and die alongside him, or you can run and live with the knowledge that you weren't enough. If you run make sure I never see you again. If you come, then bring everything you can because I want as many people as possible to die because of you. Oh I'm so excited to find out what you'll pick." She explains, with a snarl, and then drops him at last when she's done. He's barely conscious but he still tries to pull himself back up and so she grabs his arm, smacks it back against the wall, and drives a shard of glass straight through his palm to keep him in place. He shrieks in agony and she cackles. He claws at it, trying to free himself, and so she smacks him with the base of the umbrella and finally he blacks out.

She quietly dusts herself off and crunches her way over the broken glass. She stops at the door and looks back over her shoulder, again smirking to herself.

"End scene."

Part VIII: Love and War

Chapter Sixty-Five.

I've always been fascinated with stories. Where would we be without them? They entertain, they inform and they teach. A good story can do all that and more. Stories shape how we see the world; whether it's a fairy tale we're told as a child, a book we fall in love with as an adult, or an article in a newspaper that helps shape our political belief. Someone telling you their story can change yours. I'm telling you a story right now and it must be one you're enjoying because you've made it this far. They are so powerful. Humans are told fairy tales to help them understand the world, and so are Custodians. Like I said earlier, we began to learn about the world of Used-to-Bes and Custodians through storytelling. Whether it was the retired Agents who taught us, the active Custodians who came by, or even from the Superior One himself. His were always the most engaging and I suppose it makes sense that he was a great storyteller; considering the amount of work that goes into maintaining the story the outside world is told.

All of his stories, and I don't know how true they were, were told to teach us a lesson. There are so many of these lessons that stick in my mind vividly, to the point I can probably recite them.

"When the Demon was driven from this world, he left behind only fragments of himself. Wicked traces clinging to anything they could, be it a place, an object, or even an innocent soul that they could corrupt.
The one thing that's stopped the world being consumed by this infection? Our Army. Our Warriors. Our Champions. Our Agents of the Good. The children of the Order of One. The Custodians. We could not wage this war and hold back the darkness without you."

It was always the same, more or less. It was always simplistic. The stories always followed the same rules. We were good, and they weren't. There was only one that deviated from that. It was a warning about us and the power we have. This is probably an appropriate time to mention it… Because many years ago. Thousands, maybe tens of thousands, of years ago there was one Custodian who didn't stay true to the cause. He approached the Order of One and begged them to gift him with more power. There were fewer of us then. Only dozens of Custodians across the globe. His reasons were sound; he wanted the strength to liberate a nation from a tyrant who's mind had been twisted beyond all recognition by Demonic energy. The Custodian was strong and true of heart, and so they granted his request and gave him that extra power because they believed in him. He took on the tyrant's army, with a small group of villagers brave enough to stand with him, and he decimated them.

The story goes that he met them head on, slashing and stabbing his way through them in a flurry that couldn't be stopped. Arrows couldn't touch him; they disintegrated before coming close to piercing flesh, because that was the extent of his new power. Swords shattered against his skin, and the sea of enemies was parted by the force of his will alone. But the more he used his new found power the more it drained from him. He slaughtered the armies of his enemy but they kept coming, and coming, until finally the Mad King himself stepped onto the battlefield. The warrior tore through yet more soldiers. He was exhausted and pained, he was drenched in sweat and blood, and his skin was discoloured from the toll this sudden increase in power was taking on his body. His allies were long dead behind him, but he fought on. His sword got stuck in the body of an enemy soldier and so he continued with only his hands and the powers of his mind. He was gravely wounded because he was overwhelmed by the onslaught of attacks coming at him. But, he persisted. With arrows sticking out of his flesh and blood dripping from his body he continued to fight. He should've died from those injuries but with the level of power he now had he simply refused to. Finally he reached the King and he tore his head from his body, and ended his reign of dark tyranny. He stood victorious before the enemy army, who bowed to their new ruler.

By then, it was too late for him. The power had consumed him and he was driven by only his insatiable thirst for death and despite their surrender he continued to attack. They fled but he summoned all the power he could muster to destroy them as they did, sending out shockwaves of destructive energy to murder them for their allegiance to the dead King. He destroyed the entire army, the castle the King had ruled from, the very lands he'd sought to free. The power, and his determination to win at all costs, consumed him. He had been corrupted. His body and his mind were lost, and he died.

"That story is not meant to frighten you, my children. It is only intended to serve as a reminder of what you carry from today." The Superior One had told us, as he held up a vial of glowing white liquid to show us. "For those of you who are given these gifts today must also carry the burden of them. You must not let them consume you in your quest to fight evil. You must carry them with only good in your heart." He continued. This was the lesson we learned on the day we got our powers; that they are limited, and they are limited so that we don't create destruction in the pursuit of good.

It had been only minutes since Hazel left, taking Danny with her and leaving behind a broken and beaten Louis, but she is already long gone. He slowly swims back to consciousness as he hears a thud, thud, thud coming from the other side of the wall beside him. It intensifies as he stirs and he feels the sharp pain of the glass in his hand, pinning him to the wall. He reaches up and pulls it free, and screams from the burning pain. The wall beside him turns back into a door and Amber tumbles forward through it, her fists bloodied from trying to smash her way back to him. She's primed and ready for a fight, and charges to the door and out into the street in the hope she can chase Hazel down. Louis tries to protest but his words are caught in his throat. Lauren comes rushing from the War Room too, and is at his side instantly; scanning for where he's hurt and zeroing in on his bleeding hand. She scoops it up in her own and channels her power into healing him. Wade hovers awkwardly in the doorway and Amber storms back inside, more furious than he's ever seen her. She punches the wall with all her strength and pent up rage and leaves a chasm of a dent in the plaster.
"Louis? Are you alright?" Lauren asks, focussing only on him. He stares silently and shakes his head; desperately trying to hold back his tears and the overwhelming feeling of hopelessness.

Chapter Sixty-Six.

It wasn't long before Chris joined them, but for once even he seemed to be stunned into silence. They'd brought him up to speed and he sat there, wide-eyed and panicking as he tried to process it all. There had been lots of acknowledging sounds, and deep breaths, and head shaking, and then he'd gone quiet. Now, the four of them sit, speechless and despondent, around the table in the War Room. At Lauren's suggestion, Wade is waiting upstairs, away from Chris so that it would be that little bit easier to break all of the bad news they had to him. It was bad enough telling him that a human knew their secret; they didn't need the human to be present too while they did it.

"Okay. I think I've got a plan." Chris says, though quietly, at last.

"Great. What do we do?" Amber asks; and that speaks to the desperation of their situation. She's eager to hear a plan from Chris.

"You do nothing. You've all done enough." He says, coldly.

"Excuse me?" Lauren snaps, looking as if she's surprised even herself by being the first to protest.

"I think you heard me." He says, and stands up in what can only be an attempt at a tedious display of authority. "I'll alert Olivia's team and have Noel try to track the vehicles that were here tonight. Once we know where they are I'll take that team in and capture the UTB. But you will all be staying out of this. I blame myself, of course, because for whatever reason the four of you have no respect for me or my orders." He says, shaking his head as he looks across at the three of them. Lauren and Amber glare, but Louis doesn't even acknowledge him. "I won't be including you in this."

"Chris, that's a little unfair..." Lauren begins, but he leaps in to cut her off.

"Lauren, shut up. I won't take this from you. I won't take any more rebellion from any of you. It's cost you enough already. Danny's life is in danger and I'm going to have to rescue him, and all because you couldn't stop prodding at this investigation and goading this Used-to-Be. It's 4XM all over again and you haven't learned anything."

"You can't stop her." Louis says quietly but matter of factly, continuing to stare down at the table. It's the first thing he's said since Hazel left. Chris rolls his eyes.

"Oh, of course you'd have to weigh in. Louis, I've finished considering what we discussed. I will be sending you back to your old assignment. You're quite possibly the worst thing to have ever happened to this team."

"You're doing what?" Amber asks, the threatening tone a little too obvious.

"Now I'm thinking about it, I'm going to split all four of you up. Or, maybe three of you, depending on how tonight goes..." He says, with a cold insinuation. Louis slams his fist down on the table and finally looks up, with fury in his eyes.

"You arrogant..." He begins, before pausing and trying to take a second to compose himself. He knows it's important he gets Chris to listen to him. There's too much at stake. "You can't stop her. You've not listened this whole time. None of us could get near her." He tries to explain, knowing absolutely that none of them are enough.

"I'll be taking Olivia's team in. They're better equipped, more skilled and better at following my lead. I will also be with them, and I'm certainly more experienced than you." He retorts, because he still doesn't understand what they're dealing with.

"It won't be enough. You're still underestimating her. You have been all along. Finding her should've always been our top priority."

"I decide what the priorities are, Louis. Why do none of you get that? And what else do you propose I do? Take you along? How exactly will that help? You've had, what, three attempts at stopping her and failed every single time? The fourth time will not be the charm." He says, with a sneer. It's like he's enjoying this. Things have gone so incredibly badly wrong, and Danny's life is in danger, and Chris is taking this as an opportunity to be smug and Louis really doesn't understand it. Chris has done nothing and he's acting like that is some kind of victory. Hazel had made it clear that this was coming no matter what. Whether they'd have continued to investigate her or not she'd have still come for them, and for revenge. From the moment they captured Joseph this was always going to happen, Louis has been warning him about this and yet Chris has done absolutely nothing about it. But of course, he's still happy, because he seems to have got what he wanted. Chris reaches in his pocket and slams a train ticket down on the table with a grin.

"Here. Pack your things and be ready to leave." He tells Louis; but he's had enough. He's not getting through to him and he's certainly not going back to Jongleton while Danny is in danger. He stands, grabs the ticket, and tears it in two.

"I'm not going. Not while she's out there and not until…I want…to know Danny's safe." He says, and his voice cracks. Chris moves forward and right into his face. He's slightly shorter than Louis, but of a much larger build, and so as a form of intimidation it should work. It does; but not effectively enough to get him to leave Danny to die.

"One more act of insubordination and I'll be sending you for retraining." And that almost does it. Louis feels a pang of fear. No Agent wants to be sent for retraining. It's the ultimate act of punishment, to be tossed aside like a broken toy. But he's still unwilling to give up. He couldn't live with himself if he did.

"I'm still not going. I'm not going to run away and leave him to die…"

"Get on the train Louis, last chance." Chris growls, so close that Louis can smell his breath.

"No. I…" he begins, intent on refusing again. Chris doesn't let him finish; he reacts instantly and tackles him to the ground. He pulls a syringe from his pocket and jabs Louis with the same sedative they use on Used-to-Bes. It's quick and it's effective, and Louis once again slips into unconsciousness before he has the chance to do anything to fight it. Chris cuffs his wrists together. Amber moves to stand and intervene, but Lauren reaches over and stops her. She looks between the two of them, utterly torn and wanting badly to stop this. Lauren gives her a look that begs her not to.

"Don't even think about it." Chris barks at her. "I'm taking Agent Louis Smith for retraining at the Home Base, due to his inability to follow orders despite repeated warnings. You two will follow my orders and stay here or the same will happen to you. Are we clear?"

"Yes, yes we are Chris." Lauren says quickly.

"Amber?" He demands, staring at her for confirmation. Amber bites her lip in anger and nods. "Good. I'll send some Cleaners to collect the Human, and I'll let you know if we're successful in retrieving Danny. I'll decide what happens to this team when I know that…" He says, clambering back to his feet and hoisting Louis' unconscious body up with him. The other two watch on in a stunned silence as he drags him out of the house, and they lose one of their team for the second time that night.

Kim gets home and slams the door behind her. She ran up the stairs so quickly after getting out of the taxi; partly in fear and partly excitement. What she's learned today is unbelievable but if she can verify it in some way and she can get the details out there…what that would mean for her career and for the world would be massive. Demons exist. That's insane. She needs to speak to Wade and get him to help her make sense of all of this. She needs to check the facts and make sure that Hazel Hardcastle actually exists, or existed, and that she is the same person who she met this afternoon. There's so much still to do but she's on the cusp of the biggest story ever. She knew this whole time there was something about this thing but she never imagined it'd be this massive. She thought at best it'd be a story that'd grab attention, expose some wrongdoing, and then fade away. But this? This could change everything.

She takes a deep breath and composes herself so that she can take this one step at a time. She sends Matthew another text. 'Please, just call me. I really need to speak to you.' She then sets her phone down on her kitchen

counter, grabs her laptop, and plays the recording. She wants to start typing this all up. That feels like the first step.
"You see, it all started in the 1940s," The recording of Hazel says.

"No, that's probably not quite right. It began before that. 1933, my first time on the set of a movie. The Dastardly Dame."
On that set there was a beautiful, blonde, heroine. She's dressed in all white, a long flowing dress, and is mid way through arguing with the handsome, chisel-jawed, male lead of the picture. His name is Billy Houston, he's a burly looking man standing against the backdrop of a bar. Her name is Harriet.
"Oh why don't you just beat it, I know that's what you want to do." She says to him, delivering her line loaded with the emotion of a woman in love.
"It ain't like that Evelyn, you know it ain't. Two more days. We can wait that long can't we?" Billy replies, in character.
"No Eddie, I can't. I feel like I've been waiting my whole life for this and I don't wanna do it any longer." She delivers, and tears fill her eyes. She tries to pull away but he grabs her, roughly, sternly and above all, passionately.
"I promise you. Two more days for the lawyers to look over it. Then we can be together. I can't have you just beat it like that. Not when we're meant to be together. What about Mexico City huh? Me and you, together forever." He says pulling her in close and Evelyn can no longer resist. She swoons and leans in.
"Oh, Eddie…" She sobs, and there's a musical crescendo to build up to a Hollywood style kiss, and the director ends the scene.
"Cut! That was wonderful." Dick shouts. The director is a large, balding man called Dick Johnson. He's in a suit that he's sweating through because under those studio lights it's stupidly warm. "I think we got it. Hatty, you're done for the day darlin'."
"Thanks Dicky." She says, with a sweet smile. Harriet walks away from the pair, as Dick begins to bark orders to the crew about what scene to film next, and they start to frantically move props and change the backdrop.
"I was fourteen years old; and I idolised her. Harriet Hardcastle. One of Hollywood's leading ladies." The recording tells Kim.
Harriet walks over to a group of young extras, searching for one in particular. She makes a beeline towards a young, plain looking, dark

haired girl.

"Hazel." She says, greeting her daughter warmly

"Mom. You were stunning." Hazel replies.

"Thank you darling, how're you feeling?" She asks

"Nervous." She replies, shyly.

"Oh that's wacky kid! You got your mothers talent. Go out there and enjoy yourself." She kisses her daughter gently on the forehead. "Now I gotta go…"

"You're not staying?" The kid replies, sounding a little deflated.

"I can't, I've gotta run my lines for tomorrow. You'll knock 'em dead, I know you will." She tells her, with a wink, before walking away.

"Okay, background actors for the park scene!" Dick bellows from the set. "Shake a leg, c'mon." He roars. Hazel and the others move forward, and dot themselves around the scene as instructed. Unfortunately, she sticks out. The others all look a lot more natural than she does, playing their small roles well. But she still looks nervous and stiff, like she doesn't feel comfortable and she doesn't look like she knows what she's doing. For the others, they're regulars. This isn't their first time in front of the camera. Dick calls action and Billy and another actor walk across the scene, they've barely started when Dick takes issue with something, and begins to get angry. "Cut!" He snorts and points directly at Hazel. "You. Girl! Your face is directly in shot. You're ruining it. That mug's distracting. Stop looking at the camera!" He orders, cruelly.

"Sorry," She squeaks and nervously shuffles to her left, so that she's not as far in the shot. The actors return to their starting position and prepare to go again,

"Okay, and…action!" He says and the scene starts, and again, it's only seconds before he gets frustrated by something. "Argh! Cut! You, girl. Again. Your nose looks huge. It's stealing focus. I can't work with this. We need to change the lighting." He snaps and clicks his fingers as if that's a clear instruction to do exactly what he's thinking of. Several of the crew run around frantically trying to do something, but none of them dare to ask exactly what he wants. Hazel, utterly embarrassed, starts to cry. She tries to keep quiet but she's upset and nervous, and this is going terribly.

Everyone around looks sheepish and some give her sympathetic looks but no one dares to move. Not Dick though. When he sees that she's crying he is incensed. "Oh! She walks onto my set, tries to ruin my movie, and now she's the one cryin' about it." He roars, standing up from his chair and

marching over to her." He grabs her roughly by the wrist and practically drags her away from the set. She's whimpering the whole way as she's hurried off set, she's embarrassed and he's hurting her. Everyone else watches on but no one dares to step in. He marches her all the way to a quiet and currently unused part of the set. It's a small room and a contained space. There's no one around. Finally, he lets go and rounds on her angrily, cornering her.
"Please…" She whimpers through tears and pain, rubbing her wrist.
"Now look here. You only got this part as a favour to your god damn mother and I already regret it. Someone with a face like yours is never gonna make it in this business, so this is the only break you're gonna get. If you don't stop ruining my shots you won't even get this one. Do you understand?" He says and stares down at her as she whimpers and struggles to find her words. They're in such a small, claustrophobic space that there's nowhere for her to hide from his gaze. He towers over her because he's tall and wide and she's short and skinny.
"Yes sir." She sobs.
"Good, now apologise to me for wasting my time." He growls.
"I'm sorry sir, it won't happen again." She says, with a snivel.
"You're damn right it won't." He says. He steps aside, allowing space for her to leave. But, as she tries to, he grabs her by the shoulder. "That's not a proper apology though." He says, and he reaches to undo his pants.

Sometime later they both return to the set, where everyone has been waiting for them. He marches straight back to his chair, looking pleased with himself, and plonks himself down. She slowly and sadly shuffles back into position.
"What're you all waiting for? Positions, people!" He snaps looking around. They all rush back to their mark. "Action!"

Chapter Sixty-Seven.

There's an old theatre that stands in the centre of Endsbrough. It's called the Royal Theatre. It's a part of the town's history and had once hosted performances of the biggest stage shows and bands of the time. The Beatles themselves had once played there. But, like everything, the glory of the Royal had faded and for decades it was closed and neglected. Some thought it would never open again. It was left to rot, and stood as an eyesore in a once vibrant town centre. There were rumours it would be demolished to make way for student housing. It all changed again a few years ago when the money came through to renovate it. It cost millions and took nearly two years to restore this historical building to something that resembled its once former glory. Now it stood as a centrepiece of efforts to rejuvenate the town; and it once again attracted the biggest touring productions and international artists.

Tonight, though, it was hosting a performance from a small community theatre group. It's called 'King Balor's Last Stand,' it's the story of the final days of a wild pirate king, and has been produced locally, with the hope that it can be a launching pad for bigger and better things for the group responsible. The performance is in full swing, as two pirates fight on stage, crossing cutlasses whilst others stand on watching and jeering. Some of the bystander pirates are played by kids; the children of the organisers cast as extras, because they couldn't quite get enough adult actors invested.

Unfortunately, the audience are far from enthralled, with some shuffling in their seats, others chuckling under their breath at the poor writing, and some already checking the time and wishing they were somewhere else.

"Arrrr. I'll run ye through ye…" One of the 'pirates' says, without much conviction, until his performance is interrupted by the doors to the theatre slamming open loudly and dramatically. Hazel strolls in coolly, as if she owns the theatre, flanked by policemen.

"Sorry I'm late." She announces as the inhabitants of the theatre glare at her. AJ, a volunteer usher for the evening, rushes towards her.

"Hi, sorry, have you got a ticket?" He stutters.

"No. Do you know who I am?" She asks, with a mocking tilt of her head.

"I'm sorry Madame, you need a ticket, I'm going to have to ask you to leave…" He says, trying to usher her back out through the door. She remains where she is and, once again wielding it like a bat, smacks AJ so hard with her umbrella that it breaks. He collapses to the ground, unmoving and she tosses it aside. The audience members shuffle awkwardly, unsure what they should do.

"Please, remain seated. The real show is about to begin." She says, and strolls down the aisle and towards the stage. Behind her PC Nadin carries Danny, who's still unconscious, through the doors. Another of the policemen is carrying Hazel's bag. She takes off her boater hat and pops it onto the head of an elderly audience member as she passes. "Suits you.

Really adds something to that ensemble." She tells her with a grin, much to the woman's confusion. She finds herself at the front and hops gracefully up onto the stage, and then takes a moment to drink in her surroundings. The actors look utterly baffled by her appearance and are clearly unsure how to handle the situation. One of the pirates, still clearly desperate to stay in character, speaks.
"Arr, ye can't be here ye…" He begins. She whirls around, grabs a fist full of his shirt and pulls him in close.
"Give me the map." She demands with wild eyes.
"What?" He asks, breaking character. Her face falls and she looks disappointed.
"Cutthroat Island." She explains, looking around at the others. "Geena Davis? Anyone?" She sighs, exasperated, and violently headbutts the 'pirate,' knocking him unconscious. The second 'pirate,' with whom he was duelling, retreats in a panic. The audience gasp, and some, realising this isn't part of the show start to stand. They are met in the aisles by police. The actors remaining on stage, particularly the children, look both scared and confused.
"I said remain in your seats. Audience participation will be at a minimum this evening." She demands, projecting her voice out to the entire theatre. One woman has her phone out, and that in particular attracts Hazel's attention. "Madame, who are you going to call? The police are already here." She explains, with a mocking and exasperated tone. One of the officers moves quickly over and punches the woman in the face and takes her phone. Hazel turns to the three child actor extras, who are whimpering and cowering. They are in cheap looking, homemade costumes, some have facial hair drawn on. "I despise working with children." She hisses to herself.
"Hey! Leave them alone." Says one of the other adult actors, stepping in her path. With a flick of her wrist a rope drops from above the stage, wraps around his neck, and pulls him back up and out of her way. She tilts her head as she surveys the terrified troupe of child actors and smirks to herself as she gets an idea. With another wave of her hand they all begin to transform before her eyes, and the three of them become what they are dressed as. With grunts and growls of confusion, real adult pirates stand before her. "Pirates. I have treasure." She explains, and gestures to a toy chest to her left filled with plastic coins that transforms into real gold. "Help me and it's yours; all you have to do is keep these fine ladies and

gentlemen in their seats. If they get up then make 'em bleed." She says, with a deliberately dramatic cackle. The pirates nod and grunt their understanding, then jump down from the stage to get closer to the audience. PC Nadin and the others lift Danny up onto the stage. "String him up somewhere boys." She demands of them and then turns again to face the audience and drink it in. She waves her hand again, and a single spotlight appears on her.
"Oh how I've missed being on stage. You know, it's true what they say." She says, drinking in the fear radiating from her new captive audience and letting it wash over her. This is the first time in decades she has been on stage and it's made that much sweeter by the feeling of terror in the air. "There's no place…like home."

Louis forced his eyes back open, fighting off the drug induced haze that wanted to keep hold of him for longer. His head is groggy and his vision is blurry, and for the second time that night he recovers from forced unconsciousness. His brain is still in a fog and he has to really focus to try to work out what's going on. His lips part and he lets out a small groan, which is meant to be a question. He recognises the place he is but he can't quite connect it to the memory. He tries to move his hand to wipe his eyes but he realises he can't. It stops at his side. He mumbles another question but it doesn't quite come out. That's when he realises that he can't move either of his arms; because there are leather restraints binding them in place. A little bit more of the fog lifts and he realises where he is. He's in Chris' office back at the Home Base; and he's strapped into a chair, with restraints across his wrists, arms, legs and ankles.
"Hi Louis." Chris says, stepping from behind him. Louis pulls at the restraints but there's no give in them.
"Chris…I…" He begins, starting to panic.
"Agent Louis Smith, I've assigned you to the retraining programme." He explains calmly. Louis thrashes against the restraints again, with the fear he already felt heightened by that announcement.
"What? No! You can't…Chris please…" He says, the panic evident in his voice. If Chris goes through with this then it's over for him. He won't be able to do anything to help Danny or the others. Chris pulls a chair in front of him and sits down. He speaks calmly and with a sympathetic, regretful tone.

"Louis, I don't want to have to do this but I'm new to this role. I need to prove myself, and you've made it so difficult for me. You're making me look terrible, like I can't control my subordinates. You've not been able to follow an order from the start. Then, despite being inexperienced and, frankly, useless, you bumbled your way into capturing 4XM and you and everybody else thought you were brilliant for it." He explains, and there's a hint of a sneer.
"I didn't at all. That's not what I thought." Louis blurts out, desperately trying to appease him.
"I tried to work with you, but you couldn't drop this whole Hazel thing. I just asked for a bit of time but you couldn't even give me that. I tried to just send you back and get you out of the way, and do this nicely, but you wouldn't cooperate with that either." Chris continues, as if he's not spoken at all.
"I will. Chris I will. Just, let me help Danny first…" He begs, and he means it. If that's what it takes then he'll go back and stay there for the rest of his life. He just wants to get through this, to find a way to save Danny from Hazel, first.
"And take the credit for that?" Chris scoffs. "No. I'm not rewarding your unwillingness to do your job properly. Not to mention you shared the truth with a human. I don't care what the reasons were. We never tell humans who we really are."
"I had to…" Louis tries to explain, with a lump in his throat. He's scared. More scared than he's ever been. He's scared about what his future looks like if Chris goes through with this. He's trying to stop himself from crying, through fear, through anger, and through all of the other emotions that are firing through him right now in a complete and utter cloud of messy feelings that he doesn't know where to start with.
"No you didn't. You could've dealt with it differently."
"And you could deal with this differently." He tries, hoping that he can reason with him.
"No, Louis." Chris says, shaking his head, and Louis' heart sinks. It's obvious that Chris has made his mind up. He wants him out of the way and has decided this is the most efficient way to do it. Whatever logic is currently running through Chris' mind for his horrific decision, he won't be dissuaded from his choice. "You've backed me into a corner here. You've undermined me at every turn and you've caused so much trouble."
"I'm sorry." Louis says, meaning it. He never meant for any of this. He just

wanted to come here and fulfil his purpose. "I know that I've screwed up. I know that I'm bad at this. But I'm just trying to do some good. I'm trying to do what we're supposed to do. I'm sorry, Chris, I didn't mean to screw it all up, but please, not this." He says, and the tears finally come. He's been holding this in for so long. Since he arrived he's been told so many times that he's useless and that he's inexperienced. No one thought he was good enough and all he wanted to do was prove that he was. But he couldn't. He failed. He slumps in the chair, giving up.
"It's too late." Chris says and stands up, and Louis knows it is.
"What happens now?" Louis asks, realising there might be some relief in this. At least he doesn't have to fight to feel like he belongs any more.
"This." Chris says, picking up a large, metallic, sphere and showing him. He opens it up and it's hollow inside. He moves in, and puts it around Louis' head so that when it's closed again it'll engulf him and he'll be trapped. "I'm told it takes about two hours. I'm sorry. It will be painful. I wish I could say it wasn't, but it will be. I don't fully understand it, but I think a lot of that time it's mapping your brain and so you'll still be you. Towards the end of the process that's when…"
"When I'll start to forget…?" Louis asks, trying to steel himself.
"Yes. And then at the end of the two hours when the Cleaners come to collect you, you'll just be…" He looks into Louis' eyes, sharing a look of sadness that suggests he does regret this. But again, it's clear that he's not going to change his mind. He's trapped himself into the decision, in the same way he now has Louis trapped. "Empty." He says at last. "At least you won't remember the pain, though?" He offers, trying to make them both feel better. Louis inhales sharply, trying to maintain composure in the face of having his memories and everything about him completely wiped. Once this process is finished he'll be a completely blank slate, and he'll become one of the Cleaners. That's what retraining is. It's clearing everything you are, everything you know, away so that it can be replaced with something new. That's who the Cleaners are. They're Custodians who had to be retrained.
"Do you at least know where he is? Where Hazel took him?" He asks, wanting to at least go into this believing that Danny will be safe.
"Yes." He says, and that brings him some relief. Chris silently closes the sphere and as it clicks Louis lets out a whimper that echoes loudly. It's completely dark inside and he's so scared; especially as he hears a scraping as Chris connects wires to it, and in turn connects that to the

machine that will wipe his brain. Everything about him is about to be cruelly ripped away, and there's nothing he can do about it. He fights against the restraints again, even though he knows it's hopeless. "Goodbye, Louis." Chris says, so quietly that he can only just hear it through the thick metal. There's a distant click and the sphere is charged with electricity. Louis screams as his head burns.

Amber, Wade and Lauren sit in complete silence. There are full, untouched, cups of tea on the table in front of them. None of them can meet each other's gaze. They've been sitting like this for some time, because none of them are sure what to say or do next. Eventually it's Wade that breaks the stalemate, albeit reluctantly.
"What are we doing?" He asks, shaking his head. He's not sure if it's even his place to speak. It's not his world. But someone has to say something, someone has to do something, and so it's fallen to him. Amber instantly lets out a frustrated grunt and rolls her eyes.
"Nothing. Absolutely nothing." She says, exasperated.
"But that's what I mean. Shouldn't we be doing summit?"
"Did you have a bright idea?" She snaps; and snatches a biscuit from the plate in front of her and aggressively bites it.
"Well I guess not but one of your guys has been kidnapped by a Demon, who's working with my boss, and your boss has…what suspended another? There must be something we can do to help."
"He's taken him to be retrained." She corrects, shaking her head and refusing to look over at the human sitting around their table.
"Right, so he'll have to sit through a crappy course, so what?" He says, because he doesn't understand it, and that is even more infuriating to her.
"Will you shut up? It's not that. He's gone. We won't see him again. He'll have no idea who he is. He'll have his entire memory wiped, and be trained from scratch." She explains, growling, slamming her fist on the table and then snatching another biscuit and snapping it in half.
"What the hell? We can't let that happen." And now that he understands the severity of it he's horrified. He'd worked out these people could screw around with people's memories, he expected that's what was planned for him, but he didn't think they'd do it to one of their own. Amber's fiery gaze snaps over to him and she looks like she wants to do to him what she just did to the biscuit.
"Lauren, can you just deal with this!?" She says, as if he can't hear her.

"Amber, please..." Lauren, the peacekeeper of the group, tries.
"No! This is dumb. I'd love to just roll in and pull Newbie out, then all run off and save Danny, come back here and celebrate with a group hug but it's not going to work like that. This is shit. This is over." She says, and there's clearly so much pent up frustration and energy inside her that she's dying for a way to let it out. She slams her hands down and stands up. Then, not really sure why she's done that, sits back down again.
"...why not?" Lauren asks her quietly, taking her by surprise.
"What? Because it'd never work?" She snaps in response.
"Maybe not. I don't know. Chris doing this...it's not right. I can follow orders, even when I don't agree with them, if I understand them. I can do it if I can see why it's for the best. I don't see that here. That poor boy...I don't understand, and I'm not just going to sit here making cups of tea while that happens. I've got to at least try to stop it." She says, and stands up, puffing her chest out and composing herself. "I'm rescuing Louis, and then I'm saving Danny. And then we're coming back here and we are having a group hug." She explains, her face determined, despite how impossible she knows it is. "Are you with me?"
"Can I punch Chris in the face?" Amber asks, with a tilt of her head.
"Yes." Lauren tells her, making it sound so simple. Amber shrugs and gets back to her feet. That was all she needed to hear.
"I'll grab some weapons." She says, like it's no big deal, and wanders out of the room to gather whatever she thinks will be useful.
"Matthew...I..." Lauren begins.
"I wanna help." He grunts.
"Thank you. And we'll need it. But...our odds aren't good...yours are even worse." She explains.
"I still wanna help." He tells her, because he owes Louis his life and to him it really is as simple as that,
"I know. I just had to let you know." She tells him with a respectful nod. Just like that, it's decided. They're going to rescue Louis, and Danny, and then have a big group hug.

"That's...really awful. I'm sorry that happened to you."
"Oh honey, it wouldn't be the last time. Hollywood is full of perverts, and this was a long time before all that Weinstein drama. That was just how things were in those days. I bet that's how it still is."
"Did you tell anyone?"

"I told my mother, but she didn't care. It's just what happened. Men like Dick Johnson held all the power. If I'd have told anyone else it wouldn't have mattered. It would've only meant I couldn't get work."
"That's really sad."
"You don't know the half of it. The movie flopped anyway. My mother found it difficult to find work after that. She was over forty and no one was interested in casting her. The Dastardly Dame was her last big part. Me though, I was just starting out. I got a couple more small roles, did a few roles on the stage, and then bigger parts in films. Nearly a decade of working my way up and I was on the cusp of really making something of myself."

"Which is what takes us to 1942, to Beverly Hills. And believe me, the fantasy matched the reality."
Hazel, now older, walks from a car that has just dropped her off. It's a bright and sunny day and with her loose fitting silky dress and sunglasses she more closely resembles the demeanour of her modern day counterpart. Harriet is with her and she looks a little less poised and graceful than she did those years earlier, though she is still a beautiful and radiant woman. There is a crowd clamouring for the two of them at the gates to the studio; these women are both stars and, although for many years all the attention has been on Harriet, Hazel has inadvertently started to steal the limelight. Harriet soaks in the adoration she can get, and while Hazel follows her lead she does so with caution.
"Okay, mother, that's enough. We'll be late." She tells her, and Harriet reluctantly moves away from the crowd, calling back to them and blowing air-kisses as she does.
"Thank you my darlings, mwah! Mwah!" They pass through a gate, manned by a burly security guard, who gives them a nod of recognition, and the cheers of the crowd fade into the background as they approach the set. "That was rude. You couldn't have allowed me even a moment more with my adoring fans?" Harriet hisses to her daughter.
"I just didn't want to be late." She explains calmly.
"Pssh. When you're a leading lady, there's no such thing as being late." She says dismissively, and stumbles slightly as she waves her arm dramatically. Hazel grabs her, subtly, and steadies her.
"Well that's the thing mother, I'm not the lead." She says, shaking her head because she's told her this a bazillion times.

"Pah. Well you should be. Which bitch have they got in the lead for this?" Harriet replies, a little too loudly. Several crew members turn to look at them and then hastily pretend they haven't heard.

"Mother! Be quiet." She says, mortified in case her mother's poor conduct reflects badly on her.

"I will do no such thing. You need to be bold." She tells her, raising her voice even louder. "You haven't got long left. By the time I was your age I was already a star, and you, well…" She snaps.

"I'm just waiting for the right opportunity…" Hazel mumbles, hanging her head a little. They've had this conversation before. The longer she goes without that breakthrough role the more of a disappointment she becomes to her mother and her own waning star power.

"Well, as luck would have it, my old friend Dick Johnson got in touch. He's working on a new movie and he's got a role he thinks you'd be perfect for."

"No, absolutely not. I don't want to work with him again." Hazel tells her, shaking her head and trying to hide the look of disgust on her face. She has told her mother why but that knowledge was seemingly discarded almost immediately.

"Think yourself too good, do you?" She says, pulling away from her daughter's steadying grip.

"It's not that…" She tries to explain, but stops because she knows her mother won't see sense.

"C'mon Hazel. We're runnin' outta cash. You're barely making anything from the tommyrot you're doing now. This could be big. Just meet with him? Please? For me?" She says, fluttering her eyes and whining the last few words. It's true. Every bit of it. Hazel has been offered bigger pictures but she's been trying to be selective about the projects; only picking things she knew she'd enjoy doing. But, enjoyment doesn't pay the bills, and her mother had sacrificed a lot for her over the years. She could at least give her this.

"Oh fine." She relents.

"Just hear him out, that's all I ask. That's a good girl. I've arranged a meeting at his office tonight."

"Tonight?"

"Yes darling. Now, get yourself ready. Your mother needs to go find a drink…" She says, as they arrive at the makeup trailer.

"It's not even…" She begins to protest, but Harriet is already walking away, not listening.

Chapter Sixty-Eight.

Trapped. Alone. And in unimaginable pain. All he can do is scream and thrash. It's all consuming, it feels like thousands of needles being rammed through his skull and into his brain and oh god it hurts so much.
There are echoes of the past, much like how they say your life flashes before your eyes when you die, and he loses himself in them. It's an escape from the pain, and he is, in a way, about to die. He remembers the kiss with Danny, capturing Joseph, encountering Hazel for the first time, and so much more of what's happened in the last few weeks. They flick past like his brain can't quite settle on one, until finally it does and plucks a memory from deep, deep down.
"Are you ready, Louis? Now is the time to receive your gift…." The Superior One asks on a day many, many years ago. He's covered in sunshine and light and it all feels so warm. He's holding a vial filled with a glowing white liquid. Louis doesn't remember this, or rather, he didn't think he did. But it's there, locked in some dark corner of his brain and shocked out by the pain.
"I am." Louis remembers himself saying in the small, nervous, squeaky little voice of a young child. One hands Young-Louis the vial, and he drinks it, and for a few seconds everything remains the same. He stands, staring at the being before him and waiting. Then, it hits him. First as a cramp in the stomach, and then he doubles over in pain.
Another minute passes and all his senses come alive like they never have before. It spreads through him like fire, through his veins, through his entire body. It hurts and it burns, and it's akin to the pain he's in now. This pain is making him remember that pain; but it was the pain of his body coming alive rather than his brain being murdered. In his memory he remembers seeing wisps and trails of red energy circulating. He saw people, darkened by the red, infected and coloured by it. He saw the world spread out before him and sensed all the demonic energy out in it, and all the Used-to-Bes. He screams. It's too much for him. His head is burning, and that pain tears him back to the present.

Hazel is sitting at the edge of the stage, casually talking at the people of the theatre, as if this is all part of some casual one woman show. An audience with a demonic psychopath.
"…didn't even have a hat. She was less wicked witch and more irate secretary. Oh and the apple trees! They were just scantily clad women with

umbrellas. And this was only a few years ago. Why do we need to sexualise trees? That's…honestly why I say avoid community theatre. I have an appreciation of the arts, but you just never know what you're going to get, what strange choice the talentless director is going to have made in the name of standing out. Isn't that right Andy?" She tells them, and looks to her right, where there's a fat and balding man who's the director of the show standing awkwardly. He's scared and he's sweating. She wafts a copy of the script for King Balor's Last Stand at him, which she'd demanded a few minutes earlier. "I mean this whole thing is drivel. Still, at least you're not banjaxing a classic. I have a little bit of respect for you for that Andy. Wait. No. I take it back. I just got to the nudity. Did you all know there was nudity? I bet you didn't." She says, laughing and nodding towards a specific woman in the audience. "You look like you'd have been horrified. But of course it's art isn't it Andy? Exposing a woman's breasts for all to see. It's art. Not at all some dirty little man wanting to live out his sordid little dreams on stage. Then again, that's not something that's exclusive to community theatre. That's basically all the acting world is, or at least it was in my day." She says, rolling her eyes and tossing the script aside. Behind her Danny is bound in the centre of the stage. His wrists are chained together and suspended above his head; hooked on to some rigging that was supposed to be for props. She sees that he's beginning to wake, so she gets up, realising there's other entertainment to be had. "Take a seat." She says, dismissively as she pushes Andy off the stage and marches towards her next scene partner. She scoops up a discarded eyepatch and places it on her face. "'Ello poppet." She says, in her best pirate voice. He doesn't react, he just stares at her, somewhat apathetically. "What is with you people tonight?" She says, taking the eyepatch off and tossing it to the side. Danny stares right past her, trying to take in his surroundings and work out where he is. His gaze passes over the terrified looking humans, the police officers guarding the aisle, and even the real life pirates who are pacing up and down, eager to quench their growing thirst for blood. He considers and catalogues it all. "Out with it then." She demands of him, a little sore he's completely blanked her.
"Out with what?" He asks, raising an eyebrow.
"I'm expecting lines somewhere in the region of "you'll never get away with this," or a good "what do you want with me?" She explains. Danny continues to look nonchalant and does his best to shrug.
"No, I'm good." He says, going back to looking around.

"You're good?" She practically spits.

"Yeah. I think I get it." He explains, still looking quite unphased by the situation. "We're in a theatre. You said lines. And playing a role. I get it. You were an actress, right?"

"Am an actress. Once a thespian…" She says, striking a dramatic post.

"Sure." He says with a sigh, and nods politely. He understands enough to know that it'll irritate her to not have anything to play against; and if there's one thing Danny understands it's how to annoy people. She responds by jabbing him in the ribs; which are sore, and potentially cracked.

"Oww. Fuck." He blurts, not being able to hold that in.

"Oh good, you are capable of some emotional range." She quips. "But that's nothing compared to what I have planned." She says, trying to goad him. He groans in response, but not from the pain. No, this is more from disinterest.

"Look. Whatever this is, I'm not interested. I don't really want any part of this delusion you have going on, so you carry on and I'll just hang here." He says. Several of the audience members shuffle uncomfortably. They've all seen what she's capable of and they've all been cowering in fear for the last hour. They now look worried they're about to see someone else be murdered before their eyes, all because this cocky young man didn't know what to keep his mouth shut. Hazel, however, laughs at him.

"I'm not going to kill you." She says, responding to what she wants him to have said rather than what he actually said. "Not immediately, anyway. That's not the plan." Danny rolls his eyes at that.

"Great, you've got a plan. Nice. Good luck with that." He says, looking around again.

"Well, I'm glad you asked." She says; evidently just deciding to continue with what she's decided to say, despite him not playing his part in the scene with any commitment. "Your kind are always willing to rush in guns first, thoughts second. You've proved that time and time again. So, it's only a matter of time until your friends follow my breadcrumbs and come to rescue you. Especially since one of them carries such a torch for you." She turns to smile at the audience, hamming it up for them. Danny grimaces at the allusion to Louis, his emotionless expression cracks ever so slightly. She spots it. "There we are. I know all about your little romance. So he'll definitely come." She tells him, with a sly smile and a wink. Danny bites his lip in frustration. "And believe me, the more people they bring the better." She lowers her voice and leans in to whisper to him, no longer playing up to the crowd. "That's why they're all here. You see, the more fear I can create, the more pain I can create, the more blood and death, then the more demonic energy will be drawn in. That'll make for a real show." She gestures to the people behind her, Human and Used-to-Be alike. "Every single one of them could die. I kind of want that. The bigger and more terrifying I can make this battle the more inviting it'll be. The bigger the battle, the more demonic energy will be drawn, and the crazier things will become. Who knows what consequences we'll be looking at. It could all be drawn to me, and make me even more powerful. Or, fat, lumpy Andy could end up infected. Even you could."

"I can't be infected, none of us can." He snaps back, derision evident in his voice as he seizes on the part of the plan he can argue with. The bit he can outsmart her with. She smirks, and gestures for PC Nadin to join her. He gets a swiss army knife out, and runs it along his palm, drawing blood. The Used-to-Be doesn't even flinch.

"Are you sure?" She asks as she raises Nadin's bleeding hand and pushes it towards Danny, who flinches. "Would you like to test it? Would you like to see how quickly they turn on you? How quickly they go from coming to save you to trying to put you down. They'll turn on a dime." She lets the outstretched hand hover there for a moment, with the blood dripping, just inches from Danny's face. He tries to pull back but there's very little give in the chains. He's visibly shaken now. He was always told he couldn't be infected; but here, confronted with it, he's not sure enough to put it to the test. Especially with the impossible demonic energy laced drugs that Brick was selling in the back of his mind. Finally, she lets Nadin's hand fall, and he steps back. "I will end tonight more powerful than ever, or I will end tonight dead." She tells him.

"I'm hoping for dead." He replies quickly.

"Of course you are. Because I'm evil. I'm terrible. I'm awful. My very existence is unworthy. That's what your people think. That's what you've always thought. Always with the men with guns in cars turning up. From the very first night you've been hunting me and I've been running.

"I'm sure that's nothing to do with all the killing…" Danny bites back, instantly getting a little annoyed with himself for being dragged into this ridiculous back and forth.

"That doesn't matter!" She says, with a mocking laugh as if it's the most ridiculous thing she's ever heard. "Do you think everyone they cart off has killed someone? What about your one from last night?" She asks with a knowing look. "Do you even know whether he had or did you just round him anyway?" It takes Danny a minute to think back, to that soggy trip through the park and Louis' stupid jokes about a narcoleptic serial killer. It seems like a lot longer ago. Being kidnapped by a monologuing psychopath can play havoc with your sense of time. "You don't, do you?" She says, triumphantly. She's right. He doesn't know what 5DG had done, just that they needed to capture him. He hates when he doesn't know something.

"No," He admits, quietly. "But I know when they take you away you'll deserve it." He adds, a little desperate to claw back some ground in this verbal sparring match he didn't even mean to be in. She laughs again and it thunders through the theatre.

" C'mon then wise guy. What do you think happens to us when you send us away in a white van? Rehabilitation? Do you think they cure us and send us back out into the world, all better? Or do you think they murder us? Slowly creeping closer and closer to genocide day after day because we happen to fit the label of 'evil'?" She says

"It's not like that…" He starts, but again he doesn't know and for Danny that's much scarier than any threat to his life. She's rattled him, she's made him uncertain about his position and about some of the rules he's always been sure of.

"Isn't it? It's not too late, we can try infecting you and then all hand ourselves in when your friends arrive and see what happens? No?" She says, with a laugh of derision. He remains silent, avoiding eye contact. He was determined to stay composed but there's something about this that's thrown him. Her plan, for starters, is simply to create chaos and violence and any attempt to rescue him will do just that. Custodians, and Used-to-Bes, and Humans, and there's bound to be casualties on all sides and if a rescue attempt is made then the odds aren't particularly good. Once he and the rest of his team are out of the way, she'll be free to make even more mess. That's not to mention humans that could be infected along the way. "Exactly." She continues, seeing the doubt creeping onto his face that was so unreadable only a few moments earlier. He screws up his face and glares at her, but she's unphased and continues. "Whether 'tis nobler in the mind to suffer the slings and arrows of outrageous fortune, or to take arms against a sea of troubles, and by opposing end them? Shakespeare. I would've loved to have done one of his plays. I'm tired of suffering. You taking Joseph away was one arrow too many. I'm taking arms. Am I evil? Does it even matter?" She asks; and Danny keeps his mouth firmly shut. He doesn't know the answer and he doesn't care about the answer. "Don't worry. I know it's not personal. You don't know any better. You're just the flying monkeys. But I'm still going to enjoy plucking all your wings." She lets out a sigh, and changes her tone. "Time for a costume change. I'll be back soon. I've still got plenty more revelations to share." She tells him as she marches off stage.

"I don't feel like we've got a plan." Amber says. They have sat in silence for the entire drive here and yet it's only now that reality actually hits her. Now that they're sitting here, parked just outside the boundary of Home Base, and about to go charging in blindly.
"We don't." Lauren confirms, because they don't. They don't have a clue what they're doing or how they're going to do it, or even if they can still save Louis.
"Okay. I'm glad we agree."
"We've never done anything like this before. I think we just need to get in, and see what happens. We do whatever we can, whatever we have to." Lauren explains, with a heavy sigh as she thinks out loud. She's completely out of her depth but she's determined that won't stop her trying.
"Always." Amber says, but something about that makes her pause. "I don't wanna…kill any of our own." She says, sounding worried. This is already getting away from them all.
"Oh god, no. Absolutely not. No, that's not what I meant." Lauren blurts, very quickly clarifying. "No, no, no. No killing anyone. We try this quietly. I hope we don't have to fight. I don't see how we could, there'll be so many and…oh let's just go." She says, degenerating into babbling a little.
"What do you need me to do?" Wade asks from the driver's seat.
"I suppose just stay here and keep the engine running." Lauren tells him.
"You don't want me to come?"
"No. There's less chance of getting noticed if it's just the two of us. They'd be alerted the second a human stepped onto the grounds." She explains, trying to give him a reassuring smile. "But there's every chance we'll need to leave very quickly. So please be ready."
"Sure." He nods. And with one last glance to each other Amber and Lauren get out, trying very hard to ignore the enormity of the task before them.

Louis wanders, happy and carefree, through Jongleton village. It's a bright summer morning, the birds are singing, and the place is so alive. It's early, but everyone here is up early. There's already people out walking their dog, or just taking a morning stroll, or even just having a cup of tea in their front garden. Everyone gives him a friendly smile and that's what first made him feel at home here. It's beautiful, and it's peaceful, and he's missed it so much. Wait, no, he hasn't missed it. He can't have missed it. He's been here the whole time. He pops into the local shop, as he always does on his morning rounds, and hands the shopkeeper a handful of letters.

"Here you go…" He starts; but he can't remember the person's name. He looks down at the addressee on the envelope, but he can't read it. It's just a mish-mash of shapes that don't form any real words.

"Thanks Louis!" ??? says brightly, and he takes the letters from him. "Looks like it's all bills again. Don't suppose you'll just take 'em back?" He jokes. Louis laughs politely at ???'s joke, but he's still panicking that he can't remember the man's name. "'Fraid not sorry! My work here is done." He says, with a forced smile to hide his panic. He backs out of the shop, shaking his head to try to clear whatever brain fog he's having. He carries on with his rounds, hoping that was just some weird anomaly and trying to forget about it. He passes the local park where there are children playing on the swings. Or, there were. When he looks back they've disappeared and he does a double take. Now he's not sure if there ever were children there. He shakes it off again. There's something strange happening but no, he must be imagining it, right? Either way, he has post to deliver, because that's his job. He's a postman, and there are people relying on him. He greets a pensioner tending to her garden and plasters that warm smile back on his face. This is one of his favourite stops.

"Good morning Mrs. McGinty. Someone's popular today." He says, as he hands her over a handful of letters. She chuckles in response, a kind and welcoming glint in her eye, as she takes the pile from him with her muddy gardening glove.

"Thank you, love," She says.

"You are welcome! Have a lovely…" He says, but then he freezes because Mrs McGinty's smile melts away. Her whole face melts away. "What? No…that's not…"

"What's the matter lovey?" She asks, but he doesn't understand how because she's got no mouth to make the words with. Her face is just smooth and featureless and he can't remember if she ever had a face, or comprehend what it would've looked like if she did. She reaches out to him and he backs off, not wanting to be touched by this strange, faceless creature. "No!" He shouts, tripping over and falling backwards. But then, she's gone, and he wonders whether she was ever there at all. He looks around and the very town is fading away; like someone is gradually turning the lights down and it's dimming into nothingness. Mrs McGinty's house fades away, the street fades away, and even the ground under him is replaced by endless nothing. He screams, because he's scared and it hurts, and the scream echoes endlessly around him.

And then, suddenly, he's in the War Room and the screaming has stopped. "Well, maybe that's why you're here." Danny says, from nowhere.

"What?" Louis asks, because he can't remember what they were talking about or why they're even here. Danny rolls his eyes.

"You're right. It's not my biggest strength." He explains, looking up at him with those big brown eyes. "Maybe we...maybe I..." He pauses, obviously picking his words carefully. Whatever it is he's trying to say it can't be a good sign that he's taking the time to choose his words. "Okay. Yes. I need help with that part. That's where you fit in." He admits and Louis is stunned. As his stomach leaps he remembers what this is and what they were doing. This was the first time he really felt like he belonged. It was the first time Danny had really admitted that he fits into the team in any way; and he was panicked about how to respond because he was afraid that anything he would say would ruin it.

"Oh," Was the best he could muster at the time. He wants to say so much more.

"So what do you think we should do next?" Danny asks; but when Louis looks up he's not there any more. Danny is gone.

"Danny?" Louis asks, panicked. He can't lose this moment. He can't lose Danny. Not now.

But then he's not even in the War Room any more.

"I want it to hurt." Hazel says, from within the void that he's now standing in again.

And then he's in an alleyway; but it's one he doesn't recognise. This isn't one of his memories. It's not like earlier, where it was one from the deep forgotten parts of his brain. No, he knows where this is even though he wasn't there. This is an alleyway in Manchester in 1997. It's dark and it's cold and Hazel's hands are covered in blood, because she is there.

"But, you wouldn't be you. You wouldn't be kind." She explains to the dying boy on the floor. She gently removes her necklace and pops open the vial of blood she's been keeping. "But then, look at what this world does to kindness." She tells him, and Louis watches as she pours it into one of his many open wounds and his broken body convulses.
"This isn't…" Louis says to himself and suddenly it stops and they disappear, as if his brain realised it was playing the wrong movie and shut it off. Now he's just standing in the void again and he's so scared.
"Many years ago a Warrior came before us begging for more power. Begging for the strength to liberate a nation from a tyrant, who's mind had been twisted beyond all recognition." The voice of the Superior One explains; and Louis sees it play out before him, and that makes no sense because he wasn't there and he doesn't know what these people look like but he can picture it as if he was. The Warrior is on his knees before the Mad King, held in place by the swords of his soldiers. But then suddenly Louis is that Warrior. The Mad King holds a woman by the throat and he knows it's a woman he loves. A human woman he'd pictured spending his life with. The Mad King runs her through with a sword and the Warrior roars through Louis' mouth. He screams in despair as she dies before his eyes. The Mad King Laughs. Now, she's Hazel and the dead woman is Danny. It makes no sense; and yet all the sense in the world.

They hear the bloody curdling screeching from the corridor and all attempts to be subtle and go unnoticed are cast aside. Amber throws herself at the door, bursting through it and ready to fight. Her eyes widen at the sight before her. Louis is strapped into a chair, pale, convulsing and drenched in sweat. His head is locked in a heavy metal sphere that's connected up to a machine that's pumping and hissing away maniacally, and there are Cleaners hovering around him like vultures ready to swoop in. They round on her and she doesn't wait to explain or talk; she just pulls out an extendable baton and rushes them, because she knows they don't have long to stop this and she's not going to waste a second talking. She takes them both out quickly and effortlessly. Lauren rushes forward before they've even hit the floor and is at Louis' side, calling out to him.
"Louis! We're here." She cries, grabbing his hand and squeezing to try to comfort him. "I don't know what to do!" She shouts in a panic, trying to get a good look at the machine and work out how to safely stop it.
"Fuck it." Amber says, dropping the baton and joining her. She grabs the

wires connecting the sphere to the machine and rips them out. The machine powers down and Louis stops screaming and convulsing, but his body goes limp. Amber grabs hold of the sphere with both hands and pulls it apart, snapping the locking mechanism and ripping it open. Louis slumps forward, face and hair drenched with sweat. Together they undo the straps and lay him down on the floor. "Louis, wake up." Lauren tries, shaking him gently. It's then they notice blood coming from his ears and his nose. "Lauren, I think you need to…" Amber begins, but Lauren is already rubbing her palms together and bracing herself. She places her palms on either side of his head and breathes deeply.

Hazel hovered reluctantly outside of Dick Johnson's office. She came alone, and suddenly that felt like the worst possible thing she could've done. But, the alternative would've been bringing her mother and that would've offered no more protection. She braces herself, hoping that she can keep this brief. The thought of being alone with that man makes her skin crawl but she promised that she would do it. She knocks on the door. "Come in." He says from the other side of the door. She hesitates, and wonders if it's too late to turn and run the other way. But instead she enters, a friendly smile plastered on her face because she's a fantastic actress. She sees him sitting behind his large oak desk and holds back a shudder. He's even wider than he was the last time she saw him, and the shirt he's wearing looks like it's about to burst a button or two. He's lost his hair too. Not that it shows, but because he's wearing a very obvious hair piece.
"Hazel, doll!" He says, his chubby face lighting up as he stands up and moves around the desk towards her. "Come here and give uncle Dick a hug. You look great, kid." He says, and she feels as if she has to oblige. He pulls her into a hug and squeezes her tight and she gets an uncomfortable nose full of the smell of his sweat.
"Mr. Johnson. How do you do?" She says, pulling away from the hug the very second it's appropriate to do so.
"Grab a seat, let's talk. This is my associate, Sol." He says, gesturing to a rat-like man with curly grey hair sitting the other side of his desk. "He's producing the picture with me." The other man gets up from his seat and reaches out to shake her hand. She does so, courteously, and takes a seat as instructed, very glad that at the very least they aren't alone together. Dick strolls excitedly back to the other side of his desk and lights up a

cigar. He throws a script down on the desk, next to two empty cut-glasses that she has no doubt contained whisky moments earlier. "This is the one. 'Love and War.' We've got some big names attached already. Bill Davis, Apollo Banks, and here we were talkin' about who to cast as the female lead. We talked to Garland, and considered Crawford, but then I thought, no. I want little Hazel Hardcastle in on this. I was telling Sol here, this kid needs her big break and we can be the ones to give to her. And that's when I called your Mom. She said you were in!" He says, his tone full of friendliness of joviality that really doesn't match the horrific man she knows is lurking under the surface. She also knows that a lot of that is a lie. There's no way that Garland or Crawford, or most other people, would work with him right now. He was coming to her because he was desperate. Everyone knew he was having money problems andt that his name no longer came with the same power it had ten years prior. He needed to make another hit, but all that means that no one would touch him. He had no money and very few favours to call in.
"Well, that's mighty kind of you Mr. Johnson…." She begins.
"C'mon, call me Dick. I've known you god knows how long." He laughs.
"Dick. That's mighty kind of you. But, I'd really like to read the script before I commit to anything…and of course I'll need to talk to my agent…" She explains, and he roars with laughter again, banging his fist on the table like it's the most hilarious joke he's ever heard.
"Listen to this kid, Sol! Read the script. Talk to my agent. You're funny, doll."
"I assure you I'm deadly serious." She says; and his mood changes suddenly when he realises he can't laugh his way into a deal. So, he resorts to another of his favourite tactics. Bullying.
"Listen here, you oughta be grateful for such an opportunity." He says, leaning forward and sneering at her. "This picture's gonna make you a star, and here you are throwing it back in my face."
"Mr Johnson, I'm very sorry if I've offended you, but I'm certainly not throwing it back in your face, it's just…"
"Well I don't hear you saying thank you either! Do you Sol?" He says, and her heart begins to thump that little bit faster. She tries not to give it away. She doesn't want him to know he's scaring her.
"I certainly don't." Sol adds.
"Dames like you…they're dime a dozen…and they'd do anything for an opportunity like this…and here you are not showing any god damn

gratitude whatsoever." Dick snaps.
"I assure you, I am grateful, it's just..." He stands up, looming over her like he had all those years before.
"You don't seem it." He says, angrily.
"I am, it's just..." She squeaks, being forced back into the role of the young, nervous girl.
"Well...maybe you could show me how grateful you are." He says, and then blows her a kiss and grabs his crotch suggestively. "Like I said, there's girls who'd do anything for a role like this. I told Sol here you were one of 'em..." He says and her eyes widen in horror as Sol, giving her a lecherous look, reaches across and grabs her breast through the cardigan she's wearing. She shrieks and slaps him before she can really register it.
"Absolutely not!" She snaps, indignantly, standing up and trying to leave. Dick thunders out from behind his desk and races her to the door. "Get out of my way, please." She says, unable to stop herself adding the pleasantry despite her fury.
"No way. You don't get to just come in here and be so god damn disrespectful to us. You need to apologise to Sol right now." He explains and Sol looms behind her, she turns around to face him, sandwiched between the two men. She takes a deep breath, desperate to get out of this situation as quickly as possible.
"I'm sorry Sol, now please, just..." She's interrupted as Sol grabs her, and forces his dirty tongue into her mouth. He tastes like whisky and cigar smoke and it's all she can do not to vomit. She struggles in his grip and knees him in the crotch to get free. He shouts in pain, swearing loudly and she pushes him away from her. She turns back to Dick and tries to slap him too, because she's too far in for a polite escape now. He catches her hand and backhands her, knocking her to the ground. She scrambles to try to get back to her feet but Dick grabs a nearby golden statue of a tiger and smacks her over the head with it again and again until she stops flailing. All the fight is gone from her and only the pain of her cracked skull remains. She struggles for breath, trying to plead with them but not able to form words. Dick and Sol loom over her, staring down as she fights to stay alive.
"What did you do?" Sol whimpers, with eyes so wide they resemble a frog.
"She had it coming." Dick growls, still clutching the bloodied statue.
"What do we do now?" Sol asks, and Dick stares down at her, contemplating it. His eyes narrow as he makes his decision.
"Well, she's still breathing ain't she?" He says.

A little while later Dick's car pulls up at the side of the road, outside of the city and the two men drag Hazel's limp body out and toss it to the side of the road. It's raining. She's still alive, but barely. She lands face down in a puddle. They quickly get back into the car and speed away, leaving her lying there, face down, and struggling to breath. She's covered in blood, and mud, and splatterings of their DNA. She gurgles in the water as more rain lashes down on top of her broken body.

Chapter Sixty-Nine.

Louis opened his eyes, slowly and with difficulty, to find Amber and Lauren staring down at him. He blinks as he realises this is the third time he's been knocked unconscious tonight, which really can't be good for his brain long term. But then he realises that he can remember that it's the third time and, given that he expected to remember nothing, that's a very good sign.
"Fuck." He says to himself, and Amber snorts with laughter.
"Louis, are you…?" Lauren asks as she stares down at him with wide eyes.
"I'm still me. But, ow." He confirms. His head feels like it's been through a washing machine.
"And you remember who we are?" Amber asks. He nods. "That's good. How many fingers am I holding up?"
"You're not holding any up, Why're you checking for a concussion? I'm not concussed."
"I'm not, I was making sure you still knew what fingers were."
"I know what fingers are." He says, sitting up a little too quickly and getting a head rush. Lauren lurches forward in concern. "I'm okay." He says to placate her. "I remember everything. Or, I think I do. I remember what Chris tried to do and I remember that we need to save Danny."
"That's the next part of the plan." Lauren says, reassuringly.
"No, the next part is leaving before we're all hooked up to these machines." Amber adds.
"Well, yes, wonderful idea." Lauren says, getting up and helping Louis do the same.
"No." He says, simply.
"No?" They ask in unison.
"I've got an idea. It's a crazy one. But can you two just go with me?" He asks, because it's going to require a massive amount of trust. The

machine, and the flashes of what he saw, gave him a terrible idea. They look at each other and consider it.

"I think it's a little late to start rejecting crazy ideas." Lauren tells him, and that's all he needs. Without another word he rushes to the door, still a little unsteady on his feet but letting his determination carry him. He steps over the defeated Cleaners, not having to even ask what happened to them because he's certain it's Amber's handiwork. Amber and Lauren follow, albeit hesitantly and he sprints down the corridor of Home Base. He's absolutely exhausted and is still soaked with sweat. He catches sight of himself on a reflective surface and it confirms that he looks utterly insane; his hair is sticking up at all kinds of weird angles, there's dried blood on his face and neck, and his eyes are a weird bloodshot red. If anyone sees him it'll instantly raise alarm bells, but he can't think about that. Chris' office isn't far from where he wants to be. Behind him the other two call out, following him but with no idea of where he's going. He doesn't want to explain. Not until he has what he wants. He reaches it, and throws himself at the door. He forces the door open, and bursts inside. Behind him Amber and Lauren scramble in too as they look around and try to place exactly where they are. There's a large marble table just in front of the window, and there's a large stone bookcase filled with ancient texts. Louis moves straight to a large grey stone cabinet against one of the walls and pulls at the door. It's locked. He tugs and tugs at it but it doesn't budge and he groans in frustration. Amber, without even knowing why he wants to be in there so badly, joins him. With her strength she's easily able to force it open and stares at the contents. It's filled with dozens of ancient peculiar objects; strange trophies and weapons of the past, but he ignores them. He snatches at a small case and grabs a handful of small vials that contain a luminous white liquid.

"Let's go." He says. Lauren is both suspicious and confused, but she nods and follows him out of the room. Amber hangs back for another moment, fascinated by the contents of the cabinet. Her eyes linger on a scimitar hanging in its sheath. She takes it and follows the other two. From a crack in the curtains that lead to his sleeping quarters, the Superior One watches them all leave.

The time had come to end this, Chris thought to himself as he pulled up alongside the van that contained Olivia's team. They were exactly where they'd agreed to be at exactly the time they were supposed to be there. He appreciated that. In the weeks since his promotion he had wasted far too much time and he'd not allowed himself the opportunity to shine. This was it. His chance. He was taking back control of this situation, apprehending this Used-to-Be before the situation got any more out of control, and then he was going to get his old team back in line. It was regrettable that he'd had to take such extreme action with Louis, but in the drive over here he'd been going over and over it in his head and he knew he'd been left with no alternative. Sure, Lauren and Amber wouldn't be happy with him, and he'd probably have to do a little managing to his superiors about why he'd taken that action so swiftly, but he'd work through that later. In truth, if he secured this particular target he didn't think they'd be too bothered about an Agent or two being lost or retrained along the way. Bigger picture, and all that.

"That's the last sighting, so they'll be somewhere around there…" He overhears Noel saying as he enters the van, which actually doubles as an impressive mobile War Room. Chris lets out a sigh of relief as he sees a spot highlighted on a map. He was right to place his faith in this team.

"Perfect timing, boss." Olivia says as she sees him enter. "Noel's isolated a location and, look there…" She says, pointing to a theatre in the centre of it. "Didn't we get a couple of 999 calls from there a few minutes ago?" She asks.

"Actually, yeah." Noel counters, tapping a few more keys and accessing the human police systems. "And I don't see that any officers have been dispatched. It's completely dropped off their radar."

"Maybe because they're already there?" She says.

"Definitely worth checking out. Excellent work." Chris says, beaming. This is going to be easier than he thought.

"Should I give Lauren a call, get her and her team in on this too?" Olivia asks, and Chris shakes his head very quickly.

"No." He says simply. He'd briefed this team that Danny had been captured, and that he was taken by Used-to-Bes who had infiltrated the Human police; but he wasn't prepared to share all of the details with them. He wanted to tread carefully until he knew what to do with his old team.

"Are you sure, we could probably use the back-up, and I'm sure they'd love to…" Noel says, eagerly.

"I said no." Chris replies, cutting him off in a manner that was perhaps a little too harsh. But he's tired, and he doesn't have the patience for any more insubordination.

"The six of us will be plenty. We're well armed. We can have this wrapped

up within the hour. That's the plan." Picking up on Chris' obvious anger Noel and Olivia both shoot him an apologetic look and he gives them a nod to let them know it's okay. "Let's go." He says, before any further discussion can arise.
"Josh." Olivia says, calling to the driver. "You heard the man, let's go."

Hazel still hasn't returned from her 'costume change,' and that's given Danny enough time to get his big clever brain whirring. He's counted his opponents, as they've been wandering through the aisles and keeping an eye on the humans. He's spent time looking over the cast and crew and fully assessing the situation, and now he's got a really stupid idea. He zeroes in on PC Nadin, who's hovering around the front row.
"I recognise you." He tells him, and as planned Nadin turns and sneers at him.
"Yeah, you would." He says.
"Where from?" Danny asks, just trying to draw him in. He doesn't care where he recognises him from.
"All the crime scenes your lot turn up at, always thinking you're better than everyone." He says, taking a step up towards the stage.
"Well, generally I am better than everyone else, so that's probably right." He tells him, being as dismissive as possible. PC Nadin climbs up onto the stage and starts to get in close.
"Yeah? It doesn't look like it, from where I'm standing." He growls, in what should be threatening. Danny smirks and tilts his head.
"Well, I'll get out of these chains eventually. You'll always be stupid."
"Ha, you're the one who had an entire police force full of us right under your nose and didn't see it. Some demon hunter you are."
"What can I say, you never really seemed like much of a threat. Even now, I'm chained up, and I'm still more intimidated by…well…the old lady in the front row." He says, nodding towards the least threatening human he could see. PC Nadin punches him in the gut and Danny takes it with a grunt. He was expecting it and had tensed for it.
"How threatening am I now, you smart mouthed little shit?" The Used-to-Be asks him. Danny smirks to himself, and responds. He quickly pulls himself up on the chains and wraps his legs around Nadin's head, and uses the lift to unhook his wrists and free himself. Sitting on Nadin's shoulders, he twists, throwing him to the floor. He fumbles around in his pocket, his wrists still bound, and grabs at his phone. Using his powers he communicates

with the phone, and it takes only a split second to get it to send a message. It's lucky, too, because that's all he gets. Hazel snatches it from his hand and kicks him hard in the leg. With a crack his tibia shatters and he lets out a cry of agony and collapses to the ground.
"Clever Dan; but that's not the plan." She says in an annoying sing-song type voice as she looks down at him.
"Don't care." He spits through pain and gritted teeth. She shakes her head and reaches down to grab him. He tries to fight her off but with a broken leg and his wrists chained together he's not able to put up much of a fight. She hoists him back up onto the hook.
"Some people just don't appreciate good storytelling. You should care. It's all about you, and the people you care about being brutally murdered before your eyes. And that little stunt doesn't even matter. I want them here. I've left plenty of clues to lead them here. So if you were telling them where you are, you wasted your time."
"I told him not to come." He grunts, because it's true. It's the only way to stop this descending into chaos. For those idiots to stay away.
"And you think that'll work?" She laughs, looking like she is at least a little surprised. "That's brilliant. It won't change anything. They'll still all rush in here. It's always the way. It's your little hero complex. And he'll definitely come. Love makes you dumb. Look at me, I might've organised my own suicide because you took away the only person I love, and all over something that isn't even really our war." She says, clearly finding the ridiculousness of it all hilarious. Danny doesn't share her humour. PC Nelson (who was at the cemetery in part two, by the way. Looks like Louis didn't need that story about grave robbing planted) gets up on the stage and approaches.
"I think they're here. A van just pulled up outside." He tells her, looking pleased with himself.
"Excellent. Have you…heard from dear Timothy?" She asks, showing a little genuine concern.
"Yeah. He's fine. Hidden himself away like you planned."
"Good." She says, shooting a glance back over to Danny and giving him an explanation. "Got to have plans for the sequel, just in case things don't go my way. Oh, and Dan?" She says, and pulls a small gun from a holster on her hip. "Speaking of, here's another part of the plan." She says; and the sound rings out through the silent theatre as she shoots.

Chapter Seventy.

They're ready, and so it's time to end this. Chris, Olivia, Noel, and the others, Brian, Josh and Phil, are standing in the car park of the Royal Theatre. There is very little sound coming from inside, but there are also a couple of police cars parked adjacent to their mobile command centre which suggest their hunch may have been right and that Hazel's police officers are already inside. They're all prepared, armed with guns and wearing stab vests, and they stand silently awaiting his instruction.
"I'm authorising lethal force." He tells them, and though that may have been obvious from the weapons they'd been assigned, he still wanted to say it. "There are several UTBs, multiple human hostages and one Custodian. Neutralising the UTBs is the priority, but let's try to keep human casualties to a minimum. We need to get in and get this situation under control quickly. Are you all ready?" He asks. They all nod and murmur in agreement. It's so nice to not have anyone argue with him. "Olivia, do we have Cleaners?"
"Standing by, sir. They'll wait for word from us."
"Excellent. Then let's go." He says, and they start to make their way towards the building. With their numbers and the weaponry they've brought, he doesn't expect this to take long. A gunshot rings out as they advance on the building; and now, at least, he's certain it's the right place.

Their getaway was surprisingly, and worryingly, simple. Even with Louis looking like something that had been brought back from the dead, with his pale, sweat-soaked and blood stained skin and bags under his eyes that were so big he could've carried the other two in them. Even with their stolen contraband and their obvious desperation to be out of there as quickly as possible. Even with the fact that they seemed to pass everyone in the corridors and have to mutter friendly greetings to them while none of them could hide the fear on their faces. Even then, they were not challenged or even looked at with any suspicion.
They made their way out of the huge camouflaged gates that hid the Home Base from the view of wandering humans, back to the cold autumn night that felt very good against Louis' clammy skin, and practically hurled themselves into Wade's waiting car. He sped away with the tyres making a screeching sound that suggested even the vehicle was eager to be away. But even then, there was no sign of anyone pursuing them, and that made

them all uneasy. Perhaps it spoke to the trust of the Custodians and all the Agents. Perhaps the idea that any of them would do anything like this, insubordination and theft, was so unexpected that no one had thought there was anything out of the ordinary. The idea of breaking that trust made them all feel bad. But, not doing it would've been so much worse.
"I think we're okay." Lauren says, taking one last look at the deserted country road behind them.
"For now…" Amber mutters.
"Well I will take for now." Lauren replies. She's in the passenger seat in the front of the car, and turns back to face Matthew as he focuses on the road. "I think you can pull over for a moment." She tells him. He does, and brings the speeding car to a gentle stop in a layby. They all breathe a little sigh of relief as they realise that part of their plan is done. They hadn't even been sure they'd get this far. They've escaped one danger and now need to figure out how to throw themselves into another. "Louis, are you definitely alright?" She asks, turning around again and staring at him with a mixture of concern and caution.
"Yes." He answers, putting as much decisiveness into his tone as he can. Of course he's not alright, but they all have more important things to worry about. "Thank you, all of you. I…can't tell you how much I appreciate you getting me out of there." He says, leaving the 'before it was too late' part unsaid. But they all know.
"Well, we've got to look out for each other. Especially now." Lauren says, with sadness creeping into her voice. The magnitude of what they're faced with is clearly hitting her. Even if they survive the night, there might be no going back after this.
"Yeah. And I'm only just starting to warm to you. It would've been a shame for you to forget who you are now." Amber says, with a smile that Louis returns.
"I never thought I'd hear that from you. I'm glad I didn't forget you before you admitted you like me." He retorts, lightening the mood a little before refocusing them on the next part of the plan. "We need to find Danny now."
"Are you sure you're okay to…" Lauren begins to ask but, even though he hates to, he cuts her off.
"Yes." He says, forcing steel into his voice. "And I've got a plan. We just need to find them. Do we have any clue where they are?" They all think about it, and there's a desperate silence as they do. Wade looks a little lost and out of place. "This is the part where an annoying know-it-all would be

really useful." Louis adds, so acutely aware of how much he's missing Danny being part of this. He still doesn't know how he feels about him. He's not even had time to process that kiss and what it could mean. But he knows he never will if they don't act fast. Rescue Danny now, figure everything else out later. It's not a great plan, but it'll do.

"Well, I'm definitely not a know-it-all, especially about all this stuff…but the detective in me says we start by reviewing what leads we do have? Who is this Hazel we're looking for?" Wade asks.

"Oh!" Lauren blurts excitedly. "Yes, that reminds me. Noel found her, we think." She grabs a tablet from the glove compartment of the car, and quickly logs into her email. She pulls up an old black and white photo headshot of Hazel and shows it to the others. "It was the 'actress' clue in the journals. Hazel Hardcastle. An aspiring actress who disappeared in 1942."

"That's her." Louis confirms; the more he thought about it, it definitely makes sense that she was an actress. Everything about it made sense, especially thinking about the way she'd talked about being cast as a villain. It made her make a little more sense, too. "She kept talking like she was playing a role. Like she was acting."

"Hmm. All the worlds a stage, or whatever it was Shakespeare said." Wade adds, thoughtfully.

"Who's that?" Amber asks.

"Shakespeare. A famous Human writer. But yeah, it sounds like that's how she sees it." Louis explains.

"Right but how does that help us?" She asks, in that same dismissive tone he knows Danny would've been using weeks ago. It makes him smile, which he also knows is stupid.

"She said I'd cast myself as the hero. I think she wants some big, movie style showdown."

"That makes me a little uncomfortable." Lauren says.

"Because it sounds like she'll be ready for us? Like it's a trap?" Louis asks, and both she and Amber nod. "Yes." He confirms. "But that also means she wants us to find her. So there's got to be a way."

"This is really dumb. I don't like that we're sitting here talking about one of these creatures like this. They shouldn't have plans and traps. They should just be like angry dogs. We should be the ones…I just don't like it." Amber growls, unable to properly articulate her thoughts. But she knows there's truth to it, too. For all her protesting in the past, she's seen it for herself.

She saw it with Brick. He was more than just an angry animal. They've all had to alter their world view in the last few weeks.

"I agree, Amber. It's uncomfortable, we've lost all control over this. It's obvious we're not just dealing with some thoughtless creature any more. She's clearly set the stage for this." Lauren adds, shaking her head.

"Set the stage…It'll be somewhere she can attract attention!" Louis says, having an epiphany and immediately sharing it.

"Wait." Wade says, and reaches into his pocket. He pulls out two theatre tickets and shows them to the group. They read "King Balor's Last Stand," and have the name of the Royale Theatre on them. "Tim gave me these." He explains. "Seemed insistent I go. I hate the theatre. But when he was about to try to off me he said that if I'd gone the problem would've sorted itself out. What if that's where she is? What if that's what he meant?"

"That could be it." Louis says, with a nod. It's the best idea they've got."I didn't think it'd be an actual stage, but yeah, let's go." He says. If they arrive and it's not the right place, well, they can think of something else then. Again, Danny would be really useful here. He's sure he could hack Chris' phone or something else stupidly clever.

"I can get us there in about forty minutes?" Wade adds, looking at the address and starting the car and pulling out before waiting for any more approval from the group. No one argues. And now that they think they know where she is, it's time to discuss the next part of the plan. The thing that none of them want to face.

"Louis…what's your plan when we get there? What did you take from the base?" Lauren asks him, with a stern look. He suspects she already knows the answer, she just doesn't want to know it. He avoids her eyes and pulls out one of the vials he grabbed.

"This is…" He begins, searching for a way to not make it sound insane and desperate. "I saw it last time I was there and…that machine, it made me remember things. I can't describe it, but it gave me an idea. This is what gives us our powers."

"But we've already got powers?" Amber asks.

"And I ain't taking that stuff." Wade adds.

"No! I'm not asking you to. I'm going to take it. I think they give us a small dose. Do you remember the story of the Warrior who asked for more power? With the Mad King? We were told it on the day we got this. It was one of our kind who was given more. So it's possible. He used it to win a war and…look I don't think it's a good idea, at all." He explains, because

it's not. There's no way to make it sound like it's a good idea. But, he doesn't have any others. "Hazel is really powerful. I don't think we can stop her. Especially on her terms. You've seen a taste of what she can do."
There's silence again, and then it's Lauren that speaks, and her voice is so filled with concern that it almost makes Louis physically ache.
"That story…the Warrior went mad and ended up destroying himself." She says.
"I'm hoping for a different outcome, I'll be honest." He says, not reassuring anyone. "If we don't go, Danny dies. Chris and everyone he's taking with him will die too. If we do go, right now, we'll die. She's powerful and she's not alone. We are. There's just the four of us. I don't really think going back to Home Base to try to muster any reinforcements is a good idea after…well after…"
"Assaulting a couple of Cleaners, breaking you out of there, and taking some magic potions that'll give you more power but drive you mad?" Amber asks, laying it out much blunter than he could.
"I am so grateful." He reiterates. "But that means we can't go back there, and even if we could it'd take too long to get a team together. So we have to go and find Danny, and it has to be with just the four of us. Which is exactly what she's expecting. She's probably even expecting you to come, Matthew." He says, and Wade nods.
"Aye. Tim knows me well enough to know I won't be going anywhere except straight for where the action is." He agrees.
"So the one bit of this we can control, the one bit we can change, the one tiny part that she can't have accounted for, is this. It's just how much fire power we bring. I don't know if it'll work. I don't know if I'll be able to control it. I don't know if it'll just make my head explode. But I don't see anything else we can try." He says, and his desperation is apparent to them all. He can't hide it. This is a last crazy effort and it's the only bit that stands a chance of working.
"I'm on board with more fire power." Amber says after way too long of a pause; and he's so grateful for her.
"Okay." Lauren agrees. "But I'm taking it." She adds, and he shakes his head.
"No. It has to be me. You can literally save our lives, we can't afford to lose you. And Amber, you're the strongest, and the best fighter, and if any of us stand even half a chance against her it's you.

"I agree," Amber says, cracking her knuckles symbolically. So, that just leaves me. I'm the weak link. I'm the expendable one..." He says, and it hurts to say it outloud because it's how he's felt all the way along.
"Louis! No. No you're not."
"We didn't risk out necks for you just to kill yourself."
"Expendable my arse. I wouldn't even be here if it weren't for you."
They all protest at once, and it means so much to him to hear. But in this particular case his logic is sound. It has to be him. He's about to tell them that when his phone vibrates. It's from Danny.
"Theatres a trap, don't come. Bye." His voice cracks a little bit as he reads it outloud. Of course that is how Danny would say goodbye to him. "We're going to the right place, and it's definitely a trap. So, I need to do this." He says, looking around at them all. That confidence, that steely resolve that he had to fake, is back. But now it's true. He is determined because this is the only way he can see to stop Hazel.
"It's our best option. I trust you." Amber says, at last. .
"Okay." Lauren agrees. From the front seat Matthew silently nods. And so, having got all their agreement he pops open the first vial before anyone can change their mind and swallows it whole. He moves to the second and swigs that back too. He groans as it starts to work. He doubles over in pain as it feels like something is about to burst out of him; like there's some horrific explosion going on inside him.
"Louis, stop!" Lauren whimpers. But he doesn't. He quickly swallows a third. He gasps and whimpers as the pain spreads and it feels like he's on fire.
"Louis!" Amber growls in protest from next to him, grabbing at the vials. He tries to drink a fourth but she snatches it away before he can and it falls to the floor. It begins to bubble and fizz and melt into the fabric of the car. Louis tries to protest but his blue eyes gloss over into a pure white colour and he babbles because he can't form a full word. He collapses, gurgling in pain and unable to hold himself up.

The foyer of the theatre is deserted, so they're able to move swiftly through it. They've already looked at the plans for the building, and decided it was best to go in through the front door. Chris decided to go in quick and heavy, and try to take her down before she knows what's hit her. She will be expecting them, they knew that; but hopefully she'll underestimate their numbers, their skill, and their fire power. They move towards a set of double doors into the performance area; they pause and the others look to Chris for guidance. He presses his ear against the door and listens, but there's no sound coming from inside. He signals that they'll enter on the count of three, and begins to count down with his fingers. He feels excited. He feels confident. He's certain that this is his chance to show why he was put in charge.

On his mark they tear through the doors and into a large incredibly dark room. They can see shapes of people in the darkness and Chris and Noel cautiously fumble for torches and quickly illuminate the faces of the captured audience on all sides of them. They scan around the room quickly, with the others bringing out torches too, and looking for any sign of a Used-to-Be; anyone who fits Hazel's description, or who's wearing a police uniform.

The doors behind them slam closed and are barricaded shut by two figures dressed as pirates.

"What the...?" Noel says, staring into the face of someone wearing an eyepatch. There's a loud click of someone's fingers and a single spotlight appears on the stage. Hazel stands centre stage, grinning and surveying the team. She's wearing all black, form fitting clothes; and stands with a black sequinned top hat perched on her head. They all point their weapons at her, ready to fire.

"Good evening, ladies and gentlemen, and everyone else. Welcome to the show!"

"Freeze!" Chris demands.

"You talkin' to me?" She replies, with a thick New York accent. "Wait. No. I should've gone with something else. Can we try that again?" She asks, breaking character. "Don't move." Chris barks at her.

"You're going to need a bigger boat..." She laughs at herself after that one. "No, that one's definitely wrong. I'm normally so good at this. There should be more of you though, shouldn't there? I think that's throwing me off." She explains, leaning casually against a cane in her hand. Chris maintains his focus on her, but the others start to look worried as they hear movement and shuffling in the shadow all around them. Chris fires. The spotlight goes off and the stage is back in darkness.

"Everyone, form a circle, back-to-back. Don't let her sneak up behind us." Chris says, gathering the rest of the team in close as there's the sound of more movement around them. Their torch light illuminates more pirates and men clad in dark clothes. The spotlight lights back up, this time on the

six of them and all of their torches suddenly die. Hazel's voice echoes from above.
"I count six. The script calls for nine…" She says.
"What are you talking about? Show yourself?!" Chris growls back, brushing elbows with Noel and Olivia in their circle.
"No matter, we'll make do…" She sighs. Chris is growing increasingly frustrated and losing any sense of cool. "Stop talking and show yourself." He shouts into the darkness. The team are all standing back-to-back trying to see what's happening. They can't hear anything except their own heavy breathing and a light shuffling around them as shapes move in the dark. They can't tell if it's the human audience or something else. The spotlight goes off once more, and when it comes back on Hazel is standing in the centre of their circle, hovering menacingly behind Chris. She leans forward and he feels it; the chill down his spine.
"I see dead people." She whispers in his ear. Chris reacts; spinning to face her but by the time he turns she's gone and the lights are killed again.
"Stop playing games!" Chris roars desperately; and he gets his wish. All the lights are raised and the team get a full view of what they're facing. They're surrounded by six police officers in full riot gear. PCs Nadin, Nelson, Morris and Henderson, as well as Sergeant Lister and Desk Sergeant Appleby. They're already too close and the team doesn't get the chance to react before they're leaping forward, truncheons in hand, to attack. They're overwhelmed quickly as they're beaten to the ground with no chance to launch a defence; and now back on stage Hazel surveys it cackling with glee. She walks back to where Danny is, still chained, still alive and still vaguely conscious. He's bleeding heavily from the bullet wound to his non-broken leg and is still hanging from the stage hook on the ceiling. She stands next to him and looks down at the chaos.
Olivia is the first to manage a counter; using her telekinetic abilities to throw the Used-to-Bes back. It takes a lot of her energy, but it gets them a small reprieve, and they all scramble back to their feet. Chris scoops up his gun, gets his barings, and begins to march towards the stage, leaving the others to fend for themselves. His gaze is locked on Hazel because he's determined he'll be the one to bring her down. He's sent flying forward as Nelson barges into him, and knocks him, sternum first, into the edge of the stage with an audible crack.
Meanwhile Noel has thrown himself at Lister. They scuffle, Lister initially gets the better of him but Noel manages to fight him off. He manages to rip

his helmet off and then knocks him backwards, putting some distance between them. He finds enough distance to be able to fire several bullets into Lister's head, killing him, and briefly tipping the numbers.

"Ouch. One point to the good guys." Hazel announces, making a show of the commentary for Danny, who is pale and weak and struggling to keep his head up.

As Noel catches his breath from the fight, he glances around to his teammates. He rushes forward to help Josh who's been tangling with Nadin. Nadin has him pinned to the ground and is choking him. Noel tries to break it up, and manages to wrestle Nadin off him. The Used-to-Be stumbles backwards to where one of the pirates is standing guarding the entrance. He snatches the pirate's cutlass and charges forward, and before he can even react he's plunged it through Noel's chest. He cries out with a half gasp, and half gurgle, and then Nadin tosses his already limp body into Josh and they both collapse in a heap.

"I felt that one." Hazel says, licking her lips. "Really, I did. The pain. It's a little intoxicating. Can you feel it?" She asks Danny, lifting his head gently so that he can watch. Both sides are locked in combat but no one is really gaining much ground, though it's obvious that the Custodians are taking more of the damage. Their lightweight body armour doesn't offer the same protection that full riot gear does.

Some of the audience members, now terrified by the fray, see this as their opportunity to flee. They start to get up and rush towards any door that is unguarded. They're all locked, though, and the pirates snarl and stalk them, excited at the prospect to cause some pain.

Hazel is thoroughly enjoying herself and laughs as she takes in the chaos. Danny's head sags next to her, and his eyelids start to droop. She quickly digs her finger into his bullet wound. He whimpers and his eyes shoot open.

"I want you awake for this. I want you to feel every glorious second of it." She coos, gesturing at the fighting going on all around her. Then she pauses and contemplates. "Do you think he'll come?" She asks him, suddenly with a lot less exuberance in her voice. "Maybe he decided to run. That'd be an unexpected plot twist." She says, and pauses again, as if considering her options. "No. He'll come; and I'll murder him in front of you. Or you in front of him. I'm still open to that. It's an overused trope, I know, but…well these things are clichés for a reason aren't they?" She asks and stares at him. He scowls back at her, trying to save his energy. Her focus is taken back to the floor when Josh has his neck violently snapped by Nadin, and the crack even causes her to wince a little.

"It's not working!" Lauren says in frustration. The instant they pulled into the Royal Theatre's car park she leapt out of the passenger side door and into the back so that she could try to heal Louis. He's been in and out of consciousness, groaning with agony whenever he's lucid. But for the first time in years, since she first learned to control it, her power is having no effect. "I don't understand." She says, almost desperately. Amber puts a comforting hand on her shoulder and shakes her head. "I'm sure I just heard another gunshot." Wade says, leaning against the side of the car and watching the building.
"We need to get in there, now." Amber says, locking eyes with Lauren.
"But I can't…" She says, helpless looking down at Louis who whimpers as he swims back into consciousness and tries to sit up. "Louis you're burning up." She practically shouts at him.
"I can feel it all." He whimpers through gritted teeth. "I'm on fire."
"You can't do anything for him." Amber tells her, and it sounds cold. But it has to.
"But…" Lauren starts to argue.
"No." Louis splutters. "She's right." And he lets out an animal like screech and convulses. Lauren lurches forward to try to heal him again, but Amber gives her a gentle squeeze on the shoulder and she stops.
"This was the point, remember?" She tells her. "If this didn't work, then he needed us. We have to get in there so that you can help the injured and I can be the one who stops her." She says; and now it's her forcing herself to play a role. She has to be the level-headed one. Lauren nods quietly, and stands up.
"What about me?" Wade asks.
"Do you know how to use this?" Amber hands him a pistol and locks eyes with him.
"Yes."
"Good. Stay here. Be ready. Lauren, let's go." She says. Lauren tuts and shakes her head, and then finds the resolve to follow Amber around to the boot of the car where their weapons are located. Wade sits back down in the driver's seat, a little despondent. He looks back at Louis too. He reaches into his pocket where his police badge is and stares at it, thinking about what it means to him. He runs his fingers over the numbers, 329,

and shakes his head. Louis tries to sit up, but he still can't quite control his own body.

"...You have to..." He tries to say, and moans from the pain again. Wade understands. He nods, and gets back out of the car.

"No." He tells the other two, who are still rummaging through the boot.

"No, what?" Lauren asks.

"We're all in this together, right? I'm not just waiting outside like a dog you've left while you go buy a pack of fags. I'm coming with you." He holds up his hand as Lauren looks like she's about to argue with him. "I know I'm not fully to grips with what's going on; but we can just be real simple about it, there's something bad going on in there, and we need to stop it. I'm not as young as I used to be. I'm certainly not as fit as the pair of you, but even if I can help a little bit it's better than nout."

"Good." Amber says, even though Lauren still looks like she wants to argue. She wants to tell him no, to tell him to stay where it's safe. That's one of the most important rules. Protect humans. But they've broken so many rules tonight, they might as well throw another one out of the window too. "But if you die, that's on you." Amber concludes.

"Agreed." He nods. She tosses body armour to him and grabs the sword she stole.

Chapter Seventy-One.

The pirates gleefully hack at the humans who dare to try to escape, one having retrieved his sword from Noel's corpse only to brutally ram it into more screaming victims. And the moment that started, the moment her performers-turned-pirates had started killing it was like the terror kicked up a notch; and Hazel is revelling in it. Then, at one side of the room Olivia, Brian and Phil are working together to try to fend off Nadin, Morris, and Henderson. They're struggling, and they're unarmed. While at the other side Chris desperately fights against Appleby and Nelson, and he too is losing energy, already having to battle an intense pain in his chest from what is likely a fractured sternum. He lurches forward to try to grab Nelson, but he side steps. It's like they're toying with him. Nelson hits him hard in the face, knocking him back into Appleby who smacks him with a truncheon over the back of the head. They're both enjoying themselves. They've all been waiting for an opportunity like this for a long time, having to hide when all they wanted to do was fight.

The others are having a little more success, only because they're not outnumbered. Olivia digs deep and throws Nadin backwards to block an attack on Phil. She's determined to not lose any more of her team and digs deep to find a new level of protective ferocity. With a launch from Brian, she throws a kick into Morris, adding some telekinetic strength to it and sending him far enough away so that only Henderson remains. Olivia uses another burst of her power to toss one of the pirates across the room and away from one of the humans he's about to attack. Phil leaps up over Henderson as he charges at him like a bull, his power has manifested as the ability to levitate so it's very easy for him to get out of the way, and the Used-to-Be careens forward towards a group of humans who all leap out of the way as he crashes through their seats.
"This isn't working." She tells Brian, as Phil rejoins them.
"Yeah." He agrees; looking around for the next attack.
"Let's switch this up. You two attack, I'll take defence." She says, taking the brief gap to reassess the plan. They nod. Phil launches himself forward as Henderson recovers and ploughs into him, carrying him straight back to the ground. Olivia uses her power to pull another human out of harm's way, and then pulls one of their discarded guns over to Brian who catches it and starts firing.
Chris is really struggling now, unable to get back to his feet after the last shot to the back of his skull. They take turns kicking him.
Phil's skirmish with Henderson turns, as the Used-to-Be overpowers him and grabs a broken chair leg to beat him with.
Brian fires at Morris; but the Used-to-Be dodges with animal-like quickness and then growls and leaps through the air and it's only Olivia's intervention that protects her teammate as she plucks him out of the air and tosses him to the side. She's over exerting herself now; trying to protect the humans and her team and having to split her focus too many ways.
Brian tries to intervene to help Phil, but Morris is back on him as soon as he recovers, and Henderson continues beating down on him with the chair leg. Nadin marches back towards Olivia; and her eyes snap to him too, the memory of Noel impaled on a sword fresh in her mind. She drops the defensive strategy, and she attacks.
"Your side isn't doing so well..." Hazel tells Danny, on stage. "I wonder where that boyfriend of yours is?" She asks him.
"Not my...Not coming." He spits, weakly.
"Sure." She tells him sarcastically. "Shame. We could really do with..." She

stops, mid sentence, and dives to her left as Amber bursts onto the stage and fires at her. She rolls gracefully and pops back to her feet with a grin. "...new characters." She finishes. Lauren and Wade rush past Amber as her eyes remain locked on Hazel and the two women stare at each other, squaring up. They had entered through the stage door in an effort to take her by surprise, and it had worked.

"There's no wall to hide behind this time." Amber tells her, lowering the gun.

"Hide?" Hazel laughs. "That wall kept you alive. Let's see how you do without it." Amber puts the gun away and slowly pulls out her stolen sword. Hazel raises an eyebrow, a little impressed at the drama.

"Come on then?" She says. Meanwhile, Lauren rushes towards Danny.

"No." Hazel snaps, without taking her gaze from Amber she raises her hand and a wall of green flame rises out of the stage to surround him and prevent her getting to him. He's bleeding and he's weak, and he groans at the heat. Hazel reaches into her pocket and pulls out two plastic army men and tosses them on the floor. They grow and come to life, still plastic, but life sized and sentient. They move to protect Danny, taking aim at Lauren and Wade with their rifles. She pulls Wade down behind cover with her, off the stage and behind some scenery, before they can fire. "My hostage." Hazel clarifies and rolls again as Amber lunges to attack. She swings her sword viciously and cuts through the air where Hazel's neck was a second ago. She's going straight for the kill; and when she straightens up Hazel looks at her with something akin to admiration. "I like you." She says.

"Don't care." Amber retorts, readying herself for another attack. Hazel grabs a prop cutlass from the floor and raises it. It starts off plastic, clearly having been bought cheap to be part of the background, but by the time she's charged it with her power the steel blade clashes with Amber's own. Hazel, it turns out, is skilled with a sword, but Amber is too. She dodges and blocks, and they both take a thrill from the evenly matched fight. Wade shoots at the live-toy soldiers and the bullets chip chunks out of them, but it doesn't stop them, and they return fire. They're pinned down behind a flimsy piece of scenery and unable to get out to help Danny or anyone else. Down on the ground Nelson and Appleby continue to beat a collapsed Chris. He's no longer putting up much of a fight. Phil has become another casualty, dying at the hands of Henderson and the chair leg. Nadin and Olivia are clashing viciously, and Morris is slowly choking the air out of Brian.

Amber and Hazel continue to cross swords. There's a frenzy of metal clashing, and they both appear to be equally skilled, despite having trained in completely different environments. They go back and forth, until amazingly, Amber is able to score an advantage and Hazel starts to lose her footing. She stumbles backwards and is forced to climb up some unsteady looking background rope rigging to give herself some space. Amber hacks and just misses lopping off half of her leg as she climbs. Hazel leaps from the rigging, soaring over her head and trying to attack from behind; Amber dodges and strikes out with her free hand, landing a punch and sending her stumbling again. Hazel grins at her with a split lip and a look of excitement at actually having been struck; and she attacks with a burst of hard hits which Amber struggles to block. She slashes again, and again, and again, and now it's Amber on the back foot. On the fifth hit Hazel is able to dislodge her sword, and the weapon skids across the stage, and now that she's unarmed Hazel looks at her like she's prey and jabs forward. Amber dodges it, but it was a feint, and Hazel headbutts her and kicks her onto the floor. She hits the ground hard and Hazel raises the sword high above her head, ready to bring it down and stab her. Amber can't do anything as the blade plummets down and is a split second away from piercing her heart...

Kim finishes making herself a coffee, because it's the middle of the night and she needs it, and returns to her laptop. She's determined to finish transcribing the interview, if only so that she can hear it again and convince herself that it really happened. When she returns to her laptop it's open on an article that she found through Dick Johnson's wikipedia page. It's all about his gruesome murder in 1942 at the hands of a spurned, drunken, lover. She stares at the photo of him, feeling so much contempt for a man she's never met. Then, she switches back to her open document and presses play on the recording once again.

"It's always there, circling like a dark cloud and the second you're at your most vulnerable it strikes. And it hurts Kimberly."
Hazel lays perfectly still, face down in the mud, unable to move or even breath. She's on the cusp of death and there's nothing she can do about it, and what's more, she has accepted it. And then, when there is no air left in her body, and just as her heart stops beating, everything changes.
"I'll never forget it. It was like…something being stuffed down into my lungs

and expanding...it kept expanding..."
Her body starts to spasm violently, thrashing around in the mud, she flips over and arches her back, as if pulled upwards by some invisible force. She continues to throw her arms and legs around, with no control over her limbs and splashing dirty water everywhere.
"...until it felt like I was going to burst...and I couldn't breathe and I couldn't move and I couldn't stop it and all I wanted to do was die."
She stops moving suddenly, and lays perfectly still. And then she finds her voice again and screams into the night as she feels a pain unlike anything she has ever experienced.
"And then it was like my entire body was burning...like instead of blood pumping through my veins it was fire. Scolding and melting away who I was."
The wet mud around her starts to boil and she lays in it, still screaming into the night.

Back in Dick Johnson's office, he and Sol sit back at the desk with their shirts a mess and their ties undone, they look exhausted and Sol looks haunted as the reality of what they've done sets in.
"So, what do we do now?" He asks.
"I don't know." Dick replies with a sigh that sounds like a growl. "We need a big name to get this thing off the ground. She was our last option, and she's only a name because of her old hag of a mother."
"I didn't mean...forget it. Maybe we just can this picture? The script is horse-shit anyway."
"Ah, with the right cast that wouldn't matter." Dick says, pulling out a whiskey bottle and topping both their glasses up. "Damn it, maybe you're right." He admits, out of options. There's a loud knock at the door and they look at each other suspiciously. Their eyes scan the room, looking for anything incriminating, and Dick grabs a bottle of cleaning product and stuffs it in his desk drawer. "Come in." He says, cautiously. The door flies open and a bedraggled looking Harriet stumbles in. She is clearly drunk. "Where's my daughter?" She slurs, and they shoot each other a suspicious glance. "Hatty...what're you doing here?" Dick asks.
"I'm looking for that ungrateful spawn of mine. I was expecting her home hours ago." She says, and they both relax a little, realising she doesn't know anything.
"Oh...erm..." He gets up, and tries to divert her back towards the door,

knowing the quicker they can get rid of her the better. "She never turned up. We're gonna have to find someone else for the part, sadly..." Harriet brushes past him and sits down in the chair next to Sol.
"Well, what's the part? I'll do it! I mean...I'm sure I can fit it in, for you Dicky." She asks, clawing desperately at the script that's still on the desk.
"I'm not sure it's for you...we're looking for someone who's a little younger...a little more desirable. I'm sorry Hats, we'll keep you in mind for the next one..." She grabs his glass from the desk and tasks a swig, glaring up at him.
"Bullshit. You all think I'm washed up." She snaps.
"Now listen here, that kinda language is unbecoming of a lady Harriet. That's why you can't get work in this town no more. That foul mouth and your love of the sauce." He snaps, towering over her in the chair. She is unmoved and begins to leaf through the script.
"Well, I don't see anyone else queuing up to work with you Dicky," She slurs. He inhales, ready to reply, but there's a loud rumble of thunder and the lights flicker. He shakes his head in disgust.
"Now you really oughta be going. It's late. Your damn daughter ain't here, and I'm glad. She was more difficult than you." He says, and grabs her arm to pull her up. She takes another swig of whisky, draining the glass. Sol looks nervous and shakes his head, shrinking back in his chair.
"Fine, I'll go. This whiskey tastes like piss anyway." She says, tossing the empty glass aside. There's a crash; but it's not from her. Lightning strikes the building and all of the windows shatter, throwing glass everywhere. The lights black out and Harriet shrieks in shock. A second later the door to the office is blown open; and the haunting, bedraggled silhouette of a woman steps through it. Mist accompanies her and there's a chill in the air all of a sudden; the kind of entrance that special effects would struggle to replicate. The lights flicker back on and show the muddy, wet, blood stained figure of Hazel standing before them. She stands staring at the three of them through soaking wet hair. Dick doesn't miss a trick, he tosses Harriet aside and bolts around to his desk drawer. He pulls out a revolver and points it at her.
"Stay back!" He orders, his voice steady.
"What in the hell happened to you?" Harriet croaks at her, stumbling unsteadily back to her feet. Hazel ignores her mother and strides forward towards Dick. He panics and fires a shot into her chest. Harriet screams again as the impact of the shot knocks Hazel backwards and she crumples

to the floor. She rushes forward to her daughter, collapsing, weeping, at her side. Dick moves forward, stepping back out from behind the desk, to inspect her too, as she lays unmoving and bleeding on his carpet once again. Sol panics and grabs the phone on the desk. He dials the police. Dick rounds on him, revolver still in hand. "What're you doing?" He roars.
"Hello? Police. We're being attacked by a ghost!" Sol says, his breathing shallow and panicky.
"Hang it up Sol!" Dick demands, raising the gun to his friend.
"I…" He stutters, scared and unsure what to do. He considers it, but then does what he's told. He hangs the phone up but then gasps sharpley as he looks back to Dick and sees Hazel rising back to her feet. The colour drains from his face and he tries to stutter a warning. Dick, somehow getting the message, spins and tries to fire again but Hazel snatches at the barrel of the gun and knocks it away. He pulls it back and fires at her again and it goes off but nothing comes out.
"You're firing blanks." She hisses; knowing that she's changed the gun to nothing more than a prop. She backhands him in a way that mirrors what he did to her earlier, but she is far stronger and he soars over his desk.
"Hazel, what are you doing?" Harriet gasps, clambering unsteadily back to her feet and staring at the monstrous sight of her daughter. She backhands her too; sending her mother flying across the room and into the shelving unit that contains a number of awards and statues. It tips over, and they all come tumbling down. All of Dicks accomplishments scattered all over the floor. The bronze tiger that she was bludgeoned with earlier falls at her feet. She smirks, fully embracing all the anger she feels and pouring it into the tiger. The small statue grows and grows, and changes from bronze to flesh. It roars as it comes to life. Dick scrambles to his feet, seeing the animal, panics.
"That bitch has a tiger!" He screams, and dashes out of the room. Hazel's eyes follow him as he makes a break for it. The tiger however, only has eyes for Sol. It growls and leaps; tackling him to the ground and biting down on his neck. Hazel watches it with a smirk, and then paces out of the room and after Dick.

"It just all made sense. In that moment, all of the hatred I'd built up for that man through the years, all the fear he'd made me feel, oh it made me so strong and I knew exactly what I was doing. It came so naturally. I wish you could feel power like that, Kimberly, I really do. It's intoxicating."

Hazel stalks through the corridor of the studio, away from Dick's office. She can tell which way he's gone. It's like she's able to follow that stomach churning smell of sweat, whisky, and stale cigar smoke. Her eyes are drawn to the posters that adorn the corridor. Posters of the studio's biggest hits. She stares at them, drinking them all in as she passes. She stops at one of them, a beautiful, well made up femme fatale, and she's drawn in. She stares at it, suddenly aware of how very different she looks from the woman on that poster. Her clothes are dripping with filth and her skin is no better. She feels dirty in so many ways and that makes her blood boil even more. But she realises she doesn't have to look dirty. She breathes in and runs her hands over her face; initially just smearing the filth even more. But, when she takes her hands away she's transformed. Her mug has gone from being bloody and muddy to a full face of make-up, a bright red lip and smokey eye, identical to that of the femme fatale. The same happens as she runs her hands through her hair; it becomes clean, and dry, and hangs flawlessly in the way she's never been able to achieve herself. Next come the clothes. Gone is her stained cardigan, soiled and torn blouse, and ruined sensible skirt. They're replaced by a blood red evening gown and jet black gloves to match. She lets out a small moan and soaks in it. She feels so much better already. It's like this is who she's always been.

The next poster she stops at depicts the Grim Reaper, hovering over a woman as she lies asleep. It seems fitting. Hazel smashes the glass of the frame and tears off a part of the poster. She waves it in the air and the scythe that's pictured grows to life. It gleams menacingly in the dim hallway lighting. She continues her slow and methodical hunt along the corridor; knowing that he chose to ascend the stairs rather than run down and towards the exit in the hope it would throw her off. She slowly follows his path, dragging the blade along the wall and finding the sinister scraping very pleasing. The first door at the top of the stairs is locked. She knew it would be. He's not that dumb. But it doesn't stop her, she throws her weight at it and it pops open very easily as the frame splinters. She's so very strong now. She paces inside. It's another office.

"I know you're here." She coos, popping a hip and resting against the scythe. "Come out, Uncle Dick." He tries to stifle a whimper, but she hears it, and knowing he's been made he climbs unsteadily to his feet from behind one of the cabinets. He holds his hands up in surrender as he steps out, with a pathetic look on his face.

"Look, Hazel, doll, I'm sorry." He stutters. She tilts her head, struggling desperately to remember why she was ever afraid of this man. This pathetic, simple, little man. "Let's just forget this whole thing. I'll make it up to you. Any movie you want. I've got lots of friends who owe me lots of favours. I can get you whatever part you want...I'm sorry okay." He begs, and she lets him finish his snivelling apology.

"That's not a proper apology." She tells him and without another moment of hesitation she drops the blade down and swings the scythe upwards hitting him straight between his legs.

A few minutes later Harriet stumbles into the office, drunk and concussed. The tiger, once it had eaten a chunk of Sol, had returned to its normal form because Hazel had never intended it to be her end as well. She's brandishing the revolver and stops dead as she sees her daughter standing over Dick's bisected body. The scythe is now just a piece of ripped paper on the floor next to his hand. She cocks the revolver.

"What the hell have you done you stupid girl?" She snarls. Hazel turns to face her, but doesn't answer. "What the hell are you?" She demands, but she still gets no answer. Harriet keeps the gun aimed at Hazel. "Say something!"

Outside, two black cars screech up in the parking lot of the studio and several gun toting Custodians rush out. But before they can enter there's a scream from above them and Harriet's body crashes down in front of them with a splat.

They rush inside, and up the stairs to the room she fell from, and they find the two halves of Dick's body, but no one else.

Chapter Seventy-Two.

I've struggled with the decisions I made that night so much over the years. I've replayed it again and again, trying to think about how I could've handled it better, how I could've got there quicker, or just done something differently. Turbo charging myself with way more power than I could handle wasn't the best plan I'd ever had, especially because it took me out of commission for valuable time. But even after all this time I'm not sure there was a way to get a better outcome at that time. Maybe, if it had been someone else in my situation, they'd have found a way. I've wondered about what would've happened if it was me she'd have taken me instead of Danny. What would he have done? Not something quite as stupid, I'm sure. Would he have even turned up? Was that, ultimately, the biggest mistake I made. I couldn't have run. Not even just for him, but for everyone who's life was in danger, and, if I'm honest, for me. I would never have been able to live with myself if I'd not gone. I also absolutely would've died if I'd gone as I was, just plain old Louis who was nothing special. So even now it feels like I didn't have a choice. .

And so, there we were. Chris was being beaten down, with no hope of mounting a comeback. Noel, Josh, and Phil were all dead. Danny was bleeding out, guarded by living toy soldiers and surrounded by fire. Brian was being choked by Morris, and he flailed and fought and tried to use his powers, but it was no use. Olivia wasn't in a position to help either, she was locked in a vicious fight with Nadin and she was waning. The pirates were running free, attacking screaming humans as they ran and tried desperately to get out. Lauren was lost, surrounded by all of this and pinned down. She wasn't even sure who she'd help first if she could. Wade was uselessly firing at plastic soldiers brought to life by magic that he didn't understand, and he would run out bullets before those things would stop. Amber was about to be stabbed through the heart. There was chaos and death, and Hazel's plan was working beautifully. If nothing changed, then within another five minutes they would all be dead.

…but something did change. The barricaded doors explode and the room freezes as everyone is taken by surprise. The smoke clears and they all stare.
"Now that's how to make an entrance." Hazel says with excitement, as she sees Louis standing there at last. He's still not me. Not yet. But he's a hell of a lot closer now that the power has taken hold.
The three children-turned-pirates rush at him in a panic and somehow, behind the facade, he can see what they really are and he can hear their cries for help underneath. He holds up his hands and they halt and squirm as he tears the Demonic energy from them. It's painful, but it's necessary, and they collapse to the ground as children again. He takes the energy that she poured into them and changes it; he smashes it together in his hands and it creates a shockwave that rips through the theatre and collides with Nadin and Morris and fires them through the air, saving Brian's life in

the process. On stage Hazel is transfixed. She drops the cutlass and walks away from Amber, watching him with an arched eyebrow.

Henderson is the next to attack and he charges forward, still wielding the bloodied chair leg that's already caved one skull in. He swings it, intending for Louis to be his next victim, but it doesn't go to plan as the wood shatters suddenly in his hand and his momentum carries him straight forward into an outstretched fist. Then, with a wave of his hand in a way that mirrors Olivia, Louis sends Henderson flying over the heads of cowering Humans and crashing into a wall. With him out of the way, he continues his single-minded advance towards the stage, and Hazel.

Amber picks up the discarded cutlass and tosses it as hard as she can at Hazel, hoping to hit her in the back. Instead, without turning she nonchalantly waves her hand and turns it back to a prop. It bounces off her, having returned to plastic. Amber tries to attack her again, Hazel swots her out of the way and throws her down from the stage. She's not interested in her any more.

As Amber lands she rolls back to her feet and is immediately there in front of Appleby and Nelson who are still beating Chris. With the strength of the attack she'd aimed at Hazel, and the frustration at not landing it, she immediately lashes out and launches herself at the two of them.

Louis continues to stride towards the stage. The tide has shifted. With no barricade, and no pirates to stop them, the humans begin to flee through the open door. Some of them even stop to scoop up the former pirates, now back to children, and carry them out. Olivia and Brian have regrouped and are using their combined force against Nadin and Morris. She uses her telekinetic abilities to throw objects at them to keep them back and he summons explosive discs of plasma that he couldn't use before when the room was so crowded. They both cover the humans as they make their escape; keeping the Used-to-Bes away.

Hazel reaches out with her power to stop Louis' advance.

"He stops." She whispers, giving him his stage directions. He briefly stops, groaning in pain as he fights every muscle in his body, and then he continues, pushing through her hold.

"No, he doesn't." He snarls. He moves forward. Much slower, as if he's wading through water. But he continues nonetheless, and that intrigues her more than anything else. She stops trying, plants her feet, rolls her shoulders, and gets ready to meet him head on.

"Well then here we go, looks like we're onto the real final act." She says, bracing herself. He stares her down as he reaches the stage and climbs up onto it. Internally, he's still terrified. He still doesn't think this will be enough. He doesn't know if he is enough. But he knows at least now he stands a chance; and he takes all of that fear, all that anxiety, and forces it out and into raw energy. She can feel it too. They exchange a look and there's something in her eyes that's completely different to last time. He can't quite tell what it is. It's not quite fear, but it's a world away from every time she's looked at him before.

"I guess this is it. It's time for the real violence." She practically spits. She waves her hand and a row of stage lights to drop on him. He responds in the same way, by reaching and and forcing it to split in two so that it falls either side of him. She dives forward, trying to attack, but he dodges, grabs her, and smashes her into a piece of scenery. "Temper, temper…" She mocks, gleefully and with a nod of her head music starts to play. More toys, hidden around the stage grow and come to life. They creepily march towards him. A Jester, a Raggedy Doll, a Clown and a Nutcracker. They surround him, grabbing and clawing at him, and chanting in unison as they do.

"Temper, temper, that was your crime." They sing as they encircle him. It's one of the creepiest things he's ever seen, giant stuffed toys brought to life and encircling him as they stare at him with oddly dead eyes. They continue the song as they close in, swinging their heft limbs and trying to beat at him with heavy fists. He ducks and rolls out, and grabs Amber's sword. "We knew that you'd appear…" He takes a wild swing. He'd never been the most proficient with a sword during training, and so it's a sloppy swing born out of desperation. But it does the trick and he takes the head clean off the Nutcracker. Then with another wild swing he chops the Clown in half at the middle. He throws the sword into one of the toy soldiers guarding Danny and it lodges in it's head, and sends it stumbling back and into the fire. The stench of melting plastic fills the air. The Jester eerily wobbles towards him, swinging it's cane as a weapon. Louis pushes all the emotion he's feeling together, all the fear and the desperation, and uses it to reach out and blow the Jester's head up. It sends stuffing flying out over the stage. He looks to his right, where he sees the green fire still ablaze, with the soldier flailing in it as it tries to remove the sword, and he realises exactly what he's doing. It's like he can see the connection between Hazel's white hot rage, which still emanates from her, and that fire. He can feel the fear and the pain all around the room, the echoes of the deaths and agony of the survivors who know they're not done yet. He can feel Hazel's hatred for him and her deep sadness. It's what's been there all along. It's his ability to feel. He thinks back to Joseph, and how that deep red of emotion overwhelmed him. He remembers Lisa and how, faced with his and Danny's deaths, he was briefly able to channel her scream back at her to save them. This is what he's been capable of all along, he just hadn't been strong enough. He lets it all wash over him, but now it doesn't overwhelm him. Now, in his supercharged state, it's like he's finally able to swim rather than drown. He can see how all the demonic energy, tied in with all that emotion that feeds it, can be used to create and to destroy. How it can be channelled and used and how it can be controlled. He takes some, intertwines it with the green flames and blasts it towards the Raggedy Doll, setting her ablaze.

He turns, just as Hazel attacks him. Her blood red nails have extended into talons and she scratches at him, drawing blood from his face and chest. She tries to stab him with them, but he catches her hand and snaps them off. She backhands him, and he punches her. They both lash out, blow for blow, for blow, and they're evenly matched. She's powerful, yes, but now so is he, and the fact that she's resorting to punching and clawing is very telling. She tries to shove him back into the flames and he narrowly avoids it and launches himself back at her. They're tearing chunks out of each other; she tries to stick a broken nail straight into his eye and he's able to catch her arm and toss her to the ground just in time. She screeches and kicks at him and he tries to punch at her. She bites him and scratches at him and suddenly they've gone from two powerful beings to two brawling children. They're both battered and bleeding and rolling around the stage. She kicks him off and scrambles back to her feet, desperately putting a little distance between the two of them. She pulls out her gun.

"Enough tricks." She hisses. He pauses, his mind racing to try to find the way out of this. He's about to leap forward when she points the gun at Danny instead. She fires. The bullet whizzes through the air and it connects with its target. It ricochets off the chains. He realises too late that it was a distraction; and by the time his focus has turned back to her, she's already dug the knife deep into his abdomen. She pulls him in close.

"Okay, maybe I had one more trick." She cackles, and pulls the knife out.

Chapter Seventy-Three.

"It was one hell of a romantic gesture." She chuckles, as Louis stumbles back, clutching at his stomach and dropping to his knees in the middle of the stage. "Dosing yourself up and bursting in here for a daring rescue." She glances over at Danny. He too is bleeding profusely, and looks faintly over to Louis. Their eyes meet across the stage, through the dancing green flames. Louis can see that he's weak. His brown eyes look glazed over and his body is limp. His mouth curves into a vague smile; but it's nowhere near the same annoying vibrance it normally is. "I do see the appeal." She says. "He is cute. A little James Dean. I mean, I've never been too into pretty boys but each to their own." She squats down in front of Louis so they're on the same level, so that she can taunt him face to face. "I told you both this would happen." He pushes and a wave of energy hits her, making her stumble a step back. He falls forward onto all fours, because that took more out of him than anything. She laughs it off. "Oh, you've still got some power in you. Won't do you any good. Just sit back and relax. Let it all seep back out. Let all that fresh demonic energy you've rammed into yourself loose into the world as you die in a disappointing little heap on the ground." He closes his eyes and he soaks that in. That thing she just said about being a disappointment, and the idea that he's a failure. He takes that, and he adds to it everything that Chris said and did earlier that night, and every time everyone else told him he wasn't enough. Then, he throws in all the times he told himself that too. All the times his own thoughts tore him down and told him that he didn't belong in this life; that he wouldn't be good enough. He takes all of that and mashes it together because he knows he is enough. He's the one who gave her a fight that none of the others could. He's the one who stopped Joseph. He's the one who rescued Wade. He's the one who Danny kissed. He's the one who Amber and Lauren broke every rule to rescue. He's felt for so long like he's not good enough, and that's all she sees too. But he is. He knows he is. And so this time, when he takes all of those feelings and puts them into the blast, it rockets her backwards and she screams as she's launched through the back of the stage. He drags himself back to his feet, straining harder to do it than he has anything else in his life but knowing that he can and that he has to. She's back on her feet too, though much quicker than he managed.

She looks back at him with amazement. She did not expect this, and she

definitely didn't expect what comes next. He focuses on the painful hole in his stomach and he pours every bit of concentration into forcing his body to pull itself back together in the same way he's seen Lauren do to others so many times. Hazel stares, wide eyed, and watches as the stab wound on his stomach heals itself and the flesh knit itself back together only only the bloodied hole in his t-shirt remains as evidence it even happened. Now her face reads dramatically differently, and now it is fear that he sees. She's scared of him and, amazingly, she turns and she runs from him. She flees deeper into the building and as she leaves the effects of her powers diminish. The flames die and the toys littered around the stage revert back to their normal form and size. Louis bolts over to Danny, throwing himself at him and lifting him down off the hook.
"Told you not to come." He says weakly as he sets him down on the floor and tears off the chains. .
"I ignored you."
"That was stupid."
"I'm an idiot." Louis laughs and Danny gives him another weak smile. Louis has to fight back tears, because in this tiny moment he's so incredibly happy. He's done it. Danny is safe. That's all he's wanted from the moment she took him, just to make sure Danny is safe. There are so many emotions crashing over him and it's a little overwhelming. There's so much they need to talk about and he doesn't know where any of them go from here but now it feels like they'll actually get a chance to work that out.
"Louis, let me." Lauren says, practically throwing herself down onto the ground beside them. The remaining toy soldier that had her and Wade pinned down is now back in it's original tiny form and she's free to help. Out of the corner of his eye Louis sees Wade stamp on it for good measure as he stares around the stage in disbelief at the things he's seen. It's all okay. It's all going to be okay. Louis gives Danny's hand a quick squeeze and backs off to give Lauren the space she needs to heal him. She swoops in on the bullet wound first. But, despite the crashing of relief he feels, Louis knows the night isn't over yet.
"Wait." Danny says, with a panicked desperation because he can see what Louis is thinking. "Idiot, don't." He pleads.
"I have to." He explains, because he knows she's still here. He can feel it. She retreated, but she didn't leave.
"No, but, I need to tell you…"
"Later." Louis says, because he can't have that conversation now. If he

starts, if he lets himself be there with Danny then he won't be able to continue. So, despite everything telling him not to, despite his desire to just lose himself in those deep brown eyes, despite wanting to just get everyone he cares about away now, despite his exhausted body screaming at him to just stop, he draws himself back to full height and marches off to find Hazel and to end this. He moves cautiously through the corridors; but he's drawn to one particular room by the low thrumming song of her sadness and the classic melody of Billie Holiday.

A few weeks ago…
…can you? Move, I mean?" Joseph asks with glee. He already knows the answer and Agent Alex Smith's eyes widen with the realisation that they're frozen to the spot and the even more terrifying realisation of what that means.
Hazel's well manicured hand comes to rest on Alex's shoulder and, at the bottom of the hill, Joseph claps his hands with glee. "She's here." He says.
"Alex, dear." Hazel says as if she's greeting an old friend. "You really are quite persistent. I've had my fair share of stalkers, but followed us across continents and it's a little excessive."
"It's stopped being fun, honestly." Joseph says, squealing with glee and climbing back up to the path where the two of them are standing. Hazel's head snaps towards him and her face is filled with anger.
"I told you not to attract any attention for a while. And yet we are again with me having to swoop in and save you." She says, her tone sharp.
"I'm…" He begins, bottom lip pushed out like a petulant child.
"Save it! Get out of here while I deal with this." She says, gesturing towards Alex.
"And just to clear the air." He starts to sing.
"No."
"I ask forgiveness."
"That's not going to…"
"For the things I've done you blame me for!" He tries to sing over her.
"I am too angry to sing Wicked with you." She growls. "And also you're stealing my part."
"But then I guess we know there's blame to share…Okay, okay. I'll stop. Later?"
"Yes. Just go back to the hotel." She says, and even now she's softening. She can't stay mad at him, no matter how much trouble he gets himself in.

He grins at her, then waves at them both, and wanders away, as if he doesn't have a care in the world. "How do you keep finding us?" She asks, turning her attention back to Alex. She waits, expecting an answer until she realises that the hold over them is preventing that. "Oh, sorry." She says, before dialling it back just enough so that they can speak.
"Him. He's easy to track." Alex says.
"It's never going to stop, is it?" Hazel asks, sadly.
"No. You're both murderers, and we'll keep hunting you for as long as you're alive…" They explain; and they're cut off mid-sentence as Hazel shoves them into the river. Since they're still paralysed by her powers, there's nothing they can do to stop themselves from drowning.
"An excellent point…" She says, and waits, keeping her hold over them locked in place until she's certain they're dead.

Chapter Seventy-Four.

He enters.
Exactly as she'd planned. Billie Holliday, I'll Be Seeing You, is gently playing in her commandeered dressing room. She sits in front of a mirror, touching up her make-up. The blood and the wounds are gone and she looks impeccable again. She's changed too, and she now wears a long, flowing, off the shoulder black gown.
"Hello, Louis." She says, without turning.
"Hazel."
"Please, have a seat." She says, gesturing to the empty chair next to her that she has set up for him.
"I…I'm not here to sit." He stutters, a little taken aback by the change in her demeanour.
"No, but I wanted to enjoy a drink first. So, would you like one?" She asks him, taking a sip of the martini she's already made herself.
"No, thanks." He doesn't sit.
"Can't say I didn't offer. So, are you going to kill me?" She asks, finishing powdering her face and turning to look at him.
"You'd kill me, wouldn't you?"
"Absolutely. I've made that clear. But that doesn't answer my question."
"After everything you've done…" He says meekly, shaking his head. He didn't expect this from her. He expected to find her and to continue their

battle; to tear each other apart until he could subdue her or she could kill him. He didn't expect cocktails and chit chat.
"You've only seen a fraction of what I've done." She chuckles.
"Well, it's all over now." He tells her, trying to sound as sure of himself as he can.
"There's one of those classic good guy clichés. I wasn't sure, heading into tonight, if I was ready for my final bow but now…now it feels like a relief." She says, with a heavy sigh.
"Why?"
"You wouldn't get it, my dear."
"I'd like to." He says. He means it, and she can see that. She takes another sip of her martini, and the song changes to Glenn Miller 'In A Sentimental Mood.'.
"I'm so very old now. I should already be dead and buried. But here I am, fighting. I've spent most of my life fighting people like you and after this long I'm not even sure why. I'm just so very tired." She looks him up and down. "And look at you. You're amazing. So fresh and full of life and now there's probably more demon in you than there ever has been in me. You sacrificed so much, and for what? To stop me? For someone you think you might love? Or was it just some skewed view of good and evil?" She snorts and he realises that she's laughing at him. It's not to taunt him, she's not in that role any more, no the look she's giving him now is one of pity. "That'll all change. I'll be gone, you and him won't last, and eventually you'll realise the world isn't as black and white as you think, we're in technicolor, darling."
"You don't know that, and you don't know me."
"I do." She says, with absolute certainty. "That's the point. I've known a hundred of you. Generic, straight out of the mould, do-gooders. All this time I've been able to play the villain because you've been a white hat away from a perfect good-guy cliché. I should've brought hats for us. That would've been quaint." She says, and takes a quick look around the room as if she's searching for something that will suffice. Louis pauses and thinks about what she's said, and then finally takes a seat next to her.
"Pour me a drink then." He says, with a shrug. She smiles, surprised.
"I'll give it to you, that's not even the first time tonight you've surprised me." She grabs the cocktail shaker, pours him a drink, and tops hers up.
"What did you mean, about me being more demon than you?"
"Do you not understand it yet? You're infected too. Now ain't that a fly in

your ointment?" She says with a smirk, as if that should shatter him. It doesn't.
"That makes sense. I think I knew, really. It's like I didn't want to look at it, but it's always been there." He says, because honestly, that was the truth. No one had ever expressly said that their powers came from demonic energy but it made sense.
"Whatever happens to you it's watered down. Controlled. It's forced, and unnatural. Not like the way it happens with us. But that means we're the same."
"I'll never agree with you. It might not be black and white, but whatever way you justify it, you're still a murderer. You've killed people. I'm not trying to be self-righteous, but that is never okay and you should pay for that."
"Come back to me the first time you kill someone, because it'll happen." She says. "That answers whether or not you're going to kill me I suppose, if killing is just so wrong, so what are you going to do?"
"Make sure you're locked up, I guess. Where you can't keep killing."
"That's the same thing, you idiot. What do you think happens to us when we're locked up – or have you just never thought about that either?"
"I haven't, exactly." He admits, because that's just another thing no one really talked about.
"See? That's the thing I can't stand about you. Your dumb innocence. I play the villain because I know who I am. I've known it since the first time I dragged myself out of the mud. But you, you have no idea. You just mindlessly hunt us because someone told you enough stories that you believe it's the right thing to do. Your white hat has blood stains all over it, but you tell yourself it's part of the pattern. You look at it in black and white and so you can't see the red. You're not the hero in this story. Pay attention to the man behind the curtain."
"So what is the right thing to do?" He asks, sipping his own drink.
"Louis, I think this is the beginning of a beautiful friendship." She says with a smirk.
"I think we're a long way off becoming friends."
"I know, I was just quoting Casablanca." She knocks back the rest of her martini and stands. Louis does too.
"There's part of me that's sorry, for all of this." She tells him; referencing the chaos out in the theatre. The fighting isn't over, but the tide has firmly changed. Olivia, having recovered a gun, ends her battle with Nadin by firing several rounds into his head and putting him down for good. Even for

a Used-to-Be once the brain is that damaged there's no coming back. She intervenes to help Brian, and fires another shot into Morris' knee. Brian follows it up with a syringe to the neck, and that's another down.
"But then there's part of me that's sorry I didn't do more. You took away the only companion I've ever had and I wanted us to fight a bloody bitter war until the very end."
Amber takes on Nelson and Appleby, saving Chris from the once sided beatdown. She takes a chance to dive back onto the stage and snatch her discarded sword, then she leaps down and drives it into Nelson's skull.
"All's fair in love and war, so they say. And that's why we'll never really know who's good and who's evil, because when there are no rules how can you tell who's breaking them? Love and war are the same…"
As Nelson's body falls she takes the chance to check on Chris. He's covered in his own blood and he's badly beaten, but he's still alive. Appleby sneaks up behind her, realising she's taken her focus off him, and raises his truncheon ready to clobber her from behind. Wade fires several rounds from the gun she gave him and his former colleague swears loudly in pain and runs before any of them can do anything to stop him.
"…Because nobody ever really wins in either. And I'm tired of never being able to win."
On stage, Lauren is still tending to Danny's wounds. He's strong enough now to force his way to his feet. She tries to get him to stop.
"No, let me. I've got to find Louis. I need…I need to tell him…" He says, desperately.
"What is it? What do you need to tell him?" She asks. He pushes past her, hobbling on his not-fully-healed broken-leg in the direction that Louis and Hazel went.
"She's not done."

Back in the dressing room Louis and Hazel stand facing each other. Now Doris Day is singing about a sentimental journey.
"For what it's worth there's a part of me that wishes I could let you walk away. But, you're a killer, and I don't think you'll ever stop that." He tells her, sadly. He's not sure what the right thing to do any more is. But he knows it's not to let her kill again.
"What if I pinky swear?" She giggles, offering her finger out. He laughs too, and shakes his head. "No, you're right. I am and I won't. But, I've had a lot of time to think about my final scene, especially lately. I'm not coming with

you. If I'm going to be written out I at least want to control how my character goes."
"Hazel, you don't get a choice. You can't fight us all off." He says, because they can both tell that the battle outside is winding down and he'll soon have back-up. They can both feel it. She lets out a deep, sad, sigh and turns back to the mirror again. She takes a last lingering look at herself and he sees her subtly reach and grab something small and black. He can't quite tell what it is and he tries to get a good look as she rolls it in her hand. She makes a small gesture and the music changes to a version of 'Somewhere Over the Rainbow,' and she smiles and takes a moment to soak it in.
"I'm going out with a bang, not a whimper." She tells him; and she tips her hand to show a small toy bomb that becomes real as it's charged with her power. He tries to grab it, but he's too late. "And you're coming with me you stupid little monkey."

Chapter Seventy-Five.

Lauren isn't done healing him. There's still a bullet lodged in one leg and the other still has a deep ache from a bone that isn't over the violent snap it suffered about an hour ago. But he's desperate because he knows what's coming next. She told him. She'd whispered in his ear how she planned to go out because she was never going to let herself be captured. Danny limps off the stage, and drags himself through the old backstage corridors as quickly as his broken body will allow him to move. Lauren follows quickly, begging for him to stop and explain himself. But he can't. He doesn't have time. He knows what's coming and he has to stop it. He doesn't know exactly where he's going but he can hear voices and music and he rushes desperately towards it.
But that's when it happens.
There's a thundering boom and heat that tears through the air. He doesn't want to stop but before he knows it Lauren has him pinned down on the ground to keep them both safe. There's fire and smoke and he cries out. "No!" He screams because it's happened exactly like she said it would. He's breathing heavily and trying to stare through the smoke and fire and crumbling debris. He's trying to see any sign of life, he needs to see some kind of hope that it hasn't worked but can't see anything. The stench of the smoke fills his nostrils and his vision is blurred because his eyes are

watering. The fire is spreading and he struggles to fight Lauren off him. There's no way that Louis could've survived that but he needs to look.
"Danny, we need to…" She tries to tell him.
"No!" He croaks back. He won't leave. Louis didn't leave him, even though he should have, and so Danny can't leave him either. Even if he's dead. He's inhaling so much smoke, and it makes him wretch, and the water streaming from his eyes is getting worse. It's chaos and the ramifications of Hazel's last destructive act ripple out like a shockwave through the building and through his life.
The sprinkler system overhead kicks into life and he's so grateful. He finally wriggles free of Lauren and scrambles over to the wall to find the strongest source of electricity he can. He's exhausted, he's been through so much and lost so much blood but in his desperation he feels so alive and so powerful. He does everything he can to channel his power into the sprinklers and ask them to please, please give everything they can.
There's a noticeable boost in the downpour of water as they're pushed beyond what they should be capable of. The spreading of the blaze is cut off and the smoke begins to clear just a little. He wipes his eyes and he can see the night sky where there was once a concrete wall. He can see the flickers of flames on the ground, and the chunks of rubble that now litter the place where there used to be a whole room. But, in amongst all of that, he sees something he doesn't expect to see. He sees the outline of a sphere in the middle of the chaos, with the vague figure of a man inside.
Louis drops the protective bubble he summoned, because he can't hold it any more, and falls to his knees, exhausted. Danny rushes over to him, also collapsing to his knees beside him. Lauren hangs back and watches the two of them.
"What the hell did you do?" Danny shouts at him.
"This wasn't me!" He argues.
"No, I knew about the bomb. I mean everything else." He snaps, and he's so angry and so happy all at the same time.
"You're welcome." Louis says, forcing a smug grin.
"I didn't…" He begins in frustration, but stops, shaking his head and smiling back at him. It's over. They lock eyes, nervously staring at each other. The look lingers and neither of them are really sure what to do. It's broken up as part of the ceiling falls. Louis grabs Danny, pressing his body into him, and forms a bubble again to protect the two of them.

"We need to get out of here." He says.
"Finally, a good idea." Danny agrees.

"And that's it. The end of my story."
The recording ends, and Kim stops typing. She's got it all. She takes a moment to sit back and reflect, because hearing it for the second time was just as harrowing. The rape, the murder, and everything else. It's a horrible enough story without the supernatural elements. She's verified what she can; Hazel Hardcastle did exist and she's been watching footage of her online in-between transcribing blocks of the story. Harriet Hardcastle existed too. She rocketed to fame and then plummeted just as quickly. Dick Johnson was a big time Hollywood director and producer who threw too much of his money around and left himself on the cusp of bankruptcy. He died, murdered in his office, and the murder was attributed to Harriet who was his scorned lover and killed herself just after. Her daughter Hazel had disappeared, never to be seen again, officially. Some believed she'd simply stepped back from public life following her mother's crimes. There were sightings of her, supposedly, but never anything official. There was no record of her death, ever, and eventually the world had stopped caring. It's possible that's the truth, that the tragedy had just caused her to shun fame and live out a quiet life, but Kim is certain that the 1940s actress and the woman she met today are the same. She needs the others, and she knows that. This is too big just for her. She needs Matthew and she needs Marc. Her little team. She goes back to her phone, closing the finished video. It's nearly morning and she's still wired from this. 'Huge breakthrough. Call me the second you get this.' She texts to Marc. 'Call me you stubborn old bastard. I need you!' She sends it to Matthew. She knows she'll get a response from him eventually, but she's desperate to tell him all of this. Marc, too, will love it.
And just like that there's a knock at the door. She smiles to herself. It's ridiculously late, or early, so there really is only one man it can be. She takes off her glasses and sets them down next to her laptop before hopping to her feet and rushing over to the door.
"Finally, you stubborn ol…" She opens it, but it's not Wade that's standing there. It's a group of three figures that she recognises instantly. The Cleaners. They lurch forward, forcing their way into her apartment. "Stop! I'll call the police!" She says, but none of them respond. Two of them grab her. "Get off me, I'll…" The third jams a sedative into her arm and her head

starts swimming. She tries to protest but all she can do is make a vague gurgling sound as the words catch in her throat and she swims out of consciousness. Her body goes limp as she passes out..

Chapter Seventy-Six.

Outside of the Royale Theatre a large crowd has gathered as day breaks, because despite their best efforts there is no way that gunshots, explosions, and fleeing hostages wouldn't attract attention. The scene is contained, as much as it can be, by three teams of Cleaners. Hazel may be dead but there is so much to do. Some of the Human hostages have been detained and are being debriefed, some of them fled and will need to be tracked down. Morris, the only surviving Used-to-Be, will be transferred to a secure location and interrogated. Then, there are dozens of bodies to dispose of. An explanation will need to be created for what unfolded here, so as not to reveal the truth to the general public. It will be a cover-up operation that is running for months. Whatever story they come up with will have to be a very convincing explanation. But that's not a job for right now. For Louis, Danny, Amber, Olivia, Brian, Lauren, Chris, and DCI Matthew Wade the job is done, for tonight. There are ambulances there to attend to the humans. There are fire engines too. A delicate balance of involving the human emergency services without giving them the full story.
Near the entrance, Chris is sitting against a wall, out of view, as Lauren helps him by tending to some of his wounds.
"We can treat the rest later. I'm exhausted." She says as she finishes up. He was pretty badly banged up, the more concerns being a fractured skull, a punctured lung, and broken sternum. She's taken care of the worst of them but that's all she has the energy for. He still has a few scrapes and bruises, and a couple of cracked ribs, and they can be taken care of later. He's lucky to still be alive. .
"Thanks. I need to coordinate this mess anyway." He grunts, and starts to get to his feet.
"Wait. There's something else." She says hesitantly. She looks over at Louis, who is in the distance speaking to one of the Cleaners, and that gives her the motivation to say what she needs to. "He saved your life tonight." She says sternly.
"That's not import..." He begins angrily. She cuts him off.

"Yes it is. He was right. Your attempt at this was a disorganised mess because you weren't listening to what he was telling you. Noel, Josh, and Phil are dead. That's, in part, on you. Chris, we've worked together for years and you've got so many strengths. I've so much admiration for you. I would follow your lead on so many things. But tonight, I hate everything you did."

"Lauren you're out of order." He snarls.

"Yes but I'm right. You rushed in for your own glory. You tried to wipe Louis' memory because he disagreed with you. You're a crappy leader, and Rachel would've been furious with you. Drop the re-training. Drop the transfer. Start again."

"Why should I? You've got no…" He starts, and she calmly holds up a hand to silence him again.

"Like I said, I've been with you for years. I know you can cut corners when you're in a hurry because I used to be the one who cleaned up after you. I also know that for re-training you need several levels of approval. You didn't have that. Re-training should be our last option and you rushed to it because you didn't like that he kept disagreeing with you. An attack on a fellow agent like that, well, the consequences for you could be awful. Much worse than what they should've actually been for him. If I raise this to the right people, through the right channels, which you know I know how to do, then it could well end up with you being the one sent to be re-trained." She explains. He remains silent and looks sullen. He knows she's right. "Leave Louis alone. Got it?" She concludes.

"Got it." He says, barely audibly.

"Good. You need to do better." And with that, she stands, and leaves him, hoping that he really will reflect on what she's said and take it on board.

Wade breaks off from trying to reassure some of the humans who are waiting to be debriefed by the Cleaners. He feels a little guilty, and can't quite get on board with not being able to tell them what actually happened. He hates lying to them, the way he was lied to for a long time, but he also wants them to remain calm and do anything he can to make it easier on them. There's nothing good that will come of telling these people the truth. He catches Amber's attention once he's done.

"What happens now?" He asks her, as she watches Morris being loaded into the back of a van.

"They all need to be tested. In something like this the risk of infection is high. The Cleaners will do all of that."
"What about what they've seen? Being taken hostage by police and…everything else. I dread to think how this'll look…"
"Cleaners can take care of that, too. For everyone who isn't infected they can alter short term memory and send them back to their life. They can forget what happened here tonight and live normally. More than we get."
"Like what was gonna happen to Louis?" He asks, feeling very uncomfortable with the idea. He finally has the answer to those people like Cain, who couldn't remember his last few hours with his sister, and it doesn't feel good. But, it does make sense. Maybe they're better off not knowing what horrors they've seen tonight.
"No, no. It's different. They'll remember everything except the last few hours." She tells him, and that fits alongside what he already knows. It explains why he'd found people with seemingly important parts of their memory missing. He nods. "You should probably get out of here. Chris will definitely want us to do that to you, too." She explains, looking around to make sure she's not overheard.
"Might be better." He says with a sarcastic chuckle. "The world's a lot scarier than I thought. Finding out a good chunk of the lads at work are…well not who I thought. Speaking of, I didn't see Copper here tonight…"
"She wanted to keep him away from this. I heard her say it." Danny explains, as he and Louis join them. They both look battered and bloody, and there are dark bruises starting to form on both their faces. Louis has a black eye, Danny is coughing occasionally from the smoke, and they're both still soaking wet from the sprinklers. They look utterly exhausted. But, none of that hides how happy they look as they stand, just a little too close together, a little amazed to still be alive. "She told me he's a back-up plan." He explains, though right now he doesn't have the energy to be worried about that.
"Oh great, she had a back-up plan." Amber says with an eye roll.
"It wouldn't surprise me if she had a few." Louis says. They pause for a moment and let that sink in. It's not a nice thought knowing that, even though she's gone, there's still a nasty surprise or two from Hazel that they're yet to find out about. There would be a ripple effect to her death, the same way there had been to Alex's all those weeks ago. But that was a problem for later, because they actually get to have a later, and that is a

nice feeling. "For now let's just be happy we made it. We won." He says, and sneaks a look sideways to Danny. He's alive. They both are. That's all he wanted from tonight.

"Yeah. We really didn't plan for that, did we? What the hell do we do now?" Amber asks, and he laughs because that's exactly what he was thinking. He hadn't dared to hope they'd survive. There had been a cost, Noel, and Josh, and Phil and the toll it had taken on the rest of them. There was also a serious risk that some of the Humans had been infected by what had transpired. But they'd made it, and now he and Danny could work out what they did next.

"Well, first thing is first." He looks at Wade. "Amber's right, we need to get you out of here. You're not safe until we catch him." He explains. Whatever part Tim Copper played in Hazel's back-up plan, there was a very real worry that he'll attack his old friend again if he's given a choice.

"I don't wanna run…" He begins to argue.

"Even if you don't want to run from him then the Cleaners will want to take you." Danny says. The last few hours have made him shift his perspective on this human knowing their secret.

"And I don't think it'll just be taking a few hours of memory. There's a limit to how far back they can go and you've been on to us for weeks." Louis adds, with a chuckle that isn't unkind. He's incredibly grateful for this grumpy old human man and he badly wants to protect him. The rules don't matter, they've already broken enough of them tonight.

"I can transfer you anywhere you like. New name. New job, if you want." Danny offers and for the first time there doesn't seem to be any contempt towards the Human from him. "Neither Chris nor Copper will be able to find you."

"I think a change would be nice after all this…" He begins to concede, but there's still a look on his face that says he's on the cusp of protesting.

"We need to protect you, and this is the best way. Copper wants to kill you, Chris will want to contain you. Please, trust us?" Louis asks him, and Wade does. He nods, because after everything they've been through over the last few hours he does. They've all fought together. They've all nearly died for each other. Nothing builds trust quite like that. Louis hands him his phone. "Give me the address your wife is at, and go there. We'll stop by tomorrow with everything you need."

"I…thank you. I'm glad you're all ok. I'm glad you told me what's really going on and that I'm not gonna forget it. Thank you for letting me be a part

of this." He says as he hands the phone back, having added the address, and then he leaves, suddenly realising just how tired he is and how much a break sounds like the perfect idea. Amber stares at the building. There's a fire crew around the side where the explosion went off.
"Is she definitely…?" She asks, once again voicing something they're all thinking.
"Yes." Louis says, with more hope than confidence. "I think so. I dunno…she called it a scene. So, maybe…"
"She's dead. She has to be." Danny says. Those words, and the doubts they all have, linger for a moment. They all hope that she's dead; and this wasn't just some act, but they know that's a possibility. Amber looks at the two of them, standing shoulder to shoulder, both of them leaning in slightly.
"I'm going to leave you two to…talk or whatever." She says, shaking her head and marching off to find some other way to help clean up. She's tired too, but she wants to keep being useful for as long as she's still upright, because she too is quite grateful she survived the night.
And finally, for the first time since this all started, for the first time since that kiss, the two of them are alone. So much has happened since then. The kiss feels like a lifetime ago and all those questions of what it meant didn't matter when they were at risk of dying. They've been through so much and the two of them stare semi-awkwardly at each other. Louis has so much he wants to ask because all of the questions of what they are to each other matter again now. Danny beats him to it.
"What do we do now?" He says, actually looking a little shy.
"I dunno." Louis replies, not really wanting to fully meet his gaze. He's suddenly terrified. "Go home?" He asks. "Sleep, maybe?"
"I didn't mean that." Danny says. His stomach lurches. "I meant us."
"Oh. Well…what do you want to do?"
"You know I'm not good at this."
"Well, how do you feel?" Louis asks, not sure if he wants to know the answer.
"I feel like I'm glad you didn't die." Danny says, and only he could make that sound so nonchalant. Louis laughs at him, because he's such a dick and somehow he finds it so endearing.
"I'm glad you didn't die too." He laughs.
"I felt…" He begins, and takes a noticeable gulp as he picks the right words. "…like I was scared that I wouldn't see you again. I like seeing your stupid face."

"I like seeing your stupid face, too." Louis says; and now he can't help but look at him, and his stupid face, and his beautiful brown eyes.

"My face isn't stupid. It's very intelligent, actually."

"Then I like seeing your very intelligent face." He corrects, with an eye roll.

"Okay, good, so you should because…" He begins, and Louis interrupts him with a kiss. It's the best possible way to shut him up and he wishes he'd realised that much sooner. Danny kisses back. It's hungry, it's lustful, and it comes from being grateful to be alive. When they separate, they both laugh and look around because it was stupid to do that where they could be seen. But they don't regret it because it was something they needed to do.

"Okay." Danny nods, as if agreeing to something.

"Okay?"

"Okay, yes, let's do more of that. I'm going to need to stick close to you anyway so we can work out exactly what you've done to yourself."

"How close?" Louis asks, flashing a mischievous smirk.

"Let's…go home." He says, returning the grin.

"Good idea." Louis says, with an eyebrow raise. Yes. He suddenly very much wants to take him home.

"No, really. We can talk more at home." Danny says, as if reading his mind. Hazel Hardcastle told me a lot before she blew herself up that night. She knew I'd find a way to survive. I think it's what she wanted. She loved telling a story; and I think she wanted someone to witness her final moments and tell other people of them. She didn't do anything without an audience and I don't think she'd have chosen me to hear her final lines if she thought they'd just be forgotten with my death moments later. The thing that sticks with me the most is what she said about love and war, because I understand and the older I get the truer it becomes.

"I'll feel better once we're home anyway…" Danny continues, taking one last look back at the theatre where there had been so much pain, chaos, and fear.

"…'cause you know what they say…"

Everyone compares love and war, she'd told me, because no one wins in either.

"…there's no place like home."

The End

Author's Note

Before I say anything else, thank you for reading. I really hope you enjoyed it. If you take the time to read this incredibly self-indulgent little section I hope you enjoy this too.

When I said at the very start that this story had taken far too long what I meant was that it has taken me twenty years to tell. Louis started life as a character I used for online role-playing as a kid with my friends. He was a vampire hunter avenging his deceased wife. He then got an origin story; a film I planned to make with my friends. It had an Evanescence soundtrack and there was dialogue lifted directly from Buffy the Vampire Slayer. I don't know why I thought no one would notice that. In it, he married Hazel, a fellow vampire hunter who was murdered by the vampire "Morsirius." I've clearly always relied quite heavily on cliches in my work. From there it was a book, or, a series of books.

Louis evolved as I did. As I got to grips with my own identity I got to grips with his, too. I always wanted to tell the kind of story that I would've loved growing up and that nerdy little neurodivergent queer kids would love too. This spent about ten years as a TV series - something I've tried to retain with the eight episodes throughout - but for the longest time I was too unsure of myself to continue it. Like so many other creatives I was too anxious to simply create. When we hit the global pandemic in 2020 I was finally able to move my own fear to the side and write again; and by the end of 2022 I had two series of Louis' adventures. But that was when I realised I wanted it to be a book again, because that was the way I would have the most control over the story being told, and it was my best chance of making something that people like me would love.

So I suppose I want to tell you all to get out of your own way, the same way I will be constantly encouraging myself to, and the same way I will make Louis. If you want to create, create. Even if it's just for you. Or share it with the people you love, and if you have creative friends encourage them to do the same. Let's inspire each other because there is room for us all to thrive.

This book isn't perfect; I know there is still another mistake in here somewhere that I just can't see any more. But I no longer need it to be perfect. I wasted far too much time obsessing over perfection when it's unobtainable. We can always be better but that doesn't mean we aren't amazing. I remember as a kid my dad would want to know about the one thing I got wrong on a test, rather than the nine things I got right; and now I'd much rather focus on what I've got right. There are parts in here that made me emotional, and I hope they did you, too. There are also parts, like the use of the word 'stiffy,' that made me cringe and I hope they did you too. I hope you felt something, because that's all I've set out to do here. Thank you for giving me that chance. .

And I also want to mention a few more people that have been an invaluable part of this journey:

Thank you Joe, @joeeasonart, for your amazing cover art. It's everything I dreamed of.
Thank you Noah, for being so good that you inspire me too.
Thank you Nate, your encouragement meant so much to me, and because you told me about Amazon books.
Paul, Guapo, your friendship, even from a distance, makes me feel incredible and has helped me find my creative power.
For Kirsty; who encouraged me to push myself in every aspect of life.
For Neil, who taught me to be authentic.
For my Balor Cat who was a constant companion and never climbed on the keyboard when it mattered.
For everyone who has ever been excited when I've told them I was writing a book. To Adam, and Sam, and Ruth, and Martin, and every other member of my chosen family. You encouraged me.

I'm in awe that this is finished. This is the very last thing I will write in The Custodian Chronicles: The Tragedy of Hazel Hardcastle. Please let me know what you think; @garethwat or @cosplaywithme on instagram.

Oh, and yes, I did subtly drop in that a draft exists already for book two. So hopefully it won't be another twenty years before…

Louis and the Custodians will return in
'The Custodian Chronicles: The Beast Behind the Curtain.'

Printed in Great Britain
by Amazon